T0115468

WHAT I LIVED FOR

NOVELS BY JOYCE CAROL OATES

With Shuddering Fall (1964)

A Garden of Earthly Delights (1967)

Expensive People (1968)

them (1969)

Wonderland (1971)

Do with Me What You Will (1973)

The Assassins (1975)

Childwold (1976)

Son of the Morning (1978)

Unholy Loves (1979)

Bellefleur (1980)

Angel of Light (1981)

A Bloodsmoor Romance (1982)

Mysteries of Winterthurn (1984)

Solstice (1985)

Marya: A Life (1986)

You Must Remember This (1987)

American Appetites (1989)

Because It Is Bitter, and Because It Is
  My Heart (1990)

Black Water (1992)

Foxfire: Confessions of a Girl Gang
  (1993)

What I Lived For (1994)

Zombie (1995)

We Were the Mulvaneys (1996)

Man Crazy (1997)

My Heart Laid Bare (1998)

Broke Heart Blues (1999)

Blonde (2000)

Middle Age: A Romance (2001)

I'll Take You There (2002)

The Tattooed Girl (2003)

The Falls (2004)

Missing Mom (2005)

Black Girl / White Girl (2006)

The Gravedigger's Daughter (2007)

My Sister, My Love (2008)

Little Bird of Heaven (2009)

Mudwoman (2012)

The Accursed (2013)

Carthage (2014)

The Sacrifice (2015)

A Book of American Martyrs (2017)

Hazards of Time Travel (2018)

WHAT I LIVED FOR

A Novel

JOYCE CAROL OATES

An Imprint of HarperCollinsPublishers

WHAT I LIVED FOR. Copyright © 1994 by The Ontario Review, Inc. All rights reserved. Printed in the United States of America. No part of this book may be used or reproduced in any manner whatsoever without written permission except in the case of brief quotations embodied in critical articles and reviews. For information, address HarperCollins Publishers, 195 Broadway, New York, NY 10007.

HarperCollins books may be purchased for educational, business, or sales promotional use. For information, please email the Special Markets Department at SP-sales@harpercollins.com.

The quotations found in Part I, Chapter 7, on page 187 are composites taken from passages in the essays "How a Supernova Explodes" by Hans A. Bethe and Gerald Brown and "The Magic Furnace" by Harald Fritzsch, from *The World Treasury of Physics, Astronomy, and Mathematics*, edited by Timothy Ferris (Little, Brown & Co., 1991).

The phrase "A fight between an 'It' and an 'I'" occurs in *The Man Who Mistook His Wife for a Hat*, by Oliver Sacks (Harper Perennial Library, 1987), p. 93.

The work of art described in Part III, Chapter 5, is Joel Lipman's *Jesse Helms' Body*.

The quotation "The event horizon . . ." in the Epilogue is from *A Brief History of Time* by Stephen W. Hawking (Bantam Books, 1988).

Chapter 2 of Part II, "Romance: October 1989," was published in *Playboy*, October 1994.

A hardcover edition of this book was published in 1994 by Dutton Adult, an imprint of Penguin Books USA Inc.

FIRST PLUME PAPERBACK EDITION PUBLISHED 1995.
FIRST ECCO PAPERBACK EDITION PUBLISHED 2019.

Designed by Michelle Crowe

Library of Congress Cataloging-in-Publication Data has been applied for.

ISBN 978-0-06-279576-2

19 20 21 22 23   LSC   10 9 8 7 6 5 4 3 2 1

—for Billy Abrahams, editor and friend

He rests. He has traveled.

—James Joyce, *Ulysses*

CONTENTS

PART III:
Sunday, May 24, 1992

PART IV:
Memorial Day 1992

PROLOGUE

December 24, 1959–December 27, 1959

God erupted in thunder and shattering glass.

God was deafening, out of the winter sky heavy with storm clouds above Lake Erie.

God was six staccato bursts of fire, and glass flying like crazy laughter, and the skidding of a car's tires as a car accelerated rapidly going eastward on Schuyler.

God struck so swiftly, and without warning. No mercy. In the lightly falling powdery-glinting snow of Christmas Eve.

In fact it was just dusk of Christmas Eve: the brief day, overcast like ashes, was darkening early at 4:20 P.M.

Timothy Patrick Corcoran, hanging an evergreen wreath to the front door of the residence at 8 Schuyler Place, his back to the narrow street, caught the first of the bullets in the lower back, and the second shattered several vertebrae and ripped through his lungs, and the third went wild and the fourth struck the nape of his neck and lodged in the base of his skull and by this time pop-eyed in the astonishment of Death he was falling, yanking the heavy wreath with him to the fan-shaped stoop that began to glisten immediately with his blood.

He was coughing blood, choking in blood. The wreath too would be soaked in blood: a massive, heavy, ornamental wreath, purchased just that afternoon, rich and pungent-smelling, a beautiful wreath for the beautiful new house at 8 Schuyler Place, thirty inches across, with sprigs of berries so shinily red they might have been synthetic berries and a gaudy red satin bow so shinily red it might have been plastic.

A wire from the wreath, dislodged by the weight of the dying man, would catch him in the left cheek, piercing the skin. When he was lifted, and turned, the wreath would lift partway with him before falling back.

Timothy Patrick Corcoran, thirty-six years old, six feet two inches tall and 212 pounds, was a large, muscular man, a man impatient with physical incompetence, and he fell heavily and without grace, clawing first at the door against which the sledgehammer blows of the bullets had thrown him and then at the wreath and at his chest which had exploded in a pain beyond pain, collapsing, his left leg beneath him, onto the concrete stoop he'd shoveled clear of icy snow that morning and which was covered now in a thin coating of fresh powdery snow.

The third, fifth, and sixth bullets struck the door, breaking the leaded-glass window that curved like a rising sun, lodging in a wall of the foyer inside and in the thick oak wood of the door itself.

There was height to this door, and conspicuous pride. It boasted, beside the leaded-glass window, an oversized wrought-iron knocker in the shape of an American eagle, and a brass doorknob bright as if illuminated from within.

The door too would be splashed with Timothy Patrick Corcoran's blood. The vivid brass doorknob, smeared with it.

As if the dying man, in a final spasm of his fierce and inviolable will, had seized the doorknob, meaning to open the door and reenter his house.

His house, though he had not built it, only renovated it.

8 Schuyler Place: the "new" Corcoran house.

Always in family legend and in the speech of those who knew the Corcorans it would be the "new" house in Maiden Vale where Timothy Patrick Corcoran died on the eve of the first Christmas he would have spent in the house. God striking the man down on his very doorstep in a section of Union City where you would not expect God to interfere with the affairs of men at all.

Timothy Patrick Corcoran had brought his wife Theresa and his eleven-year-old son Jerome to live at 8 Schuyler Place in January 1959. Their "old" house was 1191 Barrow Street in Irish Hill, in southwest Union City: Our Lady of Mercy parish, the sixth police precinct: bounded by Grand Boulevard to the north and the waterfront of Lake Erie to the west and the city limits of industrial Shehawkin to the south and Decatur Boulevard and the railroad and stockyards to the east. But even in Irish Hill, in these post-War years, it was rare for a man to die riddled with bullets in the back on his own front step on Christmas Eve.

Timothy Patrick Corcoran, born Union City, New York, on November 7, 1923. Died Union City, New York, on December 24, 1959.

Timothy Patrick Corcoran, baptized and confirmed and married in the Holy Roman Catholic faith but deprived at the hour of his death of extreme unction, the last sacrament of the Church in which in any case he had not believed since childhood though in fact when the first bullet tore into his body and he understood that this was Death, this was the explosive fiery Death he'd several times escaped in Korea, in the mute astonishment of those quick-staccato seconds preceding the obliteration of his consciousness like chalk marks erased from a blackboard he did pray *God help me!*

Understanding at that moment for the first time in his life that it does not matter if you believe in God or not. Or if there is God or not.

For what *is* passes so swiftly and irrevocably into what *was*, no human claim can be of the least significance.

God erupted, and was gone. After the deafening thunder and shattering glass, a terrible silence.

And in that silence, rapidly retreating, diminishing, the sound of the invisible car sharply turning the corner at Schuyler Place and careening north on Summit to the Millard Fillmore Expressway and so out of Union City as if speeding off the edge of the world even as the dying man too slipped over.

Inside the house, a woman began to scream.

The child heard the gunshots, and the careening car, and he knew at once, but he hadn't heard, hadn't known, just stood there paralyzed.

He was eleven years old. Now his life would be rent in two.

What you know but can't comprehend. What tears through you changing you utterly.

Thunder?—and no lightning? Can there be a thunderstorm in the winter, in falling snow?

You wanted to think it came from the sky. Not from the street.

The fiery explosive cracks of a gun, too swift to be counted though he heard each separate and distinct and terrible, and the sudden acceleration of a car out on the street, little more than a shadowy blur glimpsed through the window—he knew, and didn't know. He was panting, sweaty inside his clothes. Not standing at a window but back from it, maybe three feet away, having just run into his room tugging off the heavy cable-knit sweater his Grandmother Corcoran had knitted for him that left him breathless—having just bounded up the back stairs heavy on his heels, his cheeks stinging numb from the cold and snowflakes melting in his hair and eyelashes and his nose running he'd been wiping on his fingers—he heard and he knew, but he hadn't heard and didn't know.

He'd just entered the room that after nearly twelve months did not seem familiar to him, nor comforting, like the new house to which his father had brought them, for which he felt a kind of frightened defiant pride, but no liking, and he hadn't switched on the light, he hadn't intended to stay in the room but just to get rid of the heavy sweater and use the bathroom and hurry back downstairs, his head was flooded with Christmas, Christmas Eve and Christmas morning and the twelve-foot evergreen in a corner of the living room with its high churchy ceiling, glittering ornaments he'd helped his mother hang and tinsel crisscrossing like exposed nerves and silver icicles and gaudy colored "bubble" lights he'd helped his father attach by tricky springs and screws to the boughs where they were meant to simulate (last night Jerome had seen, suddenly, what everyone else must know, what was so obvious) upright flames. He'd tugged off the heavy green sweater snug and airless as armor his face flushed and nose damp and he'd tossed it carelessly in the direction of his bed, yes he'd been facing the window but seeing nothing, not a car but a vague impression of a car's shape, a vehicle moving slowly or in fact stopped, out by the curb, beyond the snowy rectangle that was a part of the front lawn, no headlights, in the dreamily falling powdery snow, but none of this made any impression upon him, for why should it?—he was not a child who looked hard or sharply or with an impersonal curiosity at things which seemingly did not pertain to him and in that suspended moment before the stillness of Schuyler Place was rent it could not have been possible for Jerome Corcoran to guess that a shadowy vehicle at the curb could in any way pertain to him.

(If he'd thought about it, which he had not, he'd have supposed that friends of his parents were dropping by. It was Christmas Eve, and the big day for the Corcorans was Christmas Day, forty guests for dinner? relatives, friends? and God knew how many others dropping by casually for drinks, as in previous years they'd come crowding uproariously into the house on Barrow Street, mostly men, business associates of the Corcoran brothers Timothy and Sean, wholesalers, suppliers, customers for whom Corcoran Brothers Construction Co. had built buildings, union officials, politicians, police officers, the Mayor and his family—that would be to-morrow, the Corcorans' first Christmas Day in the new house, but this afternoon, someone might be dropping by to see his mother, or his father, in another minute the unfamiliar startling dolorous chimes of the front doorbell might sound, that was what he'd have supposed if he'd thought about it. Which he had not.)

Standing rooted to the spot incapable of thinking at all.

As if the incomprehensible noise, its sharp cracking volume, had blasted his head empty.

The green-glowing numerals of the clock radio beside his bed, a kid's toy of a clock, red plastic spaceship, his eyes took them in—4:20. Yes but he hadn't seen. Would not remember.

And then the car, the abrupt gunning of the motor, the skidding protest of rubber tires on pavement that, at other times, thrilled the child in the pit of the belly so he grinned with anticipation of the time when he'd be old enough to own a car like the older guys at Our Lady of Mercy, and to drive it in just such a way, burning rubber, racing other drivers from ground zero at stop signs—hearing the car take off on Schuyler Place where no one ever drove like that the panicked thought came to him *They don't belong here* and *Something's wrong* and his heart began to pound so his body shook and there was a pinch and a loosening in his bowels so he nearly fouled his pants but still he hadn't known.

Until, downstairs, his mother began to scream.

He ran to his mother, where she called for him. Though not calling his name, nor any name. Only raw anguished sound like an animal in pain.

The floor tilted beneath his feet. His breath was ragged, panting.

He knew, now. But could not know what he knew.

His knees were weak, he was in terror of falling headlong down the stairs. He grabbed at something—a smooth-polished railing they called, in this house, a banister.

A fleeting glimpse of a child's parchment-pale face in a mirror rimmed with sprigs of holly. Tall red candles with wicks not yet burnt, to be lit for Christmas Eve. A glimpse too, through the arched doorway of the living room, of the immense gorgeous Christmas tree and the shining presents stacked beneath.

What was the present Jerome Corcoran anticipated—a pair of new ice skates, for ice hockey?

Already none of it mattered. It was over.

This was not a stairs he descended in such panic but a staircase. He'd seen his father's carpenters working on it, he'd seen the thick plush crimson wool runner hammered down, and the plasterers, one of them a black man, troweling in the elegant oyster-white ceiling and walls, still none of it looked familiar as he ran panting and whimpering. Mommy?—Mommy? *Daddy?*

A scrawny undersized kid, a look of the father about the eyes and the mouth, the left front tooth just perceptibly larger than the right and serrated, and the tight-curly red-russet hair like Tim Corcoran's, but physically he took after Theresa who was small-boned, five feet one inch, it was his secret terror that he would not grow to be of even average height among the boys of his class and of the rough and sometimes frantic schoolyard, praying to God, and to Jesus, and most passionately to Holy Mother Mary, that he would grow, he would grow inches in a single year, never would he beg for anything again. Spindly arms and legs and his ears sticking out like a donkey's from his head when his hair was newly cut, how that infuriated him, mouthing silent obscenities at himself in the mirror which he dared not utter aloud, even to himself, because to utter such words aloud was sinful and each Saturday afternoon in the confessional he was obliged to confess all his sins to Father Sullivan for in the confessional he could not lie because to lie would be to compound the original sin and remedy nothing. And even as a young child Jerome Corcoran had inherited his father's stubborn pride and contempt for lying, for what was lying but an admission of cowardice at being fearful of speaking Truth?

Scared cards can't win, a scared man can't love.

And, the droll tossed-off phrase Tim Corcoran would say out of the corner of his mouth, *Never race a train.*

At the bottom of the staircase where the steps fanned out and widened he felt the shock of cold air (the front door must have been wide open?) and heard his mother's breathless screams which pierced the air like a continuation of the shattering glass he now realized he'd heard at the time of the gunfire and he realized was the glass of the window of the front door only when he saw that the window was broken, glinting shards of glass on the tile floor of the entryway they called, in this new house, the foyer.

Mommy—?

On this afternoon of Christmas Eve 1959 there were others in the house at 8 Schuyler Place—Timothy Corcoran's sixty-two-year-old widowed mother, Theresa Corcoran's cousin Agnes visiting from Albany, the shy gat-toothed Deirdre from Ballyhoura, Ireland, who helped with housework—but it was eleven-year-old Jerome Corcoran who first discovered his mother kneeling over his father's lifeless body on the front stoop of the house amid the lightly falling snow, her hands shining with blood and blood soaked into the long tight sleeves and the pleated bosom of her lavender wool-jersey dress.

Theresa's eyes were opaque and blind and mad as she screamed, staring at Jerome without recognition.

J ust tell us what you heard and what you saw, son."

"I heard the gunshots and I heard the car."

"You saw the car?—from this window here?"

"No. I didn't see the car."

"You heard the car, eh? The car taking off."

"Yes."

"You didn't hear the car pull up, you didn't see the car, before the shots started?"

"I guess not."

"How many shots were there?"

". . . a lot."

"Did you hear six shots?"

"I guess so."

"Then you heard the car start up. Pull away."

"Yes."

"Going in which direction?"

"That way."

"That way, right. So you saw the car?"

"I guess I saw it then, I don't know."

"You saw it, or you didn't see it, son? Which?"

"I saw it move . . . I don't know."

The child's voice might have been a girl's voice, thin and taut. There was the male fear that he might burst into tears, and no woman in the room to comfort him.

McClure, the eldest of the four men in Jerome's room, spoke in a kindly voice to him; from time to time, as now, he let his warm, heavy hand fall upon the child's thin shoulder. Jerome had been told he'd met Detective McClure at family gatherings, McClure was a distant cousin of his mother's, but Jerome had no memory of having met him as he had little memory of the faces of most adults.

"Show us where you were standing again, son," McClure said.

Jerome wiped his nose on his fingers. Went to reposition himself near the edge of the rust-colored shag rug at which, until the morning of this day that was, yet was not, Christmas Day, he did not believe he had as much as glanced.

It was a new rug with a rough grassy texture selected by his mother for his new room in the new house but he'd had no purpose in considering it until now. Had he not known that this was the rug he'd been walking on sometimes barefoot for the past eleven months he could not have identified it in a display of rugs.

How the world now was being slowed down and opened up and all you'd never looked at and never thought of was revealed as there, waiting, all along.

His knees were shaky, the men could see his legs trembling. He moved slowly like a man eager to give the impression of being sober while prepared, from past experience, to discover that he is not.

"There?" McClure frowned. "Before, you were standing a little more over this way by the window."

He did not move. He was feeling the subtle strain of adult male kindness, patience, pity. He knew it had a sudden breaking point. Still, he did not move. ". . . I took off the sweater, and threw it on the bed."

"This sweater, eh?—your grandma knitted it? I got one just like it. Except mine's some other color, I forget." Jerome's Uncle Sean, who was sitting on Jerome's hastily made-up bed, leaned over with a grunt to touch a sleeve of the green cableknit sweater folded now atop a bureau. In a curiously tender gesture he lifted the sleeve, then let it drop. "And larger, eh?" He made a hissing sound meant to be laughter.

Sean Corcoran had not slept the previous night, you could see he'd been drinking. You could see he was dazed by the murder of his younger brother Tim and the shock of it allowed him not to be thinking at the moment that he was terrified as well.

There had been threats made against both the Corcoran brothers' lives over the years but such threats had, in the past, dissipated, or had been caused to dissipate. This, the child knew without knowing a single fact pertaining to it.

Sean Corcoran, forty-one, had a boy's high-colored slapped-looking face, ravaged incredulous veiny pale eyes like peeled grapes. He had a high round belly and an exposed pink scalp across which wisps of fading red hair were combed. Like Tim Corcoran, and like their deceased father before them, Sean Corcoran always wore a freshly laundered starched white long-sleeved shirt and a necktie no matter the occasion, and no matter his condition or grooming or disposition, and so, on the day following Tim Corcoran's murder, he was so dressed, though unshaven and unwashed.

Jerome looked to his uncle for solace but Sean was chain-smoking Camels knocking ashes about the floor and bed. In his right hand he held a pint of Johnnie Walker which out of courtesy or ritual he offered to the three other men, and, when they were obliged to decline, he sipped from it himself and wiped his pale fleshy lips with his knuckles. Some time ago Uncle Sean had been a bricklayer, his hands showed the wear.

"Jerome, y'want some?"—Sean lifted the bottle in the child's direction.

The child would have said yes, he'd tasted whiskey, and many times beer, in the past, offered him by his father. But he shook his head, no, as McClure's fingers on his shoulder subtly yet unmistakably urged him forward.

"Step closer to the window, son. Right about here."

Jerome did so. He too had not slept the previous night. He had to narrow his sore, swollen eyes against the glaring light. Outside, the world was vividly white with snow and thrumming with the hurtful clarity of an overexposed photograph. Yesterday's dusk of snowfall and shadow was vanished as if it had never been and could not ever be again. A bright frigid-blue sky, a hard wind off Lake Erie blowing snow fine and sinuous as sand across the sidewalk in front of 8 Schuyler Place and the narrow street and the dune-like snowy contours of the little park, of about the size of an acre, across the street. A dozen or so handsome old brick or stone or stone-and-stucco houses overlooked Schuyler Place and the child had the unmistakable sense that these dignified houses were contemplating 8 Schuyler Place which, on this Christmas Day of 1959, was the only property here to be cordoned off by order of the Union City Police Department. The only property in whose driveway and at whose curb black-on-white vehicles emblazoned UCPD were parked.

"That patrol car at the curb—it's pretty clear to you, isn't it? To your eyes?" McClure spoke kindly; when Jerome did not reply, his kindness deepened. "Son, I know it's hell. Oh Christ, I know. But you need to re-member now before you forget."

Sean said, in a voice on the verge of a sob, "Jerome, you're our only witness."

Jerome shook his head to clear it. He'd heard the question but could not remember it. His mother had been hospitalized the night before at Holy Redeemer Hospital downtown for what they called shock and his grand-mother too had been hospitalized there for what they called a stroke. His father's body was at Donnelly's Funeral Home on Erie Street because he had been murdered, shot in the back, but it was possible to think, in fact it was quite natural to think, with the hallucinatory ease of an open-eyed dream, that Tim Corcoran was simply out of the house as he was so often, yes even on Sundays and a day like Christmas, down at Corcoran Broth-ers Construction Co. which the family called the business meaning both the business itself and the buildings and lumberyard that housed it. Or he might be inspecting a work site. Or driving one of his own trucks.

Many times the child had ridden in the cab of one of these trucks with Tim Corcoran at the wheel. Once, in a cement mixer. You were in terror that the heavy truck would overturn, the globe containing the liquid ce-ment might cease its grinding revolution, but of course that did not happen.

Many things holding the promise of terror and grief did not happen.

McClure said again, now easing his arm around Jerome's shoulders, "Son, just tell us what you heard and what you saw. Take your time if you need to."

"I told you." His lips which were raw and chapped moved painfully but no sound came. He was needing to pee again. Sick too with dread of crying as of fouling his pants and of doing these things without being con-scious of them even as others winced at his shame. There was no woman in the room, only men, another plain-clothes detective beside McClure, and a uniformed officer with a badge and a smartly gleaming holstered pistol, and the angry befuddled stubble-jawed drunken man who was his Uncle Sean sitting, big, burly, so out of place there, on Jerome's bed. By the twitching squinting way Sean Corcoran repeatedly glanced over his shoulder toward the door, you could tell he half-expected Tim to enter the room and stride inside and, smiling, perplexed, ask in that way of his, *O.K., what the hell's going on here?*

McClure said, in a lowered voice, "A man like Tim Corcoran shot in the back by human scum, we're gonna get them, they're dead meat. We know that, and they know that. You're our only eyewitness, son. Just tell us what you saw."

Jerome drew away from the detective's arm. He said, not looking at any of them, nor even at the street where the UCPD vehicles were parked, but somewhere, inviolable and stubborn, inside his head, "I told you, you don't listen. I came in here and took off my sweater and . . . it happened."

"The gunshots."

"The gunshots and the car."

"You didn't see the car?"

"I thought it was thunder at first. I don't know. I didn't know it was from the street."

"O.K., then the car took off, fast, and you saw?"

"I couldn't see! It happened too fast! It was too late!"

McClure was a man in his fifties, with a face that, like Sean Corcoran's, was flushed and slapped-looking, though his hot, humid breath did not smell of drink. His inheld fury and the tension of his smile reminded Jerome of his father's passion at being thwarted, if only by a stiffening of posture and a shifting of the eyes, and the danger you risked in thwarting him, especially before witnesses.

The other detective began to speak, but McClure cut him off with a rude gesture. "Son," he said, "the car you saw out there yesterday was for a fact a black DeSoto four-door, 1958 model, and the front and rear license plates were covered in ice or frozen mud but they were New York State plates, for a fact, black on orange, you could make out that much and maybe part of the number which was eight eight one two MCF."

McClure paused, then went on, "And one of these filthy cocksuckers is likely to be the man who shot your father in the back."

McClure thrust into Jerome's face two photographs at which, uncomprehending at first, the child stared. McClure held a photograph in each hand and each hand was trembling just perceptibly. One was of a young-ish insolent-eyed man with a downturned scar of a mouth and the other was of an older and heavier man with a V-shaped hairline and a full, fleshy nose and close-set eyes like something dead and skinned. The photos must have been police mug shots, grainy black-and-whites of about the size and quality you would get in the self-service booth at Woolworth's. McClure was holding them unnecessarily high and close to Jerome's face as if he believed Jerome nearsighted or slow-minded.

Jerome stammered, "Wh-who are they?"

"You wouldn't know their names, son," McClure said, "—we know their names and we know the name of the scum of the earth who hired them. That's our business. If you got a look at the one with the gun, he'd've been in the back seat with the window down, or the driver, that's what we'd hoped to hear, but if you can't . . . the main thing is the car, son, you saw the car, eh? Right out there?"

The other detective spoke now. His voice was excited, urgent. "The DeSoto, sedan, black car, eh? 1958 model? A kid your age knows cars, Jerome, right?"

And Sean Corcoran said loudly, "Jerome? Do what you can for your father. Just tell us?"

There was a silence. McClure repositioned the photos in such a way that he could contemplate them himself. "You wouldn't know their names, Jerome," he said carefully. "They're known to us. And the man who they work for. You maybe got a glimpse of their faces when the car was starting up."

Slowly Jerome shook his head. "No."

"No, what?" McClure asked.

"I didn't see the car, and I didn't see the men. It happened too fast."

There was another silence. It was silence like a deep crevice in the mountains (Jerome was thinking of a scene in the movie *Shane* of a few years before, it was a movie he'd loved and wept over) into which you could fall and fall.

Then Sean Corcoran lurched to his feet. He came to squat clumsily in front of Jerome who shrank from him fearful of being struck but his uncle was sobbing, as a man sobs, not in sorrow but in anger, and in the befuddlement of anger, crushing Jerome in his embrace. His breath was like fumes. His arms were hard, tight, desperate. "They killed Tim Corcoran, shot him down like a dog, but we'll get the filthy bastards, Jerome, we know who they are, send them to hell to rot, just give us a hand for Christ's sake!"

Jerome whispered, "Uncle Sean, I didn't see it."

"—The fact of it is known, the identities of the men are known, and the car, you were standing here and you saw it, you must have seen it, you're not blind are you for Christ's sweet sake? for Christ's sweet fucking sake, Jerome, you're not blind?"

It went on like this for some time, Christmas Day of 1959.

5

Y ou would not guess a man had died in so quiet a setting. The snow again falling, thicker now, like sleep coming on.

Always Jerome Corcoran would recall how nothing that *is* has the power to evoke what *was*.

How Time, not like a clock's hands that circle the hours forever, runs in one direction only. Like a river, or an arrow. The trajectory of a bullet.

Though Tim Corcoran had tried, taking Jerome each Memorial Day to Our Lady of Mercy Cemetery where for an hour or more father and son would move along the rows of markers sticking six-inch American flags into graves of veterans some of whom Tim Corcoran had known. What strange faltering uncharacteristic language issued from the elder man's mouth, what vague strickenness of manner came over him as at no other time, the child tried not to contemplate. He loved Daddy and was privileged to accompany Daddy on any excursion but the embarrassment and tedium of Memorial Day chafed at him like the scratchiest of woollen shirts.

And now, the snow falling upon the fan-shaped front stoop of 8 Schuyler Place which had been scrubbed clean of Tim Corcoran's blood and which no one would cross, leaving the house by the side door, to be driven to the funeral.

The snow falling, flakes the size of blossoms, into the park across the street.

Maiden Vale in northwest Union City had long been closed to the Irish of the south side. The Irish were considered like Negroes, Tim Corcoran had said, not bitterly so much as bemusedly, with his quizzical dented smile. We were considered shit on their shoes, kid.

Whose shoes? Jerome had asked, astonished and incensed.

Well he knew what *shit* was, well he knew the unspeakable insult.

A volatile, restless, quick-tempered child, some would say a spoiled child, the only issue of parents who'd wanted more children but whom God had thwarted. Making his father laugh unabashedly with love at his outbursts of Corcoran temper, Corcoran pride.

They liked it too, as families like, love, cherish, prize, any sign that seemingly links the generations, suggesting how the past never yields to the future but in fact directs it, determines it, and is in turn preserved in it, how the little boy resembled, in hair and facial features, the old man. Even to the slightly oversized left front tooth with the milky ripple to its enamel, and the serrated lower edge he would run his tongue over, and over, and over, through his life.

The s.o.b.'s already living there, Tim Corcoran said. His smile broadening so now you saw his teeth. That thought they were superior to us because they had more money.

Now it isn't so? Jerome demanded. They don't believe that, now?

Snow covered Schuyler Park uniformly except for the narrow curving paths which had not been shoveled since the last snowfall, only trodden upon, footprints over footprints. In warm weather the park was a rectangle of close-cropped very green grass of the type grown on golf courses. There were beds of roses and a creeping ground cover like silver moss and trees of that tall, peeling species called plane trees which Jerome had never seen in Irish Hill and which to his scornful eyes looked diseased, tin-colored bark in strips like rotting wallpaper. But Theresa said how beautiful, so quiet, so few people ever there unlike Dundonald Park on the south side. Unlike any park she'd ever lived near. Yet what a pity— and this uttered in Theresa's breathless, vehement laugh, signaling one of her teasing or daring or provocative remarks—Jerome's too grown now for a baby, or I could push him there in his stroller! that sweet stroller with the candy stripes!

Yes, and Theresa saw the very bench she'd sit on, beneath one of the plane trees, rocking Baby's stroller with one slender foot as shutting her eyes she let her head fall back and lifted her face in gratitude to the sun.

At these words of Theresa's, Tim Corcoran grew very still and made no reply.

Nor did Jerome, who understood that, when Mommy was in one of her breathless laughing moods, her eyes shining with deceptive joy and her fingers picking at one another, it was wisest to remain silent.

No swings or teeter-totters in Schuyler Park. Few other children his age. And if there'd been, would their parents have allowed them to play with Jerome Corcoran?

Shit on their shoes, kid. So they thought.

But no longer, Daddy? They don't believe that, now?

The first and only summer he'd lived at 8 Schuyler Place in Maiden Vale he'd gone back numberless times to the old neighborhood, to Dundonald Park which was a real park and where he'd played all his life he could remember. The wading pool, the swimming pool, the softball diamond, the hilly patches of scrubby littered grass, his friends. He was a boy with friends. Kids like himself whose families all knew one another or were in fact related by blood. Living in Our Lady of Mercy parish in woodframe, brick, stucco houses with small neatly tended lawns on Barrow Street, Roosevelt, Dalkey, Dundonald. If neither Daddy nor Mommy was free or in a mood to drive him back he'd take city buses. *Summit* to *Union Blvd.* then a pink transfer to *S. Erie.* The same route he took to school. In the years beyond childhood he would recall the Union City Transit buses with a distaste verging upon fury but in fact at the time he'd liked them well enough as children like well enough, or more than well enough, the circumstances of their childhood which have made them happy.

Or even unhappy. For the childhood is your own, in any case.

As a dream, even a nightmare, is your own.

Taking the rattling city buses, a quarter dropped into the till back into the old neighborhood. Irish Hill. *Why did we ever leave?* Just as Daddy, Mommy, Grandma Corcoran who insisted upon eight o'clock mass at Our Lady of Mercy every day except Sunday (Sundays, they went to high mass at eleven) were always going back. And of course Corcoran Brothers Construction Co. was there.

And all the family, and their friends. Everyone, everything, was there.

So it was: Theresa Corcoran the beautiful wife of the aggressive Irish construction company co-owner Tim Corcoran, a new and proud resident of the former Keiffer home at 8 Schluyer Place, might sit beneath the great plane tree in the little park across the street, in a white puckered cotton dress, frowning in concentration at the knitting needles flashing in her fingers, she might sit there for a long summer afternoon, or for a year, or the rest of her life, a round-faced young woman with wavy dark hair and a quick eagerness to her, something both hurt and hopeful in her eyes, but no, no one in this new and so strangely quiet and seemingly underpopulated neighborhood was likely to approach her to exclaim, "Well

now, hello, isn't it a fine day?" and still less were women of the neighborhood likely to drop by her house of a morning to welcome her as, in Irish
Hill, they would have done nearly as soon as the curtains were up in the
windows signaling the new family was moved in.

As Tim Corcoran might have told her. Kissing her, and teasing her,
in his laughing way so she would not hear the fury in his voice, *Why set
yourself up to be humbled?—you're a ridiculous woman!*

Why then did you marry a ridiculous woman?—you're the fool.

Because I am a fool, why else?

Staring at her with such love, such hunger, if the child Jerome happened to see he'd have to look quickly away.

The wake for Tim Corcoran at Donnelly's which was the most crowded
of wakes in Irish Hill since that of the notorious McNamara the ex-Police
Commissioner in 1957, and the following morning at eleven o'clock the
funeral at Our Lady of Mercy which was more crowded still.

Hundreds of mourners from Irish Hill and other parts of Union City
including Edgewater on the lake where well-to-do Irish-American families like the Slatterys lived yet not a single person from Maiden Vale except the female real estate agent who'd sold Tim Corcoran his new house.
For though there were neighboring houses on Schuyler Place there turned
out to be no neighbors living in them, still less friends.

6

Like a dream of dark rippling water the funeral passed leaving him untouched.

It was his first funeral for Theresa had shielded him from the others—elderly aunts, uncles, Grandpa Corcoran six years before.

It was his first funeral for in fact Death had never struck so near.

Strange then to be seated, and everyone staring while pretending not to stare, in a pew at Our Lady of Mercy not the Corcorans' own but at the very front of the church. Where you had no choice but to stare at the casket, the flowers, the dazzling glittering altar, the priest in stiff gold-threaded vestments who was Father Sullivan who'd married Tim Corcoran and Theresa McClure and who'd baptized their baby Jerome Andrew and who, halting and swaying in grief, the sonorous Latin phrases slurred in his mouth, flushed cheeks clumsily shaved and stipples of scarcely coagulated blood on his jaw, was now saying a solemn high requiem mass for the repose of Tim Corcoran's immortal soul.

Drunk and sick, poor Father Sullivan, well you couldn't blame him, so close to the Corcorans and he'd known Tim all of Tim's life, a spasm of coughing at the introit so it seemed he might break down entirely and his young assistant would be obliged to take over, but the old man hung on, stubborn as a bull, damned strong for his age and condition, never would relinquish the sacred chalice at such a time.

None of this was a dream yet it passed like a dream and like a dream too it held the risk of terror, a feather's touch could do it.

For he'd been staring hypnotized at the casket which was massive, gleaming black, sleekly shaped like a seagoing vessel and so how horrible it must be laid in the earth instead. And the lid shut close over Tim Corcoran's handsome face. . . . The horror of this too swept over Jerome, that his father might open his eyes to pitch blackness, buried alive, waking only to suffocate, trapped in a box, in the earth, the unspeakable horror of it of which Jerome could not bear to think even as he could think of nothing else.

At the wake the previous day the lid of the casket had been open. What terrible injuries had been done to Tim Corcoran, to the base of his skull where a .45-caliber bullet had entered, no one could see.

Jerome had contemplated the man in the casket which was lined with puckered white satin like the inside of a candy box, lying in such a way that Tim Corcoran would have scorned, in a pose of sleep, angelic sleep, a somewhat puffy face, smooth-rouged cheeks, lips manipulated into a faint puzzled smile, and a rosary of amber and silver beads twined in his clasped fingers.

A rosary! Tim Corcoran! Who had not said a rosary in twelve years.

You wondered how Tim's friends, seeing him in such a pose, could keep from laughing.

At the same time there was the presence of the rouged dead man in the candy-box casket there was the uncanny sensation felt by all that, knowing Tim Corcoran, you wouldn't have been surprised to see him show up at his own wake, the real man, tall and ruddy-faced from the cold, and snowflakes melting in his curly-crinkled hair, and his eyes bright with drink, pushing his way into the overheated flower-choked room clapping his friends on the shoulders, taking the women's hands and kissing their cheeks. Here I am, what's going on? It's Christmas, isn't it?

Jerome was urged at last to approach the casket and to kiss his father goodbye. There were so many weeping, choking women, women who'd loved Tim Corcoran, Jerome set himself apart from them defiant and dry-eyed. He leaned over the casket, he shut his eyes and held his breath and kissed the waxy rouged cheek. His heart slammed against his ribs. His bowels clenched. He thought calmly, This is not Daddy, this is someone else.

So it was all right.

Just tell us what you heard and what you saw, Jerome.
  Not blind, son, are you?
  Our only witness.

His mouth was so fucking dry, he swallowed repeatedly. The sour brackish stink of his breath rising in his own nostrils as when he woke from sleeping hard, open-mouthed, and his breath was stale.

He paid no heed to the Latin phrases, numbly he knelt with the others, he rose, and stood, and knelt again, and again stood, as the organ thundered overhead and voices sang with a yearning, hungry urgency rising to the curved painted ceiling of Our Lady of Mercy, and none of this he heard, it passed leaving him untouched.

Swaying above the altar railing, in his stiff gold-threaded vestments, the old priest Father Sullivan turned to bless the congregation, his hands pudgy-pale. This was a high mass, a solemn high requiem mass, slow, ponderous, the first solemn high requiem mass of Jerome Corcoran's life. But he scarcely noticed. Recalling how once he'd torn pages out of a comic book, *Tales from the Crypt*, to stop himself from staring at ugly drawings of a man buried alive, he hadn't been able to resist turning back to those pages, the horror of it.

He'd thought, yes it might happen to him. He would never have thought it might happen to his father.

"Jerome?—are you all right?"

His aunt was whispering in his ear. He must have whimpered aloud unaware.

On the far side of Aunt Frances his cousins were sitting, and since his father's death he had not spoken to them, nor looked them in the face. He could not imagine speaking to any of his classmates or friends, now his father was dead. Their pity for him would choke him with rage.

Strange, and uncomfortable, to be sitting here between Uncle Sean and Aunt Frances in the front pew, center, at Our Lady of Mercy. This was not the Corcorans' pew. He had to resist the impulse to glance back at his family's pew, to figure out what was wrong.

Sometimes Tim Corcoran accompanied his wife, son, and mother to mass, but most times he did not. When he did, he hung back in the vestibule or out on the sidewalk to shake hands with his friends, to talk. The women and the little boy went inside, Tim took his time, like the other men in no hurry to enter the church and bless themselves with two fingers of holy water and genuflect and be seated. You half-expected him to hurry inside, to take his place in an unobtrusive corner of the church.

Just tell us, son.

What you heard, and what you saw.

Jerome's guts churned moistly. It was pain caused him to whimper aloud but he steeled himself and did not double over. His anus burnt from scalding shit, he'd been diarrhetic for forty-eight hours.

Aunt Frances, and his mother's cousin Agnes, and Sister Mary Megan Dowd who was an older sister of Tim Corcoran's, an Ursuline nun, had been at 8 Schuyler Place to take care of Jerome. They'd drawn a bath and made him bathe. They'd dressed him in the navy blue wool suit that fitted his shoulders loosely, they'd fastened the snap-on tie at his neck. They'd combed his snarly hair. They'd hugged him, wept over him, prayed in his presence so he stood miserable waiting for it to end. Your mother will be home for the funeral, they said, then later they said, Your mother isn't quite strong enough, the doctor doesn't want to discharge her, maybe you can visit her tomorrow.

Jerome had not asked a word of Mommy. He would not.

They told him his mother loved him and was thinking of him but she wasn't quite strong enough to leave the hospital yet, in a few days maybe, when the doctor said she was ready.

And still Jerome hadn't asked a word of her. Not truly believing he would ever see Mommy again, not even her body stiff as a wax dummy in a casket.

He's in a state of shock, you see, Sister Mary Megan Dowd had whispered.

God damn them to hell for forcing him to sit in a steaming-hot tub, liquid shit had erupted from him, a spasm of gut-pain that left him whimpering and helpless. But fortunately the bathroom door was locked from inside.

Since Christmas Eve everything inside Jerome threatened to turn into liquid and drain away. If he gave in and ate, he vomited it back in a soupy acid gruel. If he drank water or fruit juice, he no sooner swallowed than it forced its way out, burning, as piss.

Tim Corcoran's bowels too had loosened, in the shock of Death. When Jerome had found him, and Theresa bent over him, his nostrils had been assailed by the stench.

There were things you could not believe, for no words can accommodate them.

Theresa had been screaming, and continued to scream, staring at Jerome without recognition. When the ambulance came, and the attendants helped her to her feet, urging her toward the ambulance, she'd screamed at them and tried to claw at their faces.

Jerome did not truly believe he would see her alive again, thus shrewdly he refused to ask a word of her.

He's in a state of shock.

As are we all. Oh, Jesus!

You're not blind for Christ's sweet sake are you?
Our only witness.

At Donnelly's Funeral Home there had been crowds of mourners, and so many flowers, and, here and there, plainclothes policemen.

A rumor had spread through Irish Hill, there would be another killing. For was not Sean Corcoran the next likely target?

Tall vases, gigantic floral displays, white lilies, and white roses, and white carnations, and most spectacular of all white gladioli, you saw the logic of flowers in such a place as the viewing room at Donnelly's, for the eye leapt at once to the dead man in the casket and then moved outward, elsewhere, anywhere else.

Faces swollen with grief, faces ravaged with shock, eyes alit in disbelief and fury, the many Corcoran relatives, the Dowds, Muldoons, Culligans, McClures. Jerome stiffened himself against their rough hugs, their fevered embraces. The tears of the women. The heat of the men's breaths.

There was the rumor, too, Jerome had *seen*.

Jerome was the sole witness, Jerome had *seen*.

Uncle Sean pointed the plainclothes policemen out to Jerome: But don't stare.

People did stare bluntly at the several Negroes who came to the wake, for there were no blacks in Irish Hill and it was not a section of Union City in which blacks were made to feel welcome.

Look!—look. Why are *they* here?

It would be said that many Negroes came to Tim Corcoran's wake but in fact there were six Jerome counted. They came, not with their wives or families, but alone, singly, self-conscious, furtive, stricken too with shock at Tim Corcoran's death but not comfortable sharing their feelings with the whites.

Tim Corcoran had hired these men, carpenters, bricklayers, plasterers, nonunion labor, for off-site noncontractual work, after hours. He'd used a black truck driver for one of his gravel trucks for maybe a week until the Teamsters tossed a firebomb through the window of the man's house in Shehawkin.

Tim Corcoran had said, A black guy saved my ass in Korea, fuck the unions I'll hire anybody I want.

Won't the unions let them join? Jerome asked. Why not?

Why? Tim Corcoran laughed derisively. Because they're assholes, kid. White asshole cowards.

Telling him then about Jack Dempsey who wouldn't fight a black heavyweight, knowing he'd lose the title.

In Korea, he'd been a POW and this black kid from Georgia had helped him when they had to march, he'd had a sprained swollen ankle and couldn't have made it without this kid helping him, so fuck the unions I'll hire anybody I want.

Jerome observed one of the black men staring at Tim Corcoran for a long time, a look on his face of horror and regret and amazement and hurt. This was a tall burly plum-brown-skinned man of no age Jerome could guess, eyes protuberant and livid with broken capillaries, a splayed nose, lips wide and thick as if swollen as, once, stung by a bee in Dundonald Park, Jerome had felt his upper lip swell like a balloon, tight to bursting. When at last the black man turned, to approach him, Jerome recognized him as one of the plasterers who'd worked on renovations at the new house.

Ignoring the stares of others, who were not hostile precisely so much as rudely curious, the man expressed his sympathy to Jerome, said how sorry he was, what a nasty surprise, at Christmas, too, what a good man Jerome's father was, nobody would forget what a good man he was, and Jerome mumbled thank you, he'd learned that day to say thank you, it was all you could say, thank you, and the black man said again, louder, what a good man Mr. Corcoran was, nobody like him in Union City for sure, and Jerome said thank you, he was swallowing repeatedly, his mouth dry as caked dust, and the black man finally just stared at him with a look of inarticulate grief, grief sharp as hunger, there was nothing further to say in the presence

of Death so he mumbled goodbye and backed off eager now to escape and
Jerome wiped at his eyes unable to remember the man's name but it was a
fact: every Negro worker his father had introduced him to over the years,
Jerome had forgotten the name almost immediately.

Is that one of them? someone asked. One of *them?*

Jerome's uncle Mike Donnelly was speaking to Sean Corcoran the two
men staring after the black man, and Sean said, not lowering his voice,
Who else?—no good reason for any nigger to come to Irish Hill, except
he helped get my brother killed.

You knew certain facts without knowing you knew. Without having
to ask.

Bricklayers' and Allied Craftsmen's Local Union No. 19. Carpenters'
Local Union No. 6. Plumbers' and Steamfitters' Local Union No. 11.
International Brotherhood of Electrical Workers Local 273 AFL-CIO.
Glaziers' Local No. 8. Insulators' and Asbestos Workers' Local 71. International Union of Operating Engineers Local No. 42. Painters' Local
Union No. 112. Roofers' Local Union No. 52. International Brotherhood
of Teamsters Local No. 161. The Mohawk County Central Labor Council of the AFL-CIO. The Western New York Trade Union Council. With
all of these at one time or another there had been disputes, negotiations,
threatened or actual slowdowns or strikes, and contracts; and yet again,
when these contracts ran out, disputes, negotiations, threatened or actual
slowdowns or strikes, and new contracts. (The newest contract, the largest Corcoran Brothers had ever negotiated, was for $12 million to build a
twelve-storey addition to City Hall, downtown at Union Boulevard and
Brisbane.) Corcoran Brothers Construction Co. was thriving in the late
1950s and Tim Corcoran was in the habit of rubbing his big-knuckled
hands together saying aggressively, Hell, I like a good fight: I'm a counterpuncher like my old man.

Son, you're our only witness.
Not blind are you, son?

They had not questioned him this morning, and would not, for this was
the morning of his father's funeral. They had questioned him for two

hours on Christmas Day and they had returned to question him the following day, though there was female screaming in the house Let him alone! Let the child alone! which he seemed not to hear himself, let alone acknowledge. And in the interstices of these exhausting and confusing sessions Uncle Sean shut the two of them away to speak with him in private, gently and even tenderly at first with the air of an adult nudging a sleeping child awake, then more insistently, impatiently. Sure you saw, Jerome, it's a fact they were there, who d'you think shot him if there wasn't anybody there, c'mon shut your eyes you can summon it back plain as day, 1958 black DeSoto, part of the license number, MCF, a kid your age knows cars for Christ's sweet sake.

And in the limousine driving to Our Lady of Mercy this morning, down from Maiden Vale, Uncle Sean was whispering to him, not very coherently for he'd been drinking much of the night, and Aunt Frances leaned over, incensed, and gave her husband a shake, Leave the child alone! Are you mad, are you drunk on this day of all days, for shame, for shame, the day of your own brother's funeral!

To Jerome she'd said, Pay no attention to that man, he isn't in his right mind these days. None of us are but he's the worst.

You know. You saw, and you know.

For Christ's sweet sake.

Detective McClure was at the funeral mass, Jerome had seen him enter the church, and genuflect, and take a seat inconspicuously at the rear. He wondered if the other detective was here, too. There were uniformed policemen out on the street and a UCPD cruiser would escort the procession of hearse, limousines, cars to the cemetery.

Though he'd died in mortal sin yet Tim Corcoran would be buried in sanctified soil. Catholic soil. In the Corcoran family plot.

Knowing what you know, seeing the effect close up, could you use a gun on a man? Fire bullets into the base of his skull, into his back? his lungs, heart? So that he coughed and vomited blood, and spilled his bowels, his insides exploding out?

For your father's sake, Jerome. Just tell us.

A bell was ringing briskly. The Holy Eucharist was being raised that God might see it, and rejoice.

Time for communion. Until this moment Jerome had not thought of communion. Had he not violated his fast by drinking water that morning to cleanse his mouth of vomit?—yes but he did not care, not in the slightest. These many minutes he'd been gazing at the casket in the aisle, before the communion rail, this strange beautiful polished black vessel that contained what was called Tim Corcoran's earthly remains, and it was not possible to know of other things, still less to care.

"Jerome, dear?—are you all right?"

Anxious, and fussy, like all women, his aunt peered into his face, gently waking him from his trance. He mumbled a reply. He did not lift his eyes to hers.

And now he was in the aisle, urged along, Uncle Sean leading the way and it was not Jerome himself but his body on numbed legs shuffling forward to the communion rail where the old priest, eyes ghastly as Death, stood waiting.

It was the supreme moment of the mass. It was the sacrifice of Jesus Christ. It was a mystery, one of the sacred mysteries. Jerome knew his catechism, Jerome had been taught and had memorized, this is my body and this is my blood, the body of Christ is present in the communion wafer and the blood of Christ is present in the wine drunk by the priest. You must be in a state of grace cleansed and absolved of all sin to take communion to take the body of Christ into your mouth but he was not in a state of grace and would never again be in a state of grace and he did not care, now his father was dead. He'd paid not the slightest attention to the Latin mass, and this too was a sin, his gaze drifting unseeing over the glittering flower-bedecked altar, over the tall slender figure of Jesus Christ crowned in thorns and bright droplets of blood on His plaster forehead, His crimson heart exposed, well fuck Jesus Christ who hadn't saved Tim Corcoran from dying, fuck God who was helpless or indifferent or not-there, fuck old Father Sullivan with bloodshot eyes, palsied fingers, fuck Bishop Healey who would come to Our Lady of Mercy to say mass for Jerome's confirmation class next year, yes and fuck Pope John XXIII. A spasm of laughter threatened. But if he laughed he'd shit his pants.

Tim Corcoran had not died in a state of grace, he'd died in a state of mortal sin, you knew that. Theresa had teased and begged him about going to confession so he could take communion, if for no other reason than to please his mother, the old woman took such things seriously and why not, who knows, play it safe, my God the man hadn't done his Easter duty from last March, Theresa laughed, call yourself a Catholic?—though in truth she preferred men who showed no great concern for the Church, weak men made her impatient. What if you die in a state of mortal sin, Tim, ever think of that? she'd poked him in the ribs but of course she hadn't meant any of it, hadn't believed he would ever die, nor had Tim Corcoran, winking at his son over Theresa's shoulder as he'd hugged her stopping her hands from slapping at him, Then I'll go straight to hell, eh?—plenty of Corcorans already there.

His aunt was guiding him, it seemed she must love him though he was not her child, they were kneeling at the communion rail like a family except instead of his father there was Uncle Sean and instead of his mother there was Aunt Frances and he understood that the house at 8 Schuyler Place of which his parents had been so proud would be sold and he would return to Irish Hill to live with his uncle and aunt, this time on Roosevelt Street which was just around the corner from the old house at 1191 Barrow Street and maybe his mother would come to live there too, and maybe she would not.

He was kneeling. It would be all right. Behind them others were lined up to take communion, even a solemn high requiem mass was a celebration of the Roman Catholic faith, this is my body and this is my blood, it was what must be done, you did it like the rest and it did not matter because none of it touched you. Jerome let his head fall slightly back as he'd been instructed, it was his body and not him, as the dead man in the coffin was his father's body and not his father, he shut his eyes obediently and opened his mouth so that the tasteless dry wafer could be placed on his tongue, he heard the old priest muttering the words his father had scorned as a dead language, he smelled the old priest's breath which was like fumes, it was all right, it was fine, fuck you all, he got through it without laughing, yes and without shitting his pants.

7

He understood what was needed from him, yet he could not lie. He understood, yes he was the only witness, yet he could not lie.

He ran away from them, from their eyes, climbing steep stairs to find himself at last at a high window in an unheated attic of his uncle's house on Roosevelt Street where never in his life had he been before, and so suddenly happy.

With his fingernails he scraped frost off the windowpane, then breathed on the glass, so that he could see out. Beyond snowy rooftops, beyond the descent of Irish Hill to the lake, were thick, swollen storm clouds at the horizon, above Lake Erie, where lightning winked and flashed with no sound.

Or maybe not lightning: the glow of the industrial sky, the tall fire-rimmed smokestacks of U.S. Steel, Union City Rubber, the chemical refining plants, floodlit high-tension power lines. It was dusk, quickly darkening to night, the boundaries between earth, lake, and sky were ambiguous. And he was drunk.

I can't, he told them, again and again he'd told them, you don't listen, I didn't see it, and they said, You saw, Jerome, but you don't remember, if you were standing by that window and looking out that window you saw, and he told them, his voice rising in despair, and in anger too, I didn't, it was too dark, it happened too fast, *don't tell me what I saw.*

And finally they gave up, the hell with it, and with him.

Not that they were angry with him really—an eleven-year-old kid who'd just lost his father. But they saw the futility of it, coaching Tim Corcoran's son who was too much like Tim Corcoran, bulldog-stubborn, a mind once made up and not to be changed by persuasion.

Always he would remember their disappointment in him, adult male pity tinged with exasperation and disgust. Fuck you, he thought, wiping roughly at his eyes.

He thought, Would it bring my father back from the dead, if I lied?

Downstairs, two floors below, voices rose, beginning to get loud. Occasional laughter. A crowd of them jammed into the house, for the funeral dinner, so-called. It had begun shortly after 1 P.M. and was going strong, indeed gaining momentum, as the day too veered drunkenly to dark. Jerome, fatherless and motherless, had eluded his aunt's anxious eye and accepted from his uncle a glass one-quarter filled with ale, dark, powerfully bitter, Tim's favored drink, and many a man favored it, Twelve Horse Ale it was, a barrel of it brought over by Davy Kiernan who owned Seneca House Bar & Grill. He'd drunk it swiftly down and this pleased the men and Uncle Sean laughed and poured him another, this time half-full, and this too Jerome drank, a little more slowly yet not less purposefully.

Just like his old man, oh sweet fucking Christ.

Later, unwatched, he drank from glasses set down and forgotten, beer, ale, wine, whiskey, a giddy mix of tastes in the mouth and the surprise of fumes rising like twin white-hot wires through the nasal passages and up into the skull and the yet more profound astonishment of the sensation of heat, burning, going down, coating the throat with fire. He had little appetite for food (so much! a feast! the Corcoran women had prepared most of it but others from the neighborhood had brought a good deal too, the table in the dining room opened to its full length and warmly illuminated by both tall Christmas-red candles and the Irish crystal chandelier overhead, bowls of food, steaming casseroles, roast beef and leg of lamb and a gigantic roast turkey and an enormous Virginia ham, loaves of freshly baked bread) but the appetite for drink, he quickly discovered, had no need to be stimulated: it stimulated itself, a thirst that grew in intensity even as it was seemingly satisfied.

Through Irish Hill and no doubt through much of Union City in those frigid waning days of 1959 there were few topics of conversation other than the murder of Timothy Patrick Corcoran, the newspapers too were full of it, even among the man's detractors there was a keen sense of loss and outrage and an impatience that would grow as police reported they were questioning many people, there were indeed suspects, yet no arrests yet, for there were no eyewitnesses to the murder or thus far none had come forward. There were rumors that Tim Corcoran had been gunned down because he'd thumbed his nose, and publicly, at Al Fenske who was president of the Trade Union Council, everyone knew you did not challenge Fenske, or was it that Tim Corcoran had crossed the Teamsters too many times, and this publicly as well. Or had he reneged on a deal (this, Sean Corcoran furiously rejected) to pay off one of the mob-connected aides in Mayor Buck Glover's administration after the City Council voted to award the contract for the addition to City Hall, the biggest local contract in years, to Corcoran Brothers Construction Co. . . . for the contract had gone to the Corcorans, as the *Union City Journal* had revealed in headlines, though their bid had not been the lowest, but, in a short list of six, second highest. (To which implied charge one of Buck Glover's aides issued the statement: *The Mayor knows that quality costs. A low bid means low-quality work.*)

These things Jerome knew, and ran up the stairs to escape knowing. Carrying with him a bottle of Schlitz beer which boldly he'd opened in his aunt's kitchen, for by late afternoon the crowd was such through the house, the very air porous with the bluish gray smoke of cigarettes and cigars, no one was likely to take notice of anything he did if he acted, not with childish subterfuge, but with adult purposefulness and authority.

In the attic he groped for a light switch, shut the door with his foot. But no one would be following him. No one knew he was here.

He stood at the window, he drank, and when the bottle was empty he set it carefully atop an old piece of furniture where somehow it fell and rolled aggressively over his foot.

Never race a train.

He giggled, hearing that voice, and drew his sleeve roughly beneath his God-damned nose which was running again. The funeral was over, the specter of Death shunted aside. There were places that knew nothing of it, this attic for instance. The massed storm-heavy clouds with their lightning flashes and their look of mute impacted rage.

Of Jerome's mother it was evasively said that she was not quite strong enough for visitors, even for Jerome, and he did not ask a word of her, for he knew better. Even before this catastrophe he knew that you did not freely ask to hear news which you did not want to hear for all good news is told you without your needing to ask.

Theresa had been hospitalized in the past. How many times Jerome chose not to recall. She'd had what was called, so oddly, *mis-carriages*, he'd mouthed the strange word aloud, *mis-carriages*, thinking of a horse-drawn carriage overturned and falling into the road, and each had been more terrible than the one preceding, and had required a lengthier stay in the hospital, so he did not ask a word, he stared down at his feet and stood dry-eyed, sullen. Once, he'd told a friend of his what was wrong with his mother, not knowing fully what the word meant, but having an idea, *mis-carriage* he'd said, and the other boy had looked at him in fearful derision, A what? what? and shortly the two were laughing wildly and punching each other. And never did Jerome tell any of his friends again why his mother was in the hospital, nor did he ask any adult about her condition except in the most general terms.

He did recall how, when Mommy was in the hospital those other times, Daddy was likely to get drunk.

Which would not be happening now, would it.

When they'd told him Theresa would not be coming home for the funeral, nor was she ready for visitors, Jerome's muttered response had been a quick O.K.

He was a little dizzy from drinking but it felt good, it felt just right. He pressed his warm forehead against the windowpane and took true comfort from the freezing glass.

He understood his uncle and the detectives would not trouble him again about the car he had not seen, all that was over. Yes and fuck them for he knew they'd been complaining bitterly of him beyond his earshot, well it wasn't to be helped.

Scared cards can't win, a scared man can't love.

Westward the lake lay flat and dully gleaming. At this distance of about a mile and a half its surface appeared featureless, like tin, though, in the perpetual turmoil of wind out of Canada, it would be rough, choppy. Strings of cheap-looking red and green Christmas lights on Dalkey Street dipped toward the waterfront to dissolve in a snarl of glaring, winking lights at the Millard Fillmore Expressway. Those mutely flashing lights beyond might be lightning, or just the lakeshore factories, he squinted but couldn't see. And did it matter. Fuck it, it didn't matter.

The buoyant sensation in his skull so like a balloon filled not just with helium gas but with light and warmth. And his veins coursing too with light and warmth. So the cold up here in the attic, his breath in puffs of steam, did not matter. He understood why his father had liked to drink and why the men downstairs were drinking and why, when at last guests rose to leave, Sean Corcoran grabbed at their sleeves and bawled at them to sit the hell down, it was early yet. Yes and fucking Christmas too, if anybody remembered.

How heavy his eyelids suddenly. He slid to the floor, seeing pinwheels of sparkling lights. Thunder erupted but this time it was muffled as in cotton batting and he saw again the shadowy shape of the car, tires spinning against the icy pavement, then taking hold, the car leaping forward. He saw no faces, he saw no license plate numbers, he stared but did not see, he was blind and could not see, yes and paralyzed too, on the cusp of sleep and then over and inside and safe there until such time as a light would be switched on overhead, hours later, and a man's voice would cry half in reproach, "Poor little bugger, there he *is*."

PART I

FRIDAY, MAY 22, 1992

"NICEST GUY IN UNION CITY, NEW YORK"

What the fuck's holding us up?"

Bright gusty morning like flags flying, the kind of day you're God-damned glad just to be alive and breathing and what's this: a traffic jam?

Corky's more incredulous than angry. Hitting his horn with his fist. Held up?—*now?*

He's driving south on Brisbane, a familiar route, in a familiar nerved-up state along this route meaning sex is imminent, delicious in anticipation, and suddenly God damn a Fed Ex van just ahead of his car brakes to a stop, and Jerome Andrew Corcoran, "Corky" to people he trusts, hits the brakes of his newly purchased $35,000 Cadillac De Ville, lowers his window and leans out—"Hey, shithead, what the hell?"

Corky Corcoran's what you'd call an aggressive driver. Doesn't like surprises on the road unless they're his own.

The one place a man's got to be in control for Christ's sweet sake is his car. Right?

Beyond the Fed Ex van, though, there's a snarl of traffic. Looks like a complete fuck-up through the intersection at Fourth, up the block as far as Corky, leaning out his window, squinting, can see. Must be an accident? God damn, just his luck. 10:48 A.M. and he's on his way to Christina's, wants to get there by 11 at least since he's got an important lunch date, fuck it he's going to be late and it pisses him to be late when it's somebody else's fault not his own.

Out on the street there's this lone cop, young guy, trying to deal with traffic jammed in four directions. Where's his backup? The UCPD's undermanned, last year's budget cuts hurt like hell, but this is ridiculous: one cop! The problem can't be street repair, Corky knows this stretch of Brisbane like the back of his hand and there's no roadwork going on.

Corky knows his way around Union City, New York, like it's the back of his hand, it's *his*. That time the Mayor told one of his new staff members, new to Union City, at a postelection lunch. You want to know about Union City, go hang out with Corky Corcoran, eh Corky?—he's your man.

Jerome Andrew Corcoran, Democrat, City Council member, business-man, a popular guy, "Corky."

Forty-three years old. Not young but anyway not *old*. And he looks a lot younger, a virtual kid sometimes, still.

Assets at about $2 million. Maybe more?

On a terrific morning like this, spring in upstate New York after a wet rainy-sleety winter, rainstorms all last week, as far as Corky's concerned, his life's just getting started.

He's got Christina Kavanaugh, and he's got plans. Even she doesn't know about yet.

That song of the Stones Corky'd be humming under his breath, sopho-more year at St. Thomas Aquinas—*Time is on my side*.

Traffic moves forward a few jerky yards like hiccups then stops. Shit! Corky's all but stalled his heart pounding in a fury as if he's been person-ally insulted in his gleaming-glittering Caddy that's the sexiest car he's ever owned (Corky says this about all his cars and always means it: this one *is*) on his way to an *assignation* with Christina Kavanaugh who's the sexiest woman he's ever been involved with (Corky says this about all his women and always means it but in absolute truth, Christina *is*), God damn he's got to watch it his blood pressure's up. That weird tightening sensation in the chest, not pain, more like a shadow of pain, or a hint of it, a warning, pain to come.

But no, don't think of that now, shithead.

Where's he? Brisbane below Fourth? A new mini-plaza off this busy street, developed by a business rival of Corcoran, Inc.'s, and Corky sees with satisfaction two of the stores are vacant, FOR LEASE. Bush's recession, fucking high interest rates, IRS on everybody's ass except the big money boys the top *Fortune* fucks tight as two fingers up the ass with the Admin-istration, don't tell me this is a free country. Bailing out the savings and loan scumbags, should chop their fingers, ears, balls off, like in—where?

Turkey, Burma. Eye for an eye, tooth for a tooth. You don't fuck around with that kind of justice.

There's a Gap store in the Brisbane Mini-Plaza, though—trendy place, that kind of funky-sexy big-sweater look, cotton knits, pants with fly fronts for girls, when Corky was a step-Daddy (sad, how long ago: he misses it) he'd take his lunch break in the fashionable downtown stores, what's the word, "boutiques," buying things for Thalia, sometimes for Charlotte though Charlotte's taste was hard to predict. Shopping for women's clothes, lingerie, the very word "lingerie" a turn-on, Jesus. Christina lying back on that sofa of hers in the silky-lacy black slip he'd bought for her, sexy as hell and meant half as a joke but, Jesus, it's no joke the power of a woman like that over a man, Corky's sick with love for her and anxious something's going to happen, he's had bad luck with women Christ knows. And no fault of his own.

Corky punches the car horn again. Reflex action like a boxer's jab. Sheer nerves. The Caddy's horn is impressive as a bull elephant trumpeting displeasure but what the hell—Corky knows this, he's a reasonable guy—hitting the horn's futile in a situation like this. You got to feel sympathy for the poor cop out there, blowing his whistle, flush-faced and sweating.

The patrolman's just a kid in his twenties. That freckled-Irish look like Corky Corcoran in fact but he's nobody Corky knows. Though Corky knows, and is known by, a number of UCPD officers, especially at the top. Plus the Police Commissioner. Plus the D.A. Not least the Mayor. And others in the "power elite"—you got to love that term, if you're in it!—of Union City.

Sure, after what happened to Tim Corcoran, Corky'd had fantasies as a kid of becoming a cop, a detective, like McClure, the guys on the TV *Untouchables*, Steve McQueen in the movies, but common sense told him no it's not for you, not enough money and too much shit you have to take, especially in the late Sixties when anybody in uniform was a fascist pig. Just as bad now, maybe worse, more media exposure, those TV "Action News" teams out patrolling the streets looking for trouble. Corky Corcoran would've had to be an honest cop and Union City's a tough place for that, the UCPD hierarchy tight-controlled as the Roman Catholic diocese, lots of secrets you can only guess at when big budgets are involved. And every day harder for the lower-ranked cops. Neighborhood-beat cops, guys on squad patrols or even on the streets. Hard to exert their authority, to get proper respect. And the fallout from the Rodney King verdict in L.A., and a similar local incident, a worse local incident since the black victim died. *Devane Johnson, 12, shot fatally in the back by UCPD Sergeant Dwayne Picket, 34. November 1991.* Christ, what a mess!

Corky's been involved in a City Council review of the UCPD's investigative handling of the case, there's pressure on the Mayor's office from the Policemen's Benevolent Association on the one hand and the Citizens' Crime Commission on the other, pressure from the black community for sure, that's an understatement, plus all sorts of "rainbow" coalitions, would the Council's proposal to set up a new board to investigate not just the Pickett case but the UCPD's Internal Affairs Division violate the City Charter forbidding the Council to change the powers of any elected official without a referendum . . . and so on, and so forth. *Don't think of it now.*

Corky Corcoran's on the record as a liberal Democrat solidly behind every liberal cause there is, for sure he doesn't defend racist killer cops but he figures, he's been interviewed on local TV and radio saying this, calmly and reasonably and fair-mindedly so how could anyone disagree for Christ's sake—If you're a cop on the beat in some of our inner-city neighborhoods where there's open drug dealing and crack houses and turf wars and shootouts between gangs of kids as young as fifteen, plus "domestic violence" that's escalating, and you're up against it every hour you're working, you'd be at risk using "deadly force" in the wrong circumstances, too.

For which utterly reasonable statement, God damn, Jerome Andrew Corcoran has taken heat of his own. *Him!*

Called a honky ass-kisser by black guys whose hands he's shaken in friendship, guys he's gone out of his way to be nice to. For Christ's sake.

(Corky, old family friend and longtime political supporter of Union City's Mayor Oscar Slattery, even closer friend and supporter of Oscar's son U.S. Representative Vic Slattery, wouldn't want it known that he himself owns a gun. Publicly, on the record, Corky's for gun control laws. Any sane citizen is, right? Fuck the NRA. Fuck that crap about citizens bearing arms, that's a red herring set up by the firearms manufacturers, simple as ABC. But, living in Union City, like any big American city, you're crazy not to be realistic. Corky owns just one gun anyway, but it's a sweetie: a Luger automatic 7.65 mm, eight-shot magazine, German-made, a rarity and a collector's item a UCPD detective once handed over to him in a poker game in lieu of cash and like a good citizen Corky's got it registered—homeowner's protection—keeps it in his bedroom in his bedside table. For self-defense. Exclusively. True, a few times he's violated the law, and a pretty tough New York State law it is, carrying the Luger on his person, for a while he carried it in the glove compartment of his car, a specific while and for good reason, but he's never fired the gun except at the target range, never waved it in anybody's face. Charlotte disapproved of the gun on principle but got a charge out of it close beside the bed, sexy Corky with his gun, not that it's *his* gun really, he'd explained to her it's homeowner's protection, for both of us, let's hope we never need to use it, right? Corky has to admit, he likes the Luger. A lot. The classy heft of it. The history. World War II souvenir worth, how much?—thousands of dollars now in 1992. And there's the simple fact of a gun, a gun in your hand, the sexy charge. *A gun in your hand, you're Death with a human face.*)

Still tied up in traffic. Fancy digital clock in the teakwood dash jumps to 10:49 A.M.

Why doesn't he call Christina, he's got a phone right here in the car, explain he'll be late. A few times, waiting for him, she'd said she was worried. Never yet a true quarrel with Christina but once they'd come close, Can't you be considerate of me, can't you think of *me* waiting for *you*, Christina keeping it light, smiling, teasing him running her hands up and down his body so they'd ended up wrestling, kissing, the issue deflected. Corky's on the phone a lot but Corky's not the kind of guy to explain, nor to apologize, just not his nature. None of the Corcoran males. Never show a woman you're anxious, any sign of indecision, weakness, especially regarding her, women despise that in a man.

Reminds them too much of themselves, maybe.

"Fuck it"—Corky hates being stuck like this, trapped in his car. Restless, antsy. Like in church in the old days. In school. Too much adrenaline. Hates being forced to think, bad as his nighttime insomnia, stone cold sober can be a real bummer.

Thinking, *Jesus: I'm almost eight years older than my father lived to be.*

Daddy he'd called him, but afterward *Father*. *Daddy*'s too baby-sounding.

He's three years older than Theresa was when she finally died. Always remember: August 2, 1967. The week after Detroit went up in flames and twelve days before Union City was hit, a black "social club" down by the docks raided by cops and some heads busted and all hell broke loose, three days of "urban unrest" until the cops, the State Troopers, and the National Guard restored order. Not that Theresa knew or cared about "urban unrest." Poor woman so ravaged those final months at St. Raphael's, hearing voices, screaming voices she said, her beauty long eaten away as if by cancer and life a misery to her and everybody around her *Holy Mary Mother of God help me! help me!* Poor Mother in a frenzy stabbing at her wrist with a dull fingernail file, desperate to die. That time I took flowers to her, pushing the vase onto the floor. Having to be restrained snatching up the glass. Not recognizing me at the end. Anyway not acknowledging me.

When you hate your life you come to be hateful. That's why Corky Corcoran's so upbeat. What's the point, otherwise?

Meet my price or it's no deal.

"Schizzy" Corky's come to call Theresa, his way of summing her up, putting distance between them. "Fucked-up" he learned to think of her. Why not? Wasn't it so? Talking of his mother in such terms to Charlotte Drummond whom he was going to marry, how shocked and disapproving Charlotte had been, or pretended to be, hearing a man speak like that of his dead mother, so Corky shrugged and grinned saying, Look, honey: the fucking woman was *my* mother, *I'm* the expert. Right?

Which shut Charlotte up, fast. The rich man's daughter, her widened eyes on Corky Corcoran, assessing.

Yes and liking what she saw. When his clothes were off especially.

Charlotte Drummond, for eleven years Charlotte Corcoran. Never seemed quite real to either of them, that name. Like Charlotte's daughter Thalia Corky adopted, her name Thalia Braunbeck changed to Thalia Corcoran but that never took either, somehow. Why not call the kid Drummond. Cut the bullshit.

Corky'd rather not think of Thalia right now. He's getting hot enough as it is. Sexed up. Charged. Like static electricity is charging his prick and he's stuck here, how many minutes, in fucking traffic when he could be with Christina Kavanaugh. *Hey Corky: do you know what I love about you best? Mmmm?*

Last night when Corky got home (1 A.M. which is early for him: he'd had a few drinks, dinner with an investor interested in developing, with Corcoran, Inc., some riverside property) there was a message from Thalia on his voice mail, twenty-five years old but Thalia can sound like a child over the phone, breathy, mysterious, Corky was alarmed hearing from her after so many months when they've been estranged (Thalia's choice, not Corky's: she's a young woman of unpredictable moods, caprices, grudges) *Corky this is Thalia please call me immediately it's serious I need your help* but, God damn her, when Corky tried the number he has for her, no answer.

Which put him into a cold sweat right away. She's playing games with him. Or *is* she in danger.

This morning, Corky tried the number again. Five, six times. From home, early; and from his office. No answer.

There's an old history of Thalia messing with step-Daddy's head, messing with step-Daddy's marriage in fact. God damn, Corky isn't going to think of her right now.

Chrissie?—know what I love best about you?

Mmmmmm. And that, too.

Corky's drifting into a horny-dreamy reverie like in church as a kid. But he isn't going to jerk off in the fucking Caddy is he.

Hears a siren. What is it?—ambulance? Pretty sure it isn't a firetruck.

Somebody's injured, might be dead. Traffic accident. That's it?

Ahead of the Fed Ex van is a Union City Transit bus, spewing exhaust. Worse idling than in motion. Diesel fuel. Grimy white and snot-green wheezing along the streets like Union City's a Third World country. Corky's pushed for stricter pollution control with city transport, but that costs. Too many years of riding these buses when he was a kid and now he hasn't set foot in one of them in twenty-five years.

10:51 A.M. Corky's mesmerized by the digital clock, Time ticking away, your heartbeat ticking, brains cells popping one by one. That book he's been reading, *A Brief History of Time*, the crippled English guy what's his name, what *is* Time, everybody's got a theory but nobody knows.

What *he* knows: Christina Kavanaugh's waiting for him. Wanting love. Wanting *him*. His cock in her hand, pearly-wet at the tip, astonished when she'd touched him like that, held him, that time in Corky's car when they were so new with each other it scared him to touch her or to be touched by her, and in his car parked across the street from 8 Schuyler at dusk she'd caressed him not so he'd come in her hand which for sure neither of them wanted right then but just to caress, to comfort.

And the last time they'd made love, in Christina's loft on Nott Street. Last Thursday. Late afternoon. After squash at the U.C.A.C. and before dinner with a lawyer-friend of Vic Slattery's and his wife. Christina gripping his back her hands clenched into fists, covered in sweat her hair gleaming black on the pillow whipping her head from side to side *Oh Corky! Oh God! Corky!* her face contorted in a look almost of agony, you'd swear it *was* agony.

Wondering what women feel. Like a steel trap sprung. But it keeps springing. The cunt's contractions, you can feel. Totally out of control. Delirious, raving. Convulsions, when it's really strong. Whereas Corky, sometimes, with some women, many times with Charlotte those last years, it's like his head is at one end and his prick's at the other and there's a detonation sweet and explosive going off he can sure appreciate but isn't inside of. Like that time driving the Expressway with some girl he'd been going out with, name forgotten now, a real tramp, they'd been sharing a joint and she'd masturbated Corky in the car fifty miles an hour in the right-hand lane and Corky swore he never veered out of his lane: *that's* control.

Yes but with Christina it's different. Christina's no tramp.

Christina Corky'd like to marry. Maybe. Never been so happy with any woman as with Christina. *I swear.*

Yes but you wouldn't like me quite so much, lover, would you?—if I were free and unattached.

Surprising Corky with this remark. Out of the blue. Just past the Christmas holiday when (he'd gathered) there'd been tension in her family, and Corky'd been at the Key Biscayne Club, Florida, for eight days, and Corky hadn't known how to reply, suddenly hot in the face. Kissing

her, stroking her, what to say to Christina when, it must be, he doesn't
know the answer to her question.

Look, honey, the main thing is: being alive.

Life *is* sweet if the fuckers meet your price.

"Hey, officer, can I help?—there's an alley here, I'll route 'em through
here, O.K.?"

Corky's cut his engine and is out of his car calling to the harassed
young cop, glad to be of service. It's occurred to him that this one-way
alley off Brisbane goes right through to Front Street and an impromptu
detour can take traffic that way then over the Third Street canal bridge
and back a block or two to Brisbane—why not? It's worth trying.

The cop must be amazed, a guy unknown to him volunteering to help
with traffic control, climbing out of a $35,000 cream-and-cocoa Caddy
willing to get right out in this mess and on a windy day blowing grit and
crap into your eyes, sure he's game, why not—"O.K., mister!" he calls
over.

So this happens: for five minutes or so Corky's in the street having the
time of his life directing traffic!—that's to say, bossing people around.
He's good at that, as his ex-wife Charlotte would say. Capable, quick,
springy on his feet like an athlete (he *is* an athlete, though always an amateur, squash, tennis, softball, for a brief while boxing in high school),
basking in the attention, innocent as a kid. With his easy smile he's the
kind of guy people rarely question but take as he presents himself. You're
an American, you're good as you look.

Corky's ex-wife knows too he's the kind of guy who thrives on emergencies. It's real life that constantly fucks him up.

"—Down this alley, right—to Front Street, right—sure it goes through,
friend!—just *go*." Corky waving his arms, pointing, even whistling. That
ear-splitting whistle perfected when he was a kid.

"Yes, c'mon, ma'am, just turn your wheel, like that, right!—fantastic. *Go*."

Revved up, hot. Like on the squash court. The hotter the action the
more the adrenaline pumps.

And his fellow drivers follow his directions. A stream of cars, vans.
UNION CITY FLOWERS delivery girl behind the wheel giving him the eye.
The first several are hesitant but the others follow like sheep. Terrific feel-

ing, taking charge like this, Corky loves it, like at certain crucial Council meetings he's got the agenda orchestrated with the Council president and Oscar Slattery's other allies primed to steer discussion to the Mayor's advantage then call for a quickie vote or a vote to adjourn, whatever. Never fails. Or almost never.

So the gridlock's broken on Brisbane above Fourth, backed up for blocks but now moving. Some of the drivers grin at Corky and make the O.K. sign with thumb and forefinger, possibly they recognize him, Corky Corcoran who's in the papers occasionally, on local TV. Not the best known of the City Council members but a straightforward guy, a one hundred percent reliable guy, no bullshit from Corky Corcoran who's come up from Irish Hill and no bullshit about *that*. If only, fuck it, he was *taller*.

He's maybe five foot nine, maybe a little shorter, conscious of his height so he always stands tall, proud, cocky, a middleweight's solid, supple body, an Irish kid's face still smattered with freckles. Fading, but still there. Sometimes it seems Corky's so good-looking women will look after him in the street, sometimes he's battered-looking as an old football, just plain homely. Depends on how he's been sleeping, and with who. Whether he's hungover. Right now he guesses he looks pretty good. His hair that's still a dark red, a winey-russet red, in corrugated waves lifting from his forehead, and his widow's peak that's the consequence mainly of a receding hairline but striking, dramatic, Corky *is* a good-looking man and has every right to take pride in his looks. Hot-skinned, intelligent, foxy-shrewd. Even people who don't recognize him can guess he's a local celebrity.

And his clothes: always stylish and in good taste, not flashy, not nouveau riche. Sure he'll go as high as $1200 for a custom-made suit like his charcoal gray pinstripe and he's got two tuxes for formal wear one of them a cool $1500 (not custom-made, but by Valentino—he'd picked it up on a New York City junket, at a men's boutique in the Trump Tower) and some elegant straight-guy Perry Ellis wear and a terrific-looking Burberry coat and today which is a special day he's wearing his new Armani "sport jacket-coat," double-breasted to give his narrow torso some bulk, it's a sexy color somewhere between fawn and khaki, and with it a white-on-white silk-cotton shirt and a classy striped Cartier tie and good expensive

Italian shoes looking just-polished—as in fact they were, in the lobby of the Hotel Statler this morning. (Weekdays, Corky eats breakfast out: he's a regular at the Statler, and at the Hyatt, and at the Union City Athletic Club, among other places.) You see him and you register a guy who thinks well of himself who's proud of himself and no apologies for a little healthy vanity.

A guy not needing to think about his first drink of the day.

So he'll say to gorgeous Christina *Hey you'll never guess what I was doing on the way over here* and Christina will say smiling *No, darling, what?* and Corky will say with a big grin, *Directing traffic, like a cop* and Christina will say astonished *Corky, what—?*

More cops arrive, sirens blasting. The situation's under control. The young cop Corky's helped out waves at him as he moves on through the intersection—"Hey, thanks, Mr. Corcoran!"

Mr. Corcoran!—music to Corky's ears. His morning is made.

It's 11:04 A.M. and he'd been due around 11:00 but it's O.K. Punches in radio station WWAZ to catch the news, five after the hour. Corky's hooked on the news, a real addict. Especially local news. Fed up with Washington politics, that shithead Bush and absolute asshole Quayle, makes you ashamed almost to be an American, at least the Democrats got through the energy bill, bucking Bush's man Watkins, *that's* good news for once but mainly Corky's caught up in local news, even the sensational stuff broadcasters like "Richie Richards" of WWAZ focus on. Never know, turning on the radio, how the news is going to touch you. Might even, if you're Jerome Andrew Corcoran, hear your own name.

Not today, though. Today it's all depressing crap. This "Richie Richards" Corky loves to hate. Frenzied yammering between ads. Latest bulletins which are in fact pseudo-bulletins. Why the fuck does the fuckhead harp on the same themes day after day: Union City is in a fiscal crisis, Union City is in a crime crisis, Union City is in a moral crisis, Union City *is* a crisis. Rust Belt casualty. Depopulating. Whites to the suburbs. So what else is new? Crime, drug use on the rise. AIDS deaths. AIDS babies. Tax base eroding. Once the third largest city in New York State, now dropped to fifth. And fast falling. Corky Corcoran who was born in Union City and

raised in Union City and loves Union City and happens to own $1 million
in property in Union City bitterly resents this kind of shit. Not the truth of
it exactly, for maybe it is true, but the selectivity, the unfair bias.

Next time Corky runs into this traitor "Richie Richards" maybe he'll
punch the fucker in the mouth.

Today's typical: the guy starts out phony-sad reporting the weather-
man's prediction of a generally lousy Memorial Day weekend, thunder-
storms expected early Monday, still the annual parade's scheduled until
further notice—you can almost hear Richards gloating, the parade's for
suckers, sure to be washed out. Then the usual firecracker recitation: one
fire, two break-ins, three drug arrests, a grandmother of nine wounded by
gunshot in a "domestic disturbance" on South Erie Boulevard—meaning
ninety-five percent black now, the stretch of Erie beyond Grand, all that
was once Irish Hill and is still quaintly and misleadingly so called. (A little knot of whites still remains. Too poor or too disorganized or too stubborn to move. And among them Sean Corcoran, still in the old woodframe
house on Roosevelt, Aunt Frances dead for years and the old man must be
seventy-seven at least, long retired, living off a city pension to which, by
a confidential arrangement, Corky contributes $300 each month. Corky
feels guilty anyway, so rarely drops by to see the old man, or even calls
him. Sean Corcoran took him in, treated him like a son, or anyway no
worse than he treated his own son Peter, and Corky's a guy right now
without a family of his own, certainly no kid of his own. Corky thinks:
I'll swing around to Sean's tomorrow, or Sunday. Hoping to Christ it isn't
too late.) Next the news is of Thursday night's demonstration at the Mohawk County Courthouse and for this Corky turns the volume up.

The demonstration, mainly of blacks, was led by a local black leader
and activist named Marcus Steadman, one of Corky's fellow City Council members and a preacher in something called the African-American
First Church of the Evangelist—a notorious troublemaker who's himself
under indictment for raping a young black woman. Steadman's the kind
of black man who depresses liberals and gladdens the hearts of conserva-
tives. *The kind of nigger,* as Sean Corcoran and his friends used to say, *to
give even niggers a bad name.* Corky isn't prejudiced against blacks, nor
any race, creed, religion, but he sees the logic of such a sentiment. God
damn, Corky can't stand Marcus Steadman. And everybody he knows,

from certain of his black City Council colleagues up to the Mayor and his aides, feels one hundred percent the same way.

Steadman's an opportunist, a rabble-rouser. Taking up the cause, in itself a worthy cause, of protesting the Pickett-Johnson incident, and mixing it in with the Rodney King verdict, and weird religious mumbo-jumbo of an upcoming Black Apocalypse—the black races of the world are going to rise up, like a giant tidal wave, and drown the effete white races, in the year 2000. WWAZ replays passages from Steadman's ranting speech of the night before, on the steps of the courthouse, *Where's justice?* Steadman is shouting, *where's black justice? Where's* our *justice?* Corky, driving his car, listens in fascination, Jesus Christ he hates that man, hates him like poison for turning every City Council meeting into a shouting match, dividing the inner-city blacks who owe so much to Oscar Slattery, plus insulting Corky personally whenever he has a chance. (How did Marcus Steadman most hurt Corky Corcoran? By refusing to shake hands with him, the first time they met. Leaving Corky with his hand stuck out, like an erect prick. *Nobody snubs Corky Corcoran!*) Even though he has to admit, Steadman's essentially right. It *is* a racist society, no doubt. And maybe Pickett did shoot a twelve-year-old kid without sufficient cause but, if so, that's for a jury to decide.

The trial's been scheduled, postponed, rescheduled. Now it's set for mid-June. Just a few weeks. With Steadman fanning the flames, it's going to be a nasty time. (And Steadman himself is soon to stand trial.) Corky doesn't like to think what might—what will—happen if Pickett is acquitted, like the L.A. cops. Union City could go up in smoke like L.A. Listen to Steadman, the guy's a true preacher, makes even a sworn enemy like Corky shiver hearing him, voice like a tenor sax, leaping and wailing, keening, Biblical cadences *Rise up O my brothers! O my sisters! Where is* our *justice?*

Next, "Richie Richards" winds up the 11:05 news in a phony-scandalized voice, keeping the most repulsive "news" for last. It's recycled crap which Corky's been hearing for at least two days now: a twenty-nine-year-old Union City resident named Leroy Nickson, married and the father of a five-month infant boy, not only beat the infant to death with his fists for "crying too much when he was trying to sleep" but disposed of the body by—

Corky punches the radio *off*.

Fuck that shit—he's heard enough.

Noticing now, now traffic's moving normally again, on the down side of Pendle Hill, an ambulance moving away. No siren now, and no flashing light. Meaning a corpse inside, not a customer.

No sign of an accident on the street. UCPD sawhorses cordoning off a driveway and part of a sidewalk, a UC Fire Co. van in a No Parking zone, uniformed firemen and cops out front. Corky's curiosity is immediately aroused. What's going on?

Pendle Hill Village is one of those townhouse-style condominiums built in the 1980s in "gentrified" islands in the downtown sector you'd have written off as dead-end zones in the 1970s. This one was built, as Corky happens to know, on the site of the old Pendle Hill Brewery. Only a few blocks from St. Vincent's Mission on Front Street where the winos line up three times a day for free meals and the occasional delousing. Less than a mile from that stretch of Canal Street the downscale pimps have staked out for their hookers. Still, it looks swanky. Yuppie-swanky. Each condo unit with its own front entrance and garage below; all buff-beige brick and curvy wrought-iron railings and red geraniums in clay pots. And bars on the lower windows so classy you might not guess their practical purpose. Synthetic like a movie set, but with a look of romance: a "village" for well-paid young professionals, computer programmers, lawyers, money people, PR and media girls, a swinging-singles kind of condo it would've been in the crude happy innocent days before AIDS. Even has its own Pendle Hill Laundry & Dry Cleaners, its Pendle Hill Florist, its Pendle Hill Fashion Boutique, its Pendle Hill Video. Corky's reminded of the place Thalia lived in for a while when she'd worked for Family Services as a caseworker, that high-rise "luxury" apartment the Dominion Towers, farther downtown, with a view of the river and the bridge and Fort Pearce, Ontario, on the other side. Thalia just out of Cornell, twenty-two years old and think-ing she's going to devote her life to "helping humanity" and it's just one of those shit-jobs idealistic kids sign on for not knowing what's ahead. Still, Thalia lasted longer than most. Her mother worrying all the while she'd be mugged, raped, murdered "down there."

None of those things had happened to Thalia, but other things had happened to Thalia.

Corky parks behind the firetruck, No Parking but he figures this is a special occasion, rules suspended. He's a curious guy, pushy you might say. Gives himself a quick check in the rearview mirror, sees he looks O.K., five hours' sleep the night before which is pretty good for him, and his eyes not noticeably bloodshot. Climbs out of the Caddy seeing the Caddy too looks good, impressive, nobody's going to notice that scratch on the right side, traversing both doors, thin as a pencil stroke he's been too busy to get it touched up but will, soon: next week.

"Hello, officer. What's happened here?"

Corky's addressing not one of the uniformed cops but an older guy obviously a detective. In fact, Corky knows him, vaguely—the name's Beck? He can see Beck recognizes him too, or almost does, there's that pinched look in the detective's face for a fraction of a second, *I know you, you know me,* fleeting and vanished immediately and Corky's thinking how for sure you don't get to be a Union City senior detective by being a nice guy, knows Beck won't answer any question of his but will block it with one of his own, so he's prepared. Beck asks, not returning Corky's smile, but politely, "You live here, mister?" and Corky says, frank and concerned, "I used to, officer. I know the neighborhood, and some people here. I was just driving by, and . . ." It isn't entirely a lie since the Domin- ion Towers is less than a mile away.

"There's been what you'd call an emergency situation," Beck says. "It's under control now."

"Not a fire—?"

"It's under control now."

Staring at Corky like he's grinding his back teeth to keep from telling Corky to go to hell. Boiled-looking face, a German stolidity to it, rhino horn for a nose, no bullshitting this guy. Maybe fifty years old. Packing a Beretta inside that bulky off-the-rack sport coat, you got to wonder how many times he's fired it.

"Yeah? O.K., I was just wondering." Corky's got his car keys in hand, rattling them, smiling. "Like I said, I used to live—"

"But you don't now, right? You're not a resident of this condo complex, right?"

"That's right, officer. I'm what you'd call a . . ." Corky smiles to show this is a sort of a joke, nothing for Beck to jump down his throat about, ". . . concerned citizen."

"Well, this area is sealed off. See? No names and no details are released until—they're released."

This means a death or deaths, but Corky isn't going to push it. Must be a dozen cops here, firemen, police radios yakking, an air of upset, grim looks, worry, sure somebody's died, the body's just been carted away, probably not a natural death, Corky will learn what it is eventually. Registering the address that's been sealed off with yellow UCPD tape: 1758 Brisbane. Townhouse condo, attached single-car garage below, Venetian blinds drawn tight on the windows, mail and flyers stuffed in the mailbox like it hasn't been picked up in days. That sad stark look of a place where something's gone wrong that won't ever be made right. Like a photo that's overexposed. You look. You can't see what's wrong but you can't not look.

Corky thanks the officer and backs off, he's a good-hearted guy not meaning to intrude. Quick to leave before Beck hasn't any choice but to order him to move on, which he guesses Beck would rather not do sensing not how they're connected to each other but that they are, in city politics dense and clotted and lushly symbiotic as algae covering a pond.

What they say in boxing, *What goes around comes around.*

Corky drives on. Knowing that the cops are already checking him out, his license plate, on the computer. Routine police procedure. Doesn't bother him. He *is* a concerned citizen.

And Corky likes cops, always has. The cops that like him, in any case. Though it's a fucking shame as everybody said for years everybody said Tim Corcoran's murderers were never arrested, never tried. Just not enough evidence. D.A. couldn't make the case stick.

Though in fact Al Fenske was killed, gunned down himself gangland style, Easter 1962. And the hired killers in the car Corky hadn't quite seen were arrested on other charges, sent to prison eventually. So there's justice. Isn't there?

Corky's at Union Boulevard already, it's 11:17 A.M. and he's smiling, his easy smile, sure Corky Corcoran likes cops, likes everybody, his reputation's he's the nicest guy in Union City, if you don't cross him.

"HE'S HERE NOW, BUT HE'S LEAVING"

Pussy, thinks Corky. Licking his lips. Jesus, beautiful.

He'd picked it up at the China Import Emporium in the Lakeview Shopping Mall, where Corcoran, Inc., owns office property.

Never sees Christina without bringing her something. A habit pleasurable and maybe addictive, Corky's apt to impulse buy for any number of people he knows, women especially (in the rear of the Caddy there's a pink potted begonia wrapped in silver foil tied with a big crimson bow, Corky picked up Wednesday with every intention of bringing it to his elderly aunt Sister Mary Megan Dowd who's been in Holy Redeemer Hospital for at least a week: God damn, he *means* to get there). This item for Christina, Corky knows she's going to like: a gorgeous ceramic figure halfway between a cat and a fox, vivid russet-red and intricately painted in brilliant colors, slanted gray-green eyes, feminine features, clever damn thing stands about six inches high and you discover you can pull it apart and there's another even more beautiful cat-fox inside, you pull that apart and there's another inside that, and so on—six in all. Must be hand-painted, tiny little brushes. Oriental art. And not that expensive—under $100.

Every time Corky gives Christina a present, she seems embarrassed, says she wishes he wouldn't. But why not? How's he going to show her he's crazy about her otherwise, in ways she can see, touch, weigh in her hand?

Corky parks the Caddy where he usually does: not in front of Christina's brownstone at 331 Nott, where she rents a third-floor loft, but up the block and around a corner by an Italian bakery. He's wary by nature. And by design. Don't let the bastards get you by the short hairs, right? An old-fashioned Irish Catholic gallantry too, which is to say a concern for appearances. Wants to "protect" Christina, who's a married woman. Anyway until they work it out when she'll tell her husband (who's, unfortunately, a pretty sick man) about Corky and when she'll be free to marry Corky—if ever they work it out.

Sure, Corky's crazy about Christina. She's really in deep in him like no other woman. But does he really want to marry her, or anyone?

Wouldn't like me quite so much, lover?—if I were free and unattached.

That's bullshit, Corky thinks. He does want to get married again, and soon. And it's going to be to Christina.

Weird, though—he's always lapsing into this dream. Not a dream exactly because he's usually awake when he has it. Lots of times, driving. Especially the Expressway, the Thruway. Suddenly he's thinking of this wife of his, kids, two or three kids, big white colonial in a lakeshore suburb like Chateauguay . . . like it's *real*, this is Corky Corcoran's actual *family*, only where are they exactly, and where's he? Almost, it scares him. That tightening sensation in his chest. Like Time is running out. Tim Corcoran was only twenty-five when *his* son was born.

Yet in the dream the wife doesn't seem to be Christina. Doesn't seem to be anyone he knows. (Not Charlotte, for sure.) Corky tries to see her face but can't. The kids too—blurred. He can hear their voices, almost—like music—airy, tuneless, teasing. *Can't buy me love.* Old Beatles song, must be thirty years ago.

What's it mean, Corky hasn't a clue. He's not a guy comfortable inside his own head.

Peering into the rear of the Caddy as he locks the doors. Jesus, how'd the inside get to be such a mess? There's the begonia plant, but also newspapers, paperback books, even empty beer cans and Styrofoam cups, a variety of crud he's accumulated without being aware of it like the crud on his razor blades, the inside upper rim of his toilet bowls. Charlotte was right: every car Corky drives he turns into a pigsty, but how's it happen?

Walking back, not fast not slow but like a guy who knows his destination and's looking forward to the very process of getting there, to 331 Nott, Corky's noticing the street life: Hispanics, blacks, shoppers, kids, pretty normal-looking folks so what's this bullshit, Union City is in a crisis?

The spics and the blacks, the guys especially, they really stand out: cool dressers. Cool dudes. And Corky too in this "sport jacketcoat" he likes the look of, silky-wool fabric lighter than camel's-hair but soft like camel's-hair, and that color. Prosperous-looking, but conservative-prosperous. Not pimp-prosperous like some of these studs.

At lunch he'll ask Greenbaum how much money Greenbaum thinks he's worth, approximately. Two million dollars is the bottom line, Corky thinks.

He likes the way people glance at him, women especially. And their eyes snag. Men sizing him up. He's a cocky guy but not belligerent; quick to smile; sometimes, if he's nervous, he can't help smiling. In public like this he walks with his shoulders squared, head up, casual in his gaze, easygoing, a manner he cultivated as a kid, transferred as a scholarship student, aged fifteen, to the private boys' school St. Thomas Aquinas. Rich classmates, and Corky from Roosevelt Street, Irish Hill. The Corcorans down on their luck since Tim's death. Except: Uncle Sean poked him in the shoulder one day, told him there's a surprise in the works, a friend's thinking of you, and next day a certified letter came to "Jerome Andrew Corcoran" from the director of St. Thomas informing him he was the recipient of a privately endowed scholarship. And no more information forthcoming than that, for years.

Corky's scholarship was for need, not grades. His grades were average at the parish school, except in math where he'd score sometimes as high as one hundred percent. Not until after he graduated did he learn, and then accidentally, that his scholarship to St. Thomas was paid for by Oscar Slattery *in memoriam* Tim Corcoran. Even Vic Slattery, who by chance became Corky's friend, hadn't known.

Corky looks up at Christina's windows, facing the street. Is she watching for him?

Corky'd like to think that Christina rents her loft in the old German-town area a five-minute drive from his South State Street office for his sake, or for her own, a convenient place where they can meet on neutral ground: not her house (Christina lives with her husband and a thirteen-year-old son in Chateauguay, a half hour's drive on the Millard Fillmore Expressway north of the city), and not his (Corky lives alone, still in the house his ex-wife coerced him into buying). But in fact Christina has had the loft for years, she's a freelance journalist and seems to believe she needs private space in which to work. Corky's wondered more than once whether other men have visited Christina here, by her invitation; whether they've made love to her on her creaky sofa bed, or on the floor; showered with her afterward in that antiquated stall with the jaundice-yellow tile so finely cracked as to suggest as immense spider's web. Not that he'd ask: never. And Christina has never said. Eleven months now, and all of it serious, but there are some things they've never discussed.

Corky's feeling excited. A balloon near to bursting. Only twenty-five minutes late. It's a gusty-sunny-glaring day, massed clouds in the east above the river, that look of somber, brooding, palpitating gray brains, but the rest of the sky a hard clear eye-piercing blue. Jesus, life *is* sweet.

There's a sexual charge just driving into Germantown. This old section of Union City, which others avoid. Winding his way through potholed streets in the shadow of thunderous Expressway overpasses and ramps—entering a seedy no-man's-land of solidly built old brick buildings now given over to discount furniture, electrical appliances, factory outlet stores—taverns, X-rated book and video shops, porn theaters, those "luncheonettes" you find only in such neighborhoods in American cities, front window greased over as if with steam, so spectacularly crummy there's a mystery in their very existence, how they continue, where their customers come from. And, along the riverfront, the section Corky's considering investing in to develop, there's this wilderness of boarded-up factories, mounds of trash, scrub trees and thistles cracking through pavement behind the ten-foot chain-link fence and graffiti-covered signs WATCH THIS SPACE! FUTURE SITE OF UNION CITY MARINA!—a federal project killed years ago for lack of matching city funds.

Up on the Expressway billboards glare in the sun like neon. A panorama of them, a look of prosperity. WELCOME TO UNION CITY CENTER CITY NEXT EXIT. Corky narrows his eyes seeing that fucking-familiar ad he hates HEINZ MEULLER LINCOLN-MERCURY SALES RENTAL & LEASING, a crude drawing of "Heinz Meuller" with beaming eyes, pipe, friendly smile, Meuller's an old classmate of Corky's from St. Thomas whose guts Corky has hated for thirty years and no doubt, the memories they share, the feeling's mutual.

Sometimes, Corky thinks, Union City even with three hundred thousand people is too damned small for him. He's lived here all his life and maybe that's too long.

Also everywhere he sees the shiny familiar red-white-and-blue signs for ROSS DRUMMOND REALTY. Drummond, biggest realtor in the region, happens to be his ex-father-in-law.

Shit, Corky misses *him*. Corky's got nothing against *him*.

Christina's slate-blue Volvo, 1990 model, is parked at the curb in front of 331 Nott. Corky smiles upward, shading his eyes trying to see if she's at a window waving. Can't see, sky's reflected in the glass, broken clouds, pieces of blue, opacity. Like stained glass seen from the outside.

Beneath the grime the brownstone at 331 Nott is a handsome, sturdy old building, German-built, 1922, to last a hundred years. In this neighborhood it won't last another five. Now, if Corky owned it and could transport it to, say, Pendle Hill, it could be reclaimed, sandblasted and overhauled inside and out, new windows, new roof, trendy skylights, divided into condo units. But here, no. Next door, an identical brownstone's boarded up, abandoned. Looks like shit. The sidewalk's littered at 331 Nott, there's graffiti, Day-Glo white, on the front door, and a pissy stench to the stoop—how Christina's nostrils must pinch, she's such a fastidious woman.

Corky gives her another year or so, she'll be gone from Nott Street.

Living where?

One thing you learn fast, in Corky's trade, in fact Corky'd picked it up as a kid, nothing's fixed or permanent or *real*, in real estate. Everything's location, context. Ever-changing.

And inside the vestibule the smell's stronger. One time, Corky surprised two black kids, really young kids, smoking what he'd guessed must be crack, staring at him, bursting into high-pitched giggles. Not at all afraid, or giving a damn. The row of aluminum mailboxes is scratched and dented from frequent break-ins. Why Christina's husband lets her rent down here, Corky can't understand. If she was *his* wife, absolutely no.

C. BURNSIDE 3A. "Burnside" is Christina's maiden/professional name. An old Union City name, in fact. Like "Kavanaugh," the husband's.

Shit on their shoes, kid.

No longer?

Corky buzzes 3A to let Christina know he's here, and opens the inner door with his key. Christ, he's excited.

But, shit: it's almost eleven-thirty. And he has that lunch date at one with Greenbaum. Why the fuck he had to stop at Pendle Hill to stick his nose in business not his own, he doesn't know. Nothing means more to him than these times with Christina.

"Chrissie?—it's me."

Up the creaking, battered old hardwood stairs Corky runs, smiling, eager, he's an upright flame, the flush in his Irish kid's face and that lover's glow in his eyes, seeing Christina Kavanaugh waiting for him. For *him*. In snug-fitting well-worn jeans, outlining the curve of hips, ass, the embroidered dusty-rose pullover cashmere sweater Corky'd bought for her at Christmas, and barefoot, despite the cold, and the crummy cracked floor of the landing—she's staring avidly at him, or toward him, forehead creased, worriedly and, at first, not quite smiling, in that instant their eyes meet, as if she doesn't see him.

Fleetingly, quick as a short thread pulled through the eye of a needle, forgotten at once, Corky has the uneasy sense he's a man rushing to fill a space, the way liquid fills a container.

The actual space, the container, will remain invisible, as much after it's filled as before.

And Corky feels immense relief, too, always at this point, seeing Christina, understanding he's come down to Nott Street with a vague superstitious dread of what he might discover in 3A. Say she isn't on the landing. Say he opens the door. Say the loft's quiet, empty—until Corky finds Christina's lifeless, broken body.

Hadn't he had the same superstitious dread regarding Thalia, who'd laughed at him.

Corky grabs Christina, kisses her. Hot, breathless, so hard she staggers a little, grabbing him to keep her balance. She too is breathless and seems tense, maybe she's been worrying about him, too? Corky says, "God, you're beautiful! I love you."

Christina laughs. "Corky, you're beautiful, too."

That sweet sound of "Corky" in this woman's mouth. Like her love of his body, his cock—unexpected.

"Yes, but I mean it."

"*I* mean it, lover."

Up in the loft Christina examines the Chinese cat-fox Corky's given her, kisses him again and thanks him, maybe she's embarrassed and maybe it pleases her, anything of his. Corky glances around the loft, always a little antsy stepping in here, always the fleeting thought *something will happen, somebody's waiting for me* for after all what's he doing but fucking another man's wife. And by premeditation.

The stab of adrenaline, like being injected straight to the heart. The sweet rush of blood into his cock. The first few times Corky came here to see Christina, they'd grabbed at each other and begun to make love practically as soon as he'd stepped inside the door, Christina partly undressed, waiting. Hot-skinned and taut as a bow and already wet for him. And only time to talk, breathless and dazed, afterward.

Now they have more to talk about, sometimes too much. Christina telling him, as she is now, of how she'd begun to worry about him . . . just a little. Of an accident she'd witnessed on the Expressway, that morning. How she'd begun out of the blue to cry—"And you know that isn't like me."

Christina offers Corky a glass of red wine, she's been sipping some herself, the corners of her lovely mouth just perceptibly stained. They stand for a while at the rear of the loft looking out the plate-glass window, arms around each other's waist, Corky not wanting to ask Christina about her husband but knowing he has to, it's expected of him and really he wants to know, needs to know. How the—what's it?—prednisone's working out. This cortisone-like drug, new on the market, highly potent, an anti-inflammatory agent prescribed for certain multiple sclerosis patients. (Harry Kavanaugh, a former federal court justice, has had MS for the past nine years. Corky gathers it's progressing rapidly, or Harry's deteriorating rapidly, he feels guilty as hell about the situation, yes but there's a sweet sort of revenge in it, why not admit it, Corky's relations with the husbands of the women he's had affairs with have always been rivalrous, tinged with spite. But secret. For sure, secret.) Christina never says much about Harry but always seems grateful when Corky asks, like a mother asked about an ailing, precious child. She says, "It's one of those wonder drugs. You know—'counter-indications' that scare the hell out of you if you read the fine print."

"If you're going to use it, maybe you shouldn't read the fine print."

"Harry doesn't. I do. But, anyway, it's been helping him—builds up his strength, boosts his morale." Christina pauses. Laughs. "We don't need to talk about it any longer, lover. O.K.?"

Corky's thinking, say Christina was his wife, and another man was here, like this, meeting her in secret, fucking her, all very methodically, on the average three times a week for the past eleven months—how'd *he* take it, if he found out? He thinks of the German Luger, the heft of it in his hand.

Except Corky'd have a hard time using a gun. On anyone. Even in self-defense.

From Christina's window at the rear of the loft Corky can see as far west as the Dominion Bridge downtown, and upriver as far as the suburb of St. Claire, the vague white blur of sailboats on the river. Closer in, the gold-glinting basilica of the Byzantine St. Mary Assumption Church, and, though you wouldn't know what it was now, the ruins of the old Moneghan Pottery Works—where entire Irish families, including a number of Corky's ancestors, emigrated to work in the 1880s. His Great-grandfather Donnelly and Donnelly's several sisters and brothers, from County Kerry. The youngest was only ten years old and they all worked twelve-hour days. When they were lucky.

The wide glittering river, the steep sky you could fall and fall into, no end to it. What's the world but motion. The Universe. Immutable laws you can't guess at. And, if you stop, the motion rolls over you indifferent as waves or clouds, you're dead meat.

Christina says, squeezing Corky about the waist, "Isn't it beautiful! On these clear days, it's like . . ." pausing breathing quickly, she's an impulsive passionate woman prone to extravagant proclamations, ". . . some kind of God. I mean—not God as a person, but God as a presence."

The Chateauguay does look alive. The more you stare at it, the more mesmerized you become, it's impossible even to determine which way the river's current is moving, it's so choppy in the wind glittering and winking like clusters of eyes; the darker troughs rippling like muscles. Union City is famous for its five river-spanning bridges and the experience of each bridge is different from that of the others as if each bridge traverses a river different from the others.

Corky laughs happily. "What the hell do we need God for? *Us?*"

He points out to Christina the hazy shape of a building miles away downtown, just visible beyond swanky aqua-blue high-rise towers and the ramps of the Dominion Bridge. It's the Griswold Building, a Union City landmark, designed by Louis Sullivan and built in 1917 as the first skyscraper—what a terrific word, "skyscraper"!—in upstate New York. "See it?—I'm thinking of buying it," Corky says casually, "—if they meet my price." Christina expresses surprise and interest, "What a great idea, Corky, but . . ." her voice trailing off in doubt, so Corky says, as if presenting his case, "At Rensselaer I did a project on Sullivan, I actually studied the original drawings for the Griswold Building. I took photographs, I did drawings of my own. It was the first time I came into contact with . . ." Telling Christina what he'd never told Charlotte, whose enthusiasm for Corky's schemes was tempered by her predilection for judging them, and hearing his voice Corky wonders is he saying too much, confiding too much, but what the hell, Christina is his mistress not his wife not a woman to coldcock him asking where he'd get the money even for a down payment on such an extravagance, such a whim, nor why, in this recession, anyone in his right mind would want to sink $6 million into downtown Union City when office rentals even in the high-tech upriver parks are down. "And another place I'm going to buy, y'know The Bull's Eye? I've got this plan . . ."

Can't buy me love, can't buy me love, oh yeah? why not?

Before they make love, Christina examines the Chinese cat-fox Corky brought her more closely, appreciatively. If Corky's gift-giving embarrasses her, or puts a burden on her, of feeling the necessity not simply of gratitude but of scrupulous interpretation, she's charming enough in complying. Leaning against Corky as she turns the thing in her fingers, brushing her hair out of her face, smiling, laughing, it's a fact that gifts reduce us to the state of being children, and in some of us this is charming, even seductive. "It's beautiful, Corky, but what *is* it?"—close beside Corky whose erection is painful as a hemorrhage into his cock, two or three inches shorter than he, barefoot, a woman of thirty-six neither slender nor plump with taut rounded buttocks, good-sized breasts, her glossy black hair almost too glossy and too black in the dazzling unsparing sunshine flooding through tall curtainless windows so Corky's lost in contemplation of her sometimes, how physical she is, how *real*. How can it be, *Atoms are mostly emptiness, the Universe is mostly emptiness*, our bodies are so *real*, our being *irrefutable!* When Corky and Christina make love on the sofa bed, sometimes more acrobatically on the matted gnarled and yellowed "Peruvian sheep-hide" rug on the floor, everything, all flesh, is dauntingly enormous, in close-up, like fucking beneath the lens of a giant magnifying glass. Corky says, stroking Christina's breasts through the luscious cashmere, "It's you, sweetheart, sweet pussy take a look," nudging his head against hers as she laughs, "Oh, right! I see!—" having discovered how cleverly the cat-fox divides into two, comes apart, to reveal another, smaller cat-fox inside it, like a parody of pregnancy—and how that cat-fox too divides into two, to reveal a still-smaller cat-fox—and that too, and so on—six cat-foxes in all, each smaller and more delicately featured than its predecessor, the last only about two inches high. Slanting female eyes, luxurious whiskers, exotic markings. "I see—it's like a Russian doll. One inside the other. It's an ingenious idea, it must be as old as—" Christina may be about to say, *the human race*, but Corky takes the cat-foxes from her and drops them onto a table and kisses her, hard.

Grips her shoulders, hard. As she grips him—his arms, his back. Suddenly, and passionately. As eager as he. As hungry.

And what relief now, no words now, no words requiring syntax, Corky's profoundly relieved, grateful, as grateful for this as for the sexual pleasure itself, passing into pure sensation where he's happiest, and most himself.

Knowing, in Christina, direct in her appetites as Corky in his, he won't confront, as he has so often in other women, even as they melt against him, their female rage liquified for the duration of lovemaking *Yes I love you and you've said you love me, why then can't I trust you?*

Hurriedly, a little roughly, Corky pulls the sweater, *his* sweater, $300 at I. Magnin, up over Christina's head, the two of them laughing breathless as runners, bunching her thick hair, thick black glossy spillage of hair in his face, impatiently Corky fumbles to unhook her brassiere, the warm satiny feel of it, and Christina's breasts heavy, always it feels to Corky's fingers there's milk in women's breasts, a liquid heaviness, density, Christina's breasts just slightly flaccid, but beautiful to him, strangely cool in his hands, the nipples honey-colored rising erect and knobby as little buttons, skin dead-white and so soft it's astonishing, such softness such vulnerability the female so vulnerable to hurt, Corky kisses, sucks, bites, she's told him she nursed her son when he was newly born and the thought excites Corky, they stumble together as in a clumsy dance, he tugs down her jeans, her underpants, removing his clothes with shaking fingers, he groans and presses his face against her belly, against the patchy black pubic hair, the heat between her legs, the secret moisture, kneading her thighs, her buttocks, the surprise of that fleshy solidity, Corky shuts his eyes in bliss, Oh Christ he's happy, never so happy as at such a time, lips, tongue, teeth, fingers, his cock erect and bobbing and ropey-veined, it's the current of the river that carries him, the bright mad tattered sunshine, the wind, many winds, pure sensation and no memory of Jerome Corcoran now, no memory of anyone and even this woman has become abstract, he enters her in triumph, exclaims as he enters her, the sharp incandescent pleasure of it, and the shock of the pleasure, always new, though so utterly familiar, so inevitable, he pushes himself into her, deep, and deeper still, falling upon her as from a dizzy height seeing her face filmed with sweat, beads of sweat at her hairline, the tense set of her jaw and the waxy-white tip of her nose, a fleeting crescent of convulsive white rimming her eyes above the irises dilated and flattened, glassy with strain, his excitement quickens as he feels her inward tightening, tighter and ever-tighter, she clutches him murmuring "Corky, my God—" the words which might be any words, a prayer, an incantation, arrhythmic and fearful, her hands clenched into fists against his back, the quicksilver rippling of her muscles, thighs gripping him with surprising strength, always he's surprised at a woman's strength, the urgency of it, the mounting desperation, as he plunges into her she lifts herself to him, pelvis, cunt, against him, as if into him, and at the same time hungry to swallow him up, he hears the sticky slap of their skins, he hears her, and himself, at such a time what's required is discipline, a style, *Never race a train!* but Corky begins to lose it, no words and no memory and his body pumping in a frenzy as his consciousness lurches toward extinction, an upright flame flaring up, up, incandescent heat, searing white heat, the sun expanding in the bright empty sky like the eye of God, All-Seeing God, and he feels an old dread of the woman's paroxysm, her mounting tension, the terrible violence in her as if, arching her back, grasping at him with elbows, arms, fists, she might swallow him up inside her, yes but doesn't he love her, doesn't he love this, this is why we're born isn't it, fucking, like this, the crude mute pumping, the lurch of the flesh, smelling of sweat, damp hair, tendrils of damp kinky hair on Christina's forehead, and Corky's arms, legs, chest, even part of his back, like wings, covered in fine frizzy red-brown hairs, patches of it in armpits and crotch, his pale pumping buttocks, the crack of his ass, how vulnerable, how exposed, something comical in the vision, sad and funny at once, Corky Corcoran too, a man's body too, defenseless as a woman's at such a time, it's a perspective he can't maintain, his brain in a swoon like frothy water swirling down a drain, he doesn't want to come too quickly, it's an old anxiety of his, yes but he's urging Christina forward, in quick leaps and lunges, a woman so unpredictable, laboring sometimes for many minutes as if swimming upstream against a tough current, yet sometimes coming almost at once, the lightest touch, he feels the tension in her as a hot stabbing sensation, the way extreme heat or cold, to the touch, is pure sensation at first, not yet pain, Christina clutches at him as if to stop herself, turning her head from side to side too distracted to kiss Corky, a strange halting shyness in her often at this moment, having rushed forward impetuously and even mannishly and now hesitating, as if fearful, there is terror in such surrender of the will and Christina is a willful woman, yes but she wants it too, she wants it from Corky, hasn't she said how she wants it, loves it, from him, yes she knows there is no way to go but forward, the Chateauguay's swift treacherous current, the thunder of the falls downriver, no turning back, there's a tension in the woman's body that communicates itself to Corky, to all the cells of Corky's body, he's galvanized with it, he *is* the tension, supremely in control and guiding her even against her will, leaning on his elbows above her, cupping her thrashing head in his hands, kissing her eyelids, her forehead that's both sweating and clammy, sucking at her mouth that seems bruised, her tongue, he feels himself floating in sky, in the reflected sky of the river, never so happy as now, if only now were forever, and no Jerome Corcoran waiting on shore, that perpetual witness. He feels Christina's spine tightening, arching, a bow being tightened, and yet more cruelly tightened, near to breaking, and what cries will issue from her throat then, what soft-choked sobs, how she'd wept dazed and delirious that first time in Corky's car, a wild crazy thing to do but they'd done it, and afterward she'd told him blunt and frank and unembarrassed it was the first time for her in how many years, since Harry's condition, she spoke of it as a condition not an illness, a mysterious degeneration of the central nervous system and Corky had wanted to know but hadn't wanted to know how long the man had been impotent *No! for Christ's sake don't tell me!* fucking Harry Kavanaugh's wife was one thing but hearing of his doomed shrinking prick was another, with Corky, like that, coming so powerfully as that, the first time in years, her face streaked with tears and her wide gray-green eyes threaded with blood, he feels that strain in her now, the rising of tension, her hesitancy and shyness in the face of its rising, rising and now sinking and again rising, she's helpless to stop, Corky loves this moment, these many moments, not minding her nails raking his shoulders, her blind grasping fingers in his hair, he sees the woman's fine-boned face distended as if in a paroxysm of the air, the eyes rolling white, even white teeth and gums wetly exposed, Corky sinks himself more deeply into her, forcing himself, and forcing her to his rhythm *Yes! yes! like this!* gripping her tight now by the ass, kneading her ass, and how small it is in his hands, Corky's strong impatient fingers, his penis is hammering, hurtful, he wonders how the woman dared open herself to him, spread her legs for him, so trusting, so exposed, in a woman's place Corky would never risk it, his penis is all of him, engorged with blood, triumphant, he feels Christina on the crumbling precipice of orgasm, murmuring incoherently, a thread of saliva across her chin, strange to think this is love, love's terrible exertion in mimicry of death, *is* this love?—*this?* Corky whispers, "Chrissie, c'mon sweetheart, c'mon I love you," seeing her face, her straining features, in close-up, beneath the lens of the magnifying glass, fucking is so intimate, it's a wonder anyone has the courage for it, yes but you don't think of this beforehand, yes but you don't think at all, Corky's face splits suddenly into a grin, a savage laugh threatens to overcome him, he shuts his eyes and a vision flies to him, quick, instantaneous, the short thread pulled through a needle's eye, yet he sees it complete—Christina of fourteen years before, Corky hadn't at that time known her, only her name, Burnside, and married to a Kavanaugh, he'd seen her at a crowded party, his restless eye scanning the crowd and snagging upon her, a handsome young woman with a pale skin, very black hair, wide-set eyes and sharp cheekbones and a downturned smiling mouth, but the shock of the vision was her belly, a rounded, swollen belly, an eight-or nine-months' pregnancy in that belly, and yet how beautiful, how beautiful, Corky hadn't been able to look away, an elegant young woman, a pale heated skin and something intense, imploring about her features, she wore a white silk maternity dress, a layered tunic over an ankle-length skirt, this whiteness seemed to Corky to have drawn all the light of the room, a cavernous room lit by candles, and around the woman's neck was a single strand of pearls, her hair was smooth-brushed and tied at the nape of her neck with a white silk bow through which a single white rose had been threaded, Corky stared, Corky stared rudely, a classy broad he assessed her, old Union City society, *Shit on their shoes, kid!* with what dignity the young woman carried herself amid the crowd, the center of gravity of her body securely in that belly, Corky drew in a sharp breath seeing her half-consciously stroke that belly, he felt that touch in his groin, saw a fleeting wince in the woman's face as if the baby had kicked her, Corky drew closer, a little drunk and happy and willing to be pushy, take me at my price Corky Corcoran tells Union City, I know who I am and I'm no fucking hypocrite is his boast, he's a vain cocky son of a bitch with a few drinks in him maneuvering his way around in front of the young woman in the dazzling white costume, catches her eye, smiles, is about to introduce himself when she regards him calmly, coolly, a just perceptible half-smile, then turns aside, passes by, joins a group of people one of whom is her husband, and Corky Corcoran stares after her, his face reddening, quickly he lifts his glass to his mouth and drinks, *Bitch! stuck-up cunt! Nobody snubs Corky Corcoran.*

    Corky had been gripping Christina tight, maybe too tight, their lovemaking has bruised her in the past, yes but she loves it, she loves it from him, she has told him so, beginning now to writhe, lifting herself against him with mounting desperation, Corky recalls having heard that an intense orgasm can trigger labor in a woman in a state of advanced pregnancy, the powerful contractions of the vagina, the eerie violence of these contractions, quick-frenzied squeezing like a heart gone wild, Christina cries out, in a climax that is a series of climaxes in rapid rippling succession, she moans, sobs, buries her damp face in his neck, Corky loves this, something fearful in it, the woman's convulsions, but wonderful too, his cock deep inside her and gripped so frantically tight, how needed he is, how much she does love him, no subterfuge here, no hypocrisy, never has he been so close to any woman and never so certain of any woman even if she had not told him how she loves him Corky would know, a man knows, the helpless muscular contractions are making him come too, he can't hold himself back any longer, slipping into that free fall, the precipice shattering beneath him, the vertigo, an explosion of dazzling light behind his eyelids, never is Corky prepared for the violence of orgasm, the sledgehammer blow of it, groaning, whimpering like an infant, it's an electric current rushing through his body, it *is* his body, he's paralyzed, in that free fall, suspended, the power of it, the impact, the ejaculation that is his heart's very blood, the fierce longing of that blood to reproduce itself, to live forever.

Corky's body flames up, he turns to ashes.

And only, Corky sees, when at last he can bring himself to lift his arm, to covertly look at his watch, its stylish ebony-dark Rolex face highlighted against the sweaty bronze hairs of his wrist—only 11:45.

Time for one more fuck, before he has to push on?

Telling her, cradling her in his arms, lazy and dazed as swimmers lying spent on a beach, basking in sunshine, "Chrissie honey, you won't believe what I was doing on the way over here, the reason I was a few minutes late," and she says, her voice lifting, warm, throaty, this voice Corky only hears in Christina at such times, "Yes, what?" and he says, boyish, bemused, "Directing traffic on Brisbane," and she exclaims, rising on one elbow to look at him, giving him the gift, and this too only at such times, in this loft floating in the sky above windy-gritty Union City, secret, unknown to all others, of her quickest most intimate most radiant smile, "Corky, *what—?*"

Great storyteller, Corky Corcoran, like all the male Corcorans, Timothy Patrick in his time, Grandpa Liam in his time, old Spades Corcoran who'd worked forty years on the Erie Canal, old Hock Corcoran convulsing his listeners with wild boozy fantastical tales, Corky's friends love him when he's most himself most Irish spinning anecdotes into stories, sure the guy's a little too loud especially when he's been drinking, especially when he wants to impress, sure he tries too hard, not usually with women (with women, you don't need to try hard: women are on your side) as with men.

Corky's stories have one thing in common, of course: Corky's at the center. He's the hero, or he's the jerk you have to love. He's the victim, or the worm-that-turns, or the guy-who-loses-his-temper, or the dumb-fuck who wins in the end. He's the sneaky counterpuncher. He's the mastermind. He's the man with the aces, the royal flush. He's—who? *Corky Corcoran!*

Telling Christina Kavanaugh not about Death (for what was hauled away in the ambulance but dead meat: no siren, no haste: that's how you know) nor even about standing his ground with that fuckface Beck who knew him, for sure Beck knew *him*, but only about directing traffic off Brisbane and through the alley, how he must have looked out there, dressed as he was, a civilian and not a cop, but with an Irish cop's face, the novelty of it, and Christina laughs as he knew she would, hugging him, pressing her warm face against his warmer, sweat-slick chest, the springy-frizzy hairs of his chest, laughing, "Oh Corky, I wish I'd seen you."

Corky laughs comfortably. "You're seeing me now."

The sinewy bronze-glowing length of him. Knobby toes, the big toes' horny nails, discolored like old ivory, he's wriggling them, at the far end of the creaky sofa, and his hard-muscled legs, knees upraised, lazy, sprawled, comfortable in the woman's arms, or so-seeming.

Corky asks, "What about Monday night—you'll be there?"

The jump is quick and slant but Christina gets the connection: if you want to see Corky perform in public, really perform, and really in public, seated at the head table with the Slatterys and the van Burens and maybe the Governor himself (*if* Cuomo can make it: that's pending), Memorial Day evening at the ritzy Chateauguay Country Club is the occasion.

Christina explains carefully, "Yes, I think we'll be there, I'll be sure, I'm sure, unless—" her voice trailing off as it does when she's thinking of her husband, but out of tact or that shy stubborn air of privacy Corky sometimes resents in her she won't say, Corky feels her thinking rapidly, eyelashes tickling the hairs on his chest, how strange the phenomenon of another's thinking: in one of the paperback science books in the back seat of Corky's car, he'd read about a philosopher who'd examined freshly decapitated heads during the French Revolution in pursuit of "thought"—"mind"—weird! but it *is* a mystery, others' thoughts simultaneous with your own but veering off on angles you can't follow still less predict. "—You know, I bought tickets. Weeks ago."

"Sure," says Corky, stroking Christina's hair, "—I know, you told me. Weeks ago."

So there's this sliver of a wedge between them, Corky's pride and Christina's air of apology beforehand, yes she wants to come to the fundraiser, no she doesn't want to come, hates these occasions, of course she bought tickets, $1000 a plate but the Kavanaughs have enough dough to buy out the place, that's not the point and Christina knows it and Corky knows she knows it. Even the fact that the Kavanaughs have long been supporters of Vic Slattery as of liberal Democratic politics generally isn't the point.

Christina says, "It's just so hard, sometimes. Seeing you at these public gatherings. And seeing you see me. I hate the deception, the hypocrisy. I never believe I'm playing the role right and I don't want to play the role right."

Corky strokes Christina's head, her hair that's so beautiful, black, glossy, not quite so fine as the hair of other women Corky's known (for instance Charlotte: her fading-gold hair she's fanatic about not allowing to go gray, Corky glanced up at her one morning, his own wife, saw, Jesus, that woman's getting blonder, who *is* that woman?) but thick, rippling-solid, he likes to close his fist in it, grip it hard.

Thinking, What the hell, what does it matter, shit does it matter really, the main thing is here, and now, like this, the two of them like this, and anyway Corky too feels clumsy when he and Christina are together in the presence of others.

It's been a long time, how many months, since he's seen Harry, had to shake Harry's hand. Poor bastard. Tried to walk with a cane for as long as he could, forestalled a walker, the inevitable wheelchair, multiple sclerosis a disease attacking young adults, the central nervous system, Corky read about it in an old paperback book *The Family Medical Encyclopedia*, guilty and a little sick learning of Kavanaugh's chances, this mysterious condition MS, the insulating tissue that covers the nerve fibers degenerates in patches and is replaced by scar tissue, who knows why, so nerve messages from the brain are blocked getting to muscles and organs, the only hope is, like Kavanaugh in the past, you can go into remission, but that's mysterious too, and temporary—Christina doesn't talk about it much, but she's said being hopeful really hurts, it's hope that hurts, you want to believe you're ready for the worst and you settle in for it then suddenly there's a change, there's actually improvement, you're on a roller coaster up and down and can't get off except at the very end. Corky hates that sensation of not being able to wake up fully (when he'd drunk more heavily than he does now, that happened frequently: scared the shit out of him), lying crooked or crumpled where he'd passed out sometimes even on the floor of his bedroom like he'd been headed for the bed but couldn't make it, sometimes in his car waking at dawn in a parking lot behind a tavern and how strange how unreal yes how mocking like a cartoon seeing these places Corky knows mainly by night exposed by day sometimes in acid sunshine like an aging woman plastered with makeup, he hates that and he's terrified of it, Christ the horror of being paralyzed really, trying to wake but not being able to, trying just to move your leg and you can't, Christina said it began when Harry remarked his legs were tired all the time, pins and needles in his feet and hands and Corky's thinking suddenly of poor Sister Mary Megan in Holy Redeemer, seventy-two years old, she'd had surgery to remove a uterine tumor the family is saying is "benign," Corky winces thinking of it, of her, how kind she'd been to him, that terrible time, that time of which Corky tries not to think, yes and months and years afterward when Theresa was sick and in a kind of remission too, Sister Mary Megan the only one in the family to perceive what lay curled like a fishhook in Jerome's heart, no matter the kid's antic good nature and gregariousness at school *Pray to God for understanding, pray to God every hour and every minute of every day for the strength to forgive Him.* Jesus he'd better haul his ass over to the hospital to see her, guilty about so rarely seeing her, Uncle Sean too, any of them, they're proud of him supposedly but he avoids the family, has avoided them since being taken up by the Drummonds, especially since marrying Charlotte, the snobby bitch, but if he doesn't get that plant to Sister Mary Megan soon the fucking thing's going to shrivel up in the back seat of the Caddy, he hasn't remembered to water it yet.

Corky asks cautiously, "How *is* Harry, you haven't said for a while," and Christina doesn't reply at first, now the lovers' languor has lifted, too much talk, the wrong kind of talk, maybe all talk is wrong, "—He's fine. For him. You know. He's home." Meaning not in a hospital, not in a rehabilitation clinic. For now (so Corky's guessing) that's the main thing.

Beyond that, don't ask. Just, no.

Aunt Frances used to say, No news isn't good news, people rush to tell you good news.

Maybe all talk is wrong at a time like this. After love. After such lovely fucking. Floating in the sky and the river below glittering like mica in the sun, Oh Christ you want it to go on forever but of course it can't, as soon as you speak you begin to ease apart.

Sometimes, after orgasm, Christina cries, so quietly Corky wouldn't know except he feels her shaking. A secret weeping, that hot splash of tears, he senses he shouldn't acknowledge.

Thinking, She wants me to force her to leave Kavanaugh. Wants me to force her to do what she wants to do.

Thinking, But what about the kid, do I want another guy's kid *again?*

Corky asks impulsively, "Having a baby—was it hard for you?"

Christina lifts her head, looks at him quizzically. Wide-set gray-green eyes, cat's eyes, close up they're glassy as gems, with a dark circle around the iris, the pupils contracted because of the bright light, weird to think how another person *sees*, the mechanism of sight, who could have invented it?—but Christina is smiling, smiling and frowning, always a little startled by the wayward things her lover says as they lie here naked not quite ready to disentangle their limbs and not quite ready to make love again. "Corky, why do you ask?—why now?" Christina laughs, kissing his lips, lightly, in play, as if to shut him up, but Corky insists, "*Was* it hard? Would you do it again?"

His own words, so casual, or seeming-casual, startling to him too.

Christina draws a deep breath, her gaze goes inward, she says, slowly, "I was very young. I was still very young at twenty-three. I wanted natural childbirth—of course. My mother and Harry's mother tried to dissuade me, but you know how I am, yes and I was worse then, more headstrong, I wanted the full experience, the ecstatic experience, and I got it: thirty hours of labor. Even so, something went wrong and I had to be delivered but by then the anesthetic didn't work—" She shudders, Corky has spread his fingers across her lower back, kneads the flesh, he has a habit of continually stroking, caressing, kneading, hardly conscious of what he does, his fingers moving of their own volition. "So, yes. It was hard. I lost a lot of blood and I sweated a quart of liquid but in the end I had a baby—that's the reward. Yes, I'd do it again. In the right circumstances. With the right man."

There's a sudden silence. Corky's prick stirs.

A pressure of silence, like air pushing inward. A kind of deafness. Like the time, returning strung out from Las Vegas, Corky had a fierce cold, sinuses stuffed as with cotton batting, and as the plane descended to land at Union City the pressure on his ears increased to the point of excruciating pain and his fucking left eardrum burst.

There's a rash-like sensation too on the lower part of his belly, in the wiry pubic hair, smarting, burning, Corky scratches it vigorously and the awkward moment passes.

How Charlotte would wake, beside him in bed, Corky insomniac and angry, scratching himself raising welts in his belly and ass, *Jerome, what's wrong*, her sleepy voice, on the edge of being frightened, the poor cunt always knew. Sure, look at Corky's wide guileless grin, look at his prick filling up with blood like a faucet's turned on, that easy and that healthy. Sure, something's wrong.

Casually Corky says, as if to change the subject though maybe really he isn't, his instinct is to back up into something serious with the caution with which you'd back up a trailer truck, "My stepdaughter Thalia, she and I've been sort of estranged since the divorce, haven't been in much contact but this strange thing, last night she called me at home, left a message, and this morning at the office, and when I tried to call her back no one answered." Corky hears his voice like an aggrieved lover's and gets to the point fast. "You ever run into her, or hear about her, Chrissie? I'm sort of, I guess, worried."

Corky's relations with his stepdaughter, begun happily when Thalia was eight years old, and broken off by degrees, jagged stops and starts, when he and Charlotte were divorced, are too complex for him to contemplate sober. He swings from feeling he's been treated badly by Thalia to thinking he's been a shit to her.

Christina says, carefully, knowing this is a touchy subject with Corky, "The last time I saw Thalia to speak with, it was a year ago, or more, she'd just quit her job with the county—I think it was Family Services?— she talked about being 'burnt out,' 'spiritually exhausted.'"

Corky says, "Right."

"Well, it's such heartbreaking, impossible work there, I've done a series on the department, I've interviewed caseworkers and clients, I know," Christina says. "The idealistic young people, like Thalia, fresh out of col- lege, all theory and goodwill—they're like birds crashing into plate-glass windows. Flying high, and hopeful, and then—"

"Their necks broken."

"—but you know all this. About Thalia."

Subtly rebuked, Corky says, "Hell, I don't know the first thing about Thalia. Where did you see her?"

"In the art museum. I was there, in fact, getting material for that piece I did for the *Journal* on the de Kruif collection, you know, the new wing—" Christina speaks hurriedly, you wouldn't guess, as Corky knows, that the de Kruifs, wealthy old Union City stock, are related by blood to the Burn- sides, Christina's family, "—and Thalia was there, having lunch with two girlfriends, and a man, they asked me to join them, in that court- yard restaurant that's like a medieval cloister, you know?—almost too charming?—so I did. One of the young women was a very light-skinned black, a creamy-brown black, she and Thalia seemed to be quite close, like sisters—I had the impression she worked for City Hall, but also for the museum, it wasn't entirely clear. And the man—he was older than the girls, but no more than thirty, I remember thinking with interest he was one of a new, young generation involved in politics, and connected with the Slatterys, but I hadn't known his name and didn't recognize his face. You probably know him, Corky. The four of them seem very close, very caught up with one another, passionate supporters of Vic Slattery, talking about him being governor after Cuomo—it struck me as wonderful, cer- tainly to Vic's credit, that he can inspire enthusiasm in such bright young people. Thalia was excited too about starting work as a programmer at WWUC, the evening news, I think. But you do know all this, Corky, don't you?"

Corky feels an unpleasant sense of vertigo. What do I know, what don't

I know. His kneading of the woman's flesh becomes more urgent, as it has become unconscious. What is it, his fingers' need to pummel, to hurt, no it's really to impress another with the fact of your existence, not to hurt: *Here I am.*

Fucked over, as he thinks, by cops, as a kid of eleven, Corky Corcoran has absorbed the cop's refusal to be questioned. What you do, you counter with a question of your own.

"What was Thalia like that day?—how did she act?"

Christina hesitates. Yes, she's tactful.

"Thalia was very sweet, very friendly, I remember being touched by how friendly she was, though she didn't know me well, doesn't know me, nor am I a friend of Charlotte's—though maybe she thought I was. She was what you'd call high-strung—excitable. She talked rapidly and not always coherently and she shivered a good deal, though she didn't unbutton her coat. Very lovely, of course—though maybe a little thin, pinched-looking in the face. She'd cut most of her beautiful hair off the night before so it was about an inch long at the crown of her head and spiky. It made her eyes enormous. You had to look twice to see was she a young woman, or a precocious boy. What struck me most was how she seemed to need to touch us—a hand on a girlfriend's wrist, a hand on the man's, on mine. The black girl especially—they seemed very close, as I said, like sisters."

Corky winces, hearing this. Poor Thalia, poor kid. Strung out on amphetamines, it sounds like—but Christina's so discreet, it's "high-strung."

"That black girl—d'you know her name?"

"I don't. I'm afraid it went by too fast. Thalia introduced me to them and the names just flew past."

"If it was Marilee Plummer—you know who that is, don't you?"

"The name *is* familiar," Christina says, "—oh, yes: my God: the young woman who accused Marcus Steadman of raping her—?"

Corky makes an incensed snuffling noise. Wriggles his toes, twists about on the sofa. He's getting charged up, a hard-on, just thinking about this shit, no doubt in his mind that Steadman did rape the girl, threatened to do worse, and Corky himself knew her, liked her—didn't know her well, not as well as he'd wanted.

The night he'd been with her, one of those long party-nights a year or two back, it'd been before Christina, and anyway nothing had happened. No need to go into details.

Corky'd made an asshole of himself and no need to delve into it.

Corky says, guardedly, "Well, it might have been her. I never knew Thalia and that girl were so close but then, hell, I don't know lots of things about my stepdaughter I'd've liked to know when I could have done some good for her." Talking like this is getting him hot, he can feel the blood coursing into his cock, nudging it against Christina, the scratchy hair between her thighs, not quite knowing what he's doing, as Christina, distracted, caresses him too, his upper arms he's vain about, the rocky-hard compact biceps, no slack skin like you see on other guys his age, or younger, at the Club, she's thoughtful, she's thinking, Corky can feel her thinking and wants to shut it off, to shut off his own fucking thinking, too. It's taking him in a direction he doesn't want.

Still he hears himself ask, "Did Thalia say anything about her mother, about the divorce?—about *me?*"

"Corky honey, I don't know, I don't remember," Christina says, kissing his mouth, drawing her tongue along the edge of his lips, smiling at him, teasing, "—I wasn't in love with you then, was I?"

"What, you're in love with me now?"

"Can't you tell?"

Sharply Corky draws in his breath, the way this woman is touching him, what she intends to do with him, yes he can tell.

As if the volition were taken from him, the push and thrust of it, the sharp stabbing sensation, the urgency. As if now it's her volition, the woman's, seizing his cock, caressing the tip, that feathery-fluttering motion he almost can't bear; easing herself against him, onto him, "Mmmm, Corky! My God," guiding him into her, something gracious and startled and radiantly sweet in the gesture, the warm wet ease of her vagina, her cunt he's crazy for. Yes it's a real craziness, he'd kill for it. The back of his skull hollowing out, his mouth dry as sand, a quick braided light flying across the white wall beside the sofa. The sounds he'd been half-hearing—an airplane high overhead, a tug out on the river, noises from the street—fall rapidly away, he's aware of nothing but the woman's damp teasing gaze brought close to his, the sweet rhythmic warmth of

her breath, her fine-pored face too immense to be seen. She's whispering, "God, Corky, you're nice, oh lover you're nice, like this, oh like this,
oh Corky, wait—" halting suddenly, gripping him hard, nails dug in his
shoulders, that tension in her so quick, she's about to come, her eyes roll
up and she ceases breathing, ceases all motion, the way she'd been rubbing herself against him, her thighs closed on him, she'd done this in the
past and Corky feels a wild frantic joy gathering in him, it's a lighted
match brought closer and closer to a flammable substance, so seemingly
without effort, without force.

"Oh. Lover. Sweet Corky. Oh *wait*."

Sweet Corky waits.

Against his burning eyelids seeing a flash of cards, so strangely and unexpectedly a waterfall of flawlessly shuffled playing cards, the only card
trick Timothy Patrick Corcoran could do and it was a lovely one, lifting
his hands like a magician like Harry Blackstone in his Magic Show, the
sleek cards flying from left hand to right hand, from right hand to left
hand, in perfect equilibrium, not a card would fall, Jerome stared hypnotized wanting the miracle never to end, the most radiant of tricks.

Corky strokes, grips, kneads Christina's flesh. The slender curve of her
waist, the ample flesh at the small of her back, the smooth buttocks. She's
half-lying upon him, frozen, motionless, her breath too withheld, only a
strand of damp hair slipping forward against Corky's cheek. He's a stiff
rod upon which she's balanced. His blood courses hotly into her. They
share the same heartbeat. As with Theresa, long ago. Before he was born.
Snug and secret upside down breathing not air but blood, fueled by blood,
Corky has never been so happy. "Is it nice? *Is* it?"

"Corky. Don't let me go."

Yes he wants a kid, it's time. More than time.

A son, he'd name him Timothy Patrick Corcoran. A daughter?—who
knows. Theresa might be bad luck.

That's the secret luck of the Irish: bad luck.

The craziness of Fate, what's called Fate. What God wants to do with
you you never thought He'd have in mind.

The craziness you inherit in the genes, in that mix of chromosomes
that's set at the time of ejaculation. Sperm and egg and heat cataclysmic
as the Big Bang they say started the universe—so extreme, the immea-

surable temperatures, the density of matter, it's impossible to track Time back before then.

Corky murmurs, "Hey: d'you love me?"

Christina murmurs, tight as a bow, "Oh, lover. Oh God."

Near-flattened, her breasts against Corky's chest. Her quickened heartbeat against his ribs. After a moment she begins to move again, cautious, concentrated, just barely moving, easing back into her rhythm, the rhythm she's imposing upon Corky. Squeezing and releasing him with her vaginal muscles, squeezing and releasing him, he tells himself he has never loved any woman the way he loves this woman and it may be true, all memory of other women has been washed away, obliterated. A tall stark window opening out onto a sky—dazzling light, a blue into which he could fall and fall, weightless, forever.

Christina cradles Corky's head in the crook of her arm, leaning above him. His lips suck at her breast, lips tongue teeth, the nipple hard and erect as a miniature stem, he's in a delirium of pleasure, wordless bliss. Inside the woman, inside her dark heated womb, yet nursing her too, what ecstasy, Christina's fingers in his hair, stroking, clenching, she brings her face to his, her wide-set eyes glassy and the pupils dilated, such an intensity of sensation makes us blind, now open-mouthed Christina kisses him, the way that first time in his car driving back from Maiden Vale, parked above the river's edge she'd kissed him, unexpectedly, to his great happiness, yet such hunger in her kiss, such terrible need, it was as if they were already fucking, their stunned bodies already poised shuddering at climax. Christina whispers, "Corky I love you, I love love love you, Corky don't leave me," and Corky whispers, "Honey, no—why would I leave you," and Christina repeats, "Don't leave me, oh please," her voice rising, tightening in what seems like pain, face contorted like pain, she's shy, fearful, shrinking even as she brings the lighted match closer and closer teasingly close to what must explode in flame before their sweat-slick bodies are released. "Corky. *Oh*."

Again it's a heartbeat, a pulsebeat away. A squeeze will do it. A pinch. Corky sees against his eyelids the lovely lightning-flash of cards. Left hand to right, right hand to left, rising, falling, a waterfall it was called, Tim Corcoran's only card trick but a damned dazzling one.

Shit on their shoes, kid.

But no more.

No more?

Oh!—you mick bastard. Fucker.

Corky laughs, loving it. Suffused with sexual pleasure that's keen as theft, stolen from the woman's body and that body the possession of another man. Corky Corcoran, a firecracker about to go off, he *is* a fucker, yes.

A space blinded with light, blown and rocked by the wind out of Canada, out of the Arctic, ceaseless. The winking mica-glittering river reflected in the sky. The nubby fabric of the blanket or quilt or is it, for expediency's sake, a giant bath towel carefully laid upon the sofa before Corky's arrival, Christina Kavanaugh is a careful premeditated woman, even her hunger is premeditated, this terrible deep yearning of her womb, her mouth, she's taken the phone off the hook so no one can interrupt, "—Oh! Corky—oh please wait—no—" she's blind and distracted and desperate, wanting it, but not wanting it, yes but of course she wants it, her arm around Corky's neck desperate as that of a drowning woman's and there's no going back, Corky grips her buttocks, tight, hard, begins thrusting himself up into her, deep inside her, Christina moans, gives herself up to him, she's about to go off and these last quickened seconds are excruciating, how Corky would love to be able to make the woman come without coming himself, those violent helpless spasms, the vaginal contractions squeezing milking at his cock yet his cock remaining hard, Corky remaining in control, then by degrees bringing her to another climax, and another, it's an old fantasy of his but not possible, he hears himself moaning too, "Oh—Chrissie," he's losing it too, a stab of pleasure searing as flame, he can't hold back, the pendulum clock begins its liquidy soprano chime and Christina presses her clenched teeth against his neck to keep from screaming, how it is for her he can't imagine, can't imagine any sensation more powerful than his own, rushing through him, groin, spine, back of the skull, he feels her orgasm, the astonishment of it, never can you be prepared for it, each time the first time, no way out but oblivion.

Gently Christina detaches herself from Corky, kisses his slack lips and rises from the sofa, he's asleep, dropped into sleep like Death the way an infant sleeps the body wholly given up to sleep so intense the skin is clammy-chill, yes but shrewd Corky believes himself fully awake and in control because he has the power to make Time cease when he sleeps, for instance hasn't the pendulum clock ceased its ticking, hasn't the traffic down on Nott Street ceased, all outer movement ceased, he's afloat bathed in radiance and utterly utterly happy, and safe.

Hears Christina in the shower, feels a fleeting urge to join her, but only fleeting. So utterly happy. Safe.

Scared cards can't win, a scared man can't love.

But that doesn't apply to Corky Corcoran.

And then with wifely solicitude, stooping to kiss him awake, Christina gets Corky up, for a moment he's sleep-dazed as if hit over the head with a sledgehammer (how many hours' sleep did he get the night before?— three, four?) but of course he has to wake up, sees to his alarm it's 12:35, he'd better move his ass.

"—Or you could call Greenbaum and postpone your lunch," Christina says, "—and stay here and have lunch with me."

But Corky's already headed, naked, for the bathroom, "Chrissie, honey, there's nothing I'd like better," he says, "—but you know I *can't.*"

Christina laughs. "Oh, I know."

Under the shower, lavishly soaping himself, it's the second time this morning Corky has had a shower but this is the luxury one, this the unspeakable exalted pleasure, he's thinking how sweet of Chrissie to laugh, so rarely to speak in reproach. Other women, most of all Charlotte, hadn't laughed.

Corky Corcoran, a man in motion. No sooner gets to one place and loves it than he's restless and bored and can't bear to stay another minute. *The truth about you,* Charlotte once said, furious, tossing something (his car keys?) at him, *you should live in your God-damned car.*

Charlotte Drummond, no she'd been Charlotte Braunbeck when they met, the woman of all Corky's women who knows him best. The brutal intimacy of the formerly married.

Married eleven years. Twenty-eight when he'd gotten into it, thirty-nine by the time he'd gotten out. A lifetime. Vowed he'd never stick his head in such a noose again.

Yet it's Charlotte he's thinking of, more soberly now. Needs to call. To check about Thalia. That look in Thalia's face the first time she'd over-heard Charlotte and Corky quarreling, poor kid like she'd been slapped, even now Corky feels a stab of grief.

It's children who get hurt, children who can't get out of the way fast enough.

Our only witness: you.

Well, he'll have to get Thalia's telephone number, new address, from Charlotte. Or maybe have his secretary call Charlotte?—unless that would insult her.

You only get to know another person thoroughly, Corky thinks, to the degree to which you've fallen out of love with that person.

Except: he's crazy about Christina Kavanaugh, and he's certain he knows *her*.

Hey: d'you love me?

Oh, lover. Oh God.

That second time she'd come, Jesus how beautiful. Open-mouthed kissing and he'd swear he could feel the contractions rippling through her. Wondering, Do their hearts contract like that, too?—must be the nearest thing to dying.

Except: if Christina doesn't show up at the Memorial Day fundraiser, where Corky's scheduled to speak, Corky's going to be hurt, Corky's go-ing to be seriously hurt, he can only be hurt by people he loves so sure as hell he's careful not to love many people now he's an adult and in control of his fate and if Christina hurts him he isn't going to like it. Which is an understatement.

It was through a fund-raising program for the old, original Maiden Vale Library he'd met her. Contrived to meet her. A proposal for $200,000 for extensive renovations of the library came up before the City Council and was vetoed derisively within minutes but Corky scanned the list of names on the petition, the names of the rich, and one name leapt out at him *Christina Kavanaugh!* so civic-minded Jerome Corcoran made it a point to show up at the next Friends of the Maiden Vale Library meet-ing one windy June afternoon of the previous year, approximately thirty well-to-do men and women, a predominance of women, Corky singled out Christina Kavanaugh at once, looked at her frankly, smiled at her in his way that never fails to coax a smile in return from virtually any

woman and most men: *Here I am, I'm a good-hearted guy, trust me!*
Christina stared at Corky, her face coloring slightly, as if embarrassed she
should know him and didn't: or was he a friend of Harry's?

Corky was introduced to the gathering as one of the few City Councilmen with an interest in the preservation of Union City historical buildings and this was in fact the truth, Corky's weakness is for buildings like
the Maiden Vale Library he's grown up seeing, at least from the outside,
and doesn't want razed, obliterated, suddenly *gone.* You had to love the
old Maiden Vale Library, deteriorated as it was, built 1836, a local mas-
terpiece of Classic Revivalism, airy rooms and high ceilings and somber
Ionic columns and a parlor-sized reading room impractical as hell; badly
warped hardwood floors, a rotting roof, leaking basement and windows,
a $2-million deficit at a time when the budgets of new, modern branches
of the public library were being cut back; only forty-eight hundred card-
holders, compared to thirty thousand at the larger Maiden Vale branch.
(Corky, ever-scrupulous in such details, had done his homework.) Still,
Corky spoke warmly and enthusiastically to the group, Corky's a guy who
loves to talk if he's in the right place at the right time, he'd impressed his
audience listing pros and cons of fund-raising for the library, suggesting
that he, in his capacity as a Councilman, try to arrange for a state allot-
ment of the $200,000 under the New York Historical Buildings Fund—
there's an emergency fund for just such purposes. Corky explained why
their cause was vetoed at City Hall but declined to speak ill of his fellow
Council members or of Mayor Oscar Slattery, clever Corky took the opportunity to point out how supportive Slattery was regarding the public
library system, public health, education, police. Seeing Christina Kavanaugh's eyes upon him how knowledgeable Corky was! how frank! courteous! with that Irish ardor and glow in his face that isn't always the effect
of alcohol and afterward as he'd anticipated a half dozen women vied for
his attention and here too Corky was clever and courteous making his
way purposefully to Christina Kavanaugh who stood holding her coat
watching him as if simply waiting for him, with a tight-jawed calm that
excited him. Happiness flooding to every part of Corky's body including
his cock: *Here I am, trust me!*

He asked her her name, and she told him. They shook hands. Corky
gripped her hand, hard. The color up in his face, the glisten in his eyes.

He said, "You're Harry Kavanaugh's wife?" and Christina said, "Yes, and he's my husband," staring Corky down, as if he'd said something to offend (Jesus, he hadn't meant to!—he'd've fallen at the woman's feet, grabbed her ankles inside those smoky-silky stockings) or to tease, "—but he isn't here now, is he?"

They walked out together. The Maiden Vale Library was in an old part of the district, on a once-prestigious boulevard of large, pretentious houses, some of them now divided into condominiums and offices, the elms had long since been cut down and even in the windy dusk the area looked raw. As Corky shoved open the heavy outer door, Christina's hair blew against his face, he shut his eyes weak with a wave of desire he couldn't believe she couldn't feel, too.

Outside the overheated library the world was blunt and stark. A place of little comfort unless you risked rejection by seeking comfort.

Corky asked, "Would you like to drive somewhere?—for a drink?"

Christina said, "Yes. Corky. You know I would."

Corky!—it's as if the woman has laid her lovely hand on his prick. Corky stared at her, sick with love.

Seeing her eyes fixed on his. A little scared, and excited. Her eyes a luminous pebbly transparency, the mouth beautiful, he'd thought of kissing her, what it would be like, a quickening sensation in his body, oh Christ. Remembering how that evening downtown he'd trailed this woman, drink in hand, yes and probably half-drunk turned on by her big, pregnant belly as much as by her beautiful face.

Later Corky was to learn Christina remembered him, too. How obvious he'd been, watching her. Good-looking Irish-faced guy a minor Democratic politician, she hadn't known his name at the time. And hadn't inquired.

Bitch. Stuck-up cunt. Nobody snubs Corky Corcoran.

No longer.

Impatiently Corky shuts off the shower, damned thing leaks, hadn't he given Christina the name of a first-rate plumber but weeks go by, months, and it still leaks. Just like a woman. Charlotte pretending she couldn't deal with plumbers, electricians, the lawn men, the furnace repair man, they only respect another man, *you* don't know. Shit, thinks Corky, the excuses women make!—drying himself with a towel Christina's already used, other towels on the rack luxuriant and spotless (you don't forget, with Christina, this is a high-class woman) but the damp towel is good enough for him.

Jesus, why's he always running late?—Corky's a guy who'll be late for his own funeral. What time *is* it?

Yes but obviously Corky needs that edge to his life. Always on the move, Corky Corcoran's your man, traversing Union City by day, by night—expressways, avenues, streets. Keeping pace with his own fast pulse. Too restless to stay in one place for very long. Metabolism like a God-damned monkey Charlotte used to complain, envious of him he never gained weight like her.

Can't slow down, the bastards will catch up with you.

Eat my shit. Who's to stop me?

Fucking Christina the judge's wife—what you live for, eh?

Corky rubs steam off the mirror, peers critically at himself. It's a weakness of his, O.K.—vain of his good looks, if you got it flaunt it, you learn young, girls casting no-mistaking-it looks at him even as a kid, eyes locking eyes. Corky's darkish red-brown curly hair, great hair for a guy but, shit, it's definitely thinning, no hiding the fact when it's wet and flattened against his scalp. *My scalp? Showing through?* The sight of it makes his prick shrink. Baring his teeth in a mirthless grin to examine them: teeth are O.K. if just slightly discolored (from smoking; but he's quit). Left front tooth is bigger than the right, buck-tooth, saw-notched, like he'd been punched by some cutey, but nobody can see, probably. Except close-up like Christina.

She'd think it was sexy. Anything about him. If they love you, you can't lose.

That early time together, Christina drunk and randy, laughing like a young girl then suddenly her face crinkled and she's crying, Jesus!—how fast they switch from one to the other, blows your mind. Telling Corky he was the only man she'd ever known who had the gift of happiness—her words: "gift of happiness"—just his smile, you changed my life with that smile. And Christina pressed herself into his arms hot and guilty saying it—this—meaning them: being lovers—was nothing she'd ever believed could happen in her life let alone planned, contemplated. And it must have nothing to do with the rest of her life. Her husband who needed her in a way Corky could never comprehend, that had to do with his very worth as a human being: should he live? should he surrender, die?—and her son, too. Her son whom she'd loved as a baby with a ferocity she hadn't known she was capable of, a ravenous mother-love it had been, and now the memory of it lodged deep inside her, and did not, could not, exactly attach itself to the adolescent boy the baby had grown into *out of my own body*, Christina said, marveling, it's something you live through but can't understand and you can't speak of it, there aren't the words. So Corky who hadn't been following all this precisely, Corky in what's called post-coital bliss, guessed some question was being put to him, some proposition of a moral kind defined and unsentimental as a legal contract, saying grandly, "Any way you want it, baby. You call the shots."

Corky examines his eyes, the left eye bloodshot as hell, and bruised-looking dents beneath his eyes, tonight for sure he's got to sleep, six, seven hours at the least, turn off the phone and get undressed and actually go to bed, into bed, not sprawling half-clothed slantwise across the bed or downstairs on the sofa the TV on or worse yet in his car as he's inclined to do, God knows why.

Why?—*to make a quick escape if required.*

Fucking fed up with being an insomniac, since the age of eleven but what's to be done. The doctors and the therapy and the rest of that shit hadn't helped Theresa erase from her memory the way Tim Corcoran had looked lying broken and bleeding and dead and the electric shock and prescription drugs for sure hadn't helped, Corky is filled with rage and disgust and knows nobody can help him and knows he wouldn't trust anybody who could help him, fuck that, he's a private man, nobody screws with his head. When they were first married, though, and he was trying to lead what's called a normal life, sleeping in a bed with his wife (whom he loved, then, hell yes he did love Charlotte) Charlotte got him to go to her doctor, get a prescription for barbiturates, Corky tried them for a few days then flushed them down the toilet. His brain zapped, cotton batting muffling everything and flashes of weird dream-pictures during the day, fuck that. Pills are for women, he'd told Charlotte. Any time I want seriously to knock myself out I'll get drunk.

Except you have to wake up, eventually. Sick as a dog.

Read, the other night, in his paperback *A Treasury of Science Lore*, the longest a human being has been known to survive without sleep is nine days. Poor bastard must have been raving mad by then.

Corky has brought most of his clothes into the bathroom. Dresses swiftly. With impatient fingers looping his tie around his neck seeing by his watch the time's 12:50 P.M.—which is pretty damned good, considering.

Steps out of the bathroom into cooler air and is about to call out something to Christina when he hears her voice, she must be speaking on the telephone, Corky pauses knotting his tie to listen, edges a little closer, barefoot and noiseless, to where she's standing, back to him, a short distance away at a rear window, sunshine in her black hair like it's on fire, he sees she's wearing a maroon-checked jacket and maroon flannel pants, a smart getup, Christina Kavanaugh too is ready to leave her brownstone loft at 331 Nott for the rest of her day. Corky hears her say, not guardedly exactly, but quietly, in an undertone, these words that pierce his heart like a blade, yet so swiftly and so without warning there's no pain, "—yes, he's here now, but he's leaving." A pause, and then, "Yes." Another pause, and, "I will, honey. Of course. Around six. I have to drive out to Indian Lake for this piece I'm doing on the Children's Center, that new therapy for autistic children, I think I've told you? Then—" Another pause, and then, in a tone of intimate appeal, of familiar placating, "Yes. You know I do."

By the time Christina hangs up the phone, turns back, Corky's sitting on the sofa bed (it was a bath towel she'd slung over it, an old bleached-out towel she's used many times before) yanking on his socks, forcing his feet into his shoes. His face is composed, clenched as a fist.

Corky Corcoran the locally celebrated poker player, the gambler, innocently vain in his imagining that no one can read his face if he doesn't want them to read it, and now he doesn't want this woman to read it, but he doesn't seem to hear her ask him something, then repeat it and still he doesn't hear, he's suspended, no-feeling, a distant roaring in his ears. *He's here now, but he's leaving.*

Christina, incongruously dressed for the city, yet still barefoot, has taken up a hairbrush and briskly brushes her hair, static electricity crackling in the long sensuous strokes, hair smooth as a single black substance framing her face that's lightly flushed from so much emotion, a pink cast to it, and she walks forcefully on her heels, with that ramrod-straight posture Corky associates with the very rich or the very arrogant. She pauses, looking at him. "Corky? What's wrong?"

Corky raises his eyes to hers, empty of all expression.

Asks, coolly, "Wrong how? With me, with you?—or generally?"

"You look angry."

"Why should I be angry? Shouldn't I be happy?"

Corky continues jamming a foot into a shoe. At home, he has a fucking shoehorn.

Christina stands before him, no longer brushing her hair, staring at him.

The pendulum clock's pert toy-ticking has become louder and if the thing starts chiming, Corky's going to smash it with his fist.

"Corky."

Christina drops the hairbrush onto the sofa, comes quickly to him, a knee on the sofa beside him, leaning over him and her arms wrapped around him, she kisses his cheek, it's a fierce loving gesture but Corky, furious Corky, doesn't respond. She whispers, "Corky?—oh, lover." He feels her quickened heartbeat but still he doesn't respond. Down on Nott Street a garbage truck makes a series of sudden noises like staccato farting.

Christina leans back to peer anxiously into Corky's face. "Were you listening, just now?"

"You mean, did I hear."

"You did—?"

Christina touches Corky's warm cheek and he flicks her hand away. It's the first rough or even impatient gesture this woman has experienced with Corky, he sees her eyes widen in that kind of alarm that has excited him frequently, with other women, that female anticipation of physical upset, violence, but Corky gives no impression of being excited now, on the contrary Christina's baffled by his steely calm, Corky Corcoran who's by nature so affectionate and demonstrative and talky, rising stiff to his feet, ready to walk out. He picks up his boxy-sporty jacket and thrusts his arms into it with the impatience with which he'd jammed his feet into his shoes and he'd be on his way except Christina stops him. "Corky! Please wait—"

Still calmly, Corky says, "I told you, Christina. I have a date for lunch at one."

"Corky, you can't walk out like this. Darling, please. I'm not sure what you heard me say, but—"

"Call me, we'll talk. After Monday."

It's as if Corky has slapped her, she steps back. Disadvantaged on the heels of her feet. Appearing, so suddenly, rather short, diminished, a not-young woman in this bright pitiless light, forehead crinkled and thin white lines at the corners of her eyes and the eyes unnaturally bright with tears, worry. Numbly, she repeats, "I—I'm not sure what you heard, but—Corky, I—"

Again she plucks at his sleeve and this time Corky reacts spontaneously: pushes her away.

A quick unerring reflex like a boxer's, the flat of his hand, right hand shoving against her left shoulder, not hard, yes but hard enough to push her away.

"Fuck you, Christina. And Harry Kavanaugh."

Corky walks out, out of the loft, taking the stairs at first calmly and then, halfway down, with the rushed fury of a wounded-hearted kid, he's in a fever of disbelief and rage and it isn't until he reaches the vestibule that he pauses, his heart pounding in his ears. *Isn't she going to call me back? There's never been one of them who hasn't called me back.*

Thinking too, he's a practical-headed guy, he's had scenes like this, at least resembling this, the hurt and the rage and the adrenaline rush, in the past, *I can't walk away, the rest of the day will be fucked.*

Wheeling back then cursing to himself and climbing the stairs, in a sweat inside his good clothes *And she's going to pay for this, too: the bitch* and upstairs on the third floor there's Christina Kavanaugh standing where he'd left her, flat-footed, stunned, a rash-like flush mottling her pale skin, tears spilling over onto her cheeks but she's defiant too. "He's my husband. Of course I love him. I love him too."

"Let's get this straight, Christina," Corky says. "Harry knows about me?—us?"

"Yes. He does."

"You told him?"

"Yes. I did."

"Since when?"

Christina hesitates. Her tear-brimmed eyes lose their focus for a moment, she's considering lying then reconsiders, tells Corky, "Since last June."

"Last *June?*"

"Yes."

"From the *start?*"

Corky hears his own rising voice, Christ this would be funny if he wasn't involved.

Staring at the woman as if he'd never seen her before, never really seen her before. Let alone, only a few minutes ago, his cock deep up inside her where, it'd seemed, it had been so right.

Christina moves to touch Corky again, to make him hear. The way she'd said Thalia was touching her friends. The fingers' raw pleading appeal, the appeal of flesh. *Listen to me, believe me, here I am: I exist.*

"Corky, please don't be angry. I should have told you. I was going to tell you eventually. Harry is my husband, we've been married for fifteen years, I couldn't deceive him. I don't want to deceive him. I share most of my life with him. His own is so—" She pauses, pleading, hoping for the right word, but the only word that comes to her is flat, inadequate, "—sad."

Corky says, "What the fuck do I care, his life is 'sad'! What's it got to do with me! As I see it, I'm the sucker—the asshole. I'm the one who doesn't know what's going on."

Seeing the door behind him is wide open, anybody could be out there on the landing getting a good earful, Corky slams it shut, so hard the place shudders.

Now to Corky's disgust Christina begins to seriously cry. An aggrieved, incredulous weeping, and the flush in her face deepening, crimson as a birthmark.

Now in front of Corky's eyes the transformation he's witnessed so many times, too many fucking times, beginning in fact with Theresa, how many times with Theresa, the woman will make herself ugly to him, the most cunning and cruel of their strategies, throwing back in your face like vomit the emotion you've felt for them, what you'd believed was love now jeering mockery. *And this too she'll pay for: the cunt.*

Christina says, "Corky, why does it matter so much?—Corky, please," and Corky says, "You're telling Harry Kavanaugh each time we fuck, it shouldn't matter so much? What do you take me for?" and Christina says, "But I don't! I don't! It isn't like that, nothing so crude as that," and Corky says, "It sounds to me pretty crude, it sounds to me pretty sick, d'you do this with all the guys you fuck, or only with me?" and Christina says, "Corky, I tell Harry about my life, I share my life with him, don't you understand?—I just want the rest of his life to be as happy as I can make it. He's seriously ill, the MS is out of remission, it's beginning to attack his—" and Corky interrupts, "Don't tell me! I don't want to know! It's got nothing to do with me! Harry Kavanaugh isn't my friend, I'm shit on his shoes, what the fuck do I care about Judge Kavanaugh, any more than he'd care about me!" and Christina, shocked at this, says, faltering, "'Shit on his shoes'?—what do you mean? Corky, that's crazy," and Corky says, "You think I don't know how you feel about me?—about guys like me?— from Irish Hill? You think I'm that much of an asshole, I don't know?" and Christina says, "But you're wrong, honey, you're wrong, what are you saying? You must know I love you, of course I love you, but—I love Harry, too," and Corky says, "Then love *his* prick, suck off *his* prick," and Christina says, pleading, "Corky, stop! The things you're saying! It isn't just that, I love you very much, I thought you were my friend," and Corky says, enlivened by rage, and his rage delicious to him, as to all the Corcorans, for what is more delicious than your soul flaming up, a big ball of flame you want to fan bigger, and bigger, "I'm not your friend, Christina, I'm not anybody's friend, *don't touch me*."

Corky is about to lose it, on the hairsbreadth edge like going over into orgasm, delicious to him, but terrifying, too, as Christina pleads with him he's been pacing about the crowded space, colliding with things, gives a chair a kick and when the God-damned clock on the mantel begins its sugary-whirring chimes he knocks it off with one flat-handed blow and that shuts it up for good, a clatter of breaking glass as Christina screams, Corky'd smash the Chinese cat-fox in his fist too but it's out of his reach on a table, he neither knows nor cares what he's doing only that he's do-ing it, such rage burns and in burning justifies itself, consumes itself, since boyhood he's had a wild temper, Christina Kavanaugh has never seen him erupt, yes but she's seeing him now, her eyes are being opened now, the bitch, the lying cunt, deceiving Corky Corcoran of all men, yet she continues to plead with him, as if words might save them, words in the face of such passion, trying to touch him, even to caress him, he shoves her away half-shielding his face as if revulsed by the sight of her. Corky's going to explode and hurt this woman if she isn't careful but still she approaches him, she can't believe she has no power over him as, within the past hour, she's had such power, and such magnificent power, Corky sees it as arrogance, a woman's arrogance and in this woman the arrogance of the rich, she's not only right but in her rightness mature, adult—"Corky, honey! For God's sake how can you be so narrow, so ungiving? Is it some Catholic thing?—some remnant? Nothing has changed between us, has it? Tell me what has changed between us?"—a woman throwing herself upon a child, a child in a fury of a tantrum, she's his mother, is she, is that it, needing just to get her arms around Corky and hold him fast, still, warm breasts against his face, fingers clutching his head, yes then she'd have him.

Then it happens, it's the paradox of such situations, Corky's experienced them many times before, older but no wiser, well maybe a little wiser, an ex-married man is always wiser than a kid starting out knowing nothing, it happens that Christina herself loses it, the lighted flame flares up in her head too, she slaps at Corky when he shoves her away, she begins to scream, sobbing, "Damn you! Damn *you!* I can't believe this! *You!*" catching him a good smarting blow on the side of the face, and in a reflexive motion quick and unthinking and unerring as a cat's Corky strikes out at her in return, he's a counterpuncher and counterpunchers love to take a hit because it pulls the trigger, gives them permission, all of the Irish you might say are counterpunchers, shrewdness in desperation, enormous joy in cunning, *Watch your back!* Corky hits Christina on the shoulder, not hard, but hard enough to stagger her backward, to let her know this is serious, and she flails back at him like in fact he's her thirteen-year-old kid, yes but Corky isn't Christina's kid or anybody's kid, he hits her again, a little harder, and this time she cries, "God damn you! I hate you!" slapping and clawing at him, and Corky crouches in a quick defense like a boxer, at St. Thomas he'd had a few lessons, skinny lightweight with a good jab but no real punch in either hand still he was quick on his feet, and he's quick now, ducking now, and his face distorted in a grimace as he balls his fist and punches Christina, this time catching her in the ribs, and again in the ribs, he hasn't lost it so much he'd hit a woman in the breasts or the belly or the face, certainly not the face, and this woman's face wet and slippery like rubber with tears, contorted, ugly, she makes one last frantic try at holding him, wrapping her arms around him, still she must believe that if she can hold him she'll have him, pleading, begging, "Corky, I love you, don't hurt me, don't leave me, I love you, don't," now in her desperation that's like a drunken woman's tugging at his belt, his trousers, she knows he's hot for it as he hasn't quite known in his rage he's hot for it too, and as at other times in his life, these other times of which he doesn't think nor wish to think except when good and soused and then he's incapable of thinking, as at other such times Corky gives in immediately, all his fury is in his cock, all his brains, his blood, like a hemorrhage into his cock and Christina pulls at his clothes, greedily at his crotch, and at her own clothes, begging, whimpering, this desperation in her she won't believe herself capable of afterward nor wish to recall afterward but now in the terrible exigency of passion can't halt, clutching at her lover like a drowning woman, the two of them abruptly on the bare floorboards clumsy and panting in manic splotches of sunshine and Corky has his fingers in her, she's moaning thrashing from side to side her face contorted, reddened eyes shut, a glisten of spittle on her chin, blindly she reaches for him, her fingers grasping at him, she must have him, no way out of this except she must have him, and quick and deft and coldly furious Corky straddles her, mounts her, with the brute efficiency with which, decades ago, as he and other fifth-grade boys at Our Lady of Mercy watched in speechless glee, a male mongrel German shepherd mounted a female mongrel setter in an alley behind the school, Corky's hot and mean as a pistol, veins standing out in his forehead, veins ropey and tight to bursting too in his penis, he shoves it into her, it's what she wants so he's giving it to her, hears her scream, grunt, whimper his name, he grips her hard and purposeful enough to bruise, just below the waist where you can get a solid grip, at the woman's waist and torso she's lean but here she's fleshy, female, beginning to get flaccid, a thirty-six-year-old woman in the body if not in the face and after all she's had a kid, she's pushed a kid through it, the birth canal, the vagina, the cunt stretched to bursting like shitting a watermelon a woman once told Corky, that's the romance of delivering a baby so no wonder Theresa quit being a mother to him as if incapable of recognizing him except to know his name and his relation to her but incapable of feeling it, Corky doesn't blame her, Corky doesn't blame any of them, Corky on his bony knees like praying his sinewy thigh muscles he's so proud of operating the lower part of his body like a jack-hammer, and as much tenderness in the operation as in a jackhammer's, a half dozen short quick hard thrusts and Corky comes, an anguished-sounding grunt forcing itself through his clenched jaws, a splash of dazed light behind the eyelids, that eruption of sheer sensation in the groin no sooner done than done. Like a decapitation.

—————————————

3

THE SHADOW-OFFICE

B y the time Corky gets to the Athletic Club downtown at Union City Square, fuck it, he'll be thirty minutes late, maybe forty, he envisions Greenbaum's crinkled-turtle face and shrewd pouched eyes, the liquid sharpness to those eyes Corky associates with Jewishness which to his Catholic imagination is as much a quality of IQ as of race or religion or whatever Jews are, yes and another thing about Jews, not that Corky's experience is deep or wide-ranging but he's been around, maybe in fact his father used to say this, with Jews there's a brain independent of and in no way hinted at by the face as with every Irish person you're likely to meet, faces you can read simple and clear and self-incriminating as a baby's bottom. Every emotion rising to the surface and the most shameful ones, above all shame itself, oozing oily at every pore.

How could she!—all these months! He'd been so crazy about her.

Sucker. Asshole. The one who doesn't know what's going on.

Corky's suffused with shame. Corky will never forgive Christina Kavanaugh. From this hour on, he's done with her.

Used Kleenex. Toilet paper.

Fuck a married woman, you'll end up getting fucked over yourself.

Whose warning was this, drunken ebullience masking utmost sincerity, Corky half-recalls it was old Drummond himself, of all people. Ross Drummond. Corky's boss for years and his father-in-law for years though not exactly the same years. Warning Corky who was after all married to Ross's own daughter at the time so it might be interpreted on the face of it a strange or even an insulting thing to say except if you knew the guy.

Treacherous old bastard, yes but he'd always liked Corky Corcoran and trusted him and that's all that matters.

End up getting fucked over yourself but how could Corky have guessed, cautious about keeping their affair secret, not so much as a hint to his friends, and Corky's friends are always pumping him about his women, and all along, from the start, she'd been deceiving him, Corky can't believe it, yes but you'd better believe it, asshole.

He's my husband, of course I love him, I love him too.

I share my life with him.

Now the fury, the sex part of it, is over, what he's feeling is hurt, shame. Driving his car too fast, swerving slightly, on a littered ramp of the Fillmore Expressway. Jesus you'd better push it out of your head, better clear your head, you're going to crack up the car and you never will make it to the U.C.A.C. for lunch or anything else.

Enough to know from this hour on he's done with Christina Kavanaugh. With both the Kavanaughs.

Clumsy to do this while driving, one arm on the wheel and a hand groping out, he gets the glove compartment open just to check is there a pint of anything inside though knowing of course that there isn't. After his last near-accident, when he'd scraped his beautiful new car along the right side, Corky made up his mind no more pints in the car thus no temptation to drink while driving no matter his mood and his need.

For whenever there's a mood, there's a need. But no more.

The last time Corky felt such shame, he can't recall. A long time ago.

Of their many quarrels none with Charlotte had gone so deep, so worked him up, sweet Jesus what if he'd lost it completely and hurt her, what then, one solid punch can smash a woman's jaw, teeth, nose, thank God he'd pulled back in time, nor had any of the quarrels with Thalia been quite so bad, of course with Thalia it was a different story, another kind of testing of Corky Corcoran. Sweet-faced little Thalia in eighth grade walking in the upstairs hall barefoot and gliding in what they called a baby-doll nightie, pink cotton to mid-thigh and childish puff sleeves and lacy collar and her little bush showing shadowy through the fabric, yes and her little breasts, no larger than peaches, the dark nipples, and Corky stared and blinked and for sure blushed and Thalia whispered, "Oh! excuse me, 'Corky'!" She'd called him "Corky," too, not in her mother's voice but in her own: shy-seeming, startled, almost inaudible: and her gaze, the thick-lashed dark brown eyes, dropping away as she turned, to hurry back to her room.

So he'd imagine, or maybe in fact he did hear, her giggling in there.

Well, fuck Thalia, fuck them all. Making an asshole of him.

Except: he's worried about her, he should call her, yes but he hasn't got her number. Yes but he could call Miriam at the office and have Miriam get the number from Charlotte, why doesn't he do that, but no he's too agitated right now, Miriam's like an old wife she can detect the faintest tremor in her employer's voice, remember her stiff disapproval though utterly wordless, discreet, when he'd been drinking in his private office, her prim worried mouth and averted eyes.

Corky's late for his lunch with Greenbaum but fuck it he's so sweated up and freaked he has to stop by his Pearl Street office to wash up a bit, his crotch for sure, and run cold water to splash on his face which looks fevered, not like a guy who's been fucking all morning but who's been royally fucked, in the ass. Changing also to a fresh white shirt identical to the one he was wearing.

You're an American, you're good as you look. Right?

Opens then a closet door, considers the bottle of Johnnie Walker on the shelf—"No thanks." It's good for a guy's morale to say no even if just to himself at a time of great temptation.

(Corky's rule of thumb is good whiskey shouldn't be drunk like medicine and never by a man alone in any state of hurt, shame, confusion wrought by a woman. For it's happened in the past that a single mouthful in such circumstances engenders a powerful thirst for another, and that for yet another, till the bottle's empty and you wake up twelve hours later your face flat on the desktop or worse yet on the floor.)

This place is Corky Corcoran's "shadow-office." So he thinks of it though no one else knows its name. Three fairly large but near-unfurnished rooms on the second floor of an old brick building at Pearl and Tannenbaum, within sight of the Expressway, with a view here too, slantwise, seen through traffic haze, of the river. Miriam the office manager of Corcoran, Inc., on State Street is aware of the shadow-office but knows virtually nothing about it not even its location. Maybe she thinks it's staffed with a shadow-Miriam, but it's not—there's no staff at 274 Pearl, Suite #7, at all. A single telephone, the old-fashioned rotary kind. But no listing in the Union City directory. The office furnishings are minimal, inherited from the previous tenant who departed in haste. A few years ago Corky acquired not only these furnishings but the entire mostly vacated building in a marathon poker game at the Mayor's residence one New Year's Day. (Not worth much at the present time, the property might be worth a lot one day, if, say, the $100-million Riverview Project ever comes through. The building at 274 Pearl, five floors, twenty "suites," built 1922, is officially condemned and was slated for demolition in 1984 but spared through a convenient clerical error in the City Hall Department of Records; through another error, the property is off the tax rolls.)

Corky uses this shadow-office to keep certain financial records it would make him uneasy to keep in his State Street office, not that there's anything illegal about these records but they're of a private nature, many having to do with cash-exchange deals and gambling wins and debts, Corky's known in Union City as a game, sometimes reckless, sometimes very lucky and sometimes very unlucky gambler, a guy who'll take a chance, a guy who'll give a friend odds, a guy who always pays you back and no bitching or self-pity, thus the records which constitute to him a kind of diary of his days and nights, but in code, and a code he periodically changes. These accounts are kept in old-fashioned ledgers with numerous listings fastidiously inked out, obliterated with a black felt-tip pen—interludes Corky wishes forgotten, and has forgotten. When some scores are settled, it's wisest to forget.

Corky also keeps in this office, in an old safe, approximately $5000 in cash—never know when you might need ready cash.

Also he keeps here a few fresh shirts, neckties, a pair or two of trousers, underwear; in a closet-sized lavatory, towels, soap, shaving and grooming supplies. Never know when, on your way rushing from one appointment to another in downtown Union City, you'll need to freshen yourself up, fast.

The best thing about the Pearl Street office, which in fact is a crummy place, is, when Corky Corcoran comes here, for however long he requires, nobody knows where the hell he is.

Back in the Caddy, speeding along the Expressway, Corky's feeling a little better. It's past one-thirty P.M. but fuck you Greenbaum if you don't like it.

He's my husband and I love him, I love him too well fuck that, Corky has better things to think about than that, now. What's a woman but Kleenex, toilet paper, you use it and as soon as you're done, you're done.

Punches on the car radio to fill his head with noise. Sees with distaste that God-damned billboard HEINZ MEULLER LINCOLN-MERCURY SALES
RENTAL & LEASING, every time he passes it he thinks of Meuller and the
other guys from St. Thomas and Corky Corcoran with them, a hanger-
on, a kid from the south side, riding in Meuller's car, and something that
happened one night when he was sixteen of which he isn't proud, Christ!
when you've been shamed every other memory of shame emerges, yes but
Corky isn't going to think about it now, any of it, he's thinking instead
of the grand pink-limestone facade of the Union City Athletic Club at
Union City Square, in the very heart of the "historic district," facing the
City-County Courthouse two long blocks away at the northern edge of
the park, close by City Hall (with its $20-million addition built, not by
Tim Corcoran, but by a rival), close by the stark white First Church of
Christ, Scientist, close by the elegant new forty-floor Hyatt on the site of
the imperial old Hotel Empire, Union City's prestige hotel where the St.
Thomas parties were held and where, for Corky's senior prom, he'd taken
a plain-pretty cousin of Vic Slattery's to whom Vic had introduced him,
a sweet scared girl whose name Corky has forgotten but how keenly he
remembers the desperation of needing to borrow $75 for the occasion,
$75 which was to him what $10,000 might be now, if, on the rush, he had
to borrow it, poor Corky! poor bastard! the terrible desperation but then
the euphoria that followed, the drunken elation, yes but it's the Union
City Athletic Club, the U.C.A.C. it's called, about which he has the stron-
gest emotions, that evening in September 1975 the membership chairman
called Corky to say he'd been voted in, beyond that the way the building
looked in all weathers, the heft of it, the stateliness of it, a neoclassical
portico and a Technicolor flag at the end of a gleaming brass pole and
the trademark crimson-striped awnings at the windows and the crimson
canopy at the front entrance and the broad sweep of the stone steps, and
the way, how many years ago, Corky Corcoran a skinny kid aged twenty
stood sometimes in the park sometimes even in the rain smoking cigarettes and looking at the Union City Athletic Club, he'd just started working then for Ross Drummond Realty & Insurance, those evenings Corky
crossing through the park pausing to stare at the men and women arriving
at the club, the rich of Union City, gentlemen and ladies they looked to
be, even in his Corcoran cynicism Corky believed them to be, handsomely

dressed men and women arriving in Caddies, Lincolns, fancy foreign cars beneath the canopy and handing over these cars to the uniformed parking attendants, then ascending the steps into the vast unimaginable interior, all of them members of the Union City Athletic Club, and how did you get to be a member, for it was a rarity for anyone from Irish Hill to be invited to join, for never had any Corcoran been invited to join, not even Timothy Patrick Corcoran the most successful of all the Corcorans, not even in those prosperous last years before they killed him.

4

CORKY DINES AT THE UNION CITY ATHLETIC CLUB

And here at the U.C.A.C., where with his trademark ridged-rippled red-brick hair and spiffy clothes and quick warm grin, forever a man in a hurry, Corky Corcoran's known by all.

"H'lo, Mr. Corcoran!"

"H'lo, Mr. Corcoran!"

"H'lo, Mr. Corcoran, real beautiful day isn't it—"

Exchanging greetings with the kid who parks his Caddy, the black doorman Archie, the house manager A. G. Rickett, the Elm Room's maître d' and the wine steward and God knows who all else, the uniformed pack of them, brass buttons and braid and black tie and smiling their sunny expectant smiles seeing it's him, Corky Corcoran, one of the "new" type of U.C.A.C. member, businessman, City Councilman, civic-minded friend and associate of the Slatterys, a good-natured guy with no pretensions or airs and, not least, generous with tips—he's feeling good already, like the air, leaked out of him, is being blown back in.

The English-churchy interior of the U.C.A.C., heavy plush carpets and chandeliers and great leather ottomans and settees and a ceiling of dark-walnut paneling in carved squares—it's a solace to him, too. This place where, since 1975, when he comes here, everybody knows who he *is*.

"Mr. Corcoran, hello!"

"Mr. Corcoran, fine day isn't it!"

"Here for lunch, Mr. Corcoran?"

And there's Red Pitts, the Mayor's aide, head of what's called the advancement team, meaning PR, bodyguard, counsel, loyal friend, as devoted to Oscar Slattery, who requires fierce and unqualified devotion, as his own son Vic—here's Red Pitts stuffed into a double-breasted beige blazer with gray slacks that don't quite match the beige of the blazer, a

speckled silk handkerchief bunched into a not-quite-perfect pocket flourish, but a fine figure of a man, battered-freckled face, snub nose, shifting
worried eyes but, waiting for an elevator, sighting Corky Corcoran on
the run to the Elm Room, he breaks into a smile, you might call it a smile
of recognition, as if his mind's been elsewhere and Corky has netted it
back—"Hey, Corky, how's it going?" and Corky greets Red in the same
convivial manner, pumping handshake, each man has a tough grip, Red's
bigger and surely stronger but Corky's got that sly-Irish deftness in his
fingers, he can make a grown man wince then back off before getting
his own fingers mangled in turn. Corky inquires, "Oscar here?"—with a
gesture toward the upstairs, for when the Mayor dines at the U.C.A.C.
at this time of day it's usually in a private dining room on the mezzanine,
Corky is sometimes included in these lunches, serious-minded but rowdy
affairs that beginning at one P.M. can last beyond five P.M., and he sees
Red hesitate before saying, "Yes," then adding, as if Corky's thin-skinned
enough to require an explanation for not being included today, "—the subject's finances, more budget shit—" and Corky nods, looks sympathetic, it
is shit, Union City forever on the brink of bankruptcy, with so much private money, the tax base falling and the conservative Republicans in the
State Legislature making it hot for the three-term Slattery administration,
not much a liberal-minded mayor can do with a $50-million budget cut
forced down his throat, sure Corky's sympathetic, but what's to be done?
"O.K., say hello to Oscar, to all of them, for me," Corky says, backing
off with a smile even as the elevator arrives and Red Pitts who's forever
on the run too steps hurriedly inside, his smile already fading, switched
off, cheap bastard doesn't want to waste it like Corky's uncle Philly Dowd
who'd go around the house unscrewing light bulbs so they wouldn't get
used up too fast and Corky guesses Pitts won't pass along his greetings
to the Mayor. Late as he is, Corky pauses to watch the arrow above the
elevator: not the mezzanine, but the third floor. Is there a private dining
room on the third floor? Must be, though Corky's never been in it.

   Later recalling, how Pitts had hesitated just saying yes Oscar was here,
going on then to say it was finances, budget, later Corky will recall this but
at the time he's brooding thinking Pitts will never forgive him, there's an
old rivalry between the two men, not a rivalry exactly but the ghost of one,
for Corky had been given to know, as far back as the early 1980s, that the

Slatterys were feeling him out for the position that would eventually go to Pitts, an undefinable but essential and in its way immensely powerful position in the mayoral administration, if you cared about politics so much, if you were fanatic in the ways these men are fanatic but Corky isn't, Corky has always had other interests not just politics nor even making money, Christ any weird thing orbiting by him can capture his attention, for a while at least, and to have Pitts' job with Oscar Slattery you have to care about nothing really except politics, the shifting sands of it, daily and even hourly seismic changes, who are your friends and who are your enemies, power's about choosing sides and hoping your side wins and keeps winning but Corky's more drawn just to friends, friendship, apart from being a lifelong Democrat he'd be as close to the Slatterys if Oscar was out and Vic lost his seat in the House, maybe closer, politics wouldn't get in the way.

Still, Corky can't help but feel just slightly stung, he knows it's ridiculous but since boyhood the knowledge that somewhere some of his friends are meeting together, for whatever purpose, however removed from him, however necessarily removed from him, Jesus! it makes him envious, it makes his guts squirm. *Why not me, what've they got against me?*

Breathless and expectant, Corky arrives at the carved arched entrance of the Elm Room. Scans what he can see of the dining room (and it's a full house today, Friday afternoon of Memorial Day weekend), looking for familiar faces, yes and here too steeling himself for the inevitability of seeing certain parties together, friends, acquaintances, business associates, women, alliances that jolt you into wondering what they mean and why are you excluded and what does it mean that you are excluded or maybe does it mean nothing?—Corky wants to see and wants to know but doesn't always want to see and for sure doesn't always want to know. (Christ, the time he'd walked in here and saw Charlotte, around the time of their divorce, having lunch with a woman named Yvette Packard with whom Corky'd had a brief but passionate affair—he'd had to walk right by their table on dazed swaying legs and the women had lifted cool mysterious smiles to him—"Why hello, 'Corky.'")

Still, the Elm Room is one of Corky's sacred places.

Every man has to have places that, the very thought of them, no matter how demoralized he is or how shitty his circumstances, makes him happy.

Business deals are forbidden in the Elm Room, not gentlemanly, but of course all the currents here, palpable as static electricity, have to do with business: the business of politics, the business of money, the business of adultery. Who's hooked up with who and who's screwing who and who's getting screwed and does he know it yet or not and some of this is in full daylight but most of it in secret which is why the blood begins to quicken when you step foot in a place like this where in your innermost heart you know you don't belong.

"Good afternoon, Mr. Corcoran!"—the beaming maitre d' hurries up, eyes shining like patent leather when he sights Mr. Corcoran, one of those club members so generous even when stone cold sober he'll slip anybody in a service uniform a ten-dollar bill and in the maître d's case a twenty-dollar bill. No special reason, just to get good prompt courteous service. What the hell, unlike old fart-in-a-bottle Philly Dowd, Corky can afford it. "May I show you to your table?—your party Mr. Greenbaum is waiting."

Corky has already seen Greenbaum at the table he'd reserved, Corky's favorite table for two there in a farther corner beyond the enormous hand-painted mural of Admiral Oliver Hazard Perry "The Hero of Lake Erie" and his men triumphant aboard a full-masted frigate in the great sea battle against the British of 1813, Corky always asks for that table so he can sit relaxed with his back to the corner and in fantasy as least, for the space of a meal at least, know that his back is protected.

At last, he doesn't want to think how late, Corky is led through the maze of tables amid a waterfall-din of voices, laughter, and the happy clatter of silverware, crystal, bottles, pausing to say hello and in several instances to shake hands with friends, men who call him "Corky" as warmly and in as brotherly a way as any man might wish, yes and there's handsome white-haired Father Vincent O'Brien waving hello, big smile for Corky Corcoran who's been a generous donor to St. Thomas Aquinas since graduating in 1967, and there's Todd McElroy the sharpie criminal lawyer, trained at Harvard Law but once too of Irish Hill, dirt-poor the McElroys, eight or nine of them living in a rowhouse on East Welland at the very edge of the shabby black neighborhood, and now McElroy, younger than Corky by a year or two, friend too of City Hall and chief legal counsel of the Union City policemen's union, is slated to defend Dwayne Pickett next month against charges of second-degree murder—McElroy nods at Corky and grants him a tight, measured smile, like he's giving something away just acknowledging Corky for whose father his own father used to work as a bricklayer when he wasn't incapacitated by drink, and here, practically in Corky's path, impossible to avoid, old Buck Glover thrusts out a palsied hand to be shaken, "H-Hello, C-Corcoran!" having forgotten Corky's first name—Glover was Union City mayor through the 1950s, mayor in fact at the time Tim Corcoran was murdered, a friend of the Corcorans or so it was claimed: Corky stares appalled at the old man, once hefty and energetic as a steer, now so aged, Corky has heard rumors of cancer but isn't about to inquire, he returns Glover's handshake and says smiling yes he's fine and all the family's fine and yes Sean Corcoran's doing pretty well, why don't the two of you get together sometime? play a few cards?—and at last Corky makes it to his table and to the patiently waiting Greenbaum breathless and exhilarated, like a football player who's run the length of the field for a touchdown.

Extending his hand to shake Greenbaum's heavy, stubby-fingered ham of a hand, seeing it's 1:48 P.M. and he's almost an hour late!—God damn it. Murmuring, "Christ, Howard, I'm sorry. I would have gotten here almost on time except things came up—" as he sits down, rapidly scans the scene, seeing that Greenbaum, a fleshy man in his mid-fifties, yet with fastidious ways, has been drinking, not wine, but Saratoga water, yes and devouring rolls, half the hard rolls gone from the basket and all of the pumpernickel, Corky's favorite, gone. Greenbaum's been looking through a sheaf of financial documents while waiting for his client and these he now slides discreetly aside, all attentiveness focused on Corky who's faltering stammering some kind of half-assed excuse. "The fucking traffic—"

Greenbaum laughs. Corky hears it as forced, unconvinced. Those sly hooded turtle's eyes, that look of patient irony about the loose lips, Corky wonders if Jews of Greenbaum's sensibility disapprove of profanity. He should learn to watch his mouth as Charlotte used to warn him, maybe Jews associate such language with ill-bred *goys*, or is it *goyim*, maybe the word itself means *unclean?*—but Greenbaum surprises Corky with a sudden paternal smile, an obliquely teasing smile, saying, "Jerome, please relax. Hasn't it ever come to your notice, you're always late? You must know you have that reputation."

Corky blinks. Corky's astonished as if this is a radically new notion, one he has never heard before from anyone, never in his life.

"I am?" he asks dumbly, a hurt kid. "*Am* I?"

Greenbaum shakes his head, his jowls quiver with a curious forgiving gaiety. "You've been late for each of our three meetings so far, but it doesn't matter in the slightest. Sitting here, with no telephone, I've been double-checking some of these figures, and I've been thinking about your accounts, and about you, Jerome, and it's all to the good. Really."

Corky's glad to hear this, though he feels rebuked.

What a relief, though—Greenbaum's comforting tone. And the ponderous sag of his face. The man has come highly recommended to Corky as a broker and general financial advisor, Corky'd had to fire the son of a bitch who'd been advising him previously and in the process he's lost a lot of dough which maybe, if he'd gone to Greenbaum, a Jew, in the first place, he might have avoided. Since the 1986 Tax Reform Act when real estate limited partnerships went all to hell, which is where Corky has much of his investment still, he hasn't been able to make the kind of profits he'd made all through the 1970s and 1980s without knowing how high he was flying and how lucky he was.

Corky signals the waiter who's been hovering near, a familiar face, too, how sweet to Corky's ears that eager query, "Yes, Mr. Corcoran?" which must impress Greenbaum who isn't a member of the U.C.A.C. (never been nominated?—or maybe has no interest in joining?—well-to-do and civic-minded Jews have been invited in for twenty years now, not long after the south-side micks like Corky Corcoran and Todd McElroy and not long before the four or five showcase blacks) though the man's expression is unreadable. Maybe he thinks we're all assholes, they're the Chosen People. Could be right.

Corky orders a scotch on the rocks. Doesn't specify any brand not wanting Greenbaum to think he's a *goy* drinker who takes it all seriously. Greenbaum's alluding to Corky's reputation has made Corky ill at ease wondering what his reputation *is*.

As the waiter walks off, Corky calls him back. "Any pumpernickel rolls?"

"Yes *sir*."

As if Corky'd entrusted him with a mission.

The thought of Christina low in his guts, like the first stirring of diarrhea.

Saying with a grin to Greenbaum, who's been watching him closely, "Howard, you wouldn't believe what I was doing just now, the reason I'm late getting here," and Greenbaum says, "No, what?" and Corky says, "Directing traffic," and Greenbaum says, lifting his heavy eyebrows, "*What?*"

So Corky tells, this time more extravagantly, his tale.

Hey: d'you love me?
  Oh, lover. Oh God.

Had it been real, any of it?—Corky lifts his glass to his mouth, first drink of the day, *this* is real, this is something you can depend upon.

That good burning sensation going down. That good airy-elated sensation going up through the nasal passages and into the brain.

So narrow, so unforgiving, is it some Catholic thing?—some remnant?
He's here now, but he's leaving.

Listening to Greenbaum lecture him. Municipal bonds, securities. Real estate limited partnerships. Real estate here in Union City: Corcoran, Inc., owns rental properties, offices mainly, one apartment building of thirty-five units on Schoharie Street near the city hospital. It's been Corcoran, Inc.'s, strategy to acquire rundown property and even in some cases property condemned by the city or virtually given away at bankruptcy auctions, then put money into it, borrowed money, the big deal here is tax depreciation and IRS has been challenging Corcoran, Inc.'s, claims since 1989: Greenbaum has been conferring with Corky's tax lawyers and "isn't too happy" with what he's learned.

Corky, staring at the menu, says, with an affable sigh, "Shit, I'm not too happy about any of this. That's why you're here." Which isn't the truth exactly: Corky had been looking forward to this lunch at the U.C.A.C., the first time he's brought Greenbaum here, hoping to get to know the guy who's a prestige money man for all his modest downscale ways (Greenbaum's dull-brown suit looks off-the-rack at, say, Macy's) and about whom Corky's heard things that have made him sound interesting: he's a widower who lives alone in spartan surroundings in a brownstone on Front Street close by his office, he's an amateur cellist and music lover with a very generous commitment to the Union City Chamber Music Society, he's childless and sending relatives' kids to college, medical school, like Corky himself, a cousin's daughter to nursing school and another kid to Georgetown Law School, Corky figures they have certain traits in common though externally—say anybody's been glancing their way, right now—they couldn't look more unlike, the fair-skinned red-haired blunt-faced mick and the swarthy-skinned pouchy-eyed rabbinical-looking Jew. Two different species?

Corky thinks fiercely, what's needed here isn't fucking financial advice but fucking *wisdom*.

Greenbaum is oblivious of the waiter and of the time, lecturing Corky further on local property investment, Corky's plans to buy (that is, to borrow money to buy) two old Union City landmarks, the Griswold Building, which will require a minimum of $1 million to renovate. The Bull's Eye, an Art Deco architectural oddity on lower State Street built in 1929 and badly needing renovations too: is this the right time, considering Corky's other commitments, and the interest rates on those commitments, for him to buy? Greenbaum also brings up the subject of Corky's four $50,000 investments in Viquinex Financial Corps. in California real estate: it's a sinking ship, the syndicator wants to combine, "roll up," all their partnerships into one, and Greenbaum's advice is yes, go along with it—"They've got a gun to your head, Jerome."

Just what Corky, his eye adrift down the columns of fancily named appetizers, first courses, entrées, specials on the Elm Room menu, wants to hear. Joking, with a twitchy smile, not looking up, "A smoking gun, it sounds like."

Corky's feeble joke is a whisper of a plea not to know, not to be told, the probable truth, which is that the entire $200,000 is gone to hell, an investment in a limited partnership he'd leapt at in 1987 when Viquinex first went on the market and Corky's then-advisor was talking it up as foolproof. Yes but don't tell me now for Christ's sake at the very start of lunch but Greenbaum, unheeding, shrugs his shoulders as if to indicate, You said it, my friend, not me.

Under ordinary circumstances Corky loves to study this menu, a beauty of a menu, by now he's sampled most of the items, more than once, though never yet *les escargots*, the thought turns his stomach, a sharp recollection of sticky gray thumb-sized slugs on the underside of an old rotted barrel behind Uncle Sean's garage, Christ! no thanks! and at $8.95 a throw, nor has he ever ordered any variation on one of today's Elm Room specials, sweetbreads *en brochette*, no thanks. A stirring in his gut. Yes but the scotch will help. Soothing, narcotizing. Brains, guts. What they call, on the menu, *tripe*. Dear God, the things human beings will take into their mouths willingly, yes and pay high prices for! That time at the Chop House Charlotte ordered honeycomb tripe, a rich buttery sauce over it, and Corky hadn't known what it was, and she got him to take a taste and all the table watched (they were there with two other couples, of the Drummond social set) and when Corky figured it out and went dead-white in the face and left the table for the men's room they laughed at him—not cruelly but worse yet fondly, patronizingly, Corky's so sweet and so *funny*.

Years of that fond patronizing familiarity, yes but he'd courted it hadn't he, how otherwise to take his place among them, Charlotte's world, and the women coming on to him too, or trying out the idea of coming on to him, then backing off quickly when they saw what he might be like, not like their husbands but direct, blunt: *You want to fuck, or not?*—*just don't play games.*

Yes but they'd rather play games.

Rarely does Corky see any of these old friends except maybe on neutral territory, big parties. The women's eyes still lingering on him but, to be frank, they're Charlotte's age, Charlotte's three years older than Corky, women that age are invisible to him.

Vic Slattery too with an eye for younger women, a loyal married guy with a terrific wife but, hell, what can you do if the younger women have an eye for you. Impossible to resist one hundred percent of the time though with Vic, as with any public figure, Clinton for instance, it's dangerous. Corky's thinking of certain postcampaign parties, the wild ones without the wives, that Fourth of July two years ago at Lake Placid where he met Marilee Plummer, that other girl what's-her-name Vic's aide's assistant—Kiki. And Thalia turned up too, came and went and was gone and he hoped to Christ she hadn't seen him. Still, by then, he *was* divorced from her mother.

Thinking cruelly, Christina at thirty-six, soon to be thirty-seven: how many years remaining to have another baby?

Yes I'd do it again. In the right circumstances. With the right man.

Greenbaum orders a salad lunch, no appetizer though Corky recommends the deep-fried crab cakes, another bottle of Saratoga water, poor bastard must be on a diet, forty pounds overweight, a whistling wheeze sometimes audible in his breathing, still he's been devouring bread, maybe out of nerves more than appetite, compulsive: they say you never get anywhere in life without being compulsive. Are Jews' IQs higher on the average than non-Jews'? Corky wouldn't want to think how Jews and Irish would stack up. Exposed in some public place like the science page of *The New York Times.*

Shrugged his shoulders just now and the man's entire body was in it, slack walrus-body, sizable in the hips. That shiny dented-looking almost-bald head packed with brains.

"That's all you want, Howard? A chef *salad?*" Corky's faintly offended. "We'll share a bottle of wine, though, O.K.? White? Red?"

Greenbaum says, with forced enthusiasm, "Either, Jerome. Fine."

Corky, trim enough at 150 pounds, except for that slabby-fatty stuff around the waist, has a blood-pressure problem. Curse of the Corcorans. What the doctor calls hypertension. Saying, deadpan, knowing Corky's appetites, just cut out the salt and the red meat and the alcohol, before we try medication.

Hearing the guys the other day in the locker room, after squash, blood-pressure pills make you impotent. Christ, fuck *that.*

Corky shifts uneasily in his seat. His penis is sore: fiery at the tip: mangled-feeling: like after that long weekend bender at Las Vegas, coming home with the clap. Scared as hell he had AIDS. The shame of that, he'd've had to blow his head off, not just dying a horrible death but people saying he's a fag.

Hasn't eaten since breakfast at the Statler hours ago, seven-thirty and then just coffee and Danish pastry so he should be famished, he's a guy who loves to eat, his Aunt Frances teasing him he's got a cast-iron stomach but, right now, that isn't so. Still, Corky refuses to be cheated of the pleasure of lunch: orders the deep-fried crab cakes, the Elm Room salad (that's doused with heavy-creamy dressing), London broil which is a specialty of the house, a side order of oven-roasted potatoes.

"And a carafe—no, make that a bottle—of the house red wine."

Corky closes his menu and hands it to the waiter, a job well done.

Christ, how he loves it here!—in the Elm Room of the Union City Athletic Club of a Friday afternoon, at his favorite table. Back to the wall.

"The faster you travel, the slower the clock. Did you know that, Howard?"

Greenbaum glances up from a document at his elbow. He's got his bifocals on, squinting at Corky as if Corky's out of focus.

"Know what?"

"The faster you travel, like through space, the slower clock time. They say it's a fact."

"That only pertains to subatomic particles, doesn't it?"

Corky's only fazed by this remark for a moment. Sipping his wine, savoring the rich-fruity red taste, Corky feels his eyes moisten with pleasure. He says, "No, it's real. I mean—it pertains to us. If for instance you had a twin, Howard, and he left Earth and traveled by rocket at the speed of light, when he returned to Earth you'd be older than him."

Greenbaum's one of those guys, can't take anything on faith, a look like there's a corkscrew up his ass. "Why?"

"Why?" Corky stuffs his mouth with pumpernickel. That's a good question. "Einstein formulated it, and it's been confirmed—the theory, I mean. Of course, I wouldn't know *why*." A pause. "I studied architecture in college, not physics."

Greenbaum's loose lips smile suddenly, it's a quick wistful look, you can see the kid he was, fifteen years old, bookish, straight-A, moony when it comes to such thoughts. "The mystery of the physical universe," he says, "is as opaque as the mystery of the human soul."

"You said it," Corky says emphatically. "I'll drink to that."

Disappointed that Greenbaum has had only a sip or two of the wine and it's God-damned delicious—something French called Château Pigoudet.

Disappointed too that Greenbaum is back to business. Just when they were getting to know each other. Breaking the ice. Of course, this *is* a business lunch, and Corky's paying for it.

He'd called Greenbaum at the recommendation of one of his squash partners, I'm getting the shitty end of the stick from too many sons of bitches, I
need help and from what I've been told you're my man. A moment's silence
before Greenbaum answered, carefully, Maybe I'm your man.

Now Greenbaum brings up the subject, painful to Corky, of the money
Nick Daugherty still owes Corky, after how long: three years? *four?*
Nick's supposed to be repaying it at $500 a crack, interest-free, but the
payments are irregular and Corky doesn't like to come down too hard on
the guy, a sweet guy, not stupid but hit by bad luck, one of Corky's few
remaining old friends from parochial school days and a link to those days,
a memory of when Tim Corcoran was alive and trucks marked CORCORAN
BRO'S CONSTRUCTION barreled along the streets of Irish Hill. It was only
$5000 Nick borrowed from Corky, a cash-flow problem with the Daugh-
ertys' family-owned printing press, he'd offered Corky a share in the business but Corky said no, that wasn't necessary, pay me back when you can.
He says, now, "What Nick owes me is small potatoes, compared to this
Viquinex shit. But I'll talk to him: I'll call him. After Monday."

Greenbaum says, "Get him to sign this promissory note. That's all."

This, sounding like an order, sets Corky's teeth on edge.

Greenbaum hands him a legal-looking form. All prepared? For Nick?

Without examining the document, quick as if not wanting anyone to
see him, Corky takes it, folds it, slips it into his pocket. "I trust Nick. But
I'll talk to him about this."

"Get him to sign it. Talk's talk."

O.K., smart-ass. Jew-boy. You're the authority.

Corky's crab cakes arrive. Steaming hot. He douses them with Tabasco
sauce. At the first bite, he feels a resurgence of nausea. At the second bite,
he feels a stirring of juices, appetite. A swallow of wine, and at the third
bite he's ravenously hungry.

Food and drink, you can depend upon. Women, money, politics, shit.

Could be, loving to eat as he does, Corky Corcoran will one day blow
up like a balloon. Like Stanislaus Corcoran, Tim's great-uncle, Union
City Police Captain, Sixth Precinct, 290 pounds packed into a five-foot-
eight frame and he'd sired nine children, bloated cagey face lopsided in
secret mirth and they'd found him floating in the canal one Sunday morning beyond the Erie Street locks, fully clothed and peaceful-looking they

said as a big man relaxing in his bathtub except for the hole in his face
bullets had blown away. The year was 1928, Stanislaus was a victim of
the rum-running feuds, but only one of the victims and until that time
he'd done all right. He'd done more than all right. One of the aristocrats
of Irish Hill and after his death his widow and kids discovered $28,000 in
a mattress in the house.

Greenbaum's chef salad arrives. Pink dressing on the side, but he uses it
all, trowels it over the fancy rolled-up slices of meat, hardboiled egg quarters, lettuce. And more thick-buttered bread. If this guy's on a diet, his left
hand doesn't know what his right hand is doing, Corky can relate to that.

Eating, the men chat more casually. Eating's the principal effort.
Corky devours the crab cakes, rubs a chunk of pumpernickel on the
greasy Tabasco-smeared plate, devours that. Orders a second bottle of
wine. More food arrives: the London broil, so-called. Some kind of steak,
Corky orders it for the name, "London Broil," first time he'd ever heard
of it was here in the Elm Room, a guest of Ross Drummond his father-
in-law to be. Never been to London or Europe and hasn't any urge to go,
Charlotte tried to talk him into it, in fact they had plans for a honeymoon
in Rome but in the end Corky was too busy, Corky's always been too busy
and he likes it that way. Christ, buying properties and repairing and renovating and hooking up with the right kind of tenants (i.e., they pay rent
on time and don't wreck the premises) and even more important the right
kind of managers (i.e., they don't fuck you in the ass) and making your
own bank payments on time, it's a full-time occupation like being a priest,
Corky thinks, or a nun. You own property, property owns *you*.

Corky says, nudging Greenbaum, "See that priest over there?—by the
window? That's the head of the St. Thomas Aquinas school, y'know, private school for boys? Out on Lakeshore Drive."

Greenbaum says, "I've heard of it."

Heard of it!—St. Thomas Aquinas is the number one high school, private or public, in all of western New York State.

Maybe he's joking? Jewish-type humor, sly and ironic. Sign of a superior IQ.

Not discouraged, Corky launches into one of his tales. Never so happy
as when telling one of his tales. A Corcoran family trait, others called it
running at the mouth, Theresa teased Tim, listen to you!—half of what

the man says is blarney and the other half b.s. But she'd loved it just the
same.

As if it's a confidential aside, never before uttered aloud, Corky tells
Greenbaum, "—When I was a young guy just starting out, I knew I had to
impress the right people. There was a big fund-raising campaign for the
school and Father Vincent—his friends call him that, I mean I call him
that now, I didn't when I was a student—was the head of the campaign,
one of these Jesuits who's invited to parties even by non-Catholics, he's
so popular, and he'd see to it that anybody who gave money to the school
got his picture in the paper and a lot of publicity, if you gave enough, I
mean—for sure, it *was* a worthy cause and I'm damned glad I graduated
from the school, the Jesuits taught me everything I know—" he's breathless, talking and chewing and saying things he doesn't mean, but what
the hell, "—I made up my mind to give the school a big cash donation.
Except I didn't have any extra cash. This was 1974, I was running kind
of scared. Getting in over my head in some ways, y'know the way you do
when you're just starting out? So—I came up with this wild idea, actually
it's simple as ABC: I borrowed five thousand dollars from an older guy
I did business with, saying I didn't want to go through the bank but I'd
pay the going interest rate of course, and a week or so later, I came back
to him with the money *and* the interest, for a month—I'd computed it to
a penny. Told him, 'This big deal came through for me I didn't expect,
but thanks a lot, I really appreciate it.' Turned around a few weeks later
and did the same thing with another guy, an influential guy in the city,
but six thousand dollars this time, and again I repaid it within a week or
so, interest exactly computed, told this guy, too, I'd had some good luck
with a deal I hadn't expected, I was really grateful he'd helped me out. So
then I was feeling, like, really lucky and prosperous, like it'd all been true,
y'know?—and I waited awhile and then borrowed ten thousand dollars
from a third party, exact same terms as the others, and this"—Corky
pauses, seeing how Greenbaum is staring at him, listening closely—"I
take in its entirety—and to me this is an enormous amount of money—
and now I'm counting on sheer luck, I don't believe in prayer or in God
or any of that religious shit but I'm sort of what you'd call superstitious
like a lot of Irish—I figure this is what you'd call a *good deal*, eh?—I can't
lose, eh?—though my history of betting on sports, especially fights, is un-

even, but I told myself, 'Corky, c'mon, this is a chance of a lifetime.' So—Howard—you'll never guess what I did with that ten thousand dollars."

Greenbaum's heavy jaws pause in their chewing. His shiny, dented head is held perfectly still, as if the thinking, inside, is in suspension, too. "Jerome, I'd never be able to guess."

"No, probably not," Corky says, laughing, delighted, "—you'd have to be crazy like me." He lowers his voice and leans toward the older man, says, "I took the ten thousand dollars, every penny of it, and bet on the Ali-Foreman fight where I got, through my bookie, I mean the guy who was my bookie then, he's since deceased, odds of eight to one. That's to say eight to one in favor of Foreman because he was the heavyweight champion and Ali'd been beaten by Frazier once who'd been beaten by Foreman and you know how it is in this country, everybody quick to say a guy's washed up, over the hill?—so they were saying that about Muhammad Ali, the jerk-offs. But *I* figured, Ali's a great, true champion, not a flash in the pan like Foreman or Leon Spinks, and he's hungry as me, niggers and micks got a lot in common, both kind of crazy, eh? So I knew he was going to win, I just *knew*. And he did."

Greenbaum had ceased chewing. A tawny incredulous light in his eyes. "He did? He won? *You* won? Eighty thousand dollars? Like that?"

"Of which I immediately gave twenty thousand dollars to St. Thomas Aquinas," Corky says, the memory bringing a flush to his face as if it had taken place, not fourteen years ago, but yesterday, "—the biggest private donation, not counting the really rich alums, up to that time. In the *Journal*, maybe you saw it, a big photo of Father Vincent shaking my hand. I was telling him sort of half-kidding, I had to confess I didn't get to mass much anymore, and he says, 'Corky, next time you do go, put in a good word to Our Father for me.' My stock went up overnight and it's never come down." Corky laughs like a braggart kid, sheer pleasure, it's a fact to him, not a theory. In Union City you make your mark when you're young and you make it in the right quarters or you never make it at all. He adds, "A few years ago when my friends got me to run for City Council, endorsed by the Democrats, they told me people still remember that twenty thousand dollars I gave to St. Thomas, though I've done a lot since, given away a helluva lot more since, Christ knows. What I never told anyone was how I'd cleared a cool sixty thousand dollars on the deal, minus interest."

Corky's cleaning up his plate the way he'd learned to do as a kid, every morsel of the flank steak, which was delicious, except bones and the most obvious gristle. And the roasted potatoes, his favorite kind of potatoes. Theresa used to make them, the aroma filling the downstairs of the house on Barrow Street. And fried potatoes too, with onions, deep in grease, in a giant black skillet.

Greenbaum exhales air through his wide nostrils, a whistling-wheezing sound of amazement. "Good God, Jerome!—do you mean you commonly bet such sums of money? And you *win?*"

At this, though, Corky clams up. He's the kind of guy, don't push.

Says, coolly, "That was then, this is now. Now," he says, reaching for the wine bottle, "—I'm what you call established in this town."

There's Tim Corcoran, at a table near the window looking out toward Union Square. Backlit by shimmering light. The man has aged with dignity, not slack-skinned and pasty like so many others who'd been young when he was, yes and he's a big, solid man still, with wide sloping shoulders, a handsome face, gray-grizzled eyebrows and gray hair brushed back neatly from his temples. Sharp color in his cheeks, a glisten of merriment in his eyes, slaps the tabletop when he laughs, a man who enjoys a good time. He's in the company of three other men and he wears a dark sharkskin suit, white shirt, striped tie. His son stares at him mute with longing.

What were the last words we said to each other, I never knew.

Then, in the midst of laughter, Tim Corcoran turns, lifts a hand to signal a waiter, his neck creases above his collar and he's coarse-faced after all, a stranger.

Not the first time Corky has seen Tim Corcoran in the Elm Room at the U.C.A.C. In the twilit polished-wood Allegheny Bar next door he's seen him yet more frequently.

White-haired sunken-cheeked Buck Glover, grown elderly, lurches to his feet at a nearby table, somebody helps him with his chair, helps him shuffle away leaning on a cane. Vain old Buck baring his dentures in a TV smile thinking the entire Elm Room is watching and about to cheer though in fact only a few diners take notice, and these frown at him in pity or vexation. Buck Glover—a defeated ex-Mayor, eased out by his own party. Dead meat. Not even history.

It's a shitty fact of life, Corky thinks, a man gets to be that old, no matter who he is or whose friend he was, there's the prevailing sentiment the fucker's getting what he deserves.

Mayor Buck Glover *was* Tim Corcoran's friend, wasn't he. That's a fact, isn't it. Risking his neck, it was said, pushing for the arrest of the man who ordered Tim Corcoran killed, causing a political division in the city, a feud between the Mayor's and the D.A.'s office but what can you do, how much can you push, Al Fenske had his lawyers and there was no evidence linking him with the crime, not even circumstantial evidence, no informers, and no witnesses to the shooting, not even to the Death Car speeding away. Our hands are tied, we're powerless without witnesses.

You don't fuck with the president of the Western New York Trade Union Council unless you know you can nail him.

One night about four months after Tim Corcoran's murder the Mayor came out to Irish Hill to address a gathering at the Knights of Columbus to answer questions and "dispel rumors" about the police investigation. For his troubles he was heckled, cursed, spat at. Sean Corcoran stood up in his defense but the angry crowd paid him no heed. Hurriedly, probably it was funny, like a scene in a movie, the Mayor's aides and bodyguards ushered the Mayor out of the hall, a rear exit and into his limo and away they sped, three shiny black City Hall limos like hearses, with two cops on motorcycles as escorts. On a corner of Dalkey Street Jerome Corcoran and his cousin Cormac Farley and Nick Daugherty stood watching, three kids, yelling and jeering, running after the limos in the street and they'd have thrown rocks except for the cops, they were wild rough kids sometimes, if they could get away with it.

Had Jerome ever confided in anyone, even in Cormac, even in Nick who was his closest friend of that time, about the Death Car he hadn't seen and could not identify. Had he ever spoken of it voluntarily to any living soul.

Son, you're our only witness.

Do what you can for your father?

Yes but he hadn't seen. He saw, but only the blurred rushing shape of the car. He said, *I told you, you don't listen.*

Mayor Buck Glover, Tim Corcoran's friend. Friend of the Corcorans, was he. A friend of Irish Hill where they'd helped elect him three times running. Charge of voting "irregularities" in Union City going back to the 1800s. To the victor go the spoils.

Buck Glover, who'd begun as a ward politician on the near south side, his father a dockworker and a union man, had come of age in Union City when the party machine, that's to say the Democratic party machine, for the Democrats then as now outnumber Republicans by a sizable majority, traded services openly, delivered and collected favors. In certain notorious cases demanded favors. A favor for you, a favor for me. An eye for an eye, a tooth for a tooth. Shrewdly the party machine played segments of voters one against the other. Working-class, middle-class, "rich." Whites, Negroes. South Union City, Shehawkin. Citizens of English, Dutch, German ancestry aligned against citizens of Irish, Polish, Hungarian, Czech ancestry: Protestants versus Catholics. And then there were Jews, and Socialists. Unknown numbers of Communists.

In 1911, the Wobblies—the Industrial Workers of the World—were so strong in Union City, or were so perceived, there was a strike-breaking riot, police violence, eight strikers killed and many injured. "Big Bill" Haywood came to the city to unfurl the IWW red banner and was arrested for sedition. In 1919 an Irish Hill Wobbly organizer named Tumulty was elected to, but barred from, the New York State Legislature. The Corcorans and their many blood kin, Dowds, Muldoons, Donnellys, Farleys remained faithful to the Democratic party. For the party, especially during Prohibition, delivered all it promised, and occasionally more. The party was the more practical arm of the Catholic Church. You could start out dirt-poor and with a fifth-grade education and wind up with $28,000 stuffed in a mattress. You could start out shanty Irish and wind up lace-curtain Irish. You started out living and wound up dead but that was a small price to pay.

Always it was assumed that the men who won the Party's nominations for offices would win the offices. And that was so. It was assumed that the men who'd done and promised to do most favors would be rewarded. But after Tim Corcoran's death, and charges of graft, corruption, nepotism, no-show jobs and Party favoritism and "negligence," the old era ended. The Slatterys came into ascendency, first the elder brother William, then Oscar who was a college graduate, their father a prosperous merchant, born in Irish Hill but emigrated to the north side, a big house on Riverside Drive, seven children and blessed by the Archbishop but not the kind to grovel on his knees before a plaster-of-Paris Virgin Mary. In the new decade of the 1960s, all was changed. A new style, a new way. A new music in politics. Not what you've done (the awarding of lucrative city contracts, beefed-up pensions, no-show jobs, a quick telephone call to the Bricklayers & Allied Craftmen's local to make of someone's twenty-one-year-old kid a Class-A bricklayer) but who you were, how you looked, talked, moved, came across to the League of Women Voters and the NAACP and on television. Not even the promises you made (for all politicians make promises) but your tone of voice, your vocabulary. Buck Glover lost the votes of even the loyal Democrats he'd paid off for there was Bill Slattery, forty-one years old and a two-term U.S. Congressman and one of his strengths was, he'd had no city-politics experience, no murky record his Republican opponent could throw in his face. Two years after John F. Kennedy won the Democratic nomination for President over Lyndon Johnson, Bill Slattery won the Democratic nomination for Mayor of Union City over Buck Glover. A new style, a new way. A new music.

Corky points out Buck Glover to Howard Greenbaum, who blinks and stares after the old man. "That's Glover?—God, I wouldn't know him." Then, a wistful grimace, "I voted for Glover, first time I ever voted."

Corky asks which term of Glover's, he'd had three.

Greenbaum says, "His third. Last."

Corky calculates, that election was 1958, say Greenbaum was twenty-one then, he's fifty-five now. Actually looks older.

Corky's feeling mellow, this second bottle of wine and Greenbaum with his fastidious ways hasn't yet finished his first glass. Are Jews genetically susceptible to alcohol, like Native Americans and the Irish?—no, it's the opposite, Jews have a high tolerance for alcohol? Stone cold sober, Corky'd be pissed off, his luncheon companion refusing to join him in this good French wine but, right now, that isn't a problem.

Corky says, "It's shitty how the Party treated Glover, tossing him out like they did. Sure, he had his faults, they all do, 'politics is the art of compromise,' I forget who said that maybe FDR?, but he did a helluva lot of good, he was a good man in his heart, lots of things the Slatterys inherited Buck began. People forget that." Corky ticks off public schools policy, health services, better-trained police and firemen and people nobody thinks of like building safety inspectors, water sanitation engineers, the city coroner and his staff. He's speaking with an urgency that must seem, to the bemused Greenbaum, out of proportion to his subject, sounds like a Democrat on TV, a Party apologist, a City Councilman being challenged. Unable too, it's the wine gone to his head, to resist adding, "—And an uncle of mine, my father's partner in the business, y'know we had this family business, after my father died—" rushing past this not meeting the older man's eyes, maybe he doesn't know and now's not the time to go into it, "—my Uncle Sean had to sell at a loss, got sick, I mean he was sick off and on for years—" not wanting to confess his uncle was a chronic alcoholic, couldn't hold a job even when he'd wanted one, it's a wonder he's lived as long as he has is everybody's take on the old bastard, "—and Buck saw to it that my uncle was on the city payroll till he retired—Department of General Services." Corky has ended lamely, like a man veering off a sidewalk into a mucky gutter. Shit on his shoes.

Greenbaum says not a word.

Corky says, just this side of belligerent, "Hell, it's the way things were done then. Buck Glover was a fucking generous man." Seeing Greenbaum impassive, unsmiling, do your older Jews, rabbinical-type Jews, take a high moral tone in everyday life?—look upon a man doing a favor for another man hard hit by family tragedy?—Corky goes on, "It's the way politics go. In Union City, for sure. Or, anyway, used to be. Now, there's a different ethics, now, I don't know." And lame here too, vague and faltering, asshole'd flunk a lie-detector test. Of course Corky knows: how'd *he* acquire certain city properties, close certain deals, at his price and not his competitors', if not with the help of City Hall? how do certain of his rental properties pass Health, Fire & Safety inspections, if not with the help of City Hall? how'd he get on the City Council which takes up too much of his time but which he loves if not for the endorsement of City Hall?

Corky says, "Your people have a different tradition, do they?"

"'My people'?"

"The Jewish people."

Greenbaum smiles, startled. He's in the midst of removing a large neatly folded and impeccably ironed cotton handkerchief from his inner coat pocket, with which he wipes his forehead, a fussy gesture. His large head does in fact seem dented, thinly covered with strands of dark hair that look as if they've been laid in place separately. His earlobes are long and look stretched. "A tradition of ethics, or of political expediency? Of course, we have both."

It's an elegant answer. It's a classy answer. Why he hired this guy, you pay the right price and you get high class.

Corky wonders, though: has he been placated, or put in his place?

Their luncheon plates have been cleared away, they're waiting now for coffee. No dessert. Greenbaum emphatically declined, even the perusal of the menu or the celebrated Elm Room pastry cart, Corky's disappointed but better not, he's invited to a dinner party tonight, so late and so heavy a lunch will interfere with his appetite. Also, he'd better watch his gut. Showering at Christina's, stooping to tenderly soap his genitalia, he'd been disgusted by the creases, hell they were bulges, in his lower gut.

Why that woman, and other women, too, over the years, have called Corky Corcoran beautiful, he can't know. Homely freckled mick face like a baby's ass and stunted-short, and, since forty, growing a gut.

Not that it's a put-on, a ploy, as with prostitutes. Really, they seem to mean it. Poor bitches, cunts. Making as much as they can out of what they have.

And when they stop loving you, the flattery stops too, and fast.

Charlotte saying, and this only one of her remarks, you think you're so good at fucking?—you're all over everywhere like a twelve-year-old, all that rough, fast stuff, it's *boring.*

Greenbaum glances at a list, he's been checking off topics, says, "We haven't gotten through one-third of what I need to talk to you about, Jerome. Have your secretary call and set up an appointment for next week. In my office."

"You'd prefer not, another lunch?"

"It's more expedient, in my office."

"O.K.," says Corky affably. Then, "You like that word, huh?" and as Greenbaum looks at him, "'Expediency.'" Corky laughs, empties the wine bottle into his glass except, shit, he's already emptied it.

There's Greenbaum's wine glass, two-thirds full. Corky eyes it but no, better not.

But, calculating: how much is he paying for the wine in that glass?

The Elm Room's notorious, the U.C.A.C.'s notorious, jacking up the prices of wine, liquor. Fuckers don't think we know our asses from a hole in the ground.

"Hell," says Corky, grinning, "—it's a good word. Classy. I use it all the time, myself."

How's it feel to be here, kid?

Past three P.M., half the tables in the Elm Room are still occupied. Friday before a holiday weekend, anybody going away for the weekend's gone and anybody not, is in no hurry to cut lunch short. That good humming buzz of voices, mainly male voices, laughter. It's a signal, when you can hear the piped-in Vivaldi, the dining room's emptying out.

Feels just great. Now Corky Corcoran's here, he's here.

The Elm Room of the U.C.A.C. One of Corky's places. Uptown, swanky. Corky's a guy familiar at any number of local clubs, restaurants, cocktail lounges, bars. Welcomed, well liked. Faces light up when he's sighted. Sometimes he overhears his name as he passes a table—the murmur, the lilt—*Corky Corcoran!*—music to his ears.

Greenbaum's talking earnestly about things Corky should care about but, shit, it's hard to make the effort. Kicked in the balls by Christina, what a joke *he'd* wanted to marry *her*, O.K. but don't think of her now, a cunt's a cunt, forget it. (In fact, when Corky first came in the Elm Room, he'd seen—and she'd seen him, cool and deadpan—a woman he'd been seeing, that's to say fucking, maybe six, seven years ago, wife of a local businessman, fellow member of this club and of others to which Corky Corcoran belongs; a social friend of Charlotte's, too. Now this woman's a virtual stranger to Corky and he to her though friendly enough, both of them, in public—Corky makes it a point to stay on good terms with his ex-mistresses, not to mention their husbands. Never know when you need a friend, right?)

How Corky loves the Union City Athletic Club: though guessing, now *he's* here, it isn't the same U.C.A.C. he'd stared at from the park.

The dignified old building had been designed by a distinguished local architect under the heady spell of American neoclassicism. That era of grand buildings, both private and public, like monuments to the dead. Tombs, sepulchers. "Classical Greek" detailing: pediments, tall slender columns, lofty ceilings, and, as in the Elm Room, a showy mixture of styles, gilt ornamentation drawing the eye up to the ceiling that's floating like something in the sky, with enormous chandeliers and filigree moldings like wedding cake. You've got to love it, so over-the-top—the stately, ponderous wall murals executed by long-forgotten artists, scenes of American patriotism, Corky's gazed at them so many times he knows them by heart, wooden-faced pioneers being greeted by stony-faced Iroquois Indians in full feathered headgear, 1791; the founding of "New Amsterdam" at the confluence of Lake Erie and the Chateauguay River, 1798 (the name later changed to "Union City"); Captain Oliver H. Perry after his Lake Erie victory over the British-Canadian enemy; the completion of the Erie Canal, 1825; a Civil War scene, Union officers and enlisted men, exclusively white.

Nothing wrong with being patriotic, thinks Corky. From colonial days to Operation Desert Storm.

Not that *he* has ever served in any war, nor even served in the Army. Hard to realize he's too old, now. His father in the Korean War, his Uncle Sean in the Second World War, older cousins of his in Vietnam—if Corky let himself think about it, he'd be ashamed. Like he's been a coward, a man not really a *man*.

Wonders if Greenbaum served. Too smart, probably. When they get to know each other better, Corky can ask.

In Israel, he's read, every man's a soldier. Women, too?

Jews stick together, micks stick one another in the back.

Corky's got a cousin on his father's side, last name Farley, said to be in the IRA. In County Armagh, on the border. Or is that just rumor?

Still, the Irish people don't support the IRA. Back-stabbers. Ninety percent of contributions from the United States. Corky once gave $1000 cash to what he'd been told was the "Irish cause" but in retrospect he thinks he'd been screwed and in any case it was an asshole thing to have done, what if he'd been caught? exposed? a liberal Democrat giving money to an outlaw terrorist army?

Also, Corky Corcoran doesn't believe in terrorism. Not that kind, innocent people blown up. Women, children. Even men. No thanks.

From where he's sitting he can see the park, windy, wind in the trees, mid-spring and the leaves are all out, those plane trees, elegant species, tall now, that solid deep-chested look. Dozens of trees the U.C.A.C. planted at its own expense on city property when every elm practically in Union City died of that fucking Dutch elm disease.

Plane trees, the peeling bark: Corky feels a stab of hurt, then he's angry. Schuyler Park, where Theresa sat. Knitting, waiting. On that bench, waiting.

Feels just great, thanks. Fuck you all, thanks.

Now Corky Corcoran's here, he's here.

It burns his ass, though, to see McElroy, over there, with *his* party. McElroy too much like Corky himself except he got a law degree, had better breaks. No smarter than Corky Corcoran, though.

Corky's trying to figure out who's with McElroy, what the connections are. Two of the men are maybe older partners in McElroy's firm?—Corky recognizes the faces from around town, but doesn't know the names. And there's Police Chief Ben Pike and Budd Yeager, a homicide detective, next in line, it's said, as chief of detectives—Yeager's a member of the poker-playing group to which Corky belongs, a loose, shifting group, though with Oscar Slattery at the center. Maybe once a month they play, at the Mayor's residence on Riverside Drive, small stakes, no serious gambling, though some serious playing. Corky's just an average player, but a good sport when he loses.

Recalling that Yeager owes Corky for one of the games, it's been weeks now and Corky knows he isn't going to collect. That fucker.

Corky guesses he likes Yeager well enough, you have to admire the son of a bitch, educated in the Marines, crewcut hair the color of metal filings, jaw like the heel of a boot. Detectives, plainclothes cops, carry guns with them all the time, don't they? Even in the swank Elm Room?

Yeager's not a member of the U.C.A.C., of course. But Ben Pike is.

Weird to think, Corky thinks, shivering, how there're guys in this room, white linen tablecloths and a single red rose on each table and classical music in the background, everything elegant, decorous, who've killed people. In the line of duty, so-called. Yeager, for sure, and maybe

Pike—he doesn't know about Pike. And other men, scattered and anonymous, well-heeled diners enjoying lunch, who've maybe killed, in a war. In uniform, with issued weapons. In the line of duty.

Corky raises a glass, blindly drinks. He's thinking, how can you shoot another person knowing what the bullets do, going in the brain, in the soft vulnerable helpless guts.

Yes, Corky likes Budd Yeager well enough but doesn't really know him and, at Oscar's, tries to keep out of his way. Beating him at cards, all their friends witnesses, was surely sweet, but maybe shouldn't be repeated too often.

Corky says, interrupting Greenbaum who's been talking rapid-fire business for the past ten minutes, "—You see that table of men over there?—by the window? Eight-to-one odds *I* know what they're talking about."

"Yes?" Greenbaum peers over his bifocals at Corky quizzically, not as if he's interested in Corky's statement but surprised and a little disdainful of the fact Corky's made it. He's been waving another legal document, fucking depressing shit, but Corky's been drifting off in self-defense. Along with coffee and these Swiss chocolate mints they bring on a three-tiered silver dish which Corky can't resist Greenbaum's been sweetening him, it seems like, praising him for the high-interest bonds he bought in the early 1980s (some of them paying ten percent interest, good solid conservative investments Ross Drummond advised for him) the way you'd praise a dim-witted kid for not shitting his pants. Sweetening him, Corky's been thinking uneasily, for some bad news. Is that it?

Corky's decided not to come out pointblank and ask Greenbaum how much he's worth at the present time. If Corky really wants to know he can find out from his accountant. And add in on his own the extras, the properties and cash and loans out he deals through his Pearl Street office.

Greenbaum's gazing with hooded froggy eyes at the men at the table by the window but doesn't seem much impressed.

Corky says in an undertone, "—That guy with the gray hair is Ben Pike the police chief, you must know him from his picture in the papers, and that guy next to him, Budd Yeager, one of the top UCPD homicide detectives, Yeager's a friend of mine, and the guy next to him is with the Internal Affairs Division, and the youngest guy, back to the window, he's an old St. Thomas classmate of mine, the lawyer who's going to defend Dwayne Pickett next month. You know—Pickett?" Corky's getting pissed off, his companion so slow on the uptake, and so deliberate in it, like he can't be fucking bothered with this trivia. Corky's busting his balls to be nice to the guy in his own private club and this is it?

But Greenbaum seems to know who the men are. At least, the name "Pickett" rouses him.

Saying, with a shudder of revulsion, "If that murderer is acquitted, it will do for Union City what the Rodney King verdict did for Los Angeles. We'll go up in flames. Every advance we've made in race relations will be destroyed. Uh!—it doesn't bear thinking about."

Corky's surprised hearing Greenbaum so emotional, like he's personally involved. This is Corky's way of thinking, too, but he says, "Pickett and the two other cops swear the kid had a gun. That is, they saw a gun. Just because the gun never got found doesn't mean it didn't exist and didn't get carried away by the other kids running with Devane Johnson. Or, if it didn't exist, *something* existed that looked enough like a gun maybe by accident and maybe not to be mistaken for a gun. I've heard these cops in person, at the Internal Affairs hearing, and they sound like they believe what they say one hundred percent. I'm not defending Pickett, but—"

Greenbaum interrupts contemptuously, "Shooting a child in the back! Between the shoulder blades! That's where the bullet went *in*. And claiming self-defense!"

"Yes, but—"

"It's despicable. That the policemen's union—this ridiculous 'Benevolent Association'—is defending those men makes them all accomplices in a murder."

"Yes, Howard, but—"

"It doesn't bear thinking about."

Greenbaum's been speaking so loudly, his large soft lips quivering like jelly, Corky's worried the cops might overhear. But disappointed too when Greenbaum returns to the business at hand.

Corky says, "Howard, you seriously think Union City cops are racists?" as he's unwrapping another of the mints, he's lost count how many of the damned things he's had, Charlotte used to conspicuously push the tiered silver dish away from him at such times saying he'd had enough,

"—I don't, I just think they're antsy, y'know—trigger-happy. I think they have a tough job." Eyeing Greenbaum's wine glass too, two-thirds full. If it isn't dispatched soon the waiter will clear it away.

Again Greenbaum glances at Corky with that quizzical look of his. Like, asshole, you're paying me to talk about this crap, and not finances?

Greenbaum shrugs, smiles. Says, with barely audible concealed contempt, "Sure, the Union City police are less overtly racist in 1992 than they were in the 1960s when they voted to support George Wallace for President. Or in the 1920s, when half of the force belonged to the Ku Klux Klan. I suppose it's a real moral achievement that they haven't gone out on strike to support Sergeant Pickett."

"That's kind of extreme," Corky protests. "I mean, shit, Howard—isn't that kind of extreme? Our cops aren't racists."

"'Our' cops?"

"D'you know sixteen percent of them are nonwhite? Patrolmen, out on the streets, it's twenty percent nonwhite? Oscar Slattery's been pushing to bring the numbers up higher and it's going to work."

Greenbaum shrugs and gives Corky that glazed-bored look that means he's stopped listening. But Corky isn't a politician for Christ's sake he's a citizen speaking the fucking truth.

"—Anyway, Howard, blacks can be racists, too. Right? This Reverend Marcus Steadman, who raped a girl—a black girl—a black woman—the things he says, he's a black racist, right? What about that?" Corky's getting excited, hot under the collar.

"What about that?" Greenbaum retorts, "—I'm not defending Steadman."

"Blacks are anti-Semitic, too. I mean—some of them. A lot of them. Right? You know about that? Like what's his name Faker—"

"Farrakhan."

"Yeah, him! What about him? *He's* black, O.K.?"

Greenbaum stares at Corky puffing up like a frog. There's a terrible silence, the men breathing hard staring at each other across the white linen tablecloth. Corky's been hearing his voice raw and aggrieved and adolescent as on the St. Thomas debate team. At the state tournament in Albany where Father Dolan the debate team's advisor told Corky he'd won his debate but lost the decision because the judges ended up hating his guts.

And Corky'd protested, You mean it isn't enough to be *right?*—they have to *like* me, too?

So Corky decides to cool it. Back down a little. He's coming on too strong, Greenbaum won't want to be his friend. Two bottles of wine and two scotches and Christina kicking him in the balls the way she did, he'll be out of control if he doesn't watch it. Saying, "Of course, two wrongs don't make a right. Steadman has nothing to do with it. I see your point, Howard." Though, did Greenbaum have a point? "Any one of us, our souls were examined, like with an X ray, he'd have prejudice, race hatred, nobody's perfect, but"—asshole, what're you saying now?—"that doesn't give us the right to shoot somebody in the back. Or," Corky finishes lamely, "—to be shot in the back."

A twitch of Greenbaum's lips. A noisy stirring of his coffee (which Corky sees is practically whitened with cream) and it's back to business.

More praise for Corky for having dumped his Utah Power bonds a few years ago. Also for bailing out of a nuclear power plant in the State of Washington which has subsequently folded. Also for cutting his losses in a partnership with a Union City developer with whom Corky'd planned a "condominium village" on Meridian Avenue on the site of a block of condemned rowhouses—"The man is headed for bankruptcy court. I mean that literally."

Corky laughs. "You mean, I'm not?"

Greenbaum ignores this. Moves on briskly to praise Corky for his choice of a tax lawyer to help him with his case with the IRS, which is challenging Corcoran, Inc.'s, pension plan tax structure, demanding $400,000 in back taxes. (Corcoran, Inc., established 1981, consists of one person, Jerome Andrew Corcoran. Once a year, Jerome Andrew Corcoran, president of the corporation, makes out a check for his annual salary to Jerome Andrew Corcoran, vice-president, secretary, and treasurer of the corporation. On that same day, Jerome Andrew Corcoran, treasurer of the corporation, makes out a check for his annual salary to Jerome Andrew Corcoran, president of the corporation. A high percentage of the income flowing into Corcoran, Inc., is designated for the corporation's pension fund, thus untaxed; what remains is emptied out once annually, in the form of these salaries.) Corky winces, thinking of the fucking lawyer's fees, $300 an hour, how he hates lawyers, producing nothing for the society, raking in big percentages, he should have been a lawyer himself, at least he's sending his nephew Rickie to law school and maybe someday Rickie can help *him*.

"I can't sleep nights, worrying about the IRS," Corky says, rubbing his eyes, "—what's to stop the fuckers from auditing me, screwing me, every year from now on? Assuming I win this case, which I can't assume." Raps his knuckles on the tabletop, a reflex that's unthinking and a little loud.

Greenbaum snuffles. Indignation. He's on his client's side, though— "You have a right to be upset, Jerome. It *is* unjust. Your corporation is legally constituted and your pension income will be taxed after you retire, as income. The IRS has no grounds. We happen to know that there are trillions, I mean literally trillions of dollars in pension funds in this country held by, for instance, unions, the most notorious being the Teamsters, but the government's afraid to pursue them, bad publicity and, of course, the unions can pay top dollar for legal counsel. So the IRS goes after the small pension funds, the small fry. For peanuts." Even in the sympathy of his outpouring, Greenbaum's lips twitch.

Small fry, peanuts. Me.

Corky laughs, "I thought I did have 'top legal counsel,'" even as he reaches for Greenbaum's wine glass, "—You're not going to finish this, Howard? May I—?"

Corky carefully pours the wine into his own glass. He figures, a glass averages out to maybe five dollars. He's paying.

Greenbaum says, apologetic, "Since my wife died eight years ago, I rarely drink. To me, wine is celebration, ceremony, and . . ." His voice trails off but Corky gets the point: *this* isn't celebration or ceremony.

Thinking of the first time he'd gotten drunk. After his father's funeral. His head going up like a helium balloon even as his knees buckled and the attic swam. And the lightning flashing in the darkening sky unless it was just Shehawkin, fiery shit pouring out smokestacks into the air.

Corky says, quickly, "Yeah, I know. I mean—I can guess."

Next, to Corky's annoyance, Greenbaum has another legal document, this time for Corky's signature. Greenbaum has advised him, and he's agreed, to take part in a class action suit against the Bender Financial Group, Inc., of Portland, Oregon, another of these limited-partnership deals he'd invested in, like Viquinex except this one *has* gone belly up, filing bankruptcy out in Portland, taking Corky's $175,000 with them if they can. (The secret reason for the bankruptcy claim is it's a way to escape fines and cleanup for certain of the group's companies, imposed on them by the Environmental Protection Agency. So Greenbaum has informed Corky.) A number of investors are uniting to sue and this form is from the United States Bankruptcy Court for Oregon and Corky figures what the hell he'll sign, more money down a rat hole, only he won't sign here—"I'll take it, and sign it back in the office, and mail it to you," he tells Greenbaum. Folds it, puts it in his pocket with the promissory note for poor Nick Daugherty. A gentleman might talk business in the Elm Room but a gentleman doesn't *do* business in the Elm Room.

Recalling all he'd heard of the Union City Athletic Club's tradition of *no Jews*. And then, in the 1970s, a *quota on Jews*.

Next, Greenbaum's on the subject, to him crucial, of Viquinex, and why Corky as an investor should vote yes in the roll-up proposal. By this time, mulling the last of the Château Pigoudet in his mouth, reluctant to let it leak down his throat, Corky's agreeable, Corky's cool. Beginning to realize that when Jerome Corcoran deals outside Union City, New York, it's other men's prices he has to meet, not his own that others have to meet. He's the one likely to get fucked, not the one who does the fucking.

Corky swallows the last of the wine. Why has it taken till now, May 22, 1992, he's forty-three years old and divorced and no kid or kids and no woman he loves or can trust and, asshole, you're not getting any younger, or smarter—why has it taken him till now to realize this simple fact?

Union City, New York. Born here, lived all his life here. Here, everybody knows his name.

Recalling how he'd stood at Christina's rear window. All he could see, he loved. His gaze drawn like a magnet to the modest spire of the Griswold Building miles away. The only Louis Sullivan–designed building in western New York State, the first skyscraper for hundreds of miles and what a weird, bold, beautiful building with gargoyles and terra cotta so in advance of its time—and the fuckers, the City Council, the Chamber of Commerce, yes and City Hall, would abandon it to be sold to some developer who'd surely raze it and build another office tower or worse yet a high-rise parking garage on the site, Corky Corcoran's going to buy it and restore it, fuck anybody who tries to stop him, Corky's the man.

Yes, and the old Bull's Eye, too. On lower State Street surrounded by discount furniture stores, pawnshops. But still does a good business, weekends especially, a jazz combo sometimes and a mixed crowd, whites and blacks, Corky has terrific memories of late nights at The Bull's Eye after high school games, dances, yes and for her sixteenth birthday he'd taken Thalia there, just the two of them, on tentative good terms, peace between them, tentative and precious and the kid had liked the place, Corky wonders if she ever goes back, all grown up now.

The Griswold Building, The Bull's Eye. Two landmark Union City properties. He'll buy, and Greenbaum's not going to be involved. Can read about it in the paper.

Corky asks Greenbaum what a roll-up is, how's this going to fuck him in the ass further, not that, feeling so mellow and so cool, he seriously wants to know, he'll take Greenbaum's advice but he wants Greenbaum to think he wants to know, Jerome Corcoran's a sharpie, too. His reputation around town is strong as it is because Corky's got the habit of quizzing people closely, making them sweat. While Corky frowns in skeptical concentration maybe not half-listening. Eye contact's the trick.

So Greenbaum warms to his subject, and yes he's convincing. Explaining why a general partner, or a syndicator, requires a roll-up at certain crucial times, the enhanced economic power, the fluidity, and Viquinex is in serious trouble, might have to file for bankruptcy, so they're going to their ninety thousand investors in eleven partnerships for help: vote yes, give us a new, big unit. Corky sees the logic of it. Sees too his back's against the wall. If Viquinex folds, he's out his $200,000; if he goes with the roll-up, he'll have to pay a fee. And he could still lose. But Greenbaum says, "Assuming the proposal goes through, the new partnership will be managed by Hallwood, a merchant bank solid as the Rock of Gibraltar. Shares will be listed on the American Stock Exchange."

The Vivaldi's getting sharper now, sounds like one thousand violins sawing away out of the ceiling. Corky says, "O.K., Howard, you're the expert, I'm in for yes, except what's needed isn't fucking financial advice but fucking *wisdom*." Corky's words sound alarmingly slurred. His face feels like a neon sign. Here comes the waiter, smiling, with fresh piping-hot coffee. Greenbaum smiles that twitchy startled smile. But it *is* a smile. "The question you ask yourself in the middle of the night," Corky says earnestly, "is *why are we here?* I mean, you know, on earth? I don't know about the Jewish people, but, I used to be Catholic, our catechism taught us *we're here to know, love, and serve God in this world and be with Him in the next* but that's a lot of bull, right? I was eleven years old when I figured that out for myself." Corky leans forward, elbows on the edge of the table. Keeping his voice low, level. There are only a few parties remaining in the Elm Room and one of them is McElroy and his companions. "The other night, Howard, I was reading this paperback book, *Whither Life?* is the title, about the origin of the universe, there's some cosmologist, in fact he's a Jewish person, at Princeton University, believes we're here, *Homo sapiens*, in the universe, because we're *conscious*." Corky speaks with boyish ardor but Greenbaum the wise old patriarch listens gravely, as if this is dubious news. "See what I mean? The universe is mostly empty stuff, just nothing, a vacuum, or rock, dust, debris, but we human beings are conscious, and one of the things we're conscious of is the universe." In Corky's head, this sounded impressive. Uttered aloud, in the Elm Room, voices and laughter at a nearby table and the violins sawing away and Greenbaum regarding him with that inscrutable frown, it falls flat.

Greenbaum, stirring his coffee, sipping it thoughtfully, says, "Yes, that's a theory."

"A theory?—it's a fact."

"Hmmm."

"It's a *fact*, we *are* conscious—aren't we?" Corky in his excitement raps his knuckles on the tabletop. Even muffled by the white linen tablecloth they make a sharp enough noise to alert the waiter, who's been in attendance close by. Corky signals him, no, not yet.

Corky says, "Howard, can I ask you something? frankly?"

"Yes?"

"What do Jews think of the universe?"

Greenbaum laughs. Such straight white perfectly aligned teeth— obviously dentures. You can see he'd been a good-looking guy twenty years ago, give him a full head of dark curly-kinky hair. But Corky isn't sure he likes the laugh, it's maybe insulting. "What do Jews think of the universe?—which Jews?—which universe?"

Corky doesn't know what to make of this. He knows, but it isn't the response he'd hoped for. Too much like those fucking high school debates, answer a question with a smart-ass question, ask your opponent to define his terms.

"Well, like," Corky says awkwardly,"—the Jewish people? As a people? They believe in God, don't they?"

"Some do, some don't." Then, seeing this is too blunt, in the face of his companion's eagerness, Greenbaum adds, with pedantic equanimity, "Orthodox Jews—fundamentalist Jews—naturally have beliefs very different from, say, Americanized Jews. Reform, liberal, humanist, secular, agnostic—all different. To the Hasidim, a Jew like myself would be no better than a heathen."

Corky persists, "Yet you're all *linked*. You're all *Jews*."

Greenbaum says, ironically, "Through history, yes, we have been perceived in that way."

"I mean it's a deep blood tie, it's race. There's pride in it. The 'Chosen People.' With us—" Corky flails about, not knowing what he's saying or even what he means, "—it's all fucked up, we hate one another's guts. There's no *unity*."

"If you're thinking of Israel," Greenbaum says, as if to be helpful, "that's a unique political-religious phenomenon. An artifice, unthinkable without American support, in a perpetual state of war expectancy. Of course, Israel appears unified."

Corky says, "Yes, but you could go there, you'd fit right in. They're your *people*."

Greenbaum says, again laughing, "And why would I want to emigrate to Israel? It's about the size of New Jersey, did you know?"

"New Jersey! Christ." That's a sobering thought. "But, look, you're linked by history, that's the main thing. A history of being 'superior' people—I mean that, sure!—and of being persecuted because of that. Other people, like for instance the Irish, my father's family came over from County Kerry, they're persecuted, but they're not superior." Corky says, hotly, "The Irish Catholics are the niggers of Great Britain. The question you ask yourself, you're a 'nigger,' is was I born this way, or did some fuckers make me this way?"

Corky's head feels like a balloon detaching itself from his body. He's stopped drinking, he's had a cup of powerful black coffee, but is he getting drunker? Maybe the chocolate mints are doing it. Chocolate's addictive as tobacco, Corky has read. Screws up the brain's chemistry.

Greenbaum says, sympathetically, "Personal history is painful enough, racial history can be crushing. That's so."

Corky says, "It must be so fucking hard, being Jewish. I mean, just to think about. You know?—just to get through a day without hearing 'Hitler,' 'Holocaust'—that depressing shit. I read in *The New York Times* the other day, in Germany there's these young kids who call themselves Nazis." Corky pauses, not meaning to get onto this subject, but he can't seem to stop. "I'd want to kill, *I* was Jewish. I'd go off my head. My daughter Thalia, actually she's my ex-wife's daughter, a serious, high-strung girl, she went to Wells College for a year then transferred to Cornell, took art, history, philosophy, one of the courses she took was about the Holocaust, she said it changed her life forever. She says the world really *is* good against evil, a madman like Hitler you're either for him or against him, right? you either stop him or get stopped by him, right?" Corky's breathing hard, unconsciously gripping Greenbaum's arm. "Well, I'm not telling you anything you don't know, Howard, am I."

Corky signals for the check. Time to move on. Greenbaum has an appointment at 3:30 P.M. and Corky's got to get in touch with Thalia. Only two other luncheon parties remain in the Elm Room, one of them is McElroy and his friends but they're about to break up, too.

A changed light, through the tall windows facing the park. Corky can see those heavy massed clouds, like brains, covering the sun. They call it the *lake effect*, in Union City—one minute sunshine, the next a fucking overcast sky.

While they wait for the check, Greenbaum finishes his coffee, fastidious slow sips, the man's lips fleshy, sensual, here's a man who appreciates food and appreciates life, not rushing, all over everywhere like Corky Corcoran. Corky has heard the Yiddish *mensch* but isn't sure exactly what it means. Anyway, Greenbaum hasn't opened up to him, there's civility and distance between them. The Elm Room's too formal, elegant? Corky says, evenly, "So, Howard, you'd rather meet in your office, instead of have lunch? Or, look, why don't I meet with you first, then we can go out somewhere? Next week? I'll have my secretary call."

Greenbaum says, politely, "Fine, Jerome."

"You know, you could call me 'Corky.' I've asked you."

"'Corky'—yes, fine."

An awkward silence. Corky recalls how, that first lunch here, with Ross Drummond, the older man had done all the talking, talking at Corky, leaving him breathless.

A sick stirring in his gut. Groin. How she'd torn at him, sobbing, near-hysterical thrashing her head from side to side on the floor, spittle on her chin like semen and he'd known he was hurting her but hadn't cared, and Christina's nails raking his shoulders, sides, buttocks, wanting to hurt him too yes but wanting his cock deep inside her too. Begging him then not to walk out. *Corky, no. Corky, I love you.*

Can't believe it's over. But it's over.

The nuns in grade school scaring them about Hell. Which was a place. You got in, like in a cave, and you couldn't get out. Did you ever scald yourself, did you ever burn yourself on a hot stove, do you know human flesh burns and melts, like fat?—well, it can. In Hell, it does.

The nun who taught Jerome's sixth-grade class told them that the most painful punishment of the damned is being forever deprived of God but the child Jerome Corcoran thought it would be just fine to be deprived of God if he wasn't burning alive.

Scanning the items on the check, calculating the tip, twenty percent of $115.95, Corky asks Greenbaum, casually, "One more thing I always wondered: do Jews believe in Hell?"

Now that the strain of the lunch is over, and Greenbaum's about to escape this intense, hot-skinned character Corcoran, he says, as if the question has engaged him too, "Actually, no."

"No—?"

"The Old Testament doesn't deal with it—there's too much going in the real world. Much later, in the rabbinical era, in the Christian-medieval era, ideas of an 'afterlife' seep into Judaism, but don't get developed." Seeing Corky's mildly incredulous look, Greenbaum laughs. "You think Jews missed the boat, Jerome?—I mean, 'Corky.'"

"But how did you—do you—keep people in line? Without Hell, how do you scare them?"

Greenbaum lifts his stubby fingers in a delicate hands-off sort of gesture. "*I* don't want to scare anyone. Do you?"

Corky says, frowning, for him this is serious talk, "I mean, look, in religion, I thought the idea's to scare people into believing in God, and in being good? Without Hell," Corky laughs, "the Catholic Church would be lost."

Greenbaum says, "Judaism seems always to have focused upon ethics. There's the promise of the Messiah to come, and a new world, and there's a strain of mysticism, but in mainstream Judaism, the focus is upon ethical behavior, human responsibility. Human beings dealing with one another."

"And no Heaven, either? Jesus."

"The idea is there, as I said the idea of the 'afterlife,' seeping in from outside influences. But it never really gets developed."

Corky has handed back the check with his scrawled, near-illegible signature, he's accepted the waiter's beaming "Thanks, Mr. Corcoran!" and he and his guest are headed for the door, somewhat awkward now on their feet, as if each is being forced to take a new measure of the other—Greenbaum is a large, thick-bodied, slope-shouldered man, making no effort to keep his spine straight, yet well over six feet tall; Corky, for all his flamey-haired energy and persistent goodwill, is inches shorter. And he hates being shorter.

Corky asks, skeptically, "How'd you people get so advanced, so fast? You started out primitive in the desert, then what?"

"You know, 'Corky,' I'm not 'you people.' I'm not all Jews." Greenbaum speaks, as he'd spoken earlier, almost gaily; merrily; on his feet, affable and unhurried, he does seem to be lording it over Corky. He carries a scuffed brown leather briefcase under one arm; the handle is broken. Brown shoes with the dark suit, and not recently polished. A middle-aged Jewish widower and music lover and top money man and a total mystery to Corky. "Do *you* speak for all Christians?"

"Hell no, Howard," says Corky with a shrug, "—I don't even speak for myself."

Greenbaum thanks Corky for the lunch, and the two men shake hands saying goodbye, when Corky sees a startled expression on Greenbaum's face, and turns—it's Budd Yeager, big smile, looming over Corky too, one hot heavy hand clapped on Corky's shoulder and the other, fingers dexterous as in a secret caress, slipping something (folded bills?) into the breast pocket of Corky's jacket. "How's it going, Corky, I've been missing you," Yeager says, but not wanting to talk, no time to talk, he's in the company of the others and has walked up to Corky just to make this gesture, already turning away, big toothy smile, pewter eyes and pewter crewcut and it's a friendly gesture, man to man, a secret between them (Greenbaum *is* surprised) that links them as friends, buddies, so familiar and comfortable with each other there's no need for the formality of handshakes, greetings. Corky grins and thanks Yeager and waves to the others, Ben Pike and Todd McElroy smiling toward him, too, and makes it a point to continue out of the Elm Room with his companion not remarking upon Yeager's gesture, nor the mysterious contents of his pocket, he senses Greenbaum's intense curiosity but this is private business.

"O.K., Howard, thanks, thanks a lot, I'll have my secretary call you next week, we'll set something up, O.K.?"—smiling and backing off seeing the puzzled expression in Greenbaum's face, the shifting assessment. Corky walks briskly away, his destination the men's room (not the first-floor men's room but the mezzanine) reveling in the ease and warmth and rightness of Budd Yeager's unexpected gesture, perfectly timed, hinting to Howard Greenbaum Corky Corcoran's stature in Union City, in quarters where Greenbaum for all his brains and Jew sagacity wouldn't have a clue.

Corky's grinning. Not taking the elevator but bounding up the stairs. *How's it feel, kid, to be established in this town?*

Seeing, in the privacy of a toilet stall, that Budd Yeager has paid the poker debt he's owed Corky for six weeks. Not a check but cash, nine crisp freshly minted hundred-dollar bills.

Nine hundred dollars! Terrific. Corky presses his nose to the bills, sweet Christ what a smell. Women should wear it, as perfume.

Except: Corky seems to recall the loss wasn't this much, more like $700. Corky was a little drunk at the time, not to the extent his mental capacity was impaired, he's never, or rarely, *that* drunk, so he can't be sure. He'll look it up in his ledger.

The trick for Corky is to achieve that delicate equilibrium between sobriety and shit-faced drunkenness that's his optimum poker-playing time. When he plays cards—or do the cards, like magic, play him?—with an unerring instinct. *I can't lose! I'm here to win!* At such times Corky's afire, Corky's gifted with second sight, his opponents' faces are transparent and readable as the front page of a newspaper, *can't lose! here to win!* but—unfortunately—this state's temporary. It might last an hour, it might last ten minutes.

That night, at Oscar's, Corky'd had a run of at least forty minutes. He'd fucked Budd Yeager over royally, Yeager an aggressive, bullying poker player, thought for sure he was calling Corky's bluff and then, the look on his face, seeing the cards in Corky's hand fanned out before him—four aces. "Cocksucker!" he'd whispered.

In that context, no sweeter term of endearment.

Later that night, Corky's luck faded, he'd been fucked over in turn by others, not that he minded losing to Oscar Slattery, old Oscar laughing with greedy childish pleasure fanning out his own winning hands, the Mayor happiest at such times, or so he says, when he can relax with his friends, let down his guard, rough and careless and profane and cunning as he wants, yes and he's especially fond of Corky Corcoran, always has been, Corky likes to think Oscar thinks of him as a kind of son, a nephew maybe, more like Oscar than Vic who's always been a source of tension, and hope.

Corky puts Yeager's bills in his wallet. Must be, if Yeager thinks he owes Corky $900 it's $900. Corky isn't going to complain.

How's it going, Corky, I've been missing you.

Meaning what? There've been other poker nights at the Mayor's to which Corky wasn't invited? Or, there haven't been any recently, which is why Yeager hasn't seen Corky?

Washes his hands energetically at one of the fancy marble sinks, douses his warm pleasantly throbbing face in water cold as he can get it out of the faucet, tries to tamp down his springy hair. Like Tim Corcoran's: rooster's comb. In the fluorescent light that seems a magnification, Corky sees random steely-gray hairs.

I can believe I'm going to die but, shit, not that I'm going to get *old*.

Which reminds Corky: get down to see Uncle Sean tomorrow, why not take him to visit Sister Mary Megan in the hospital?—two birds, old birds, with one stone.

Terrific idea.

Give me something to do, to take my mind off Christina Kavanaugh.

Corky prefers this men's room on the mezzanine floor since, this time of day, it's likely to be deserted. And no uniformed black attendant hovering close by with a linen towel, *H'lo Mr. Corcoran! Nice day Mr. Corcoran! Thank you Mr. Corcoran!*—to be frank, that shit turns Corky's stomach, handing out ten- and twenty-dollar bills like he was made of money, not fucking worried about his financial future. Also, Corky has been a busboy, parking attendant, in his late teens, knows how those guys hate your guts, anybody depending upon tips hates your guts and you can't blame them, Mr. Hot-Shit Money-bags leaving big tips. That Frenchy maitre d' downstairs with the shiny black eyes'd slit Corky's throat with his teeth for his money if he knew he could get away with it.

"Well, screw you, too."

Corky speaks aloud, loudly. Grins at his reflection. What he'd like, it's only in the privacy and secrecy of an empty men's room at the Union City Athletic Club the thought strikes him, is to climb high enough so he can shit on them all.

All of Union City, friends, enemies, and noncombatants. And that's the truth.

Still Corky wonders, Is there a poker game tonight at Oscar's? that I'm not invited to?

And who was at the luncheon today, upstairs?

Corky wonders too when Vic Slattery is arriving from Washington. The banquet's Monday evening at 7 P.M., obviously Vic will be up earlier, probably for the full weekend. In fact, he's probably back right now.

Possible (though how probable?) there's a message waiting for Corky at home or at the office, inviting him out to Chateauguay Falls for a drink. The last time he'd been out to Vic's and Sandra's, just a few close friends, and Vic speaking frankly of the low morale among the liberal Democrats, and the kinds of letters from his constituents he's been getting, it isn't just the recession but a malaise of the spirit, Americans are fed up with lies from politicians so how to make them listen to the truth?—that was back in February, snow on the ground. And Vic thanking Corky for coming out, and Sandra kissing him on the cheek. Next time I'm up from Washington, before Memorial Day, we'll have to get together, O.K.?

O.K.

O.K., Vic Slattery, I'm with you one hundred percent, I'm your man.

By the end of the decade, if all goes well, of course it might not go well but say it does, Vic Slattery might be a U.S. Senator. Might be Governor of New York State.

And Oscar Slattery should still be Mayor of Union City by then, why not, tough old bastard's in the prime of his career. Mid-sixties and in great health.

Know why I trust you, Corky? Oscar Slattery once said, rye whiskey on his breath which meant he'd be telling the truth, *You don't take any bullshit and you don't hand it out, just like your old man. That's why.*

Corky finishes up, walks out of the men's room, he's feeling less rocky now he's washed his face, splashed cold water on his blood-veined eyes. Maybe? or no? yes? going to punch the elevator button for the third floor, check on things up there, when he hears his name called, "Mr. Corcoran?—Jerome?" Turns to see a man in his mid-thirties, shorter than Corky by an inch or so, though wearing gleaming Cuban-heeled black shoes, a face unknown to Corky despite the guy's friendly-forward manner and the way he thrusts out his hand to be shaken, giving his name as Teague, or maybe Tyde—"I believe we have at least one beloved friend in common, Jerome? Father Delucca?" he says earnestly, and Corky says, "Father Delucca's dead, I thought," a dumb response since Corky knows the old Jesuit, Corky's high school math teacher, *is* dead, he'd gone to the funeral three, four years ago, Teague, or is it Tyde, nods with grave vehemence, "That's one of the reasons I hope to speak with you, Jerome."

This second "Jerome," so emphatically uttered, signals Corky the guy wants something from him, and anybody who wants something from Corky Corcoran, Corky hasn't got time for *him*.

Also, Corky guesses that this character, who's rattling away about a memorial project, Riverside Park, "mausolem of the local, deserving, much-mourned illustrious dead," is not a member of the U.C.A.C. The Club has about five hundred members and Corky doesn't know them all but he knows this guy isn't one of them.

Teague, or Tyde, has a sharp reedy voice, a pronounced western New York State accent, more nasal than Corky's own. His face looks squeezed together. And his head's too small. Moist protuberant eyes, small grayish squirrel teeth, an air of zealous-salesman conviction Corky can't stand. Jesus! The guy's wearing a boxy black-on-beige checked sport coat and is it a tin-colored leather necktie, maybe two inches wide?—Corky's never seen anything like this in the U.C.A.C.

The earnest little man is speaking in such an urgent, rapid-fire way, Corky hasn't any choice but to interrupt. "Look, sorry, I'm in a hurry, now's not the time for this," Corky says, backing off with a smile of a kind not to be confused with a smile; and Teague, or Tyde, looks after him with stricken eyes. Crying, "Mr. Corcoran!—Jerome! 'The Union City Mausoleum of the Dead' is a project of the utmost importance—I'm approaching only a few select benefactors—when *will* be the time to discuss it?"

At the stairs, Corky calls out over his shoulder, indifferently, "Contact my office." Thinking that will be the end of it, but here's the little guy at his elbow, accompanying him downstairs. "Mr. Corcoran, just a few minutes of your time, right now! Father Delucca spoke so warmly of you! Once you grasp the significance of my project, I know you'll be a one hundred percent supporter—" Corky can't believe this, the pushy little bugger. Corky says, "Fuck off, will you?" They're at the bottom of the stairs, in the lobby, Corky glances around to see no one's within earshot, says, with a menacing look at Teague, or Tyde, "And get the hell out of the U.C.A.C.—you're not a member."

"G'bye, Mr. Corcoran!"
  "G'bye, Mr. Corcoran!"
  "Have a real fine day, Mr. Corcoran!"
  "Thank *you*, Mr. Corcoran!"
Corky emerges blinking into the sullen, wintry-glowering light. A strong damp-metal smell of the river and where the hell's the sun?—it's May, not March. Corky feels cheated. The way the fucking day had looked, felt, tasted back at Nott Street when he'd first arrived, run up the stairs to Christina—Christ! might have been weeks ago.

Valet parking. The Hispanic-looking kid in the U.C.A.C. uniform doesn't need to be reminded which car belongs to Corky—"Yes sir, Mr. Corcoran! Coming right up! Caddy De-Ville."

Sometimes you wonder if they're jiving you, all of them—even the young ones. At least, the jobs Corky had as a kid, he'd never had to wear crimson pants and brass buttons and braid.

Recalling the photos of Tim Corcoran, and of Sean, too, in their U.S. Army uniforms, they'd looked good. So young. Sassy, proud. Corky wishes, knows it's stupid but wishes anyway, he'd gone into the Army, Private First Class like Tim Corcoran and maybe a medal, too, he'll never have that experience now, know what it's like. A soldier, a man among men—except now, they have women, too. Corky's war was Vietnam, nothing to be patriotic about. Theresa made him promise not to enlist, confusing him (maybe) with Tim; convinced he was going to die, be shot down, like Tim, poor Mother. For sure, Corky'd had no intention of going to Vietnam and getting his ass shot off. His luck, he'd be rolling down this ramp here (a wheelchair ramp parallel to the U.C.A.C.'s front steps) crapping sideways through a tube into a plastic bottle. Like poor Harry Kavanaugh.

He's my husband, I love him too, I share my life with him.

And Corky'd loved her! Fantasized about marrying her: Having a kid! Jesus.

Corky's guts squirm, that sensation that means hot liquidy shit.

That heavy lunch, and two bottles of wine. And scotch. Is he trying to kill himself?

Thinking what shame to come, what public humiliation, everybody in Union City knowing about him, Christina, and Harry. Judge Harold Kavanaugh, retired. The third party to the love affair, the voyeur, and now, looking back, Corky's forced to think of the man as an eyewitness, a presence, those numberless times he and Christina made love, and the things they said to each other, the things *he'd* said, so isn't Corky himself a voyeur?—talk about *sick.*

It isn't just Corky's pride that's offended, it's his morality.

Lucky he didn't lose it back there, and hurt her. A woman's vulnerable, the nose easily broken. Eyes easily bruised. He'd hit a few women in his life including Charlotte (who'd hit *him*) so he knows.

"Fuck you, Christina. And Harry, too."

Corky's been noticing a gleaming black stretch limo idling in the drive. One of the City Hall fleet. He can't make out who's in the back seat, the windows are tinted too dark. The Mayor's contingent is leaving now, too.

A rear door of the limo swings open, and Red Pitts climbs out. Calls Corky over, and, the kind of coincidence that happens if you're in the right place at the right time, it's Oscar Slattery himself calling over, "Corky?— need a lift?" Corky's flattered to hell, sure.

A quick handshake with the Mayor, and exchange of greetings.

Corky hasn't actually seen Oscar Slattery this close, face to face, in how long?—weeks. The last poker game he'd hosted, back in April. Glimpsed on television lately, he's been having a hard time, the fiscal crisis, but mainly the Devane Johnson shooting, Marcus Steadman's attacks, "racist" charges—untrue, outrageous, but freely made; at City Council meetings, he manages to keep control, good-natured as far as his good nature will take him, gets most of his proposals voted in, but then two-thirds of the Council members are loyal supporters of the administration. Corky's struck now by the strain in Oscar's face, the pale blue eyes threaded with blood, as bad, he's thinking, as his own. And Oscar's cheeks lined, splotched-looking. But Oscar Slattery is a handsome guy still, sixty-eight years old, thin fine filmy-white hair, strong bones, pride in his posture, if a little stiffness. Smiling up at Corky, out of the sumptuous rich-leather-smelling interior of the limo: "Well! We'll be seeing each other Monday evening, right? In Chateauguay?" Corky says, "Right! Absolutely." Though making a droll face as if he's just slightly apprehensive of giving a speech, which in fact he is. Oscar asks after Corky's family, as he invariably does, and it's ritual, but not wholly ritual, since, during and after Corky's divorce, he'd inquire about that too, and specifically; Corky gives the usual swift-upbeat answers, everybody's fine, he's fine, his nephew Rickie Payne at Georgetown Law is doing pretty well—the connection being that Vic too went to Georgetown Law School. All of which Oscar is glad to hear, glad to hear. With Corky, he's likely to be kind, but there's a playfulness to his words, an edge of banter, so you can't forget for long that this is, for all his smiling, a public man, a man of power, a shrewd politician, impatient if things don't move along at his own brisk pace and according to his own, sometimes secret, agenda.

Though today Oscar seems distracted. There's an uncharacteristic old-mannish pursing of the lips and uncertainty. Corky asks is Vic up from Washington yet, and Oscar nods vaguely but doesn't seem to have heard. Repeats he'll be seeing Corky at the fund-raiser Monday evening, right?—

"Every ticket's been sold, terrific, eh?" Corky asks again, about Vic, a little louder, and this time Oscar says, a flicker of worry or annoyance in his face, "My son has never learned to campaign. He's afraid of getting his hands dirty." Corky mildly protests, "Hell, Oscar, Vic was great last time out, what d'you mean? All those crossover votes?" so there's a brief exchange about this campaign, two years before, in which Corky'd been involved, mainly as a consultant, and talk of the upcoming campaign, but Corky judges Oscar isn't following even his own words very closely. The animation's there, fueled by, of course, a few drinks, but not the concentration. Oscar peers up at his son's friend from high school with oddly searching eyes, an air of anxiety beneath. As if he has something to ask Corky which, for all the almost familial intimacy of this exchange, he can't bring himself to ask.

Which shrewd Corky Corcoran's going to remember, for sure. How, knowing what he does, at this moment, and seeing that Corky doesn't know, Oscar Slattery lets it pass. A handshake, and goodbye for now.

Red Pitts has been standing close by, smoking a cigarette, he's edgy too, so Corky asks him, in a lowered voice, "Red, is Oscar all right?" and Red says, coolly, "Mr. Slattery's fine, Corky. How about you?"

5

CORCORAN, INC.

trange how by day sometimes a brittle shell of moon, luminescent as aged perforated bone, is visible in the sky. Riding the crest of clouds fleeting and insubstantial as human thought. Borne by high, invisible winds. Appearing, disappearing. And reappearing. Seeing the moon where he doesn't expect it, Corky squints thinking of Our Lady of Mercy Cemetery where his parents are buried. TIMOTHY PATRICK CORCORAN. THERESA AGNES CORCORAN. What unimaginable flesh still clings to what brittle bones, what soft-rotted grave silks and linens. *Death-lace:* the word comes to Corky out of the sky as he's stalled in traffic by the God-damned fucking pedestrian mall blocking Second Street.

Guilty son. Must visit them soon. No son any longer. Would they know me?

Never "Corky" to them. And now losing my hair.

In fact it was Democratic Councilman Jerome A. Corcoran who helped promote the campaign for "Union City Revival '89" part of the $15-million package of which was the blocking off of certain downtown streets as pedestrian malls. So Corky has himself to blame, among others. That solid Democratic voting block on the Council, outnumbering any opposition (and the opposition's always shifting) two to one. So a three-block five-minute drive from the Athletic Club to Corky's office at 773 South State will take him fifteen minutes. Trying not to feel anxiety about Christina. About Thalia.

Why the fuck should *he* care about Thalia. Another man's daughter.

No son any longer. And never a father.

Nor a husband: you get divorced, you *get* divorced. As in *getting fucked over.* Something done to you.

Except: how to divorce a daughter even if she's another man's daughter adopted under your name but never your own who nonetheless lived with you and your wife in a semblance of "family" for eleven years. How's it done? how's it done *right?*

In Irish Hill, in the old days, nobody got divorced. Had kids and the Church forbade divorce so you didn't think of it. Nor of abortion. Getting a girl *in trouble*, you married her for life.

Lucky that never happened to Corky Corcoran. Just plain luck, the screwing around he did. Waiting to put his head in another kind of noose.

Corky's thinking: if he can't get hold of Thalia on the phone, he'll drive to the most recent address he has for her, Highland Avenue near the State University campus. Crummy neighborhood, and her the granddaughter, and an heiress, of Ross Drummond. Corky'd only visited Thalia's apartment there a single time. And that not a visit exactly, since Thalia had no idea he was there. Cruising by in the street.

Corky, let me alone, you're not my father.

Corky, just fuck off! Why keep up the pretense?

Bullshit, you don't love me. And I sure as hell don't love you.

"Sure, Miriam—call Mrs. Slattery back and confirm, yes I'm free."

Sometimes, life *is* sweet.

Corky calls Miriam at his office a dozen times a day when he's in his car as most days he is making his Union City rounds of business appointments, squash games, lunches, drinks, visits to certain of his properties, check-ins with building supers sometimes announced but more frequently not. Terrific invention, the car phone. Cellular phone. And voice mail. Corky'd bought stock early in these but fuck it the wrong stock. Fell right out the bottom, October 1987.

This morning early, 7:55 A.M. he'd been at his office and stayed till 10 A.M. but hasn't been back since. Trusts Miriam Dunne with running the office, women make the best office managers, devoted to you. Corky'd feel guilty about keeping Miriam working late Friday afternoon of a holiday weekend—the other girl, Jacky, is off—except Miriam never seems to mind. And she's married, too. Mid-fifties. Not bad-looking for her age but hefty in the ass. Powdered and rouged and her hair "permed" as if that makes a difference, she has grown children and a husband Corky's managed never to meet. Adores him—"Mr. Corcoran."

When Corky calls in, Miriam reports the call from Sandra Slattery a glimmer of excitement in her voice, never has met the glamorous young Slatterys but once the Mayor when accompanying Corky to City Hall her cheeks suffused with color shaking Oscar's hand. Corky tells her yes though in fact dropping by for drinks at the Slatterys' tomorrow at 6 P.M. isn't ideal. Corky has another date he'll have to get out of.

Glancing skyward, the thin sickle of bone again for a moment exposed then hidden by cloud. *See how far I've come! See if you can stop me!*

Reading in *The Universe and You* how iron dust from the farthest stars exploded in the Big Bang millennia ago inhabits our bones. The very marrow.

Smiling at his reflection in the rearview mirror, he *is* a good-looking guy could pass for thirty-five, maybe younger. Join up with a health club somewhere in the suburbs where his face isn't known, see what kind of pussy he'd attract. Never fails: let them cruise *you*.

Two years ago, before Christina, that tennis club in Riverdale—fucking one of the female instructors, cute-butchy freckled all over like Corky himself and orangey-red-haired, she'd led him into a private changing room for instructors, locked the door at 5 P.M. of a dark-snowy December day and they didn't emerge again till 8 P.M.

Miriam's running through the calls that have come in and Corky's half-paying attention, routine business, nothing crucial, then Miriam pauses (and Corky knows her pauses: bad news) to say a call had come in at 2:10 P.M. from his daughter Thalia that sounded more upset than the first. Corky says quickly, "O.K., Miriam, fine. I'm on my way and I'll take care of it." Stiff with Miriam whenever anything involving his personal life comes up, private domestic life, or any of his women, none of the old girl's business.

But forced to turn west on Second which reroutes him practically to Front Street, waterfront loading docks then across to Nott, slowed down then at the construction site at Union and Fifth, that new eighty-storey glass-steel-and-aluminum office tower, *that* pisses Corky off—there's so much fucking office space vacant in the center city, some of it owned by Corcoran, Inc., but a lot of it, too, in other new high-rises, the situation's crazy unless you know the tax breaks these guys get, financiers they're called, few of them locals, no interest in Union City at all. New York City–based companies, Toronto, even Tokyo. (A lot of stink, local publicity, about some Jap company taking over the bankrupt First Fidelity Bank tower.) Corky hates their guts, these fuckers, crooks, still you have to admire them—calculations on such a scale, it's cosmic. Ivan Boesky, Michael Milken. Trump: who, even when he's bankrupt, his creditors come on their knees to suck off *him*. Thinks Corky, That's big-time, that's real class.

Not small fry like Corcoran, Inc., scrambling to save a few measly hundreds of thousands of dollars from going down the toilet.

Small fry!—that prick Greenbaum, insulting Jerome Corcoran his own client, to his face. And Corky buying him lunch, which wasn't cheap.

Corky decides suddenly he has been insulted. Maybe Greenbaum was humoring him, too, about his gambling?—his investments? Wouldn't surprise Corky, Greenbaum has some deal cooking, some scam, of his own.

Ross Drummond's joke: *Know why you can never trust a Jew lawyer?* and Charlotte winced, and Corky bit, asked why, and Drummond said, barking with laughter, *Because you can't trust a lawyer—any lawyer.*

Corky'd laughed, too. So, he was crude?—is? The joke *is* funny.

Downtown Union City. Friday afternoon of Memorial Day weekend. Traffic. Buses. Corky's eye is snagged by people waiting for buses, out of ten there's only two whites, one of the black women is tall and what they call statuesque, breasts big as both of Corky's outspread hands, terrific ass, fits in those gold lamé slacks like she's been poured in them, yes but she's too tall: must be six feet: looking down at him, and, in bed, just too much. Not that Corky's had the experience of finding any woman too much for him, too much flesh, he's avoided the problem.

And never any black woman, either. Not one. All these years.

He'd come close, with Marilee Plummer, but she's the kind of bright young ambitious woman, the kind coming up now, even the black ones are white. And Marilee's skin so creamy, so much white blood in her, ridiculous to call such skin *black*.

At Union and Sutter there's the old Woolworth's, still in business. Where for a wild nightmare three weeks, one Christmas-shopping season, Corky'd worked, aged fourteen, hours at a stretch in the crummy ill-lit concrete-walled basement unpacking crap goods, Christmas shit, inhaling dust and chaff-like bits of excelsior. Up the block is the regal old Hotel Statler, in receivership in the mid-1970s then bailed out, renovated and refurbished and now a classy place again, Corky drops by for breakfast two or three times a week, sits in a booth reading the papers, sipping coffee, plotting his day. Uses the barbershop there, the shoe-shine service. One of the numerous places around town where Corky Corcoran's known, and liked.

American flags flying along Union Boulevard, whipping in the wind. All the larger merchants, the hotels, banks. Memorial Day that meant so much to Tim Corcoran, a day he'd for sure get drunk, out of happiness and grati-tude for being alive a man gets drunk. Embarrassing to a kid, a grown man crying in the cemetery amid the rows of little flapping flags, just cloth on a stick, yes but if Corky could have his father back, now: his father: *his*.

Corky's passing the site of the old Slattery Bros., razed in the 1960s and replaced by a new building, all of it Slattery-owned property still, prime Union City real estate. Up into the late 1950s Slattery Bros. was Union City's high-quality department store, an emphasis on women's clothes, fine furs. The ranch-mink jacket Tim Corcoran gave Theresa that Christmas-before-the-last came from Slattery Bros., and the fox stole, with the fox head, beady-glass eyes, for Grandma Corcoran, from Slattery's. Theresa and her women friends shopped at Slattery's. It was known that Oscar Slattery's father and uncles, wealthy merchants from the 1940s onward, had made their original bundle during Prohibition, had a hand in bootlegging and rum-running out of Canada like certain of Corky's kin, though on a grander scale. With more conspicuous results. Like old Joe Kennedy, patriarch of America's first family. Yes, and why not?—even the awed first settlers must have caught on, this New World is here for the grabbing.

"H'lo, Mr. Corcoran!"

Corky gives the keys to the Caddy to the attendant at Empire Park-ing around the corner from his office, it's the second time today Corky's driven in here, a man in a hurry, a man with appointments, a man who, if you were a parking garage attendant like Bix, a greyhound-lean young black man, you'd want to emulate—wouldn't you? So Corky sees himself, not always at ease with the vision, mirrored in others' heads. "Right, Bix. How's it going?"—a grin and a wave as Mr. Corcoran's walking away.

Shit, he *is* worth $2 million. And maybe more.

As soon as the recession lifts, and property values bounce back up—for sure. As soon as it's a seller's market again.

It's a half-block and around the corner to 773 South State. Past a wig shop, a discount video-CD store, some dusty vacant windows, a peanut vendor in dark glasses, and, on busier and more prosperous South State, a men's clothing store and a restaurant-bar called Smithy's where some of the City Hall crowd eats, not upper management, nor the clerical staff, but midlevel, assistant prosecutors, deputy mayors, detectives. A good place for a quick meeting but, most days, Smithy's isn't classy enough for Corky Corcoran.

773 South State is one of the older buildings in this, the old business sector of Union City. The financial district since the mid-1800s. Corky's proud to be located here, it's what you mean when you say you have an office *downtown*. Though the building in which he rents is probably not going to last out the decade. It's only nine floors which makes it a midget amid the glassy high-rises, Bank of America, First Fidelity, Union Trust, still the place has dignity, Corky thinks, built in 1922 in that style known as Chicago Commercial—big, broad windows, square pilasters, even (hidden beneath the grime and pigeon shit) geometrical brick patterning in the facade.

Corcoran, Inc., is on the ninth floor. Located here since 1977 when Corky decided, in the face of much pressure from both his father-in-law and his wife, no thanks, he didn't want to be a junior partner of Ross Drummond's, despite the obvious advantages. (Drummond must be worth somewhere beyond $20 million. Once you've got that much, you have to be a real asshole to lose it, and Drummond, for all you'd say about the old bastard, is no asshole.) But Corky for sure didn't want his father-in-law, or anybody, looking over his shoulder.

Corky loves 773 South State, loves the offices of Corcoran, Inc. But mornings are the best time, arriving here early, before the office staff, before even Miriam Dunne who sometimes arrives as early as eight A.M.—"Just to get a head start on the day." (Miriam has a degree in accounting and bookkeeping from St. Rose College. She does routine office business while Corky reserves for himself the bigger and trickier projects.) Corky's day begins as early as he can manage, with or without the residue of a hangover, yes but he's been cutting back on his drinking lately, since Christina, since he had a close call maybe a year ago cruising at four A.M. on the Expressway and his car swerved out of its lane and nearly struck a concrete wall, he'll get to the office before eight A.M., loves the look of the stately four-inch gold-leaf CORCORAN, INC. on the frosted-glass outer door marked 901.

A man needs his own office, his own space. A sacred space.

A man among men, in the money-world. Which is (maybe) the real world.

Corky figures, there's the love-world, and there's the money-world. A man has got to have his space in both but, if it's a choice, maybe the money-world's *it*.

So he'll arrive at Corcoran, Inc., early, and always he's excited, he's hopeful. It's disappointing that one by one other tenants are moving out of 773 South State, the ninth floor is only half-occupied now, four other tenants and the antiquated lavatories Corcoran, Inc., shares with them are getting seriously shabby. But Corky can rent three moderately good-sized rooms here, the rent's reasonable for *downtown*. His inner office has a corner view, two windows, through a narrow slice of space he can even see some of Dominion Bridge, a southern exposure so on clear days the brightness pours warm as honey against his face, hands. Sometimes Corky will sit there and, odd for him, who's so restless by nature, stare out, dreamy, content. *Now I'm here, I'm here.*

Where he is he doesn't know, or why, or where he's going, but, shit, he *is* here. And content.

Except when he rushes in late, delayed by traffic. Or when he's frantic and furious yelling over the telephone. (He calls this "expediting.") Or in a wild, aggrieved state pawing through folders, documents, computer printouts, anything from IRS. Miriam Dunne, long devoted to her employer, whom she persists in calling "Mr. Corcoran," has frequently answered a summons to his office to find him sobbing with frustration, yanking at his hair—"Miriam, they want to bust my balls! Everything's going to hell!" Then, within an hour, Miriam might overhear him laughing on the telephone, chatting with, who knows who, a pal, Mr. Corcoran seems to have a lot of friends of the kind you laugh with, and sometimes, she guesses, they're women. Much of Corcoran, Inc.'s, business is done by telephone, and much is done by Mr. Corcoran out of the office, but Mrs. Miriam Dunne is sure, she'd swear, and the same thing goes for the secretary-receptionist Jacky, that all of the transactions are legal.

Why are Miriam Dunne and Jacky Ferenzi so devoted to Jerome Corcoran?—well, the man's sweet, he's funny, he's a little crazy, he's kind and generous and even a little spendthrift, takes them out to lunch every few weeks and always for Christmas, Valentine's Day, birthdays, gives them time off with pay when they need it, asks about their families and seems to remember what they've said, he's a tease, in fact a terrible tease, sometimes it's almost too much, "Don't fax with me, girls!" Mr. Corcoran has called out breezily more times than you could count since the new fax machine was delivered, he's short-tempered too as a spoiled child, and secretive, used to be he'd lock himself away in that inner office of his drinking till he passed out, yes and it's pretty clear he has another office somewhere in the city and another business, part of his secrecy, he has affairs with married women, he's a gambler and mixes with low-life, he'll work you too hard forgetting what time it is and next day won't show up until afternoon, he's always losing things on his desk and blaming you, he's careless but thinks himself fastidious, forgetful but thinks his memory is perfect, yes but he *is* generous and kindhearted and in a man, for a woman, that's the main thing, and of course his battered-handsome freckled face, his wide-set hazel eyes, so hopeful, women have fallen for *hopeful* since the world began.

All this, or anyway much of this, Corky knows, and takes advantage of.

Though never, now, not for the past ten years, has he come on to any hired help. Before Jacky there was Kim, and before Kim there was Bonnie, and Bonnie, sullen-pretty gum-chewing Bonnie was the last secretary of his Corky fucked, the first time right there in his office, on the old elephant-colored leather sofa once the property of Corcoran Brothers Construction Co., amid the girl's breathless squeals and giggles and Corky's groans, God you're beautiful! beautiful! which was true, her young big-nippled breasts, her smooth-fattish stomach and thighs and platinum-blond bush, or anyway true at the time. Like rabbits they'd fucked on the creaking sofa, and in Corky's car (at that time a Mustang convertible, lipstick-red), and in the Hotel Statler, and in the new tacky-glamorous Marriott on the lake, and in suburban motels, and once by romantic moonlight in Dundonald Park beyond the old rotting baseball bleachers where as a kid Corky'd played softball with his old, lost friends, and then, a few quick months later, when the fucking soured and Bonnie spoke with alternating hurt and sarcasm of *commitment*, and wasn't so beautiful, nor even in a mood to pretend to be so, Corky'd had no choice but to goad her into quitting, yes he paid her off generously, he isn't that kind of male chauvinist prick, but the strain of the affair was too much, in this small office, where he had to worry about Miriam Dunne knowing, as at home with Charlotte, where he had to worry about Charlotte knowing, Christ! too much.

So Jerome Corcoran is an employer who makes it a principle never to date anyone on his payroll. Never never, it only explodes in your face. He speaks of *sexual harassment* with disdain and distaste, that buzzword of the media since the Clarence Thomas–Anita Hill hearings—in fact, at the time of the hearings, Corky came out strong for Anita Hill.

Surprised, though, that Miriam Dunne took a prissier, more skeptical stand. She'd said a woman should have more pride than Anita Hill had—"A woman should be a lady and if she can't be, if it's that kind of office, she should quit. Right away."

Which leaves the matter ambiguous: did Miriam know about little Bonnie, after all?

Corky uses the men's lavatory on the ninth floor, unleashes a cascading stream of burning shit, he *is* anxious, he's been anxious all day, maybe through the night after Thalia made that call, left that garbled message on his tape, *It's me, Thalia, I* . . . and then a long pause so Corky thought she'd hung up, then *I need to talk to you* . . . her voice faint, almost inaudible.

And this deceit of Christina's, he'll never forgive.

When Corky enters Corcoran, Inc., there's a waning afternoon light slantwise on the receptionist's desktop, no one at his desk since Miriam's at her own in the second office, he can hear her talking on the phone, querying, "What? Please say that again? *What?*" Corky's eye takes in, admiring, can't help but admire, the stylish office furniture in this outer office, room, forty percent discount from a wholesaler he knows, never pay top dollar for anything: repeat, *anything*.

Aged eighteen, elected treasurer of his senior class at St. Thomas, Corky'd been shrewd enough to bargain for, not kickbacks exactly, you wouldn't call them kickbacks, *arrangements* is a more accurate term, dealing with the jeweler who supplied the senior rings, and the printer who printed the yearbook, and the caterer for the senior prom, and one or two other local merchants eager to get contracts with St. Thomas. Where there's a tradition of kids' parents (or anyway most of them) having money they're not reluctant to spend for high quality.

On the wall behind the receptionist's desk is a blown-up map of Union City and suburbs with big red pins, and quite a few of these, prominently marking properties owned by Corcoran, Inc. On a side wall is a large bulletin board lavishly layered with eye-catching items: a feature from the *Journal* depicting Corky as one of six "Good Citizens of 1989" as chosen by the Union City Chamber of Commerce; glossy photos of Corky smiling and dapper as an Irish maitre d' in black tie shaking hands with, among others, the chairman of the New York State Democratic Caucus, the president of the Union City Mission Society, the Jesuit head of St. Thomas Aquinas, the officers (lovely, rich) of the Union City Junior League, the head of the Mayor's Advisory Committee on Human Resources, such VIPs as New York Governor Mario Cuomo, Massachusetts Governor Michael Dukakis (the occasion was a fund-raising dinner at the Statler for Dukakis's ill-fated presidential campaign, to which Corky contributed $5000), the majority leader of the New York State Legislature Whitney Post, and of course Mayor Oscar Slattery and U.S. Representative Vic Slattery. Prominent too in the room, quick to catch the drifting eye, are shiny brass plaques, framed certificates and citations, a two-foot pseudo-bronze bowling trophy atop a bookshelf, a cluster of snapshots and Polaroids, some new, most faded, of victory celebrations, charity bazaars, church suppers, firemen's picnics, New Year's Eve at the Mayor's residence, excursions on the lake, a Fourth of July in the Adirondacks, each with Corky Corcoran smiling happily at the camera. So many terrific occasions! So many terrific friends! One of the Polaroids, taken at a fund-raising auction for the Maiden Vale Library last fall shows, as if by chance, Corky beside a striking woman with black hair falling swath-like to her shoulders—Christina Kavanaugh, with others.

This is Corky's single photo of himself and Christina together and he's standing here staring at it, fingers twitching, wondering if he should take the fucking thing down, rip it to shreds.

The morning he'd taped it to the wall, sharp-eyed Jacky at the receptionist's desk asked, "Oh Mr. Corcoran, who is that?—she's so strange-looking," and Corky, annoyed, said, "'Strange-looking'?—why?" and Jacky said, scratching her throat with her long red curving nails, "Oh I don't know, Mr. Corcoran," giggling embarrassed, "—like she's Egyptian, or something. The hair. The eyes." When Miriam saw the Polaroid, she said, with a sniff, "There's a hard-looking woman! Brrr!"

Corky looks now, and sees only what he'd seen before: Christina is so beautiful, and, in high heels, Corky's own height. Damn.

Corky's been approached by influential Democrats, including Oscar, over the years, sounded out about running for public office, something more ambitious than the City Council—for instance state senator. When Vic moves up (Vic's sure to move up: one more term in the House and that's it), Corky could take Vic's place, U.S. Representative from the Thirty-fifth District. Or, when Oscar retires . . . who knows?

Corky always disclaims political ambition, *I'm a businessman not a politician* but, sure, he likes the public exposure, the applause, the heat of elections and the way you feel, when you win, you've put something over on somebody. The kinds of people you rub elbows with when you're on top.

Corky pokes his head into Miriam's office, signals her he's back, Miriam's on the telephone seeming vexed, schoolmarmish, bifocals on her nose, her powdery-grainy skin more lined than Corky likes to see: he and Miriam Dunne have been together so long, she's like an older sister, almost like a mother. The kind Corky should have had instead of, poor Mother, the one he'd had.

You. Our only witness.

Miriam, on the phone with, it sounds like, one of Corky's supers, sits at her desk the way a cop mans a squad car, head aggressively forward, a bulldog resilience to the jaws. Corky gathers it's some sort of trouble about a stopped-up toilet, or toilets—he signals Miriam *no*, he doesn't want to take over. Corky admires Miriam Dunne, sweet to him, maybe sweet on him, but a tough gal with others when required. "Then try another plumber. You have Mr. Corcoran's list. No, he isn't here. *No,*

I have *no* idea." The supers who in theory manage Corky's buildings for him are forever calling the office with problems. Plumbing emergencies, heating emergencies, leaking roofs, windows, basements, falling plaster and bricks, vandalism, tenants causing trouble, tenants behind on their rent, or disappeared overnight—Corky's familiar with it all. Basically it's a matter of who gets fucked by who and sometimes Corky halfway likes it, pitting his will against others', or against the tug of the world's weight, but now he isn't up for it, God knows. He goes into his office and shuts the door and wonders has he time to take a quick drink before Miriam comes in, or hasn't he. The scotch, Dewar's, is locked in a desk drawer.

The desk, pride of Corky's inner office, is Tim Corcoran's old rolltop, dark mahogany, massive, with numerous pigeonholes and slender drawers and, on either side, three deep drawers. A solid, beautiful piece of furniture of a kind no longer made, and sometimes the very weight of it, the feel, the aroma of the old wood sends a violent happiness coursing through Corky's veins. Tim Corcoran's desk! Not lost, not destroyed, but saved. And *his*.

Corky'd managed to acquire a few pieces of office furniture from Corcoran Brothers Construction Co. that had been sold with the business years before, but bought by an Irish Hill merchant, a friend of the Corcorans, and maintained in good condition until Corky came of age, went in business for himself, and bought it back. Theresa had died years before but somehow, hazily, Corky has the idea she knew—when he sits at the desk, he seems to feel her presence, too.

There's a bottle of Old English Furniture Polish Corky keeps on hand, uses on the old mahogany. For weeks, when he'd first acquired the desk, Corky searched through the drawers, poked in the pigeonholes, imagining he might discover something of his father's if only a scrawled note, an invoice or a receipt. But nothing. In one of the deep drawers there is in fact a "secret" sliding panel, but it too yielded nothing.

The gray leather sofa too is a solid, weighty piece of furniture, with claw feet. Ugly. But ugly with dignity.

Tim Corcoran himself had bought this furniture secondhand, from an Irish Hill attorney of a high reputation who, dying in young middle age of leukemia, was forced to retire and sell his handsome office furnishings.

Uncle Sean was the one to tell Corky this. Laughing his snuffling nasal laugh—"You know the old Irish saying, Corky: *one man's sorrow is another man's bliss.*"

Corky'd never heard that one before. But, for sure, he knows the sentiment.

Now the rolltop desk is so cluttered, the pigeonholes and drawers so stuffed, there's hardly room to breathe. Corky's the kind of guy reluctant to throw anything away, never know when you might need it, this IRS audit's proof of that. Anything pertaining to business, yes but it isn't just business material Corky saves, filed away in folders, but all kinds of other crap, City Council minutes, notices of fund-raisers he knows he won't attend but maybe should write checks for but hasn't gotten around to yet, hefty unread reports (on, for instance, air quality control in the state, or the status of civilian-police complaint review boards, or federal unemployment relief programs) issued by the New York State Legislature. There's an ever-increasing accumulation of financial records, of course. Legal records pertaining to properties owned by, or once owned by, Corcoran, Inc. Duplicates of forms issued by the numerous city departments and bureaus with which Corcoran, Inc., has to deal. And bills—always, a flood of bills. Corky spends a lot of time on the phone investigating these bills. He's known as a hard-nosed customer, won't take any shit, if materials or services aren't precisely what he ordered—repeat: *precisely*—he'll negotiate payment, and it won't be to his own disadvantage.

Miriam Dunne is forever worried about lawsuits, Corky laughs and assures her these people, the ones he has his quarrels with, won't sue.

Some of them are Corky's enemies, permanently. Others turn up again, as business associates, even friends. Union City's too small a place to hold grudges, for practical reasons. And Corky Corcoran, for all that he's a bastard, with a furious short temper, is rarely unfair in his demands.

What goes around, comes around.

Corky sits heavily in the old, creaking swivel chair at the desk, it's one of those hardwood chairs with the seat shaped to your buttocks except not to *his*. Has to sit on a cushion, a mashed, flat cushion from Woolworth's. He's had hemorrhoids, off and on, for years, since the age of twenty, still remembers the way his scalp froze, heart thumped, *knowing* it must be cancer, when, wiping his ass, he'd happened to see the toilet paper smeared not just with shit but with bright red blood.

Now, Corky deals with the likelihood of seeing the real thing, in toilet paper or in the toilet bowl, by never looking. Never.

Corky removes the documents Greenbaum gave him, reads quickly through them, the promissory note, the form from the bankruptcy court in Oregon, he's decided against taking a drink, better not, too much to think about, Thalia, and Christina, once he gets started he won't be able to stop. Luck of the Irish: weak genes for metabolizing alcohol.

Now, he remembers: Jews *do* metabolize alcohol well. Another advantage. No Jewish alcoholics?

The court form only requires his signature so he signs it, tosses it in his wire tray OUTGOING, Miriam can mail it back to Greenbaum next week. He supposes it was silly not to sign it at lunch but, hell, you don't do business in the Elm Room.

The promissory note's for Nick Daugherty to sign. That's going to be painful. An admission on Corky's side that he doesn't trust Nick to repay him the loan, no way to disguise it. Unless Corky can say his accountant insists?—sounds lame. Nick knows, from boyhood, nobody *insists* with Corky.

He'll have to take the note to Nick in person, maybe to Nick's house?—or would that be crude? The Daughertys have so often invited Corky over, Corky's their kid Ryan's godfather, he's ashamed he never gets out there, Nick his old friend, yes and a true friend, anyway for a while—those years, kids together, in Irish Hill. Never make those kinds of friends again.

Never fall in love again.

"Shit."

Thinking of Christina who'd wanted to come visit Corky's office, the pretext being she was interested in some property he owned, or maybe just the wife of a friend shopping downtown, but she'd never come and Corky thinks it's just as well: Corcoran, Inc., isn't that impressive. Not to the wife of a federal court judge. Not to a daughter of the Burnsides. A relation of the de Kruifs. Christina said, kissing him, I want to know everything about you, Corky!—I love you, and Corky said, I want to know everything about *you*. And they'd exchanged much information, but scattered and haphazard and always there was the clock, the time, to watch. And always, Corky's thinking, furious, Harry Kavanaugh at home, watching the time, too.

"Fucker."

Corky lifts the receiver cautiously, Miriam's still on the line. At another time he'd eavesdrop, or break right in, but not now. Doesn't give a damn—a *shit*—about somebody's stopped-up toilet.

Seeing the office through Christina's eyes, this inner sanctum Corky loves, he's deflated, depressed. The windows need cleaning, the view's nothing. Tinted-glass windows of Union Trust rising opaque for forty floors, a fragment of pearly-mottled sky, no sun remaining, not even five P.M. and it's dusk. *This* is May?—*this* is the climate, the city, Corky loves? Sucker. And the room crowded with three long steel-and-wood filing cabinets and, in bookshelves and atop windowsills, Corky's miscellany of telephone directories for cities throughout the state, *Information Please* almanacs since 1981, a shiny new and mostly unread *Encyclopaedia Britannica*, volumes and manuals on tax law, property law, insurance law, inheritance law, Union City building inspection and fire inspection codes, real estate guides and brochures like the glossily self-promoting *Union City, New York: Past, Present & Future* printed by the Chamber of Commerce. Plus books on city planning, architecture, local history, trade unions, *Urban Economics, Economics of Property, Economics of Labor, Artificial Intelligence and Human Cognition, From Ozone to Oil Spills: Our Endangered Species, Political Theory and Public Policy, Elites, Leadership, and Society, The Origins of Western Civilization*. And the framed photos and clustered snapshots on the walls, more of Corky jaunty and smiling in black tie shaking hands with politicians familiar to Christina, she'd hardly be impressed by, Democratic party professionals, hacks, State Senator Dwyer now under indictment for bribe-taking, yes but Christina does admire Vic Slattery, she and Harry Kavanaugh have contributed to his campaigns, there's a great snapshot above Corky's desk of Corky with the Slatterys, Vic and Sandra and the kids, at their summer place at Racquette Lake, sailboat in the background, Corky sitting on the beach in bathing trunks, hugging his knees, lopsided grin, bronze-glinting hairs on chest, arms, legs, looks like a chimp. Beer can in hand—a Corcoran signature. Vic in white shorts, T-shirt, blond and brawny and columnar in his height and his smile blurred, must have moved as the picture was snapped. Tough for a politician of Vic's seriousness, he comes across publicly as stiff, wooden, he's a good-looking guy but not photogenic. And Sandra Slattery, just behind Corky, sitting in a lawn chair, a knee visible over Corky's shoulder, as if she's touching him, nudging him, but she's not, Christ knows they've never touched so that it counted. And the Slattery kids Mark and Angelica, what good-looking kids, Smiling America's the caption, Vic could campaign for President, but nothing pretentious about any of them, and Corky so much at home with them, he'd have liked Christina to see *that*.

Suddenly Corky sees, in Sandra Slattery's handsome tanned somewhat moonshaped face, her wide dimpled smile, even in the heft of her breasts in a paisley halter top, something that reminds him of Christina.

Jesus Christ: was Christina Kavanaugh Corky's Sandra Slattery, was that it?

Anyway, it's over. Used Kleenex.

Corky's just locking up the lower right-hand desk drawer, just absorbing the warm rich medicinal taste of the Dewar's, only a single mouthful, though large, going down, when he notices, atop a stack of letters in his INCOMING tray, a pink slip with a name printed on it in Miriam's careful hand: *Teague*. What, that asshole? It's a joke! Miriam has checked the please call box and there's a telephone number and a message but, furious, Corky crumples the slip and tosses it into his wastebasket. Teague! Recalling how, when Corky was talking with Oscar Slattery in front of the U.C.A.C. he'd seen, out of the corner of his eye, Teague, or Tyde, nosy little jerk-off in his checked coat, creeping down the steps looking in their direction.

Maybe hoping Corky would introduce him to the Mayor of Union City?

So when Miriam Dunne comes into Corky's office, flushed from her argument on the phone, and peering nearsightedly at Corky over the tops of her bifocals, that habit Corky hates, makes Miriam look ten years older, Corky pounces on her at once: "What's this shit?—this 'Teague'? You talked to him? Wasted office time on him? Said I'd call him back? You know I don't have time for even what I have to do! God damn it, Miriam, I'm days—weeks—behind!" snatching up a handful of papers for emphasis, and letting them drop. Miriam regards him calmly. The more agitated her employer, the calmer Miriam. Corky's ashamed in the face of the woman's patience, kindness, tact, still he can't help himself, it's a Corcoran trait, the men exploding in fury and the women there to regard it calmly, calmness a kind of sanity you learn to rely on in others. Miriam says, frowning, "—Oh, him: that little man? I'd have sent him away except at first I thought he was a friend of yours, Mr. Corcoran, from high school. It was sort of confusing—something about a priest? De-Lucca? Then he got to explaining what he wanted, his 'mission' he called it, he seemed so sincere and sweet and, I don't know, *simple*—like a seminary student, you know, except he's too old for that. He wants, he said, to 'erect a monument to honor the dead'—in Union City—must be local famous people, I suppose—it did sound like something you'd be interested in, Mr. Corcoran. You're always giving money for—"

Corky interrupts impatiently, "When did all this take place, Miriam?"

"A little after noon. I had lunch in the office, and Mr. Teague showed up, I gave him coffee, we talked, he showed me his drawings of the 'temple' I think he called it—"

"And you told this operator I was having lunch at the U.C.A.C.? Jesus, Miriam!"

Corky's excited because he's fearful of the message from Thalia, which he knows follows next. Sometimes his emotions are so transparent, he can read them himself.

Offended, Miriam draws herself up to her full height of maybe five foot three. A dense, bosomy, compact woman, but sharp-eyed, reminds Corky of his aunt Mary Megan Dowd, Sister Mary Megan of the Order of St. Ursula, when she was younger. Miriam says, "*Of course* I didn't tell him where you were, Mr. Corcoran. You must know that."

"Then how did he know?—the fucker shows up at the Club, embarrasses me in front of my friends, what the hell?" Corky's on his feet exasperated; knows that Miriam can smell the scotch, for sure, and this pisses him off, too—women poking their noses in his private life, why marriage is a noose around the neck. "Trying a scam with me, Corky Corcoran! The nerve."

"Mr. Corcoran, I'll call him back next week and say you aren't interested. Where is—?"

Miriam's looking for the pink slip, but Corky says, "Fuck 'Teague,' forget it."

"But—"

"Tell me about my daughter."

"Oh—yes." Miriam's tone softens, but her warm powdered face shows worry. Quickly she removes the bifocals, pink indentations in her nose, that air of feminine hurt (there's a tradition between them that Miriam is forever startled by, shocked by, her employer's language—after twelve years), but solicitude, too; frequently in the past Miriam has conveyed personal messages to Corky, some of them in fact from Thalia, at a time when Thalia was not speaking with her mother nor in a mood to see her stepfather in person but wanting, needing, to speak with him, if only to upset him; calls too from Charlotte, and from other women—Corky doesn't want to think how many other women, and what *really* they said to Miriam Dunne which Miriam Dunne out of tact would not repeat. Saying, now, fussing with the glasses, "Like I said, around two, she called, the second time, and, oh dear, I couldn't make out who it was at first, I kept saying, 'What? What?' and maybe I'm getting hard of hearing but your daughter's voice sounds different every time I hear it, Mr. Corcoran, and there was static or something on the line, finally she said who it was, she said she was afraid, and I asked her why, and she didn't answer for so long I thought maybe she'd hung up, then she said she was waiting to see *you*, and—"

"Wait," says Corky, excited, "—where? Highland Avenue?"

"—Oh, I did ask her, I did but she didn't seem to hear. Then—she said this strange thing—" Miriam licks her lips nervously. Her eyes brim with sympathy, something like pity, that scares Corky, you see it in people's eyes at certain junctures of your life you want never to repeat, at Tim Corcoran's wake, that big bruiser of a black man staring down at Corky, a sorrow that can't find words. Now Miriam's saying, "—I think I heard right: 'Don't believe it's suicide, it isn't.'"

"What?"

Miriam repeats, a little louder: "'Don't believe it's suicide, it isn't.'"

Corky's appalled. "Don't believe what's suicide?—*what?*"

Miriam says helplessly she doesn't know, of course she asked but doesn't know.

Corky's pacing around, when he's scared it comes out as anger. Saying, as if talking to himself, "Thalia's an emotional girl, she's not stable, she says things she doesn't mean or even knows what she says," looking at Miriam, in disgust, "She didn't leave a number—again? You didn't get a number from her—again?"

Miriam protests, "Mr. Corcoran, I asked. But she hung up."

"That's all she said—'Don't believe it's suicide, it isn't'? That's all?"

"I was saying 'Hello? Hello? Thalia, hello?'—I've never met your daughter but I feel like I did, so I called her by her first name," Miriam says, as if this required explanation, apology, at such a time, "—but she was gone. I never heard her hang up, the line was just dead."

"God damn her." Corky runs his hands through his hair. If it isn't one woman fucking him up, it's another. He wonders if they do it on purpose.

Thalia wouldn't kill herself without saying goodbye to me.

How do you know?—I just know.

Telling himself, too: he's survived scary emergencies involving Thalia in the past, and this is just another.

Corky thanks Miriam, urges her to go home, he feels like a shit keeping her so late, yes but Miriam is happy to be here and to be helpful where she's needed. As she moves off she says, "—I took the liberty of calling Mrs. Corcoran—ex-Mrs. Corcoran, I mean—and left a message for her, to call you back right away, here, or at home, to give you your daughter's number. And where she's living now. And I called that television station, WWUC, you mentioned Thalia was working there?—but the only number they had for her, and the address, you already have."

"Jesus, Miriam, what would I do without you?" Corky says, staring at her, and he means it. "You're the only one with any brains around here. Thanks." He does then this odd impulsive thing, hugs her, fingers sinking in warm fatty flesh at her waist, inhaling a talcumy scent. Hugs her and releases her and, ruddy-cheeked, she steps away, looking at him startled.

Too nerved up to sit at his desk, Corky makes a few quick calls of his own. The same number he'd tried earlier for Thalia, and again no answer, though now he's thinking uneasily, Thalia *is* there, only just not answering the phone.

Why she isn't, or can't, he doesn't want to speculate.

Next he dials a number scrawled in pencil in his address book, *Plummer, M.*, but no answer. Then another number of another girlfriend of Thalia's but it's years old and he gets a recording, Sorry this number is no longer in use. Thalia did volunteer work for Vic Slattery's campaign two years ago, but those headquarters are long gone and Corky would be embarrassed to call mutual associates, men, hunting down his wife's daughter from whom he's estranged, a messy family situation, Aunt Frances used to say primly *We keep ourselves to ourselves, thank you*, and so we do, or try. Last, Corky calls Ross Drummond Realty, the old man isn't available which is what Corky was counting on, instead he speaks with Agnes the office manager, Miriam's approximate counterpart, and as capable, and friendly to him, Corky's a favorite of the invisible network of women, most of them middle-aged, maternal, underpaid and -valued, who run, behind the scenes, Union City's male-dominated business and government offices, loves to hear their voices lift in pleasure when they learn who's on the line, "Corky?—Corcoran? Oh he*ll*o."

Sometimes he thinks that's all there is to life, really: if, when you identify yourself on the phone, or run into a friend, there's genuine pleasure in it. Smile, handshake, He*ll*o!

But Agnes, husky-voiced and warm as she is, can only supply Corky with a telephone number and an address for Thalia, fuck it, Corky already has.

Since he has Agnes on the line, Corky inquires into The Bull's Eye, the property is cross-listed at Drummond's so Agnes reads off the specs, asking price is steep—$485,000—but this will come down, Agnes thinks, since the owner, that's to say the widow of the owner Demetrius Crowe, has had only a few offers well below the list price and she's turned them down flat but the expectation is she'll be getting desperate, the property's a hard sell in this market, been listed eleven months now. In a surprised voice Agnes asks Corky if he's thinking of buying and Corky says smoothly, "Me? Christ, no. That part of downtown is dead. I'm inquiring on the behalf of a client."

One man's sorrow is another man's bliss.

Before hanging up Corky asks Agnes a favor: not to tell her boss about the call, O.K.? Either that he inquired about Thalia or The Bull's Eye.

"I'd just feel more comfortable, Agnes, if the old man doesn't know," Corky says, and Agnes says quickly, with a conspiratorial air, and a touch of reproach that he should even ask, "Corky, of course I won't tell Mr. Drummond, or anybody," and Corky says, "Agnes, you're a sweetheart, thanks!" knowing for sure the old gal will tell Ross Drummond as soon as she hangs up just as, in any similar situation, Miriam would tell Corky Corcoran. That's what these women are for.

Corky's eager to get out and going but Miriam waylays him, plucking at his sleeve, she'd almost forgotten and of course Corky had forgotten—the wedding present for Mike Donnelly's daughter Rose who's getting married in early June. Bought it at Presson's, the only high-quality department store remaining downtown, Miriam hopes it's all right—"Beautiful, and real silver, just look," Miriam says, lifting the glittering finely engraved tray out of a mass of tissue paper in a gilt-lettered box, and Corky stares at the damned thing for a moment registering it. At this time! Right now! So much on his mind! A fucking silver tray! And for the daughter of one of Corky's shit-faced Donnelly cousins, Mike pisses Corky off every time they meet and no doubt it's reciprocal, that branch of the Donnellys has always been tightfisted and spiteful and envious of the Corcorans, pretending grief, shock, outrage, when Corky's father was murdered but secretly gloating. For sure, secretly gloating. Tim Corcoran was getting ahead of himself, Tim and Sean both, serves them right, what else can you expect, thinking they're so high-and-mighty, now look. Corky knows, he's Irish. Nobody has to tell the Irish their relatives are whispering behind their backs and gloating at ill fortune, they know.

Miriam's looking at Corky awaiting his judgment. Seeing the look on his face. Which she can read perfectly—the tone, if not the details. For years now Miriam has been in charge, and very capably in charge, of buying most of Corky's obligatory gifts. For weddings, baptisms, anniversaries, birthdays, Christmas. Relatives, friends, business and political associates, yes and for a while she'd bought presents for Charlotte when Corky couldn't be bothered, you stop loving a woman you stop being able to think about her long and seriously enough to buy presents. Also, there's no time. Miriam sends flowers to funeral homes and hospitals at Corky's instruction, she's forever selecting the appropriate cards for him to sign. If

Corky ever goes into politics seriously—which, Christ knows, he doesn't want truly to do, does he?—he'll need a full-time secretary for this kind of crap. Like the Mayor's got, plus Red Pitts. Like Vic. Somebody to do PR for you so even when you're sincere, you know it's worthwhile to be sincere. You're not just wasting your time like a private citizen.

Corky asks how much the silver tray cost, and Miriam says $139.98 which is within the price range he stated, not under $100 and not above $150, and Corky nods satisfied, "O.K., Miriam, thanks a lot, that's great. Just so the asshole knows—I mean the girl's father—that Corky Corcoran has good taste, and can pay for it."

He signs the card with a flourish. For this quick moment, he's feeling good.

Heading back then to Empire Parking. The second time that day.

Jesus!—he's sweating inside his clothes, an itch like lice in his crotch he's so worried wondering what he'll find at 8397 Highland.

But she wouldn't, would she? Without saying goodbye?

Corky passes a shivering sidewalk vendor, same guy with the dark glasses, spiky hair and goatee, poor bastard from some tropical climate—Pakistan?—Guatemala?—they all look alike—Corky buys a can of club soda which, at the car, he uses to water the badly wilted pink begonia for Sister Mary Megan. He figures, water's water, isn't it?—even if it's carbonated? To make sure he doesn't get the back seat damp he sets the plant onto some newspapers, *Wall Street Journal* he'd skimmed that morning at breakfast and there's a front-page headline that really pisses him off—DEVELOPER FILES FOR BANKRUPTCY IN DISPUTED $300 MILLION HOUSTON PROJECT.

Hot-shit financiers up to their asses in other people's money—how do they do it? how get away with it?—while Corcoran, Inc., only just manages to stay afloat.

The price you pay, Corky's thinking, for being honest.

6

CORKY RESISTS EVIL

t's 5:20 P.M. and downtown Union City is emptying out.

Corky in his car, east on Fifth Street, a back route to avoid the bus routes on Union Boulevard and State, he punches on the radio, out of nerves, listens without comprehending to a staticky gabble of news reports, global oil boycott urged by the European Community to help force an end to Serbian intervention in Bosnia and Herzegovina, mortar attack on a breadline in Sarajevo, Christ! every week a new disaster area in the world, and now the countries, the very names of the countries, are unknown and unpronounceable, Corky's wondering what has happened to the ex–Soviet Republic, rarely hear about that any longer, not to mention Northern Ireland, what about *that* struggle?—but basically, the sad truth is, there isn't enough time and compassion to spare. "Fuck it"—Corky punches another station, WWTZ, mellow jazz, sounds like Brubeck. O.K.

Hearing, though, Thalia's voice, six years ago: "The world really *is* good against evil, either you stop evil or are stopped by it."

That voice bell-like and accusatory. Her hair, dark and limp and without luster, spread like a drowned woman's on the dazzling-white hospital pillow.

They'd thought she might die. Yet there was arrogance in her bruised eyes, a defiant set to her parchment-pale lips. Ignoring Charlotte and staring at Corky as if, shit, *he* was supposed to do something about the world's evil?—in the next ten minutes?

Corky and Charlotte were inclined to blame Thalia's professors, especially the one, a Jew of course, who taught "Visions of the Holocaust" unleashing terror and morbidity on impressionable young minds. You have to blame somebody for Christ's sake! have to sue somebody! so Corky made a few quick belligerent calls threatening to sue Cornell University but it was mainly to let off steam, scare a few of these academic pricks, Professor, Dean, Provost, take themselves so seriously well fuck that shit he's the father of a sensitive girl who has almost died as a direct result of an undergraduate course there and who's responsible?

How alarmed they were, everybody Corky spoke with. Scared shitless he *was* going to sue, not knowing how he hates, is terrified of, lawyers.

Well, somebody's responsible. And it's not the parents.

In the hospital Thalia said, unable to raise her head from the pillow, "—They really rubbed our noses in it," and Corky asked, "What?" and Thalia said, with a faint, pleased smile, "The evil of the world that's our own shit out there we don't dare acknowledge." And Corky was shocked into silence, as was Charlotte. The calmness, matter-of-factness of the remark making their blood run cold.

And the way Thalia ignored Charlotte who trembled with love for her. As if anyone who loved *her* was by that love contemptible. Concentrating her attention on Corky, step-Daddy Corky, needing to be punished too for the lust in the poor bastard's heart for her, he's never acknowledged?

How Corky replied stammering, or if he'd managed to say anything, he can't remember. Gripping Charlotte's hand hard. Husbandly, in control. Except he wasn't in control, and never has been. Poor Charlotte: *Anorexics are repudiating the mother's nourishment. The condition is a daughter-mother struggle sometimes to the very death.* And Charlotte sobbing but what can I do? what can I do? I want to be a good mother what can I *do?*

The psychotherapist was a man, smug cocksucker. Corky'd felt the injustice, had a quick glimpse of what it is, to be a woman judged by men.

Except there's no other judgment they take seriously. Is there?

The first time Corky knew of Charlotte's daughter he and Charlotte were already sleeping together and he'd been frankly pissed, she had her hooks in him pretty deep. It all happened fast the way these things did in Corky's younger life. Corky was crazy about Charlotte Drummond his boss's daughter, not just he's a mick hustler from Irish Hill with an eye for the best bet, but Charlotte was a knockout in those days and carried herself in so classy a way, you had to love her even if, by the rules of common sense, you couldn't always like her.

So being introduced to Charlotte's eight-year-old daughter Thalia

Corky was on his guard *what the hell am I getting into? another man's kid* but as soon as he saw the little girl he fell for her. Love at first sight. Couldn't resist. Those big long-lashed brown eyes and fine soft brown bangs to her eyebrows, hair brushed back and tied with a red velvet ribbon, she'd been dressed by her mother in a red tartan jumper, white stockings and black patent leather shoes like a child-mannequin in the show window of the fanciest store in town. And what a sucker Corky Corcoran himself young then, twenty-seven, staring and blinking at this beautiful little girl shy with two fingers in her mouth staring and blinking up at *him* like there's some special understanding between them instantaneously, some destiny.

Which will turn out to be true. Could Corky have known, maybe he'd have run like hell.

The first meeting—the first time Corky'd met, too, Charlotte's mother Hilda—was at the elder Drummonds' house, a French Normandy mansion at 19 Lakeshore Drive, one of those big beautiful baronial homes in the Edgewater district of Union City just far enough away from the southwest industrial section to be prime property. Those millionaires' houses on grassy slopes overlooking Lake Erie that Corky knew from how many drives along the lakeshore, his heart stirred by raw yearning, like staring at the regal facade, the canopy and uniformed doormen of the Athletic Club—What must it be like, to live in one of those houses! To be even a guest, to be known by such people!

Even after you know what it is, you still feel that thrill of expectation. Like it's your old, lost self, your forgotten soul.

As a young child Thalia was already taking piano lessons, and that first evening Charlotte encouraged her to play for Corky and her grandparents, and so, shyly, she did, clearly excited by the adult attention, and eager to please her lovely glamorous mother. (Of Thalia's father, Charlotte's first husband, Corky had been told very little at this time. Except he knew the marriage had been a disaster and Braunbeck, the husband, had walked out when Thalia was three and Thalia never asked about him, behaved uncannily as if nothing had happened as if maybe there'd never been a father, which Corky understood might not be healthy but for which Charlotte was grateful. For she too preferred silence on the subject.) And after little Thalia played her piano exercises and the adults clapped enthusiastically there went, to the Drummonds' surprise, their guest Corky Corcoran to the piano himself, the big handsome Steinway grand like nothing he'd ever approached in his life, and unhesitating, in childlike good spirits, played "Chopsticks" and "Glow, Little Glowworm" sitting beside Thalia as companionably as if he was an uncle, or an older brother. For in Irish Hill this was common. In Irish Hill, you drank quickly (as, in the Drummonds' house, Corky certainly did, not Twelve Horse Ale to which he was accustomed but Ross Drummond's fancy French wine) to get to that state where you liked everybody a lot, and everybody liked you.

> Glow, little glowworm!
>   Glimmer, glimmer!
> Glow, little glowworm!
>   Glimmer, glimmer!

—Corky Corcoran's flat nasal funny voice that made Thalia giggle, playing piano with two or three fingers, no pedal, not the slightest self-consciousness. And Thalia clapped excitedly, and demanded to be taught "Glow, Little Glowworm," and also "Chopsticks." Saying to Corky she didn't know piano could be *fun*.

And Corky said, with a wink over Thalia's head at Charlotte, "Hell, everything's meant to be *fun*."

Afterward, Charlotte remarked, "You've made quite a conquest, Jerome. Usually, Thalia hates my—" pausing then, wanting to choose the most decorous word, "—male friends."

So Corky thought belligerently, I'm not a male friend, sweetheart. I'm the one.

Years later, after Thalia was twelve, thirteen, how many times Corky came away from a scene with her frustrated and angry, regretting he'd ever put his head through the noose, taking on another man's kid. Those scenes, the specifics long forgotten, veering into clumsy flirtation or snotty archness on Thalia's part, and on Corky's uneasy banter. And beneath that banter Corky's quick terrible temper. (But never, not once!—did he hit Thalia. Nor even slap her, nor shake her. Knowing once started it might be hard to stop.)

Corky's instinct is, when things get too serious, to crack a joke. Thinking even now if he could just get Thalia to laugh at his jokes as in the old days wouldn't everything be all right?

That time in Killian's Red Star he'd gotten on the subject for him a subject of which he never spoke though thought almost constantly, putting it to his friend Nick Daugherty like a joke, sure it was a joke, Do you ever get, y'know, sort of—antsy, excited—your own daughter running around the house in her nightie or panties?—at that time Nick's girl Angie was about eleven, and Thalia already thirteen, and Nick snorted with laughter a little too loud, wiping beer-froth from his lips, Christ, Corky, you're a dirty old man, eh? And you're not even *old*.

The whispered tales of the old country, rural Ireland, the Dingle Bay relatives, how fathers and even grandfathers, yes and certainly brothers, "bothered" girls. And whose fault was it, whose fault exactly. In Ireland, right now, May 1992, incest is only a misdemeanor.

Corky's gripping the steering wheel so tight his hands ache. Sweating inside his clothes, anxious about Thalia and angry, too. Not knowing what the fuck's waiting for him. If anything's waiting for him. If maybe he's wasting his time.

Then again, remember: that midnight telephone call from Thalia's hysterical roommate at Cornell. Thalia had just been taken to the hospital by ambulance, she'd collapsed on the stairs. She'd had bronchitis for three weeks and it turned into pneumonia but the surprise, the shocker, what Corky won't ever forget, was when he and Charlotte walked into the intensive care unit unprepared to see what Thalia had become—flat and wasted and deathly-white as an Auschwitz victim, a girl of twenty whose normal weight was 115 pounds (and this too, the doctor told them, was low) now weighing, even with the fluids pumped in her, 89 pounds.

Seeing, Charlotte burst into tears.

Corky'd just stared, frozen. Scared shitless.

A radiant sickness it was, an icy-cold calm, teasing-starving, the mimicry of Death, very different from Theresa's helpless tearful-raving sickness, the voices in Theresa's head, the dreams striking her open-eyed, sometimes in her son's very presence, yes this sickness of Thalia's was in the girl's control, her mastery, her pride.

Displaying her bones, the stark collarbones almost poking through the translucent skin, the ribs, jutting pelvic bones, child-sized wrists, ankles, and the tiny muscles of her upper arms attached, it seemed, so precariously to those bones, the pride in her face Corky recognized he'd last seen in one of his nieces showing visitors her ten-day-old baby.

A glisten to Thalia's eyes, fixed on *him*. Always he'd thought them beautiful eyes, dark and thick-lashed and expressive, Dreamy-Eyes he used to tease, back when Thalia was teasable, what's Dreamy-Eyes thinking about now, huh?—at the dinner table liking to make the kid blush, and the kid liking it too, or seemed to. And now, the triumph in those eyes. A yellowish tinge to the eyeballs as to Thalia's skin generally, like old ivory keys, jaundice it was, and this too she was vain about, you could tell. *Am I beautiful now? Am I? Is it easy to love me, now?*

Charlotte fell quickly into the old groove, once the crisis was past. Saying all the wrong shithead things you could count on Charlotte to say—"How *could* you, Thalia! Not telling us a *word!* What you've *done* to yourself!"—as if the kid had shit her pants instead of almost dying. And Corky, tongue big and clumsy in his mouth, head packed with cotton batting, fumbling, "Honey, you know we love you, don't you? Why would you want to hurt yourself, honey?" thinking how you crave magic, words of beauty to pierce the heart like a soprano's aria or as in Shakespeare, the way the words rolled off the actors' tongues in the two or three plays Corky'd happened to see, but when it's your turn, poor dumb prick, when the spotlight's on you, what rolls off the tongue is TV-movie-of-the-week crap and the girl just looks at you.

Honey you know we love you don't you.

Do I? If you say so.

In any case, Thalia didn't die in Ithaca General Hospital. Her kidneys held out, and her liver. And her stubborn ecstatic will.

And then once she was home, a semester's leave of absence from Cornell, home to rest up, *fat up* she called it, with a wan resigned smile, *Yes I'm eating again, see?—for your sake, yes* Thalia began to speak nostalgically about her sickness, as of a place she'd visited, a journey that ended too soon, and this with a frankness and directness new to her, who had been, through adolescence, so circumspect. Saying to Corky and Charlotte (in fact, in the embarrassing presence of others, Corky'd taken a party of friends and family out to dinner, never so happy as when he's hosting a big table at Brauer's Steak House, or The Cloverleaf, or London's Seafood Restaurant, or the Mohawk Room at the Statler, or the Elm Room at the U.C.A.C., settling the bill with the maitre d' before anybody knows what's up), how people, average people, have erroneous ideas about fasting, really they do—"We're all eating now, stuffing our bellies, we think this is terrific, feeding the body, like the body's a baby, you know?—but fasting is even more terrific, you won't believe this but it's better than sex." Pausing then innocent and big-eyed glancing around the table to see how these adults are taking it, and of course they *are* taking it, their own voices stilled indulging her who'd almost died, and now her bold eyes on them, Thalia in her glory, a saint, a martyr, no Catholic training but she had the knack of it, Corky thinking how he'd love to wring the spoiled little cunt's neck talking like that in company, "You fast at first of your own volition, it's your choice, your decision, but then it starts to take over, like pushing out in a river and the current takes you, it's better than sex really, there's nothing so radiant, I know you find this hard to believe, you two," now speaking only to Corky and Charlotte, her voice lowered, "—you two, but it is. Better than sex."

At a traffic light, Corky's wanting a drink, but no, no you don't, not in an emergency.

Ran off at the mouth with Greenbaum because he'd had two quick stiff ones, then the wine, Jesus!—making the poor guy listen to maudlin shit about the Holocaust, Hitler, evil. *Then commiserating with him because he's a Jew and has to listen to this shit.* Should be ashamed of himself. Fact: a mick can't metabolize alcohol fast enough, when the poison hits the brain it's lights out.

Corky's thinking it'd almost be better, healthier, to be a bona fide alcoholic (which he is not). You go to AA, give yourself up, cold turkey, take the pledge.

Plenty of serious drinkers among the Corcorans, Dowds, Donnellys, McClures. Even a few women. Mary Megan's mother, was the rumor. Of course, it wouldn't be said aloud.

Not many in AA, though. A different kind of religion from Catholicism.

The example of Sean Corcoran. A bad example.

Scraped off the sidewalk in front of the Seneca House half-dead and carried by ambulance to Holy Redeemer and later went into the hospital's outpatient Recovery Program, which is allied with AA, and he went to maybe five meetings then quit without telling Frances or anybody in the family and Corky happened to run into him at a tavern buying drinks for half the bar, a flaming-faced but still good-looking old guy in his sixties, one of those loud laughing drunks everybody likes as long as he's buying. He saw Corky, and pulled a guilty face, slinging a heavy arm around his nephew's shoulders and saying, loud enough for all the taproom to hear, "Jesus, kid, a man's got to have something to look forward to, to make him tie his god-damned shoes morning after morning."

Corky laughed, "Hell, Uncle Sean, I'll drink to that."

Thalia so intolerant, as a teenager, of the drinking adults did. The parties Corky and Charlotte hosted, and attended. So many! That New Year's morning, Thalia about fifteen, her cat Ruffles was sick and who but step-Daddy with a violent hangover headache had to drive her and the cat to the vet's and there Thalia sat stiff and tearful in the rear of the car with the cat in her arms saying how Corky's breath stank, how could he and Charlotte abuse their bodies so, it was disgusting! it was immoral! *She* was never going to drink.

Corky laughed but he'd been pissed off.

All those years of laughing when he'd been pissed off. That's family life.

He'd made a joke of it, all Irish vowels and diphthongs—"'Jaysus, kid, a man's got to have something to look forward to, to make him tie his god-damned shoes morning after morning.'" Silence in the back seat as if he'd said something obscene, or farted. Then, a hurt shocked little voice, "Oh, that is disgusting! Oh, Corky!"

Corky protested, "Hey, I was only kidding, sweetheart. Only kidding, kid."

"Oh no you *weren't*."

And now, an adult, Thalia takes Percodans, or their equivalent, powerful painkillers prescribed when she'd had two impacted wisdom teeth removed a few years ago and how's she get them, legally or illegally? Plus amphetamines, Corky's convinced. No actual proof but he knows the signs, excitable and irritable and speedy-minded in her talk, her voice trails off and she forgets what she's been saying, quick to cry, or to laugh, poor Thalia. Next, her looks are going to go.

Burnt out, spiritually exhausted. At twenty-five, that's too young.

Hadn't Corky tried to help her?

Only just not enough.

Wondering who that man was, Christina had mentioned. At the art museum. One of Thalia's lovers? (If Thalia has lovers. Hard to imagine her physically involved with a man.) If there's a man it must be someone Corky knows. Connected with Vic's office, maybe. Young professional. Lawyer, maybe. Everybody's a lawyer today, God damn them. And so young. Anybody under thirty-five's a kid now in Corky's eyes and sure, he resents them. *He* used to be the kid.

Corky resents the guys, that is. Not the girls.

The girls, Jesus. Got to love 'em.

PR glamor girls, TV girls, environmental law and women's rights and pro-choice and social welfare and each season a crop of rich men's daughters putting in their time at shelters for battered women, hot-line crisis centers, Feed the Homeless. Corky's been on a commission to get funds for a pet program of the Mayor's, Out-Reach it was called, very popular with the local media, young kids with B.A.'s teaching in the inner-city public schools for a year, putting the screws on the teachers' union to get some zealous idealistic energy into the moribund system, and most of the teachers were girls, young women you have to call them, sweethearts. A girl you'd mistake for maybe a student at St. Rose, professional virgins at St. Rose was the joke in Corky's day, she'll turn out to be a lawyer with a major law firm downtown or an investment banker. And for sure she's no virgin. And, with her salary, no joke. Got to love 'em.

Even Vic, eh?—even Vic. Of course that's confidential. Hard to keep your hands off when it's so plentiful, ripe delicious fruit hanging from trees, and no fence around the orchard.

The girls, and Thalia for a while among them, drawn by the heat of politics, where it has heat, not the old pol Party hacks but the younger guys, Vic Slattery for instance, rising fast in the Party and acquiring that most precious of all commodities the *national image.* Much of this is media bullshit but the strange thing is, you fall for it even when you know better. When you've helped create it yourself.

That night Thalia turned up at the party at Lake Placid, must have been with a guy and maybe somebody's husband, it was that kind of party, guys without their wives, no press invited. Corky wonders who it was. She'd left hurriedly learning Corky was there. Stepfather. Ex-stepfather. Wisest to keep out of each other's way.

Don't believe it's suicide, it isn't.

A woman doesn't speak of suicide, even to deny it, unless there's a man involved. Somewhere, somehow. The trouble with women is, they think because a cunt has a conscience, so does a prick.

Still Corky's thinking, speeding north on Ballard Street in a drizzle just light enough to fuck up his windshield wipers, If anything has happened to Thalia I'll find the bastard and I'll kill him, I swear to God.

Passing the Ballard Street depot in the gloom. It's a massive old building still dignified like a cathedral, though layered in grime, porticos and Gothic arches and somber granite figures bracketing the great clock above the front entrance, slated for demolition until the Historical Register people got on the case. Corky's eyes lift automatically to see what's the time, but shit, he should know, the old clock's Roman numerals haven't been illuminated for ten years. No time, for ten years. Up into the early 1960s the depot had been a busy place, then a steady decline, much of the building's unused now since there are so few trains daily, dim-yellow interior lights and only two taxis at the curb and homeless sprawled in the doorways and this long depressing stretch of crumbling brick wall plastered over in posters, shredding and rotting paper like leprosy. Fucking mausoleum.

On the Council, Corky Corcoran always votes to retain the old city landmarks, keep 'em standing as long as we can because once they're gone, they're gone.

No, there's no money for such sentimental crap, not in Union City, not in 1992 in the deep of the Republican recession. But Corky votes with his heart, not his head.

Corky hurries beneath a railroad overpass. In and out, fast.

Never drives beneath any underpass in neighborhoods like this without remembering a summer storm in 1981, flooded underpasses and commuters trapped in their stalled cars and black kids, *gangs of marauding black youths* as the media excitedly phrased it, robbing, plundering, using fists, booted feet, knives, guns. Corky'd known one of the victims, poor bastard, shot dead.

What can I do about Thalia renting a place on Highland Avenue, Charlotte had called Corky, breaking a hurt angry silence of weeks, and Corky said, Let me try talking to her.

So he'd tried, but not that hard. Sure he was worried about her but he has his own life, doesn't he. There's a limit to how much shit you can take from a kid who used to be your daughter.

Another close call with a red light, Corky's feeling hot, mean. In Detroit, you don't want to cut another driver off, he's likely to have a gun and blow you away and in fact for months after the terrorizing of 1981 Corky'd carried his German Luger automatic in the glove compartment of his car, but no longer. The Mayor's drive to get firearms out of Union City, take back the streets for law-abiding citizens, Corky was one of the outspoken City Councilmen in support of the measure, the least he could do was remove his own concealed weapon from his car and return it to his house. He *does* have a license for homeowner's protection.

On Highland Avenue now. These wide windy avenues of Union City, something about them, even the desolation, the shut-down shops and sidewalk litter and tall weeds and saplings in vacant lots, makes the heart expand. Reminds him of Erie Boulevard, those years. Rain-washed cobblestones down by the docks, warehouses. An underlying smell, a weird kind of a pleasant smell, of the old stockyards. Animal terror, slaughter. Rancid blood. Miles away, here on Highland, a humid evening and wind from just the right direction like now and you can smell it. Union City soil, soaked in blood. And not just animals, either: the Irish and the Chinese laborers, digging the canal, back in the early 1800s. Dying like dogs of influenza and their bodies buried in mass graves on the canal banks. Lime poured over them to hasten decomposition. For reasons of general health, sanitation.

What the historical guides don't tell you. Nor *Union City, New York: Past, Present & Future.*

Still, Corky has to admit, he likes that smell. He's got his window down in spite of the drizzle, doesn't mind his face getting a little wet if he can breathe it in. A deep almost shuddering breath and his nostrils flaring.

It's almost freaky how, it comes down to it, Corky Corcoran has loved his life.

The old streets of Irish Hill, the old neighborhood. The 1940s, the 1950s, the 1960s until about the time of Martin Luther King's assassination when everything began to change, shift like quicksand under your feet. Hell, Corky himself had fled. He's no fool.

But: where you come from, whose kid you are, that can't be changed by any history. It's a gift, not God's gift but, hell, a gift. In a weak moment he'd told Christina that, and she'd kissed him and said, *Oh Corky, yes. I can see that in you.*

Passing now on his left a dive called The Hot Spot. Zigzag-loony red neon. That manic look of failing businesses. *GO-GO BAR! LUNCH DAILY!* *LIVE ENTERTAINMENT!* *GIRLS! GIRLS! GIRLS!* *TOPLESS GO-GO!* Half the stores along this strip are vacated or burnt out (incendiary fires, meaning arson, meaning landlord-arson, are up a whalloping twenty-seven percent this past year and this affects everybody's fucking fire insurance, including Corcoran, Inc.'s) but only five or six years ago The Hot Spot was still a good jazz nightclub, a competitor of The Bull's Eye, and Corky has some terrific memories associated with it except *Jesus, why think of that: why now* one memory isn't so terrific. Corky was still married to Charlotte at the time, maybe it was even during one of their shaky reconciliation interludes, like walking on eggs around the house and saying *yes* instead of *yeah* or *O.K.* and saying *please* and *thank you!* and *I love you* and making love on schedule suspecting every twitch and moan and the degree of explosive intensity of every orgasm was going to be eagerly reported to Charlotte's therapist, *My husband is trying, is my husband trying, do you think?*—and under this pressure Corky naturally cheated whenever he had the opportunity, and, downtown, he had the opportunity fairly often, though restricting himself to women not in Charlotte's social set nor in any way likely to be associated with them. And so one evening Corky took a young woman, you wouldn't have called her a girl, from the D.A.'s office out for drinks at The Hot Spot, he's forgotten her name, maybe blanked it out, but she'd come on to him strongly and it was impossible to resist. One of the assistant prosecutors for the county, probably no more than three or four women of a staff of fifty lawyers and the rap on her around town was she was a first-class lady lawyer. (The joke being that, of course, no lawyer can be a lady—no lady a lawyer.)

This woman was in her early thirties, Corky guessed. Hard as nails in court but girlish, almost coy, around men. Not bad-looking for that dark, trim-wiry, athletic type, coarse skin but carefully made up, darkish-purple lips then the vogue. She'd made no bones about it, she *was* attracted to Corky Corcoran. Not just the provocative things she said, the salty language sprinkled with *fucks* and even a *cunt* or two, a real liberated woman she wanted you to know but at the same time feminine, or maybe it was mock-feminine, laughing up into Corky's face and widening her eyes, brushing her breasts against his arm, touching him for emphasis as she talked. Corky's old fantasies from adolescence were all of dirty-talking aggressive women, women coming on to him, literally on him and screwing him robustly, but in real life, in literal fact, he's uneasy in such a situation, starts cracking his nervous jokes, drinks too much. The lady lawyer interrogated him about his marital status and his work and any number of mutual City Hall acquaintances, matching him almost drink for drink, and Corky inhaled her sharp perfumy smell, for all he knew it was underarm deodorant, thinking this was terrific luck wasn't it, an attractive intelligent youngish woman practically falling into his lap, in fact in the leather booth at the shadowy rear of The Hot Spot she was practically in his lap, a fond familiar hand on his thigh, teasing his groin so the blood rushed into his cock not in lust but in a kind of panic. Corky Corcoran *was* in a mood for fucking. Always in a mood for fucking. So horny as a kid, even during mass in enforced silence and relative immobility he'd had to keep his eyes from straying onto women, girls, the tender exposed napes of necks, swells of breasts, thighs, asses plump in hardwood pews, the shuffling up to communion the most dangerous time, Corky's eyes burning red and his cock so animated he was in terror that the slightest friction would make him come in his pants even as Father Sullivan elevated the Host and the damned bell rang, a ticklish-teasing sound that put him in mind of girls' giggling, yes and this was the worst, the most precarious and the strain of it went on for years until aged fifteen he worked up his courage to tell Aunt Frances, no, he didn't believe, hadn't believed since his father's death *so let me the fuck alone!*

Corky in his controlled panic asked the lady lawyer about the case she was currently preparing, she told him it was confidential since the pretrial hearing was still ahead gazing at him deeply and meaningfully with her eyes that seemed to glisten with a knowledge of him and of the very root of his being secret from all save her and she leaned close to him and laid a forefinger on her lips and then on his as if swearing them both to silence, saying, with a nod toward her briefcase, that a representation of some of the case's evidence was in there though she could not show Corky, no she couldn't show him, no, no!—then with a wink saying, Excuse me, I'll be right back, got to take a pee, and Corky aroused and curious watched her make her way not very steadily to the women's room and as soon as she was out of sight, naturally he opened the briefcase and boldly pulled out some documents including a dozen black-and-white glossies of a sight that made his scalp freeze even as he whispered, *No.*

The glossies, he can see them clearly, vividly, now, years later, except he's too sober to handle it, photographs of a badly beaten naked woman, young, maybe twenty, lying on her back in what appeared to be a marshy ditch, eyes starkly open, mouth open, blood-encrusted mouth and nostrils, blood smeared across her heavy slouching breasts, the curve of her belly, wiry pubic hair, fattish thighs, each of the photographs from a different angle, and at different heights, Corky swallowed and stared and could not look away and could not stop himself from examining each of the photos in turn, as the horror of it passed yet more deeply into him of what he was seeing he had no right to see and would regret and be ashamed of seeing and perhaps never forget, lodged deep in memory with other such sights long passed into visions of such profound luminosity and human hurt they seemed to belong not to him but to the race. Corky did not want to see, yet he saw. He did not want to be a witness, yet he was a witness. The sorrow and ignominy of an unknown girl's death, her puffy bruised-battered face and startlingly lucid-seeming eyes, *No!* he whispered, *no, no!* staring a fist jammed against his mouth and saliva leaking onto his knuckles as suddenly close by a jazz trio struck the first sweet notes of "You Made Me Love You" and The Hot Spot shifted its tempo to night.

7

CORKY COMMITS A FELONY

Thalia, honey?—it's me, Corky."

No answer. All he hears, pressing his ear against the door, is the accelerated pulse of his own blood.

"Honey, are you there? It's Corky. Hey, Thalia—" Rapping his knuckles another time on the door, trying the handle another time. As if, asshole, the door's unlocked itself, just now?

Corky draws a deep breath. What to do?—well, he'd been expecting this, hadn't he.

Behind his eyelids, a glimmer of something naked, fleshy, openmouthed, open-eyed. Yes but Thalia wouldn't, not without saying goodbye, she's an emotional girl and you could say self-destructive but not despairing, you have to be dead-ended to kill yourself. Corky can't believe, he'd vow to God he *knows*.

Knocks on the door a few more times, leans his head to it, no sound inside. Which doesn't prove she's not there, or there. She might be out, she'll be back soon. She might be moved out. Or inside listening calmly to him, he pictures her on a kitchen chair her long legs drawn up to her chest, she's barefoot, still, very calm, her face composed. Listening to him.

"Hey, Thalia? It's Corky." A pause. He's scared, sweating.

The last time they'd spoken together, over the phone. Corky'd called her. At Charlotte's suggestion. Try to talk sense to her, she won't listen to me, you know she hates me. Corky'd protested, No, not really, Charlotte, it isn't that simple. Charlotte said, choked with rage, Yes but I wish it was.

That last time, Thalia told him please to let her alone, thank you for your solicitude Corky but you're not my father, Corky fuck off, do you get it?—you don't love me and I sure as hell don't love you.

True that, in Corky's daydream of a wife, a family, himself as Corky

Corcoran yet not exactly himself, and who the guy is, he doesn't know, there's no room for Thalia.

Corky tries the doorknob again. Just don't lose it, he tells himself. If you lose it, you're fucked.

Elsewhere in the building, downstairs, there's a sound of voices, TV noise. Kids screaming. A young family, Thalia's fellow tenants at 8397 Highland, half-timbered semidetached old house from the prosperous 1920s when the University was private, much smaller, no more than five thousand students, and Highland was a street of solidly middle-and upper-middle-class houses, upscale apartment buildings, doctors' offices. Now the University is SUNY Union City, sixteen thousand students, overbuilt in the 1960s boom and retrenching now, for years. Highland is part of a typical university fringe area, some streets more residential than others, boasting to be "safer"—the usual bullshit of city people kidding themselves. Corky's sold off his near-north side property, won't invest in any more for a long time. Rising crime rates, declining property values. A high-risk mortgage zone. Rent to students and other transients, you're going to get fucked.

Why Thalia, granddaughter of one of the richest men in Union City, real estate wizard, chooses to live here, on a street of shabby-genteel houses, in an area of all-night laundromats, secondhand bookstores and pizzerias and bars and Burger King and video rentals and photocopy services and the Birthright Clinic (abortions) and the Art Forum (a crummy old theater with a marquee advertising a "One-Week-Only Godard Festival"), Corky can't guess. When he made a stab at it, what he got back over the phone, *You don't love me and I sure as hell don't love you*, was not encouraging.

Corky descends a step or two, pauses, cocks his head again to listen. He'd tell himself he heard a voice, a muffled cry, but it's kids screaming downstairs.

Still, he goes back, knocks on the door again, tries the buzzer which doesn't seem to work. "Thalia, sweetie?—hey. C'mon." His buoyant voice, a faint Irish lilt to it at such times, of stress and phony optimism.

Thinking of, Jesus he's got to get this out of his head, those glossies in The Hot Spot. A murdered girl, no beauty in such nakedness. The human body, once dead, its luminosity gone, a match flame blown out and, dear sweet Christ, it's *out*.

Dead meat. Used Kleenex, toilet paper.

Shit, Corky's kidding himself about that, too. Christina. Loves her, sure he does, maybe he didn't exactly understand, maybe it isn't true exactly about Kavanaugh. Hotheaded and he'd lost it fucking her hammering her against the bare floorboards wishing he could tear her cunt, her uterus, all of it, his cock hurtful as a knife.

Corky gives up and starts back downstairs shielding his eyes from a bare 100-watt lightbulb. There's a smell of fried potatoes and something garlicky wafting up from downstairs. Maybe Thalia's friendly with her neighbors?—Corky peers at the name in the slot by the door, it means nothing to him: *Esdras*. He checks the mailboxes, aluminum with sunburst slots through which you can see mail inside. There's something in the box marked *Thalia Corcoran*—envelopes, fliers. Maybe more than a single day's accumulation. Corky pries the mailbox almost open with his thumb, then releases it. Better not.

Kids' tricycles in the vestibule, a baby stroller, an adult bicycle, handsome, expensive-looking. Thalia's? Strange, the two of them are so out of touch now, he doesn't know. (Doesn't know if she still has her car, the Saab. There's no car on the street that resembles it.) The bicycle's chainlocked and it's one of that new hybrid kind, with deep-grooved tires. A dozen speeds, complicated hand brakes, handlebars set at a moderate height, not so low as a racer's. A man's bike, but Thalia always wanted men's bikes. The frames are sturdier, you go faster. Superior design.

The last time Corky'd bought a bike for Thalia she was in high school. They drove out to that enormous Sports World at the Niagara Mall and Corky was a little dazzled by so much gleaming merchandise. America is play, expensive play. High-tech for kids. Thalia chose a top model, nothing but the best for Corky's little girl, but he'd winced seeing the price tag—$320 for a kid's bike? "Gosh, Corky, welcome to the twentieth century!" Thalia teased, nudging him in the ribs with a sidelong smirk at the salesman, a kid not much older than herself. Corky shrugged and laughed, what the hell he could afford it. Though unable to resist telling Thalia on the way home about his bikes when he was a kid, how much they cost, secondhand Schwinns or no-name and no-color bikes gritty with rust. One with a wide wire basket for delivering groceries. One he stole, removing the fenders and painting it a robin's-egg blue including the rusted handlebars.

Thalia said, "Oh!—how could you *steal?*—from another *boy?*" as if Corky'd committed murder. Corky shrugged, "Plenty of things got stolen from *me*." He wasn't joking.

Corky returns now to his car, parked at the curb. Should he call the police? They'd come, for him. Break down Thalia's door. Except then the door would be broken down. The episode would be on the police blotter. Any intervention by law enforcement officers. Any use of force. The name *Corcoran* would be involved. Maybe *Drummond*.

Corky telephones his home number from his car phone, enters a series of code numbers and gets access to his voice mail. Fast-forwards through a half dozen recorded messages and not one of them is Thalia. (And not one of them is Christina.)

But one *is* Charlotte, giving him Thalia's telephone number and the Highland address, a pause then she says she hopes to God it isn't more trouble and will he please call her back as soon as he can?

Charlotte who once confided in Corky, even as they were estranged, A mother's worst fear isn't just that she will lose her child, but she'll lose herself, as a mother. She'll wish she'd never given birth.

Charlotte, now remarried. Her third husband and Corky hopes to hell this one works out permanently.

Well—maybe he'd hurt her, and maybe he'd hurt Thalia, but not deliberately. Never deliberately. He's a man who loves women and never hurts a woman deliberately.

Corky hangs up the receiver. Starts the car. An idea has come to him, he'll need to move the car. Up the block. Around the corner. Away from 8397 Highland.

Excited and nervous like, as a kid, and not exclusively as a kid, he'd know he was going to jack himself off only not just yet. Soon.

Corky's thinking how, when Thalia worked at Family Services, one of her clients was a welfare mother with a twenty-nine-year-old unemployed son who hung out at her apartment, coerced drug money from her, beat her

and terrorized her, and Thalia helped the woman to get a court injunc-
tion against him, and soon he began stalking Thalia, she knew it must be
him, not speaking to her nor coming too close, just waiting for her, following her, with an improbably fair, rosy round face, and corn-silk hair,
a fattish guy, obviously deranged, dangerous. And after weeks of this—
the fucker waited for Thalia across from City Hall when she left work,
strolling in her parking garage, or in the foyer of the apartment building
she lived in at the time (downtown, overlooking the Dominion Bridge and
the river) and several times in the very corridor outside her apartment—
Thalia called Corky, not desperate in her tone or words, careful in her
choice of words, with a forced logic. She had a problem, she said, and she
knew the police couldn't help until the stalker actually did something to
her and in the meantime, she guessed, she didn't know what to do: how,
in her thoughts, to ever be free of the man, awake or asleep. Corky, who'd
known nothing of this, but who'd never much liked the idea of Thalia as a
social welfare worker, said without hesitation, blunt and furious, "O.K.,
Thalia, leave it to me."

Corky'd deliberated approaching the stalker himself. Stalking the
stalker—he liked that idea. The Luger in his pocket. Then decided no,
better not, you're a respectable citizen worth two million bucks, and this
fucker's shit on your shoes, blow him away and the D.A. won't have any
choice but to indict, friend of the Slatterys, loyal Democrat, protecting
your daughter, no matter, first-degree manslaughter at the least, and
carrying a concealed weapon, fuck that. So Corky hired two hefty guys
he knew who worked down at the docks, paid them $500 each up front
and $500 each when they delivered, and was an eyewitness, from his car,
to the fact that they did deliver: dragged Thalia's stalker into an alley
explaining as they punched, kicked, kneed, banged him like a cymbal
against the garbage cans, that they were U.C. plainclothes cops assigned
to protect City Hall staff and if they had to deal with him a second time
he'd be dead meat. And following that, the stalking stopped.

Of course, Thalia never knew. And Corky wants it that way.

She knew only that, overnight, the man who'd been terrorizing her disappeared. One day there, the next day not. And the next day, and the
next. So she was free in her thoughts of him; of the self-absorption, as she
called it, of paranoia.

Did you have anything to do with it, Corky? she'd asked, but Corky pretended surprise, no he hadn't done anything yet, you mean the bastard's stopped following you?

Expediting Thalia's stalker. *Sweet.*

Thinking of that now, and liking the memory. Maybe he'd been a little reckless, hiring guys like that you're setting yourself up for blackmail, but, for Thalia, it was worth it.

Shrewd Corky Corcoran has parked the big Caddy around the corner from Highland, on a side street called Richmond. (Noting that the alley that runs behind Thalia's house intersects close by.) He unlocks the car trunk, locates an eight-inch screwdriver amid the tools and other crap and slips it inside his coat. Whistling quietly to himself, getting his adrenaline high. Like stepping into the ring in the gym at St. Thomas, his twelve-ounce boxing gloves on, his body, cock to brain, afire.

Who's your man?—I'm your man.

Returns to 8397 Highland. A casual stroller. The neighborhood's moderately busy. Cars, kids on bikes. Activity enough so no one's likely to notice him and if so, so what?—Corky Corcoran's a prosperous businessman and looks it.

Decently maintained semidetached brick-and-stucco houses, and older Victorian woodframes, fire hazards but attractive, three storeys, turrets, gables, verandas, what remains of old rotting cornices, the kind of architecture Corky as a kid associated with elegance and mystery—the prominent citizens of Irish Hill built such homes for themselves on Dundonald Street. These houses, though, have long been partitioned into rental units. Some of them are rooming houses, run-down, sad to contemplate. A few years from dereliction.

Shit, thinks Corky, as if personally affronted, once the big old Victorians are gone from America, they're gone.

Once his America's gone, it's gone.

Like Irish Hill: virtually no Irish still living there, and even the hills look flatter.

At Thalia's house, Corky makes his way unobtrusively, he thinks, along the driveway, badly cracked asphalt, to the rear, an old garage and a car parked just outside it but the car's one of those cheapie American compacts, not Thalia's car. (If Thalia still has a car? Old man Drummond who knew to interfere but rarely in his granddaughter's life insisted that, if she drove any car at all, it had to be a safe car—by which he meant a Volvo, a Mercedes, a Saab. Solid as a tank so if another driver hits her even side-on the steel won't buckle. These Jap cars, said Drummond contemptuously—steel soft as cooked spaghetti.)

Corky sees the back yard's surprisingly deep, a rotted fence at the rear, but there's access to the alley. Just in case.

Children's swings, garbage cans lined up against the garage. Dusk now, could be November. Wind-blown drizzle, a metallic taste. A back porch, needs repair. Window looking into a kitchen: a man's big burly figure, young guy, but nearly bald, with rimless glasses, a junior-faculty look to his harried face as he stoops to tend to a fretting child. Corky thinks maybe you don't always want kids, eh?—not when they're screaming like that.

Keeping well out of the light so the guy, Esdras, can't see him. Anyway he's feeling, in his adrenaline glow, invisible to human eyes.

(But it's reassuring: that Thalia lives upstairs from a young seeming-normal family. And that the kids' clamor is sufficiently loud, Corky won't be heard.)

Returns to the front of the house, and again enters the vestibule crowded with bikes, baby stroller, into the pungent aroma of cooking, and climbs the stairs, as quietly! silently! as possible; and, at Thalia's door, jimmies open the lock with the screwdriver; working fast, and sweating; desperate, maybe a mistake, but what the fuck else can he do?

Don't believe it's suicide, it isn't.

You don't love me and I sure as hell don't love you.

A good sign, thank God the chain latch isn't in place. If it was, Corky'd have to fracture the doorframe or break in the paneling.

Corky pushes the door open, pauses before entering. Unconsciously holding his breath.

It's true, as the cops say. You can smell death immediately, as soon as you enter death's premises. It's in the air. It's a high meaty unmistakable smell. Panic, too. You smell panic, too. Not just when the body's been dead for hours or days and it's decomposing flesh but a body freshly killed.

And sometimes too a stench of excrement, yes Corky remembers.

Corky never forgets. The final ignominy of a violent death. The final thing God does for you before letting you go.

"Thalia."

An emptiness, and no smell thank God except the cooking odors from downstairs.

Corky shuts the door behind him. Relocks the Yale lock, and slips the chain latch in place. His hands are trembling badly.

Switches on a light and sees—a surprise—that Thalia's living room isn't what he'd expected, it's so spare, sparsely furnished. Unlike previous places she's lived, and her room, her girlhood room, at home.

There are only a few items of furniture—a small sofa covered in a gritty fabric like whole wheat, some plain varnished hardback chairs, a long, low, unfinished table stacked with books and papers. The hardwood floor has only a single handwoven dove-gray carpet, Navajo-looking. This, Corky remembers from the other apartment. Artsy-craftsy stuff. Attractive, if you go for that look.

Corky's critical noting sloppy carpentry at the room's wainscoting. And those oyster-white painted walls with a look of aged, fine-cracked plaster beneath. Renovating these old houses, you either do it right or don't do it at all.

The room is narrow, windows at either end. Old-fashioned many-paned windows, the kind that collect grime fast and can't be kept clean, outside or in. Corky'd take out those windows and replace them with clear Thermopane. Thalia hasn't hung any curtains or drapes to soften the effect of the windows, that stark, raw look Corky finds ugly. There are cartons against the walls, maybe she hasn't moved in yet. Maybe she's preparing to move out.

Corky's in motion, quick, nerved up, walking as lightly as he can in these smooth-soled shoes. If she *is* here, she'd be in the bedroom or the bathroom, so he checks these rooms out, his heart beating so hard he's virtually blinded for a few seconds switching on lights, staring. But nothing. No. No Thalia in the bathroom, her naked body not sprawled bloody in the tub or on the floor, nor is she in the bedroom, her naked body atop the bed in a posture of mock sleep; nor, Corky stoops to look, blood rushing into his head, is she under the bed. He rises panting and elated.

"Christ! Thank God."

Next, Corky checks the bedroom closet, locates another closet in the hall and checks that too, a black leotard hanging from a hook startles him, he trips on black aerobics shoes on the floor. Yes and the rear door, the back stairs: checks that, too, switching on the light and switching it off again. Television and kids' yammering from downstairs and a stronger smell of greasy-fried potatoes that has a weird effect, nausea in the belly but saliva flooding the mouth. His blood beats quick in anger now too of Thalia's life, here.

She's doing it, he thinks, to spite her family. To spite Charlotte who'd wanted a debutante-country club daughter, and to spite Corky Corcoran, God knows why.

Yes, and you know why: don't bullshit.

Yes but, fuck it, he doesn't. He doesn't know why. The more he'd tried to give her, the more she'd backed away. Even her political beliefs and her activism she made out to be fueled by an idealism very different from Corky's involvement, with him it's just old City Hall influence and graft and what's-in-it-for-me, the old corrupt Union City Democratic machine, Thalia's made of finer stuff, Thalia's a new female breed. Thinks Corky, *This new breed, they don't even bleed.*

When Thalia was hospitalized in Ithaca, one aspect of her condition was amenorrhea. Cessation of menstrual periods. From weight loss, the doctor told them, when her weight goes up she'll become normal again.

Thalia joked, *Maybe I don't want to be normal?—whose "normal" is it?*

Next, Corky checks out the kitchen. And no body there slumped in a corner, long legs bared limp on the worn linoleum floor.

Well, the kitchen's a sad place. Damned drab and needing a new sink, dishwasher (this is the old, top-loading kind, must be from the 1960s). New lighting. Walls redone, ceiling, certainly the floor, they make terrific new slate-looking tiles now, mopping clean with water and no wax or even liquid polish, Corky's rental units all have these, he's gotten great discount prices, half what you'd pay up front.

Corky lifts a phone receiver to hear the dial tone. Yes, this is the number he's been calling.

Fuck that number: he's memorized it.

Corky sees there's a carton of fruit juice on a counter, a few glasses, plates, in the sink; one of the cupboard doors part open; a dishtowel (matted, grungy) on the floor. An air here, a look, as of someone in a hurry. Just stepped out? He lays his hand on the stove's burners—cold. Opens the refrigerator door and sees it's nearly empty: a carton of nonfat plain yogurt (the "expiration" date May 19, 1992—Thalia hasn't been grocery shopping in a while), a few hard-looking greenish apples (with those prissy little labels on them: "organically grown"—as if you could trust such shit), wilted head of lettuce, plastic bowl containing a few limps stalks of celery, carrot sticks. Some of that brown pebbly-textured health-store bread Thalia'd given Corky once, thick and chewy but no salt, not much point in eating bread with so little taste. Still, there's fiber. If you want fiber. Everybody talking these days about "fiber": on TV: even old Ross Drummond with his "stomach problems" (i.e., chronic constipation): weird emphasis in the culture upon shit, shitting, though if you were vulgar enough to spell it out that way (as, in fact, a few times, Corky's done, just to get a rise out of company) you'd get frowned at.

Corky checks out the freezer which is nearly empty. And layered thick in frost. How the fuck *does* Thalia live?

Corky laughs aloud, it's an angry baffled sound. Shit, she's a mystery to *him*.

Must be he's a little high. Adrenaline rush. Feels good. Sexed up. Breaking and entering: but what if he's caught?

That big guy downstairs, built like a linebacker. If he'd discovered Corky forcing his way in, and Corky with the screwdriver in his hand.

Suppose somebody comes to the door, now.

As a kid Corky'd forced locks, broken windows, a gang of kids including Nick Daugherty, small thefts mainly merchandise—weird things like first aid supplies, giant cans of Campbell's tomato soup, motor oil, used tires, once, Halloween it happened to be, a full case of beer off the back of somebody's pickup truck. Except for the beer they'd sold the stuff, around the neighborhood. And Corky's own cousin Mickey Dowd a patrolman in the Sixth Precinct giving him hell, slapping him around, y'want to go to Juvenile Hall, shithead?

Should get the hell out since Corky sees Thalia isn't here. But trailing his hand through the clothes, mainly coats, in Thalia's hall closet, caressing. That time Corky gave Thalia a beautiful red-fox jacket for her eighteenth birthday, a secret even from Charlotte and the little bitch told him thanks but I can't, can't wear fur, these were living creatures butchered for vanity, I'm sorry, Corky, and in fact she *did* seem sorry, but not enough to change her mind about the coat.

Touching now the filmy black leotard hanging from a hook. Sniffs it, a sweaty-salty smell, reinforced cotton crotch. Doggy-Corky, a nose for women's secret smells, secretions. Underarms, cunt.

Corky shuts the closet door quick, as if fearing he might be seen. Gives the glass knob several hard twists, a way of smearing fingerprints. What you've been doing in here, asshole, is getting your prints all over everything.

"Well, too late now."

It's a wild purposeless thought. And he's thinking too of Yeager, the warm, good feel of the guy's hand on his shoulder. How surprised and how impressed Greenbaum had been, the way the detective sauntered over to slip, so slyly, those folded bills into Corky's coat pocket. A secret. Secret connection. The expression on Greenbaum's face: undisguised. A man like that, brainy as he is, of a superior race as he is, he can look down his nose at politicians like the locals, who's running City Hall and who's on top, the boys with the power, and the muscle that guarantees the power, but when it comes down to it, he's impressed.

Corky returns to the front room. To his left, at the rear, in an alcove measuring maybe ten feet by twelve, there's a table Thalia uses to eat on, very plain too, but good wood, looks like cherrywood, a book opened on its spine on the table, a notepad, pen. And above, hanging from a hook in the window, is a birdcage—a hand-crafted cage Corky gave Thalia years ago and hasn't thought of since. It's empty, no birds. Corky smiles, surprised to see it. Touched.

That cage! One of Corky's countless impulsive purchases. He must have been in a market or a gift shop, the thing caught his eye and he thought of Thalia for some reason, and bought it. It's made of bamboo, real craftsmanship, made in Thailand. Ingenious how the slender bamboo strips are shaped into a graceful octagon, maybe meant to suggest a pagoda?—tiny bamboo pegs holding them together. Purely ornamental, though. At least in this country. Birds would crap up the bamboo, fast, and it wouldn't be so pretty anymore: Corky's Aunt Frances kept canaries, Corky knows. A real cage, for real birds, you'd require practical materials, like aluminum, for wiping clean.

So Thalia still has it. When, judging from the look of this place, like some Shaker display room in a museum, she's gotten rid of so much else.

Corky picks up the book, a hefty book, it's a textbook, astronomy?—Jesus, since when? He's a little hurt, Thalia's never told him she's taking a course in anything. So out of touch this past year, estranged. And Thalia knows Corky's always reading in science, he's a sucker for paperbacks about the universe, figures you can't know too much about where you came from or where you're going. Except the math, if there's math, leaves him behind. Well, he thinks, Charlotte must not know either, or she'd have said.

The textbook's titled, simply, *The Universe*. Purchased at the SUNY U.C. Co-Op. Corky leafs through it, pauses to read a passage Thalia has marked in yellow felt-tip ink—

The death of a large star is a sudden and violent event. The star evolves peacefully for millions of years, passing through stages of development, but when it runs out of nuclear fuel, it collapses under its own weight in less than a second. It might seem that this implosion would be a chaotic process, but in fact it is quite orderly. Indeed, the entire evolution of the star is toward a condition of greater order, or lower entropy.

Thalia had underscored *in less than a second*. Christ, Corky thinks, that *is* weird.

Another marked passage, elsewhere in the book, catches Corky's eye—

Where there is quantum theory there is hope. We can never be completely sure this cosmic heat death will occur because we can never predict the future of a quantum universe with complete certainty; for, in an infinite quantum future anything that can happen, will eventually.

Here, in the margin, there's a single yellow exclamation point: !
Thinks Corky, That's more like it.

You're an American, you're an optimist. Or you're fucked.

Corky returns to the living room area, such as it is. So damned small. Except for the books and loose papers, tidy. He tries to picture Thalia on the sofa, reading, taking notes, always a kid for reading and taking notes and Charlotte said, once, she'd found a diary of Thalia's in Thalia's bureau but most of it was in code, you'd think she didn't trust her mother! But he hasn't seen Thalia in so many months, it's scary to think he doesn't know what she looks like exactly—how long her hair is, is her skin healthy, what's her dominant mood. With him, she'd been angry. But from other people he'd heard other things.

This place, it does remind him of a Shaker exhibit. Shaker furniture, American plain style. Like the best of Frank Lloyd Wright. Clean lines, the eye just moves. Beauty that makes those overblown European styles, baroque, eighteenth-century, Victorian, look like the crap they are.

Except the Shakers couldn't have had the right idea, could they? About God, the purpose of human life, sex. For sure, not about sex. They didn't believe in it. No screwing, no physical love, no pregnancies, no kids. Corky recalls how, in theology class at St. Thomas, somehow the subject of the Shakers came up, chastity, chastity for everyone, and the good-natured fattish Jesuit who taught the course, Father Scully, got the class going, quizzical and sniggering, until, was it Corky himself?—one kid dared raise his hand and asked the question they were all dying to ask, How did the Shakers reproduce, and deadpan Father Scully sucked in his lips and gravely murmured, They didn't: they died out.

A storm of laughter, Corky remembers laughing so hard he'd nearly pissed his pants. For all beliefs not Catholic were contemptible, and the Shakers the craziest.

For sure, to a class of horny sixteen-year-olds, whose pricks were alive and sentient as snakes zipped up in their pants, any religion forbidding fucking was crazy.

Corky walks lightly on his toes, or tries to, damned hardwood floor, he knows his weight's making it give, maybe creak, he's counting on the noise downstairs. Examines some of the books on Thalia's table, mostly paperbacks, new purchases—*Famine in an Age of Glut: "First" and "Third" World Countries; Race: How Blacks and Whites Think and Feel About the American Obsession; The Unauthorized Version: Truth and*

Fiction in the Bible. A book on the sofa, with a pen for a bookmark—*The Romantic Quest: From Faust to Faustus.* Corky leafs curiously through Thalia's notes to herself, torn-out notebook pages covered in her slanted, earnest hand with its headlong plunge, *A life in Time is betrayed by mere time, if redemption is at 11 A.M. what will follow at 12?*—and similar stuff, school stuff Corky thinks it. Christ, Thalia's twenty-five years old.

On the floor beside the sofa is a neat stack of photocopied forms, with a receipt for twelve dollars from Kampus Kopiers. A plea, Corky guesses, to be sent to state and U.S. congressmen—

> *I strongly protest the wasteful slaughter of America's wildlife carried out by the USDA's so-called "Animal Control" program. I urge you, as my representative, to work with USDA/APHIS to end this cruel destruction and develop sensible programs to reduce agricultural damage without killing our precious wildlife.*
>
> *Yours sincerely,*

Also on the floor is a cheaply printed pamphlet titled BIRTHRIGHT, and this Corky snatches up with sudden interest. The abortion clinic? What has Thalia to do with *this?* Corky leafs hurriedly through it, pauses at the diagrams, the cartoon-simplified drawings, frontal and cross sections of a woman's body, focus on the reproductive organs, "the uterus in pregnancy," and upside-down fetus with a head as large as its body, a snaky tangle of umbilical cord—the identical diagram he'd seen as a boy, seeking out the mystery of *miscarriage.*

Has Thalia had an abortion?—if so, Corky would be the last to know.

Telling himself no, probably she's working at the clinic, it's only a few blocks away, doing volunteer work, telephone, backup stuff of the kind she's always done, environmental issues, Vic's campaign in 1990, Dukakis in 1988, envelope stuffing, door-to-door soliciting, the kind of thing you do when you're eager to help shape the world but have no other way of doing it than to attach yourself to someone who knows how. Or makes that claim.

For a while, Corky had been flattered by Thalia's interest in his position on the City Council. Corky too runs for public office, sees his name in the newspaper, on billboards, on an election ballot. JEROME ANDREW CORCORAN, Eleventh Ward. Christ, it's still a thrill!—no getting around it. Though Corky's position pays only $25,000 a year and of his three elections to the two-year office, he'd run unopposed the last two times. *Just think, Corky, you might be Mayor of Union City someday*, Thalia would say with adolescent enthusiasm, and Corky just smiled and shrugged, *Who knows?* In theory, Thalia was correct. The Mayor of Union City should be chosen from among the Council as their most capable and experienced spokesman. But Corky knows how, in practice, that's almost never the case. And even when it appears to be so, when, in the early days of Buck Glover, Buck was first a Councilman, backed by the Party, then president of the Council, then nominated by the Party to run for Mayor, it really isn't. Not as an outsider might think.

Politics is the art of deal-making, pure and simple. Like, say your game's poker—but you're playing it with the help of a lot of other people, doing the *game* atop the table but the *dealing* beneath, and that's where the action, the adrenaline, is. But Corky couldn't explain this to a kid like Thalia, idealistic like most kids that age, then quick to get disillusioned.

Nor could Corky explain how, hell, he's in politics for friendship, he'd be a lonely guy otherwise.

So it happened, Thalia came to just one Council meeting, Corky's first term in office. All excited beforehand and planning to take notes she could present in her social studies class in high school. But the session lasted five hours in the old fifth-floor Council room at City Hall, the rattling ventilator seemed to be pumping warm air and stale cigarette smoke in, not out, contentious, confusing, boring, the main issue being incinerators, how to budget, where to build, even the flamboyant Marcus Steadman was exposed as a long-winded bore, and Corky Corcoran's contributions came to a few scattered minutes of reasonable and forgettable talk, and the poor kid who'd arrived with such hope soon passed into a trance of stupefaction. So this is grassroots politics! So this is *it*.

And saying afterward in a snotty aggrieved voice, as if she'd been cheated, *My God isn't it all just about money, the budget and taxes and how to divide it, everybody like chickens pecking one another and everything so limited, just Union City?*

Thalia never came back. Rarely asked Corky about the Council afterward. Like it was some old embarrassment between them. Corky teased her a little, how short-lived her interest in local politics, how fickle, then let it drop.

Maybe he *was* disappointed, a little. *Is*. But, hell, let it drop.

Corky returns to Thalia's bathroom and this time he almost has a heart attack seeing a quick hallucinatory flash of a woman's naked, bloody body in the tub, beyond the plastic shower curtain which is striated shades of blue. "Jesus!"—he yanks the curtain aside and of course there's no one there, nothing. His heart's pounding like crazy.

That dead girl in the D.A.'s photos, nameless. Corky'd never wanted to know her name. Or how she came to be murdered. To be murdered like that. Better not to know, there's already too much you know you can't not know.

When the assistant prosecutor returned from the women's room of The Hot Spot, Corky was gone. Paid their tab with a twenty-dollar bill and walked out having stuffed the photos back in the briefcase clumsily enough to show that, yes he'd gone for it, he'd fallen for it, but no he wasn't turned on, no thanks. He'd driven away not caring that he was leaving the woman stranded, no car, she'd have to call a taxi, and whenever they saw each other afterward the woman fixed Corky with a stare of absolute loathing and he'd meet that look with one of his own, staring her down. Until finally, months later, at the periphery of a gathering, a quasi-official reception downtown, maybe a little drunk the woman approached Corky to say with a sneer, "What *were* you afraid of, Corky?—may I ask?" and Corky said, not missing a beat, "Some kind of disease."

That was that. The bitch never bothered him again, not even to cast him one of those cold fish-eye looks.

Corky examines the bathtub. It's old, porcelain, not the new synthetic stuff that's easy to maintain; gritty with the residue of cleanser, and not very clean. Corky pokes his finger in the rust-ringed drain and discovers it's damp. A few hairs curled there, dark brown. One's maybe three inches long and the others are short, wiry. Pubic hairs?

Those times by accident (yes: accident) Corky'd happened to see his wife's daughter naked, when she was past a certain age, he'd looked away fast. Maybe not fast enough, but fast.

Corky examines the shower curtain, it's grimy from soap splashes.

Needs replacing. If he'd known, he'd have brought a new curtain over, install it and surprise Thalia when she comes home. Remembering how she'd mention getting lightheaded, reaching up to put in a shower curtain, having to attach the hooks to the rod. Low blood pressure, and the blood runs out of your head when you reach upward.

Corky checks the sink, but the faucet's got a drip, a fat erratic drip, should get on the landlord's ass to call a plumber but no, keep your nose out of it, Thalia wouldn't like interference. Thinking, he'd read the other night, in that science paperback *Chaos*, how a drip can sound irregular, all kinds of irregular-seeming weird things can seem that way, but if you've got the key there's a pattern to it, the secret pattern of chaos.

Swiftly then, maybe just a little guiltily, Corky checks out his step-daughter's medicine cabinet. He's the kind of guy, he's in somebody's house and he'll look. But it's what you'd expect, and no surprises—jars of vitamins, vitamin C, vitamin D, vitamin E, megavitamins, plus a big bottle of calcium tablets. And Bufferin. As a kid, prone to headaches, Thalia'd lived on Bufferin. The only prescription vial contains chunky white pills, *oxycodone*. What's that?

Corky checks the toothbrush, running his thumb over the bristles. Dry.

Next, Corky stoops to check out the space beneath the sink, here's a mess, amid the clutter a package of StayFresh MiniMaxi Sanitary Napkins which he peers into, wrapped-up squares, white, he'd used to nose around in his mother's things and the thick gauzy bandage-like Kotex scared him, but intrigued him, like the thought of a woman or a girl bleeding from *there*, Jesus! from *there!* so he'd felt queasy about it, and like the other guys he'd make jokes about it, even, a few times, scavenging in the trash cans in one or another alley, and the sight of—unless he'd never seen it, really? only heard of it?—that dumb prick Mack Daugherty, Nick's cousin, hauling out some old dried-bloody Kotex from a trash bag and blowing his nose in it for laughs, or to make the girls scatter and run for shame: Corky shakes his head now, Jesus, what's to say. He's made love with women who were bleeding and the slick-slimy feel and even the smell of it had excited him, but there's an undercurrent of disgust, for sure. Even with Charlotte, those early months they'd been so hot for each other. Even with Christina.

Fuck *her*. Don't think about *her*.

Corky sees the little knob on the cupboard door's wobbly, he takes the screwdriver out of his pocket and tightens the screw. Quick and deft and now the knob's secure.

At least, thinks Corky, Thalia must be menstruating again, and that's a good thing. It means normal, doesn't it?—some kind of normal.

Corky switches off the bathroom light, shuts the door.

Was the door shut, when he'd come in? Can't remember.

Better get out of here before she comes home, Corky tells himself but here he is in Thalia's bedroom again. Sniffing the air wondering if that sweet-stale-musty odor is *her*.

Dirty old man. And you're not even *old*.

Thalia's bedroom too is sparely furnished. Narrow bed, bureau, wall mirror, by the window a desk Corky recognizes as Thalia's from years ago—her schoolgirl desk. And a carpet on the floor plain and functional. A look to the room, Corky's thinking, as if a man wouldn't be welcome here.

Like a nun's cell? Except no crucifix on the wall. Thalia isn't Catholic, she'd been baptized Presbyterian. What she believes in, or doesn't, Corky isn't sure.

As a girl in the house on Summit Street, Thalia had kept her room private, didn't want Charlotte to enter without knocking, and never when Thalia wasn't there. Corky'd kept out of it. Steered clear of such disputes. Had his own life, and a complicated life, at the office and elsewhere, months when he'd miss dinner several times a week. He regretted it, sorry as hell, but what can you do? And he'd had a drinking problem. Not serious, but a problem. So Thalia would look at him, and her eyes brimming with tears, disappointment in him, or disgust, or anger. Or maybe it was simple jealousy. They know when you'd rather drink than be with them if it means not drinking. When you'd rather fuck some woman you don't give a shit for, than be with them. They know, and you know, but what can you do? Corky'd think, weakly, Jesus, I'm just a man.

It looks to him as if Thalia was in a hurry, leaving this room. A few scattered items of clothing, on the bed, on a chair; the nubby white bedspread pulled up hastily, not quite covering the single pillow. The venetian blind on the window is shut tight and some of the slats are twisted, or broken. The closet door's ajar—unless Corky himself, poking about before, left it that way? He examines the closet again, it's dense with clothes, and shoes on the floor, a larger closet than the one in the hall, a vacuum cleaner against the wall, and suitcases stacked one atop the other behind the clothes, bulky for the space so the clothes are pushed outward. And boxes, on the floor and on the shelf overhead. Books crammed inside, papers. Corky wonders what Thalia thinks valuable enough to save, packed and hauled from one apartment to another. Since Charlotte's remarriage, Thalia doesn't store anything with her mother.

And nothing in the house on Summit though, there, her old room's unoccupied. Just one of the several rooms upstairs in Corky's house he has no use for.

Corky shuts the closet door this time, carefully. Again giving the glass knob a twist. Not practicality, maybe superstition. You're Irish, you're born guilty. Spend your life hoping to trick your way out of it.

Thalia's bedroom, strange to be here, alone here. He notices, this is odd, there's no TV set. Not in here, and not in the other room. Odd for a young woman who'd worked for a while at WWUC-TV as an assistant programmer, even did a few live news and weather spots, Corky was flicking through the channels one night, the surprise of seeing Thalia, his Thalia, on the screen, and looking pretty good, professionally capable, clear-modulated voice, but it hadn't worked out, God knows why. The social welfare job and the WWUC-TV job and a few other things she'd tried, and quit. But no TV in the apartment, only a radio on the bedside table—that's strange.

Next, Corky examines Thalia's bureau drawers. Four drawers, and he slides them noiselessly open. Knows he's a shit for doing this but it's for the girl's sake, she's alone, she needs protection. Whistling inaudibly through his teeth. Women's things have a powerful attraction for him, beginning with Theresa's, panties, brassieres, stockings, slips—that beige lacy-silky negligee of Theresa's he'd used to rub against himself, couldn't have been older than five, in a swoon of pleasure, happiness. He's touched to see, here, that Thalia has so many socks—and neatly paired, balled together, as Corky should do with his, but hasn't time. Jesus, she *is* just a kid. Does need protection.

Trailing his fingers through panties, bras, rubbing the satiny-stiff fabric of a bra, sad to see how small the breast cup, not like her mother's, hefty D-cup tits, the nipples cranberry-colored, turning hard as soon as Corky tongued them, like her clit, too, Charlotte's, a blood-hot hard little cock, and she'd never seemed to like him making love to her there, or pretended not to, with Charlotte, so different from Christina, you never knew for sure what was going on. Corky wonders if Thalia's like Charlotte in such ways, how she is with her lovers, if in fact she has lovers, this room doesn't look like a place for love, damned depressing. Corky lifts a pair of panties, sniffs—a neutral, faintly fragrant smell, or is he imagining it. He's beginning to be aroused but ignores the sensation, like a question you don't intend to answer. Wondering what must it feel like, to wear such things? Such silky-satiny fabrics? You'd be too conscious of your body? Or, not? Like he'd used to think it must be a Rube Goldberg kind of thing for a woman to pee, not direct somehow but convoluted and messy, not exactly in control, but he'd asked a woman once, asked too if he could watch her pee, but she'd been drunk and hadn't maybe understood, just laughed at him, Corky what on earth! the things you say! Recalling that poor bastard O'Rourke, thirty-five years ago, in Irish Hill, a pervert as he was called, and he an ex-seminarian, thieving women's underthings from clotheslines and when he was caught he was discovered to be wearing Mrs. Flannery's enormous pink cotton bloomers, arrested and actually sent to jail and everybody, just everybody, spoke of it, and laughed about it, an uproarious joke for years so just the whispered name could set off Corky and his friends in school, or church: O'Rourke. Corky'd thought, sweet Christ he'd rather be killed than forced to wear a woman's underthings. Though maybe what he'd meant, he's thinking now, brushing his lips against the crotch of a pair of Thalia's panties, is he'd rather be killed than found out.

In the lowermost drawer, beneath woollen sweaters, Corky's probing fingers discover something meant to be hidden?—a manila envelope, photos inside. Corky whistles through his teeth: seeing the first half dozen or so are of an outdoor gathering, a party, familiar faces, in one there's Thalia smiling, head uplifted, part of her face blocked by a man's blurred profile, in another there's Vic Slattery talking with that lawyer-friend of his George Presson, in another there's Marilee Plummer the gorgeous black girl laughing with a white girl Corky knows from around

town named Kiki and a man with his back to the camera Corky guesses
is Mike Rooney, Vic's press secretary—and is that Red Pitts in the background, fatty-muscular torso stretching his T-shirt? Corky's stung: this
was a party to which he hadn't been invited.

Yes and you know why: because Thalia was there.

Thalia looking pretty good, not healthy exactly but sexy, long milky-
pale legs, shadowed eyes, her hair brushed back from her forehead kinky-
thick, and that lovely dazzling smile of hers Corky's seen so rarely in
recent years.

Corky drops some of the snapshots, stoops to pick them up from the
floor, "Fuck. Fuck. Fuck," thinking it's no accident the men at the party
he knows are married, Vic, Presson, Rooney, one or two others, are
there without their wives. Corky's been to parties like these, for sure. He
counts five good-looking young women in their twenties and one of them
Thalia which excites him and burns his ass, fuck it he *is* jealous, counts
seven, maybe eight men, and no Oscar Slattery either, no one Oscar's age
there, the men are all in their forties except Pitts who's a little younger.
The pictures were haphazardly shot so there's a drunken tilt to most of
them. People's backs, backs of heads, elbows, blond-brawny Vic Slattery
open-mouthed in laughter, Thalia and Kiki with arms linked in a pose
of playful exhibitionism, and Red Pitts looming over them—Pitts, that
bastard. Corky recognizes the place as Rooney's summer cottage at Racquette Lake but this is an off-season get-together, the leaves have turned,
spectacular splashes of color against the evergreens. Golden-hazy sunshine spilling like coins onto the weed-ridged flagstone terrace, in Thalia's
hair and on her shoulders, rich and warm-gleaming in Marilee Plummer's
creamy-chocolate skin, what beauty in that skin, and what a figure, a high
round tight little ass, no wonder that black prick Steadman wrecked his
political career over her.

Corky's thinking: one of these guys is Thalia's lover, or was, maybe, at
the time of the party, but who? There's at least one Corky can't identify,
he's never pictured head-on, metallic-gray hair thinning at the top of his
head, sloping shoulders in a seersucker coat, the only man at the party
wearing a coat, in a fuzzy shot of Vic, George Presson, and Marilee, he's
in the background leaning across a table to hand Thalia something, or

simply to touch her arm, and Thalia's smiling at him, or it looks that way. Corky guesses the guy's one of Vic's hotshot Washington friends, one of his newer friends, Corky Corcoran has yet to be introduced to.

Corky knows he's being unreasonable, childish, but his heart's thumping, jealous and mean. Like when he'd first begun to suspect Charlotte was fucking another man, and he should have been relieved, and was, except it threw him into a rage, he'd wanted to kill. Now he's thinking, staring at the snapshots, like evidence at a trial, this is Representative Vic Slattery's secret life, is it?—is that what hurts? Vic's secret life, asshole, you thought you knew all about. Thought you were essential to it.

The snapshots are stamped Oct. 1990. Before the election, which Vic was to win by a fifteen percent majority over his Bush-backed conservative Republican opponent. So the party's a previctory celebration, why the hell not, Vic was ahead in the polls.

And Corky Corcoran, Vic's old friend and (unpaid) campaign consultant, where was *he*? Terrific-looking party he missed.

The other snapshots in the envelope are of lesser interest. Family pictures, old ones. Only a few, so, to Thalia, they must be special: Thalia as a toddler, with her parents Charlotte and Sherwood Braunbeck— what a toothy glamor-boy fuck, phony "Sherwood"; Thalia about four or five, with her doting Drummond grandparents, Ross and Hilda looking young; and young too, Christ, achingly good-looking, there's Corky Corcoran himself, squatting beside beautiful little Thalia who's about nine; Thalia a little older, sulky and thin-limbed beside her glamorous mother posed against a garden wall at the Summit Street house (Corky guesses he must have taken this picture but he can't remember, and can't remember his wife looking so good, a sweet smile, fading-gold hair to her shoulders, shit, maybe he *did* love her); and the last snapshot, a shocker, shows Thalia about twelve, in shirt and jeans, beetle-browed but smiling, beside stepfather Corky in white shirt and tie, smiling too, and there's a third figure scissored neatly out—obviously, Charlotte.

Seeing this, Corky's embarrassed. What's it mean? Some old squabble of daughter and mother? Thalia taking revenge, cutting Charlotte out? Pointedly leaving her stepfather *in*?

Corky's tempted to tear up the snapshot. It's evidence, and what it's evidence of, he doesn't want to think.

Corky has replaced the manila envelope, shut the bureau drawers as he'd found them, he's lifting the bedclothes on Thalia's bed just to see, or to sniff out, what's there, heat and tension in his groin like he's going to jack himself off into the bed and what a sick, what a perverted, what a disgusting and unconscionable thing which, for sure, he isn't going to do, not Corky Corcoran—when, suddenly, out of nowhere there's a knock at the door to the apartment. And a man's voice, muffled.

Then it's louder, unmistakable: "Hello? Thalia? Is that you?"

Corky freezes, heart racing. They must have heard him downstairs?

O.K. but don't panic, asshole. You got yourself into this and you can get yourself out.

Carefully, not hurriedly, though his hands aren't exactly steady, Corky replaces the bedclothes, smooths the bedspread of wrinkles, neater than it was, then he's at the door trying to walk soundlessly, wincing as the knocking comes louder, more nervous and aggressive the stranger's voice, "Hey? Hello? Who's in there? If you don't open this door—"

Corky guesses it's the guy from downstairs, "Esdras," must be a friend of Thalia's, protective of her too, Corky's bad luck. Bastard's maybe twenty-eight and built like an ox, outweighs Corky by forty pounds.

Corky's thinking: he can take the back stairs down, and make a run for it, as with part of his mind he'd been thinking he might have to do; or, more sanely, c'mon Corky why not, just go open the door and explain who he is, why he's here, it isn't what it looks like, Thalia did call him and she is his stepdaughter and he can identify himself.

But the guy's rattling the doorknob, threatening, "—know somebody's in there! Open up or I'm going to call the police—"

Says Corky in an undertone, "Fuck you."

The thing is, a man doesn't like to be pushed. For sure, Corky Corcoran doesn't like to be pushed.

Standing poised as on a high wire between the two doors, front and rear, freely sweating now, but cold, an icy-calm excitement, a deep adrenaline charge, another male, and a stranger, challenging him, *him*, who has every right to be here, having been summoned. Lucky for "Esdras" this isn't Detroit or Miami where everybody packs a gun, what a temptation to Corky to shoot through the door, blow fat-ass "Esdras" away.

Corky backs off, light as he can make himself, hoping the fucking floor doesn't creak, then he's at the door opening off the dining room alcove and making his way stealthily down the stairs, he's panicked but it's a controlled panic, a weird suspended panic, thinking the guy's wife could be posted at the rear or could be up front, listening to her husband, anxious about him, the risk he's taking, guy sounds like a hothead, but scared too, beneath the bluster, Corky knows the symptoms, *we're all scared so get out of our way.*

Yes a fucking good thing, Corky isn't packing the Luger.

Then his luck shifts, he feels it shift, as, in poker, the cards flying out of the dealer's hand make or break you, though you need to think it's *you*, your brains, skill, good looks, God smiling on you, that kind of shit but in fact it's purely luck and at the foot of the stairs Corky's luck shifts, nobody's there to block him or be a witness and another crappy Yale lock unlocked in two twists of the wrist, Corky's outside and on the back porch, propelled down the steps like a shot off a shovel and in the chill-windy drizzle like a damp cloth against his overheated face, enormous pleasure in it, what relief!—Corky's running like hell, knows where he's going as if he's been here before and lived through this before, head prudently ducked and elbows close to his body hearing a woman's voice behind him, scared, but angry, "—stop, mister! I see you, stop!"—but already Corky's on the far side of the garage as the meaty sinews of his legs grip in, calves, thighs, you move too with your arms and shoulders and neck, Christ what pleasure in it, always such pleasure in the body, the body plunging, flying, yearning, pumping its seed, the brain turns off and the body takes over, now behind the dumpy garage and in the debris-strewn alley running past shadowy stunted trees and shrubs and trash cans, so many trash cans, and kids' discarded crap, like running scared as hell in the alleys and lanes of Irish Hill and laughing like hell because somebody, some adult, was after them, God knows for what purpose, always there was a purpose, always Corky and his friends were in trouble, to think of those years is to feel a stab of guilt, exaltation, triumph at getting away with whatever petty crimes and misdemeanors and fucking off that constituted Corky's boyhood, the drizzle here blown more directly into his face, chin tucked in like Joe Louis in the old photos, too bad he's wearing his fancy pinching shoes not jogging shoes, and too bad his fancy clothes, trousers ready to tear in the crotch, yes but he's running panting and elated and his heart pounding hard and strong and Christ how sweet, how truly sweet, and wild, Corky Corcoran's wild, a crazy mick which is what people shake their heads and say of him, maybe he'll regret this but maybe not, for who's to know?—who's to recognize him as a City Councilman, a local businessman?—a millionaire?—nobody's seen his face not even Esdras' wife calling after him, and, the Caddy parked shrewdly far away as it is, on Richmond, at the far end of this alley, Corky's got only to emerge from the alley, like this, and slow to a walk, go to his car, sure he's sweating like a pig and out of breath and his hair's sticking on his forehead and his eyes are dilated with pupil but who the fuck's to know? who's to stop him?

PART II

SATURDAY, MAY 23, 1992

CORKY, HUNGOVER, AT HOME

So *that's* it! My God."

The headline in Saturday morning's *Journal*, the photograph—Corky's hit in the gut.

This news that hadn't been released when he'd watched the 11 P.M. news the night before: that Marilee Plummer is dead, a "suspected suicide," found by a neighbor in her car, in a closed garage, the car's motor still running and the garage filled with exhaust, at 9:20 A.M. Friday morning.

Corky checks out the address—yes, 1758 Brisbane, Pendle Hill. The condominium complex called Pendle Hill Village.

"Oh Christ. Shit. Marilee Plummer! *Her.*"

The ambulance driving away moving out into traffic on Brisbane with no siren, no urgency. *A corpse, not a customer.*

He'd been right about that. And guessing too the corpse was female.

Dazed minutes feeling his hangover deepen, plunge dragging his feeble consciousness into his very bowels Corky stands barefoot and shivering in the vestibule of his house reading the lead article in the *Journal*. Gorgeous smiling black girl Marilee Plummer, Thalia's friend but how close Corky doesn't know, it makes him uneasy to wonder since, once, he'd gone out with Marilee and yes frankly he'd been hot to fuck her but it hadn't worked out she hadn't wanted *him*.

Corky Corcoran's precious white prick, and certain advantages that might have come with it—Marilee Plummer had said *no.*

It's 8:10 A.M. Bleak, windy-rainy morning. Corky Corcoran feeling the loss of this young woman who wasn't a friend but might have been. The loss too of a person he knew, even if not well and with a measure of antagonism; the barrier of her *skin*; the mysteriousness of her private life. For when Plummer brought charges of rape and sexual assault against Marcus Steadman, and the news dominated Union City conversation for days, the first wave of sentiment was what was this ambitious attractive young woman doing with a man like Steadman?—a black man raping a black woman, doesn't seem so much a crime somehow.

Not that Corky Corcoran said, nor even thought, such a racist thing. He's enlightened, he's a liberal Democrat. Voted to create a special subdepartment of Family Services to deal with crimes of sexual violence. (Until the late 1970s, in Union City as virtually everywhere in the country, there were no provisions for crimes of sexual and/or domestic violence.) But the prejudice is hard to eradicate even if you're enlightened and Corky'd heard racist comments all around town in his clubs and in restaurants and on talk radio and in the office of Corcoran, Inc., where both Miriam and Jacky expressed a curious sort of qualified sympathy for Marilee Plummer of whom they knew only through the media. *A black man raping a black woman, doesn't seem so much of a crime somehow.*

And so, yesterday morning, Marilee Plummer killed herself.

Obviously, there's a connection?

The coroner's report says carbon monoxide poisoning, a "considerable degree" of the painkiller Percodan in the dead woman's blood. No signs of physical injury. No apparent health problems. And no suicide note.

In the photograph on page one, Marilee Plummer looks younger than Corky ever knew her. Smiling, seemingly confident, almond-slanted eyes and wide cheekbones and Afro-style hair. In life, animated, confrontational. Exotic. *Frecklehead* she'd called Corky Corcoran, teasing. Cockteasing.

There's an article too in the paper about Marcus Steadman, and his photo above the caption *controversial City Councilman indicted on charges of rape and "sexual terrorism" in January 1992.* Corky quickly skims this, wondering what will happen—now that Marilee Plummer is dead, the trial set for June will be dropped. So Steadman walks? free? God damn! Corky hates the guy's guts, for a number of reasons. He'd hoped to see Steadman sent to prison.

Don't believe it's suicide, it isn't.

Maybe Steadman killed her?—hounded her into killing herself?

Steadman, an old enemy of Oscar Slattery's, who's run against him for Mayor, splitting the black inner-city vote, might not be a murderer but Corky doesn't doubt the guy's capable of inspiring certain of his fanatic

followers to murder. Like the Black Muslims in the 1960s. Like fundamentalist Muslims today. How a smart girl like Marilee Plummer who'd
been associated with the Slatterys and with people of equal quality, white
people Corky's thinking, could have been attracted to a man like Steadman, it's a puzzle. Twenty-seven years old, honors graduate from SUNY
Union City, assistant to the curator at the County Historical Museum,
active in Union City Democratic politics and the NAACP and she's called
by friends and Pendle Hill neighbors quoted in the paper "ambitious" and
"bright" and "goal-oriented" and "friendly"—at least, before the Steadman incident. Since then, she's said to have been "more private," "more
subdued," "withdrawn." One Pendle Hill resident said of her "she didn't
smile as much as she used to."

Marilee Plummer's family refused to speak with reporters.

Marcus Steadman is said to be "unavailable for comment."

In the inner-city black community, as distinct from Union City's
middle-class black community Washington Park, many, maybe most
blacks both female and male sided with Marcus Steadman. Just as, everywhere in the city, blacks and whites have tended to choose sides in the
matter of the Pickett shooting of Devane Johnson. It's a sports mentality,
choosing sides. Hell, Corky feels that way, too—not officially and for
sure not publicly but it's hard not to. As a man, he's likely to identify with
another man accused of rape, so long as no violence is involved; as a white
man, he's likely to identify with another white man, so long as no violence, no really criminal activity, is involved. In the matter of Steadman
and Plummer, Corky'd long ago made up his mind. He was on Plummer's
side, sure. *Black bastard Steadman, black prick deserves to go to prison
for a long time.*

Which would remove Steadman from Union City politics, permanently.

No more of his spoiler campaigns, siphoning off votes from the Democrats that should be theirs by rights.

No more having to look at the motherfucker there in the Council as-
sembly room, his smirking face, insolent mocking questions. Making of
every issue a matter of *race* a matter of *black against white.*

Of course, Steadman vehemently denied Plummer's charges. Insisting
that sexual relations between them were consensual, he was being black-
mailed, extorted. There were no witnesses to any assault or coercion,

which the victim claimed took place in an apartment owned by Steadman on Fifth Street, not his legal residence but where he'd brought her to discuss "spiritual matters" relating to the African-American First Church of the Evangelist where he was minister. Instead he'd kept her captive for three hours, threatening to kill her if she resisted him. After raping her, Steadman allegedly told her no one would believe her if she accused him; and if she went to the police, "his people" would rise up and punish her. He then shoved her out onto the street. By her own account Marilee Plummer was too distraught to call the police immediately, nor even to call friends, but went home and only the next afternoon reported the assault. At first, when the news broke, Plummer's name was not given; nor was it known that Steadman's victim was a black woman. Corky remembers the first furious rumors flying around town, that Steadman had raped a white woman. And what whites were saying should be done to him.

It was only after a grand jury indicted Steadman that Plummer decided to go public. By then, in certain quarters, her identity was generally known. Outrage against Steadman lessened, ironically, it must have been bitterly for Plummer, when people learned that his victim was black.

And now, the victim's dead. "Suspected suicide."

And Thalia Corcoran, who'd been her friend. Which explains Thalia's mysterious behavior lately. The telephone calls, the disappearance. Thalia's afraid Marcus Steadman will pursue her, too?

Shaving, Corky avoids his bloodshot eyes in the bathroom mirror. His hand holding the razor's trembling so he has to firm it up with the other. How much of this is his hangover and how much worry about Thalia, shock over Marilee Plummer—who's to know. Lately, these past few months, Corky doesn't seem able to drink quite so much as he'd always done. Without feeling like shit the morning after.

Last night he'd maybe made a mistake, can't understand now why but after driving away from Highland he'd been too excited to come back to the house, dress for the van Burens' dinner party one of those fancy-formal dinner parties Corky Corcoran's grateful as hell to be invited to, these are important influential rich men and women and Corky needs them for backing if he's going to run for any office higher than City Councilman for the Eleventh District *which he isn't sure he is: that depends upon the Party.* But instead of going to the van Burens' he ended up cruising the city, his nightspots, even the Irish Bar down by the docks, restless and pugnacious and close to getting into one or two fights though restricting himself to ale and no more than three ales at each bar reasoning you can't get seriously drunk on ale with a constitution like his because you bloat up on it before you get drunk. Also you spend half your time pissing it out, it runs through you like a sieve, then washing your hands in the men's room you splash cold water on your face which sobers you up. So, Corky figures, he hadn't been drunk the night before though he *is* hungover this morning.

He's inclined to blame Thalia. Listening last night to his telephone messages and there she was again, he'd been relieved to hear her voice but pissed, too. Breathy and almost inaudible *Corky?—by now maybe you know? why I'm so afraid? If you're home tomorrow I'll come over around four* then a pause so long it seemed she'd hung up before she added *If I can.*

Corky replayed the message three times. *Corky? by now maybe you know? why I'm so afraid?* But public disclosure of Plummer's death hadn't been made yet. So how did Thalia know? It must've been at least sixteen hours between the time he'd seen the ambulance drive off from Pendle Hill Village and whenever the news was released, in time for the morning edition of the *Journal* but too late for the 11 P.M. news. The identity of a deceased person isn't released by police until relatives are informed.

And that's weird, too—that the UCPD couldn't locate relatives of Marilee Plummer for all those hours.

Corky pauses in his shaving remembering Oscar Slattery squinting up at him out of the shadowy rear of the limo. That was midafternoon and by that time Oscar knew of course and Oscar was sick about it but hadn't told Corky, in retrospect Corky thinks Oscar may have been about to tell him then decided not to. But why not. Shit, they're all enemies of Marcus Steadman aren't they. Corky Corcoran's your man.

Corky's hurt. His loyalty to Oscar, the years of their connection, their friendship—why hadn't Oscar confided in him?

He'd known Oscar Slattery since he was fifteen years old. And liked to think there was, there is, a special relationship between them. *My son has never learned to campaign. He's afraid of getting his hands dirty.* That undercurrent of worry and reproach when a man speaks of his son in such a way to a guy his son's age. Like a woman complaining of her husband to you, you know she wants to be comforted and you know what comforting means. In Oscar's case the signal Corky gets is You'd have been a truer son to me than my own son. You and I understand each other.

Last night navigating the Caddy through the buzz in his head like a hive of giddy bees Corky must've blanked out totally on the van Burens. Meant to call and explain he couldn't make the dinner: family emergency. A shitty thing to do, just not show. He knows from when he and Charlotte had people to dinner, the effort you put into it, like friendship itself is on the line, or pride, or whatever—if somebody doesn't show up it's more than a disappointment it's an insult. In the case of the van Burens, it's an insult and an asshole mistake on Corky's part since van Buren's the county Party boss, a genial guy and generous to his proven friends but if you cross the line and he's your enemy, you're fucked.

Corky's thinking he'll call the van Burens later this morning, it's still too early right now. Give them some hard-luck story about Thalia being so upset about her friend's death she'd needed care, counseling. Which is no lie, in fact.

And no drinking, today. Not even ale, beer.

Old Hock Corcoran in his last days, pissing his bed, yelling with the D.T.'s. Corky's scared as hell to go out like that.

He's too smart to go out like that.

Though staring at himself in the mirror where he's cut his jaw shaving, a bright trickle of blood through the lather and his eyes like burst grapes and thin white lines at the corners of his eyes he wonders if other people can see, Christina for instance; wonders how old he looks, how he's perceived. What Timothy Patrick Corcoran would see, seeing Jerome now.

Corky returns to his bedroom to get dressed firm in his resolution he isn't going to drink today. All day. And he'll drive down to Roosevelt Street to visit his Uncle Sean as he's been promising he'll do. And take the old man out to Holy Redeemer to see Aunt Mary Megan. Two old birds with one stone. *Yes but you love them don't you, they're about all you have connecting you with the old days.* Get rid of that potted plant he's been hauling around in the car for days.

Corky never enters his bedroom this "master" bedroom without thinking he wants Christina here. Never has brought her here. He's furious at her, he's through with her, but he wants her, here. In that bed amid the tangled sheets. Right now.

Cranking open the louver window farther to air out the room. A smell of armpits, crotch. Corky's own private smell. But the humidity's like a mouth pressing close and breathing into his. Not even any sky this morning just this crap-drizzly-gray overcast ceiling skimming the tops of the tallest trees.

So lonely. Christ have mercy on my soul.

Corky straightens the bedclothes, drags the fancy silk-quilted spread up over the pillows. Charlotte furnished the room and didn't stint on the expenses but now things are looking shabby. A cleaning woman comes twice weekly and changing the bedclothes is her task, Corky can't be bothered. Since the divorce he'd quickly reverted to old bachelor habits of falling asleep half-dressed in bed reading or watching TV drinking into the early hours of the morning when the very taste of whatever he's drinking—ale, beer, wine, whiskey—has a brooding quality, more important somehow, serious. Sacred. Wakes to find himself lying sideways atop the bed rolled up in the spread his trousers still on, sometimes his shoes. The light still burning like he's a kid scared of the dark.

Last night coming into the room Corky'd gone straight to the bedside table to check out the Luger and now he checks it out again—takes it up in his hand, weighs it. Long-barreled heavy fucker, an automatic, eight shots in the magazine, sleek polished handle, looks good. A burnished look like it's got a history.

Wonder how many men has this gun killed. And who's to come.

But could *he* shoot it? And at who?

Standing in front of a full-length mirror smirking and preening pointing the barrel at himself in the mirror like a teenaged wiseguy, then pointing the barrel at his own head. Weird sensation. Exciting. Like breaking into Thalia's apartment—the risk.

Death. In your hand. So fucking easy.

In one of his fantasies Corky'd imagined Fenske living long enough so that he, Corky Corcoran, could have killed him. Was that possible?

No. Not possible. In his heart he knows he's just an average guy, a coward.

Hopes he'll never be put to the test. In a position where he could save somebody else's life but he'd be paralyzed, or run like hell saving his own. The shame of it afterward, he'd never outlive.

Tim Corcoran always had a gun, a pistol, smaller than this, kept in his bedside table, too. And probably other guns, at the office, or in his car. Rough growing up in Irish Hill when he'd been a kid and you needed to protect yourself and you needed people to know you could protect yourself. When his parents were away Corky used to go into their bedroom upstairs at the Barrow Street house and in secret take out Daddy's gun, a Smith & Wesson six-shot, .38-caliber bullets. So excited breathing so quickly he'd almost have a hard-on. Pose with it in front of the mirror like he's doing now except then he was running the risk of Daddy discovering what he'd done and beating the shit out of him.

Also Corky'd discovered, beneath the mattress on his father's side of the bed, a box of Trojans wrapped in medicinal-smelling tin-foil packets, examining these curiously, holding the packets up to the light. Too young at the time, no more than eight or nine, he hadn't known what these things could be except being hidden they were secret. And adult.

Standing here in his own bedroom thirty years later. Memory jolting him like an electric current. God help me, I loved them so. Both of them. He puts the safety back on the Luger and returns it to the bedside drawer.

It's then the telephone rings and Corky feels his pulse leap thinking It's Christina but, damn, no, a man's voice, and not a friend's, at least not a voice he can recognize straight off and for some reason the guy doesn't introduce himself, asking urgently, "Hello? Am I speaking to Jerome Corcoran?" and Corky says, "Yes," suspiciously, and the guy says, quickly, a high reedy-nasal voice that is in fact beginning to sound familiar, "I apologize profusely for disturbing you at home, Mr. Corcoran, and on a Saturday morning!—but this is a matter of some importance, and—" as Corky screws up his face, listening incredulously, can this be who he thinks it is?—*can* it? "—if we could just sit down to confer, the significance of my project would become clear, Mr. Corcoran—'Union City Mausoleum of the Dead'—only a small, select board of trustees—" and Corky interrupts, "Look, you, 'Teague,' or is it 'Tyde'—I told you yesterday I wasn't interested, didn't I?" and there's a pause, then a rush of words, and an air of reproach and righteousness beneath, "Yes but if you *knew*, Mr. Corcoran!—if you were *informed!*—the architectural plans—" and Corky's saying angrily, "I told you fuck off, mister, and I mean *fuck off.*"

Hangs up the phone, quivering with rage. The nerve of that asshole, calling Corky Corcoran up at home, on a Saturday morning, on *this* Saturday morning, with his crackpot scam! A hot rash spreads up Corky's throat into his face.

Yesterday, at the Athletic Club, when that jerk-off was buttonholing him, had anyone noticed?—any of Corky's fellow Club members?

Corky plans a series of telephone calls. He's the kind of guy, even an emergency, or a tragedy like the Plummer death, isn't such a threat, if he's got a telephone receiver in his hand.

Now, this new invention the cordless phone: Corky loves it. Doesn't have to be restricted to one place, he can walk around, work off nervous energy. These days, talking on an old-fashioned phone, the danger is Corky will start his pacing and yank the plug out of the socket.

First he skims through the *Journal* again. Seeing how the front page is designed, unless it's an accident—four photos and columns of newsprint in a near-symmetrical pattern, the smaller photos of Plummer and Steadman balanced with the lead top-center photo of a military action in Bosnia, "Muslim Slav" forces firing on Sarajevo civilians, and an equally big photo near the bottom of the page, Carolyn Warmus with her attorney after her second trial in White Plains where she's been found guilty of murdering her lover's wife. Pathetic-looking woman, a loser. And those dopey bangs covering her forehead.

So much passion in the world. The trouble people make for one another.

Just Corky's luck, he'll wind up with a bitch like Warmus someday.

Inside, page twenty, there's more about that crazy bastard Leroy Nickson. One of those disgusting tabloid-type stories that flare up and everybody's talking about it for a few days then it disappears and you never hear again. Unless there's a trial. Corky reads the brief article though he knows he shouldn't, it just makes him angry, he's a liberal Democrat and a Cuomo man but, hell, he'd vote for the death penalty to be reinstated, just to put Nickson in the good old electric chair. Lethal injection's too good for some cocksuckers.

A good thing, though, politically speaking—Nickson's white. Everybody can get behind being outraged at him, white, black, Hispanic, Asian, you name it. Not like Sergeant Pickett who Corky sort of thinks might be a fall guy. White cop, racist? Or just scared and jumpy and used poor judgment firing his gun thinking the fleeing kid was drawing a gun to fire at *him*? Not knowing, how in fuck could you know, in the dark, in the confusion, running on foot into what might be called enemy territory down there on Welland, the kid's only twelve years old.

Corky's depressed thinking about it. The trial's scheduled now to start in mid-June. With Steadman discredited that takes some of the heat off the Mayor and his men and the UCPD but there's plenty of trouble ahead. Walking a tightrope it's called, a no-win situation. Sure to get statewide, maybe national media coverage. After the Rodney King fiasco. Oscar's been in print and on TV making terse careful statements calling for a "thorough investigation" of the shooting but if you know the code, he means an investigation by the UCPD Firearms Discharge Review Board which is under the auspices of UCPD Internal Affairs and so under the authority of the Chief of Police. So he's basically tossing it into the D.A.'s lap to figure out how to prosecute. Both the Mayor and the D.A. are elected officials (and Warren Carter's a Republican moderate—there's a Union City tradition of Republican D.A.'s) so there's the common belief that they aren't connected along lines of influence or patronage, like, for instance, the Police Commissioner is a mayoral appointee, but insiders know the two men are connected. They're rivals, they might hate each other's guts, but they're connected. In ways Corky can only guess at.

Then there's the Policemen's Benevolent Association. Polled at eighty-nine percent behind Pickett. And nobody in Union City wants to fuck with the cops any more than they do in Chicago, Philadelphia, New York City. It's a fact—Corky hates to admit it—nobody except a wild man like Marcus Steadman is willing to say publicly, the cops are a political force in America. Beyond Democrats and Republicans, an actual *force* like a tornado or a hurricane, you don't alienate them if you're a politician. Not just the crooked cops, the graft and corruption you hear about that's the tip of the iceberg for what you don't know and for your safety don't want to know but the rank-and-file union men, the average cop—white male working-class American. Some with high school degrees, some without.

In Irish Hill, the guys who liked to play rough became criminals or cops, in high school they'd been interchangeable. If Corky hadn't gone to St. Thomas, and out of the parochial school system, Christ knows how he'd have ended up. The cooked-up deals he gets involved in, the occasional kickbacks and bribes and fees and tax write-offs that're part of business at Corcoran, Inc., are white-collar stuff. Even if you get caught, you don't serve time.

The last time a mayor of Union City fucked with the UCPD, gave in to pressure in 1971 trying to install a Citizens' Crime Commission with the power to overrule the Firearms Discharge Review Board, there was a police strike, the next thing to a police riot, right at City Hall. Between three and four thousand uniformed police waving picket signs, yelling and blocking traffic and even stomping on the hoods and roofs of cars, terrifying the citizens. A sight that, if you saw it, as Corky Corcoran did from a fifth-floor window in the Criminal Court Building across the street, you'd never forget. He'd actually been scared, physically scared. Even with his Irish face, his Corcoran name, his reputation around town he'd been scared.

Thinking of Beck. That look Beck gave him. Trying to figure why Corky Corcoran's poking his nose around Marilee Plummer's place when he had no way of knowing something had happened to her. In what way Corky's connected.

The first reflex is: send flowers.

You're a politician, you're an elected official, and you *are* a personal friend: send flowers.

So Corky's first call is to his florist, Corky's got an account there, orders flowers in memory of Marilee Plummer, sent to the funeral home. Listening simultaneously to the five-minute radio news at 10 A.M., no new developments regarding Marilee just a restatement of what Corky already knows, but there's an angry taped quote from one of Steadman's aides—"Mr. Steadman in no way knows any single thing of this person killing herself, I repeat Mr. Steadman in no way knows"—then state news, national news, Bush, Quayle, asshole politics, Corky switches off the radio in disgust. He's got his cordless phone and he's set up operations in the solarium (the solarium is at the rear of the house, the last of Charlotte's additions and though Corky resisted initially now it's his favorite room, beautiful fifteen feet by twenty feet with a brick floor and curved glass overlooking the deep sloping lawn, juniper pine bordering the property and a six-foot wrought-iron spike-topped fence—so Corky feels protected): a pot of instant coffee boiled acid-potent, his frayed pocket address book, his fat home Rolodex, a pad of legal paper and a ballpoint pen and that snapshot of Thalia's he stole yesterday.

Stole?—took. Figuring Thalia will never miss it.

This is the snapshot in which Thalia's figure is blurred and she's talking with her unknown male friend in the background, and in the foreground, talk about accident, coincidence—Vic Slattery, George Presson, and Marilee Plummer.

Marilee's dressed like a fashion model, one of those classy-hooker types you see in glossy magazines, sexy but smart, hot to look at but cool, playing it cool, a red sheath dress of some slippery material so tight it shows the curve of her buttocks and her big nipples through the fabric, a half dozen gold chains around her beautiful neck and wild sunburst earrings like an African princess, the kind of earrings that look heavy but are in fact feathery-light made of aluminum or tin. Now Corky knows what's in store for this mysterious young woman he thinks he can see a sign, a hint in her face, that characteristic tension in her neck, almost-angry twist to the mouth, you can't tell is she laughing with the two middle-aged Caucasian males beside her or is she laughing at them? For sure, with Corky Corcoran, the bitch had been laughing at *him*. Two years ago, at least, in the Zephir lounge. He hopes to hell Marilee and Kiki—there were two girls involved—didn't tell anybody about him making an asshole of himself. Or, if they did, that word didn't get back to Thalia.

Next, Corky calls one of his poker-playing buddies Digby Dunne who's city editor at the *Journal*, takes him seven minutes to track Dunne down (in his car, on the Turnpike) but Dunne only tells Corky what he already knows, there's nothing the paper's holding back except a tip the police got that one of Marcus Steadman's women friends had been harassing Plummer but the information's unreliable and to name any names might be libelous so the paper's holding off. Dunne asks Corky what he's been hearing and Corky says not a thing.

Next, Corky calls a WWUC broadcaster who's a friend, Biff says all kinds of rumors are circulating but nothing substantial, it seems pretty clear Plummer's death was suicide. Corky says but what about a suicide note, in that case? Biff says he doesn't know. The cops in this town, if there was a suicide note, the investigating officer might pocket it to deliver to an interested party, that's been known to happen, or suspected. For blackmail purposes, or to do a friend a favor. Since Plummer was associated with the Slatterys, both Oscar and Vic at different times, and since supposedly she'd gone out with any number of prominent Union City white men, married and unmarried, who knows what a suicide note might have been. And if she'd left a diary, or letters she'd written.

Biff asks Corky if he'd ever gone out with Plummer. Corky says with a rueful laugh no, he'd never even got close.

Next, Corky calls a UCPD lieutenant in the Sixth Precinct and asks him what he's heard, if anything, about the Plummer death but the lieutenant claims not to know anything except what he's read in the paper or seen on TV like everybody else. Corky can tell the guy's telling the truth, so passes on to him the tip about the woman friend of Marcus Steadman harassing Marilee Plummer and hearing this the lieutenant curses calling Steadman a familiar epithet. And Corky says there's a rumor there was a suicide note the police are keeping under wraps, any truth in that?—and the lieutenant says how would he know, he's in the Sixth Precinct.

Corky makes a few more calls. It gives him a sense of power making calls, dozens sometimes in a single day from his desk at Corcoran, Inc., or from his desk at Pearl Street, or in his car, or here at home. As many as twenty-five telephone numbers he's memorized without making any effort, weird photographic memory he'd put to good use in school though it isn't of much value generally. He'd memorized Christina's number immediately and has a powerful need to punch it out now but won't let himself. He just knows how he'd sound calling her anxious and repentant like a dog kicked in the ass *Hello Chrissie?—look, I'm sorry.* And if he doesn't say he's sorry what's the reason for calling her.

Fuck Christina. He's got plenty of other women in reserve.

There's a beeping signal when Corky next picks up the receiver meaning a call came in while he was on the line, he's hoping it's Christina but when he punches in his code it's just Charlotte—poor Charlotte, repeating her message from yesterday. *Jerome, please call me, I'm so worried, tell me what's happening, and if you speak with Thalia will you ask her please to call me.* There's more to Charlotte's message but Corky punches "3" for erase.

Corky's secret feeling about most of the women he's been involved with through his sexually active life: *message erased.*

Next, Corky calls his Uncle Sean. Twelve rings, Corky's about to give up figuring the old man's out, then the phone's answered and there's this strange voice Corky hardly recognizes low and suspicious-sounding, doesn't even say hello but asks who is this, and Corky identifies himself, and there's a long pause and Sean asks again who is this, so Corky raises his voice saying it's Corky your nephew, hey is something wrong Uncle Sean, and finally the old man says Corky? it's *you?* so Corky's embarrassed, it's been so long since he's called this man who'd been like a father to him. Corky makes a joke of it but Uncle Sean doesn't laugh. Corky asks him is today a good day for a visit, is he free to go out to lunch maybe at the Seneca House and how'd he like to visit his aunt Mary Megan at Holy Redeemer. It isn't clear from the exchange whether Sean knows about Mary Megan's surgery and just doesn't want to talk about it, the men in Corky's family, including Corky, are like that, or whether he's half-drunk (this early in the day?) or just woozy or getting Alzheimer's and Corky's impatient wasting time trying to decipher his uncle's words, puts it to him like this—"O.K., Uncle Sean, it's eleven o'clock now how's about I see you in an hour?" And Sean mumbles what sounds like yes he's free.

Next, Corky calls a druggist friend, a betting buddy he sometimes goes with to the track, asks Willy what's a pill called *oxycodone* and Willy tells him it's a powerful painkiller and tranquilizer like Percodan, with a codeine base. Corky asks is it habit-forming and Willy says with that hacking laugh of his that Corky's grown to dread, it's so superior and so morbid, "Shit, Corky, that's a serious question? Anything that kills pain is going to be habit-forming."

ROMANCE: OCTOBER 1989

Mmmm*mmmm!* You know what this specimen is, honey?—a sweet ol' Freckhead, that's what he is. Ain' he?"

"What?—'Freckhead'? Wha's that?"

"No, girl, I mean 'Frecklehead'—ain' that what I said?"

"You said 'Freckhead.'"

"Say *what?*"

"'Freckhead.'"

"Nah"—shrieking with laughter, like she's being tickled, "—I never did! Never did! 'Freckhead'! *Never!*"

They were both teasing him, no mercy, Corky loved it. The gorgeous black girl giving off that ripe yeasty-plum scent, the wild-eyed hot-breathed white girl, one on each side of grinning-drunk Corky Corcoran in the Zephir lounge where somehow they'd wound up, crowded together, arms, legs, thighs, even heads bumping, and Kiki's hair in Corky's face, and Marilee's right breast nudging Corky's arm, squeezed into one of those red-leather banquettes along the wall. Practically behind the stoned-looking combo playing—is it disco music from another era?—so loud Corky can hardly register the noise as music, only as percussive waves. The three of them, laughing their heads off. Howling with laughter. Corky's eyes leaking tears, and Marilee's rich deep-bellied shriek, you could tell that girl's colored without needing to look, and you could imagine her shrieking like that making love, Oh man Oh lover Oh like that Oh mmm*mmmm just* like that. And Kiki, even wilder, she's maybe high on coke, Corky wouldn't doubt, and maybe Marilee too, along with being *wasted, smashed, bombed out of their skulls* on alcohol. Kiki's got a high-pitched girlish giggle, all elbows and hair and rolling-white thyroid eyes, skinny body and pointed breasts inside some cheap-ethnic tunic top, pretty pasty-pale face screwed up like she's in pain, or near to coming, and her rat-frizzed dyed-copper hair like Brillo wire but Corky's attracted to her, too, not so powerfully as to Marilee but, yes, to Kiki, too, to both girls, damn right.

This *Playboy* fantasy playing in lurid Day-Glo colors in Corky's head, as in one of those CineMax mall theaters, that these two terrific-looking girls in their mid-twenties are going to make love to Corky Corcoran who's old enough almost to be their father, yes the pervert's imagination is careening along at full tilt, he's practically slavering over them, Marilee Plummer on his left, Kiki what's-her-name on his right, big shot at the Zephir where they know his name and lavish tips, what the fuck that he's old enough almost to be the girls' Daddy, he's getting to be the age he thought he'd never get to be, you never think you're going to get to be, old enough that half the world's young enough to be his daughter, Jesus! What's a guy supposed to do, chase after females *his* age?—try to get it up for females *his* age? Shit, Corky's out from under that heavy bitch he married not even knowing she was three years older than him, what an asshole Corky Corcoran thinking himself so shrewd, such a stud, lucky Charlotte's a rich man's daughter and can tell him go fuck, I don't need alimony from *you*. So he's a free man now, legally divorced and free and clear, nobody's husband, nobody's step-Daddy needing to feel guilt at another man's kid regarding him with big tearful eyes when he hasn't paid sufficient attention to her or slamming her bedroom door when accidentally, *really* accidentally, he's happened to glance inside passing by seeing her half in underclothes or bare-assed or just brushing her hair in that whiplash way of hers you'd think would have loosened half the hairs on her head, or coming out of the bathroom glaring at him pouty-mouthed as if knowing (but how could she know?—fuck, she couldn't) step-Daddy's going to whack himself off inside, the door safely locked, sniffing the dry-sharp smell of her urine the fan hasn't quite carried off. Free and clear and living by himself at 33 Summit Avenue in the prestige neighborhood of Maiden Vale, maybe these two beautiful girls would like to come back there for a nightcap? a nightcap or two?—in the meantime he's celebrating his freedom, American Express Gold Card covering the Zephir tab he'll be stunned to discover, next month, the fuckers must have padded, overcharged him for drinks and, asshole, he'd encouraged the waitress to calculate her own tip, dumb prick Corky Corcoran, born yesterday, imagining all the world loves you because you love all the world, or pretend you do, yes but right now he does love all the world, his arms around these two great-looking girls, his scotch on the rocks going down smooth as if it's the first after a long cruel thirst and not, who knows, the fifth or the sixth, God knows. Asking these two boom-boom girls, "What's happier than a drunk pig wallowing in the muck?" and the girls cry out in unison, "*What*, Corky?—*what* is?" and Corky says, exploding in laughter, so that drinkers at the bar glance around quizzical and smiling hoping to get in on the joke, "*A drunk Irish pig wallowing in the muck.*"

"Ohhh Freckhead!—I mean Freck-l'-head!—are you funny!"

"*Ain'* he funny? Ohhhh I'm gonna wet mah pants!"

Marilee Plummer mimicking a Southern black, comical-sly parody of stereotyped Negro speech, purely good-natured, Corky thinks, and no malice or anger in it, Corky thinks, and Kiki falling in with it, a natural mimic too, the two girls like jazz musicians off on a riff. "Freckhead" veers hilariously close to "Fuckhead"—more squeals, howls—Marilee leans across Corky squeezing her sizable breast against him, practically in his mouth as she slaps at Kiki, "Girl, you watch yo' mouth! Yo' white girls is all the same: bold an' brazin'! this gen-mun here's gonna be shocked, yo' watch yo' mouth, hear?"

Well, hell, it *is* funny. At the time.

Which time is approximately two and a half years ago, summery weather but Corky seems to remember it was autumn at the time. The North American climate's so screwed up now with ozone holes— "greenhouse effect"?—you can't take any season for granted, even the Snow Belt's been having mild winters, not the savage snowstorms and eight-foot snowdrifts of Corky's childhood. So in fact it was autumn, that wild night. Jesus, *wild!* When, a few hours earlier, he'd picked up these two girls, or had they picked up him, at some lavish crammed cocktail reception at the Hyatt, or was it the Empire, one of those affairs honoring an outgoing president of some charity organization, or the fiftieth anniversary of the Union City Arts Council, and up on the dais speaking briefly and wittily there's Mayor Slattery, and one or two beaming officers of the organization, and maybe a vice-president from Squibb or Exxon announcing a $5-million subsidy, much applause and cheering and crowding at the bar and next thing you know you're slipping out with these two girls who call you "Corky" and laugh uproariously at your jokes, in your car (the white Audi, at this time? yes) driving to a favorite nightclub, a pretense of supper, this terrific jazz combo at The Bull's Eye except, how the hell, you who've lived in this frigging city for forty years and boast you could make your way around it blind somehow take a wrong exit from the Expressway, let's go to the Zephir instead, down on Chippewa, it's the Zephir you really meant to go to anyway, why not?

Where they know your name, they're always impressed.

H'lo Mr. Corcoran!

Good evening Mr. Corcoran!

Thank you Mr. Corcoran!

Thank *you!*

Are Marilee and Kiki impressed, too?—Marilee on Corky's left and Kiki on Corky's right, both girls drinking red wine and leaning across Corky to whisper at each other and dissolve in giggles, and Corky's got his arms looped over both, in play, only in play, you can tell it's play because he's grinning his boyish-affable grin, his arm around Kiki's bony shoulders as a way of covering for his arm around Marilee's warm solid rich-ripe-smelling shoulders, the more he gets to know Marilee Plummer the more he's crazy about her, what a figure, and her hair's in cornrows at this time, numberless cornrows, tiny braids, weird, Corky's never seen cornrows close up before, practically in his nose, and an oily-sweet scent lifting from Marilee's scalp, must take forever to braid hair in such thin braids, and do they grease it, too?—or doesn't Marilee's hair require straightening?—she's got so much Caucasian blood in her, she could almost pass for white. Something exotic like—what?—Spanish, Portuguese. Smoky-creamy skin but with a texture different from Caucasian skin, a thicker skin, doesn't age the same way, fewer wrinkles, creases. The way black boxers can take punches to the face that white boxers, poor saps, can't: the day of the white pro boxer's over forever, Rocky Marciano the last white American heavy-weight, never another. "High yellow" is what Marilee Plummer would be called by other, darker blacks and Corky's wondering is that a term whites can use, or is it racist, insulting? He seems to know that Marilee Plummer, so seeming at ease with her white girlfriend and her grinning white-man escort, is sensitive about the color of her skin, as about her identity. God, yes. You wouldn't want to cross *her.*

Strange how, at his age, knowing so many people as he does, so many connections in the Democratic party in the business sector and more generally, Corky Corcoran has so few black friends. In truth, no real black friends. God knows, Corky's tried—he really has. At Rensselaer he'd known two or three black guys, the only ones in the school and he'd gotten along pretty well with them working in the cafeteria with them but never kept up any contact afterward. And in Union City, over the years. Since the 1960s. It seems if you're white you're always courting blacks and they seem to like you well enough but they never call you back, never invite you over. Except for political connections it's the same thing with Vic Slattery, Vic confessed to Corky. *You feel like such a hypocrite.*

But Corky in his warm erotic daze isn't thinking much of these matters. Nor seriously listening to Marilee and Kiki chattering across him, their flirty-oblique allusions, teasing-taunting incomprehensible to his ear as if they're speaking a foreign language, poor Corky in his chic flannel Polo suit, metallic-midnight-blue Hermès tie, his hard-on the size of a bowling pin draining all the blood from his faltering brain, thus he can't think, isn't trying to think, it's Friday night and he's a free man a divorced man with no encumbrances save memory and *what's memory if your brain's shut down* and his American Express Gold Card is his ticket to ecstasy or at least oblivion. How Jerome A. Corcoran of 33 Summit Avenue, Union City, New York, Democratic City Councilman and next-in-line president of the Council and millionaire businessman-financier has wound up at the Zephir, this overpriced and glitzy-tacky nightspot listening to a combo like Muzak played with air-hammers and chainsaws and a lead singer gravel-voiced singing bad Lou Reed so his head's not only buzzing from scotch but vibrating and rattling, and these amazing girls on both sides squeezed into the banquette-booth, he'll be unable to recall afterward. Nor will he be able to recall the precise sequence of events that will lead him—no, propel him with vertiginous speed—to the emergency room at Union City General Hospital.

Marilee, Kiki. No need for last names in the Zephir. Sharp shrewd girls but they know how to play, too. Smart career-oriented girls, grown-up girls. Of that new breed of strong-willed young women masquerading as girls, health club members, some of them bodybuilders and all of them with an eye on the prize, not *feminine* but *female*, fashion condoms in their Gucci purses and they know how to ply them. To be frank, Corky would be scared as hell of such women except he's had so much practice handling women. And women are drawn to *him*. From the age of fourteen onward Corky Corcoran has practically had to fend females off, and of course he's a gentleman, too, or has made himself into one, a small price to pay for the prizes a gentleman gets that some crude asshole hasn't a clue he might be missing, like a man who drinks Four Roses instead of Johnnie Walker Red or drives a budget car instead of a really good car hasn't a clue what he might be missing in life, poor dumb prick.

A small price to pay, thinks Corky, dazedly grinning. Lifting his glass—"I'll drink to that!" and Marilee and Kiki raise their glasses too, drinking to whatever it is they're drinking to.

This, then: Marilee the dusky-skinned beauty and Kiki the pale-frantic beauty are leaning across Corky Corcoran chattering giggling making jokes that elude him, maybe involve him but elude him and thus the more hilarious for being uttered in his smiling presence, in his lap you might say—where both girls are leaning familiarly in, thighs warmly aggressive against his, Marilee giving him plenty of her fleshy-doughy breast against his arm, Kiki giving off a stoned radiant heat in his face, Corky's cock is so immense and rod-hard the girls can't seem to keep their hands from brushing against his knees, thighs, crotch, for conversational emphasis perhaps, the way, so seemingly innocently and by chance a woman will touch a man's arm, or wrist, or lightly tap the back of his hand as she speaks to him, so seemingly innocently and by chance. Oh God, yes. Corky loves 'em, Corky's crazy about 'em, these terrific girls, these grown-up flirty-sexy wild-reckless fantastic girls, Corky doesn't have a clue who they are really, as he'd be the first to admit he doesn't have a fucking clue, who they are as girls, as women, as fellow citizens, hard to think of them as fellow citizens in fact, like these feminists yammering on about a woman's *personhood*, a woman isn't just tits and ass and can she fuck and can she *serve*, Corky's bemused trying to consider a woman's *personhood* if it isn't her body what the fuck is it? *why* the fuck is it? Corky doesn't have a clue but he isn't going to let that worry him, not now, not tonight, fuck that heavy crap, too much talk in the world and too much "communication" Corky's thinking, "communication" of the wrong kind, Corky doesn't know what these girls want of him, he only knows, or thinks he knows, what he wants of *them*.

And oh God does he. Does he want it.

Marilee leaning across Corky from the left, Kiki from the right, Corky guesses every guy in the Zephir's staring at him in envy, yes and they'd be right, poor bastards. It's cocoa-skinned Marilee whom Corky's most dazzled by, can't keep from sniffing her, Doggy-Corky with his nose alert and sensitive as his prick, his nose *is* a kind of prick he's thinking, laughing thinking, Christ he's drunk but happy-drunk, elated-drunk, not mean-drunk and certainly not falling-down-drunk, Corky'll show 'em. Marilee's bronze fingernails tapping his knuckles so Corky's dying to seize her hand, grab hold and suck at the fingers, her exotic cornrow braids are slithering like snakes in his face, Corky's vision is beginning to go, his eyeballs misting over, Doggy-Corky who'd like nothing better than to poke his avid nose in the crevice of Marilee's neck, a plump dimpled fold of skin, yes and nuzzle the nape of her neck, and her breasts, he'd like nothing better than to bury his face between those hefty big-girl's breasts, tearing through the silvery-twinkly fabric with his teeth, then down on his knees beneath the table burying his face between her thighs, his flushed-freckled face right there between her thighs, her bush he knows must be thick, kinky-wiry, very black, and her vaginal lips fleshy—warm as her lipsticked lips, and her clit that's fat and hard and pumping-hot with blood, he'd guess it's a larger clit than any he'd ever seen or touched or tongued or even imagined, not a Caucasian clit but a black clit, this girl may be high yellow but she *is* black, black blood in her, that makes a difference, Corky knows. Practically swooning now, panting like an actual dog, not trusting himself to raise his glass to drink, he's in two places simultaneously, crowded in the booth between Marilee and Kiki and also beneath the table with his face between Marilee's fleshy-warm-damp thighs, down there between her legs where she's wet, slick and wet, and he's tonguing her like mad, Corky knows how to set the pace, the rhythm, how to vary the rhythm, it's a gradually accelerating rhythm and the pressure of the tongue must increase, he's going to bring off Marilee right here on the sticky red-leather banquette amid the air-hammer disco, yes but they'll stop you, somebody will stop you, no

Marilee won't let Corky stop, no Marilee has got Corky's head pinioned between her muscular thighs and she won't let him go, leaning back and pushing up into his face, her pelvis rocking too like mad, and the rhythm so fast now there's almost no pause between beats like that weird thing he'd read the other night sleepless and horny *10 million trillion neutrinos speed through your brain and body in a single instant! one single instant of the unfathomable instants that constitute a life!* almost no pause as Marilee leans back moaning and gasping for breath digging her bronze-polished talons into Corky's curly hair that's damp with sweat and murmuring "Mmmm*mmmm* white man, you sure do know how!" Except Corky's so excited he's close to losing it, if one of these girls so much as brushes her fingers against his thigh, let alone his crotch, he's fearful he'll come in his pants, and not inconspicuously but with a groan, a sob, a yelp, he's terrified this is going to happen coming in his pants like a kid, like that time he was sure he was going to come in the confessional, the actual confessional!—a nightmare episode that went on and on and on as Father Sullivan interrogated him in pitiless detail about impure thoughts and practices since his previous last confession the previous Saturday, how many times a night do you commit this impure act, my son? what are the impure thoughts that accompany it, my son? do you not know that such impure thoughts and acts are like thorns in the heart of Our Savior, my son?—the old beery-breathed priest wheezing and grunting, settling his bulk closer to the confessional grill, insisting Jerome lean his mouth right against the grill to speak directly into my ear, otherwise I can't hear you, my son, you speak so softly, I won't be able to absolve you of your sins and these are grievous mortal sins, my son. *Come closer.*

Clos-er.

Thinking of the old priest sobers Corky, for a few minutes at least, he feels the hot-pulsing blood drain out of his cock, his thoughts aren't so muddled, wipes his face with a cocktail napkin: Jesus, sweating like a pig. His hand's steady enough to trust with a glass. And the girls are gaily raising theirs, delicious red wine, sparkling long-stemmed glasses, a toast to you, and to you—and to *me.*

"Waitress?—another round here."

A good thing Corky's in control of himself again: this flirty Kiki nudging her sharp little chin against his shoulder, her wine-stained tongue protruding between her lips, and she's trailing her long beringed fingers against his belt buckle, the girl *is* high on something and not just red Bordeaux. Corky's attracted to her, too, Kiki's a physical type like Thalia, tall willowy-thin small-breasted narrow-thighed very young-looking and enormous-eyed girls, hectic nerved-up mannerisms, probably their pulses are faster than the normal pulse, heartbeat faster, the classic ectomorph type, or is it endomorph?—Corky can never keep the two straight, *he's* a mesomorph.

Meaning square in the middle, the most common physical type.

Only maybe just a little too short, for a man. At five feet nine.

Marilee's a bit calmed too, admiring Kiki's jewelry: her exotic earrings in particular. Corky's noticed the half dozen gold studs in the girl's ear, also a cruel-looking gold clamp on the outer whorl of the ear, sort of butch, sexy. Suddenly Corky's enthralled with Kiki's ear, it's so delicate in its contours, so naked and exposed. He says, touching the clamp gingerly with a forefinger, "Honey, this thing must hurt like hell. What *is* it?"

Kiki shivers, and giggles. The movement of her shoulders—shrinking, combative, provocative—reminds Corky of Thalia. She says huskily, "Well, Corky, maybe I *like* hurt."

Marilee takes this up, a big toothy smile. "Maybe Kiki likes *hurt*, ol' Frecklehead, you ever thought of that?"

So. Somehow it happens that Kiki removes the cruel-looking gold clamp from her ear, and Marilee, who's wearing, this evening, big amber rhomboids, eye-catching but conventional earrings, examines it with a bemused expression, and Corky's got to examine it, too, Corky insists upon taking it and fumbles to fit it on his own ear, and both Marilee and Kiki are dissolved in laughter, and Corky says, "Hey, gimme a hand, eh?" so Kiki fits, more precisely *forces*, the clamp on his ear.

And in that instant the clamp's *on*.

"Oh God."

Pain like a razor slicing the outer rim of Corky's ear. Pain like a flash of lightning blinding him. Pain like a shout, like a scream, like a shriek. Corky yanks at the clamp but it doesn't come off, God damn it doesn't come off, he knows he's made a mistake already breaking into a cold sweat, trying to laugh, muttering, "It's a little tight, it hurts—can you get it off?" Marilee and Kiki see this is sudden, serious business, Mr. Corcoran has gone dead-white in the face and looks as if he's about to pass out. How old *is* he, they might be wondering. In their forties, men start to have heart attacks.

So, biting their lips to maintain grave expressions, the girls try to pry Kiki's clamp off Corky's ear. His poor right ear. Poor Corky! They take turns, Marilee's long sharp fingernails are impractical for such a task, and Kiki's too nerved up, breathless. Minutes of mounting pain, agony, pass as the girls tug, twist, wriggle, *wrench* at the brutal thing, with no luck.

Corky mutters, his face, his entire head, aflame, "God damn, God-damn fucking thing, this isn't funny, God damn get it off. Get it off!" Hearing, he thinks, the girls' muffled giggles, though when he turns to them, tears brimming in his eyes, they look innocent enough, sympathetic and apologetic. Oh so sorry, Corky!—*so* sorry!

Corky's losing it. Corky's got a temper, and Corky's in pain, it's only the outer whorl, the rim, of his ear, but God! what pain!—like a torture instrument, like an instrument that's being tightened, so he's sweating like a pig, ashamed and panicked and in utter physical distress *that's at the same time laughable distress*, poor Corky! And so clumsily on his feet the table's almost overturned. And Kiki's part-filled wine glass goes clattering to the floor, splashing wine on Corky's dove-gray sharp-creased flannel Polo trousers. "Shit," says Corky, and, "Fuck it, get this off," says Corky, and, "God damn, this isn't funny," says Corky, his eyes leaking tears, his vision shimmering yet he can see, and he'll remember seeing, the bemused faces of other patrons, quizzical glances and concerned frowns and outright smiles, grins. *And Corky Corcoran in the most astonishing physical distress* though it's only, what?—a gold clamp of no more than two inches affixed to his ear. His ear!

Corky is tearing so frantically at the thing, Marilee Plummer grabs his hand to prevent him from ripping his very ear off—"Oh, oh! Corky, *no!*" It's the most sincere she's been all evening but Corky isn't in a mood to notice. The Zephir manager, who knows Corky Corcoran, or in any case knows him as an occasional free-spending patron of the Zephir, hurries over to see what the problem is, and to restrain Corky who's on his feet staggering blindly and cursing, "Fuck it get this fucking thing off, *this is no joke!*"—to the astonishment of other patrons, and the surprise of the combo. The Lou Reed imitator actually pauses, frazzled hair like a wig, wasted eyes staring. Kiki is crying, "Oh I'm sorry! I'm sorry! Oh dear!"—but spoils the effect by bursting into laughter and having to hide her face, and Marilee scolds, "Girl! Come on! *This is no joke!*" but Marilee too is biting her lips to keep from laughing. By this time Corky's a man so driven by pain, fury, humiliation, he pushes these cruel girls aside, makes his way blindly out of the lounge hoping to hell among these gaping bemused patrons there's nobody who knows him. He's walking hunched over as an elderly man fearing total ignominious collapse, his face dead-white and even his freckles bleached out, cheeks glistening with tears as voices call after him—"Corky!—Corky!"—but Corky pays no heed, Corky's through with mock sympathy, mock solicitude, he's too distracted by his inflamed ear, the wild throbbing heartbeat in his ear loud as the combo's drumbeat, refuses aid from the Zephir manager who with a straight face offers to get a pliers, or maybe a screwdriver would be better to force the clamp off the ear, Corky says, "Get away! Go to hell! Leave me alone!" clutching at his dignity as a man might clutch at a thread-bare towel to cover his nakedness in the eyes of strangers. And then he's outside. Reeling, swaying like a drunk except he's stone cold sober his knees turned to water and suddenly he's puking out his guts in the park-ing lot, in no condition to drive himself to the hospital so he limps up the street to a taxi stand and falls into a taxi asking the driver please to take him fast to Union City General Hospital (which is about two miles away) insisting he isn't having a heart attack, he isn't going to die in the back of the taxi, the driver smells vomit and has possibly seen the flash of the fucking thing on Corky's ear though Corky's trying his best to hide it, yet not too conspicuously, with his right hand.

And hurrying, limping, head ducked, into the emergency room en-trance at Union City General, rushing into bright lights and that unmis-takable hospital-disinfectant smell, teeth gritted against the pain in his ear that seems now a virtual blossom of pain, an irradiated tree of pain, Corky's vision blurred as if underwater yet seeing with humiliating clarity the curious, bemused glances of strangers, thank God they are strangers, no one here seems to know who Corky is. Nor does the name "Jerome Andrew Corcoran" mean anything to the middle-aged nurse-receptionist on duty at the busy hour of eleven P.M. of a Friday in downtown Union City, the woman maintains a deadpan sort of sympathy, Corky stammers explaining the accident, he knows it's trivial but it hurts like hell. A woman friend put the earring on him, *and it won't come off.*

And then a wait, a wait of how many minutes?—many. The waiting room's already filled when Corky hobbles in, a groaning young man bleeding through a roll of gauze wrapped around his head is carried hurriedly by on a stretcher, Corky's embarrassed of his own problem and spends the ninety minutes pacing and prowling about in the outer lobby, in adjacent corridors, he avoids others' eyes, he shrinks and skulks and ducks around corners, in a men's lavatory he stares astonished at his face that's pale, yet mottled, flushed, freckles standing out in comical relief like raindrops tinged with dirt, *sweet ol' Frecklehead, Fuckhead, Corky Corcoran.* He fills a sink with water as cold as he can get it, dunks his head in it, his red-swollen right ear and that side of his face, teeth chattering, and again desperately and clumsily he tries to work the clamp loose, tries to slide it up, down, considers for a moment actually ripping this part of his ear off, but the pain is so intense he loses his balance, slips, strikes his head hard against the the side of the porcelain sink, almost knocks himself out.

"Fuck! Fuck! *Fuck it!*"

Not until 12:34 A.M. is Jerome Andrew Corcoran's name called and at last he's led, weak, into an examining room, trying not to wince with pain and even to assume a measure of dignity as a tall lanky bespectacled black intern, young kid no more than twenty-five or -six, examines the afflicted ear, tugs experimentally at the clamp, maintaining an air of professional decorum no matter what he's thinking, "Hurts, huh? Wow, the earlobe's *swollen.*" Corky has to bite his lip to keep from screaming. The intern insists then he lie down on an examining table, try to relax, important to relax, mister, and he and a young Asian nurse work at loosening the clamp, you'd think they might get it off within seconds but in fact it takes minutes as Corky lies with his eyes tight shut leaking tears as what he imagines are surgical instruments are applied to the clamp. By this time Corky's ear has swollen to twice its normal size in reverse proportion to his cock which has shrunk to half its normal detumescent size and the pain has become abstract, not an extraneous and accidental factor in his life but a defining element in that life—*This is the price you have to pay for being Corky Corcoran.* And suddenly, the clamp is off.

Corky sits up slowly, tentatively. Red-eyed and sniffing. He tries to smile, does in fact smile—"Thanks! I can't tell you how much!" The black jivy intern, the pretty Asian nurse joke with their patient now, treat the injured ear with a smarting disinfectant, damned thing still hurts like hell and feels like it's balloon-sized and shredded like raw meat but Corky's anxious to show he's O.K. now, he's a good sport, his thanks are profuse, he isn't drunk now but indeed stone cold sober yet he sounds a little drunk, giddy, his voice loud, saying to the intern, "Well, Doctor, I bet you've never had to remove one of these God-damned things from anybody's ear before," and the intern says with a grin, "In fact, mister, we remove 'em all the time, from all parts of the body, y'know? It's like an epidemic out there, all kinds of kinky-funky goings-on." And he and the pretty Asian nurse dissolve in laughter Corky hopes isn't edged with cruelty. Corky hopes isn't at his expense.

As Corky prepares to leave the examining cubicle the intern asks him, "Hmmm mister, don't you want your earring?" with a curly smile holding the twisted chunk of metal in the palm of his hand, fucking thing isn't gold or platinum just some cheaply glittering crap metal now bent nearly flat, hard to comprehend how it could have caused such agony in a grown man. Corky's smiling, Corky's a guy who can take a joke, except suddenly he slaps the black kid's hand and sends the clamp flying—"Don't fuck with me! Just send me the bill!"—charging blind out of the emergency room and out of the God-damned hospital, ol' Freckhead's had enough for one night.

3

"DOWN TO THE MORGUE"

Why the hell not?—I'm on the City Council."

Headed south on Decatur on his way to visit his Uncle Sean when the idea hits Corky, excites him. Why not? The city morgue, Twelfth and Huron. He'll be passing it in five minutes.

Only 11:43 A.M.—for once Corky's running on time. So impulsively he swings onto Meridian, takes it to Twelfth which is one-way, a favorite route of his. Three moderately fast lanes and no repair work right now and traffic lights timed if you know how to pace them which Corky does, he takes the route so often. Sure, why not, the Union City Morgue. See what's being said about the Plummer suicide.

Corky knows the chief medical examiner, Brophy. Not well, but a poker contact. Weird guy, you have to hand it to these characters, they get along with dead bodies and death, build their professional careers on corpses. Got to be sick! Still, who else wants to do shit like that?—no normal guy. For sure, not Corky Corcoran.

Also that jerk-off what's-his-name, Wickler, Wexler, head pathologist, a protégé of Brophy's. Another contact.

Corky's driving on Twelfth bulling his way into the right lane for his turn, crowding out some black dude in a shit-eater Olds 88, Corky's trick is to crowd in not seeming to notice what he's doing all innocent like the guy's in his blind spot—which maybe he is—then if there's resistance he glances over startled and apologetic, lifting his hand to signal *Hey man, Christ, I'm sorry!*

Works every time. Or almost. The black dude glares his eyes at hot-shit whitey in the Caddy, but there's respect for the Caddy, and this is whitey's turf, so fuck it, no sweat. It's what you live for, Corky's thinking, hitting his brakes to make the turn, moments like this. Quicksilver—then gone.

Like that last trifecta sweep he won. Harness race out of Chicago.

Twenty-six thousand, five hundred clear on an eight-hundred-dollar bet, owed it to some guy he scarcely knew and hadn't in fact liked the looks of, or maybe the guy had halitosis, beefy cigar-smoker, and they're at Bobby Ray's Sports Bar one night and Corky's buying drinks to counteract his pissed-out mood and this guy Larry, or Louie, gets to bullshitting with him and there's the moment, it's always just a moment, a single nanosecond *Ping!* and you know you're a brother of the other guy and he knows it. So this Larry, or Louie, leans over to Corky Corcoran and drops certain loaded information into Corky's lap.

"Just keep it to yourself, paddy, who told you. Eh?"

Corky laughed. Hadn't been called "paddy" in years. Sure, he'd keep it to himself, he's not the kind of gambler shoots his mouth off around town. Clearing $26,500 on $800, a sweet deal.

Saturday mornings, especially a holiday weekend, no normal citizen will be found in the office, but these morgue men, top guys who got to the top because they're compulsive about their work, might just possibly be in.

Also, Memorial Day weekend's one of the big American weekends, if you're in the Death business.

Driving, Corky catches some spot news, WWTQ between blasts of teenaged rock, update on the Plummer suicide except not much new—no suicide note yet reported, a stepsister in Lackawanna blames the media for Marilee's death, the curator for the historical museum where she worked is quoted saying Ms. Plummer though new to his staff since last September was one of his "most valuable" "most imaginative" assistants.

Corky wonders was the job at the county museum a patronage job.

Not that Marilee Plummer, smart and ambitious as she was, needed or could have wanted a no-show job. Still, Corky makes a mental note to ask around. Just curiosity.

After the incident with the earring Corky might've called Marilee once or twice, can't remember or doesn't care to remember but in any case nothing came of it though when they encountered each other around town she behaved respectfully to him at least to his face not laughing at him nor making any playful reference to ol' Frecklehead as he'd feared she might. *The one thing a man's terrified of, is a good-looking woman laughing at him.*

Too smart for that, ambitious career girl careful in her dealings with influential men; aware of and respectful of a Caucasian male with Jerome A. Corcoran's connections. For a young woman on the periphery of power that's ninety-nine percent male power understands she's got only one really negotiable asset and that's her reputation. Smart, good at her job, good-looking, sexy—all that's assumed. But her reputation for being loyal, trustworthy, *respectful* to important men—that's her real ticket.

Cunt power doesn't exist. It's only granted by men. And that provisionally—to be revoked at any time.

Corky's feeling good making every traffic light on Twelfth, fact is he's happiest in his car, in motion. Once away from his house he can *breathe*. Like a cement sky opening up and in fact as Corky emerges from a railroad underpass at Market Street the sky actually opens up, heavy soiled-looking cloud surface breaking into chunks like massive boulders, rock-faces illuminated by sunlight so Corky stares upward. There's life on Earth, and a life in the sky. Could you love there you'd be happy. Great crevices of icy blue beyond. Blue without end. Corky's heart lifts like a lover's.

Chrissie?—it's me.

You know I love you. I'm sorry.

Suddenly Corky knows: Christina Kavanaugh is going to be *his* wife.

How does Corky know, he just knows. Instinct. Logic. She's dying to have his kid. Loves him because he makes her laugh, he's a real man seeming not to be living in his head but living through his body like his soul *is* his body and she's a woman to appreciate that. Loves his cock, too. And this thing about Harry Kavanaugh, this shocker—Corky's seeing how it will turn out for the best. Sure. For, now, Christina will have to choose between Harry Kavanaugh her dying husband and Corky Corcoran who's so fucking *alive* and what choice for any normal woman is *that*?

Corky first glimpsed Christina at a party in Edgewater, some millionaire-philanthropist's house fourteen years ago and he was married at the time but as soon as he saw Christina Kavanaugh he knew she was the one—though pregnant. First he'd seen the watermelon-belly, and then the face. Sighted her, and stared. A damned good-looking woman, self-possessed, intelligent mouth and eyes and eyebrows dark enough and thick enough to appear unplucked, and she was wearing white, a sort of quilted raw-silk fabric, and a white rose in her hair, how glossily black her hair, Corky Corcoran drew a deep breath and just stared. Rude mick, a few drinks under his belt and Charlotte had to keep an eye on him but Charlotte was elsewhere and Corky fell in love like a magician had snapped his fingers *She's the one.*

Recognizing too she's one of the Burnsides, a name meaning not just money but class. The Burnsides were wealthy landowners in the Lakeport settlement of Union City at a time in history when the Corcorans of County Kerry, Ireland, might've been living in caves, God knows swinging from trees. Burnside an early governor of New York State, somebody else a general, War of 1812. All this flashing through Corky's head as, seeing him, his rude stare, and then not seeing him, coolly looking through him, the woman whose actual name Corky didn't yet know passed by him bearing her enormous belly like a trophy ignoring his expression of dazed adoration. And he'd thought, in her wake, feeling faint, but pissed too, *nobody snubs Corky Corcoran.*

And so it's turned out. And this way too he'll be revenged on Federal Court Justice Harry Kavanaugh, another old-money high-class name. That irritation Corky like ninety-nine percent of the American population feels when you drive up and see the parking space is reserved for some cripple in a wheelchair and these parking spaces are always empty God damn it so you have to park a half-mile away, this irritation Corky feels for Harry Kavanaugh whose wife he's going to take from him. No mercy no pity. Fuck pity. *No more shit on their shoes* for Corky Corcoran whose prick at least is in working order.

Down to the morgue.

Two kinds of families in the world: those who don't have any idea what *down to the morgue* means, and those who do.

The weatherworn buff-stucco building at Twelfth and Huron, attached to the rear of Union City General Hospital, a quarter-mile from the Union City Police headquarters—high-density siren zone. Ambulances, police vehicles, constant traffic. Except the morgue faces Huron, a bleak neighborhood of discount furniture stores and used-car dealers and Day-Glo defaced fences and sidewalks. The old Loblaw's Grocery renamed Huron Fresh Foods Market (Korean) and the old Ace's Keyboard

Lounge renamed Club Zanzibar (black) and the old Fox Theatre (long empty). Since the fires of summer 1967 and the sporadic riots following Martin Luther King's assassination in 1968, much of the black inner-city neighborhood looks like a war zone, bordering the hospital-UCPD sector. Fitting, the morgue should be here.

Corky can't help shivering. Old memories stirred. Many a blood relative—Corcoran, Donnelly, Dowd, Farley—made this trip over the decades. Called *down to the morgue* to identify a corpse.

Some years ago, when Sean Corcoran was drinking his heaviest, Corky was in perpetual dread of being called down to identify his uncle, found dead in the street and his wallet gone. In fact he'd had to identify his great-uncle Hock Corcoran, about six years ago, and that was bad enough: a call came from Hock's daughter, herself a woman in her fifties, a woman who still looks through Corky at family gatherings judging him a sinner for having married a divorced woman, pleading with him to go down to the morgue in her place to make the identification, choked fury and shame even in her grief over the phone and Corky'd said O.K., what the hell. Somebody had to do it. Hock Corcoran, old drunk, flat-out brain-rotted rummy with a chronic habit of running away from home and turning up by the docks, or in Chambers Park that's the city's gathering place for people like himself. Hock's brain was long pickled in alcohol so he was rarely, at his most eloquent, able to grunt out a coherent statement, but the old bugger had a will of iron, knew what *he* wanted—which was to roam the slummy downtown by the docks, beg for quarters, maintain his red-wine coma, sleeping where he happened to pass out. And this for years. Years!

The weird thing about alcoholics is, *they keep going.* The human organism's tough as a cockroach.

Once, hauling the old bugger home from St. Anthony's Mission on Front Street, Corky actually had to stop his car and get out and puke, Hock stunk so powerfully—the profound stink, beyond the stink even of skunk, of a man who has not washed his body or changed his clothes in weeks and has in fact pissed his clothes, and worse. Poor Corky! His car at the time was a sporty red Corvette. He'd had to get rid of it soon afterward.

And when he'd identified Hock, he'd been as brisk and businesslike as possible. As soon as the morgue attendant drew back the sheet from the dead man's face, Corky muttered, "Right! That's my man." Not requiring more than an instant's glance through slitted eyes to see that the bloated-battered flamey face was a Corcoran face, no mistake.

"We'd know one another anywhere," Corky joked on his way out.

An earlier visit *down to the morgue*, in 1975, when Corky had to identify his cousin Cormac Farley, a friend of his boyhood, had been more painful. A lot more painful. Cormac was Corky's age and like Corky a bit of a gambler. Except Cormac seemed to have no other trade or profession, he'd been married but separated from his wife and young family, spent time in Vegas and Miami Beach and it was told around town he'd borrowed money from too many sources (one of them, rumor had it, was the pension fund administered by the officers of the United Brotherhood of Plumbers and Steamfitters local) and so Cormac disappeared over a weekend to be found transformed into a sort of naked flesh-balloon floating face down in the Erie Barge Canal above the Lockport locks. So damaged was the corpse, the immediate cause of death was not clear. By the time Corky made this trip *down to the morgue*, and this time, too, to spare relatives, Cormac had been missing for eight days and there was no doubt in Corky's mind that the body must be his; yet, seeing it, seeing that hideous face that had been, in life, Irish-freckled as Corky's own, Corky'd nearly broken down. Maybe in fact he had cried?—he's tried his best to forget.

The morgue is in an old municipal building that doesn't seem to have changed since Corky's last visit. Except it's grimier, more pigeon shit streaking the facade. Above the front entrance is a bas-relief of the Union City seal: two heraldic-heroic figures, one male and the other seemingly female, an American eagle above them with its wings spread protectively and symbols of farming, seafaring, and railways spread about them. On a scroll at their feet, *Magna est veritas et praevalebit* and the date 1799. Corky knows the Latin inscription means *Truth is mighty and will prevail*, not that he knows Latin. The inscription has always impressed him and scared him, a little—the best face you can put upon yourself and your actions, it's all going to be swept away.

Still, you can't give up.

Shit, you *can't* give up.

Inside, Corky's hit by a whiff of sickish air. Not all the ventilating fans in this old building working at full force can disguise the product processed here. And, for sure, the fans aren't working very efficiently.

Corky's relieved, though, the place isn't deserted. In fact it's busy. Noisy. A uniformed cop is escorting a dazed-looking middle-aged black couple through the lobby, probably parents come to identify their murdered son, the woman's crying so brokenheartedly Corky can't look, pathetic too they've dressed up for the morgue, Sunday clothes. The receptionist's wicket is open but nobody's visible so Corky just pushes on. There's an opened door through which people are passing freely, Corky figures he'll slip inside and see if Brophy's around, or what's-his-name Winkler, Wexler—the Forensics Department and the pathology labs are close by. If you look like you've got business down here, chances are you won't be questioned. For who in his right mind would come *here* if not on legitimate business?

Called *down to the morgue* on a Saturday morning in May.

Corky sees cops, both uniformed and plainclothes, one or two guys that might be from the D.A.'s office, not a single woman except the weeping black mother. Once he's past the lobby, his nostrils pinch even tighter. Christ, what a smell! Nobody seems to notice it but him.

It's like he's underground. This place is underground. Narrow grimy windows at the end of the corridors, protected by chicken-wire. But the light is all flourescent tubing humming and flickering overhead.

Corky strides along briskly. A short man knows how to *walk*.

Always knows his destination or at least look as if he does. His cousin Cormac was maybe an inch shorter, *he* knew how to walk, make himself look tall by some action of his neck, shoulders. And prowling around a ritzy apartment building on Dundonald where there was a family with good-looking daughters, Cormac and Corky, must have been eighth grade, Cormac taught Corky the simple lesson if you look like you know your destination and especially if you're carrying something (wrapped in bloodstained paper from the butcher's for instance), nobody will get suspicious.

Which was true, anyway most of the time.

Corky's over his hangover and is looking, if not terrific, for him, pretty good. Slick-combed hair and not so pasty-faced, fresh-shaven (and the cut on his cheek already healed) and very well dressed for such surroundings. The city municipal buildings fall into two categories: new and impressive, like the addition to City Hall; old and shabby, like the detention centers, the police precinct houses in the poorer neighborhoods, the morgue. You'd tag Corky Corcoran as a really top detective or a top prosecutor or a sharpie lawyer, not some poor bastard *down to the morgue* on personal business. Fresh white shirt, navy blue polka-dot necktie, navy blue broadcloth sport coat, khaki trousers with a sharp crease, not cheap khaki but upscale, a men's boutique in the Hyatt. And sporty canvas shoes with a crepe sole.

At least, if he has to run like an asshole down some alley, risking arrest and public humiliation, he'll be wearing the shoes for it today.

So when a guard asks Corky what's his business here, Corky says, "I'm a friend of Ed Brophy's," smiling, and that's enough, the guard just nods and waves him on. Young cop, respectful. Of course, it doesn't hurt that Corky Corcoran's skin is *white*.

Even at the morgue, where most of what you'd call the clientele are black or Hispanic, every cop Corky's seen is Caucasian.

Corky follows arrows directing him to the office of the chief medical examiner, trying not to glance inside opened doors, God knows what he might see. As in a hospital, but worse than a hospital. He remembers that the actual morgue, the refrigerated area, is close by. And he's getting closer. The bitter-acrid smell's getting stronger. A good thing he hadn't had any appetite for breakfast, *that* would have been a mistake.

He's disappointed seeing that Brophy's door is shut. Through the frosted-glass window it's clear there are no lights on inside.

Disappointed, but maybe relieved. Maybe he won't look up this other guy, whose name he isn't sure of; isn't even sure he's a pathologist, if that's his title. Assistant medical examiner? Assistant coroner? What's the difference? Corky's standing there not knowing what to do, maybe drive on to Uncle Sean's since it's almost noon and the old man's expecting him.

Two burly morgue attendants are pushing a rattling aluminum gurney past, talking loudly together, laughing. The tiled linoleum floor is so cracked and warped, the gurney bounces and careens like a shopping cart slamming along a potholed street. Which wouldn't matter much except there's a corpse on the gurney, carelessly covered in a plastic sheet. Enormous bare dusky-skinned feet protruding at one end and a greasy glisten of nappy hair at the other. Corky looks quickly away but not quickly enough.

He's headed back out when, turning a corner, he hears a man's voice, high-pitched and insinuating, "Well, hel-*lo*, last name's Corcoran, isn't it? What brings *you* here?"

Corky sees it's this guy he'd met once, Wexler? Winkler?—greeting him with a pretense of warmth, Corky's usual style, though the guy, carrying a can of diet chocolate soda and several wrapped slices of cheese-and-pepperoni pizza, can't shake Corky's hand. Somehow, this is funny? Why's the guy twitching and winking at him? And that wide grin? "Bet you don't remember me?—I'm Wolf Wiegler," the guy says, before Corky can say yes of course he remembers.

Wolf Wiegler?—that's a new one to Corky. He'd wonder if his leg's being pulled except, up close, he can make out the ID W. *Wiegler* on the guy's badly soiled lab coat.

Corky says, pausing slightly, "First name's Jerome."

"Yes? 'Jerome'?" Wolf Wiegler's squinting at Corky through his thick-lensed glasses, screwing up his face as if he's doubtful. "What brings *you* here, then?" Laughing, showing uneven yellow-tinged babyish teeth as if he's made a joke. Corky's sense is that this is a character he'd do well to avoid except isn't this just the kind of character who'll spill secrets if he knows any? Every municipal department has somebody like W. *Wiegler* on the staff.

Corky says, "I just dropped by to see Ed Brophy, I haven't run into Ed for a while," and Wiegler says, sneering, "Oh our resident media hero," an allusion to the fact that, some months ago, Corky'd nearly forgotten, Brophy had been interviewed on TV in connection with the Devane Johnson shooting, as chief medical examiner. Wiegler goes on to speak of Brophy in droll elliptical sardonic terms, calls him "Herr Dock-tor Brophy," the men must be feuding, Corky knows nothing of this, nor wants to know. As he speaks, Wiegler continues to squint at Corky as if there's some joke between them. So twitchy, a visible tic in his left cheek, Corky guesses this weird bastard must have some neurological problem which he hopes to hell isn't catching. Corky has a penchant for picking up others' habits, accents. Maybe Wiegler has a case of Tourette's syndrome? That angry kind of humor? Corky read about Tourette's in one of his paperback science books, his early-hour insomniac reading. The medical description struck him: *A fight between an "It" and an "I."*

Wiegler chatters in his sly, insinuating way, as if Corky was an accomplice in dislike of Brophy. He's balancing his runny pizza slices atop the can of diet chocolate. Must be his lunch, brought back to his office. Imagine eating here! Amid these smells! Corky can almost feel sorry for the guy, must be lonely amid the stiffs, doing autopsies and lab work, whatever. The kind of character who'll buttonhole anyone crossing his path. Corky's calculating the strategic moment to cut in, inquire about Marilee Plummer, when Wiegler abruptly changes his tack. He says, with an aggressive snort, "Jerome, what's this about a big Democrat shindig Monday night in Chateauguay? All the party elite in Union City? *I* wasn't invited."

Corky's surprised Wiegler has even heard of the dinner. But the guy must be a registered Democrat, he'd be on mailing lists. Corky says, "Sure you were invited, Wolf. All you needed to do was pay a thousand dollars."

Wiegler laughs loudly. Baring his damp stained baby's teeth. The tic in his cheek jumping. "A thousand dollars! Are you serious, man! For dinner! For golden boy Slattery's campaign!" The name *Slattery* rolls off Wiegler's tongue in a way offensive to Corky. "*I* wouldn't pay a thousand dollars for the Last Supper, man."

Corky, who's practiced at faking laughs, laughs. It's a habit like handshaking, back-slapping if you're meeting voters. Sometimes, no matter the personal repugnance, it has to be done.

Corky says, "It's great to see you again, Wolf. You know, I was wondering—"

But Wiegler's still laughing at his own joke. The tic in his cheek is more pronounced. "The Last Supper, you know? Jesus Christ and His disciples? I wouldn't pay a thousand dollars a plate *there.*"

"Right," says Corky affably. "Probably I wouldn't either. What I was wondering, Wolf, is—"

"Man, I wouldn't pay five hundred dollars!"

"Right—"

"You know why?"

"No, why?"

"It's too much to pay for a supper. That's why."

Corky's smile is strained. What *is* this asshole? Reminds Corky of one of Theresa's fellow patients, years ago at the psychiatric hospital at Indian Lake. Poor bastard was diagnosed as schizophrenic-autistic. Babbling excitedly to himself but refusing to look anyone in the eye. Religious delusions kept him going.

Theresa in her lucid moments, in fact there were prolonged days and even weeks of what you'd call lucidity, would speak sympathetically of her fellow sufferers, as if making excuses for them. *They're not of their right mind.*

Wiegler's saying earnestly, "Don't get me wrong, I voted for Vic Slattery, and I voted for Mayor Slattery—*I always vote for Mayor Slattery.* Otherwise, would I be here?"

Corky cuts in, before Wiegler can go off on another riff, "I was wondering, Wolf, about this young woman Marilee Plummer?—died the other day? They said it was suicide, and—"

Wiegler's eyes behind his thick-lensed glasses narrow in an exaggerated squint. His face visibly stiffens. He even takes a step backward. He says, interrupting, "Brophy did it."

"Brophy did it—?"

"Ran the tests on Plummer."

Corky has more questions, but he sees how Wiegler's changed, cagey now, wanting to get away. Yet saying, almost it's a taunt, such dopey humor, "—That colored girl, was it? You knew her, man? *I'd've* liked to know her better, but Brophy got in first."

Wiegler turns, walks on, brusque and rude and Corky hasn't any choice but to follow. He sees Wiegler's office ahead, door opened, the frosted-glass window of the door, W. WIEGLER, PATHOLOGY in black. Also a hand-lettered sign DE MORTUIS NIL NISI BONUM which is a Latin Corky doesn't know. Through the doorway Corky sees that Wiegler's office is large but badly cluttered with files; daylight, filtered through an antiquated window thick with grime, has a sickly look. On top of Wiegler's desk (which is a rolltop desk, battered but of good quality) is a dingy human skull given a startling jaunty look by the presence of a cigar stuck between its jaws.

Seeing Corky wincing, Wiegler says, with mock solicitude, "Sorry, man, is she somebody you *know?*"—and laughs loudly.

Corky laughs, not quite so loudly. He's shrewd enough—not that this situation requires shrewdness—to see that Wiegler doesn't want to answer any questions of his. He's butting his nose in where it isn't wanted, he'll have to take some shit.

Maybe later, another time, he can take revenge on this asshole?—reminds him of "Richie Richards" on WWAZ. A good solid right to the mouth. Corky's sneaky left hook Coach had praised, except it lacked punch. Yes, someday.

But to Corky's surprise—and this too is calculated, orchestrated—Wiegler isn't going into his office but continues down the corridor, carrying his pizza slices and his diet chocolate, calling out cheery hellos to colleagues, morgue attendants, as Corky trots along behind, managing to retain his affable smile. Wiegler glances back at him with a twitchy grin that looks angry, or maybe just amused. Though his black-plastic-rimmed eyeglasses and his bow tie (just visible beneath the soiled lab coat) give Wiegler a professorial air, there's something thuggish about him. His head is round and hard as a bowling ball and his steel-brown hair lifts from it in a crewcut. Wiegler sees Corky studying him and says, with sly meaning, "*You* look spiffy, man, must be headed somewhere special?—not just here, huh, am I right?"

Corky says, evenly, innocently, "Well, yes—I'm having drinks at the Slatterys' later today. Vic and Sandra, that is."

Wiegler whistles. Flashing that malevolent grin. "'Vic and Sandra'—no kidding? Man, you really move in elite circles, don't you? I'm *impressed*."

The sarcasm is juvenile, it's so crude. Corky feels his face flush but he's thinking asshole, you asked for it. Smiles, nods. He'll have to take some shit from this character if he persists here, figures it's worth it.

Except, where is Wiegler leading him?

"You want to talk, man, c'mon, you're welcome. I'm having my lunch, though. Also just starting a prep, you won't mind?"—Wiegler's cheerful and breezy, shoving open a heavy door with his shoulder, MORGUE NO ADMITTANCE EXCEPT ON OFFICIAL BUSINESS.

Corky's jaw must drop open, there's a panic in his face but Wiegler pretends not to notice, humming to himself.

The morgue? Wiegler's taking him in the morgue?

Corky's got no choice but to follow Wiegler into the morgue?

Wiegler's going to eat his fucking lunch in the morgue?

Corky follows blind, dazed, still a strained sick smile on his face. O.K., Corky will call the fucker's bluff. Nobody eats his lunch in the morgue does he?—must be the guy's only kidding. Maybe it isn't personal animosity against Corky Corcoran but just some routine they do here, pulling a greenhorn's legs. Him being on the City Council, and all. Maybe that's it?

But Wiegler's serious enough. To Corky's horror, he is.

Wiegler's striding along, biting into one of his pizza slices, strings of cheese hanging down from his mouth like collapsed tusks. Laughing and waving hello at two morgue attendants, the two burly men Corky saw a minute ago in the corridor, who are dumping the body off the gurney and onto a metal slab. A body heavy as a sandbag. A body that *thuds*. So Corky flinches feeling the pain the man inside the body would feel if he was still inside the body which of course he isn't. *Jesus Mary and Joseph* flies through Corky's head *pray for me now and at the hour of my death Amen.*

A prayer out of Corky's lost childhood, thirty years ago.

"How's it going, guys?" Wiegler cries merrily.

"O.K., Dr. Wiegler," says one young man, and the other, a good-natured shrug, "Can't complain."

Wiegler's the noisy bossy kind on the job, gives the attendants brisk instructions about "prepping" their boy. Corky stands to one side waiting, not listening. Not looking. Except he sees the oversized dusky-brown feet, tender pink bare soles, long naked legs, dark-woolly scrotum out of which something sprouts fleshy and pinkly raw like a swollen goiter. *Asshole don't look.*

Corky doesn't listen for fear of hearing too much, he's a sensitive soul in the presence of Death. Except he gathers the black man's only a kid, nineteen. Dead of gunshot wounds in the chest. And he was a junkie, arms and legs riddled with track marks.

Wiegler moves on, toward the rear of the morgue. Corky numbly follows.

"I'd offer you some of my pizza, Jerome, except there isn't much. Sorry!"

Corky mumbles it's all right.

"Yeah, man?—what'd you say?"—turning to Corky with exaggerated solicitude.

Corky mumbles louder, "Thanks, it's all right."

Wiegler grins expansively. "Some people, they don't like cold pizza anyway. Turns their stomach. And the crusts are *hard*, you got to have good gastric juices to process them."

Corky hasn't been *down to the morgue* for years but it's all familiar to him. He'd forgotten, but no he hasn't, it's all there, waiting. Cormac on that table (empty today), Hock on that table (where Wiegler seems to be headed). The smell, the smells. Despite the giant ventilator and rattling fans. Now it comes back, this chemical-bloody-bowel smell. Except there's something more, a smell of stale or rancid food. This, Corky doesn't remember.

Yes, there's evidence, desiccated pizza crusts scattered on the counters, greasy buckets from Kentucky Fried Chicken, plastic deli containers, Styrofoam cups with puddles of coffee in them, soda and beer cans—eating's a regular activity in the morgue. A pair of chopsticks on an empty autopsy table! Corky's head spins.

Corky thinks, A mistake to come here.

Corky thinks, Yes but you can't turn back.

Jesus, what if he faints? throws up? Which is what Wiegler's expecting? Memories not only of the disfigured corpses of Cormac Farley and Hock Corcoran but of Tim Corcoran, handsome in Death, a rosary twined through his fingers, sweep over Corky. And Theresa too. In a sudden panic Corky glances about. There wouldn't be a female body here, would there?

There are just two corpses in sight, so far as Corky can tell, and both are male. The young black and a white man, in fact suety-colored, with a hairless dented skull, on the autopsy table to which Wiegler's headed with his lunch. This corpse, hefty as a side of beef, is sprawled gracelessly on the tilted, grooved table, flabby arms and legs outspread. His genitals too look swollen and raw, like something skinned. The head has lolled to one side, bruised eyes open, and the jaws hang slack. For a terrible moment the dead man appears to be one of Corky's old Jesuit teachers!

Christ, no: DeLucca's been dead for years. Corky's sure.

Wiegler's been doing something to this corpse, taking swabs with Q-Tips, making slide specimens. Corky sees test tubes, a caliper, a tweezers, a cruel pick-like thing that looks like a dentist's instrument, a miniature flashlight, a pair of badly stained yellow rubber gloves. A lab report sheet on a clipboard propped against the dead man's naked feet.

Corky's swallowing to fight panic. Trying to breathe deeply and regularly as he'd been taught by his high school coach but at the same time, the air's so foul, trying not to breathe at all. Tasting bile at the back of his mouth. But he isn't going to give in to nausea and he isn't going to turn back. Not with Wolf Wiegler watching him the way he is, grinning and chewing but his eyes behind his glasses shrewdly cold, assessing.

Wiegler says, "Never been in our sanctorum before, eh, Jerome my man?" settling in on the edge of the autopsy table, nudging the dead man's buttocks. You get the idea Wiegler sits like this often, he's right at home. Even sets the can of diet chocolate soda on the poor bastard's chest between his flaccid nipples. All the while devouring his cold pizza slices with unrestrained appetite and washing mouthfuls down with hearty swigs of soda. What a swine!—it isn't just eating here, it's the combination of cheese, pepperoni, pizza dough and diet "chocolate" that turns Corky's stomach. Corky says, to set things straight, "Sure I've been down here before. More than once. You didn't grow up in Irish Hill and not get acquainted with the morgue."

"You're looking a little pale, though, man. The smell getting to you? *We* don't smell it, *we're* immune." Making a little joke, his mouth full, nodding toward the corpse. "Lately it's fresh air that bothers me, you know? God-damned wind off the lake gets me coughing."

"No," says Corky, "—I'm fine. I won't be staying long, though—"

"Hell, Jerome, you're welcome to stay as long as you like," Wiegler says, almost jeering. "What'd you want to know?—about the colored girl? That shithead Steadman's girlfriend?"

"Marilee Plummer wasn't Steadman's girlfriend," Corky says, "—I think you've got that wrong. She—"

"Whose girlfriend was she, then? Yours?"

Wiegler's so blunt, so brash, yet friendly-seeming, all grins and winks and tics, Corky doesn't know how to read him. An asshole like this, he can be underestimated. Corky's known of weirdly nasty cops and a guy or two even in the D.A.'s office who gets in a position of power so his sickness, you could call it his evil, can really come out. At the same time, Wolf Wiegler is maybe just a joker?—pulling Corky's leg 'cause he's jealous of him?—his connections around town?

"No," says Corky, as evenly as he can manage, "—Marilee Plummer was not my girlfriend. I don't go out with girls that—"

"—color?"

"—I was going to say *young*."

Wiegler laughs explosively, derisively. So enjoying himself, the attendants glance over at him with smiles and Corky half-expects the dead men are going to glance up, too. Everybody loves a laugh. Wiegler says, mock apologetic, "Man, I must've confused you with somebody else. Hot brown sugartits and cunt is *very* popular in Union City, and we likes 'em *young*."

Wolf Wiegler's the kind of guy so obviously a bachelor, even if queer he wouldn't have a clue; the kind of guy prissy and celibate as a nun. So what's this heavy sarcasm? What's he getting at? Corky says, fuming, "Fuck that 'we,' count me out. My interest in Marilee Plummer is just—" and here Corky falters a little, for what *is* it? He's reluctant to bring in Thalia. "—wanting to know. Wanting justice."

"Well, Jerome," Wiegler says, grinning as if there's an understanding, a covert joke between them that Corky's too dense to get, or to allow himself to get, "—there I'm on your side. We all are."

Before Corky can proceed, Wiegler adroitly changes the subject, and the tone. Suddenly he's serious. Schoolboy-earnest. Like he's giving Corky some slack, now Corky's swallowed his lure. Play with him a little, is that it? A son of a bitch to figure out. And Corky's worried about that queasy churning sensation in his gut. Yesterday, a bad attack of diarrhea, he hopes to hell that won't happen again. He's weak-kneed leaning unobtrusively against a table piled with hacksaws, used swab sticks, chemical beakers, carelessly folded green plastic sheets like the material used for garbage bags, discarded rubber gloves, empty cardboard containers from Gino's Pizzeria and House of Huang. Wiegler says, "—What I was saying out there, about the Slattery fund-raiser on Memorial Day?—I didn't mean, I was just shooting my mouth. Hell, I'd love to be included. If I could afford it. If I moved in those circles. Union City elite. Black tie, eh? You own your own tux, I suppose, Jerome?"

Must be bullshitting Corky, but Corky just nods, or is it a shrug. In fact he owns two tuxes, and hopes to hell the larger still fits. The last time, the waistband left red marks in his skin.

Weddings, wakes. Fund-raisers, funerals. Dress-up occasions where, out of boredom, or anxiety, or both, you stuff your face and get tanked.

Wiegler's continuing, "What I mean is, Slattery's my man, too. I'll give to his campaign. I gave in the past, and I've given to the old man, it's the least you can do on the city payroll. Vic will be a U.S. Senator in a few years, maybe? Maybe, who knows, President someday? He's decent, and he's not too dumb. I'm solidly behind him so tell the Mayor should he ask." Wiegler laughs, all twitches and tics, the notion's so far-fetched. "The Mayor's sure to ask, man, right?"

"Is he?"

Wiegler ignores this, pushing on. He *is* serious. "What I also meant, Jerome, about the Last Supper, etcetera, I wouldn't pay a dime because I'm not a believer. Not in Christ, or any of that crap. I used to be, I was baptized Presbyterian, but I'm not, now. You do your first five hundred cadavers, that's it, man,"—snapping his fingers, "—for the 'spiritual life.'" And he sniggers and winks at Corky as if he's said something daring. Corky can't believe this. "What you get truly to admire, I mean it truly blows your mind, is the physical apparatus, the machinery of brain, body: *Homo sapiens*," fondly rapping his knuckles against the head of the dead man beside him, so Corky flinches. Wiegler's saying expansively, "The more you know about it, the less. That's my personal definition of the divine. Fuck God, eh?—now it's the Big Bang. And the human brain, that can encompass it. *Mirabile visu!* Well, I'm a worshiper. No false pride. Think of it, man: Darwinian evolution could've taken any number of turns but it turned toward us. A rummy like this guy here, *he's* shit, the 'person' inside the machinery, but the machinery, wow. That's God."

Corky says quick without thinking, like he's been personally insulted, "Why's he 'shit'? Maybe he wasn't always a rummy, maybe—"

"Nah, we're all shit, man, I mean we're flyspecks, the 'persons' inside the brain, the asshole 'personalities' we think so much of. Not a one of us—and I include myself, with my Cornell med school training—could invent the bodies we inhabit, let alone the brains. We're like Cro-Magnons occupying one of those hundred-million-dollar high-rises downtown without a clue how they even got there. Don't tell me!" waving excitedly at Corky who wasn't about to say a word, "—I know. I truly know. I'm a witness to the wonder of physical creation, even with a shit-job like this in this dead-end Rust Belt city, *man don't tell me*." Corky listens amazed as Wiegler, heated as a kid in a high school debate, one of those high-IQ kids even the Jesuits were wary of, not only are they geniuses primed to trip you up but they're wild cards in the deck, never know when they might crack, starts in yammering about the human brain, and Darwinian evolution, and the Earth, and the Universe, the works—some of Corky's favorite subjects in fact, except this is all too fast and too intense, he can't keep up. He feels like a drowning man. That sick swampy sensation in his gut, starting to rise.

"*Homo sapiens*, the masterwork of evolution thus far," Wiegler continues, in a passion, "—only just arrived a few *minutes* ago, comparatively speaking. Galactically speaking—an infinitesimal crumb of a *nanosecond* ago. We're not the end, we're only the beginning, maybe? And space is so empty, like the atom, mostly emptiness. Black matter, invisible. Like Pascal said, centuries ago—'The silence of these infinite spaces frightens me.' Nobody's ever said it better. *And he was Catholic*." Wiegler laughs hoarsely, wetly, his eyes showing white. Then falls to coughing, and hawks up some greeny phlegm into a paper napkin with a sunny Gino's face stamped on it.

Jesus Mary and Joseph, thinks Corky. He's close to being sick trying now not to breathe at all.

How long Wiegler talks in his fierce sputtering headlong way, about the Universe, and Time, and the "exquisite machinery" of *Homo sapiens*, Corky scarcely knows. Probably it's only minutes but it feels like an hour. He figures this is a strategy to steer him away from the subject of Marilee Plummer but that's only part of it. Nobody could be so fierce and lunatic, nobody'd *care* so much, you can't fake it. Even an evil customer like Marcus Steadman can't fake one hundred percent, he's got to *care*.

Wiegler moves on to hard-fact statistics, pulling figures out of the air, must have a photographic memory, one of those idiot savants?—light-years and equations and percentages and neurons and ganglia and how *Homo sapiens* is composed of primeval matter exploded out of and flying from the Big Bang, and Corky's impressed, you'd think this guy was a Jew except he'd said Presbyterian.

It's an irony not lost on Corky Corcoran in even this shaky state that, given his layman's knowledge of certain subjects, outclassing most college graduates he runs into, he should be at such a disadvantage now. He knows, or should know, some of the things Wiegler's so charged up talking about. Doesn't he read himself to sleep or oblivion most nights, greedily devouring paperback books, magazines, the other night till four in the morning trying to make sense of certain consecutive sentences in *A Brief History of Time*, Christ if he could just remember some of that fancy crap if he wasn't in such a shaky state fighting nausea blinking to clear his vision *Is that dead man breathing? listening?* trying to keep in mind his purpose in being here *Wanting to know! wanting justice* this nightmare place that's a butcher shop you must never wind up in: better cremation: better oblivion but Corky can't even think of that in his rising panic and this pounding headache at the base of his skull he's thinking of the Memorial Day banquet, the Chateauguay Country Club where he's going to give a brief tribute to Vic Slattery no more than eight minutes but Corky Corcoran will really be on the spot in front of people he's yearning to impress it's his golden opportunity to impress aligning himself with Vic Slattery in so public a way and at such a crucial time God damn it everything has to happen at once like an avalanche—Christina betraying him, and Thalia fucking things up in her usual style, and those cocksuckers the IRS suing Corcoran, Inc., for $400,000 in back taxes he can't pay, Christ he's on the verge of bankruptcy with those limited-partnership deals caving in—*him*, Corky Corcoran, one of the shrewdest guys in Union City, on the verge of fucking bankruptcy! And at Chateauguay he'll have to come across as completely in control, winning and appealing and smiling and *sincere*, a politician's nothing if he can't come across as *sincere*. For maybe Corky will be elected president of the City Council and maybe Oscar Slattery will designate him the next Mayor maybe yes? maybe no? and what if Christina Kavanaugh is there Monday night? with her husband? *And what if Christina Kavanaugh isn't there?* these thoughts bombarding Corky's dazed brain like a million trillion neutrinos per second or is it a trillion million?—fuck it, that's the problem, God damn that's where Corky inevitably fails himself, his own self-expectations, can't retain ninety-nine percent of what he reads so avidly as if his life depended upon it, can't fucking keep it straight is the Earth 4.5 billion years old or 4.5 million years old, how far is the sun from the Earth and when's it going to self-destruct, in 5 million or 5 billion years? Corky's read such statistics a thousand times but fuck it if he can keep any of it straight, the age of the Solar System, the size of the Milky Way, what's a galactic year exactly, how far away and how old *are* quasars, what *is* Omega, if you keep going long enough traveling through the Universe would you wind up where you began, or—where? And what *was* there before the Big Bang? *How the fuck could something come from nothing?* That's what Corky wants to know, is that too much to ask?

Wiegler's speaking of the heat-death of the sun and the future annihilation of the Earth, winding down some, sort of sad-resigned, philosophical, for the "wonder of wonders, the human brain" is doomed to annihilation too, and Corky says, like a man lighting a match in the dark, a man you didn't expect to have a match, nor the strength to light it, "Yes, a star's history is over in a millisecond, but—where there's quantum theory there's hope. Right?"

Wiegler stares at him so startled, eyes enlarged like an insect's inside his thick glasses, Corky repeats, defiantly, "Where there's quantum theory there's hope. *Right?*"

Beyond this point, Corky begins to lose his concentration altogether. Acceleration near the point of impact. Sucked into a black hole.

He'll recall that Wiegler, roused from his trance of mystical wonderment, turns mean, shrewd. Wraps the conversation up—literally he's gathering up the remains of his lunch from the dead man's chest, tosses it flamboyantly, in mimicry of a basketball play, into a trash bin, "Well, man: what you want to know, about the Ne-gress, *I* don't know, it's got nothing to do with *me*. Brophy's report says suicide. We process thousands of cases through here a year, and they're all in one category: DOA."

Wiegler's annoyed, or nervous. Or maybe just eager to return to work. Saying, in a rapid professional voice, "Go to your buddies over at headquarters and ask them. Suicide's no problem to diagnose when you have a subject dead in her car, car's been running and out of gas, garage is filled with exhaust, carbon monoxide and some tranquilizer in her blood and no signs of force, coercion on her body—not even any semen in her cunt." Sneering, impatient. "If Marcus Steadman forced her to it, that's for somebody else to prove. Our work stops here."

Corky says, persisting, "But Marilee Plummer didn't leave any suicide note behind? You'd expect, if—"

"Shit, man, who knows? *You* know? What you read in the papers? So what, no suicide note's reported?" Wiegler speaks disdainfully, as if Corky's being willfully obtuse. "Cases like this, somebody might receive a note or a letter, or a telephone call, before the suicide, or there's been a conversation, but the other party doesn't report it. Why should they? Dead's dead. *I* wouldn't get involved."

"But the family might want to know. For Christ's sake, when a person does something so extreme, so despairing, as kill herself—we should want to know why. It's a matter of—"

"'Justice'—?" Wiegler says mockingly.

"Well, why the hell not? What's wrong with that?" Corky protests. In weakened states he tends to speak from the heart, like a real greenhorn. "What's wrong with justice? Not the crappy *idea* of it, but the *real thing?* Applied to real people?"

Wiegler fixes Corky with a disbelieving smile. All the while he's methodically wiping his hands on his soiled lab coat and brushing crumbs off his trousers. A hulking bulky guy, like there's uneven padding inside his clothes, though he's not much taller than Corky. His trousers are baggy gray polyester and his shoes are oxblood moccasins with tassels. When he moves his head in a certain dipping-twitchy way, as if there's a crick in his neck he can't quite undo, his pink scalp's visible through his crewcut. Corky gets a picture of Wolf Wiegler not only a bachelor and celibate but living with an elderly arthritic blind mother.

"Shit, Jerome, I thought you were one of Slattery's City Hall cronies, tight with old Oscar like two fingers up the ass," Wiegler says, laughing. "What's this 'justice' crap you're handing me?"

"Crap? *Why's* it crap?" Corky's more perplexed than angry. He doesn't get this guy grinning and winking at him, nor the hostility beneath. "I take this seriously, Wolf. It isn't bullshitting, believe me."

"Then *why* isn't it? What's it to you man?—if you weren't fucking the

Ne-gress, like you said," Eyeing Corky to see how this goes over, if he's pushing too far.

Corky's getting so emotional he's beginning to stammer, he's on the edge of losing it. "God damn it I told you: I'm concerned. Why the fuck shouldn't I be concerned! I'm a City Council member, I'm a citizen for Christ's sake! My stepdaughter is—was—a friend of the d-dead girl and she's taking it pretty hard." Lightheaded from the smells and the presence of Death, two dead men he can't get it out of his head *they're somehow breathing, listening.* But why bring in Thalia, asshole.

Wiegler says loudly, it's almost a jeer, "Stepdaughter? *You?*" as if there's something preposterous in this, then goes on, sarcastically, "—What's *she* say? It isn't suicide?" and the two men stare at each other, a long moment, Corky's trying not to lose it seeing his adversary through a pulsing mist, guessing he's making mistakes but not knowing how, why. And it's empty in the morgue now, the attendants have left, just Corky Corcoran and Wolf Wiegler and the corpses amid the rattling ventilators, the promise of more corpses, hidden corpses, in the refrigerated unit to the rear, shelves of corpses, yes but if you can't see you can't know. He's aware too of the tools of Wiegler's trade close by—hacksaws, scalpels, wicked-looking shears, syringes, what looks like a power drill (for boring into skulls?). His gut's giving him such pain he'd be doubled over by it except, Wiegler watching, he can't give in. Can't.

Watch your mouth, Corky's thinking, quick and cunning, for maybe Wiegler does know something about Marilee Plummer's death it isn't in your best interest to be told. Once you know a thing you can't not know it.

Corky shrugs. "She's upset. She's lost a friend."

Wiegler screws up his face so it's meditative, yet still a smirk. "Hell, girls try to kill themselves all the time. Maybe ten percent of the time they succeed. If they don't get fucked they're frustrated and if they *do* get fucked they're disillusioned." He breaks off laughing, giving Corky a nudge in the arm like the two of them are sharing the joke. "We're not like that, eh?— not 'sensitive.'" He laughs again. Corky stares at him in disgust.

Wiegler sobers up some, and says, changing the subject like he's an emcee on a fast-paced talk show, "—Leroy Nickson, man! You been following the case?"

"What?"

"This Nickson case, man. You been following it in the paper, on TV? We got in the *New York Post* yesterday. *I* was the one who did the dog."

Corky blinks slowly. "'Did the dog'—?"

"Opened the fucker up." Wiegler makes a playful yet precise motion with his fingers, like a harpist. He's grinning at Corky and Corky's trying to grin back. "They brought the guy in to headquarters—Nickson—you've seen him, right?—Elvis sideburns, floppy mustache, acting outraged, and his wife's like a zombie—'Where's your baby?' the cops are asking, and he says *he* doesn't know and *she* can't even answer, it's the neighbors who called the cops, for weeks the baby's been crying 'like a banshee' one of them was quoted then suddenly it stops, you got to conclude something happened, right?—except the baby not only stopped crying but disappeared. And there's this German shepherd dog must weigh one hundred pounds, barking all the time big nasty fucker to keep in a two-room apartment—" Wiegler snaps his fingers. "It doesn't take much brains to put two and two together, even the UCPD cops can figure this one out. So—" watching Corky slyly now, and eagerly, seeing the sick look dawning in Corky's face, "—they haul the dog over here in muzzle and restraining harness, and I do the dog. Rambo."

Corky nods. He's showing he follows this, O.K. "You do the dog. Rambo."

"Right. I do Rambo." Wiegler wriggles his shoulders like he's being tickled. This is a story you can tell he's already told many times, though it's new, and will tell many more times through his life. "I stick the fucker and it takes him maybe three minutes to die, Rambo's so tough, then I open him up on this table here, must've been ten cops and guys from the D.A.'s office watching, plus half the staff in this place, forensics, a police photographer, you name it. All we needed was a TV crew. I opened up Rambo's stomach and bowels, which are so crammed they're practically impacted, and out comes Baby Nickson, in coarse chunks. Maybe most guys would need to do lab work to see what it was, *I* didn't, *I* could tell right off. Because it wasn't all that digested. Some was, some wasn't. Nickson broke the skull with a hammer and pounded it flat, in fragments, and broke up the bones pretty well, but it was all there, or just about, an entire human baby. Sort of, you know?—like chop suey. Christ!"

Corky hears this through a buzzing haze. He hears the words but isn't sure he's hearing them. Then he's walking, he's in motion.

"You O.K., man?—Jerome? You're looking a little—"

Turning, in motion, or is he falling, his knees gone and he can't remember how he'd come in, which is the way out, the glaring light of the tall windows shifts and contracts and the ceiling begins to sink and he hears Wiegler's voice raised in mock concern or maybe it's genuine concern but the voice is far away and the floor pitches so suddenly beneath him there's no time to catch hold of anything to stop the fall, he's falling as the wave of nausea rises in him ballooning into his mouth and he's vomiting, helpless choking acid-hot vomiting but he's falling, he's gone, the sharp edge of a metal counter flies up to strike his left temple, Corky Corcoran's *out*.

4

CORKY PLACES A BET

He is being bathed by his mother. A lifetime ago in the house on Barrow Street. Set down gently in the warm soapy water. In a yellow plastic-rubberized baby's bath. In the kitchen, atop the table. It's so cold outside, wind-driven snow, rivulets of ice have formed on the insides of the windows, layers of thickness like gnarled roots. The gas oven is lit, the oven door opened. Waves of radiant heat pour out. Rippling over his baby skin. If he could see his mother's face! Her eyes! But he sees only the hands gently bathing him, squeezing a sponge over his head. He hears a voice, her voice, but he can't hear the words. Or is she singing, a voice and no words. He looks up, she's leaning over him, arms around him, the radiant heat rippling over them both. Her face, her young face, a girl's face, a face of such beauty, the shining eyes, the radiant-rosy skin—he stares, he tries to see, with every fiber of his being he tries to see, but can't.

You made me love you.

Didn't want to do it. Didn't want to do it.

"Fuck."

Corky presses his foot down, hard, on the gas pedal. The Caddy lurches forward. Tires faintly screeching. North on Huron, then over to Ninth, one-way traffic on Ninth going east and out of here.

Corky's in a wild fucking hurry to get out of here. Whether in the best condition for driving or not.

It's 1:20 P.M. He's lost an hour and a half. Where, he doesn't know. Oblivion. How do you vomit on a near-empty stomach?—it's hard.

First the gruel-like substance, tasting of acid and coffee. Then the dry heaves.

Gasping and gagging and choking like an epileptic in a convulsion, but only half-conscious, passing in and out of consciousness.

In the morgue!

And he'd hit his head, asshole might have cracked his skull, never woke up again. So, the first necessary thing, when they revived him and he could sit up, was to crack a joke—"Well, I'm in the right place for *this*." Making them laugh, or what sounded like laughing.

Tasting the vomit now, in his teeth. Rinsing his mouth didn't do it, he'll have to brush his teeth.

Fuck his necktie's stained. Expensive God-damned tie and it's stained. In a fury, while driving, not slackening his speed, racing to make a light, Corky manages to loosen the tie and rip it off and crumple it in his fist and toss it out the window, there it goes flying briefly in the wind and then falling, lost on Ninth Street amid gutter trash.

Can't face the old man now. Just can't.

Shit, he can't. It makes him almost panicked to think of it: driving to Irish Hill, the old streets, passing Barrow Street, that house, the only house of his dreams, then to Roosevelt, and *that* house, the house following his father's death. Maybe he dreams of that house too, but he doesn't want to remember.

Disappointing Uncle Sean, fuck it, can't be helped.

The Irish break your heart, break one another's hearts. It's in the blood. Can't be helped.

Anyway, Corky's more than an hour late, probably the old man gave up on him in disgust. Or maybe thinking, that age, his mind's not what it used to be, he'd got the time wrong, or the day.

An ambulance racing up Ninth—loud frantic siren growing louder, deafening. Everybody pulls over to give it a wide berth except Corky Corcoran who's driving fast too, fuck it *he's* in a hurry too. The ambulance speeds past him, on the right.

Always a wild thumping heartbeat, any siren passes that close.

But Corky keeps on, looking straight ahead. Bloodshot eyes but determined. The fuckers won't get the better of *him*.

Up ahead, on Schoharie, is Bobby Ray's Sports Bar, Corky'd had a pleasant thought of the place earlier, maybe he'll drop in. He's hungry. Thirsty. Dehydrated from losing so much liquid.

A powerful hunger sweeps over him, leaving him shaky. Hasn't eaten yet today, *that's* why he passed out. He's famished.

Must have been crazy, to go to the morgue so impulsively, at such a time. What worries Corky most, though—his overestimation of his own strength.

What the fuck's happening to him?—thinking too he could just walk away from Christina. Slam the door, goodbye, forget.

That last time like he'd been desperate to jam it up inside her wanting to hear her scream, tear her cunt, womb. Stab her to the heart like she'd stabbed him. Almost, he'd expected to see her bright blood glistening on his cock.

But it isn't that easy. He's thinking of Christina all the time. Even when he isn't conscious of it. He feels it, the loss. Shit, he knows. Wanting the woman's arms, her voice. Love. Love of *him*.

Did he dream of her, her holding him, just now?—passed out on the icy floor of the morgue? Vivid as a hallucination, a waking dream, Corky can't remember. Just the force of it, the terrible longing.

You made me love you. Didn't want to do it.

Suddenly Corky's desperate to call Christina Kavanaugh. Tell me I'm still loved, tell me everything's O.K. Don't let me die!

He'd come to, on the floor, not knowing at first where he was, dizzy, flailing his arms, trying to speak. Ammonia fumes piercing his nostrils rising to his brain like white-hot wires. It wasn't the pathologist who was reviving him, crouched over him, but a woman medic Wiegler must have summoned. Happens all the time, visitors to the morgue passing out. One minute all right, the next minute crashing to the floor. No shame to it. They'd tried to prevent Corky from getting up as quickly as he did and walking out, maybe afraid of a lawsuit. Wiegler was looking tense, worried, like he'd gone too far with Corky and Corky would see to it he was made to regret it, maybe lose his job?—did Jerome Corcoran have that much influence with the Mayor?—these thoughts running rapidly through Corky's head even as, smiling, shaking his head, he insisted he was O.K., he was fine, sorry for causing so much commotion. No, he did not want to be taken to the emergency room, no thanks no X rays for him he's late for an appointment.

He'd used a men's room off the lobby, though. Washed his face, rinsed his mouth. Dabbing wetted paper towels against his forehead where he'd banged himself, hoping to keep the swelling down. Wiping at his necktie, getting the worst of the vomit off, he'd thought, and off his coat sleeve, trouser cuffs. Cheap paper towels, standard City issue, cheapest of the cheap, like the single-ply toilet paper too, shredding when wetted. Corky stared at himself bloodshot-eyed Corky Corcoran in the splotched mirror of that dank antiquated men's lavatory, pale freckles like dirty raindrops against his paler skin. That Irish redhead's pallor. Curdled-milk pallor. A scared kid no older than seventeen inside the forty-three-year-old's face staring astonished and appalled at that face.

Is that me? What has happened to me?

Wondering, can you go crazy this way? Is this how it starts? The way a paper towel shreds when wetted, disintegrates? The thin membrane of sanity. The way, at first just alert, attentive, Theresa would glance up, hearing the start of it. The approach.

Corky's thinking it started yesterday, the traffic jam on Brisbane. Smooth sailing and he'd felt terrific on his way to Christina Kavanaugh, then suddenly—stalled. Since then, things are veering out of his control.

Embarrassed remembering how he'd directed traffic, helping out the cop. Basking in the attention, Christ what an asshole, the cop smiled and waved at him when he drove past, "Thanks, Mr. Corcoran!" and Corky's thinking no maybe the smile was a smirk, the thank-you sarcastic. And he'd boasted of this to Christina, and who else, Greenbaum, probably Miriam. All of them humoring him. *What an asshole.*

Corner of Ninth and Schoharie, Bobby Ray's Sports Bar, a popular hangout, Corky's grateful to see it though by day, like all these places, it looks diminished, drab. Fake redwood facade that needs refinishing, those fake windows, the old action-neon sign—jerky black dots in rapid motion, cartoon images of boxing, horse racing, baseball, football. Corky has terrific memories of Bobby Ray's, and Corky has less than terrific memories of Bobby Ray's. You drop $800 one week, pick up $1100 the next week, drop $500 the next, pick up $400 the next, so it goes. The trifecta, $26,500 (untaxed), was Corky's big coup. He'd lost a bundle, a cool $10,000, on the Tyson-Douglas title fight, still can't believe Tyson lost, lost like that. Greatest heavyweight since Ali coldcocked and crawling dazed on the canvas groping for his mouthpiece—a picture it's hard to erase from your mind.

Down at Pearl Street, in Corky's codified ledger, he'd have a detailed lists of bets won/bets lost at Bobby Ray's and he'd guess, if he ever did the calculations, he'd discover he was just about even up. Like his fat Aunt Mildred losing weight, gaining it back, losing weight, gaining it back, a gambler loses, wins, loses, wins, it's what you do, unless you fuck up totally and you're *out*.

Inside Bobby Ray's is near-deserted, only a few customers and no familiar faces in the bar, at least no familiar faces that matter. It's dim-lit, soothing to the eyes, especially bloodshot hungover eyes, Corky feels better already. Gives a quick drink order to the guy tending bar then ducks into the men's room to check the swelling on his forehead. Shit, the size practically of a golf ball, how's he going to disguise it?—his hair's receding at the temple.

In this mirror though Corky looks almost his old self, cocky and handsome. Almost.

Anyway he runs cold water, splashes it on his face. Feels good. Rinses out his mouth as best he can. What a taste, puke!—Corky's read it rots your teeth, too. Sheer acid. These sick females he'd read about in *People*, bulimics, gorging themselves on food like hogs then sticking a finger down their throats to puke it back up, their teeth rot, along with other bodily miseries. Poor bitches: all to be *thin*, and men hate *thin*, that flat-chested look, no more tits than a guy, no hips, shows how unbalanced they are. Corky wonders if Thalia got into that, at Cornell; or if she was strictly anorexic. Bone-thin, ghastly-pale. God-damn attention-getting behavior, but it works. *The evil of the world that's our own shit out there we don't dare acknowledge.* Fuck it, what's a kid like Thalia know about evil? Corky could tell her a thing or two.

Never has trusted her since that anorexic collapse, the hospital at Ithaca, walking in and seeing her. Starving herself, beautiful Thalia, like that crazy Frenchwoman the Jew who converted to Catholicism then repudiated her race, *God grant that I become nothing* Thalia quoted as if in approval and Corky had to bite his tongue to keep from saying what he thought about that kind of sniveling half-assed "mystic" crap.

God's gonna grant you *become nothing* soon enough, sweetheart. No need to pray to the old fart to hurry it along.

Corky checks his watch: 1:33 P.M. Thalia's coming to the house at four, gives him plenty of time. He's sure as hell not going to be late for *her*.

Out in the bar, Corky's ale is waiting for him, Twelve Horse, dark, on tap: first drink of the day and it goes down just fine, that sensation in the mouth, in the throat, rushing into the blood, that reliable shock of pleasure to the system signaling *All's well*. Like coming, almost. That good. Maybe better. The comfort of it, infantile maybe but what the hell. *Mother loves you, here's my breast.*

Corky tastes a second big swallow. Sighs.

Where there's quantum theory, there's hope!

The bartender, Lew, pushing fifty but dressed like a jock in a U.C. Mohawks T-shirt, big beer gut pushing at his belt, calls over to Corky happy to see him, "Hey Corky, podna, how's it going?—haven't seen you in a while," and Corky manages to both smile at the guy and freeze him out simultaneously, it's a trick he's perfected, "Can't complain, Lew, except I've been busy as hell," signaling he's busy now, moving briskly to the rear, to the telephones, with his ale. The last thing Corky wants is to get buttonholed by this guy right now.

Still, he overhears Lew telling somebody at the bar that he's "Corky Corcoran" and it gives him a little stab of satisfaction.

Bobby Ray's is one of Corky's cherished *places*. His reputation's known here and he's liked for who he is as a person not just the fact he's a generous guy, lavish tipper in the right mood. Bobby Ray Deck, the old man, goes back to Tim Corcoran's day, every time he sees Corky he has to shake his hand, gaze into Corky's eyes, ask how are you, son. And the mute message between them, not even words but a feeling distinct as an electric shock: *He's dead. Dead?*

Fuck it, now's not the time. If Corky sights the old man he'll avoid him.

Corky drinks his ale standing making telephone calls. The first one's to Sean Corcoran—"Christ, Uncle Sean, I'm sorry as hell, but I've gotten tied up—how's about tomorrow? O.K.? I'll check at Holy Redeemer, see how Aunt Mary Megan is—if she's well enough to see visitors—" and what can the poor old guy do but go along with it, this isn't the first time his nephew's let him down, and won't be the last, but so be it. Corky hangs up feeling both exhilarated and like a shit, recalls the last time Lois spoke with him nagging him about not visiting, my father isn't going to live forever, Corky, you know he loves you, Corky, and Corky shrugs, guilty, annoyed, these damn cunts twisting your balls in the name of "love" like they've appropriated the word, you don't "love" enough like it's your duty you're falling short of, well fuck that. He'll get down to Roosevelt Street tomorrow, or he won't.

Corky's second call, though, is a different matter. For this, he needs a second glass of ale.

Punching the numerals for Christina's Nott Street place *Hey Chrissie: I'm sorry, you know I love you* though guessing she won't be there, not on a Saturday afternoon *Christina?—Jesus, I'm sorry. You know I love you I'd never want to hurt you* hearing the phone ringing and seeing the sunlight through the rear windows, the bare smooth floorboards and the rug they'd made love on so many times *Christina, it's me, I made a mistake, can I see you, how soon can I see you* each time like the first but Corky'd never had a thought it might be the last *Chrissie my God I'm sorry sorry sorry* what a relief in knowing she isn't there. Won't answer.

Corky hangs up, hard.

Anyone observing him sees an angry man.

A minute or so recovering, before he tries Christina's home. He's sweating. Shivering. Running his tongue rapidly back and forth across his saw-notched front tooth. A nervous habit, he's not aware of, exactly. *Christina?—it's Corky, we need to talk. I'm sorry for* but *is* he sorry, isn't she the one to make the first move, didn't she betray *him*? Corky hasn't memorized Christina's home number, never calls her at home, has to look it up in his pocket address book, *Kavanaugh*, what if Harry answers, what then? *Harry this is Jerome Corcoran you know who this is, don't you?* punching the numerals and hearing the phone ring at the other end and his panic's growing what in Christ is he going to say? to her, if she answers? to *him*, if he answers? there are simply no words, no words. When Corky hears the phone being answered, not an answering machine but a living presence at the other end of the line, he quickly hangs up.

Shit, he *is* shaking. Which means he must love her. Which means she's got her hooks in him deep.

"Fuck it."

Corky's quarter drops clattering into the coin return.

This next call makes him anxious too, but eager, hopeful as a kid. Like receiving a test booklet back in high school, math, physics, chemistry where answers have to be precise and no bullshitting and you know you haven't done well, you've fucked up but still there's that stab of hope, almost a sick ecstasy of hope, the priest calling his name and *Jerome Corcoran* coming forward, taking the bluebook from the priest's hand and even now not daring to look at the red-scrawled numeral that's his fate. Because as long as you don't know for sure, there's hope.

It's Howard Greenbaum Corky's calling, the second person after Christina he'd yearned to speak with when he came to at the morgue, recalling now too he'd had a panicky dream during the night of losing all his money and his property was to be sold for taxes, which could happen, Jesus couldn't it! Calling Greenbaum at home, never has called Greenbaum at home before, maybe a mistake but Corky's in no condition to care about etiquette right now, "Yes? Hello?" Greenbaum answers in a voice so vibrant and youthful Corky thinks he's got the wrong party, but when Corky identifies himself yes it's Greenbaum, Greenbaum's voice drops, perceptible disappointment, the poor guy's been hoping to hear from someone else, a friend, a relative, someone he *likes*. Corky can't care about such niceties now, he's too anxious. Asking Greenbaum more questions about the IRS suit, will they demand interest? will they fine him? could he go to jail?—"I was only following my accountant's advice, you know that, Howard!" Greenbaum repeats what he said the day before at lunch, reassures Corky, the worst that can happen is he'll have to pay the federal government $400,000 and Corky laughs incredulously, "The worst! For Christ's sake, Howard, that *is* the worst!" and Greenbaum tries to calm him explaining they can appeal the judgment and in time they'll win, maybe three years, they should win, and Corky laughs louder, "By then I'll be a pauper! I'll be *dead!*" lurching on to speculate how he might lose everything, all the years building up Corcoran, Inc., and he might go under, this deep recession the shit-faced Republicans have led us into, should he dump some property at a loss and take a write-off? should he acquire some property (he's got one or two in mind, in Union City) and hope to hell the economy improves? a Democrat in the White House by January 1993? and Greenbaum interrupts patient and sympathetic-seeming suggesting why not sit tight for the time being and Corky half-screams, "Sit tight! I'm going crazy, Howard! I'm *drowning!*" desperate to keep the Jew-genius money man on the phone talking rapidly and not entirely coherently even hinting at one point, he'll remember this afterward with keen embarrassment, maybe he could drop by Howard's place? this afternoon? now? to go over some accounts? it's an emergency it can't wait until next week but Greenbaum discreetly blocks this saying he has family obligations today and tomorrow, a bar mitzvah to attend, his nephew's son, and Corky pauses to ask what's a bar mitzvah exactly, he's always wondered, is it like confirmation in the Catholic Church, and Greenbaum explains patient and sympathetic-seeming but Corky isn't listening, Corky's sweating thinking of how in 1982 the IRS launched an audit on Ross Drummond Realty & Insurance, Inc., and the old man hired the best tax lawyers in New York City and ended up paying both the lawyers and the IRS, Christ was it $2 million?—and that was a victory in the old man's eyes. *A victory!* Corky interrupts Greenbaum to speak of this at some length, dropping quarters in the coin slot, in the background in the bar a TV blaring and guys talking and laughing loudly one of them with a hee-haw laugh and Corky sweating and shivering wonders *is* he going crazy, *is* he drowning, and Greenbaum asks cautiously, "Is there something wrong, Jerome?—something personal?" and Corky laughs despairingly, "Call me, 'Corky,' Howard, I've asked you," and Greenbaum murmurs, not very convincingly, "'Corky,'" and Corky goes on to say, "No there's nothing wrong with me personally, what the fuck could be wrong with me personally!—a man doesn't have any *personal life* left to him in this country!—the tax laws, and the interest rates, and this latest catastrophe we discussed yesterday, Bender going under, Viquinex that was supposed to be such a terrific investment—" praying Greenbaum will take the ball and run with it, all Corky wants in his desperation is to be talked to by this superior human being with so many facts at his fingertips, mastery of the shifting miasma of economics and the wisdom of centuries, *Judaism seems always to have focused upon ethics* and thank God for that not like Catholics scared as hell about saving their own individual asses, thank God Greenbaum takes his cue and explains to Corky for possibly the tenth time the financial situation he's in with his limited partnership investments, the technicalities of the "roll-up" and the advantages of the new reconstituted partnership and of being listed on the American Stock Exchange—"And it's to be managed by Hallwood, a merchant bank—" "—solid as the Rock of Gibraltar," Corky finishes for him.

By this time, Greenbaum's soothing intelligent matter-of-fact voice in his ear for how many minutes, Corky's feeling much better. He's finished his second ale, which has steadied his nerves. He guesses things might not be so bad after all. He's hungry.

Thanks Greenbaum and reiterates he'll have his secretary make an appointment for next week sometime, wishes Greenbaum a happy Memorial Day weekend and "bar mitzah" which even as he pronounces, his tongue clumsy, he suspects he's gotten wrong, but Howard Greenbaum's too much the gentleman to correct him.

In the sports lounge, which is nearly empty except for two other parties, Corky devours a juicy part-raw ten-ounce Bobby Ray's Sportsburger (with melted blue cheese, pimentos, peppers, anchovies, mushrooms, onions, salsa sauce so hot it brings tears to his eyes) on a crusty sesame-seed roll the size of a heavyweight's fist. Always at Bobby Ray's Corky orders the Sportsburger and always it's delicious, chewing and swallowing such food you know why you were born, no fucking mystery to it. And a generous portion of crinkle-fries, a cross between French fries and potato chips but served hot, greasy salty and hot. And seeing Corky's finished his crinkle-fries before his burger, the waitress in her U.C. Mohawks T-shirt and matching baseball cap and snug-fitting miniskirt brings him, unasked, a side dish of more. And another tall glass of Twelve Horse Ale foaming from the tap.

Corky eats and drinks with such appetite, he can't keep from smiling. Obviously he'd passed out at the morgue because he was famished. In a state of nerves. Can't even remember what that cruel bastard Wiegler was talking about when, for Corky, the floor fell away.

In the bar, on TV, there's a Detroit Tigers–Toronto Blue Jays game out of Detroit, in the sports lounge, on the five giant TV screens, there's live coverage of a golfing tournament in California, a replay of a boxing match, a replay of a track meet, live coverage of a Mets game, ceaseless CNN programming. The sports lounge is a large sunken space with green-marble-Formica tables and deep-cushioned chairs, as in a slightly tatty hotel lobby; the main attraction is the wall of silent TV screens but the other walls, windowless, are crowded with posters of bygone sports events, autographed photos of bygone sports heroes, and a panel of framed photos of the U.C. Mohawks in their baseball regalia over the decades, from the team's inaugural year, 1949, to last year, 1991. Corky's followed the home team since grade school and recalls certain of his old passions with both embarrassment and yearning. In Union City there's the saying, What're the Mohawks for except to let you down?—which is maybe unfair, the team isn't bad, just unpredictable. Finished last season about dead in the middle of the American League East; this season, they've started off strong, which can't last. If they make it to the playoffs it will be the first time in six years and Corky doubts they'll make it. Anyway, what *is* a team these days? It used to be, a player stayed with a team through his career; now, he makes a few mistakes, gets injured, shows the first symptoms of aging, his batting average down and he's traded off and somebody new brought in. Not to mention the hot-shit superstars. The teams are just commercial products, why not admit it.

Still, Corky's a sucker if things get hot. Last year's playoffs and World Series he dropped more than he made, in a frenzy of betting both at home and via a connection in Las Vegas. Wound up $4300 in the hole so this year he's going to be more cautious.

Corky finishes his lunch staring at the giant TV screens. When there's no sound, human activity looks weird, purposeless. The boxing match ends with one black guy's arm being raised by the referee (who's wearing clinical-looking rubber gloves—sports in the age of AIDS) while the other black guy, bleeding from an eye, nose, mouth, is helped shakily to his feet by his handlers. Then a slow dissolve to harness racing at Belmont: Prairie Flower, Blue Vesa, Orion in first, second, third. The golf tournament continues in slow time with cuts to commentators yammering so seriously you'd think it was a World Summit meeting, Corky's grateful he can't hear those assholes, hates golf, tried it for a while under the tutelage of old man Drummond the strategy being to make important contacts at the U.C. Golf Club but fuck it it wasn't worth it, glad-handing pompous old farts, nor was Corky Corcoran much good swinging a club, admit it. Corky's craving for sports is a craving out of boyhood, a hunger for those shared moments, memories, bound up with certain of his old friends from the neighborhood Nick Daugherty, his cousin Cormac, the McGuirt brothers, later in high school Vic Slattery and his friends. The boxing team, the track team, swimming—for Corky, ways of being with his friends. *Never so happy as then. You know it.*

The track meet has ended and is replaced by, what is it?—a dogsled-ding competition in the Yukon? Fierce blue sky, blinding-white snow, yapping huskies Corky's grateful he can't hear. On the screen the Mets continue—slow time, too—against the Phillies—mediocre baseball on both sides. Corky used to follow the Mets closely but since winning the Series they've gone to hell, just another boring team, new faces and names Corky can't keep track of. On the CNN screen there's a cut from Bush grinning and waving fatuously to some Republican crowd to what looks like a desert encampment, close-ups of, Jesus, skeletal black children with swollen bellies and heads that look distended, like bulbs. Corky, chewing crinkle-fries, looks quickly away.

So, the world's unjust, there's terrible suffering, so who can help it.

What the fuck, a man's hungry he's got to eat.

Something to make you tie your God-damned shoes morning after morning.

Our own shit out there, our evil, we can't acknowledge.

"Another ale, Mr. Corcoran?"

Corky nods yes, sure—"Only call me 'Corky,' eh?"

Quick meant-to-dazzle smile, dimpled plump cheek, not a girl any lon-ger but girlish in her ways, kittenish, cute. *Playboy*-standard breasts in that T-shirt and Corky eyes her like he's interested or would be if he was free, or had the time, or circumstances were different.

"'Cor*ky*.'"

And moving away she swivels her hips for Corky, moves her ass, a generous-sized ass, tosses her streaked brown hair that's artful snags and snarls. High-heeled white boots, metallic-wet-looking stockings. Fatty knees. Thick calves, thighs. And those tits. Not Corky's type exactly but in a pinch, any type will do.

Sharing that pig-snout Polack girl with Vic, Buddy, Heinz, after one of the St. Thomas dances, when they'd taken their good-girl dates home and got together drunk and horny as hell and Vic was the shyest one worried about "ven-er-eal disease" and *he*, Corky, was the one with the experi-ence, boasting he'd been fucking pigs like that since seventh grade. More like ninth grade but who's to know.

Corky steals a glance back at the CNN screen but it's still famine in Africa, a Caucasian Red Cross officer on TV stooping over a hospital bed in which an adult skeletal black figure lies *but is speaking, moving a stick arm*. Corky swallows hard trying to concentrate on the Phillies pitcher winding up teasing-slow but the God-damned CNN screen is distracting so finally Corky cursing to himself jerks his chair at an angle so he doesn't have to look. Doesn't have to see.

"Hey, Corky? C'mon in!"

Corky should get the hell out of Bobby Ray's and drive home, Corky *should not* join these guys at the bar for still another ale, sees by his watch it's 2:48 P.M. and Christ knows he doesn't want Thalia to suspect he's been drinking this early in the day, Thalia with her bloodhound nostrils capable of detecting a beery belch at one hundred yards. Surely *should not*—but one more can't hurt.

The bar's more crowded now, an affable noisy gang of guys watching the Tigers-Jays game on TV, Corky takes up a position beside Artie Fleischman whom he knows, not well, just to say hello, Fleischman's a UCPD officer, lieutenant in the Fifth Precinct, off duty at the moment in khaki trousers, red-plaid shirt and white T-shirt beneath. Big guy in his forties, heavy jaws, pouchy eyes, easygoing manner, or tries to give that impression, like Budd Yeager. A lot like Budd Yeager.

Strange: Corky's had an overnight thought about Yeager, since yesterday, something about the way Yeager came up to him, clapped his hand on Corky's shoulder, never so friendly to Corky before, never so *interested* in Corky before, those cold eyes crinkled at the corners and the mouth meant for a smile, slipping Corky nine hundred-dollar bills like it's a love note when, Corky's sure, the debt wasn't that much. What's it got to do, Corky wonders, with Marilee Plummer?—anything? Or with Corky showing up at Plummer's place just as the ambulance moved off? For sure, Beck reported him. And Yeager's onto that.

Or is it a coincidence, maybe.

It *is* a coincidence Corky's here at Bobby Ray's, talking and laughing with these guys, Artie Fleischman who's as friendly as you'd want, for a guy essentially a bastard, who knows how many heads he's bashed or men he's shot *faced with what he believes to be deadly physical force* as the cop handbook phrases it. At the inning break there's some "flash-bulletin" local news: live TV coverage of Marcus Steadman's "reputed retreat" in Shehawkin where the City Councilman-evangelical preacher-indicted rapist is believed to be hiding out from the media. A blond female reporter with hyperthyroid eyes is speaking excitedly to the camera, there are quick bold cuts to a small woodframe bungalow in a tidy lot and cryptic close-ups, as in a suspense movie, of shut doors, windows with drawn blinds. Is Steadman really inside? Trapped, hiding? Like a beast tracked to his lair? Like a guilty man? *Refusing to show his face to WSUC-TV's crew?*

Along the horseshoe bar a dozen or so men are muttering in righteous disgust, anger, impatience, and Corky among them, sentiment's as solidly against Steadman as if he'd killed Marilee Plummer outright, or maybe their fury at the black man has little to do with Plummer, maybe it's just a righteous sort of fury, the kind of fury that makes you feel good, you're with your buddies and this is how your buddies feel, everybody at Bobby Ray's is white, and male. And when a film clip comes on of Steadman addressing the demonstrators on Thursday evening, on the courthouse steps, the muttering gets louder, nastier—"Nigger prick!" "Black motherfucker!" Corky's seen this footage before, he's heard parts of the speech, Marcus Steadman waving his arms before a crowd of his supporters protesting the Rodney King verdict and the Pickett-Johnson incident, the tall black-skinned Steadman with his extraordinary preacher's voice, big-eyed, mad-eyed, fully in control of the crowd of demonstrators all of whom are black, *Where's justice? where's black justice? where's* our *justice?* and the demonstrators crying *Yes!* and *Say it brother!* Wave upon wave of voices, keening and wailing and ecstatic, and Steadman looming over them, an ugly bulldog of a man, his face gleaming-oily with sweat, *Rise up O my brothers! O my sisters! Where is* our *justice?*

None of this is new to Corky. Corky knows it practically by heart, it's been recycled over the airwaves so much. But this time Corky's moved by what he hears. Steadman's words, and the crowd's response. Corky's thinking suddenly, Christ what if *he* was black, and hearing Marcus Steadman like this? How'd he feel then?

Thinking too, maybe skin color *is* real, a category like a separate species. Being black, yes being a nigger, if that's what you must be in others' eyes, in whites' eyes. If that's the price you pay for knowing who you are and who you aren't.

Artie Fleischman jabs Corky in the arm, vehement, grinning, "You know what I'd like to do?—rip off that spade fucker's prick and stuff it down his throat."

Corky makes a grunting noncommittal noise. Maybe yes maybe no.

Returning then to the live coverage in Shehawkin, about ten miles away. The blond reporter's wide eyes and quickened voice, WSUC-TV's "flash SWAT team" peeking at the bungalow deeded in the name of Marcus Steadman's stepmother, more close-ups of blank blind windows, isn't this trespassing, Corky wonders, harassment?—wouldn't blame whoever's inside if he went berserk and fired a shotgun at the asshole film crew. All the guys at the bar, though, including Lew the bartender, are fascinated by it, really into it. *Fuck Steadman, fuck the nigger!* All you'd need is a firebomb to toss through one of those windows.

Artie Fleischman isn't the only off-duty cop here, Corky recognizes two or three others. Bobby Ray's is a white cops' hangout which is part of its appeal.

Corky shifts his shoulders uneasily. Takes a big swallow of his ale. He can't help but wonder what it's like to *be* Steadman right now—hiding out in that house. All the talk in Union City about Marilee Plummer, and Steadman to blame. If she'd been a white woman, and if this were a few decades ago, the guy might be lynched by now.

The local news bulletin ends abruptly, fading to an ad for Miller Lite, an ad for the Dodge Caravan Mini-Van, back then to Tiger Stadium where it's the top of the third, the Toronto team up to bat and Corky tries to concentrate but he's rattled, hot in the face, thinking he should get the hell home. All his life he's been a guy in the wrong place and running late. Starts out with all the time in the world then fuck it he's running late. If he gets home in time he can shower, change his clothes, sober up some before Thalia arrives. Did she say four o'clock or four-thirty? Can't fuck up, this is going to be a crucial meeting. God knows what Thalia will ask of him. Or take without asking.

Should call the van Burens, too. Hand them some plausible excuse for last night.

What you don't want to do is get on Andy van B's notorious shit list.

As bad, or almost, as getting on Oscar Slattery's.

Corky knows he should leave Bobby Ray's . . . but he's drawn into the game, hard to resist. The mood in the bar, how Corky loves bars, and the companionship of guys like these, hard to resist. And they like him, and he likes that. Loud-laughing, profane. Dirty jokes. Corky Corcoran buys everybody at the bar a drink reciting the old Irish toast in an Irish-inflected voice—"'May the road rise up to meet you, may the wind be always at your back, may the sunshine be warm on your face, and may you be safe in Heaven before the Devil knows you're dead'"—and the guys love it, and applaud. Irish blarney, Irish bullshit, Corky's a sucker for it, too. And somebody else, infected by Corky's mood, buys another round. And so it goes.

Corky likes to think he's the kind of good-hearted guy, he inspires generosity in others. Right?

They said that of Tim Corcoran, too. But his brother Sean—tightfisted.

Corky's eating stale pistachios out of a bowl shared with Artie Fleischman and another cop, they've been trading wisecracks, baseball history, what they know, or think they know, when Dave Winfield steps up to bat. Winfield! Corky's heart trips absurdly, he wants Winfield to do well. Like he, Corky, has to prove something to his friends.

The guys along the bar, plus Lew, are hostile to Winfield, which pisses Corky who's been following his career for a long time, what seems like most of his own adult life. You got to admire these veterans of the game sticking with it when they're traded off, the shit Winfield took as a Yankee, from Steinbrenner, the guy's a hero for Christ's sake, both legs scarred from injuries in the game, a bad back, also he's black and that can't be easy even today. Also he's forty-one years old in what's basically a kid's game. "Here's my man! Here we go! Stand back!" says Corky with cheerful belligerence, knowing sentiment's strong against Winfield, against the Toronto team. His drinking buddies are silent, sullen. The pitcher's a twenty-four-year-old blond kid named Gary Redmon who'd passed through the Mohawks swiftly on his way up two seasons ago so there's strong local sentiment for him, the white kid with Elvis-style sideburns, smirky mouth, good-looking and on the spot pitching to Dave Winfield about whom there's such an aura, so much history. Corky's friends stand silent and tense not even drinking as Redmon makes a show of playing it cool but he's rattled pitching one, then two, balls, one lucky strike and then on Redmon's fourth pitch there's a *crack!*—Winfield connects with the ball and it's a high-arcing fly out into center field and into the stadium, a home run: Winfield rounding the bases smiling and easy, big guy, muscular, solid in the gut and probably feeling back pain but you'd never know; too classy to show what he's feeling except, now his teammates are giving him the high five, grinning at him, he's naturally feeling good and since there were two men on base the game's now tipped solidly toward the Jays, six runs to Detroit's two. Corky's excited and gleeful as a kid, pounding the bar as Winfield trots home. Certain of the other patrons are muttering cursing Winfield, the usual racist names so Corky says, more pleading than angry, "Look, Christ, the guy's *good*, and at his age, practically my age for fuck's sake," meaning to raise a laugh but nobody laughs, nor even acknowledges Corky's remark. Everybody's tense watching the TV and no joking, Corky sees Artie Fleischman's close-set glinting eyes fixed like a snake's and can't resist goading him when Redmon throws four balls in a row and walks the next batter, really fucking up now and the Detroit fans booing, and now comes some young Canadian new to the Toronto team and connects with the first throw a line drive deep into right field so the guy on first slides home and the batter makes it to second and Corky's laughing and pounding the bar sending the pistachio shells flying, really into it now though the others along the bar are mostly silent, sullen.

"Shit! That's baseball," Corky says, hugely delighted. "The Mo's"— meaning Mohawks—"should be half so good."

One of the off-duty cops says sourly, "Since when are you such a Canuck-lover, Corcoran?" and his companion mutters sneeringly something about "sucking black cock" which Corky hears, so he says, excited, "Yeah?—fuck you, assholes, you can't recognize a great athlete, Winfield's a great athlete I don't care what color," and Artie Fleischman says quick and hot, "Shit, that old spook won't last the season," and Corky says, "Watch your mouth, Fleischman, everybody here isn't a racist," and Fleischman says, "'Nigger,' then,—that old 'nigger' won't last the season I bet you money," and Corky says quick and hot too, "Yeah?—you do? Put your money where your mouth is," reaching for his wallet in that way he has like he's reaching for a pistol, knows the gesture will sober Fleischman and it does, Fleischman backs down muttering, "—The Jays will fuck up before the season's over, I'll bet on *that*," making a clumsy swaggering show of reaching for his wallet, "—like they fucked up last year, and before that, asshole Canucks," and Corky leaps in, "Like hell! Give me odds, five to one, the Blue Jays will win the fucking pennant in October!"

There's a pause, a beat or two, everybody staring at Corky and Fleischman, the lieutenant's at a disadvantage saying, stumbling, "—Why not the Series, Corcoran?—if you're gonna shoot off your mouth," and Corky's tempted to say yes, why not, the Series, why not, for the sake of seeing the looks on these assholes' faces wondering if Corky Corcoran has insider baseball dope unavailable to hicks like themselves, he's got connections with the Vegas casinos doesn't he, practically a professional gambler? But Corky's not going to be suckered into that. Saying instead, "Maybe the Series, but for sure the pennant: want to bet?" that delicious shiver rippling like an echo of the very words *want to bet*? like *want to make love?—want to fuck?*—Corky Corcoran standing toe to toe at the bar with Lieutenant Fleischman who's at least three inches taller than he is and thirty pounds heavier and who does in fact pack a pistol inside his coat, all off-duty cops carry their guns, Corky just now caught a glimpse of Fleischman's but Corky's no less arrogant, pushy, he's enjoying this, the others guys watching and Fleischman's baffled as a bull beset by a bulldog not knowing which way to jump. A man's instinct is to accept any challenge but Corky's bet is so off-the-wall, so unexpected, making such a bet in May when the teams are just getting started, God knows what the lineup will be by October—the Jays could be in first place, or last. Fleischman says doubtfully, "Are you serious?" and Corky says, "If you know me, you know I'm always serious." It takes Corky ten minutes of explaining, cajoling, working out odds on a paper napkin, before Fleischman sees a good thing here, or thinks he does, and agrees to the bet.

Corky's a little feverish saying he's on the Canadians' side because a mick is a kind of Canuck, right?—"You expect him to be a loser, you're surprised when he's a winner."

It isn't the actual money that excites, it's the premise, the logic. What to skeptical eyes looks like illogic. A sexy feeling too deep in the groin though sometimes Corky's blood pumps so hard he's fearful of some kind of attack but fuck that, he's flying high: pushing a racist prick like Fleischman into a corner, he can't escape without losing face.

Women as different and as little known to each other as Corky's Aunt Frances and his ex-wife Charlotte have teasingly chided him for gambling because he wants to lose because he wants his gambling friends to like him but, fuck it, that's not so, and today's bet with Artie Fleischman proves it: Corky's a gambler because he can't just haul off and punch certain bastards in the gut the way they deserve.

Corky's in for $1000 against Fleischman's $4000, he's had to reduce the odds in Fleischman's favor but it's worth it. Grinning and hot-faced then the men shake hands—"It's a deal!"—hard bone-crunching handshake, Fleischman's fingers like fleshy steel and Corky has all he can do to keep from wincing. But he's feeling God-damned good, best he's felt in the past twenty-four hours.

Since Christina Kavanaugh kicked him in the balls.

Corky's and Artie's bet is so unusual, it's like a strange-shaped object you want to examine from all sides. The other guys are drawn in, too, all of them on Artie's side, that's where the odds are, and Corky's stuck his neck out now—hasn't he? So the others get in on it and Corky accepts their bets too, chicken feed at $400 a crack; except the cop who made the remark about sucking black cock announces he'll bet Corky $8000 to Corky's $2000—and Corky doesn't miss a beat or blink an eyelash, saying, "It's a deal!"

Calculating he's risking a total of $6000 if the Jays lose, chump change for Corky, but if they win he'll clear a cool $24,000 *and he knows they're going to win.*

By this time it's 4:10 P.M. and Corky's so roused up he's almost forgotten he's supposed to be home by 4:30 when Thalia's due. He's so distracted he's scarcely taking in the TV game where now the Tigers are at bat, somebody's just connected and hit a line drive, there's a swift sure throw to first and the runner's out and the score's still 6 to 2, Jays ahead. "Another ale, Corky?" asks Lew and Corky's not hearing staring at the screen as Tiger Stadium fades to a Marlboro ad like one dream fading to another and beyond that there's still another, you'll never come to the end of it.

Scared cards can't win, a scared man can't love—which doesn't apply to Corky Corcoran, that's for fucking sure.

5

STEPDAUGHTER

*Y*ou're *not my father, why keep up the pretense.*
Bullshit, you don't love me. I sure as hell don't love you.
But I do. And you do, too. What can't be forgotten, only betrayed.

He'd gone to see her and she'd practically shut the door in his face. Eleventh-floor apartment in the Dominion Towers which he was never to see, never invited inside, that evening as a blizzard came roaring down from Canada pitch black at six P.M. he'd risked getting stuck and having to pay a tow truck for the privilege of being turned away from her door glimpsing over her shoulder a man's figure shadowy, blurred; whether Caucasian, black, or other—he couldn't tell. She'd seemed frightened seeing him. The anger in his face. Corky some other time, this isn't a good time, O.K.?—I'm sorry it just isn't a good time.

He'd hired two goons to beat the shit out of this guy who'd been stalking her, and it worked. Not that Thalia knew, or guessed—not that *he* knew. Crazy as she is, her sense of morality, she might've called the police on step-Daddy, get him booked for aggravated assault.

Yes but I'd do it again. Sure.

It's a risk but worth it. To protect her.

Corky's approaching 33 Summit Avenue south of the park, five-bedroom Georgian Colonial he's stuck with since his divorce. The house his wife had to have, on the market at $320,000 (in the mid-1970s) but sold at $285,000. Pawpaw Drummond's realtor expertise not to mention the old bastard's interest-free loan of a cool $100,000 and his help in getting the newlyweds a thirty-year mortgage.

Thirty-year mortgage!—what a noose Corky'd stuck his head into.

Not knowing he'd be able to pay it off in eight years, determined to get out from under the debt.

Out from under his father-in-law's boot, too. Only not quite so quickly.

33 Summit Avenue is two and a half miles south of 8 Schuyler Place. Both addresses are in Maiden Vale, but Corky's house faces Summit Park, the largest park in Union City, acres of hilly wooded grassy land, the neo-classical marble temple that's the Union City Museum of Fine Arts, the County Historical Museum, the prestigious Annandale Foundation for Medical Research, a number of landmark mansions some of which are no longer private homes but schools, headquarters for charities, clinics. Corky Corcoran's house is one of the smaller houses along the park but it's classy, eyecatching—the brick's the real thing, faded-rose, beautiful, over a hundred years old not the sleek modern kind. A spectacular facade with a half-circle portico, four slender white columns, white shutters on the eight latticed windows. Slate roof. Circle drive. Three-acre lot, prime property in Maiden Vale. Juniper pine, plane trees, Russian olive. That gorgeous hedge of blooming lilac. If Tim and Theresa could see, they'd be proud of him. Jerome did O.K. after all.

Of course, upkeep on the property isn't cheap. Nor taxes. Nor insurance. Waking sometimes sweating in a dream of adding up columns of figures with his pocket calculator melting in his hand like a limp prick. Dizzying columns of figures rising out of sight, endless. But telling himself it's worth the price.

When Corky arrives at the house it's already 4:40 P.M. and he's anxious he might have missed Thalia, no car in the drive and no sign of her as he lets himself in the back hearing the telephone ringing cursing and stumbling to get to the phone but, fuck it, just as he lifts the receiver there's a click. Whoever the caller was, he or she isn't leaving a message.

Corky's on his way upstairs when the phone rings again and he answers it (in the kitchen: staring out into the back, the deep sloping lawn, ten-foot lilac hedge and poplars at the rear like something in a French painting so beautiful Corky still wonders, *I live here? I own this?* even if he has trouble breathing sometimes) and it's a neighbor, one of Jerome A. Corcoran's constituents in the Eleventh District who'd prefer no doubt a Republican Councilman except nobody with such credentials not a certifiable nut seems to want to run against the incumbent, the name's just familiar enough to Corky's practiced ear so he can fake it, Hello Gordon, good to hear from you, sure I remember you, how *are* you, and how's the family?—and the rich old fart is on the blower for the next ten minutes complaining indignantly about the trash pickup on his street, trucks barreling by as early as 7:30 A.M. Wednesdays and Saturdays the purpose of which is to wake the residents, purely for spite these Negroes clanging and clattering and shouting at one another, yes and laughing too, and they make it a point to leave bits of debris in everybody's lawns purely for spite, Gordon's certain, Gordon's damned certain, and what is Jerome Corcoran going to do about it? so Corky says politely he'll call the superintendent of the Sanitation Department on Tuesday and complain and he'll bring the subject up at the next council meeting which is Thursday, yes it *is* a problem though maybe not so bad as in other parts of the city where trash pickup is only once a week or not at all but thank you Gordon, very good to hear from you, and hanging up Corky slams the receiver down screaming "Fuck you you shit-eating old asshole calling me at home on Saturday you motherfucker!" in a rage clearing the kitchen counter of whatever's there including the gleaming chrome three-slice toaster tumbling and crashing to the floor amid a deafening crash and a spillage of desiccated crumbs.

Now Corky's waiting for Thalia whom maybe he's missed. Jesus he's sick at heart, worried he's missed her.

Switches on a TV flicking rapidly through the channels, how many channels, thirty? forty?—the more channels the less there's to see, or anyway the less time you have for each, Corky often flicks the remote control so fast the TV picture's hardly more than a blur as if he's speeding past, breathless. No baseball game, must be over. No, here's one but not the one he'd been watching at Bobby Ray's, looks like Cincinnati but Corky's too restless to watch. He's beginning to regret his bets on the Blue Jays, now the excitement's dimmed down and he's left wondering why, sheer impulse, completely fabricated odds, and so early in the season. In May, for Christ's sake! And on Toronto! The last three times the Blue Jays got to the playoffs they screwed up, everybody knows they're jinxed. Dave

Winfield or not. *Nigger-lover. Suck.* And this year, with Corky's luck probably the team won't even make it to the playoffs.

A couple of years ago, dropping $10,000 on Mike Tyson. Not to be believed. Tyson on his knees on the canvas dazed groping for his mouthpiece trying to pick it up with his gloved hand. Not to be believed but there it was.

Corky's feeling anxious hears something outside, yes but it's just a car in the street, forgets the TV going to the front of the house to check his mail, mainly bills, flyers, throwaways including a Neiman-Marcus catalog addressed to Mrs. Charlotte Corcoran. An actual personal letter *but it isn't Christina: couldn't be* postmarked Washington, D.C., from Corky's nephew Rickie Payne. One of the kid's dashed-off word-processor notes bringing Uncle Jerome up to date on his latest news, or lack of it—*Looks like I won't get any summer employment but not for want of trying, I sent out 55 letters!* Corky helped send Rickie to St. Bonaventure's, now to Georgetown Law figuring he owes it to the family, always an obscure guilt about the family, not that the family gives a shit about *him.* And the younger people, Rickie's generation, with their college degrees looking down on Corky Corcoran who never went. One semester at Rensselaer Polytechnic, to hear him talk about it you'd think it was MIT and he'd gone four years.

What's Rickie hinting at in this letter? Can't get summer employment in a law firm, so he'll need a summer stipend? Wouldn't you know it, a Corcoran finally goes to law school and nobody wants lawyers, there's a glut on the market.

Well, Rickie can go fuck. Get a job at McDonald's, or parking cars. See what the world's like.

No son of your own, the least you can do is send Rickie to law school. Also Angie to nursing school in Syracuse, Pete's kid Frankie to Fresno State. Sure.

Upstairs in the room that's Corky's private at-home office, off-limits even to Mrs. Krauss, thus never cleaned, Corky makes a few calls including a call to the Slatterys' (where he's due for drinks at 6 P.M., it's 5:10 P.M. now) explaining to Sandra his circumstances: there's a possibility that Thalia is going to come by, he hasn't seen her in some time, doesn't want to miss her. So maybe they should postpone drinks for another time? Sandra Slattery sounds disappointed, which is flattering as hell—"But, Corky, we do want to see you! Vic was saying how he misses you. If Thalia doesn't come, or doesn't stay very long, why don't you come out here for dinner? Just us, just family. Will you?"

Corky Corcoran feels his very groin stir. Family dinner with Vic and Sandra Slattery!

Saying, "Well, O.K. Yes, thanks. If I can. Sure. What time?"

"Around seven-thirty. And if you can't make dinner, drop by afterward. Just give us a call, will you? Monday evening will be a madhouse scene, we won't really have a chance to visit then."

Corky hangs up smiling, can't remember when Vic and Sandra last invited him for an intimate dinner, not since Vic's first term in Congress. When Corky sees his friends, it's usually in a context of other people. Lots of other people.

Something you don't want to think about: how friendships are like love affairs, marriage itself. Always one party's deeper into it, more dependent upon the other. More jealous. As Corky's been with Vic Slattery since the age of fifteen, his first weeks at St. Thomas watching the big good-looking blond boy secretly, taking every opportunity to talk to him, get next to him in the cafeteria line, in gym class. No accident that Vic's last name was Slattery but that wasn't the main reason.

An imbalance of love means an imbalance of power.

With Corky's women, too. Charlotte, for those years he'd actually loved her. And now Christina. *Yes but you can't trust women. You can trust men.*

Corky sits at his desk that's piled with weeks of accumulated mail, papers. He's got the radio on hoping for news, a can of Bud and some stale Planter's peanuts so gritty with salt he's practically getting a buzz on from it. Studying this promissory note for Nick Daugherty that when signed requires Nick to pay the full amount of his $5000 debt to Jerome A. Corcoran by 1 September 1992. Greenbaum drives a hard bargain but, sure, he's right: you know he's right. Just that Corky Corcoran for all his pugnacity in politics and in barrooms, his reputation as outspoken, plain-dealing, hotheaded, can't imagine how he'll put it to his old friend. *Nick, I've got something for you to* . . . Fuck that. He can't!

Corky's at-home office is even messier than his Pearl Street office,

which is at least cleaned from time to time. Here, he's never wanted anybody in, not even cleaning women. Had a special key made for the lock
to keep out Charlotte for eleven years, not that he didn't trust her he said
but it makes him nervous to think somebody, anybody, might be poking
around in his office. Like poking around in his head.

Paranoid, Charlotte called him. Sometimes she was teasing, and sometimes not. Wondering if it was an Irish male trait and Corky told her
never mind that ethnic bullshit though realizing yes probably, at least a
Corcoran trait, men keeping their business affairs private and in some
cases secret even from the government and IRS.

So when Corky wants this room cleaned, he has to clean it himself in a
fury of impatient vacuuming that burns itself out in about twenty minutes.

The primary secret of Corky's home office is his *files*. Which he thinks
of, formally, as *files*; though much of the material is crammed into boxes
and cheap accordion files as well as in conventional metal-and-wood
office filing cabinets with locks. These *files* are so stuffed with data, so
intricately cross-referenced, though not yet computerized, Corky contemplates his holdings as a bemused and intimidated librarian might
contemplate the vast unfathomable holdings of a library whose very
purpose is obscure yet whose authority is unshakable.

Corky's *files* began with newspaper clippings and diary-notes pertaining to his father's death. Any documents he could lay his hands on,
including Timothy Patrick Corcoran's death certificate. And sympathy
cards—must be over a hundred of them. He's accumulated more than
one dozen twelve-by-fifteen-inch manila envelopes crammed with material once precious, now not glanced at, nor thought of, in years: the file
TIMOTHY PATRICK CORCORAN in the oldest of the filing cabinets. Files too
for F. (Fenske), T.U.C. (Trade Union Council). All this dating back to the
early 1960s, now frayed and yellowed, thirty years old.

Still, the mystery hasn't been solved to Corky's satisfaction. There's
something left out—he's sure.

To make a *file* on somebody or something is to get a handle on them
and Corky likes the idea, he's got a pack rat's mentality maybe accumulating data for data's sake. And so his *files* contain manila envelopes labeled
UCPD (Union City Police Department: data on a miscellany of officers,
some of them no longer on the force, from the Police Commissioner on

down); U.C. COURTS (County, State, Federal), CITY HALL (through several administrations, all Democratic), MO. CO. DEMS (Mohawk County Democrats), MO. CO. REPS (Mohawk County Republicans). Also U.C. LAWYERS, U.C. BROKERS, U.C. REALTORS, U.C. $$$ (Union City millionaires). Also U.C. ARCH (architecture), U.C. REL (religion, with an emphasis on the Catholic hierarchy form the Archbishop on down). There are personal files on friends, among them V.S. (Vic Slattery), O.S. (Oscar Slattery), R.D. (Ross Drummond). One of the more recent, burgeoning files is D. (divorce: hundreds of documents, photocopies, letters from Corky's and Charlotte's respective lawyers, bills and receipts). Other files are mysteriously coded—N.E. (containing data on men Corky believes to be enemies of his, whether business or personal); C. (con games, fraud—Corky's an admirer of some of these ingenious guys); W. ("wisdom"—folders crammed with articles from sources as diverse as *Scientific American, Reader's Digest, American Lawyer, Fortune, Computer World* which Corky's sure he will study some day). There are files, most of them fairly thin, marked T., S., E., R., S.D. and so forth—Corky's women. And thicker files, though kept up only intermittently, marked C. and T.C.—for Charlotte and Thalia.

In truth, Corky hasn't kept up most of these *files* for years. Nor even glanced at them. Just wants, needs, the information on hand, locked away, in secret, his.

No file for Christina: he's been keeping things—notes, snapshots, postcards, clippings—in a drawer, loose. Maybe, if they don't get back together, he'll throw it all away. *So narrow, so unforgiving, is it some Catholic thing.*

Corky's trying to balance one of his checking accounts cursing and sweating with his pocket calculator aware irritably, anxiously of the time, assuming by now, 5:35 P.M., Thalia isn't coming or she'd come and, asshole, he'd missed her when he hears a sound behind him and turns to look and there in the threshold of the doorway of this office she'd never been allowed into while growing up, this secret off-limits room of Corky's she'd referred to as Bluebeard's Castle—there's Thalia. Smiling at him.

"Thalia, for Christ's sake!" Corky says. "You scared the hell out of me."

Thalia laughs. "Corky, aren't you expecting me?"

Corky has to hand it to his adopted daughter. This Braunbeck-sired daughter, this stranger to his blood and his sensibility and his very comprehension—in the first moment of any encounter, she'll turn the blame, the need for defense, back upon Corky.

Anyway she's smiling, that's a good sign. And looking pretty good. Not healthy exactly, but then Thalia's curious beauty has never seemed healthy, her skin pale and a tawny-lemon light in her eyes, a bruised look to the eyes like she's been crying. But she *is* smiling, gypsy-festive with a sprig of lilac in her hair—no doubt torn from one of the bushes outside. Teasing, on the edge of taunting, "I'm sorry, Corky. You do look a little *scared*."

Corky jumps up to hug Thalia risking her stiff-arming him as she's done unpredictably since the age of fourteen, this time she lets him though without hugging back, stiff in the spine, and Jesus how thin—Corky feels her rib bones through the layers of clothing. Asking how'd she get here, he hadn't heard any car in the driveway, he'd been waiting for her and just about given up, hearing his voice rattle on reminding him, God damn, of Charlotte, that love-reproachful way of hers that only makes Thalia defensive, hostile, so he's quick to add, smiling warmly at her, "Never mind. I'm god-damned glad to see you, honey."

Thalia says dryly, "Why?—you didn't think *I* was going to commit suicide, did you?"

"Of course not. But—"

"I'm not that easy to dispose of. You'll see."

Corky isn't sure he's heard right. "Thalia, what?"

But Thalia ignores the question. Glancing about, rueful, though somewhat breathless, as if she's been running; as if she's come a long way and isn't certain where she is, or why. "The door was unlocked downstairs, I just walked in," she says. "That isn't like you, Corky, is it, to leave a door unlocked? It's weird to be a trespasser here, where I used to be—used to live." Saying, teasing, "'Blue-beard's Castle'—where Jerome A. Corcoran keeps his secrets."

How formal, how bitter the name "Jerome A. Corcoran" in Thalia's mouth. By Corky's request she's never called him anything other than "Corky."

Corky says quickly, seeing Thalia's peering at some of the papers on his desk, "—This? This crap? It's just paperwork. Shit-work. I'm trying to balance my checking account." Adding, even as he blocks Thalia's way,

"The IRS is after my ass again. This time it looks serious, Corcoran, Inc., could go under. I feel like a rat in a maze. I'm a driven man."

Thalia asks, "Can't you get advice from Grandfather? He knows all the tricks, doesn't he? You and him, you have a lot in common."

Thalia's voice is heavy with irony, cruel, that juvenile irony that pissed Corky off for years. Living with it, for years. Like Thalia's of a purer stock, or a hippie of the 1960s—never speaks of money except to suggest there's something grubby, shameful about it, dirty. Though Corky happens to know that her grandparents are leaving her a bundle—must be beyond $4 million in investments, properties, cash. It's Charlotte's fear that Thalia will give her inheritance over to one or another of her organizations and Corky thinks that might just happen but *he's* out of it, now—no more sucking up to Ross Drummond hoping to get him to change his mind about anything.

Corky's strategy with Thalia is usually to play it straight. Pretend you don't get the irony, sarcasm. Cut through the girl's bullshit and appeal to her sympathy which every woman has, you can count on it. Corky tells her about the latest IRS audit of Corcoran, Inc.'s, pension plan plus the limited-partnership failures, and Howard Greenbaum who's going to change Corky's life, he knows it—"A truly superior person. One of the finest money men in the city but classy, too. At lunch we talk about morals, religion. He's Jewish, of course—I think we're going to be friends."

Innocently Thalia says, "I thought you didn't trust Jews, Corky."

"What, me? Of course I trust Jews."

"Didn't you used to say, 'Never trust a Jew unless you have him in your pocket'?"

"Honey, that was your grandfather. That *is* your grandfather. Don't mix us up." Corky's laughing but Corky's annoyed. And the way Thalia's standing there sizing him up like she's, what—assessing him?

Corky manages to usher Thalia out of his office, locks the door and leads her downstairs, looking at her sidelong but keeping his expression neutral. *Try not to comment on your daughter's physical appearance even when it alarms you* one of the doctors told Corky and Charlotte after Thalia's hospitalization, but, Jesus it's hard, up close Thalia doesn't look so good, bruises under her eyes, inflamed eyelids, skin sickly-pale and even blemished at the hairline, and her hair snarled and matted fall-ing to her shoulders uncombed, unwashed—Corky smells the strong sweet lilac scent but a ranker smell beneath, Thalia's oily hair. Thalia's body. The crotch of that leotard, the yeasty-cunty odor.

Thalia's nose even seems longer, narrower. Waxy at the tip and the interior of the nostrils moist, pink as if inflamed too, feverish. Her lips are bloodless and parched-looking. Corky doesn't doubt she's running a fever, she'd be hot to the touch.

So don't touch. Keep your distance.

Corky knows better but can't help himself, in the kitchen saying, "Jesus, Thalia, you look like one of the homeless, have you been sleep-ing in the park?" running his eyes up and down the length of her, she's wearing a shapeless ankle-length skirt of some flimsy black material, a maroon satin jacket of some ethnic design, not very clean, missing a but-ton, and beneath the jacket a black sweater, good quality, looks like cash-mere, stretched at the neck. On her feet are scuffed black flat-soled shoes Corky's sure he'd noticed last night in her closet which means she's been back to the apartment since then.

Thalia runs her hands through her hair, says insolently, "So what, maybe I have."

"What the fuck's that mean?"

"I've gotten in the habit of sleeping where I *am*. Where sleep over-takes me."

Thalia smiles strangely. As if there's something secret and erotic about this. As if sleep is a lover.

Corky asks, "Why? Are you afraid of staying in your apartment?"

Thalia says, fixing him with that sickly-bright look, "No more than anywhere else, Corky. Should I be?"

Now Corky knows that Thalia's place was broken into, and is she go-ing to admit it, for sure she isn't. For all Corky knows, the place had been broken into before *he* came along. "Well, that neighborhood," Corky says, stumbling a little, "—you know how Charlotte feels. And your grandparents. And—"

"And you?"

"Of course, me. You know we're all worried about you, honey."

"Me! What about yourselves?" Thalia's peering at Corky suspiciously. "What's that on your forehead, did you hurt yourself?"

"No, it's nothing," Corky says quickly, annoyed.

"It looks like a—"

"It's nothing."

In this exchange Corky hears that note he hasn't heard in, Christ how long, a child's fearfulness of an adult's injury or weakness, the adult who isn't maybe equal to his role. How Corky never knew his father to show any weakness, none. Not in Corky's presence at least.

Only the death, the dying. The blood. The smell of shit.

If that's a weakness.

Corky's concern for Thalia seems to have touched her, at least she's quiet now, broody and downlooking. Leaning against a kitchen counter as if she's storing up her strength.

The raw, reddened, grainy edges of Thalia's eyelids. A yellowish cast to her eyes, faint too beneath the skin's pallor, what does it remind Corky of, shit he doesn't want to acknowledge: that corpse flat on his back, deader than dead, a can of diet chocolate soda on his chest. Corky shivers.

Also, reminds him of his friend whose skin went yellow from jaundice, poor bastard caught hepatitis from screwing around and nearly died and maybe by now (Corky hasn't run into Foxy Ryan, a heavy drinker, in a long time) he's dead. Once your liver goes, you go. But Corky doesn't dare bring the subject up to Thalia, the slightest hint he'd like her to see a doctor and she'll get hysterical. Too many doctors and "therapists" fucking up her head worse than it was, as Corky himself agreed.

That'd be like poking a wildcat with a stick. Jesus, no.

Opening instead the refrigerator door, casually takes out a bottle of pineapple juice, pours juice into two glasses not saying a word just pushing one slightly in Thalia's direction on the counter and taking up the other himself and drinking and the damned stuff *is* good though Corky's strangely without appetite.

C'mon, kid, drink with me. Loosen up.

A quick memory of Corky and his stepdaughter, by that time a delicate-boned adolescent girl with lovely eyes, a furtive manner, a row of glittering-silver braces over her front teeth, standing in just this kitchen in just this way sipping fruit juice and talking about—what? Much of it was Thalia in league against Charlotte, tearful about Charlotte with whom she didn't get along, to put it mildly, and seeking an ally in Corky, and Corky tried to play it both ways, he's a guy who plays it both ways as long as he can. Corky wishes he could come up with some good memory of those years but the weird thing that's been running through his mind is *Glow little glow-worm glimmer! glimmer!*

Thalia's been staring at the glass of pineapple juice, swallowing compulsively, distracted as Corky continues, speaking casually, not putting pressure on her, saying he'd been a little scared by her telephone messages, why wasn't she home when he tried to call her, he must have tried to call her twenty times and no answer and no answering machine, not that he was angry, he wasn't, but he was scared, she must know he loves her and naturally he's scared when she's out of contact and behaving so mysteriously—"Even Miriam, at my office, you remember Miriam, honey, don't you?—was worried." Wants Thalia to feel just enough guilt so she'll drink the fruit juice and that will be a start, at least. If she's starving she's lightheaded and not capable of making sound judgments, if she's on oxycodone, or an amphetamine, her appetite's depressed, it's a cycle. Corky's edging toward her, wants badly to touch her, circle her thin wrists with his fingers. He's thinking, if he touches her, he'll have won.

After possibly three minutes second-by-second of a stalemate Thalia reaches out slowly and takes up the glass of fruit juice, and raises it to her mouth, Corky's careful not to seem to be watching, in fact he's looking out the window at the hedge of lilac and clouds high in the waning sky like horses' manes and he's changed the subject talking of the Toronto Blue Jays, that afternoon's game, the crazy bet he made shaking his head as if, perceiving Corky Corcoran at a distance of only a few hours, even he himself is bemused. Says Corky, "Well. I stick with my bets, I don't regret them and I never renege." The sky seems to him so beautiful, cobalt-blue darkening behind the clouds, he almost can't bear it.

This jumpiness, this edginess, you wouldn't call it exactly sexual excitement, for Corky isn't in fact aroused, seems to communicate itself to Thalia for just as she's about to drink she pauses, and lowers the glass, raises it again tentatively then lowers it as if the very weight of it tires her, God damn it, Corky's practically grinding his teeth observing this out of the corner of his eye. Doesn't say a word. Won't poke the wildcat. Just drains his own glass stifling a profound belch half pineapple juice and half Twelve Horse Ale.

God damn this stepdaughter he married himself into: this is how it's been between them, Thalia and her aching step-Daddy, for too many fucking years.

Then, these quicksilver changes are a fact of life with Thalia, as with ninety percent of the females Corky's known, which is why basically you can't trust a female no matter who it is, Thalia catches sight of the morning *Journal* scattered across a table, and goes to look at it, the front page and the photo of Marilee Plummer and the headline and starts breathing quick and audibly like she's begun to hyperventilate and she's saying, whispering, "—can't believe Marilee's dead! Just can't believe it!" and begins to cry and by now the damned fruit juice is forgotten set down hastily on the table.

Thalia cries, and Corky goes to comfort her, she doesn't push him away at least not initially, he feels his heart's breaking, poor kid, so sorry for her in her grief that's a tremulous grief irradiating her body so she's shivering convulsively. And how helplessly she cries, a harsh jagged angry weeping, her face looks longer and narrower streaked with tears, rivulets in her cheeks. All Corky can do is murmur, "—it's tough, honey, Jesus I know, it's shitty—" shocked feeling how thin she is, jutting shoulder bones like wings, knobby vertebrae, not like a woman in her mid-twenties, unhealthy, wrong, and there's the oily-rank smell of her hair, and the fleshy-stale smell of her body, faint scent of underarms and crotch and sweat half-pleasurable to Corky's nostrils as it'd been the evening before in Thalia's closet sniffing at the soiled leotard. But Corky feels no sexual stirring, only a profound unease, almost panic. The way Thalia's crying so sharply reminds him of Theresa, his cock's shriveled to about the size of a prune.

"Honey? Tell me?"

Thalia shakes her head, Thalia pushes Corky away, not roughly but decisively. Hurrying then out of the kitchen, distracted and wild-eyed glaring in grief, the sprig of lilac fallen to the floor unnoticed. Corky follows her into the solarium, she's only half-conscious of where she is but he's relieved she hasn't run out of the house, what would he do then, pursue her? drag her back inside?—he's dealt with hysterical women upon occasion in his complicated past but always Corky Corcoran was the cause of the hysteria so that puts you in an entirely different position, a position of power. Which he doesn't have here. But in the solarium Thalia begins to calm down. Makes an effort to control herself. Corky's tentative, hovering near. Corky's own eyes are moist with tears. Shit, a woman crying, female grief, it goes through you like a knife blade, nothing like it.

Yet Corky's alert enough, seeing the cordless receiver on the glass-topped table, to take it off the hook. So they won't be interrupted.

Thalia wipes her face with a tissue, and blows her nose, half-turned from Corky so he can't see her ravaged face, saying, "We were like sisters for a while, Marilee and me. Not recently but last year, and the year before. We were still friends—I *am* still Marilee's friend—only not so close—but we were close, why didn't she listen to me!—I did all I could, I swear, to talk her out of it."

"You knew Marilee Plummer was going to kill herself?"

"No! I mean, I didn't know when. I mean—" Thalia pauses, tearing at her thumbnail with her teeth, "—I was terrified she would, but I couldn't stop her."

"You mean she told you?"

"They don't need to tell you, you know."

"'They'—?"

"People in despair, people who want to die. People who wind up in such a state, it's easier just to die."

"Then Marilee did kill herself, it *was* suicide?"

Furiously Thalia says, "She tried it once before, maybe more than once, nobody knew but me. In March, it was. She called me, her voice was so weak over the phone I almost couldn't hear her, 'Thalia, I'm in trouble,' she said, 'I made a mistake,' it was five in the morning and I didn't even ask any questions, I knew, I put a coat on over my nightgown and went over and there Marilee was, in bed, she'd taken all the barbiturates she had, in this condominium of hers, all expenses paid, you've seen it, maybe?—in Pendle Hill." Thalia speaks rapidly, not looking at Corky. She's visibly shaking. "She'd vomited some of it up so I helped her, I forced her to vomit up the rest, then I made black coffee for her, I cleaned things up, I washed her, poor Marilee, I washed her hair. Fancy cornrow braids, dozens of them, takes hours to braid and it's expensive having it done the way

Marilee did because she's—she was—a fancy glamor-black, like on the cover of *Ebony*, like in *Playboy*, the kind you look at and you think, there's somebody who's really made it, no bullshitting Marilee Plummer. But she wasn't like that, that was what she tried to be but she wasn't, and her black friends were gone, she'd dropped them after college and they were gone and the blacks here in the city considered her the lowest of the low, purely shit, for turning Steadman in—whether he'd raped her and humiliated her and did you know he'd pissed on her?—the 'golden shower' it's called—whether he'd done any of it, or not. Most of them never believed Steadman had except if he had well the cunt deserved it, the cunt was asking for it, why'd she go with him to his place if she wasn't asking for it. The women especially. The black women. Not just the ones in the inner city though that's where it was concentrated—*is* concentrated. They're glad Marilee's dead! They're happy for Steadman! Even some members of her own family, Marilee said, were on his side." Thalia's breathless, speaking rapidly, angry tears in her eyes. "So I stayed with her, that day. I held her for hours, she was catatonic, her jaws rigid like lockjaw, she was freezing cold. So scared. She didn't look like Marilee Plummer but like another person. When you're depressed it's like your body is dead, and so heavy. The spirit is turned to lead inside the body. I kept telling Marilee that after the trial she could move away, go to New York for instance. I could go with her, I said. I said, 'He may have hurt you, Marilee, but he didn't defile you.' Thinking of course it was all Marcus Steadman. How life had changed for her, after what happened. And finally Marilee said, it was just a whisper, I wasn't sure what I'd heard at first—'It isn't just him.'"

Corky says, "Meaning what?"

Thalia doesn't answer immediately. She hugs herself, shivering. Cuts her eyes at Corky, her anxious step-Daddy staring at her not knowing what to do or say or even what to do with his hands. "*You* weren't involved with Marilee, were you, Corky?"

"Of course not."

Corky's response is quick and adamant but he knows his face is flushed.

"Did you ever go out with her? Call her?"

"No. I hardly knew her."

"Marilee knew *you*."

"What's that supposed to mean?—sure she knew me," Corky says, trying not to get rattled. Thalia's looking at him with that expression he wouldn't want to decipher. "Lots of people know me. So what? And even if I had called Marilee Plummer, which I didn't, so what, what's it to you? What's it got to do with her killing herself?"

"It might be," Thalia says slowly, meanly, in such a way Corky guesses she's testing him, "that Marilee told me some things, about you."

"Then she was lying."

"Was she?"

"What's this, an interrogation?—I said yes. If she told you she was seeing me, sleeping with me, whatever—she was lying."

"Marilee didn't lie. Not to me."

"How the fuck would you know?"

"She was my friend, she trusted me. Cut it out, Corky, will you? *You* don't know shit."

"Honey, why are you so angry with me? I don't get it."

"You get it, all right."

Thalia's voice so quavers in dislike of him, repugnance for him or for someone she sees in his place, Corky can't quite believe it.

"You know who Marilee was involved with, don't you?" Thalia asks, "—why she did what she did? Sure you do."

"Honey, I *don't*."

"You know, you're one of them. You share—when you can. Don't you!"

"Share what?" Corky asks, his face reddening, he knows what Thalia is getting at but can't acknowledge it, shit, he can't. "—Who was she involved with?"

Thalia backs off as if Corky's planning to grab her which he isn't, he's approaching her meaning only to comfort. She knows she can trust him, or should know.

"Your friend Vic Slattery."

Corky shakes his head, this *is* preposterous. Maybe not, knowing what he knows of Vic's weakness for women, more likely the weakness of women for Vic, but whose fault is that, not Vic's, Corky's frowning and shaking his head annoyed as if he's been accused himself, made to blame. Asking Thalia skeptically, "Did Marilee tell you that, too?"

"Marilee didn't need to tell me, I knew."

"How did you know?"

Thalia pauses as if she's about to say *I know Vic Slattery* but there's such anguish in her she can't speak, can't speak those words, which in any case Corky doesn't hear, nor want to hear; nor will he remember having heard or not heard. Corky's stern and his face is heated and his eyes slightly wild but he's this girl's stepfather close as any blood relation, it's an insult if she backs off mistrusting him, and disbelieving.

"About Vic, there are always rumors, all kinds of shitty slanderous rumors, everyone knows that," Corky says, pursuing now a palpable truth, a truth Thalia herself must acknowledge, certainly she knows. "No man in public life, a man as attractive as Vic, and dangerous, from the point of view of his political enemies—"

Thalia cries, "You wouldn't tell me the truth, would you, even if you knew? Any more than *he* would. Unless he was made to."

"Thalia, I am telling you the truth. I wouldn't lie to you."

"Wouldn't you!"

"For Christ's sake, Thalia—"

Thalia looks at Corky wanting to believe him, he sees that and it placates him a little, still he's angry, he's angry in Vic's place, some terrible gathering blame like the very sky turning opaque seems to be encroaching, though possibly it isn't, it can be made to cease.

Corky's without any doubt, or tells himself so. *He* can make it cease.

"I think you lie all the time, I think you've lied to me lots of times, I don't doubt you have your reasons and your reasons are good ones, you think," Thalia says rapidly, backing off, now against the solarium wall, nudging her leg against the edge of a planter containing a gigantic fern whose leaves have begun by degrees to turn brown, despite Mrs. Krauss' efforts to save it, "—I don't even doubt that you love me, or think you do." Her mouth works, she's pale and long-faced, horse-faced, ugly. "For instance: was it you who broke into my apartment last night, Corky?"

"Me? Your apartment?" Corky isn't prepared for this thrown into his face, but his answer comes swift and astonished, "—Jesus, Thalia, someone broke into your apartment? Last *night?*"

"It was you, wasn't it? Corky, just tell me. I know why you did it and I'm not angry, just tell me."

Corky shakes his head, wordless. Should he say? He should. He contemplates his accuser, he's close to smiling. *Once said, never unsaid.* He wonders how good a look the woman downstairs got of him, or maybe somehow Esdras himself. Christ!

Though saying, genuinely upset, "Thalia, let's get this straight: sometime last night, during the night, your apartment was broken into? And you were there?—in bed?"

Thalia eyes Corky doubtfully. As if she knows, but doesn't know. "Yes, I was there. But not in bed. And it wasn't during the night, it was early in the evening around six. It *was* you, Corky, wasn't it?" pleading with him now.

"What do you mean, you were there?" Corky asks, astonished. "When this person broke in, you were *there?*"

"I was hiding. In a closet."

Smiling at Corky, a swift defiant smile so he's stricken to the heart with terror that his and Charlotte's worst fears are exactly right: Thalia *is* unwell.

But Corky's so astonished, he can only repeat, like a parrot or an idiot, "You were hiding?—in a *closet?*"

Thalia says, "I was prepared to hide, I knew they would be coming for me. I was already hiding but then I thought, hearing him at the door, maybe it was you, because the phone had been ringing all day and I thought it might be you but I couldn't answer because it might not be you and then they'd know."

Corky's staring at Thalia. He should acknowledge the intruder was him but somehow he can't. Just can't. Though afterward to regret it and even now suspecting how afterward he'll regret it he's unable to speak, you asshole Corky, trying to do good and fucking up as usual. And now compounding one lie with another, asking, even demanding, "Jesus, Thalia, honey, why did you just hide if you heard somebody breaking in your apartment, why didn't you call the police?" and Thalia shakes her head vehemently, as if Corky's asked an outrageous question, with revulsion she says, "The police!—*them!*" and Corky asks, "What do you mean?" and Thalia says, "*You* know," and Corky asks, "Honey, what do I know?"—for indeed he's baffled, and sweating like a guilty man, all this has about blown his mind.

But Thalia won't say. She knows what she believes she knows but she won't say so Corky surmises it's paranoia, a fear of the police too, Thalia has never seemed to trust the police and Corky'd taken it to be an affectation, a radical-minded young person's affectation, as in the 1960s the belief was never trust the pigs, the pigs in uniform. And Thalia and certain of her friends believed themselves radical thinkers, so this makes sense. A kind of sense. At least, Corky wants to think so.

Asking, still upset, about the intruder—how long was he in the apartment, did he steal anything, didn't she get a look at him?—and afterward, what had she done?—and where is she staying now?—and Thalia's answers aren't very coherent, nor very audible, Corky thinks she's staying with a friend somewhere in the city, but even that isn't clear. Don't push her, don't press her, that will only make things worse, Corky thinks. He's had experience with hysterics, in this very house.

"I hid because I wouldn't be driven out by them. I was already in hiding when he came. He might have been *them*, or he might have been *you*, but I couldn't know so I got into the closet and made myself small as I could, squeezed behind some clothes, and suitcases. He opened the door, he opened it twice—and didn't see me. I didn't breathe but I heard him breathing, I thought it might be you but what if it wasn't, because Marilee was dead and they'd be coming for me because I was her friend, oh Corky we were close as sisters for a long time then things came between us, I won't say what, I won't say his name, it was my fault as much as Marilee's, I'm so ashamed. I didn't approve of Marilee's life, her jobs, living where she did, the people she'd turned her back on—it was her mistake, she set whites higher than blacks I think, without meaning to—but I don't want to judge, not her. Then after it happened in January, with Steadman, and everything Marilee couldn't control, we were close again, she needed me. But I couldn't help her, at the end. I failed her. I knew, I knew she would kill herself, not when, but I knew she would, and I couldn't stop her. I had foreknowledge in dreams. But it didn't make any difference."

Corky has let Thalia speak uninterrupted, now she's crying again, a despair so raw and open it's like Corky's own, almost. And not shrinking from him as he holds her, gently, cautiously folding his arms around her thin shivering body.

"Jesus, Thalia! Poor little girl."

Next comes an interlude of calm and Corky's given reason to feel he's back in control. Sitting with Thalia and talking soothing her and humoring her as one might a sick child for surely Thalia is a sick child, has been so for years. But so skilled in negotiating the terms of her own sickness and so intelligent a young woman, always there's the question Corky puts to Charlotte: Who's to say? You, me? Who's to say who's right, and Thalia in the wrong?

Thalia says, biting her thumbnail, her face fine-wrinkled with the effort to be precise, honest, "What I wanted most for myself was to be *not* myself. To be abstract, in the service of a principle. Not intoxicated with 'ego.' Blind with 'self' that's like a beacon shining into your eyes," and Corky says uneasily, for something about this is wrong, "What do you mean, 'wanted,' Thalia?—it's all in the past?" and Thalia says, not hearing, this selective deafness is a trait she shares with the mother she's repudiated, "—Which is why Marilee seemed wrong to me, and mysterious, for so long. I didn't understand at the time but now, since her death, I've been thinking of nothing else since her death but this, I do. You see, Corky," eager and almost elated, as a teenager she'd light up with such sudden insights, some of them obvious, others subtle, or weird, or plain mistaken, "Whites expect nonwhites to be more than just individuals. We expect them to be in the service of a principle—abstract—not selfish like the rest of us. It's a form of racism! Colonization! Like the white liberal who's so shocked and hurt by the black whose religion is hating whites. Saying 'Hey, I'm your friend, I don't hate you so how can you hate me,'" and Corky says, irritated, "You sound like Marcus Steadman, for Christ's sake—you believe that shit?" and Thalia says, still frowning, with that attitude of exquisite precision wanting or needing to get things said, and said right, as if for the record, "It isn't a matter of what I believe, or you believe, it's a matter of what *is*. Sometimes it just comes to you. It must be like God—overwhelming—blasts you through, obliterates you. A few months ago I was in that pro-choice rally that turned nasty in Union Square Park. We were marching to City Hall and the Operation Rescue people blocked us, they were screaming at us, waving their signs, chanting—'Pro-choice is a lie, no baby chooses to die,' and that stopped me cold. It went right through me, it was cold and sharp as a blade, I felt the truth of it. It wasn't an opinion, it was a truth, and I felt it, I knew." She pauses. "But I didn't change my politics."

Thalia's breathing quickly, audibly. They've been sitting at the glass-topped table in the solarium as the sun shifts toward the horizon illuminating the bank of clouds like a mountain range on fire and Corky's been earnest and fatherly, saying now, "Hell, Thalia, there are two sides—more than two—to any political position. But if you want to get anything done, any progress, you have to decide, make up your mind which side you're on and act. You can't always be thinking. You only have to act. In the voting booth—"

"I know that," Thalia says quickly, brightly. "Corky, I know that! But I need to hear you say it. I really do." There's a strange emphasis to her words, Corky can't figure it. Is he telling her to do something it won't be in Corky Corcoran's own best interest for her to do?

Thalia's curious about the house, wants to see it. What's this house she grew up in like *now?*

Corky follows her into the front rooms, rarely used now he's a bachelor, and alone. Switching on the living room lights seeing the room through Thalia's eyes, high ceiling, ornate molding, the swanky European-style furniture or what remains of it—a stage setting but where are the actors?—what's the point? Corky hasn't had anyone over in a long time. He's invited out so often, there's no need, and no time anyway. And when, married, he'd invited some of his own people over, that's to say his relatives, the occasions always fell flat. Trying to mix Irish Hill with Summit Park, the same difficulty Tim Corcoran had inviting the family to Schuyler Place, the nicer people shy and stiff and all but mute fearful of spilling something on the rug or farting and the rest of the pack, the Donnellys for instance, making sure they did spill something, and did fart. Corky recalls that Christmas open house when he'd mixed his relatives with Charlotte's and with their friends, the strain of it, Corky's cousin Lois inquiring point-blank of him do you own this place free and clear or is there a mortgage, Mike Donnelly getting in a quarrel with Ross Drummond over politics, Sean Corcoran in a disagreement too with one of Corky's neighbors, the old man maudlin-drunk, and worst of all, Corky winces remembering, a parish priest from Batavia, second or third cousin of Corky's, Father Mulvaney, passing out in one of the bathrooms with the door locked so Corky ended up having to remove the hinges from the door, fuck that, fuck that shit, such embarrassment, and Charlotte pointedly saying nothing about it, Charlotte and the Drummonds, a united front.

So, no more parties. Not till Corky gets reestablished.

Thalia says, "It's hard for me to believe that I ever lived here. Except I had to come from somewhere, didn't I."

Corky says, "Well, this part of the house doesn't look familiar, much, to me either."

"I remember the house more than I remember myself in it."

Corky says dryly, "Well, Thalia, *I* remember *you*."

French windows along one wall, a milky-marble fireplace on the facing wall, imported from Florence, Italy, according to Charlotte's fag decorator, out of an eighteenth-century *palazzo*. Creamy-beige brocade, recessed lighting, but a bare hardwood floor, needing to be waxed. Half the furniture gone. That bronze Chinese rug, hand-woven, crimson and jade and turquoise herons, beauty to knock out your eye, how could Corky let Charlotte take it, Thalia asks, childish indignation in her voice, and unfairness, and Corky says, shrugging, "The rug was a wedding present from your grandparents, as far as I was concerned it was Charlotte's, of course." Not adding, what the hell, anything Charlotte wanted of the household she could have. To get out from under that heavy neurotic bitch, so he could breathe, was all Corky wanted at the end.

Weird how, when you're in love, buying furniture for your house, each item is precious, invested with meaning. When love's gone, it's just some objects in a room and the room's got walls, floor, ceiling—what's the big deal?

Thalia says, "Grandpa tried to buy me, too. Plenty of times. But he hasn't succeeded."

"No?"

"No."

Corky thinks of the $4-million inheritance. Wondering suddenly if Thalia will even outlive her grandparents—live to inherit.

Of course she'll live: I'll make sure of it.

"In what ways has Ross tried?" Corky asks.

"Various ways," Thalia says coolly. "You know how he is, that type. And Mother, too. And, in his own way, not a very effectual way since I never see him, Mr. Pierson."

Charlotte's third husband, Thalia's new stepfather. Gavin Pierson whom Thalia always calls "Mr. Pierson." He's a highly successful Union City investment broker, an associate of Ross Drummond's, mid-fifties, wife died of cancer a few years ago and Charlotte "consoled" him and Corky knew, or half-knew, too caught up with his own affairs to concentrate, except he'd notice how at the Athletic Club on the squash court and in the locker room during those months when Pierson was swept up in Charlotte's scheme of revenge, the poor guy couldn't look Corky in the eye, stammered guiltily in his presence. "What's with him?" Corky once inquired to mutual acquaintances as Pierson hurried away and the men were blank, innocent. Pretending they didn't know.

Corky's fists are clenched, remembering. The bruise on his forehead throbs.

Corky asks, "Charlotte has told me, you refuse to see her. You hurt her feelings, you know."

Thalia shrugs. "She isn't my mother now, that's past."

"Hey, c'mon: what kind of talk is that?"

"I told her we're free of each other and it's a good, beautiful thing to be free. It's like a cleansing flame, Corky. You should know."

"I know you're talking a lot of crap. What's it, some Oriental 'wisdom' religion? Like out of a fortune cookie?"

Thalia laughs. Her laughter rises like glass reversed in falling, a happy sort of breakage. There's a faint eerie echo in the room and hearing it Thalia presses her forefinger over her lips and laughs harder.

Before Corky can press her on this, he's actually about to take hold of her arm, Thalia moves on into the next room, the dining room, a latticed French door overlooking the slope of the lawn and an elegant Irish crystal chandelier hanging poised over empty space—no table beneath, no chairs, another bare hardwood floor. As if some comically abrupt apocalyptic event had occurred sweeping inhabitants and furnishings alike away, no trace of their passing, not the slightest disturbance in their wake. Thalia laughs, and wipes at her eyes. "Christ it's so fucking sad, isn't it—any place where people've *been*, and aren't any longer."

Corky protests, "Why? I'm going to buy new furniture, for all these rooms, just haven't gotten around to it yet. I'm thinking I should wait, maybe I'll get married again."

"Married again? You?" Thalia stares at him, so blunt it isn't even rude. "It's too late for you."

"What the hell's that mean?—'too late'? I'm only forty-three years old."

"It's too late for all of you."

Thalia speaks softly, with an air of sorrow, resignation. Corky tastes cold thinking again yes she *is* disturbed, something *is* wrong, like when you're a kid and you meet another kid who isn't right in the head, just that expression *not right in the head*, how quickly you know, though you'd be unable to explain.

Corky decides to play it light, though. Maybe the kid's teasing.

"You don't know the first thing about me, Thalia. About me, let's say, as a man."

"I know you're the kind of man who has to prove he's a man by way of women. But it's other men you're proving to, like they're proving they're men to you. It's the opposite of freedom. Where freedom's fire, that's muck." Thalia makes a bemused snorting sound, a teenaged kid moving off with a sidelong glance at Corky, she's laughing at him.

Goes into the next room, which Corky wishes she wouldn't, damned nosey kid and he can't reasonably stop her.

This room's an ex-parlor you might say, once Charlotte's and now exclusively Corky's, a bachelor's den. Black leather sofa, matching chairs, curtainless windows, expensive wall-to-wall carpeting but stained, scattered newspapers, magazines—business, sports, girlie stuff. There's a gigantic TV on a swivel stand, VCR equipment. There's a CD player, state-of-the-art equipment, shelves of CDs mainly jazz, blues. Thalia doesn't remember this, looks around squinting. A kid bursting into her daddy's secret room and after a moment's startled pause she begins to smile, sly slow smile, examining the girlie magazine atop a table, Corky wishes the hell she wouldn't, fuck he's embarrassed like he's exposed as some jerk-off, drooling over airbrushed tits and cunt and whacking himself off.

How to explain to Thalia that except for *Playboy*, to which he's been a loyal and enthusiastic subscriber since the early 1970s, and which generally he reads in near-entirety, he buys these magazines off newsstands and hardly glances through them. The habit, the instinct, is in the buying: some promise, or hope, of—God knows what.

Says Corky heartily, as if he's just now thought of it, "Thalia, I have an idea: let's go out to dinner, just the two of us. It's after six. I'll make a reservation. If you want, you could take a shower, freshen up. What do you say?"

Bent over a table leafing through one of the skin magazines, Thalia doesn't hear. She's absorbed, her lips moving. Laughs, sniffs. Wipes at her nose. Then, peering at Corky through a straggly curtain of hair, forehead creased like the skin's been squeezed together, she says, deadpan, "Corky, I used to get the distinct impression, when I was in high school, maybe even junior high, that you sort of wanted to, I mean you entertained the possibility of, well—I mean—" she grins, a mean light in her eyes, "—you wanted to fuck me. Was I wrong?"

Corky's stunned at this, it must show in his face.

Saying, as if Thalia's joking, or pushing the way she does, no relationship to truth or anything actual, anything that need be acknowledged, "Yes. You were wrong."

Thalia laughs. Flicks the magazine shut, straightens to her full arrogant height, smiles at Corky. "I thought maybe I *was* wrong, I just wanted it confirmed at the source."

Corky moves on. Shaky-legged, and his face mottled, Jesus, he's shocked at this. Just the word *fuck* in Thalia's mouth in that way, *fuck me*, can't believe it. Coming out with it like that!

She hates me, Corky thinks.

His instinct is, he's back in the kitchen again, sees the cordless phone, he'll call Charlotte. Poor woman she's been frantic leaving messages for him. Worried about her daughter and with good reason.

Charlotte, help me! Maybe you could come over here, how soon can you get here, you and Gavin.

Corky laughs harshly, takes a Budweiser out of the refrigerator and drinks. Fuck Thalia, she thinks she's going to cocktease *him*.

You and that gentleman-prick Gavin. Come over here, I'm bailing out. She's yours.

She never was mine, she's nothing of mine, I was playing a part, I was pretending to be Daddy, all my life I'm playing parts, I don't know who the fuck I am and know what?—I don't give a shit.

The beer's so cold and so good going down, Corky's eyes moist over in simple gratitude. He's trembling.

Thinking of the stolen snapshot. Thalia, and some man. And Vic, and

Marilee Plummer, another man. What's it all about but fucking, either you are, or you aren't. Bottom line.

Either fucking, or being fucked. In the ass. Sure. Simplest premise of human life.

Like what that smart-ass kid said, at the debate tournament, from some genius-school in Manhattan, Corky and Vic and the St. Thomas team thrown up against these New York kids most of whom are Jews with a Chink or two thrown in, the topic is Resolved: The U.S. military presence in Vietnam is essential in America's war against World Communism and the St. Thomas team's all patriots for sure, the Holy Roman Catholic Church teaches its sons to be patriots, die for your country and God bless you and similar shit and this sly kid, last name ends in -*berg* or -*stein*, cuts through the bullshit saying the purpose of war is basically to provide food for insects, worms, scavengers, that's the ecological perspective, that's the ultimate perspective, "human" values are just part of the equation, and how the guys' jaws dropped, Corky's and his teammates', and the look on their Jesuit advisor's face, never heard anything like *that*.

That, said Father Dolan, afterward, is the voice of atheism.

Well, thinks Corky, somebody's got to cut through the bullshit some of the time, there are your basic premises in life, fuck or be fucked, eat or be eaten.

He's hungry.

Then, when Thalia drifts back into the kitchen a while later, tears in her eyes, she'd gone upstairs to look at her old room she misses it actually dreams of it a lot weird as that sounds, Corky's in a mood to be nasty himself but right away, unpredictable as she is, Thalia sounds wistful, sincere. "There's so much lost to me I wish I could retrieve. I'm coming to the end of something but I don't know where it *started*." Staring at Corky, gnawing a thumbnail so he's sorely tempted to snatch her hand away from her mouth.

Corky takes this straight, in fact he's touched. Any time Thalia makes a civilized overture to him, he's a pushover.

"Honey, the end of what?" Corky asks.

"A period of difficult adjustment."

"Meaning—?"

Thalia stiffens, a look comes over her face like she's ashamed, Corky guesses it's a man, hopes to Christ it isn't Vic even as he tells himself reasonably it couldn't be Vic: Vic Slattery fucking Corky Corcoran's step-daughter would be like Corky fucking Vic's wife Sandra, you just don't do such shit to your close friends.

Corky's convinced, Corky erases all further suspicion.

Saying, "Why don't we discuss this at dinner? We've got so much to talk about. Some of the things you've told me—" Corky's voice trails off, can't deal with it just now. Needs a drink stiffer than Budweiser.

He then rapidly runs through, for Thalia's sake, the names of restaurants they might go to—Brauer's? Italian Villa? House of Siam?—as Thalia stands listening, or seeming-so, biting her damned thumbnail to the quick. Interrupting him then as a child might, rude yet not by intention, "Corky, what *is* your life?"

"My—what?"

It's a weird moment. Corky feels like a boxer who's been jabbing keeping his opponent at just the right distance then suddenly he's hit a blow to the solar plexus coldcocking him dead.

"Your father was murdered, and the murderer never even arrested," Thalia says calmly, outrageously, "—and then your mother—didn't she die in a mental hospital? But it doesn't seem to have affected you, somehow. I mean, your personality. You seem to—well, to like life. You're *like* life. Life itself. You keep going."

Corky's shocked. Corky's angry, embarrassed.

Hell, Corky's flattered.

Saying, managing to laugh, his Irish-kid smile, "Shit, sweetheart, you know Corky Corcoran: 'Where there's quantum theory, there's hope.'"

But Thalia doesn't get it. B.A. Cornell, smart-ass kid knows all the answers, condescending to her own stepfather in his own home, she doesn't catch on he's waving it in her face practically, *I'm the guy who broke into your apartment.* Doesn't remember the very passage she'd underlined in her astronomy text.

Less amiably Corky says, "Sure I keep going, Thalia, you got a better alternative? What am I s'posed to do, fucking roll over and die?" He pauses, seeing she's looking at him in that strange assessing yet opaque way. "For one thing, I've got to look after you, don't I? If you get sick again, or freak out. Jesus, the way you've been living!"

Quickly Thalia flares up, on the defensive, "I'm not going to get sick, and I'm not going to—'freak out.' How dare you say such a thing about me! I know exactly what I'm going to do."

"Yeah you do, do you?"

"Exact justice."

The calm way Thalia says this, like it's all a foregone conclusion, Corky shivers. But Thalia's smiling.

Exact justice: Corky's words to Wiegler, tossed back into his face.

Corky shrugs. "Good luck to you, then."

"I don't need luck. It's courage I need."

"Courage *is* luck, sweetheart."

Thalia seems about to say more, then thinks better of it. Gnawing her damned thumbnail until it bleeds.

Corky checks his watch: 6:29 P.M. Immediately becoming 6:30 P.M.

Outside the sky's still light, in the west, threaded with a burnt-looking gold like tarnish, but darkness is rising; gathering in. Jesus, this day: where has it gone? so many hours seemingly open before him, a day he'd meant to do so much, truly he means to see Uncle Sean, he's *got* to see Uncle Sean, and what is he going to do about Christina? Just let her go?

So much time, and now gone. Down the toilet. Condensed into an ever-smaller space, gravity crushing in upon itself. Atoms in collapse.

Corky's drained his can of beer and collapses it in his fist, tosses it onto the overflowing basket beneath the sink so it falls, rolls clatteringly, what the hell, Corky shuts the door. Saying, stretching so his biceps bulge, "O.K. sweetie, what say we freshen up, go out to dinner? I want to take a shower, too. It's been a long day, Jesus!"—shaking his head as if fondly, but remembering the morgue, his puking, was that really *him?*—laughing mysteriously, "Wait'll I tell you what happened to me today."

Their old relationship: step-Daddy entertaining stepdaughter with tales of the big, adult world. Step-Daddy the hero of every tale. Sure.

Thalia hasn't agreed to dinner exactly yet she moves obediently, like a child, a vague dazed child, toward the stairs. Corky ushers her along, his hand at the small of her back.

"Like old times, eh?" Corky says. "Just you and me."

Which isn't entirely accurate: Corky and Thalia were rarely alone for meals in restaurants. (And rarely alone at home together, except during

those early years when Charlotte was involved with the Union City Players and had to be at rehearsals, and at performances of plays.) Not until
Thalia was an adult of twenty-two and working at Family Services, a few
times Corky took her to lunch at a Thai restaurant close by.

Now things seem to be in control, in Corky's control, he's feeling better. More himself. "Sure I like life, Thalia. Life *is* sweet—if you're alive."

Here's the plan and it's an innocent plan: they're going to take showers.

In separate bathrooms. Of course!

Thalia in a bathroom in what Charlotte spoke of grandly as the *guest
suite* which, Corky checks it out, his housekeeper maintains in perpetual
readiness—thick monogrammed towels, gleaming ceramic and chrome,
a gorgeous shower curtain whose outer layer is white lace—though no
guest has used it since Charlotte's departure nearly six years ago. And
Corky in his own bathroom. Of course.

But Thalia detains him with childlike worry—"But, Corky, what can I
wear, after I've showered? I can't put these soiled old shameful old things
back *on*, can I?"

Corky senses some mockery here, this mimicry of his own seeming
fastidiousness—must've insulted her by suggesting she take a shower at
all?—but plays it straight. He's crazy about her, he'll play it straight.

"Want to wear something of mine? A nice shirt?"

"Corky, yes! A nice shirt. Please."

"It won't fit very well, but—" Corky trots off obligingly to paw eagerly
through his closets, discovers a long-sleeved fuchsia shirt in raw silk, and
here's a gorgeous oystershell raw silk Christian Dior with textured stripes
worn only once. And two or three others Corky scoops out on their hangers too. The prospect of Thalia slipping one of his shirts on, her breasts
bare beneath, excites him enormously.

He returns to the guest suite but Thalia's already in the bathroom running the shower. The room is filling pleasantly with steam. She's testing
the water's temperature with her hand, droplets like beads of sweat have
splashed onto her face, her eyes are moist, swimming. She's kicked off her
shoes, long narrow delicious-pale feet just perceptibly grimy between the
toes *those toes he could lick! suck!* and she's removed her jacket so Corky
stares seeing the rib-knitted little black sweater so tight her small hard bra-

less breasts are outlined and the nipples as prominent as pits. Corky's come to the bathroom doorway bearing the shirts in his arms and stops dead in his tracks seeing Thalia there, so intimate there the way she's standing barefoot and partly undressed smiling and looking at him.

And the shower running hot and furious. And the steam.

"Corky, thanks!"—Thalia's flirty, wide-eyed standing barefoot almost as tall as Corky pushing her hair provocatively out of her face smiling at him as if there's a meaning in this: Corky bringing her his shirts. He lays them on the bed as Thalia calls out, "We're going to dinner, Corky, and after dinner—what?"

Corky isn't sure he's heard this correctly. Thalia's looking at him frankly as she'd done in the TV room flicking through the skin magazine. That look that goes through Corky like a blade. Sharp to the groin.

Repeating, "After dinner what will we do?—come back *here?*"

"Wherever you want, Thalia."

Such pressure in Corky's chest, he can barely utter these words.

Backing out of the room, in retreat, leaving Thalia to strip and get under that fierce-running shower naked thinking *Jesus my own stepdaughter isn't going to cocktease* me.

In haste then Corky showers. The needles of water stinging blinding his eyes. Dropping the fucking soap he's so nerved up, excited. Squeezed too much shampoo onto his head and there's a thick lather of soap on his chest, the monkey-red frizz of his torso, a thick swirl of it dropping to his groin where his cock's bobbing dumb-eager, hopeful—yes but obviously Thalia's not on an emotional keel and even if she were she *is* Corky's adopted daughter, he's responsible. Never would Corky touch Thalia, even in his wildest most lewd dreams, not Corky. *Fuck, fuck me* she'd said giving him that unmistakable look but Corky is her stepfather and he's known her and she's trusted him since she was a child of eight and Corky means to honor that fact. And he's a man of honor, he's a decent man.

Fuck, fuck me, did you want to fuck me, was I wrong? Yes, wrong.

As another time the slippery soap flies out of Corky's fingers and skids across the tub.

Corky showers, lathers his body furiously, slapping at it as if to punish. Erection bobbing between his legs like a second head, it's the fragrant steamy heat that's to blame. Christ knows he's tried to care for the girl, tried to be a true father to her. And how many times she's shut the door in his face. Turning her head when he'd tried to kiss her, that first time when she was fourteen and Charlotte said she's having her period, she's self-conscious. That first time and never afterward the same. *You don't love me and I sure as hell don't love you.*

Corky's thinking of last year when Thalia suddenly quit her job at WWUC-TV and seemed to have gone into hiding and Corky gave copies of her picture to a dozen UCPD friends asking them to keep an eye out, he'd been pretty upset. Even considered hiring a private detective except the only private detectives in Union City are ex-cops and Corky knows why they're ex-.

And yesterday. Telephoning her twenty times, worried sick about her. Risking his neck, his very ass, breaking into her apartment in dread of finding her body there. And why?—because Corky loves her.

(He's mortified to think that Thalia was hiding there, in that closet. He knows which one. The suitcases, the clothes crammed together on hangers. The shelf above. The black leotard hanging from a hook.)

But now Thalia's safe, and in his care. He's found her again. He'll protect her. The Italian Villa's where he'll take her for dinner, fancy wop place all pink stucco and illuminated fountains and Gino the manager always rushes up to Corky to shake his hand like Corky's the Mayor himself. *Hello Mr. Corcoran! How are you this evening Mr. Corcoran! This way Mr. Corcoran, your table's waiting!* And always a rear corner table, plenty of privacy, and Corky's back protected.

The main thing is to feed Thalia. You can tell by a glance she's not in a normal state. Cheeks thin, eyes so hollow and burning-yellow, and her collarbones so prominent. Even before the shock of Marilee Plummer's death, Thalia was obviously in a bad way. Corky will talk seriously to her. Corky will make a doctor's appointment for her. And maybe she should see a psychotherapist. (Though Corky himself doesn't believe in that shit and would as soon go to a palm reader as a psychoanything.) And that wild paranoid stuff about people coming after her, coming to get her—Christ, *that* was frightening.

Corky rinses the soap out of his hair, off his body. Staring in dismay down at himself, his erect cock, the shame of it. But it's a hard-on out of sheer nerves, he thinks, not sexual desire. He isn't that much of a shit.

Last time he'd had an undeniable hard-on for Thalia, in a rush it comes back to him now the way a faucet, turned on, gushes water, he hasn't wanted to recall it, or the circumstances—well, he'd dropped by City Hall to take Thalia out to lunch at the Thai restaurant up the block which Thalia liked so much for its vegetarian dishes, tiny place and no liquor license and so hardly Corky Corcoran's first choice for dining out but he was good-natured about it indulging his stepdaughter, what the hell, and stepping out of the elevator on the ninth floor outside Family Services he sighted Thalia a short distance away, in the corridor, talking with—who?—of all people Red Pitts, what's Thalia doing with Red Pitts, the bastard looming large and bulky in his double-breasted maroon plaid sport coat, frowning, grinning, that twitchy grimace of Pitts with the steely eyes untouched, toothpick between his teeth and Thalia was standing back from him, looking up at him, her slender body tense, earnest low-voiced conversation it seemed to Corky whose veins were flooded in an instant with adrenaline hot as flame as in the presence of a male predator-rival and when Corky emerged into view of the two of them, Thalia and Red Pitts, Red Pitts and Thalia, in the same instant and with virtually the same expression, looked at him: alert, guarded, blank. And Red Pitts with his twitchy grin waved to Corky, and moved on, took himself out of there discreetly and surprisingly agile on his feet as Corky's noticed in the past about him, and Thalia hurried to greet Corky happy to see him, the happiness seemed genuine, offering her cheek to be kissed, as Corky somewhat roughly did, he's clumsy in such maneuvers, asking at once, "What was that about, you and Pitts?" and Thalia said, "Nothing," and Corky said, "Yes but what, what were you talking about?" and Thalia laughed and said, "Why, you, Corky—who else?"

And afterward in the Thai Palace, dim-lit paper-tablecloth and -napkin joint, stinking of curry, Corky brought the subject up again, naturally Corky couldn't leave it alone, saying of Red Pitts, "You know Red packs a gun, don't you?" and Thalia said, surprised, "No, I didn't know that," and Corky said, keeping his voice even, "Red's the Mayor's bodyguard basically, he's an aide but he's there too to protect Oscar with his life— it's a job I could have had, Oscar initially wanted me, but I'm not the type, shit I'm not gonna pack a gun like a bozo cop," laying it on thick and mocking and still keeping his voice even, so no jealousy, no envy, and Thalia looked a little sick murmuring, "—I didn't know that," and Corky said, smiling, "There's lots of things you don't know, sweetheart," and one of the things Thalia didn't know was how Corky Corcoran knee-to-knee with her at the tiny table, her own stepfather, was feeling about her, what wild sensations were rushing through him though centered in his groin, his achy cock, at that very moment.

Thinking: if maybe things go right at the Italian Villa, a couple carafes of red wine should do it, and Thalia's in the mood, playful and mellow and flirty and Corky can slip the stolen snapshot out of his wallet and give away how he's the mystery intruder after all—maybe. It's risky but might work. He's done crazier things. Casual about it taking the snapshot out and showing it to Thalia who'll be wide-eyed and astonished at first and then he'll ask what the snapshot is, what's going on here, why these people (at a party to which he wasn't invited but Corky won't go into that) and why Red Pitts with them but not Oscar, what's the occasion and what's the connection between these people, and who's the guy Thalia's talking with, her lover?—or just one of her lovers?

Corky won't push it, depends upon the mood. Like poking a wildcat with a stick. He's had experience.

In the shower in the fragrant steam Corky's cock is snaky-hard, dangerous. Jesus, like he's fifteen years old again.

So, steeling himself, with deft counterclockwise motions of his wrists he turns the hot water faucet *off*, and the cold one *on*, colder.

"Ow!"—icy water out of the shower nozzle, shocking as if he's been kicked by a horse.

Corky's poor cock wilts, shrinks, shrivels in an instant, how swiftly the blood drains out, his flesh all but crawls up inside him cold-blasted to extinction.

A fight between an "It" and an "I."

Then for the second time that day this time tremulous with anticipation Corky shaves, rubs lotion into his cheeks, combs his damp springy hair and has to conclude, even with the God-damned bump on his forehead, he doesn't look bad. Not bad at all. Closer to thirty than forty, in the right light. He dresses swiftly pulling on white cotton Jockey shorts and Calvin Klein trousers and shaking out of its cellophane wrapper a new Calvin Klein shirt, blue cotton twill with a monogrammed JAC on the pocket. Remembers when he'd bought this shirt (at the Gentleman's Boutique in the Hyatt) it was Christina Kavanaugh he was envisioning, seeing himself in her eyes. But Christina Kavanaugh isn't on Corky's mind now.

Hasn't thought of her, nor felt the faintest twinge of regret or loss or perplexity or hurt or outrage, since Thalia walked in the door.

Whistling "Melancholy Baby" grinning not paying much mind to the rhythm, it's Dixieland he's feeling so upbeat.

Trotting down the hall then to check up on Thalia, see how she's doing, Corky's barefoot buttoning his shirt—"Hey Thalia?"—the bathroom door is still shut, the shower still on, a waterfall of sound. Corky imagines Thalia beneath the shower: naked: streaming water slippery and gleaming, the swing of her small breasts, glistening-dark pubic hair, curve of the stomach, hips. Thalia lifting her face to the shower, her eyes closed like she's being kissed, or loved. Warm water streaming over her like a caress. To think she'd been in that closet yesterday! And Doggy-Corky only inches away.

Corky swallows hard. What the hell are you thinking of, are you crazy? You shit.

Returning to his bedroom to finish dressing, fumbling in his excitement knotting a tie around his neck, once of those flat-metallic Armani ties he'd never wear downtown at the U.C.A.C. for instance, a signal you're a stud, no mistake. And his Armani jacket, boxy double-breasted, gunmetal-gray ideal with the blue shirt, the dove-gray trousers, who's Corky remind himself of—that actor what's-his-name, late TV movies, Richard Widmark?—specialized in sexy psychopaths. The best kind.

Except: the bedroom's a mess, he sees it through Thalia's critical eyes, clears the newspapers off the bed, paperback *A Brief History of Time* he's been reading, putting himself to sleep with for the past six months, plus cashew wrappers, used Kleenex and paper napkins and a Stroh's beer can rolls clattering across the floor when he yanks the bedspread trying to straighten it cursing himself in his haste. It's after seven P.M.

Jesus, he should call the Slatterys: explain he can't make it after all. But no time right now.

In haste then returning to the guest suite to check for Thalia but, damn, the shower's still on.

Still on?

Corky cocks his head at the bathroom door, listens. Nothing to hear but the shower. He puts his hand on the doorknob.

Corky goes out, Corky returns. Socks and shoes on. Discreet dabbing of *Joop! eau de toilette* on his upper body. Ready to go? It's 7:20 P.M. when he raps on the bathroom door, "Thalia?—hon? You still in there?" and there's no answer, just the roar of the shower. Which seems to him a little louder unless he's imagining it.

"Thalia?—is something wrong?" Corky finally opens the door to a blast of steam like a sauna. *She's killed herself, here* but when he pulls the shower curtain tentatively open he sees—no one's there.

No one. The tub's empty. The steaming water, powerful as if out of a hose, is falling upon emptiness.

"Thalia? What the hell—"

The thick luxury towels on the racks, untouched.

Corky doesn't want to think this is what he knows it is so he turns to see if, maybe it's a game?—Thalia's hiding behind the door?—but of course she isn't.

There's no one in the bathroom and he wonders how long she's been gone, leaving the shower on to deceive him.

Suffocating steam in here. Mirrors so opaque Corky can't even see the glimmer of a reflection, he's an invisible man.

Then, in the bedroom, in cooler air where he can at least see, Corky stands contemplating his shirts, *his* shirts, beautiful shirts tossed down carelessly on the bed, one of them on the floor, where Thalia left them. She'd taken one of them after all but in the state of mind Corky Corcoran's in, like he's been hit over the head with a shovel *and* kicked in the balls, he'd have a helluva time figuring out which.

6

CORKY CLINCHES A DEAL

You think I'm not serious?—you think I'm bullshitting? *Me? Corky Corcoran?*"

Five minutes to midnight. The Bull's Eye. He's incensed, insulted. Amid the fever-din of voices, laughter, a stoned jazz quartet hyperventilating what sounds like "Mood Indigo." How Corky got here exactly, he couldn't have said, but, shit, he's here and feeling good about it, his Corcoran, Inc., checkbook opened out on the sticky bar, his pen in hand and he's hot to close the deal: a cool thirty percent down payment on a price of $400,000, his offer, Corky's price, which is $85,000 below the price Mrs. Demetrius Crowe, the widow, wants for The Bull's Eye.

That's to say, the down payment is $120,000. Corky can make out the check tonight to Mrs. Crowe but he'll have to postdate it for May 27. Next Wednesday. By which time he figures he can cover the full amount, no problem.

No problem, Corky?

No problem.

What's capitalism in its essence but the skillful manipulation of funds? Other people's money, if you're short on your own.

The lucidity to which a few drinks, if they're the right drinks, can bring a man! *Where there's quantum theory, there's hope.*

Corky's at the bar of The Bull's Eye, wedged in among hard-drinking couples and young-wolfish males in packs, also a shrieking contingent of thirtyish females, midlevel office workers out on a Saturday night to celebrate one of their own getting engaged, or possibly divorced, or, who knows, these days, maybe a successful abortion. Attracted by Corky Corcoran's boyish-battered good looks and his springy red hair, his rumpled but stylish clothes, loosened necktie, his *aloneness*, these women have been casting flirty eyes in his direction, even boldly offered to buy him a drink, but Corky's been playing it cool, just smiling murmuring "No thanks!" and keeping his back turned. He's got it in his head to close the deal with Chantal Crowe tonight, this very night as if sensing he'd change his mind in the cold sobriety of the next day.

Also, Corky's had his fill of cockteasing cunts right now.

Arrived at The Bull's Eye lurching off the Fillmore exit ramp and up South Main till the landmark revolving Bull's Eye came into sight, neon-lit above the entryway, found a place on the street amid trashlitter, at about ten P.M. after a few drinks at the Seneca House and he's limited himself here to Johnnie Walker Red Label, neat: the best. Good whiskey clears the head of crap like it clears the sinuses. And Corky's sick of ale and beer, believe it or not, Christ he's had enough today to float a battle-ship. Pisser's about worn out from so much liquid running through it.

God damn Chantal Crowe!—Corky's a little drunk but at his most winning, making a playful swipe at her as she sidles past, "Hey Chantal, how's about you and me having a quiet session?—I'm serious," slapping the bar with the checkbook, grinning but impatient wishing the old broad would cut the shit. Chantal says in her husky smoker's voice, fluttering her spiky fake eyelashes at him, "Now, Mr. Corcoran, hon!—this is not the time or the place, is it?" How many years, decades, Chantal has been living in the United States, a French war bride of the 1940s, and still she speaks with a French accent. Corky's thinking, you live in the United States you should speak English the right way, it's the least you can do. To show respect. To show you're a citizen.

Still, the French accent is sexy. Doesn't grate against the ears like some of these other accents, Paki, Jap, Indian, Mex, whatever they are, half the time somebody foreign-looking, that's to say darkish-looking, talks to Corky, or tries to, he doesn't know what the fuck they're saying. In restaurants it's bad enough, now they're showing up in banks, as dental assistants, even at the car wash Corky uses. Even at the Athletic Club, in uniform.

Corky tries to talk Chantal into at least sitting down at the bar with him, let's have a drink and discuss this, but she's elusive, says she has to help behind the bar, has to help wait tables, maybe a little later when things quiet down. Big-boned busty woman in black sequins, brassy-dyed hair, terrific legs for a dame in her sixties at least, and her face isn't bad—

thick makeup, penciled eyebrows and fake lashes and glossy lips. In the daylight she'd look like a peeling wall, Corky thinks, but on her own turf, in this light, smiling that enigmatic smile, one of her eyes half-shut in a wink, old Chantal Crowe looks pretty good. What's that actress' name— Ethel Merman. Some wild old sexy dame like that.

"C'mon let's talk," Corky says, reaching for Chantal's fattish bare arm, and Chantal slaps at him like he's a naughty boy, "Mr. Corcoran, not just now!" and Corky says, "No better time than now, Chantal," and Chantal's behind the bar, reaching for a bottle, giving him a good look at her ass as she stretches, and the backs of her remarkable legs in black-patterned stockings. Old Demetrius Crowe's widow. Rolling her eyes at Corky, or at the fact of Corky, drunk and persistent and brandishing his checkbook like it's his cock in his hand. Sure she knows him, her husband knew him, both of them with a weakness for betting, especially on sports. Corky Corcoran's a high roller in Union City, a wheeler-dealer in local real estate, close buddy of Oscar Slattery and the City Hall crowd that's been in power for years, a friend too of Vic Slattery which puts him on a slightly higher moral plane—doesn't it? Sure she finds him attractive, he's a good-looking guy. He's got money, too. Sure she wants to unload The Bull's Eye, much as she'd loved it when her husband was alive, she must be desperate to sell Corky's thinking so what's her game?

My price, thinks Corky, $400,000. Or it's no deal.

The thought skimming his brain but his brain is too saturated with Red Label to absorb it that Howard Greenbaum's going to be incredu-lous: what the fuck is Corcoran, Inc., doing buying a heavily mortgaged jazz nightclub in downtown Union City, not even checking out the books, the insurance, the actual condition of the premises, what madness in the midst of Corky's own financial problems and in the depths of the reces-sion! Corky flinches seeing Greenbaum's pouchy eyes and shrewd frog-face, how to explain to him what The Bull's Eye has meant to Corky since the age of sixteen, how to speak of the heart's desire, impossible.

All Greenbaum would see, looking at The Bull's Eye, is it's an archi-tectural oddity, Art Moderne plunked down among dumpy foursquare buildings, South Main in the shadow of the Fillmore Expressway. Maybe he doesn't even know, or care, that it's a local landmark, built just be-fore the start of World War II, and how bold for its time—the facade's ebony porcelain-enamel with vermilion and lemon-yellow stripes, sleek horizontal lines in mimicry of the lines of the automobile; above the recessed entryway, like something in a Technicolor fantasy, there's the neon vermilion-green-yellow bull's eye, six feet in diameter, revolving. (Revolving when the place is open, that is. When it's closed the sign is shut off and shut down.) Inside, The Bull's Eye divides into two spaces: the outer is a funky restaurant, lots of tinny chrome and Formica surfaces and imitation leather seats, a 1950s diner; the inner, the rear, is the night-club, with a spectacular curved ebony bar and recessed lighting, smoked mirrors, crowded tables. For a while during the swinging 1970s The Bull's Eye was a disco, a Union City hot spot for singles. (Corky'd taken Charlotte there, showing her off. Ross Drummond's daughter doing those wild dances with him. How long ago, now—*disco!*) Demetrius Crowe owned the place for twenty-five years, kept it open through lean times out of a love for it Corky supposes, what else, you find yourself harboring such obsessions, your life twisted around some freaky thing like undergrowth twisted together. Poor bastard Crowe dropped dead, Corky'd heard, in the back room, right on the premises, screaming at some asshole delivery-men who'd fucked a delivery up. Coronary thrombosis. And the widow Mrs. Crowe inherited.

Corky thinks that, someday, places like The Bull's Eye will be on the National Historical Register. Records of their eras. Small-time, anonymous America. Not just the architecture of the rich and famous but what you'd call the *extraordinary-ordinary.*

"And I want a piece of that history."

Restless, primed for action. Sipping his, what's it, third whiskey?—fourth?—and it's going down smooth. Sweet liquidy flame mild to Corky as maple syrup. On another occasion in such a state he'd be hot for a woman, tonight he's aloof, ignores the perfumy broad beside him (a hooker?) who keeps nudging him, low-cut gauzy dress showing practically her nipples, Corky's alarmed thinking it's Kiki at first, the same frazzled-kinky hair and hyper manner nudging against him giggling, "Excuse me, mister!" but Corky mumbles coolly, "Excuse *me*," and ignores her. He's got eyes exclusively for Chantal Crowe watching the shrewd bitch deft and quick on her feet as any of the young waitresses, as at home behind the bar as the bartender. Feminine, but a businesswoman, you can see that. Eyes in the back of her head. (She's aware of Corky, for sure. Talking and laughing with other customers, but always glancing back at him.) Corky's getting excited, Corky's primed.

Few sights in life so lovely as a well-stocked bar, illuminated sparkling glasses, bottles of all sizes, shapes, and a mirror behind. Lights reflected in glass, gorgeous as a Christmas tree. Corky's eyes mist over, he's in love.

After that incredible shit with Thalia tonight. Thalia, Corky's own stepdaughter! Playing that trick on him slipping away not even taking a shower (he'd checked the towels, none of them damp), if that's what it was, a trick, and not a symptom of madness. *Fuck it don't think about it, a cunt's a cunt.*

Corky concentrates on the music. Liking the way the saxophonist, a tarry-black guy with veiny hooded eyes and rubbery lips, handles the deep alto notes. *Ain't been blue. No, no, no.* As Chantal returns to the bar flashing Corky a squinty smile, a winking smile, but Corky gets the idea she's actually afraid of him. That's it! He feels a prick of elation. Saying, "O.K. Chantal, let's cut the shit: my price is four hundred thousand dollars, a hundred twenty thousand up front," waving his checkbook, and Chantal grimaces like he's laid his hand on her pussy, "Mr. Corcoran, I have turned down six offers higher than that!" which Corky knows is a shit-faced lie but he's too much the gentleman to challenge her.

Earlier, Chantal told Corky looking him direct in the face that The Bull's Eye had only been on the market for five months, not knowing that Corky, thanks to Agnes at Ross Drummond's office, knows better.

So that's how it is. Can't trust the cunt.

So what else is new?

There's Corky Corcoran in The Bull's Eye restaurant aged sixteen, squeezing into a booth with his buddies. His bony face freckled and pimply in about equal proportion, in his nervous excitement he'll pick at his pustules not knowing what he's doing. Draws blood sometimes. Fingernails edged with it. Sixteen but so skinny he looks younger. A happy kid, good-natured kid, joking a lot and taking the brunt of jokes, you could say he's a clown, but a shrewd watchful calculating clown, grateful to be laughed with, or at.

So long as they call him, as they've started to, led by Vic Slattery's example, "Corky."

Squeezing into the vinyl booth, Corky and his friends from St. Thomas. Vic Slattery, Heinz Meuller, Eddy Darnton, sometimes the Weisbeck kid, and Vic's cousin whose name Corky has guiltily blotted out, poor bastard would one day die in Vietnam, a Navy pilot. And there might be Vic's girlfriend Sandy Sherman pretty and arch and sure of herself, Sandy from Marymount the girls' Catholic school, and Beatrice Ryan who was Sandy's friend, and who went out occasionally with Darnton, pretty wide-eyed Beatrice with her habit, which was considered cute, of bumming cigarettes from the guys, including Corky, whom otherwise she ignored. (No, Corky was never to ask Beatrice Ryan out. Vic urged him, go on, call her, she's waiting, she likes you, what've you got to lose? but Corky never called Beatrice Ryan. He had too much to lose.)

Crowded into a red-vinyl booth, their habitual booth, at the rear right, in the corner by the jukebox (The Bull's Eye jukebox!—it's still in the restaurant, unless it's a precise replica, complete with a half dozen Elvis Presley selections), Corky Corcoran and his friends.

His friends, sure. And he's a friend of theirs.

So you'd think, seeing them. Loud-laughing high school kids, not public school but private school, something special about them, in their midnight-blue satin jackets with st. thomas scripted in white on the backs. Corky's the skinny red-haired one, Corky's got a high-pitched braying laugh, he's fidgety, funny, a bit of a smart-ass, a dirty mouth to him too, as daring or maybe more than filthy-minded Heinz Meuller, at least when no girls or adults are within earshot. Corky's reputation among these rich kids is he's tough, he's short but scrappy, quick to flare up, prepared to fight. He's from Irish Hill, still lives in Irish Hill, he's the real thing. A terrific guy, everybody's friend. Everybody who matters, in any case. *Corky* Corcoran, not *Jerome* Corcoran. Sure, everybody in Union City knows how his father was killed, but with Corky it's never an issue, absolutely never comes up, he never talks about his family never even his mother who's alive but in some kind of rest home or mental hospital, you don't need to be embarrassed around Corky, *he's just like everybody else, real normal like everybody else, it's like he's forgotten his background so you can forget it too.*

Shutting his eyes seeing looming gigantic as in a dream his friends' faces, Vic's and Heinz's and Eddy's and Weisbeck's—the girls' pretty-powdered vacuous faces—that corner of the restaurant gauzy with ciga-rette smoke: yes but he can't see his own face, can't recognize his own face, my God no. *Don't look, don't risk it, asshole. You know better.* But unable not to look, and unable not to think of those moments of sick worry, the choking sensation in his throat, the fear in his gut of how, say he's meeting the guys at The Bull's Eye and hasn't come with them, or even if he's already there with them but has to go back to the john, he'll discover somebody else has taken his place in the booth: one time it's Brian Cudahy who's a good friend of Vic's, another time it's Gordon Stearns with his date from Marymount, two chairs pulled up to the table so there isn't any room for Corky and nobody notices him not even Vic Slattery distracted in the midst of happy innocently brutal adolescent-male laughter. So Corky's standing there weakly smiling his face hot with blood, Corky's standing there not knowing what to do, how even to retreat unseen. *Tough shit, "Corky." Not that we don't like you, "Corky," sure we like you, "Corky," you poor fuck "Corky," we just forgot you, "Corky," can you live with that?*

Can, and will.

The combo's drifted into a new piece so woozy, unless it's Corky who's woozy, he almost can't identify it, has to listen hard, ponderingly hard, finally hears it's an old favorite of his "Angel Eyes" a true alcohol-soaked song, Corky nods and taps his foot and feels his body yearn to move in sympathy with—exactly what, beyond the music, he doesn't know. *Don't think of it, of her. Of either of them. Don't.* He's in a state not unfamiliar to him where the present tense is all he wants to deal with, the present tense is all there *is.*

Which makes impeccable scientific sense, doesn't it: maybe on the sub-atomic level you can reverse time, not that Corky for all his insomniac reading can comprehend one one-hundredth of that shit, but sure as hell on the atomic level and all levels beyond, you can't.

The shitty trick that Thalia played on him, the shitty trick that Chris-tina's been playing, fuck them both. They're all cunts, that's the bottom line. You can't trust a cunt. Any of them.

Tiredness in Corky's bones, Christ he's an old man of forty-three, never should have lived so long, yes but fuck it he's having a terrific time grooving with the jazz, jazz-y is sex-y, jazz *is* sex, that's the secret. Telling Chantal Crowe who's sitting now on a bar stool beside him sipping a club soda through a straw how he's crazy about The Bull's Eye, since he'd been a kid he'd been crazy about the place, so many happy memories here so he's got to buy it, can't let anybody else buy it, he's determined. Eyes misting over as he confides in Chantal Crowe pouring his heart out to this woman he scarcely knows and does not in fact trust except in his woozy-mellow state he's forgotten and she's nodding encouragingly, smiling listening without hearing, waiting patiently for drunken Corky Corcoran to get down to business and meet her price, she's sensing the end is rapidly approaching, and thank God, she's been on her feet for hours only now managing to sit down, it's 1:40 A.M. and twenty minutes till closing and the place is emptying out though still loud, shrill-drunk jabbering and wheezing laughter and the jazz combo jiving like their instruments too are laughing coarse and slurred, and here's Corky Corcoran the high roller bleary-eyed and swaying even on his bar stool so drunk Chantal will have to send the poor fool home in a taxi to be delivered like a bundle of sodden laundry, but he's talking urgently, with growing desperation, waving his checkbook in Chantal's bemused face, "—Won't take four hundred thousand, O.K. then Chantal how's about four hundred twenty-five thousand?" and Chantal hesitates, about to shake her head *no* but before she can Corky says, "O.K. then I'll raise my price: how's about four hundred fifty thousand?" a look in his eyes like his balls are being twisted and seeing Chantal is still about to shake her head *no* he says, frantic, furious, face hot with blood and the bruise on his forehead throbbing, "—O.K. fuck it I'll go to four hundred sixty thousand but that's my final price," and at last after a pause and a sigh Chantal gives in, a murmured, "*Alors*, Mr. Corcoran—four hundred sixty thousand dollars is a price I will accept," batting her spiky eyelashes at him, like all these hours it's her precious cunt she's been guarding and what pleasure now to give in, to surrender, "Yes, Mr. Corcoran, four hundred sixty thousand dollars for The Bull's Eye is a price Demetrius would allow me to accept."

Corky says quickly, "It's a deal!"

Though rubbing his knuckles in his watery eyes and blinking and staring, he's disbelieving, incredulous, but God! how happy!—repeating, "It's a deal! It's a deal! *It's a deal!*" so it comes about that Corky Corcoran with fingers he has to steady with his left hand as he writes makes out a check from Corcoran, Inc., payable to "Chantal Crowe" for a down payment of thirty percent of $460,000 which is $138,000 postdated May 27, 1992.

It's a deal.

PART III

Sunday, May 24, 1992

CORKY MAKES A VOW

*O*wing money is like lice in the crotch, no matter how hard you scratch the fuckers can itch harder.

Who's telling Corky this, hot meaty-garlic breath in his face so he's close to gagging, is it Grandpa Liam?—the old man long dead but scolding and censorious, and that angry grin of his given an inflamed look by his stumpy yellowed teeth. These secrets dealt out by the dead like pinochle cards coming so fast Corky's clumsy fingers can't grasp them. He's leaning away from the old man so the back of his head's pressed hard against something metallic but uneven, a rod or a lever, God knows. He's trying not to breathe desperate to keep from puking. Stomach tilting and lurching like a rowboat adrift on the choppy river. Explaining earnest and urgent as a schoolkid *But business debts are different from personal debts! you need to borrow other people's money to make your own* and the old man derisive with his barking laugh, a wave of his fist, stub of a cigar between his second and third fingers. *Don't do it, y' hear? don't make that mistake. And if you do, son, don't come bellyaching to me.*

Through his eyelids, his eyes shut tight in the grimace of his jaws, Corky's oppressed by the glare of an arc light high overhead. And the cloud-massed night sky soaking up a furnace-y red glow from the South Union City and Shehawkin factories. Penetrating the Caddy's windshield splotched by drizzle which should decrease the light's intensity but seems somehow to increase it. And his head's jammed in this space like a nut gripped by a nutcracker. And his left ear feels shredded. And he *is* going to puke if he so much as moves his smallest toe but, toward morning, a sudden piercing pressure in his bladder, he's got to move, or piss his pants and the luxury-leather car seat.

Desperately flailing then, managing to get the car door open for (he seems to know) it's the door handle that's been making an indentation in the back of his skull, Corky finds himself groaning on hands and knees in sharp gravel his eyes still shut, begins retching even as his crazed fingers unzip his fly, vomiting in helpless spasms an acid-hot liquid bearing little resemblance to Johnnie Walker Red Label even as an equally acid-hot liquid sprays from his cock.

When he's depleted at both ends, like a sponge wrung dry, he's too exhausted to climb back into what he's forgotten is his car precisely, for it could also be, in his wayward dreaming, a hospital bed of the sort he'd glimpsed in one of Theresa's hospitals with straps and buckles and something to grip the head, so he lies where he'd fallen, amid the sharp stench of vomit and piss, *his eyes still shut.*

How, as a kid, he'd risen through dense layers of sleep clinging to sleep terrified of waking never wanting to wake to the horror of what awaited him on the front stoop of the house and so long as *his eyes are shut* he was not awake, need never awake.

"Hey mister! Hey you! You alive?"

This voice, a woman's voice, urgent but charged by hilarity, a short distance away so she's shouting—Corky's eyelids flutter open at once, no idea where he is, what the fuck has happened to him but he's alert and responsible squinting toward the figure on a pedestrian bridge, can't make out the face but knows by the voice this is a black woman and so to his profound relief not likely to be one of his Maiden Vale constituents.

"Y'need some help there, mister? Hey?"

The woman's cupping her hands to her mouth, about thirty feet from where Corky's lying in the gravel, curious about coming any nearer. Just wants to know, Corky guesses, if he's alive or dead.

He tries to lift his head that's heavy as cement. Tries to lift a hand. Tries to speak—"No I'm O.K.—" but his voice is too weak to carry and he's shivering, God-damned teeth chattering like crazy.

Evidently there's a kid with the woman Corky hadn't noticed, for this kid, a black boy of maybe eight, comes trotting over, wide-eyed, staring, thumb between his teeth, stopping a few feet from Corky and their eyes lock and Corky tries to grin now managing to sit up, and to rub at his eyes, assuring the kid he's fine—"No cops or ambulance, please." And the kid backs off, calls to his mother what sounds like, "Aw he O.K., just some drunk," and Corky hears the woman's laughter coming rich and melodious and cruel and next thing Corky knows he's opening his eyes for the second time, might be an hour later or only minutes. This time lying stiff and aching on his side and at once he's panicked hearing silence, why no traffic here close beside the Millard Fillmore Expressway where he seems to remember he parked his car, or had the car drifted off the pavement and onto the shoulder and bounced gently to a stop beneath a billboard, so the wisest move's to park it, asshole. But Corky doesn't hear the Expressway, doesn't hear the sounds of the city he should be hearing if the city is alive and the Bomb has not been dropped and all life save his extinct, an actual cold sweat breaking out on his body inside his soiled clothes and the hairs on his head stirring even as the sweet-sonorous chimes of what he recognizes as St. Mary Assumption Church begin and he thinks *That's why: it's Sunday* and a profound relief floods through him for though he's hungover as wretchedly as ever he can recall and lying in actual filth he's damned glad to be alive in Union City with all its other citizens.

It's 7:48 A.M. by the time Corky can coordinate himself, legs, arms, head, volition, to climb back inside the car, yes and thank God there *is* the car and nobody stole it, nor stole your wallet either, fuckface, and drive back home to Summit Park his head aching and eyes tearing up so he's fearful of driving beyond thirty miles an hour (and the Expressway virtually deserted, and the traffic lights blinking yellow on Union Boulevard and Summit and no cops anywhere), carrying the exquisite misery of his hangover as if it were a basket of eggs balanced on his head, how lucky you are asshole just to be alive, and *no more whiskey, nor even beer and ale*, from this hour forward.

No more, you've had it. You know you've had it.

Just some drunk.

Corky's sick recalling the car's screeching tires of the night before. Slick wet pavement, the Expressway ramp, and he'd hit the brake as a reflex, too stewed to know what he was doing like a boxer out on his feet but still throwing punches. Fucking-fantastic lucky he didn't skid in the other direction across the median and into oncoming traffic. Or didn't plow into a pedestrian turning out of The Bull's Eye lot where he'd quarreled with Chantal Crowe insisting he take a taxi home. Just lucky, no drunk-driving arrest, vehicular homicide and a mandatory minimum of ten years, or is it twenty, which is what you deserve shithead.

Shithead alcoholic.

Yes you know: you're an alcoholic you're a sick son of a bitch.

Because it's in the blood. The curse of the Corcorans, the curse of the Irish. Like, what's it called, sickle-cell anemia, the blood curse of the black race.

So what you're going to do, Corky, is this: first thing Monday morning,—no, Tuesday: tomorrow's fucking Memorial Day—you're going to AA headquarters on State Street, no better at the hospital where Uncle Sean went in case somebody recognizes you.

No more whiskey, nor even beer and ale. No wine. From this hour forward.

CORKY DISCOVERS A THEFT

I t must be the sweet-teasing scent of lilac borne on the chilly air that sets Corky off.

The lilac *Don't think of it! of her! don't* in a panoply of beauty so intense it brings tears to his eyes, tall bushes forming a hedge in the rear yard disguising the mean-looking wrought-iron fence that's Corky's height.

He's inspecting the Caddy in the driveway, he's on shaky legs but knows it must be done. Eyes throbbing taking in another long derisive scratch on the passenger's side, dents in the right front fender that look as if they've been made by a bottle opener, and there's a general splattering of mud reminding him of nothing so much as the wayward drunken applause of The Bull's Eye's patrons when the combo did not so much finish their final set the night before as abandon it, the saxophonist by this time blowing spittily and near-tuneless through his magnificent instrument.

Corky inspects the damage muttering, "Shit. Shit. Shit."

And wafting to his nostrils the mocking fragrance of the lilac.

His lilac. *His* bushes. *His* property.

Entering then the preposterous house, his house, and as so frequently at such times Corky imagines he hears, or actually does hear, echoes preceding him, whispers and murmurs and laughter emanating from the front rooms *Some drunk! just some drunk* the revenants of the very parties Charlotte and he used to give to which (he'd thought wryly) Corky Corcoran himself wouldn't have been invited if, sucker, he hadn't been the host.

In the rear hall and entering the kitchen, always a surprise, the size of that kitchen, Corky's already fumbling with his clothes eager to get them off, removes his vomit-stained sport coat and tears at his shirt, fucking cuffs he can't unbutton, in a sudden fury of revulsion he rips from his torso, arms, wrists the proudly monogrammed metallic-blue cotton twill shirt Christina Kavanaugh has never seen, the very shirt he'd put on preening in a mirror seeing himself in his own stepdaughter's admiring eyes, his stepdaughter who did not in fact see the shirt either, and never will. Corky wads these articles of overpriced clothing into a sloppy ball and throws it down onto the earthenware-tiled floor Mrs. Krauss maintains buffed to a high useless sheen. Yanks off his shoes then, the right, the left, these both urine-stained and-stinking, and throws them down, a loud noise meant not simply, though primarily, for Corky's own pleasure but also with the intention of alerting any intruders who may be in the house that the homeowner's home, and might be armed.

Except, fuckhead, the Luger's upstairs in your bedroom where the thief has already discovered it. A slender black youth with a knitted-wool cap pulled down over his forehead, gloating eyes, a big smile. Lifting the white man's fancy revolver and turning it in his hand. This piece gonna *work?*

Corky's fingers fumble to unzip his fly except—it's already unzipped. And still damp. And in a frenzy then swaying on one leg he tears at his trousers, the elegant gabardine dove-gray he'd liked so much viewing himself in the three-way mirror of the Gentleman's Boutique at the Hyatt, unless it was the Esquire Shop at the Hilton, a mannequin-handsome spic-looking kid salesman flattering him so he wound up buying three pairs, a rush order to the tailor for a next-day pickup. The trousers, which are both vomit- and urine-stained, he wads too into a ball and tosses onto the kitchen floor, then reconsiders, and snatches up, with the other garments, to stuff into a plastic trash container beneath the sink. Doesn't want poor Mrs. Krauss examining this evidence and drawing conclusions about her employer that, though accurate, will only cause her distress.

Corky then, after these exertions, stands with feet rooted to the spot, though body swaying, and waits for the powerful nausea in his gut to pass, also he dares not move his head for fear the fistful of shattered glass inside his skull will slide as well causing enormous jangling pain.

Corky Corcoran in soiled Jockey shorts and undershirt in his stocking feet in the showcase kitchen of the house his former wife inveigled him into buying and then departed, early Sunday morning and he's alone wild-eyed and trembling. A mouth that tastes and feels like it's encrusted with dried shit. Splotched vision like the TV when local motherfucker planes fly too low. *Yes, but Monday—no, fuck it: Tuesday—morning you're turning yourself in to AA.*

Imagining a bugle band awaiting him. Applause, handshakes, hugs. Corky Corcoran, at last! Like the Knights of Columbus brass welcome band in the old days before they all decided he was shit, Mayor Buck Glover visited Irish Hill celebrating his reelections.

Corky moves on. Toast crumbs sharp as gravel underfoot where (he can barely remember this, let alone why) yesterday in a rage he'd swept the toaster onto the floor, the toaster itself dented but smartly gleaming on a counter. And there's a dried sprig of lilac on the floor Corky looks away quickly not to see.

Don't! just don't.

In the sink are glasses, plates. Coffee cups with tarry pools of coffee in them. Corky guesses he should try to eat or drink something, hasn't eaten anything except crap peanuts since lunch yesterday at Bobby Ray's Sports Bar. It's a fact alcoholics never eat right. It's a fact your kidneys and liver can go overnight. There's pineapple juice in the refrigerator but the thought of it turns Corky's stomach. And the leftover coffee, days old, fuck that.

Corky pushes out into the hall, heart pounding and he's itchy with nerves and a worry that in the corner of his eye scuttling across the ceiling there's a cockroach, or cockroaches, but he doesn't want to look because he knows nothing's there. Hungover lately he's starting to see these things, not see them exactly but imagine he's about to see them. Beginning of the D.T.'s.

The way old Hock Corcoran went out, his brain rotted and babbling and clawing at himself convinced he was covered in stinging red ants.

Laid out on a slab, at the morgue. Dead meat.

Magna est veritas et praevalebit.

Scratching himself, his fuzz-matted chest, his crotch. Digging his nails punishingly into his pubic hair recalling that vivid dream, *Owing money is like lice in the crotch,* Grandpa Liam's voice so loud in his ear he'd've sworn the old guy was right beside him in the car but it's weird because Liam Corcoran died when Corky was five years old so the warning about incurring debts wasn't made to him, must have been made to Corky's father and Corky overheard.

On the stairs Corky's balancing his head to keep the razor-sharp slivers of glass from sliding inside his brain. In his stocking feet and underwear, Christina should see him now. He's gripping the banister to keep his balance. A panicky sensation that there *is* someone in the house. But he knows better: nobody could break in here, it's like a fortress, $2000 worth of burglar alarm equipment with a hair-trigger sensitivity, sometimes activated by the very wind, years ago Thalia's cat Ruffles. Goddamned thing has a deafening siren that rings both on the premises and in the Eleventh Precinct station.

"Hey? Anybody here?"

Upstairs Corky pauses to listen, his heartbeat's enormous and he's panting. A terror touches him that he's going to die, an explosion of bullets so sudden and so without warning he won't be capable of grasping the fact of his own death.

Yet, if being observed, even if only by God in Whom he doesn't believe, Corky can't weaken. He's urged forward possessed suddenly by an idea, goes to the guest suite where, still, his fancy shirts lie tossed on the bed untouched, he enters the bathroom to see nothing—no one—the thick, spotless towels as before, the sparkling porcelain sink and toilet, the tub. A bar of sculpted soap on a ledge untouched. *Fucking little cocktease, I can't believe you played such a trick on me. Your own step-Daddy!* In a fury that propels him magically before the murderous pounding of his head he slams out of the bathroom and opens a closet door in the bedroom, empty save for tremulous coat hangers on a rail and extra blankets on a shelf, he rushes into the hall where there's a closet (though only a linen closet, entirely shelves), opens this door and shuts it in virtually the same motion, then enters his own bedroom and opens closets, poor Corky choked with frustration—no Thalia hiding in here, only clothes, Corky's clothes, thousands of bucks' worth of clothes.

The throbbing in his head catches up with him like a wave breaking over a heedless swimmer. Almost blind, Corky gropes his way to the bedside table, seeming to know beforehand what he will find, or won't find— "Jesus, Mary, and Joseph!—*fuck!*" The Luger's gone from the drawer.

Corky yanks the drawer out farther so it falls out, God damn it and no gun! *no gun!*

Desperate now he stoops to look behind the table, beneath the bed—

nothing. Sweeps his alarm clock and a stack of paperbacks to the floor, yanks the bedspread off the bed—nothing. Gone? The Luger's gone? Corky's wild-eyed, panting, helpless. Sits heavily on the edge of the bed, grips his head with both hands to contain the terrible throbbing of blood vessels on the verge of bursting, he's losing it, he's going to pass out, a black pit opening before him sucking him in even as he tells himself, furious, outraged, you fuckhead, you supreme asshole, thinking she'd come to see *you* and what she'd come for was to take from you the sole object of value in her eyes you possessed: a gun.

3

CORKY BREAKS DOWN

Yeah? Wha—"

"Corky—?"

"Who's it?—*Shit!*" Groping for the God-damned phone receiver that's no sooner in his hand than it slips out and tumbles to the floor beside the bed, Corky's eyes still shut tight and his face grimaced like a Fiji war mask, he's clumsy fumbling for it not fully aware of his surroundings not the time of day nor even the day, wakened from a sleep more akin to coma than sleep by a fierce idiotic mechanically repeating noise close beside his head, the sleep of utter oblivion which the elder Corcorans would speak of as *a sleep at the bottom of a well*, "O.K., yeah, h'lo?" Corky's trying his best to respond as if he's up and conscious and not at all disturbed by the call. Opening an eye to see, Jesus Christ it's 11:09 A.M. Still Sunday?

"Corky, good morning, I hope I didn't wake you—"

"Sandra? Hell, no—"

"Or, if there's someone with you, I'm not—"

It's Sandra Slattery, not Charlotte as Corky's first thought, and she's being funny-teasing, for it's Corky Corcoran's fabled reputation among such long-married family-oriented straight-good-citizens as Vic and Sandra Slattery that he's the man-about-town he's the wild-living bachelor-womanizer hard drinker and gambler the rogue Irishman Corky, Corky the Mystery Man, never know when or where he's going to turn up or with who or what's the deal until it's a done deal and Corky's nonnegotiable price has been met, yes and you never know whose wife he's been screwing until that too is a done deal, that's Corky Corcoran for you!—lucky bastard.

"No, no—good to hear your—"

"—you're sure? Really?"

Quickly swinging his legs, he sees they're bare legs, off the bed to sit up, he's in his underwear?—sweaty-entangled with bed-clothes, and head pounding and eyes burning as if somehow while comatose he's been staring into the sun, Corky's yet shrewd enough to fall in with Sandra's kidding, it's an affectionate kidding never laced with reproach or accusation or sexual innuendo as he'd get with another woman. For twenty-one years Corky Corcoran and Vic Slattery's wife Sandra have been a fixed equation as two satellites unwaveringly revolving in orbits around a planet are a fixed equation—no sudden attractions, no missteps or mistakes, no collisions. If Sandra wasn't Vic's wife and if Vic wasn't Corky's closest-oldest friend, not even taking into account who Vic Slattery as a public figure is, and whose son, it's highly possible, even probable, that Corky-the-rogue would have made moves on her—Sandra *is* his type: classy, good-looking, smart, self-possessed—and this Corky's gallant enough, and subtle enough, to have allowed Sandra to suspect since the night of Vic's and Sandra's wedding party at the Union City Athletic Club, St. Valentine's Day 1972, when, under cover of being affably drunk, he'd kissed her a little too forcibly on the lips. "—You know me, Sandra: up since dawn working—" and they laugh together, each comforted by the fiction as by a secret password.

Now he's sitting up Corky feels a little better. Not great, but better. Trying to concentrate on Sandra's words which come at a fast clip, "—sorry you didn't drop by last night, we were waiting for you—we'd *hoped*—before tomorrow night—" and Corky blurts out, "Oh Christ, Sandra, I forgot—" at once wanting to bite his tongue he's made this admission which isn't very flattering to the Slatterys—of all people, the Slatterys!—and a fuckhead remark in any case. So he has to double back and explain, or make a show of explaining. Can't tell the truth, has to invent a plausible-sounding truth. Not what the past two days have been precisely but what they've been in the abstract, sheer confusion and hell, humiliation, anxiety, helplessness—"And there's more to come. I don't know how much more of it I can take, but there's more to come."

"Corky, what on earth is it? You're scaring me."

Corky's sitting hunched over on the edge of his rumpled bed vigorously scratching his head, his chest, his lumpy belly like a chimp with fleas. Reaches inside the tight elastic waistband of his shorts scratching. His pubic hair, his limp and alarmingly clammy testicles. Maybe in fact he has fleas. Lice? He's stammering and stumbling not knowing what to say, of course it was a mistake to make such an admission to Sandra Slattery as to virtually any woman, must be a half-deliberate mistake inviting the woman's solicitude and considerable warmth, every woman a potential mother, and a potential lover if not a wife in reserve. (Is Vic listening in to this conversation? Corky, who believes his friend a man of near-absolute integrity, certainly the most honest man of Corky's wide and dubious acquaintance, nonetheless thinks this might be a possibility.) He tells Sandra it's a personal crisis, something he'd rather not discuss, which only piques Sandra's curiosity the more, and stokes her female compassion, and this in turn weakens Corky who's dangerously close to losing it breaking down entirely like a hysterical woman confiding in Sandra his anxiety about Thalia, what Thalia has done, what the fuck's he going to do about Thalia, yes but he can't expose her for Christ's sake, no more to his friends than to the police. He can't, won't. He's got to protect her. Thalia's vulnerable having broken the law and Corky's for sure not going to report *that:* not just the theft of the Luger but she's obviously carrying it on her person, a concealed firearm, the New York State statute's rough even for first-time offenders, a mandatory two years in prison!— *two years!* The possibility of Thalia being arrested, booked, actually imprisoned, makes Corky feel faint and he loses the thread of his own subterfuge.

There's a pause. Then, gently as if she's reaching down inside Corky's shorts, past his lumpy belly and prickly pubic hair, to take hold of his genitals, gently, so very gently, not as a sexual overture so much as a gesture of sheer female solicitude, and knowing by instinct where to take hold most cunningly, Sandra asks, "Corky, what *is* it?—you sound so unlike yourself." And Corky's in a paralysis of misery wanting to confide in this woman wanting to bury his face against her breasts, he deserves some sympathy himself for Christ's sweet sake, yes and some pity, but how can he speak of his stepdaughter without betraying her? and how so much as hint of her wild accusations against Vic without betraying Vic?—so soon after Marilee Plummer's death, this would be an unforgivable insult Corky can't bring himself to make against his friend. For there's a bond of maleness that does not so much repudiate the female as transcend her:

the anxious intimacy of brother-rivals who dare never accuse one another of any *manly* sin for fear of being expelled irrevocably from that intimacy.

So Corky says, like a man in a falling elevator rushing to speak before it crashes, "—I'm in love with a woman I thought loved me, and it's over—I feel like shit—since Friday—oh Jesus, Sandra, I really loved her and it blew up in my face and I've come to the end of something—" sobbing appalled at his own sudden helplessness and unable to stop like his heart's truly broken, poor Corky Corcoran and he hadn't known that fact until now.

4

CORKY GEARS UP

ever race a train Timothy Patrick Corcoran used to say with a droll twist of his mouth suggesting the futility and self-destructiveness of such a maneuver, but now Corky's wondering if the remark also means only race vehicles you're sure you can beat.

"Anyway I'll try."

He spends the brief remainder of Sunday morning preparing for action. It's an emergency situation with Thalia, he thinks, but he can't act without thinking, he can't get desperate and further fuck things up.

At least, the shock of it, discovering the Luger gone, and the lucky call from Sandra Slattery, has had the effect of sobering Corky up.

(It's a lucky call, coming when it did, and Corky doesn't care to consider the circumstances of the call, he's dismissed the possibility there are reasons other than friendship for Sandra's having made it, fuck such suspicions. He'll clear things up with Vic when he sees him tonight. Vic would never lie, nor even distort the truth, to *him*. Sure Corky feels like an asshole breaking down crying over the phone but Sandra was tactful, didn't pry out of him the identity of his lover, which in his weakened state Corky might have revealed, only exacted from him the promise that he'll come have dinner with her and Vic tonight—"Just the three of us.")

Now fully sober, and determined to remain so, Corky takes a cool shower and shaves carefully steadying his right hand with his left avoiding his bloodshot eyes in the mirror, in fact his entire face is showing symptoms of being bloodshot, but he continues calmly swallowing down two more Bufferins and another time he gargles and cleanses his mouth to rid himself of the taste of a colossal drunk and its aftershock. Rehearsing *I am an alcoholic, I'm here to get help* which is what he's heard the AA people ask of you. Why's it supposed to be a tough admission to make *I am an alcoholic I need help*, Corky's thinking it will be a snap, like Dave Winfield hitting that homer: the *crack!* of the ball and its beautiful trajectory out above center field and into the stands and the Brownian movement of the spectators in the stadium leaning inward toward the ball's flight, drop— and that beautiful too, like a flower's petals closing. At least, for Corky, alone in his bathroom whistling through his teeth grooming himself for the day, rehearsing the words is a snap.

Shit, thinks Corky—I should've bet the Jays would win the World Series too, while I was at it.

Next combing his damp hair as flatly somber as he can. Dressing then not showily today, as if he's of a mind to attend mass (but he can't: the last mass for the day, everywhere in Union City, is at noon), but as modestly as his wardrobe allows—white cotton shirt and cufflinks, plain beige- linen tie, tan sport coat and trousers. Before leaving his bedroom he gives in to the need, though he knows it's futile, to search for the missing gun another time, maybe Thalia played her sucker of a step-Daddy a prank by hiding it in his sock drawer or in the crotch of his silk designer pajamas or in a pocket of a sport or suit coat in his closet—but no. Don't get excited, and don't get hot. Corky replaces the table drawer, replaces the alarm clock which is still whirring away, no stopping it, the red minute hand circling the fixed point at the center, now 11:38 A.M.

Still, now his hangover's lifted and he's freshened up he's feeling what you'd call *guardedly optimistic.*

Downstairs Corky takes the time to brew fresh coffee and even to drink some fruit juice steeling himself against a moment of gagging, he's whistling "Angel Eyes" thinking of last night's decision to buy The Bull's Eye not wanting to think it's a mistake and beyond a mistake a mystifica- tion, why does Corky Corcoran do the wild impulsive things he does, it's as if another man makes these decisions, yes but Corky *is* the man—isn't he? The Jesuits used to warn of the "influence of the Devil" but in their ambiguous jargon you couldn't tell really is there a Devil or isn't there. But there *is* freedom of the human will. The "age of reason" is only seven years, meaning once you have your seventh birthday you're on your own and responsible. Meaning you can condemn yourself to Hell and have only yourself to blame.

The Bull's Eye!—Corky's heart leaps at the prospect. Sure, the place needs extensive renovations, probably a new kitchen, new plumbing, new wiring, new floor, but that knockout bar! the mirrors! the diner! yes and the location, crummy at first glance, might be made into an asset, there's the Downtown Refurbishing Project that's been languishing in a City Council committee for the past year stalled by some Charter code-law and maybe, just maybe, Corky Corcoran and one or two other Council members friendly with the Mayor can get on the committee and push the project through and fuck the Charter, it's been done before and by both sides, Slattery and anti-Slattery and Corky's thinking it's our turn now and if it isn't a deal can be struck and if it's struck off the record—no record in the official minutes—the *Journal* reporter assigned to the City Hall beat won't know shit about it. And if the Refurbishing Project gets funded, and that much of that section of South Main razed and rebuilt, The Bull's Eye will be worth a lot more than $460,000 in a few years. Won't it?

Right now though Corky's got to think of covering his ass to the tune of $138,000. By Wednesday. Maybe Ross Drummond would lend it, the old man's been bellyaching he never sees Corky anymore since the divorce. I think of you as a son, Corky, not just a son-in-law, O.K. now's your chance Pops to help me out.

It must've been a wild scene last night at The Bull's Eye—Corky negotiating with Chantal Crowe amid the jazz. The sly bitch maybe thinks she put something over on Corky Corcoran but Corky Corcoran's a man you don't fuck with.

Owing money is like lice in the crotch no matter how hard you scratch but fuck that somber counsel, Corky's all grown up now.

Fat Sunday edition of the *Journal*, weighs a ton, and mostly crap— Corky tosses away the full-color advertising sections, the comics he sets aside for later, real estate and business, sports. Quickly scanning the front page seeing there's no new news of Marilee Plummer, funeral's this afternoon at 4 P.M., a "private ceremony." No new news of Marcus Steadman who's still in hiding in Shehawkin. Can't blame the bastard. Corky can imagine himself in hiding too, someday. His picture in the paper, front page: City Councilman Jerome Corcoran.

Arrest? Indictment? Obituary?

Multimillion-dollar deal clinched?

Most of the news is depressing as usual, just as well Corky doesn't have time to read it this morning, neo-Nazi firebombs in Germany, more fighting and killing in that remote region Bosnia, what's that got to do with *us*, and, God damn, yet another item on that local motherfucker-creep Nickson who fed his baby to the dog, Family Services checked him and his wife out only a week before the atrocity, and there's a photo of George Bush with his sappy-phony PR grin and dumb-fuck eyes accepting an honorary degree from Princeton University, and a long feature on this weirdo Texas billionaire Ross Perot—CLINTON KNOCKED OFF COURSE BY RISING TIDE FOR PEROT.

Just what the Democrats need, Corky thinks, clenching his fists, twelve years in the shithouse and now some kooky third-party spoiler comes along to fuck things up.

Corky shoves that section of the paper aside, he's had enough. Reads about yesterday's game in Detroit, the Blue Jays flying high in first place in the league, nice photo of Dave Winfield slamming the ball out of the park, some things do turn out O.K. That's what God made American sports for: to compensate for the rest of the shit.

Caffeine in his blood so he's getting charged, geared up, his first call's to Charlotte, can't forestall it any longer, she answers on practically the first ring and must be in a rare mood not immediately reproaching him for not having called but actually saying, "Oh!—Corky!" forgetting to call him "Jer-ome" so Corky thinks, *That's* sweet, but has to tell her the bad news: Thalia did show up yesterday, and Corky did try to talk to her, but— And Charlotte interrupts, "Oh my God, *what?* She stole your *Luger?*" and Corky says quickly, "Not so loud, I don't think we want anybody to know, do we?" and Charlotte says, alarmed, stammering, "—Oh my God, oh Corky, oh what are we going to do," and Corky says, "Don't get hysterical, I've got a plan," but Charlotte as usual isn't listening running at the mouth, "—How could you! That gun! Where was it, in the bedroom? In that drawer? Is it loaded? Oh God is she—suicidal, do you think?" and Corky says, "I—don't think so," and Charlotte lashes out, "What do you mean, you don't 'think' so?" and Corky says, trying to remain calm, picking his nose, "Charlotte, honey, I don't know, I don't think she is, I think probably it's one of her ruses, you know how she is, these attention-getting stunts," which isn't what Corky exactly means to say, he's vulnerable and Charlotte leaps in outrage saying, "'Stunts'! How can you! When she almost died of anorexia, was that a 'stunt'?" and Corky, beginning to lose it, temples pulsing, says, "Look, it *was* a stunt, that kind of behavior *is* stunt behavior, no matter it was almost fatal, stunts *can* be fatal, that's all I meant," and Charlotte says, "My God, you're so unfeeling, I can't believe what I'm hearing," and Corky says, "Don't start attacking me, we don't have time right now to attack me, O.K.?—this is an emergency situation," and Charlotte says, breathless, "I'll go to her! I'll find her! I'll bring her home with me— I'll make things right between us!" and Corky says, wiping a slick clot of snot on Ross Perot's squinty-beaming photo, "Sure, honey, but where are you going to find her? *I* couldn't find her all day yesterday and the day before," and Charlotte says, "Isn't she—that place on Highland—" and Corky says, and what pleasure in this witty sarcasm, "That's the one certain thing about your daughter, as of this moment: 8397 Highland is the single place she *isn't*."

So Charlotte shuts up for a while and lets Corky talk, it's his plan to make some calls and try to track Thalia down, he'll leave messages for her, and Charlotte should do the same, but nothing hysterical, remember Thalia loves to stir things up, yes she's a serious young woman and she's certainly an intelligent young woman but she's also an exhibitionist, Corky's tempted to add *like her mother* except that's not fair, maybe— practically every woman Corky's ever known except the homely ones are exhibitionists, and even some of them. Charlotte seems to accept this. (There's a soft snuffling sound on the line: is she crying?) Hesitantly, she brings up the subject of the police, and they both agree the police should remain out of this, God, if this got in the news! and tied in somehow with Marilee Plummer's death! and Corky says, "Don't tell anybody, even Gavin, O.K.?" and Charlotte says, in a faint, sardonic voice, "Oh don't worry, I won't tell *him*," so Corky's left to wonder pleasantly what that means. He's about to hang up when Charlotte says, in that sudden afterthought way of hers that means really she's been planning it all along, "Jerome, will you drop by? Sometime today? Regardless of whether you locate Thalia? I'd just like to see you," and Corky says, flattered but wary, "Well, maybe," and Charlotte says, not begging because that isn't her style, but urgent enough, "I'd just like to see you, we need to talk, mainly it's Thalia but it's other things too, don't you feel the same way? I'll be home all afternoon," and Corky says uneasily, "Look, don't wait around for me, you know how things are," and Charlotte says, "I didn't say I'd be waiting around for you, I said I'd be home all afternoon in case you drop by, is that too much of an encroachment upon your precious bachelor freedom?" hanging up the receiver just hard enough to make Corky wince.

By this time he's been picking his nose so furiously he's started a minor nosebleed.

Corky's strangely stirred by the conversation with Charlotte, doesn't love the woman any longer and for sure isn't *in love* with her but . . . it's weird, it's unsettling, how deep some connections go. Like trees whose roots have grown together underground. It's the last place in the world Corky's going to drop by today, the million-dollar house Charlotte and her third husband Gavin Pierson own in Chateauguay Falls, he'd rather return to the fucking morgue than wind up there, that heavy neurotic bitch, that lying manipulative cunt, no thanks! But hearing her cry just now, envisioning her face crinkled and about to dissolve Corky's baffled at his own response. Or maybe it's Thalia, the riddle of Thalia between him and Charlotte, as if in fact somehow beyond his reckoning and certainly beyond his wish or desire Thalia *is* his daughter, and so his responsibility.

Removing a wad of bloodstained Kleenex from his nose gingerly looking to see if the nosebleed's stopped.

Corky calls Thalia at the Highland Avenue address and leaves a message on her answering machine, now operating, *Honey this is just to say I'm not angry but I am worried, will you check back with me when you can?* in so frank and neutral a voice, nobody'd ever guess he'd like to strangle the little bitch.

Fuck, fuck me, did you want to fuck me yes and that's not all.

Next, Corky calls George Presson, Vic's lawyer-friend from Georgetown, technically he's a friend of Corky's too except the men can't stand each other, trying to track down Kiki whose last name Corky doesn't know but the shrewd prick Presson insists he doesn't know it either—"Isn't the girl a friend of yours, Corky?" Coolly Corky says, "No, she was a friend of Marilee Plummer's," and this stops Presson dead so there's a beat of a few seconds, just silence. Corky asks innocently what's wrong, did I say the wrong thing, and Presson starts stammering, "No, I'm— just feeling what a tragedy it is, a young woman like Marilee, gone," and Corky says, "Yeah, it's shitty, if that's what tragedy is—shit," and again there's an awkward pause, Corky's tensed up wishing he could see Presson's face, it's a pinkish-rosy face a cross between a baby's face and a football, something stitched and prim about the mouth, rich-boy Catholic schools outdistancing Corky Corcoran who may have gone to St. Thomas Aquinas but only out of Oscar Slattery's charity, and not even a full year at Rensselaer Polytechnic, Irish Hill mick. If Corky could see Presson's face he could read his cards, he's played poker a few times with the guy and what a pushover Presson is, $300-an-hour lawyer but no match for Corky Corcoran. None of the rich boys are. Corky's cocking his head grinning at the splotched glass roof of the solarium, decides to risk it, pushing a little, "—This Kiki, I don't know how reliable she is but she's been reported saying Vic and Marilee Plummer were involved somehow, you know anything about that, George?—*I don't*," and Presson says, in a voice neutral as Corky's on Thalia's tape, "Why ask me, Corky?—why not ask Vic?"

"Yeah," says Corky, sneering like a kid, "—I'm going there for dinner tonight, maybe I will."

Knowing Presson won't tell Vic about this conversation, Presson isn't the type. An upscale lawyer, Washington connections, doesn't get *his* hands dirty.

Next, Corky calls Mike Rooney who's the other guy in the snapshot he knows he can trust not to buzz things back to Vic, Rooney isn't the type either, Vic's press secretary and a speechwriter-researcher, a civilized man not like Red Pitts, say, whose connection to his boss and thus to his boss's son is tight as if his heart's ventricles are entwined with theirs, no fucking around with a pro like Pitts. And Corky has luck, too, first calling Rooney's house then tracking him down at the golf club, that's to say the Union City Golf Club, the old-money WASP club, and a Rooney in it, like a Corcoran in the U.C.A.C., shows how times have changed in America. Corky hooks up with Rooney on his cellular phone, he's still out on the course and flushed-sounding with a good morning's game and friendly enough to Corky if a little curious at the circumstances of the call, it's an emergency? 11:55 A.M. Sunday? so Corky sets Rooney straight, a story that rolls off his tongue like he's rehearsed it which he has not, he's trying to find out the last name of that girl Kiki who's a friend of Corky's stepdaughter Thalia because Thalia is at Kiki's and a mutual friend of the girls has just called hoping to get in touch with them, but Thalia didn't leave any number with Corky and Corky can't reach Charlotte, Corky just wants to be helpful, you know? Rooney says amiably, "Kiki!—I think her last name is Zaller, Zeiler, something like that, and her first name is Katherine, she's in the directory," laughing like a nudge in Corky's ribs meaning the cunt's wide open? meat on a rack? so Corky says, offended, "Hey I'm calling for my daughter," and Rooney says, laughing louder, "O.K., Corky, tell 'em both hello for me."

But before they hang up Rooney asks Corky, more serious, if he's prepared his tribute to Vic for the fund-raiser yet, and Corky says not exactly, he's working on it, and Rooney asks if he needs any help, any information, and Corky says hell no, he knows Vic and he knows Vic's congressional record, and Rooney asks if he'd received the "Vic Slattery Profile" material the office sent him, and Corky says probably, sure, he's got a file of material on Vic and probably it's in with that, and Rooney says yes but if you need any more information give me a call, and Corky says sure, and he's about to hang up but Rooney pushes it, how long's Corky's tribute going to be, remember there'll be four tributes plus Andy van Buren's intro then Vic's speech slated for twenty-thirty minutes plus Q-and-A to follow, and Corky says, "You told me eight minutes maximum so it's eight minutes maximum, what's the problem?" and there's a pause and Rooney says, in that way Corky's heard him, frowning and running a hand through his little-boy fluffy-thinning hair, "Problem? Who's got a problem? Corky, I'm just asking."

So they don't trust me, Corky thinks. And a chill comes over him—it's the drinking, maybe? Corky Corcoran drunk and running at the mouth making an asshole of himself in front of the rich Democrat donors, Irish Hill mick never went to college probably leading off with a dirty joke to everybody's embarrassment, who's that guy? who chose *him* to give a tribute to Congressman Vic Slattery? and the Slattery staff headed by Mike

Rooney wants it known *not them*, but Vic himself, loyal to an old Union City friend, Slattery's weakness is his sentimental streak, you know how Vic is, so different from Oscar in this regard, a soft touch. And maybe too, sure, maybe there's some political expediency here, the old Irish–Union City connection, big Democratic votes.

Like he's worried by Corky's silence Rooney says, "Corky? You still there? Is something—"

Corky breaks the connection with his thumb. Fuck you.

You can always blame the cellular phone for fucking up.

It's twelve noon. A powerful thirst washes over Corky, God could he go for a beer!

A half dozen more quick calls before he leaves, Corky's methodical, and philosophical, about his calls, can't live without the telephone, Christ knows how many calls he makes a day, sometimes as many as fifty if there's a deal going down, out of the house, out of his State Street office or his Pearl Street office, out of his car, out of a pay phone should he have the slightest worry about a phone being tapped, a number recorded. Like Ross Drummond when he had two-thirds of his gut surgically removed, ulcer-ridden, enough to kill a normal man, but there's the old s.o.b. propped up in his hospital bed hooked to IV fluids and blood, an actual tube in his nose, and Corky walks in and hears him yelling at somebody over the phone and after he hangs up and Corky asks amazed how he is he says he feels great, as long as he's on the phone doing business.

Also, Drummond told Corky, you feel great when everybody's expecting you to croak *and you don't*.

The final call Corky makes out of the Rolodex is to the residence hall at St. Thomas Aquinas, feeling a sudden need to know sharp as an ulcer in the gut and so calling, of all Catholic priests in Union City, Father Vincent O'Brien, having to wait maybe ten minutes for the Jesuit to come to the phone and when he does he's brusque with Corky allowing his old student and big-deal donor to the school to know that Corky caught him on his way out to a luncheon at the Proxmires', the Proxmires being wealthy Protestant philanthropists with a castellated manor house on an estate overlooking Lake Ontario, so Corky immediately apologizes, "Hey

I'm sorry, Father—" speaking to any Jesuit it's like you need to apologize for taking up their time not like a parish priest, the fuckers, "—I'm just needing to know what a Latin inscription means," and Father Vincent says in a disbelieving voice, "*You* want to know what a Latin inscription means?" and Corky says, "Yeah, if I can remember it right, '*De mortuis nil nisi*—'" so mangling the pronounciation he can hear the Jesuit hiss before interrupting, "'*De mortuis nil nisi bonum*': 'Of the dead say nothing but good.'"

5

A ROMANTIC INTERLUDE

I need a drink, and I need it right now.

Swallowing nervous and dry-mouthed running his finger down the telephone directory listings, why's the print so small, why's his vision so splotched and blurred he's stone cold sober.

Forty-three years old, maybe you need bifocals.

Corky Corcoran with his perfect 20/20 vision!

Or, anyway, almost 20/20: he's forgotten the exact numbers.

Like his height which is five feet, nine inches on his driver's license and on other documents but it's a height dependent upon shoes with a good solid sole and heel, fucking humiliating to be measured in just his socks on one of those scales at the doctor's the more humiliating when the nurse pushes the metal ruler down against his scalp, ignoring his cock's-comb hair. Like they're measuring you for a coffin already.

Sad, scary: how the old shrink, get shorter. Sean Corcoran once looming over Corky as a kid, of a height with him when Corky grew up, now he's inches shorter, not just his rounded slumping shoulders but his actual spine, shrinking. At least, Tim Corcoran hasn't had to suffer this ignominy.

(Corky thinks guiltily: I have got to see Uncle Sean, today or tomorrow. *I have got to take him to Sister Mary Megan before they both croak.*)

(Thinking too, for expediency's sake if he's in the Irish Hill neighborhood maybe he should pick up another gun. That ribs joint down by the docks, used to be The Shamrock, Corky knows from his cop friends that you can pick up guns, rifles, automatic assault weapons there, all you need is cash. But maybe a white face will fuck things up?)

Need a drink, and need it right now but Corky's located Kiki in the directory, name's Zaller, the only plausible listing: K. Zaller, 588 Schoharie. Single women living alone listing themselves in the directory with only initials, who the hell are they fooling except themselves? Thalia got an unlisted number after that creep what's-his-name started following her around. It takes a real scare to make them wise up. No playground out there, and you're Little Miss Muffet nobody's going to touch.

K. Zaller. 588 Schoharie. Meaning five blocks east of State. Corky tries to envision what that might look like but there's been so much urban renewal in that part of the city, also he's getting interference like from a rival radio station *I need a drink, and I need it right now.*

Which is shit, Corky thinks furiously. Shit! It's only 12:20 P.M. and he often goes this long without taking the first drink of the day, no problem at all, for instance the other day getting to the U.C.A.C. late for his lunch with Greenbaum and he hadn't the shakes then, had he.

The problem is, now he's quit and he knows he's quit so it's a different metaphysical proposition.

The way the Jesuits would toss around the word "metaphysical" talking of theology and nobody knew what the fuck they were talking about but it's an impressive word.

But yes he *has* quit, cold turkey and he's stone cold sober and it's going to stay that way. They teach you at AA once an alcoholic always an alcoholic whether you ever take another drink again in your life, Corky sees the grim logic of that. Sure. Anything else is bullshit, kidding yourself you're Jesus Christ when, the first time you walk on water, you drown.

The ashy taste in his mouth's so bad Corky has to stop at a 7-Eleven for a quart of grapefruit juice, sourest juice they have and no sugar in it and he's drinking from the container as he drives, no appetite for anything solid nor for thinking about it right now. Say he finds Thalia at Kiki's—a long shot, but maybe—and it all goes down O.K., he'll buy both the girls lunch, a swanky Sunday lunch at The Top of the Flame, fortieth floor of the Hyatt that revolves, one full revolution every hour. Overpriced tourist place but nice. Corky, Thalia, and Kiki. Nice.

Poor fuckhead, planning to take Thalia to the Italian Villa the night before. He'd already chosen the wine: 1988 Napa Valley Cabernet Sauvignon, fruity, full-bodied, terrific.

Driving toward Schoharie and the glittery high-rises of down-town. Fast-blown clouds like wisps of thought and the sky opening up always a surprise opening like a big, big blue eye, Corky's squinting his eyes at it, the brightness painful. Almost there's a sensation of being drawn into it, sucked. Suction. The way, who was it, Corky's cousin Lois who's got such a grudge against him, told him she could feel poor Aunt Frances sucking at the spoon being spoon-fed by Lois in the hospital in the last stages of the cancer that killed her, it's not like a baby's sucking Lois said, when the baby pushes forward nursing, it's like something inside Mother is trying to suck *me* in.

Death she was saying but nobody wanted to name it.

Corky sure as hell didn't want to name it.

Nervous and dry-mouthed though he's been guzzling the grapefruit juice. Maybe it's too late, he *is* an alcoholic and can't quit, he'll have D.T.'s and start to convulse like an epileptic. That time a few years ago during the divorce he'd gone on such a bender mixing night and day and awake and asleep and what was going on in the world and what was going on in his head, passing out at his desk and next morning Miriam white-faced and terrified shaking his shoulder *Mr. Corcoran? Oh Mr. Corcoran please wake up!* thinking he'd had a brain hemorrhage. Scaring himself too fantasizing killing Charlotte and her lawyer Donaldson, the way he'd lead them into a trap and shoot them both actually getting a hard-on the fantasy was so powerful, so sick Corky went cold turkey and it was like he'd lost God without having known he'd had God. After forty-eight hours of sheer hell Corky gave up and started drinking again but kept it under control pretty well.

But now it's out of control again. You know it is.

Why kill Charlotte, the poor dumb cunt, *he'd* wanted to be free of the marriage. His wild emotions in those days Corky'd never been able to figure out.

Wanting to hurt Christina, too. Deep in her body, *that* she'll remember. So she'll never fuck another man again.

Yes but he loves her! *He* wants her.

The God-damned Meuller billboard passes by overhead, next is the Nott Street exit, Corky's swallowing compulsively missing Christina so much it hurts. She never did call him and he isn't going to call her. He can't. *I love him, I share my life with him, he's my husband.* Why had Corky been thinking she wanted to marry *him*?

"Asshole."

Why lay yourself open to hurt, why invite it, fuck it you've had enough. The shrapnel wound in the small of Corky's father's back, plum-sized, discolored like dead skin, an ugly-puckered mouth. After so many years Tim said it didn't hurt, it's nothing, *numb*. What Corky feels is more like an exposed heart, one of those lurid moist full-color photos of open-heart surgery enough to make you sick if you don't look away quickly enough. The eight-foot statue of Jesus Christ in Our Lady of Mercy drawing Corky's eye as a kid shuffling up to the communion rail, His bleeding thorn-crowned heart exposed for everybody to gape at like it's an inflamed prick.

A man's got to have his pride.

Christ, Corky can't believe it: breaking down sobbing on the phone with Sandra Slattery! *Him!*

The last thing you want from your friends is pity.

Off the exit ramp at State Corky parks and guzzles down the rest of the grapefruit juice feeling his gut bloat like he's swallowed a balloon. Twelve-thirty P.M. and he's excited taking up the phone receiver and punching out Kiki Zaller's number, not that he'll identify himself if she answers, that isn't Corky's strategy, just wants to establish if she's home. He'd called back at the house twice and no answer and this time too the phone just rings, rings . . . Which makes him the more determined to connect.

Can't remember the last time he saw Kiki except it was a crowded party scene, maybe a reception in one of the downtown hotels. She's a PR girl, or somebody's "assistant." Maybe a photographer. Or one of Howie Norwick's junior staff at WWUC-TV. Lent by her boss to work for Vic Slattery's congressional campaign. Or did she volunteer to work for the campaign? Corky can't recall if she's, like Thalia, a rich girl, or a poor girl mingling with the rich. In Union City politics, there's practically nothing in between. What Corky does remember is that God-damned gold clamp of an earring, his ear's permanently damaged from the ordeal, poor ol' Frecklehead! Corky remembers Kiki poking her sharp little chin against his shoulder and murmuring suggestively, *Well, Corky, maybe I like hurt.*

No answer at Kiki's number, and no answering machine. Corky gives up, hangs up. His sense is that this mission is doomed but what's the alternative, he drives on. From State to Schoharie along the river it's a no-man's-land of scrubby vacant lots and disused abandoned docks and acres of cracked and weedy asphalt bordered by twelve-foot wire fences with WARNING: NO TRESPASSING signs weatherworn to near-invisibility. Warehouses burnt out in the fires and looting following Martin Luther King's assassination almost a quarter-century ago are still here, boarded up, unsold. One of the downtown banks owns most of this riverfront property, it's worthless but for sure City Hall has worked out a tax deal. You can't get insurers to underwrite anything in this part of the city.

Two blocks away, the notorious State Street Project, built in 1973, where hundreds, or is it thousands, of black welfare recipients live dense as insects in vertical hives. In the mid-1980s Corcoran, Inc., invested in a residential-rental property down here, twenty units, a brick-and-stucco building so ugly to the eye and so offensive to the nose Corky couldn't bring himself to visit it even to check up on his super who he had reason to believe was a pimp, along with cheating Corky at every turn—demanding kickbacks from plumbers, for instance, who then inflated their bills passing along the increase to Corcoran, Inc. In time, the tenants trashed the dump so badly Corky couldn't collect any more insurance and sold the property at what was filed with IRS as a capital loss, which in truth it was. Corky'd been hoping somebody would set fire to the place but nobody did and he hadn't felt he dared risk having it burned down himself (hiring a pro arsonist you're opening yourself up to blackmail, also what if somebody dies in the fire?—that's serious), to this day the place is still standing, Corky's driving by now, after a quick glance he averts his eyes.

Around the time he sold the building was when Thalia collapsed at Cornell, it comes back to him now.

Schoharie is a steep hill leading up from the river, potholed asphalt, rowhouses populated by blacks, Hispanics, welfare whites, then across Erie Boulevard it's more working-class, in fact Devane Johnson's family lives in this part of the city—Devane Johnson, the twelve-year-old black kid shot in the back by a UCPD officer. Driving in this part of Union City in a Cadillac De Ville isn't so risky as you'd think, the drug dealers and pimps all drive expensive cars so a white businessman successful as Corky Corcoran fits right in.

Where Schoharie crosses a broad, busy avenue called Werhle it changes its character, a block of duplex woodframe houses not at all badly maintained, the next block refurbished brick rowhouses smartly painted in designer colors, Corky knows the guys who developed this and they had the right idea, the west side is ripe for gentrification, like Pendle Hill. Except in this recession, are the units fully rented? Corky guesses not. *His* aren't.

588 Schoharie isn't a rowhouse but an apartment building of three floors, new-looking, moderately upscale, a young professionals/singles type of place, exactly where you'd imagine an ambitious girl like Kiki to be living while she scans the field, calculates how far she can get, who she can get, before she's thirty and played out. Used Kleenex, Corky wonders if they see themselves that way, ever? Or don't dare? Kiki's building has its architectural pretensions, it's disconcertingly similar to the Georgian Colonial facade of Corky's own house, red brick and white portico and trim, broad white shutters, that all-American look, sheerly phony. Inside it's cheap materials, built to last maybe twenty years, some of the fixtures, bathroom racks, doorknobs, coming off in your hand, and those processed wood doors that warp so they can't close—Corky knows, he owns properties like this himself, short-term investments. Sad, he's thinking, unless maybe it's funny, the architectural styles of this country, pseudo-Colonial across the street from pseudo-Victorian and close by "French Country" (those tacky mansard roofs! Corky sees them everywhere, can't stand them) and "English Tudor" and "Contemporary" and "Postmodern"—and inside, these creatures Wolf Wiegler called Cro-Magnons, with no clue how we got here, or why.

Corky enters the vestibule of 588 Schoharie, checks out the mailboxes, there's K. ZALLER Apt. 6B and he presses the buzzer but no response. "Fuck it." He hears voices, a young man and a young woman push through a door careless about closing it behind them so Corky reaches out to keep it from locking and slips through and upstairs at 6B rings the doorbell once, twice, three times—"*Fuck* it."

Back at the Werhle intersection Corky'd noticed a LIQUOR WINE BEER store, and he sees it fleeting in his mind's eye, but lets it go. Presses his ear against the door to 6B as he'd pressed his ear against Thalia's Goddamned door the other day, why is Corky Corcoran always on the outside of where he wants to be, what is his life coming to! No sound inside. Nothing distinct. Maybe Kiki, like Marilee Plummer, is dead?—but Corky won't be the one to find her.

Back in his car Corky contemplates what to do. It's a ten-minute drive
to Sean Corcoran's—a fact pressing on his chest like concrete. He loves
the old man, he supposes, only just doesn't want to see him, talk to him.
When Corky's old, who in hell's going to want to see *him?*

The prospect of getting old, being old,—that putty-colored old rummy
in the morgue with his ghastly face, skinned-looking testicles, Wiegler's
diet chocolate soda can resting on his chest—Corky's tasting panic. *I
need a drink, and I need it right now.*

But if he goes to visit Sean maybe he can pick up a gun, it's beginning
to seem obvious that Corky Corcoran needs a gun to protect himself from
danger.

Corky drives back to Werhle and parks the Caddy in a small shopping
plaza, ignores the LIQUOR WINE BEER sign and enters instead a food store
where, propelled by a compulsive thirst, he buys another quart of grapefruit juice, opens the container with shaky fingers and begins to drink it
there. The cashier, a woman in her thirties, initially attracted by Corky's
springy red hair, good clothes, battered good looks, is now staring at him.
Corky says, smacking his lips, "Real healthy for you," as if it's a joke, and
the woman shrugs and says, "Maybe." Corky's so used to women opening
up to him this is a rebuff that stings.

Corky notices there's another woman in the store, a customer, dark-
haired, with glasses, a plain pinched face, in shirt and jeans and sandals;
oddly furtive, jerky in her movements up and down the aisles, as she picks
up items, stares at them, sets them back on the shelf. Or is she stalling for
time, until Corky leaves the store? He watches her and sees, to his astonishment, how her thin triangular face becomes Kiki Zaller's—this is *Kiki?*

And she's watching him, unsmiling, face severe as a mask's.

"Hey Kiki—it's you?" Corky smiles a big hello but he's staring too,
can't help it: Kiki, whom he remembers as a reckless beautiful girl, is
hardly recognizable, in chunky plastic-framed glasses with an amber tint
that looks medicinal, her skin sallow without makeup and her lips bloodless and that spectacular frizzed copper hair now mostly brown, blunt-cut
and skinned back from her face.

And no earrings. Not even studs. Where they'd been, Corky can see
tiny puncture marks in the girl's delicate earlobes.

Clearly Kiki isn't overjoyed about running into Corky Corcoran on this balmy spring Sunday. Her smile is twitchy and fleeting and her eyes are narrowed like a cat's. "Mr. Corcoran? What are *you* doing here?" Corky laughs incredulously, takes it that Kiki's joking, saying, "What's this 'Mr.'?—I'm 'Corky,'" squeezing her limp cold little hand as if they're meeting on their usual party turf; he'd even kiss her cheek except Kiki's holding herself so stiff, seems almost frightened of him. Corky laughs again and says, "Actually, Kiki, I'm looking for you."

Kiki laughs too, harshly. Her triangular little death's-head of a face dips in mirthless mirth. "Oh no you're not, 'Corky,'" she says.

Corky's a little embarrassed at Kiki seeing him with the quart of grapefruit juice, drinking it right there in the store like a kook. But Kiki's not her old self, flirty and derisive. She'd ignore Corky entirely if she could.

Corky looks on as Kiki's purchases are being rung up on the cash register, he can see she's uneasy, or annoyed, him standing there smiling, so good-natured a guy it's impossible to shake him. She's buying a carton of Capris, one of those so-called low-tar cigarettes Corky used to scorn when he smoked, cigarettes for women, and a six-pack of Molson's Lite, Corky scorns "lite" beer too, except the very sight of the aluminum cans sets his mouth watering, and three cans of Campbell's soup, and five eight-ounce containers of fruit yogurt, and a package of something called FreshScent which looks like sanitary napkins—fumbling with her wallet (which is reptile skin, or a good imitation, expensive) so Corky leans in quickly, "*I* can pay, Kiki," but Kiki flashes him a look of barely contained rage, "No thanks, Mr. Corcoran, *I* can."

So from the start, that first exchange, it's fucked. Which Corky knows, but can't accept—for why would Kiki Zaller be hostile to *him*? He's the nicest guy in Union City, he's got friends in high places, he wants only to do the right thing.

(Near as Corky can remember of that wild-drunken night, he'd been a gentleman through the humiliating shit about Kiki's earring stuck on his ear. Hadn't lost his temper with either Kiki or Marilee as another guy would have—the bitches laughing at him calling him Frecklehead, that's to say Fuckhead. So what's Kiki got against him now?)

Corky's eager to establish contact with Kiki, that vein of intimacy or its semblance he requires the way he requires oxygen to breathe, saying in an undertone, as he follows her out of the store, "Christ! Wasn't that a terrible thing, a shocking thing, Marilee . . ." letting his voice trail off so Kiki can murmur in response, but she doesn't say a word. Not a word! Outside in the sunshine, a glaring windblown light and Corky sees Kiki isn't Thalia's age after all but years older, pushing thirty, her face is tight with strain, she's clenching her jaws, not looking at him. The chunky plastic glasses aren't flattering to her slender face, there's a reddened mark on the bridge of her nose.

How she'd leaned against him nudging her breast against him teasing and breathy, *Well, Corky, maybe I* like *hurt* but is this the same girl? Corky can't believe it.

Still there's a connection between them, physical, erotic, a sense of a shared secret. *That,* Kiki can't ignore.

But then this happens: Corky asks Kiki where's her car and Kiki says in a small cold voice she walked to the store and Corky says O.K. then get in mine, here's my car, I'll drive you back but already she's edging away gripping the grocery bag against her breasts and pointedly not looking at Corky, and Corky calls after, "Hey Kiki—what the hell? C'mon get *in.*" But the cold little bitch continues on toward Schoharie with no more than a cursory gesture as if to say leave me alone, I do what I want to do, don't fuck with me. Corky couldn't be more astounded if the girl'd slapped him in the face.

When a guy's rebuffed, though, he's got two choices: to accept it and creep away like a loser, or to pretend it never happened. Corky's made a career of going for the second option.

So he climbs in the Caddy, sure he's pissed and hurt but he's not going to show it, like losing an election (which in fact has yet to happen to Corky Corcoran) when you're gracious about your rival's success and the voters who didn't vote for you, that's just shrewd poker, everybody loves a good loser and Corky's primed for the role and he knows, he just knows, Kiki's going to come around to liking him and trusting him, and maybe more: he knows.

Wondering if, at her apartment, Kiki will offer him a beer.

Corky drives along Schoharie at five miles an hour hugging the curb, keeping pace with Kiki who's walking fast, a stiff angry look to her walk, and her head stiff, certainly she's aware of him but she doesn't so much as glance toward him like he's some guy trying to pick her up, and Corky hopes to hell a police patrol car doesn't cruise by, no telling what Kiki might say. But Corky smiles—this is all so fucking weird to him, such an insult, he's got no choice but to smile—calling out to Kiki, "Jesus, I don't want to bother you, Kiki, I guess you've had a bad time of it lately?—Thalia took it pretty hard, too. And that's why—that's one of the reasons—I'd like to talk to you? Just for a few—" Such an appeal, so straight from the heart, how can the bitch ignore it? *But she does.*

At 588 Schoharie Corky parks the car, gives it away he knows where Kiki lives by parking hurriedly at the curb before she turns up the walk, rushing then to the entrance to open the door for her. Still smiling, but his eyes are showing the strain. Kiki passes coolly through the doorway making sure she doesn't brush against him. What's he got, AIDS? Her face is so tight it's as if wires are strung beneath the thin, sallow skin, radiating outward from her eyes and bracketing her bloodless little slug of a mouth. The flirty-fucky party girl Kiki Zaller's known to be, where's *she?* Corky can't help but think there's a deliberate deception going on here aimed specifically at him.

Or is Kiki a lesbian?—that's it? He seems to remember Kiki and Marilee dissolving in peals of laughter in each other's arms. Choking with hilarity at the predicament of ol' Frecklehead.

Inside the vestibule Corky's a gentleman politely offering to take Kiki's grocery bag from her as she fumbles to unlock the inner door, but Kiki shakes her head impatiently to indicate no, no thanks, she can do it herself, she's got a routine. Corky's panicked he's going to lose her. He lifts his hands, he's throwing himself on her mercy, saying, almost begging, "Kiki, I need your help, it's got to do with Thalia," and at this Kiki gives him a furtive look, a look maybe of guilt, and mumbles, "Sorry I can't help you, *sorry*—" she's slipping through the door but Corky grabs it and follows her, "Hey please! Don't shut me out. I'm a desperate man—look at me."

His hangover eyes, the bruise on his forehead, his shaky pleading voice—this does the trick, or seems to.

Kiki sighs. A hissing sound, like Father Vincent over the phone.

Your foot's inside the door, that's the main thing. Once you get inside nobody's going to remember how you got there.

Kiki leads Corky upstairs, allowing him now to take the grocery bag from her, a small victory but it's a victory. And at the door to 6B she murmurs, "Come in, then," in a flat, dry voice, as if they've been quarreling and Corky's won out of sheer doggedness. He feels his prick stir, the first sign of life in eighteen hours.

Inside, the living room's small as Corky envisioned. A faint stink of tobacco smoke. Standard oyster-white walls, ceiling track lighting, sofa, chairs, a large TV prominent in a corner, stacks of videocassettes spilling onto the floor. Wall-to-wall carpet, too-bright electric-blue, covered in lint and dustballs. Something sad about this room, maybe it's a furnished room? "So this is where you live, Kiki!" Corky says with forced enthusiasm.

No reply. As if speaking, or making even a gesture of ordinary civility, would cost her too much, Kiki directs Corky into a cramped little kitchen where he sets the grocery bag down, feeling husbandly, on a sticky counter. His eye takes in a certain measure of grime in the sink, jagged flecks of rust on the stove, glassware and plates set on the counter upside down, rinsed and not washed. He wonders what rent Kiki's paying for this place.

Even now Kiki doesn't so much as murmur thanks but begins to unpack the bag. Breaks open the carton of cigarettes immediately, lights up a Capri without offering Corky one, how does the bitch know Corky doesn't smoke, rude bitch, enough like Thalia to be a sister, why are younger women so much less feminine than women of Corky's generation? And so brisk, matter-of-fact, the way Kiki's slamming the Campbell soups onto a cupboard shelf, then dumps the six-pack and the yogurt into the refrigerator. A mostly empty refrigerator, with a sweet-rancid odor lifting to Corky's sensitive nostrils.

He's smelling Kiki, too. Paradoxical combination of soap, dried sweat. Musty-bloody. An odor of underarms, that under-the-hair-nape-of-the-neck odor that turns Corky on—an old, old memory of the girl from Ballyhoura his father had helped to bring over, Deirdre, Deirdre's smell, her unshaven underarms, legs. Running Jerome's bath but not overly keen about baths herself.

All this cheers Corky up. Giving Kiki his warmest grin.

"Not going to offer me a cigarette, eh? Or a beer? I guess I'm seriously on your shit list."

Kiki has shut the refrigerator door but hasn't moved away. The kitchen's so cramped, they can't avoid touching. Corky sees she's smiling, or anyway her lips are twitching; for her, this is quite a concession. Seen in profile Kiki's a striking young woman, even without makeup. Her slender nose, strong chin. The bones of her cheeks. Through the open collar of her carelessly buttoned shirt Corky can see the taut tendons of her neck, a bluish vein pulsing there. Always it comes over Corky, this close to a woman, virtually any woman, a weird disorienting sense of her *being* that's somehow identical with his own.

Says Kiki, now archly, raising her eyes to Corky's as if something is prodding her *be female! female!*, "Do you want a cigarette, or a beer, Corky?"

Says Corky, smiling, with satisfaction, "Thanks a lot, Kiki. But actually I don't."

Kiki takes a deep drag on the cigarette and exhales smoke like pent-up laughter. Turns to walk away, running a hand through her chopped-looking hair. Doggy-Corky trots after, his eyes dropping to take in her tight little ass in the bleached jeans, the slightly swaggering motion of her shoulders inside the shirt. He's aching to touch her, he's the kind of guy who finds it hard to talk to a woman without touching her, a hand on her shoulder, a squeeze of her fingers. The tension between them has made him excited—maybe Kiki's planned it that way?

Kiki says bluntly, before Corky can speak, "I'm sorry I can't help you, I'm through with all that. Why don't you leave."

"But, Kiki—"

"I'd just like you to leave."

"I only want to ask you—"

"Yes, but—no: I don't know anything about her, and I don't want to know." Kiki's breathless, backing off from Corky, smoking her cigarette quickly as if she thinks somebody's going to take it from her. "I'm starting a new life on June first."

Corky says, pleading, "But I'm desperate, Kiki—I've got to find her before something happens."

Kiki stares at Corky. She pushes her heavy glasses against the bridge of her nose. "You've got to—*find* her? How can you *find* her? She's dead."

"No, I mean Thalia. Not Marilee. I'm looking for Thalia."

"I told you, I don't know anything about Thalia, either. About either of them. I'm leaving Union City on June first and going to—" a wild note in her voice, a twist of her lips as if she's daring Corky to doubt her, "—Rio."

"Rio? Brazil?"

"I've got a friend who will take me."

"Who's he?"

"Who's *she?*" Kiki laughs. "No one you know."

The telephone starts to ring. They're in the living room, there's a phone within a few feet of Kiki but she doesn't seem to hear it ringing. It's like a dream, Corky thinks, Corky himself out there telephoning, poor fucker's trying as always to get *in*.

With mild disapproval, Corky asks, "Aren't you going to answer your phone?" Of course, he's flattered as hell she doesn't.

Kiki shakes ashes onto the soiled blue carpet. "It's a wrong number."

"How do you know that, honey?"

"They're all wrong numbers. I know."

So the telephone rings, he and Kiki look at each other as it rings, Corky's thinking of the many times in Christina's loft the phone rang while they were making love, and how the ringing, the very sound, entered into their lovemaking as if it were the thrumming of their bodies, their bodies' music. The ringing ringing ringing, the hot coursing of Corky's blood, the rising and abrupt peaking of pleasure in his groin so intense it seemed to fly, not from him, but through him, a stream of liquid fire.

Kiki's scrutinizing Corky, something blind and hurt in his face. Almost gently she says, "You didn't follow me into that store, did you? Have you been hanging around here?"

"Of course not."

"But you know—knew—where I live."

"You're in the directory."

"Not after June first."

"Why are you so eager to leave? You've always seemed like such a—" Corky can't think of the exact word, and Kiki's staring at him so derisively he's thrown off stride, "—happy person."

"Happy! Yes, sure. You guys kept me in coke, sure I was happy for you." Kiki laughs, exhaling smoke in spasms. Her glasses have begun to slide down her nose.

Corky plays dumb. "Coke? Since when?"

"I'm leaving for personal reasons but also—I'm a coward."

"What do you mean?"

"When Pickett gets acquitted, this city's going to burn. I'm not even going to think about it."

Corky's incredulous. "Pickett? Acquitted? The jury hasn't even been picked yet."

"Now nobody will listen to Steadman, *he's* fucked. You guys saw to that."

"Why do you keep saying 'you guys'? What the hell's that mean? I'm not 'guys,' I'm one guy. And what d'you mean, 'saw to it'? Saw to what?"

Kiki shrugs the question off as if it's too absurd. "*You* know."

"What do I know?"

In a taunting singsong voice Kiki says, glaring at him, "*I* don't know anything about it, and *I* don't want to know anything. I'm out of it."

Corky says, desperately, "Look, Kiki, I only need to know about Thalia. Where—"

"—from you, that's a laugh!"

"—where she might be? Who her friends are—"

"*You.*" Kiki laughs harshly. "Thalia's told me plenty about *you.*"

Corky doesn't hear this. He's agitated, angry. "She needs help. She isn't well. I need to find her."

"I said no. I don't know."

"I thought you were friends—"

"No."

"You, Thalia, Marilee Plummer—"

"No." Kiki presses her hands against her ears. Her lips are drawn back from her teeth in a skull's grimace. "No no *no.*"

The telephone has ceased ringing. Except for a car passing out on Schoharie it's very quiet. Corky's hot in the face, breathing quickly. He's sexually aroused and surely that's Kiki's intention, taunting him the way she's been doing. There's a smell lifting off her that's unmistakable.

Kiki says, "You and Red Pitts. I get you confused. But *he's* the pimp. You're the gentleman."

Before Corky can ask what the hell this means Kiki goes to the telephone and takes the receiver off the hook. A gesture so languid, so matter-of-fact, it goes through Corky like an electric shock. *She's going to fuck me? My God.*

Suddenly his throat's parched to the point of pain, how badly he needs a drink.

Instead he has a cigarette, and Kiki has another, tossing him the pack of Capris she's stuck in her shirt pocket as if she knows his secret desire. Corky's hands are shaking but it's a good sensation like the adrenaline rush before a fight.

Corky lights up, the first deep inhalation takes him straight to where he wants to go. That powerful sensation, good stinging-acrid sensation, smoke expanding his lungs like a bellows. His eyes flood with tears. He could cry, *is* crying. "Oh Christ."

"How long's it been?"

"Five years." Corky's coughing, wiping at his eyes. He can't stop smiling. "I haven't had a really deep breath in five fucking years."

As if absentmindedly, Kiki kicks off her sandals; her long bare toes, dead-white, flex against the electric-blue carpet like a monkey's. Corky loves barefoot women, they're more likely to be shorter than he is.

And Kiki Zaller's looking better to him all the time. She's taken off her ugly glasses, she's smiling more easily. Flashing her eyes at him like the flirty-fucky girl he remembers. Like the dirty-mouthed girls of the schoolyard, the older girls, eyeing a good-looking kid like Corky wanting to see could they make him blush. And the heat that coursed through his face, certainly he did.

Corky smokes his cigarette in a warm erotic daze. Keeps it in his mouth, tight between his teeth, as he takes off his sport coat and drapes it neatly over the back of a chair. Kiki leads him into the next room, a shadowy room, there's a futon on the floor, what a ridiculous object Corky thinks, but he's forgiving, he's too excited to be judging, a futon, a regular bed, what difference does it make, Kiki's of another generation, *that's* exciting, too. And where Thalia was a tease, Kiki's the real thing.

Kiki's bedroom, Kiki's clothes scattered about. A closet door, open. So Corky can see inside *and there's no one inside.* He's laughing he's feeling so good.

He'll deal with not drinking by smoking again. Not three packs a day as before, when he was coughing himself sick and had to quit, but in moderation—six cigarettes, say, in twenty-four hours; one cigarette every four hours. Make that nonnegotiable. Corky knows he can handle that. And these low-tar Capris, in the past he'd consider them next to shit but actually they're not bad. Though he'll smoke another brand, a man's brand. The solution to Corky's drinking problem's so simple he wonders why it took him so long to think of it.

Kiki's at the room's single window adjusting a venetian blind saying, teasing, "—You *did* follow me into that store, didn't you—c'mon tell the truth, you prick—" and Corky's denying it, "Hell no, it was an accident, honey," liking it she's so comfortable with him suddenly she can call him such a name, though Corky has to know it *is* sudden, Kiki Zaller's reversal of attitude, or mood, if he wasn't thinking with his cock he'd surely wonder about that. Kiki laughs snapping the blind cords as a kid might, open, shut, open, shut, as if she half wants to break the mechanism, shafts of warm sunshine widen spilling onto the futon, then narrow, then widen again, and narrow. When the blind's as shut as she can get it the room's still fairly light. Colors are still distinct. Corky wonders how flushed his face is, it feels burning hot. Ol' Frecklehead!

A futon A *futon!* Corky's never fucked anybody on a futon before, though years ago, in the 1970s, a waterbed, now there's a truly ridiculous object, beyond reckoning. Smelly-stagnant water, sloshing, seasick. Corky's all but forgotten the woman, one of Charlotte's golf-playing friends, a rich man's wife but they'd met, at her insistence, in the townhouse of a young relative of hers, a nephew: the waterbed was his. Weird, sick, incestuous, but Corky hadn't investigated too closely. It had been sweet enough while it lasted.

Apart from the futon Kiki's bedroom furnishings are minimal. Another cheap wall-to-wall carpet on the floor, an old-fashioned pedestal mirror, a poster on a wall—Corky's curious examining it, what *is* it? Looks like an anatomical drawing, a magnified penis? a cross-section diagram of a man's lower abdomen, genitals? In the dim light Corky can just make out the arrowed labels—"glans penis," "prepuce," "scrotum," "testis," "epididymis," "vas deferens," etc. Kiki laughs and says, "It's from a series by a protest artist out in Ohio, it's really fantastic stuff—*Jesse Helms' Body.*"

Corky says, *"Jesse Helms' Body—?"*

"It's protest art."

Anatomical drawings, like photos of open-heart surgery, make Corky a little squeamish. A sliced-open penis, a look into somebody's abdomen—that's *art*?

Corky stubs out his cigarette in a plastic ashtray littered with butts. One last deep drag, and—here goes.

Squeezing Kiki's sinewy shoulders and kissing her full on the mouth, time for intimate contact, he's been avoiding it, *gentleman! you're the gentleman and Red Pitts is the pimp!* no idea in hell what Kiki meant by that and in no hurry to know. Where your friends are concerned, better not to know. Kiki's mouth isn't very giving, her saliva tastes clammy, gamely Corky pokes his tongue bumbling and sliding against hers, and Kiki gags slightly and ducks her head: the thing about kissing is it's too personal, like talking. Fucking's easy. Fucking's a machine. You set it *on*, it goes.

Kiki's eyes blaze up at Corky's as she unbuttons her shirt, shrugs out of it, her eyes dropping to her own breasts which are creamy-pale, fuller than Corky'd imagined; she smiles, biting her lower lip, she's exciting herself—it's a child's version of a striptease, clumsy but aware. Even her face seems fuller, as if fleshed out with blood. Next her jeans, she unzips the fly front, tugs them down, as she stoops she's looking at Corky fixing her gaze on him as if daring him to look elsewhere, but Corky looks elsewhere, touched, for a moment troubled, to see she's wearing white cotton panties, the shadow of her pubic hair is like a dark hand behind the fabric and as Corky reaches out to touch her Kiki eases away insolent, taunting, "Don't touch! Not yet! You obey *me*, this is my turf, O.K. friend?—you're my slave or it's no deal." Laughing as Corky's laughing, it's as if Corky's giddy-drunk without needing to drink, the nicotine rush did it, his cock's hard as an ax handle and about as long unfurled, detached from trousers, underwear—a gift he's proud to display to Kiki who widens her eyes at the sight! the size! "Oh Mr. Cock-or-an! *Wow*." Like a wild kooky porno film where the action's jerky and uncoordinated, you don't know if it's meant to be comic or just *is*, the very pathos comic, the shame. Kiki backs off then on her slender legs, appealingly knock-kneed legs, still she's wearing the white cotton panties riding high on her thighs as if they're an old pair, frayed at the waistband, Corky has a quick thought she might be wearing a sanitary pad, she's having her period, just his luck, no but Corky doesn't mind, Corky's an old experienced hand, an old experienced prick, nothing fazes *him*. Except in his haste stumbling kicking off trousers and shorts, breathless fumbling with the cuffs of his fresh-starched white cotton shirt with the scripted monogram JAC in white silk thread which too in his excited haste he lets fall to the floor, should take time to drape it over a chair, all his clothes over a chair, Corky's a fanatic about his clothes but things in Kiki's bedroom are happening too swiftly now to be processed. *Is she crazy? am I?* but Corky's in no mood to take warning. There's an undercurrent of gloating revenge, too, fuck you Christina, d'you think I need you Christina, just watch.

Corky says, "Hey: you're beautiful," voice cracking in surprise, but meaning it, for near-naked and shimmering before him Kiki Zaller *is* beautiful, Corky loves her. How transformed, the plain-pinched bespectacled woman in the food store, you'd never imagine, yes but it's true with so many women, beauty in the flesh, the dumb mute flesh, no face nor even head attached. Corky sees a perceptible pleasure like a flame rising into Kiki's face at the contemplation of her own body, it's as if she hasn't seen this body in a long time, and herself reflected in a man's eyes and in his desire: it isn't Corky, or not Corky exclusively, but all men, Man: a living mirror presenting her with the gift of herself.

Kiki laughs just slightly shrilly. Out of breath as if she's been running. Saying, "*You're* beautiful, friend. Except for this little—" boldly pinching some flab at his waist, "—padding. But, for a guy your age, oh *wow*."

Corky resents this, but laughs and reaches for her. Cupping her breasts in both hands, nipples tough as rubber, stoops to suck at a nipple but Kiki closes her fingers in his hair and yanks his head back—"Not yet! You obey *me*, I said, Mr. Cock-or-ran! You're my slave."

"O.K. I'm your slave. What're my instructions?"

Figuring he'll humor her, he's had experience humoring hysterical women. *All* women are hysterical, you push the right buttons.

Kiki laughs, crosses to the bathroom, and Corky's eyes are drawn helplessly after her, his cock's tremulous, his heart's racing, can he trust this girl for what if she locks herself in the bathroom? decides to take a shower, lets the water run and run? she's unpredictable enough to pull a stunt like this and Corky's in such a state he'll break down the door and drag her out, no more cockteasing for *him*. Kiki does in fact shut the bathroom door, there's a quaint sound of trickling pee and a toilet flushing like a cataract and a faucet turned on and off, then Kiki pokes her head out the door her mischievous gaze dropping from Corky's heated face to Corky's heated cock, "Still here, friend?—just checking." She startles Corky tossing him a crimson-foil package, a condom, Corky's awkward and embarrassed unwrapping it, tries to joke, what's the joke, his erection's endangered, such behavior isn't Corky's generation's style at all, nor the behavior of preceding generations, the male's the initiator, the male's dominant, the male's *it*. But Corky's a good sport and Corky sees the logic, it doesn't fail to cross his mind he's protecting himself from her, too, a wild cokehead-nympho possibly screwed by half the guys in Union City from the Mayor on down, yes and not excluding Red Pitts, that notorious pimp, Corky's eager to humor and to obey, Corky thinks it might be fun to be a slave, at least for once, at least for now, though fitting this God-damned sheath on his aggrieved cock is no simple matter, Corky's out of practice, it's been in fact years. And how like the embarrassment of, at the doctor's, the pretty young nurse handing Corky a paper cup—"For your urine sample, Mr. Corcoran"—then taking it from him brisk and bright and matter-of-fact—"Thank you, Mr. Corcoran"—as if urine— urine!—was the best Corky Corcoran could do for her.

Like a nurse too, Kiki returns with a towel, a large bath towel she folds for double thickness and drapes across the futon. She's fully naked now, flush-faced, Corky touches her in wonderment, his caressing fingers on the bumpy curve of her spine, her sweet glimmering pale ass, the crack of her ass. But Kiki slaps at his hand, hissing, "No! Don't! *You* follow orders!" Corky's erection is at half-mast but chastely sheathed as Kiki wishes, maybe this pleases her, a mere glance at it, and at Corky, as she crawls onto the futon and arranges herself on it, her hips on the bath towel, a fussy crinkle to her forehead as she tugs at sheets, adjusts pillows, it's as if she's alone arranging herself for a gynecological procedure of a sort you don't want to imagine. Lying back then, arms behind her head, head on the pillow, spreading her legs to Corky who's been crouched over her like a Cro-Magnon, and at last, with an effort she doesn't trouble to disguise, she smiles up at Corky as if only now recalling he's there. "Kiss me! My slave."

Fuck you, thinks Corky, but he's got a reputation as a good sport, and he *is* here, went to all the trouble of fitting on the condom so might as well use it.

Corky lowers himself onto the futon, even the word *futon* is ridiculous to him, it's like a gym mat and he and Kiki Zaller are paired for a wrestling match, there's a sinewy athletic look to the girl, the long legs, the surprisingly strong shoulders, a nimbleness about the thighs. Corky leans down to kiss her mouth but it isn't her mouth she means—"No! Begin here!" touching herself between the legs. Corky sees the wild eyes, black-dilated eyes, inhales the funky heat lifting from her, that musty-bloody odor, he's feeling revulsed but he's excited too, kinky stuff, Doggy-Corky, what's to lose. Scrambling with mock obedience down then to kiss Kiki's belly, it's a flat somewhat sunken belly, pelvic bones like elbows and the squish of the innards too palpable, and the fuzzy-scratchy pubic hair so much thicker than Christina's, like Corky's own. Kneeling then at the edge of the futon, bare knees on the floor but at least it's carpeted, pressing his mouth against Kiki's cunt, yes she's having her period, unmistakable, but seems to have washed there or at least swiped at herself with a wetted tissue thank God. Corky's disgusted but excited too, getting into the doggy spirit of it, it's a fact he's forty-three years old and has never done exactly this though many times making love to women who were menstruating, hard to avoid if you're fucking one of them regularly, that one weird time with a pregnant woman who was "spotting," but don't think of that now, yes and another time with a five-months-pregnant woman, a different woman, who teased Corky or was she seriously speculating that her orgasms were so powerful she might go into premature labor but don't think of that, for Christ's sake, now. Corky's gamely nudging and tonguing Kiki's scratchy mound, her moist vaginal lips that are disappointingly thin and flaccid not full, fleshy like Christina's, yes and Charlotte's, he's tonguing Kiki's slimy little clit that reminds him of a slug, wet with what's probably blood, the smell of it, the taste of it, sticky-clotty blood in Corky's very eyelashes, his poor prick's wilting, what if the fucking condom falls *off*.

And Kiki?—Kiki's stiff as a broomstick. Must feel nothing, not even a tremor. The sinewy muscles of her thighs so tight Corky's head is pinioned as in a vise, his poor ears flattened, jaws numb, God damn he's about to give up and fuck the bitch's brains out as she should be fucked, let her try to stop him, when suddenly she begins to moan, her fingers in his hair, she's alive, writhing, moving her head from side to side, "Oh—oh—oh—" as if astonished, maybe she's never come before? is that possible, Kiki's never come before? Corky's the first? inspired now, his tongue a tiny jackhammer, gripping and kneading her thin buttocks, a red mist passing over his brain so he's oblivious to his surroundings, he loves this girl whose name he's forgotten, he loves this intimacy, it's all good, supremely good, like a soaring jazz riff, up and up and up and still higher, Corky's erection returns in triumph, how could he have doubted himself, he feels the muscles tight against his ears knotting and contracting, Kiki's groaning, gasping for breath, "Oh!—oh—" a sound as if she's being strangled but Corky presses on, the escalating rhythm of his tongue, teeth, mouth forcing her forward, no turning back, now with both hands she's gripping his hair, she's lifting herself from the futon, spine arching as in an exquisite convulsion, she's coming, Corky adores her, so open to him now as if she's turned inside out, sheerly female, and his.

Kiki's cries are sharp as birds' cries, rising to a shriek then trailing off. She lies then panting, dazed. Corky wipes his face and deftly shifts into position spreading her legs farther and about to enter her when she astonishes him by pressing the heel of her right foot hard against his abdomen and saying, "No! No you don't! Rapist!" She pushes him away, squirming free and drawing her knees up to kick at him as a child might kick. Corky's first amazed thought is that the orgasm set her off, triggered something in her brain, she *is* convulsing, like an epileptic. But it's clear that Kiki's in control of herself, throwing off the aftermath of sexual pleasure as one might throw off the aftermath of a sneezing fit.

"Thought you'd do to me what you did to Thalia—your own stepdaughter! Didn't you! Get *out*."

Corky's on his knees, swaying. Wiping at something wet and sticky in his face, in his chest hair. "What?" He can't believe what he hears.

"You heard me, you pervert. Get *out*."

"What did you say? Thalia—?"

"She told me. I know all about you, mister. I didn't believe it at first but now I do."

"Thalia told you—? What—? Kiki, this is crazy—"

"How you came on to her, touched her, she was eight years old when it began, making her sit in your lap while you played piano, getting into bed with her in your underwear, kissing her, touching her, for years—and her mother knowing what was going on and pretending to be blind because she was in love with you. *You!*" Kiki's face is a mask of righteous loathing. Her bloodless little mouth is damp with spittle. "I believe it all, now. Just get *out*."

Corky's swaying on his knees, incredulous. By this time his poor cock is wilted as limp celery, hanging like a dead weight in the pale condom-sac. He says, in a cracked voice, "What the hell are you saying? Thalia? *Me?* I never did—"

"She told me, and I believe her. Of course you'd deny it."

"But, Kiki, for Christ's sake—what did I *do?*"

"You didn't get a chance to! I'm not a victim." Kiki's voice rises dangerously. "Following me home the way you did, pushing in here. Trying to rape me. A pervert like you, you'd like to *infect* me. Infect women! You're lucky I'm not screaming for help, I'd have plenty of witnesses and you'd really be fucked, mister. You and your precious Slatterys!"

"Kiki, what are you saying? What's this got to do with—"

"Just get out, you're disgusting. I loathe you. All of you. I loathe what you did to me. I never wanted to do it, you forced me." Kiki's speaking more and more rapidly, and incoherently, on her feet now, her hair in her face, breasts swinging. There are lurid smears of blood on her belly and inner thighs, glistening in the half-light. Corky gets to his feet too but doesn't dare touch her. If she starts screaming, what might he do? "You followed me, you know you did. You had this planned!"

"Kiki, no. I only wanted to ask you about—"

"There are witnesses! The woman in the food store—she saw. And along the street, how you followed me in the car, tried to force me to get in, I'll call the police, I'll file charges, you'll be as fucked as Marcus Steadman, as what you did to *him!* Keep away."

"Kiki, I didn't do anything to Steadman, what are you saying? What is this?"

"I hate you! I'm not going to listen to you! I'm finished with you! Get *out*."

Corky's speechless then in shock seeing Kiki snatch up his white shirt from the floor and, with savage satisfaction, wipe herself with it between the legs. His shirt!

Afterward wondering if it hadn't been planned, even the hysteria, that threat of female madness like a burning match brought up close to flammable material so naturally Corky panicked and fled, wasn't going to stick around and try to talk reason into the bitch not with the threat of screams, cops, charges of rape. Rape! He'd never even got to fuck her. And there would have been witnesses, for sure some righteous citizen would've stepped forward, the cashier in the store, the young couple who'd passed Corky coming in, observers along Schoharie. And what headlines in tomorrow's *Journal*—CITY COUNCILMAN CORCORAN ARRESTED ON SEXUAL ASSAULT CHARGES.

So in prudent desperation Corky flees apartment 6B of the cheesy redbrick Georgian Colonial at 588 Schoharie, 1:48 P.M. of this Sunday in May, only partly dressed, unlaced shoes and no socks and no shirt beneath the sport coat, smears of blood on his graying-red chest hair and like an aborigine's warpaint on his face and throat and even in his hair, a man in frantic haste yet purposeful in flight as if escaping a burning building. Not daring to look back.

Muttering, as he hasn't in decades, "Jesus, Mary, and Joseph!"

In his car, then, a man's place of refuge. Key jammed into the ignition before the door's fully shut, motor racing before the gear's fully in drive, Corky accelerates from zero to thirty miles per hour in a brief city block burning rubber as, as a moony kid, he'd heard drivers do, imagining what fantasies of adult freedom and adult audacity in that screeching music.

6

CORKY TAKES REFUGE

You're an American, you're good as you look.

And thank God for that simple fucking fact.

The second time in three days, Corky Corcoran takes refuge in his Pearl Street office. Running there like a dog with its tail between its legs. (Corky's had actual glimpses of Doggy-Corky's tail: mongrel, mangy, drooping at the tip.) This place where nobody knows he is, Charlotte never knew, he strips naked and washes himself out of a mere sink, there's pleasure in such cramped circumstances, asshole, fuckhead, what better do you deserve. Corky should've been one of those Catholic penitents, monks in the Southwest beating themselves with rods, wearing strips of barbed wire inside their burlap robes, sleeping on wooden planks in unheated cells offering their misery up to Jesus Christ so there's some use for it.

But feeling good as he washes, or anyway better. Can't help but feel a lot better, that crazy bitch's blood off him and this fresh white shirt he's tearing out of its cellophane wrapper—the beauty of a new shirt, the solace, thrusting his arms into the sleeves, buttoning it up, peering at himself anxiously in the mirror. The weird thing is, all the shit he's been taking these past few days, Corky Corcoran doesn't look all that bad.

You're an American, you're good as you look. You'll be judged that way so judge yourself that way, too.

Need a drink?—a drink, a drink. Corky recalls the bottle of Johnnie Walker in the closet approximately five feet away as he sits at a battered-aluminum office desk going through his ledger, at least he's got a cigarette, and he's smoking that with the air of a man long deprived, and grateful. In fact he's got a near-full pack of Capris filched from a table in Kiki's living room on his way out, in antic desperation fleeing while dressing as in the bedroom the furious young woman shouted after him rapist!

pervert! murderer! and Corky sighted the pack and swiftly pocketed it
with the reflexive finesse of a pickpocket of old plying his trade even as the
hangman leads him through the crowd to the scaffold.

Finding here, to his infinite relief, in one of the desk drawers, a box of
matches silver-embossed *The Hot Spot.*

Corky checks the ledger, Friday April 10, Yeager did owe him, not
$900, but $780. He cancels the debt with an X.

(Of this $900, which Corky distinctly remembers putting in his wal-
let at the U.C.A.C., only $360 is left. Where did he spend $540 in the
intervening hours? Standing drinks at Bobby Ray's or The Bull's Eye? If
somebody stole from him, for instance Thalia while he was in the shower,
why wouldn't the thief have taken all his money? Cash is always running
through Corky's fingers like he's pissing it so this is no new startling rev-
elation.)

Entering in code in the ledger for Sat. May 24, his several bets on the
Blue Jays to win the American League pennant: $1000 with Fleischman,
$2000 with the other cop, smaller bets of $500, $300, can't remember
exactly but the total's $6000 at four-to-one odds. Scanning the columns,
seeing he's owed money by L.S., by W., by J.K., not poker debts but sports
bets, $2350 the total Corky shivers shaking ashes into a wastebasket
thinking the fuckers won't have to pay him if he's dead.

Why the fuck are you so morbid, Corky?—this isn't like you.

No it isn't. Yes I am.

Corky recalls how old Father Sullivan was mourned in Irish Hill when
at last, deep into his eighties, he died. A lament among the men of Our
Lady of Mercy parish in particular that they'd lost a good loyal friend, a
priest who was one of them and understood their ways even to the point
(drinking, gambling) of participating in their ways, yes but the deeper if
unspoken reason for mourning Father Sullivan was the many hundreds of
dollars he'd owed them which were never then paid.

A drink, drink. Christ, Corky's throat is parched: five years away from
smoking, he'd about forgotten what it does to your mouth, sinuses. Still
the taste's so good, the nicotine rush must be what cokeheads go for, or
heroin addicts—so sweet, worth dying for.

Corky thinks: why did Yeager give him $900 when he owed him only
$780, why at that time, a few hours after Corky'd turned up at Marilee

Plummer's and that by mere chance as Yeager, Beck, any of the others couldn't know except wouldn't it have been an asshole thing to do, just turn up, asking dumb-fuck questions, if Corky'd had any actual reason for being inquisitive. And wouldn't it have been a dangerous thing to do, if there was any actual reason for it to be so. Even if Marilee Plummer died by her own hand and her own volition. *Don't think it's suicide, it isn't.*

Suicide can be murder, though. If you're forced into it.

Like murder, sometimes, is suicide. Asking for it.

Corky recalls too how that day Oscar Slattery spoke to him leaning out of the limo, anxious, searching Corky's face, what did Corky know, or guess, it was Oscar yet not-Oscar, not as Corky knows him, something must have happened that had shaken the old man as Corky'd never seen him shaken but why would the death of a young black woman matter quite that much, even accounting for the fact, or at least the possibility, that the Mayor had been fond of Marilee Plummer as, so famously, he's fond of so many people, and generous with so many people, excepting political enemies against whom he's a vindictive pitiless cunning s.o.b. who never forgets a bad turn done against him. Why not, Corky's been wondering, feel relief, a kind of relief, private relief anyway, that Marcus Steadman, who'd been maneuvering to run for mayor against Oscar, would now be thoroughly discredited. Fucked, as Kiki said. Why not.

As fucked as Marcus Steadman, as what you did to him.

And Corky shocked, amazed, naked and blood-smeared and his poor scorned prick hanging limp between his legs, protesting *I didn't do anything, what is this?*

Like not-knowing these many years about his father. Not who had killed Tim Corcoran, paid for his death, but why Al Fenske was never arrested. Never charged with anything relating to that death.

What goes around comes around except sometimes not. Sometimes the turning upon itself is endless, futile. Around and around and around, the same questions, unanswered. And not that they are unanswerable, either: for somebody knows, or knew: but it's information you can't get hold of. You live with the questions, eventually you die with them, is that it?

"Christ. I just don't know."

Corky shuts the ledger. Rises from the dented aluminum desk that

came along with the "suite" like the other substandard furnishings, filing cabinets, chairs, lamps, wastebaskets, strips of pinkish fake-marble
linoleum tile loose on the bare floorboards like throw rugs, all inherited
with the acquisition of the five-storey building at 274 Pearl which is in
fact owned not by "Corcoran, Inc." but in the name of another party for
tax purposes but not for purposes having to do with Union City property
taxes since this mysterious building is no longer on the tax rolls having
been slated for demolition eight years ago. Yet there's a Korean grocer
renting space at the corner. He's been there for years. Kim Phoo or however the name's pronounced, God damn just Corky's luck the guy's open
for business Sunday afternoons standing in the doorway of the store gazing out when Corky pulls up in his mud-splotched Caddy and parks at the
curb and, head ducked, shielding his shirtless chest with both arms like a
modest woman, hurries into the entrance at 274 Pearl.

Kim Phoo's a model tenant, however. The best. Never any complaints,
demands, questions put to his Caucasian landlord. Like he's a gift of the
Mayor's, too.

By now Corky's dying for a drink. Rising quickly having made a decision opening the closet door, there's the familiar bottle of Johnnie Walker,
a quarter-full and Corky's hands are shaking carrying it into the lavatory and swiftly unscrewing the top pouring the contents into the toilet
bowl before the whiskey fumes hit his senses. Then, *this is the measure of
Corky's desperation*, he flushes the toilet.

Making sure the fucking whiskey's gone. Absolutely.

Before leaving the Pearl Street office Corky opens his safe and removes
$1000 of the $5000 he keeps on hand for emergencies. Ten $100 bills
neatly slipped into his wallet. (If he seriously wants to buy a gun he'll need
cash, no checks or credit cards.) Thinking of Thalia, at a loss what to
think. Sure, he'd fantasized doing to her and with her certain things he'd
be ashamed anyone knew but wouldn't any normal man in such circumstances in such close domestic quarters, living with his wife's daughter so
strong-willed and emotional yes and good-looking, and teasing, Corky
couldn't help the drift of his desire any more than the sudden erections he
had to hide not only from Thalia but more significantly from Charlotte
who was jealous enough in any case, how the hell was it Corky's fault! But

just because he'd fantasized certain things didn't mean he'd really wanted to do them just as even now sometimes in a foul mood he'll fantasize raping sodomizing thrusting his cock down some female's throat deeper than *Deep Throat* so she's choked on his jism, some women piss you off they're asking for it practically begging for it some of these feminists for instance and that knockout blond bitch so gorgeous in *Basic Instinct* but that doesn't mean that Corky really wants to do such things, hell no. He guesses he's a guy who wants to do the right thing by other people, do unto others as you would they do unto you, doesn't believe in God and etcetera but that's the Gospel teaching that most makes sense.

But his lustful thoughts for his wife's daughter only began, he swears, when she was twelve or thirteen. *And they were only thoughts not deeds!*

Not once had Corky touched Thalia, in all those years. He knows. Yet Thalia's told Kiki Zaller he had. And God knows who all else. Maybe she even believes it. *Maybe she even believes it!* Corky's read enough pop-Freud to know that wishes if strong enough can become memories; or, reversing the logic, memories can disappear, repressed, and return as wishes. And from his firsthand experience a few years ago on the Union City Civilian Complaint Review Board investigating charges of "unprofessional behavior" by the police, he knows that witnesses can claim even under oath they've seen things that did not occur. It's a basic premise of criminal law that "eyewitnesses" are notoriously unreliable, in fact often wrong; the more adamant, the more likely to be wrong; yet, the more adamant, the more convincing. Especially to asshole jurors new to the game.

Yet more preposterous is Thalia's claim that Corky molested her as a little girl. Forcing her to sit on his lap at the piano, aged eight. At a time when Corky was crazy about Charlotte Drummond and the two of them hot for each other as rabbits! It's just absolutely incontestably false yet how could Corky deny it, with what words can you deny such an accusation, like poor shithead Nixon insisting he wasn't a crook—*I am not a child molester, I am not a rapist, I am not a pervert.*

What really wounds Corky is how Thalia'd always flattered him. So many years of flattering her step-Daddy. Saying he'll be Mayor of Union City someday.

But if word gets out what Thalia's saying now, Jerome Andrew Corcoran won't even be reelected to the City Council.

This is the day that, pissing into the stained toilet bowl of his Pearl Street office, holding his wizened cock that's the hue and feel of skinned chicken, and with about that degree of body warmth, in his hands, Corky feels sorry for it. Sorry for it!

He guesses some watershed's been crossed. Some invisible boundary. He isn't going to feel the same about himself as a man ever again.

7

CORKY AT THE ZANZIBAR

You want to believe in magic when you're a kid. Later on, you want to know what the trick is so you can pull it yourself.

Corky's headed south on Erie. Taking the stoplights as they come not speeding up approaching the intersections because he can taste it, how badly he wants not to fuck up what he's going to do next, it's 2:55 P.M. and the day is draining like one of those slow stopped-up toilets that keeps sucking and sucking the shitty water down so you can't believe it's ever exactly going to flush and in a way it never exactly does but finally the shitty water's gone and no more water drains in because the fucking thing is broken, and you'll need to call a plumber. That's exactly how this Sunday, May 24, 1992, is draining away for Corky Corcoran, but what the hell?—a squinty-wincing smile at himself in his rearview mirror, he's a good sport.

Southward on Erie then past Union Boulevard suddenly passing the melancholy ruin of the old Palace Theatre in a block of partly razed buildings looking like a bomb site, Christ it's true what Oscar Slattery's detractors say the man's letting the south side, i.e. the black sector, go all to hell, Corky sees the gabled and turreted structure of the fancy old "Egyptian"-styled theater, the sagging marquee behind derelict scaffolding itself abandoned for years remembering with a rush of emotion that Sunday matinee where he'd seen Harry Blackstone the magician, HARRY BLACKSTONE & HIS MAGIC SHOW, the excitement of it, the very anticipation of it like the delirium of Christmas, *Can't wait! can't wait! can't wait!* a kid's typical frenzy and Corky wishes to hell he was capable of such anticipation at the age of forty-three! Typical of him, Tim Corcoran had bought out a row of seats close to the stage, it was Corky's cousin Peter's birthday and a big noisy gang of Corcorans was included, Corky's father and mother and grandparents, Aunt Frances and Uncle Sean and their kids Peter, Lois,

Tess, and others too, other kids, like six-year-old Jerome mesmerized by Harry Blackstone's magic tricks you understood were tricks but, Jesus, *how?* Blackstone the Master Magician, inky black pointed goatee, "piercing" eyes, crimson mouth and brilliant white teeth bared in a smile like Satan's with the power to hypnotize you against your will, to steal away your soul. Corky remembers his young cousins squealing with excitement, Jerome himself clenched with tremulous concentration astounded by the fantastic sword-swallowing tricks, the lethal flaming torches whirling in the air, a beautiful blond girl in a star-spangled bathing suit smiling as she's locked into a glittering coffin-box and sawed in half by cruel Harry Blackstone *truly sawed in half you could see for yourself* and the two halves rolled horribly apart so how *was* it a trick?—not scary but equally dazzling were the card tricks, the gold watches that leapt from Blackstone's white-gloved empty hands, the living doves snatched out of the very air fluttering and cooing about the stage, the living rabbits out of the black satin top hat. "Jesus, the guy is good!" Tim Corcoran had to acknowledge, wondering how the hell he did it, how much money he made too with these traveling shows, was he a millionaire like he deserved.

Corky's grandparents said yes Blackstone was pretty good but couldn't hold a candle to the Great Houdini who they'd seen in this same theater in 1923, now *there* was a magician.

The greatest mystery about that day of mysteries—forever afterward the family teased Corky *he'd* been hypnotized by Harry Blackstone, *he'd* actually been up on the Palace stage hypnotized in front of a thousand people!—when, in fact, as Corky well knew, he never had.

The hypnosis part of the program had excited him far less than the other parts, the true magic.

Corky guesses they confused him with Peter Corcoran, maybe, or another child, as adults will. Not that Corky remembered Peter being hypnotized, either. But *he*, Corky, sure hadn't been.

Corky tastes cold, remembering. So many years. All that elder generation of Corcorans long dead and gone to dust, and of the middle generation only Sean Corcoran remaining. In whatever shape Sean Corcoran was. No matter what bullshit people want to believe and want everybody else to believe the fact is you die, you don't have a clue when or how or to what purpose. Bullshit too about Time not existing well the only solid fact *is* Time, a conveyor belt like in the slaughterhouses carrying us all along. The only difference is between those who know they're going and those who don't.

After the magic show on the way home to Barrow Street Jerome asked Daddy what is "magic" and Tim Corcoran driving his big shiny black Caddy smoking a cigar the ashes flying back out the opened window laughed and shrugged saying you want to believe in magic when you're a kid, later on you want to know what the trick is so you can pull it yourself, and Corky's thinking God damn, yes, fucking-A correct, but you never do learn, do you.

And that includes Tim Corcoran, too.

Need a drink, Jesus do I need a drink. South on Erie past Decker and over the canal bridge at Welland, old two-lane rattling bridge should have been replaced twenty years ago but now the neighborhood's gone mostly black and nobody gives a damn. Crossing the placid mud-colored Erie Canal high from last week's days of rain, Corky thinks of how as a kid he'd swum off the banks here, mud-shitty water even then but he, Nick, Cormac, the other kids swam in it anyway, and in the lake, too, stinking of fertilizer from the Cayuga plant. Quick glimpse of the backs of shabby rowhouses strung out along the weedy canal towpath, flash of wild-growing lilac, so familiar to him it's like he's seen it last week, with a kid's eyes, unjudging. Corky grips the steering wheel tight to control the shakes.

Too fucking sober for Union City. That's Corky Corcoran's problem.

If he continues on Erie another two blocks he'll be passing Barrow Street. But if he turns onto Welland then doubles back he'll be passing the old site of Corcoran Brothers Construction and the lumberyard his grandfather Liam owned. A block to the east is Roosevelt where Sean Corcoran's still living in the old house, weird and crazy to be back in the old neighborhood but it isn't the old neighborhood, it's someplace else and another time and Corky's seeing with envy how on this warm-balmy overcast spring day everybody's out on the sidewalks and streets blacks of all ages and attire bright colors spilling out of the African Zion Church in a woodframe building formerly a branch of the Union City Public Library, up the street the public grammar school and today kids

are swarming like beetles in the playground, everywhere black kids on bicycles, skinny-gangly boys with weird zonked-up flattop hair like wedges
atop their heads, beats anything white kids can come up with even those
asshole punks with their waxed spiky hair. Seeing Corky Corcoran driving his Caddy cautious as he can along the busy street (he doesn't want to
run over one of these kids!) their eyes follow him, screw you, whitey, yeah
you, whitey, we're looking at *you*, whitey, you got it?

Corky swings around on Dalkey, cuts back to Erie, then Welland
again, approaching the Zanzibar from the potholed stretch of pavement
descending to the docks. There's the warehouse Corky'd worked at, one
of his shit-jobs hauling crates and barrels for the Great Lakes Freight Co.,
looks like it's still in business. Summers the heat was so bad mixed with
the stench of fertilizer nitrates and oil he'd come close to puking, sweat
stinging his eyes and soaking through his clothes and every muscle in his
skinny body aching, and his hands, had to pay for his own fucking gloves
that wore out in less than a week. Summer was bad enough but winter
was worse, winds off Lake Erie dropping the temperature to as low as
minus ten degrees Fahrenheit and still he'd be sweating working inside
then coming outside the fucking gloves would freeze on his hands so he
couldn't get a good grip and a sudden tear in the fabric was like a razor
slash in the flesh so like the other guys Corky tried to work without his
gloves for as long as he could until his skin split and cracked and even the
blood froze.

Must be mainly blacks down here now, you couldn't get a white man
to work like that. Like the city sanitation crews where the only white guys
are the ones driving the Dumpster trucks.

Corky parks across the street from Club Zanzibar. A look of tattered
half-melted grimy snow on the sidewalks and in the gutters here but it's
not snow, it's litter, it won't melt away. Raw-looking pink neon sign, unlit, CLUB ZANZIBAR, used to be THE SHAMROCK, there's a sleazy video rental
store up the block open on Sunday but everything else looks shut up or
permanently out of business. Weird thing seeing these billboards advertising cigarettes, beer with black models, good-looking light-skinned
blacks, gorgeous women on display, like one of those kids' games *What's
wrong with this picture.* How you know a part of the city is black. Seriously black.

Parking the Caddy and locking it Corky's aware of black guys observing him, they're hanging out on the corner close by the Zanzibar where maybe it isn't that unusual for white men to come, on private business. A certain kind of white man streetwise and with dough to spend. Corky flashes his big-toothed smile and gives these guys the high five like the team giving Dave Winfield the high five and they look at him like he's some kind of asshole from Mars and this pisses Corky off but he doesn't let on, he's got too much class to let on, just pushes inside the dump where there's a sudden terrific mouthwatering smell, barbecue, Corky guesses, hot greasy French fries, God he's starving he realizes he hasn't had anything solid to eat in maybe twenty-four hours. *That's* what's wrong with him!—no wonder he's got the shakes.

Need a drink, a drink his throat's so fucking parched but first thing Corky does is go to a cigarette vending machine and buy two packs of Camels, lights a cigarette inhaling deeply feeling a helluva lot better already, a man's tobacco. He's aware of eyes swiveling onto him out of the smoky interior, a sudden startled hushing of voices except for the TV on loud. Everybody wondering who he is, a mick-cop look about him maybe, undercover cop but it's Corky Corcoran with $1000 in his wallet in his back pocket he's serious about spending.

And if he gets his ass busted down here, or worse, when she hears about it Christina is going to feel like shit. Knowing she's to blame.

And Thalia, and Kiki. Yes and Charlotte too, bitch never gave him a chance to be a real husband to her, that steady flow of interest and dividends into her bank account, protested it didn't matter to her but it mattered to him, he's never forgiven *her*.

But Corky's smiling taking his time choosing a table, one of the small diner-style Formica-topped tables where he can sit with his back against the wall facing out toward most of the room. Surprised how inside Zanzibar's is a disappointment more a café than a tavern still less a funky cocktail lounge where there might be jazz weekends, and glamorous black women. And fuck it there's a distracting racket of video games, a half dozen of them and guys dropping coins into them, Corky can't stand those video games, goofy comic-strip screens and belching-farting-blipping-chirping noises, you expect it of half-assed mall-rat white kids with nothing better to do but not blacks. Like Thalia said, whites expect blacks to be better than we are, dedicated to a principle meaning the principle of being black in a white racist society thus perpetually alert and perpetually outraged unwilling to be suckered into squandering their best energies. Seeing black guys at video screens is just so damned depressing.

What Marcus Steadman should do is preach against such brain-rotting crap. Get it banned from black neighborhoods. That's what Corky Corcoran would do if he was a black Councilman.

"Hey, what's it take to be waited on?"—Corky's question is good-natured, just a little impatient but that's only natural, he *has* been sitting long enough for the waiter (if that's what that black guy is hanging out at the back) to notice him. There are maybe twelve tables in the place of which eight are occupied and everybody's been served and whatever they're eating, Jesus it smells good. Corky's question hovers in the air not so much unanswered as unheard, unacknowledged. "Any menus?" Corky asks.

Noticing then at a nearby table a guy Corky knows from City Hall, mustached middle-aged black man with a head shaved bald like Marvelous Marvin Hagler, he's a Democratic alderman from the Fourth Ward so Corky calls out, "A.G., my man!—how's it going?" and A.G. contemplates Corky just a beat too long before replying, with the faintest of smiles, "Ain't bad, Mr. Corc'ran," and no query put to Corky in return. The black prick!

A.G.'s with a table of black men, beer bottles crowding chunky blue plates heaped with this delicious-smelling food, baking powder biscuits, heavy gravy, what looks like pork chops, some kind of fried fish, corned-beef hash maybe, Corky's mouth is watering so hard it's like his saliva buds are weeping. He's so hungry by now he'd forgo a drink for food.

TV's on loud broadcasting another baseball game but Corky isn't in the mood to get into it, and those God-damn video games sending up an interference, and somebody's got a transistor radio tuned to a local rock station, so when the Zanzibar patrons get back to talking with one another and laughing like this pissed-off white man isn't there or if there invisible Corky knows it's maybe a mistake for him to be here but fuck it he's not going to give up.

Maybe anyway you don't need to be waited *on*, maybe you walk up to that open counter looking into the kitchen and give your order direct to the cook, this is fine with Corky who's too restless to sit still, he's on his

feet affable and smiling threading his way through the crowded tables trying not to be spooked at how he's being looked at or resolutely *not* looked
at, a good-looking young couple cutting their eyes at him like he's giving
off a bad smell, a table of older black men and women playing cards who
fall silent as he passes their faces blank with what Corky senses is withheld mirth, but it's the younger men who eye him coolly and appraisingly
then look away leaning together grinning and murmuring words he can't
decipher, Corky wants to protest, Hey, cut the shit, I'm one of *you*.

The Irish are the niggers of Great Britain, that's a known fact.

The Irish used to be the niggers of Union City, shit on the WASP shoes,
that's a known fact.

Corky leans his elbows on a counter at shoulder height looking directly
into a kitchen where a stout black woman with her hair tied up in a head
scarf is frying something in a heavy iron skillet—butter, onions, chicken
wings and legs covered in breadcrumbs. There's others in the kitchen too,
busy or anyway acting busy and paying Corky no heed. Corky can see
through an open door into a rear storage room and guesses that's where the
firearms are kept, it's possible that deals are made exclusively from the rear
and you approach by the alley, *that's* the signal?

Corky leans forward smiling inhaling the rich cooking odors. Hoping to hell he doesn't look as dazed as he feels. *Christ on a crutch!—I'm
starving.* The dizzy memory washes over him, like a bad joke, he'd actually had a fantasy of meeting up with Thalia at Kiki's and taking the two
out to Sunday brunch! Of all his dumb-fuck notions, that's the saddest.

"Hey, h'lo? Can I order some dinner?"

Seeing he's there and not going to go away the tall lean black guy who'd
be the waiter if there was a waiter asks Corky politely but unsmilingly
what does he want, and Corky says he wants a couple of things but to
begin with how's about some coffee, and how's about a menu?—and the
waiter shakes his head, polite as all hell, a fox-faced light-skinned guy
with insolent bug eyes, sorry, no menus, "—So how d'you know what to
order?" Corky asks reasonably, and the black woman handling the skillet
lifting it effortlessly with a muscled arm as she stirs the sizzling chicken
parts laughs without so much as glancing at Corky. It's the kind of rich
laugh makes you yearn to join in whether you know what's funny or not.

The idea is, Corky guesses, if you don't know what to order in a place like this you got no business being here.

Corky sucks on his cigarette. Says, with a smile, "Something smells good, that's for damned sure."

Says, "You got, uh, barbecue?—ribs, chicken? How's about pork chops? Colored greens, grits, cornbread, gravy, that kind of, what's it, catfish—fried catfish? Black-eyed peas, chitlings?" He doesn't know for sure what colored greens, grits, chitlings are but in the state he's in it all sounds good. "Sweet potato pie?"

The woman at the stove laughs now scraping the still-sizzling food onto a plate, biscuits too on the plate, and a mess of greens that's possibly what Corky means by "colored greens," and the guy who's the waiter takes up the plate and a thick white mug containing coffee and without a glance at Corky sidles past him and out into the restaurant to serve some lucky son of a bitch but Corky's trying to keep civil, knows he's got to win these people's confidence if he wants to be fed let alone sold a gun.

"Sure was sad about Marilee Plummer, wasn't it," Corky says somberly, "—I knew Marilee, she was a good girl—woman, I mean—I imagine everybody around here is pretty upset—" though it occurs to Corky even as he speaks that in this neighborhood with so many welfare blacks, blacks on probation or parole or just out of prison or on their way in, sentiment would be for Marcus Steadman and not Marilee Plummer. "—And I know Marcus Steadman, too—not well, but we're what you'd call colleagues."

Colleagues!—what kind of an asshole word is that?

"—I mean, we run into each other pretty often. At City Hall."

Now this is calculated; Corky's playing poker here and he's shrewd; but "City Hall" comes out sounding wrong even to his ears. So quickly he adds, frank as he can be, "Look, I'm not a cop. No bullshit, for sure I'm *not*."

The waiter's back conferring now in an undertone with the woman in the head scarf, there's another black guy there too, and a puffy-faced sullen girl of about fifteen with lips so swollen thick and shiny Corky can't keep his eyes off them, and what, red-fleshy as they are, blood-hot, they remind him of he'd just been mashing his face, teeth, tongue against so very recently, he's trying not to think. Corky sucks at his cigarette exhaling smoke furiously, wonders if he's losing it, hell no he isn't losing it, these black folks can perceive beneath the color of his skin he's the man he is, he's their friend he's on their side he's one of *them*.

"A.G. over there—A.G. can tell you who I am. I'm no cop."

This gets no response Corky can gauge, the waiter and the cook are still conferring, and when he looks over to where A.G. was sitting he sees the chair's empty. And the plate at that place empty too, wiped clean—the fucker!

Corky says, more pleading now, "Maybe I look like a cop, but I'm not. I swear. In fact I'm what you'd call"—rubbing his knuckles in his eyes like a guy suffering a colossal hangover—"the opposite of a cop."

Still no response.

"I've got cash, I need to make a purchase. I know this is the right place—there's only one Zanzibar on Welland, right? And I need to eat, too. And—did I ask you for some coffee? Please?"

The big-boned no-bullshit black mama in the head scarf is looking at Corky Corcoran now. Not like she's been listening to him but she sure is looking. Something so raw and yearning in the honky motherfucker's face any female human being no matter the color of her skin, and this lady's skin is the color of black raspberries, is going to take pity on him. Saying, with a sweep of her hefty arm, like she's the boss here, "O.K. y'all go sit down, mister, somebody take care of you." At least this is what Corky thinks the woman says, her words run together like syrup and her voice is a deep throaty growl. A quick baring of her big broad teeth with a glimmer of gold that's as much of a welcoming smile as Corky's going to get.

So Corky sits down. Seeing the shifting of eyes from him as he turns, quick as darting minnows.

Look, God damn you, I *am* one of you.

He's pissed by the way that spade A.G. froze him out. As if they weren't on the same side at City Hall, in a manner of speaking. God damn, Corky Corcoran will get his revenge if and when he can, wishes he could remember A.G.'s last name but there's only one of him in Union City Democratic politics, one fucking spade alderman from the Fourth Ward.

Corky lights up another Camel. The table of older blacks is breaking up, card game's over, Corky's been looking on trying to figure out what the game *is*, not poker, not euchre, not gin rummy, one of the old ladies has kept the score in a notepad and there's a murmurous exchange of coins and bills but Corky can't figure out who won since everybody's cool and expressionless and suddenly eager to be gone—"Hey, don't let me chase you away," says Corky impulsively, "—I'm *not* a cop." Smiling and lifting his hands palm outward like a character in a movie showing he isn't armed. Or anyway hasn't got a gun in sight.

The elderly neighborhood blacks look at Corky as if he's spoken to them in fucking Sanskrit or something. Conspicuously packing up their things, and leaving.

Corky laughs, annoyed and hurt. Says, for as many of the other patrons as want to hear, "What, I've got AIDS? 'Cause of my skin? I should be in fucking quarantine or something?"

This gets the attention of a table of loud-laughing youngish blacks, three women and two men looking like they're dressed for Sunday church, the women in frilly floral spring dresses like balloons, the men in pastel-colored sport coats and silk ties, they regard Corky soberly for a few seconds then look away murmuring to themselves, and Corky steels himself waiting for them to laugh, and when they don't maybe it's worse—"In fact I *don't* have AIDS," Corky says. "And I'm *not* a cop."

The young black guys at the next table are finishing up their beers watching Corky over the upward flash of the brown bottles, looks like they're pushing on, too. Corky's dismayed. He knows he could relate to these guys if they'd give him half a chance if they could get into a discussion of Dave Winfield for instance, or Mike Tyson, or Ali—if they were all at The Bull's Eye, on Corky's own turf. He'd make *them* feel welcome.

Corky says, reasonably, "—*You* know, right? Any kind of an undercover operation, down here, it's black detectives, not white. *You* know." Trying to draw them into this half-joking and half-serious but the guys aren't any more interested in conversing with Corky Corcoran than the others were.

Five more minutes and another two parties have cleared out leaving the Zanzibar mostly empty tables. Corky's reminded of some dream he used to have of finding himself in a public place naked, and everybody staring at him, laughing and edging away. A young kid at the time, his cock start-ing to grow, hairs sprouting on his body, a terrible wildness in his veins he'd known he could never control.

Corky sits, waits. It's 3:23 P.M. by his watch, it's 3:30 P.M. The TV baseball's between innings but nobody turns the volume down, one ear-blasting ad follows another, some zonked-out teenaged kids are playing the video games a few yards away—*they're* not spooked by the strange white man—and Corky Corcoran's sitting in his good clothes fresh-groomed and hopeful at a sticky Formica-topped table in a nigger soul food restaurant in a dead zone on West Welland trying not to freak out waiting for that delicious-smelling rich black coffee that's taking a hell of a long time to arrive at his table let alone the delicious-smelling bar-becued ribs or chicken or pork chops or catfish or corned-beef hash, gravy-soaked baking powder biscuits, sweet potato pie that's taking even longer. Corky's a reasonable man he's a good decent loyal Party man he's an elected Union City official he's a millionaire property-owner and busi-nessman and family man with responsibilities *he is not going to freak out.*

For sure, last night scared him. Blacking out, and waking in the gravel by the Expressway, light in his eyes blinding him like he's meant not to open his eyes again stinking of piss and vomit—*him*, Jerome Andrew Corcoran!

How Tim Corcoran would be shamed, if he could know.

If he could have known how his son he loved so much would turn out.

Corky's uneasy smoking his cigarette knowing he's being watched and whispered over, he's been staring at a poster on the wall directly in his line of vision, an ad for Coors beer, there's a sleek muscled black jock and a gorgeous light-skinned black woman with her hair in snaky min-iature braids, sexy, the woman's damned good-looking reminding him of Marilee Plummer around the mouth that flirty-fucky swollen-mouth look. And there's the smooth-muscled black jock smiling lifting his can of Coors as the gorgeous black model gazes up admiring, Corky's read that in these shrewdly calculated ads the psychology is the male is the center of interest so the female looks at *him*, so everybody ends up looking at him, that sleek cocoa-brown stud swigging Coors like it's his own cock, that's the secret—black cock, supreme. A white man feels uneasy seeing a black guy so good-looking with a good-looking black woman, the two of them connected, completed together, no need for anybody else. Can't help but think that, a white woman's given the choice of a white man, or a black, the two of them equal, she'll choose the black for sex—that's the secret, too. Or maybe not a secret. The average American white man's erection measures 6.1 inches but the average black man's measures 6.4 inches.

When Corky read this statistic, just the other week, maybe in *Playboy*, he'd felt almost a panic attack. He was sure he didn't measure 6.1 inches, let alone 6.4 inches.

Thinking then, what kind of asshole statistic *is* this! Who in Christ's name has been measuring the pricks of American men and worked out an *average?*

And after that, Corky stopped thinking about it.

God-damn posters displaying hunk models, fantastic females, must make everybody uneasy. What're you supposed to do, jerk off in homage to them? For sure, you can't *be* them. And blacks, seeing these models with Caucasian features, straightened hair—must be even worse for them.

Selling beer, tobacco mainly. "Targeted" ads. The black consumer nobody gave a shit for, till they got spending money.

What Corky'd do, is take down these fucking poster ads. Strip the walls. Put in some plasterboard, and an acoustical ceiling. Recessed lighting. Good solid no-polish tile floor instead of this wornout crap linoleum. Get rid of these shitty beat-up tables. Get rid of that counter opening into the kitchen. Close off the kitchen, break through the wall into the next-door building he'd noticed is vacant, put in a classy bar. Good leather bar stools, mirrors. Blacks like excess so how's about some gold fixtures, crushed-velvet drapery, velour "banquettes." Mirror-topped tables. Paint the walls in blue carbon steel, and the exterior, too, funky-cool. And the neon sign CLUB ZANZIBAR in tropical colors like citrus fruit sweet on the tongue, the most elegant tubing Corky could find. And they need a parking lot—raze the derelict building next door, pour in asphalt. Valet parking, maybe. When CLUB ZANZIBAR catches on with the uptown trade, the trendy yuppies who snort coke weekends, yeah you'll need valet parking.

Corky's mind is racing. It's the nicotine, and it's doing him good.

Should he stake the owner of the Zanzibar?—or buy the property out from under him? If so, should he fire the staff to teach them a lesson in good manners? And include Aunt Jemima who's obviously a terrific cook? Or make an exception of her?—she'd at least talked to Corky. One thing's for sure, Corky Corcoran will pay his crew of loyal black workers twice the wages or anyway one and a half the wages anybody nonunion is making in this dead-end zone of Union City. That's why they'll be loyal, and defend him against black racist agitators like Marcus Steadman.

Maybe, though, Corky should go into a partnership in Club Zanzibar with a black man. He knows a black realtor . . . Not a fifty-fifty partnership of course, Corcoran, Inc., will have controlling interest.

Jerome "Corky" Corcoran the legendary Union City entrepreneur.

Jerome "Corky" Corcoran honored as one of those Union City citizens whose faith in their city transcends . . . whatever.

Jerome "Corky" Corcoran the Democratic candidate for Mayor of Union City . . .

The tall lean black guy has been taking customers' money at a cash register up front, now the place is about empty and he's clearing the table next to Corky's his sly fox-face betraying not the slightest awareness of Corky's existence. And the girl with the fat sullen lips is clearing another table like the dishes and cutlery had insulted her momma, ignoring Corky too. Still he's watching them dignified and with his faint hopeful I'm-giving-you-a-chance smile thinking for sure he'll fire these two, kick their black butts right out on the street. "Excuse me, when is somebody going to take my order? I've been waiting for a God-damned long time," Corky says. Speaking clearly and politely like a man with a legitimate complaint, not some troublemaker on the verge of losing it. Obviously there's some misunderstanding here it's in everybody's best interest to clear up. "And where's my coffee? I ordered coffee." Corky has his wallet out on the table wadded thick with bills.

The waiter finally looks at Corky sliding his eyes like grease without moving his head. "What, man? What're you saying?" His voice is just this side of jeering, like he's a high school kid incredulous at something some old guy is asking. "Zanzibar's closing. Sunday afternoons, we close, man." The girl at the other table doesn't glance at Corky at all slamming plates and cutlery together and swiping at the tabletop with a discolored sponge.

"Why'd you say you'd serve me, then? You said you'd serve me," Corky protests, though he can't remember whether anybody actually said so, "—and now you're not going to? Now you're *closing?* What the fuck is going on here? Is this a restaurant open to the public or isn't it?" Corky's trying not to get excited but he's like a child with a just grievance, he's feeling almost elated. "You know what, man? *My civil rights are being violated.*"

Corky's on his feet and the waiter's standing there eyeing him, taller than Corky by two or three inches but giving Corky maybe twenty pounds, Corky's hot in the face and ready to fight though he guesses it's a mistake. He sees there's nobody in the kitchen—the woman in the head scarf, who'd seemed to like him, is gone. The last of the kids playing video games is trailing out the front door. The sullen girl does look at Corky now, a little scared and backing off.

"I've got money," Corky says, opening his wallet so the black prick can see, "—I'm willing to spend, man," riffling through the bills, the $100 bills conspicuous, "—I'm here to spend, man, so what's the fucking problem?" like he's unzipping his pants displaying himself.

The waiter shakes his head as if he's getting scared, too.

"Nah, man, we closing. Sunday afternoons, we close."

Corky's about to protest louder when up out of nowhere like a magic trick of Harry Blackstone's, like he'd popped up through a trapdoor, there comes this fierce little bulldog character, a touch to Corky's elbow so Corky freezes like it's a gun shoved at him, turns and sees a little man no taller than five feet with the ugliest pouched, wrinkled, wizened face he's ever seen—"O.K., mister, what's the problem?" this guy asks, in a high-pitched voice like a saw, "—What's *your* fucking problem?"

Corky's so taken by surprise he can only stammer, "Wh-Who are *you?*"

"I'm Mr. Beechum the pro-pri-etor of Club Zanzibar but never mind who'm *I*, mister, who're *you?*"

Corky stares blinking at this runty little bulldog he guesses means business. This is the guy who sells the guns in back, this is the "Beechum" Corky recalls now he's heard of, just the name, "Beechum," "Beechum's the man to see"—Corky thinks he's heard this. In the confusion of the moment, though, he isn't thinking very clearly.

Corky tells Beechum how he's been treated, he's a man with money to spend and not used to being treated like shit, man you better believe it, displaying the bills in his wallet to Beechum too, who's frowning and squinting at them and up at Corky like he's trying to place Corky, undecided how to deal with him. Beechum is solid in the torso as a keg with skin black as pitch and oily-rich, quick intelligent fierce-yellowish eyes and a flattened pug nose, no telling how old, might be forty, might be sixty, Corky's Caucasian eye can't judge. Corky's put in mind of Johnny the Philip Morris cigarette kid, the same kind of weirdness, something you can't figure out, is this a midget?—a dwarf?—but in no visible way misshapen, and not small exactly, only short. Beechum is showily dressed, a dude, is that the word, dude, pimp-style too except he has too much class to be a pimp, not that Corky knows about such things really, he prides himself on his street smarts but in fact he doesn't know much about the inner-city black population except what he reads in the papers, sees on TV like everybody else. What to make of the proprietor of the Zanzibar in a maroon suede jacket, a collarless ivory shirt, a heavy gold medallion on a gold chain around his neck. His fore-shortened legs in checked trousers. Gleaming black shoes with a Cuban heel like a dancer's. A soft-brim creamy-ivory fedora on his neat-nappy hair, bulldog head. And those squinty no-bullshit eyes taking Corky's measure like they're the same height, not to mention the same color.

"Maybe you better put yo' money away, mister," Beechum says somberly. "We sure do believe you, you rich."

But this is delivered in such a solicitous drawl, with a sly screwing up of the bulldog face, it's obviously jiving.

"I'm not rich," says Corky, "—but I need to be treated with respect. I've been *dis*respected here, God damn it."

"Man like you, driving a Caddy De Ville, you sure do deserve not to be *dis*'d."

"That's right, God damn it! I *do*."

Corky's feeling lightheaded like none of this is exactly real but he has to play it as if it is, he's got no choice. Sweat breaking out under his arms and on his forehead and he's got the visible shakes now, dying for a drink and if only he had a drink, he'd know how to deal with this bulldog-spade who's like nobody Corky has ever met up with. Usually for a guy Corky's height looking *down* at an adversary is so unexpected such a change so welcome he's invigorated by that simple fact but for some reason Corky doesn't feel that now, it's more like one of those big lummox heavyweights like Gerry Cooney confronted with one of those tough, squat, compact killers like Mike Tyson who's short and going to crouch shorter who's going to duck every good blow while nailing his opponent low in the body, breaking ribs and fouling.

Corky tells Beechum in a voice more whiny than he'd like how he was promised service, promised coffee, how he's got serious business here at the Zanzibar but he's been treated like some punk with no cash or connections at all, he's here on the recommendation of a mutual friend—not naming the only name that comes to Corky's mind, which is that of a white cop. And maybe Corky isn't so sure of all this, either.

"That so? Hmmm!" Beechum fixing Corky a look like he still can't figure out how to assess him. "And you ain't gonna tell me that friend's name, eh?"

Corky hesitates. Then shakes his head irritably. "No."

Meaning, I don't trust you either, man.

Meaning, nobody's going to bullshit Corky Corcoran.

Beechum's been edging Corky toward the door, that's pretty clear. Like you'd ease a jumpy-nervous dog in the direction you want him to go without him exactly knowing what's going on. Though with a part of his mind his stone cold sober mind Corky knows. And Corky's going to remember. A stunted little spade manipulating *him!*

Except maybe, just maybe, this thought's been blipping in Corky's head like the Pac-Man video, Beechum's carrying a gun.

For sure, Beechum's carrying a gun.

Anybody selling guns illegally is sure to be carrying a gun.

Corky says, stammering slightly, "—L-Like I'm not wanted here for one reason and one reason only—that's what pisses me off."

"Which reason is that, hmmm?"

"You know what it is."

"Hey, mister, this poor fool don't know—*you* tell *me*."

Corky draws a deep tremulous breath. Ridiculous, how he's trembling. "I'm—*white*."

"Man, no!" Beechum pops his eyes and shakes his jowly little face like he's never heard anything so surprising. "You're *white*—? *That's* yo' problem?"

The TV's been switched off by this time and the silence in the Zanzibar is profound like something rising up from the earth through the warped floorboards. Corky's idiot words hang in the air—*I'm white! I'm white!*—and the wild thought comes to him, *am* I white? how do I know?

If it was just Beechum and Corky Corcoran alone together of all the earth's inhabitants, no "Caucasian race" standing outside Corky to give him definition and claim him for their own, Jesus, he *would* be scared shitless. Not a snowball's chance in hell standing up to this motherfucker the crown of whose hat comes to approximately Corky's chin.

Corky adds earnestly, like he doesn't mind how he's being jived, "And I'm not a cop. *You* can figure that, can't you, Mr. Beechum? I was an undercover cop, here at the Zanzibar, I'd be black. Right?"

"Man, you too quick for me. Why'd you be—what, black? How come?"

Beechum screwing up his face so it's a layered mass of tarry-black flesh out of which his eyes gleam yellow like reflectors.

Corky stares at the belligerent little bastard. Gun or no gun, he's asking to be slugged. Pure meanness. The waiter and the girl are gone, so he isn't fucking with Corky for their amusement. Corky says, like a man sweating under a cross-examination on the witness stand, "'How come'—? This is a black place, in a black neighborhood, the cops do an operation they use black detectives. A white guy like me—obviously he'd be under suspicion the first he steps in the door. You wouldn't deal with him."

"Hmmm! 'Deal with him'—what? Coffee, spareribs, sweet potato pie?" The bulge of Beechum's eyes suggests how he's enjoying this.

Now it's out in the open, Corky thinks. O.K., man.

By this time Beechum has edged Corky up to the cashier's counter. There's an eerie scintillating in the corner of his eye and more of that bleeping and farting—another video game. Corky glances around and sees no one's there. He says, lowering his voice, "—That's right. You're right, Mr. Beechum. I didn't come here for food, I came here because I need protection. I need it now. I can't wait. I've got money like I showed you and I'm interested in"—lowering his voice still further, and bending toward Beechum so there'll be no margin for error—"a gun."

Beechum widens his eyes. "Eh? Say what?"

"A gun. Fucking *gun*."

"A gun, my man!" Beechum's looking grave, shaking his head slowly from side to side, a ponderous kind of head-shaking, his torso involved too, the gold medallion gleaming and winking between his suede lapels. The bas-relief is a lion with enormous mane and bared teeth. "What kinda gun?"

"Show me what you have."

"Mister, you know what you want or you don't know, hmmm? And if you don't know, ain't much purpose hanging out here."

"—A Smith & Wesson fifty-seven, forty-one Magnum six-shot."

Corky answers quick: this is the gun of choice, he's heard, of the UCPD, the kind certain of the cops own though the Department is issued another model.

Beechum bares his gums in a grin that possibly registers surprise. Corky thinks, I've impressed the bastard!

"How yo' know that straight off, my man? *I* never heard of the motherfucker."

"Look, Beechum—Mr. Beechum—don't jive me, O.K.? Like I say, I've got the cash. And I'm in a hurry."

"Hurry—goin' where?"

"—I've been putting up with a lot of shit from you and your friends and I've had about enough of it."

Beechum's standing with his arms folded across his chest eyeing Corky in that way Corky can't figure—does he just not trust him, or does he not *like* him? Corky can accept not being trusted but not being liked—that hurts.

Whichever, Beechum's bulldog face tightens as he makes his decision. Shaking his head gravely and ponderously, "Hmmmm! Mister, I'm sure you're speaking the truth, but, shit, I'm afraid Beechum ain't the man to help you. Go tell yo' friend, there's no guns at Club Zanzibar."

"What? Hey, come on—"

"*You* come on, mister. Nobody here in possession of any gun let alone selling 'em."

"—I can pay up to five hundred dollars. Like I told you, I—"

Corky's got his wallet out again and Beechum raps sharply at his arm. "Nah, *no*, mister. Best you leave now, Zanzibar's closed."

Corky's incredulous. "What?"

"Best you leave now, mister. Get in yo' Caddy and drive back where you come from and tell yo' friend he's full of shit—you got it?"

"Look, Beechum," Corky says, excited, "—I'm a serious customer. You do business with me now, maybe we'll do business another time. If I told you my name, you'd recognize it! I'm not leaving here without what I came for."

Beechum laughs. Raises his eyebrows so high his fedora lifts.

"Oh you ain't, my man, eh? You ain't leaving? Eh?"

"Look," Corky says, pleading, "—I'm your friend, I'm on your side. Politically—I'm on your side. At City Hall—"

"City Hall?—where's that?" Beechum asks in mock earnestness. "Which city?"

"—the Mayor and his—"

"Mayor who? C'mon man, *you* jiving *me*."

Beechum's edging Corky backward and God damn it he's stumbling into a chair, almost falls but rights himself in time, Christ he *is* light-headed, famished. Hearing himself say, aggrieved as a kid, "—If I was black you wouldn't treat me like this," and Beechum shoots back quick as a TV comic, "How'm I gonna treat you, then?" and Corky says, "Like a brother," and Beechum laughs crinkling his face so his eyes are yellow slits, "Shit, man, you ain't my brother!—and if you was, how you so certain you know how I'm gonna treat you? Might be, I been bustin' my brothers' balls since they grew 'em."

It's then Corky makes his mistake: takes hold of Beechum's arm as Beechum pushes at him, and Beechum pushes at him harder, quick as a coiled-up spring unsprung, and next thing Corky knows he's on his ass on the floor. How'd it happen? *What* happened? It's like in the boxing ring, you're jabbing at your opponent you've got your opponent in your sights, then suddenly you're on your ass seeing stars or crawling on the canvas trying to pick up your mouthpiece with your gloved hand, and your opponent looking at you from above. Beechum's not smiling now looking at Corky from above his yellow eyes flashing pure meanness. The sheen of his black oily skin is like flame beneath the skin's surface. "Nobody puts his hands on me, man. I don't care what color you are or think you are. This is Roscoe Beechum!"

Corky persists, stammering, "L-Look, I—I'm desperate—I need to do business with you—Somebody took my gun, I need protection—I'm afraid I'm going to be—"

Shrilly Beechum says, "What's that got to do with Roscoe Beechum, I'm asking you, man?—what the fuck's any of you got to do with Roscoe Beechum?" crouching over Corky in such fury Corky begs, "Jesus, don't shoot!" shielding his face with his arms imagining he sees, or in fact seeing, a gun in Beechum's fingers drawn out from inside the suede jacket, Corky's ingloriously scrambling back on his ass feeling Beechum's hot breath in his face like the very breath of a lion, king of the carnivores. And those eyes! "I'm leaving, hey don't shoot!"—grabbing a lightweight aluminum chair that almost topples over on him trying to get to his feet, still Corky's saying as if, God help him, he can't not say it, as if the point of his being here in Club Zanzibar for whatever harebrained purpose knocked on his ass is his saying this, uttering these words, in a voice almost too choked for Roscoe Beechum to hear, "—My f-father was Tim Corcoran—d'you know that name—d'you remember him—'Tim Corcoran'—Corcoran Brothers Construction—we all lived here, in Irish Hill—he died because he hired nonunion Negroes—in 1959—he was killed—my f-father—" not knowing what he's saying as the words tumble from his mouth as, afterward, Corky won't recall much of what happens in Club Zanzibar this afternoon, just as he was never able to remember being hypnotized by Harry Blackstone being volunteered by Daddy to climb up onto the stage in response to the magician's request being cheered on by the gang of relatives and ascending with childish bravado to the stage and the man with the Satanic spiky black beard and black shining eyes asking Corky to count with him backward from ten and with the pronunciation of the very word "ten" there came washing over the child complete oblivion, complete not only in itself but with the power to obliterate memory even pertaining to it, surrounding and defining it. And Corky hears Beechum grunt what sounds like, "Who?—'Corcoran'—" but in the next instant the door of Club Zanzibar is open and Corky's outside on the pavement. Swaying on his shaky legs but, at least, he isn't on his ass.

Corky wipes his eyes with his knuckles. He's aware of a half dozen black boys gaping amazed at him and he's aware he has to not only get to his car but unlock it, not only unlock it but climb inside and drive it away without being mugged, he's smelling rain before he feels it on his overheated face, he's smelling a familiar mixed odor, something metallic in the air, the sharp sour smell of fertilizer, but a ripe fragrance of garbage too, and lilac beneath—a smell as of home, his lost home. He has his car keys out seeing that his tires are slashed. He's unlocking his car seeing, Jesus, no, his tires are not slashed—not the ones on this side, anyway. Nor are his hubcaps gone. The black boys with their oddly sculpted flattop hair are observing him closely, murmuring and giggling among themselves, but maybe Club Zanzibar is in a buffer zone and patrons of even the Caucasian race are privileged not to be harmed, nor even touched—is that possible, Corky's thinking. Is that possible.

At any rate nobody touches him. He's O.K. Inserting the key into the lock with surprising dexterity considering the condition of his nerves, easing himself into the Caddy that's like a cocoon-womb receiving him, and the fragrance herein too of the pink begonia for Sister Mary Megan he means still to deliver to her bedside, so help him. Corky's safe!

Except as he's about to drive away, one of the black boys hurries to the car, "Hey Mistah Cor'crin," he calls out, and Corky turns to see something in his hand seemingly nonlethal, "—Mistah Beechum say this for you, and no charge, O.K.?"

It's a big wedge of sweet potato pie wrapped in aluminum foil, and a Styrofoam cup of black coffee, lukewarm.

8

CORKY ON MOUNT MORIAH

You, Jerome. Our only witness.

It's a private funeral not only closed to all outsiders but its actual location meant to be a secret, except Corky Corcoran knows. One of his TV-news contacts. No media please, please no media at our daughter's funeral the Plummers begged but fuck the family of the deceased, right? Fuck the mourners where there's a hot story.

Even before Corky arrived to scout out the neighborhood there were TV vans in the street, a narrow residential street off Decatur called Washington, all but blocking traffic spilling glaring-white lights, cameras, cables. Film crews, photographers, reporters milling around hoping to engage the mourners as they arrive and hurry into the church, what leeches they are, these "media people"!—Corky, who's addicted to the news, who's at this very moment punching stations on his car radio hoping for a news announcer's voice, nonetheless feels disgust. This *is* a funeral, after all. For Christ's sake someone has *died*.

Corky's discreet enough not to cruise past the church, he's parked up the block, he's bothering no one. Just about the only white faces here are the media people, and Corky doesn't want to be mistaken for one of them. He's a mourner—at a distance. Smoking his cigarettes, picking gummy sweet potato pie from his teeth. Trying to think. The death of somebody you don't know intimately nor even well, not a friend not a relative not a lover, but you've had some contact with, is a shock like a minor earth tremor—you feel it, but there's no emotion.

Corky wonders if Thalia is at the funeral, if she'd been invited. If he sights her, what he'll do.

Thalia, Marilee. And Kiki. What's the connection?

Corky's in such a state of nerves he's susceptible to thinking *he's* the connection.

The Covenant Evangelical Free Church where the private funeral for Marilee Plummer is held this afternoon of Sunday, May 24, 1992, is a modest white-painted woodframe building that more resembles a house than a church, in a neighborhood of similar modest neatly tended wood-frame and stucco houses. This is southeast Union City, Washington Park. Now almost entirely black and Hispanic working-class where until the late 1960s it was 100 percent white working-class. Corcoran, Inc., used to own property here, office rentals on Decatur, but no more. It looks to Corky as if Washington Park is holding its own, though if it unravels it will be along wide windy Decatur Boulevard where crack houses and prostitution are prospering.

When Corky was growing up in Irish Hill, Washington Park was Polish, Italian, solidly Catholic. Locally renowned, or was it notorious, for its citizenry's unflagging resistance to the post-War phenomenon of urban social change "integration"—until the riots of 1967 and the eruption of inner-city vandalism, looting and fires of the following year in those days after the assassination of Martin Luther King threw the community into a panic, and Washington Park lost its white population to the suburbs. Like Irish Hill, equally scattered. Corky remembers working for Parks & Recreation in late summer 1967 saving money for tuition to Rensselaer and how one evening at the Seneca House with some of the guys from his crew he'd run outside to see the sky go up in gassy orange flames just a few blocks south of Irish Hill, it was a few days after the Detroit burning and he'd wondered *Is this the end? the end of Union City? the end of America?* Almost, he'd felt a weird kind of elation. He wouldn't have to go to Rensselaer after all where he'd probably flunk out. He wouldn't have to take care of nor even see again his crazy mother, shuttling back and forth between her wearying kin the Corcorans and the McClures, and St. Raphael's Hospital. He wouldn't have to be Corky Corcoran, Tim Corcoran's son.

Through his streaked windshield where the wipers are timed slow Corky watches the facade of the little church, the hearse at the curb, the dozen or so mourners' cars. Wonders if his "funeral floral display"—*in memory of Marilee Plummer, with sympathy Jerome A. Corcoran*—was delivered to the right address, and if anybody took note. Not thinking of Tim Corcoran's funeral, nor of that hearse which was the first and will

remain the only significant hearse of Corky's experience. For what purpose to such thinking, what but a perpetual laceration of the heart, and
Corky's nerves are already strung so tight his eyes feel like they're about
to pop out of their sockets. If only *a drink! a drink!* if only Christina
hadn't betrayed him if only Roscoe Beechum had sold him a gun!—the
devious little prick. (Yes, Corky devoured the sweet potato pie, sugary-
syrupy and chewy and the heavy crust too one of the most delicious tastes
he'd ever had in his mouth, he'd wolfed it down like a starving animal
chewing and swallowing large mouthfuls washing them down with coffee
his hands trembling and his eyes flooding with tears of gratitude as he sat
in the Caddy at the foot of West Welland overlooking Lake Erie on this
gusty-rainy spring afternoon God-damn happy to be alive seeing how the
entire western sky above the lake was a single mass of cloud, clotted and
ribbed, covered by a hulking shadow that seemed somehow to be the very
shadow of the earth, cast upward.)

By 4:45 P.M. nobody's yet emerged from the church. The showy shiny
hearse at the curb. The mourners' cars. A half dozen burly black men, in
suits, neckties, hats, standing about the front of the church as if guarding
the premises, but not cops. Corky's sure they're not cops. There's a UCPD
patrol car cruising the area, two officers inside . . . passing by Corky for the
third time they give him a hard stare seemingly without recognition. It's a
free country isn't it, he's got a right to be here. Fuck you. Corky's antsy and
bored and scared *a drink, need a drink* but look: if you can hold out till
Tuesday, the AA clinic. And Tuesday, too, the stores will be open, there's a
sports store on Union, you've got a homeowner's gun permit, you can buy
a gun legitimately and no fucking around like at the Zanzibar.

Corky's been punching radio stations up and down the band a squawk
of static and heavy-breathing Stone Age rock and some prissy asshole
preaching *Are you washed in the Blood of the Lamb my brothers and
sisters* and ads delivered at top volume finally hitting upon a news update
but it's WPOR Oriskany seventy miles away, even weather predictions
there don't interest him. Corky wants to know what's going on in Union
City, what's the latest news, the news-about-to-break, he's dying to know.
Sensing that something imminent is gathering, an electrical storm gathering to discharge itself.

Yes but why do you think you're going to die at any minute, what the fuck's wrong with you, *other people die but not Corky Corcoran!*

Just can't sit in the car any longer so he's outside stretching his legs, it's a mistake maybe but Corky's strolling in the direction of the church smoking his cigarette in the rain bareheaded and liking the cool feeling against his heated skin. All those reporters, media sucks, standing around in the rain waiting for something to happen. Waiting for mourners of a dead girl to emerge from a church. A coffin to be photographed, a hearse. Death. There's a TV truck in the street bearing a gleaming white satellite dish like an upended flying saucer, several camera crews with their equipment like artillery. Glazed-eyed reporters, standing around with nothing to do but interview one another. One of them, blond glamor girl for WWTC-TV Evening Action News in a little red career suit and snazzy white boots, looks like a baton twirler and Corky's eyeing her with interest when unexpectedly she recognizes him and cries, "Oh! Jerome Cochrane?—is that who you are?—one of the Mayor's aides?" and Corky feels simultaneously a thrill of pleasure at being so singled out, for many others are milling about in the street, and a deeper and more profound pang of regret, now his cover's blown.

As always, when you're beset by the media, on their terms and not your own, things happen too swiftly to be processed. Corky sees a little red light pop on as a TV camera is wheeled at once in his direction, the blond in the red suit and boots who's Peggy Crofton as she proclaims herself thrusts her microphone into Corky's face as she fires away questions suddenly fierce and professional as any man: was Corky a friend of the deceased Marilee Plummer? is he acquainted with the Plummer family? what is the Mayor's relation to the deceased? what is Vic Slattery's relation to the deceased? what does Corky think of the fact that only blacks, no whites, were allegedly invited to Marilee Plummer's funeral? what is Marcus Steadman's role in this? what of the coroner's verdict of suicide, does Corky have any opinion?—and Corky's standing blinking and trying to speak his mind blank as if he's been struck a succession of hammer blows to the head, this woman is all over him jabbing her microphone practically into his mouth like it's a cock she's wielding like a weapon, and what Corky manages to say, stammering and squinting into the camera dazed by lights and sweating berating himself *Asshole! how'd you get yourself into this!* he doesn't know, he does manage to say the death is a "tragedy" and he does manage to correct the woman's misidentification of him but the rest is a blur. And thank God then the doors of the church open, mourners begin to emerge, Peggy Crofton and WWTC-TV abruptly terminate the interview with Corky Corcoran.

Stunned Corky practically limps back to his car. Jesus, it's as if he *has* been fucked, in the face, by a vicious bitch he'd mistaken as a bimbo baton twirler!

Corky's strategy next is to drive not *behind* but *ahead* of the funeral procession, to Mount Moriah Cemetery which he happens to know is their destination. Not that he means to intrude, for sure he doesn't. Just that he can't give this up.

Like that guy stalking Thalia. Corky's forgotten his name.

The one, for her sake, he'd had beaten half to death.

Shortly before 5 P.M. then of this day rough and saw-notched as the underside of Corky's tooth against his tender tongue, which in nerved-up states he compulsively touches, as compulsively, when alone, he picks at his nose and mutters to himself, Corky sets off for Mount Moriah Cemetery. His head does feel as if somebody's been hammering on it. And his stomach!—the sweet potato pie, so delicious to eat, lies heavy in his gut as undigested body parts.

O.K. asshole don't get thinking of *that*.

You want to make yourself sick, don't get thinking of *that*.

And what had that sadistic prick "Wolf" Wiegler said sneering of Marilee Plummer—*Nah it isn't so fresh, it'll be buried tomorrow*—like spitting in your face, the shock of it, you're talking about a human being who has just died and he's talking about a corpse.

Dead meat.

Corky thinks, he'll get his revenge on "Wolf" someday. Like that asshole "Richie Richards." These guy poisoning the world with their cynicism. Negativism. You're an American you're an optimist. You're an elected official you're for sure an optimist. Corky remembers a sermon in the St. Thomas chapel, fancy stained-glass place with beautifully carved rosewood pews and Spanish tiles on the floor the bequest of a wealthy alum and in the pulpit there's this big-deal Jesuit from Loyola of Chicago a theologian he's called an old buddy of John F. Kennedy it's boasted and this guy is as different from a Union City parish priest like Father Sullivan as John F. Kennedy's different from old scumbag Buck Glover delivering the most passionate sermon the St. Thomas boys in their navy blue blazers and red-striped neckties have ever heard *The atheist seeks to poison God's world out of despair of loving Him and by Him being loved.*

Now Corky Corcoran's an atheist. But God damn it, he still loves the world.

Shrewd Corky invisibly leading the funeral procession takes Decatur to Meridian, Meridian to Seneca, this is a part of Union City he knows like the back of his hand, so many years layered in driving it, a succession of cars and the commercial buildings changing with time and Corky Corcoran himself changing with time though unwitnessed by himself thus invisibly. Corcoran, Inc., owns property along this stretch, an office building at Decatur and Ninth, another office building at the Meridian intersection, undistinguished decent-looking slightly shabby and weatherworn brick buildings of the late 1950s though modeled after the old Chicago Commercial style—the large steel-framed windows topped by smaller transom windows in the upper storeys, the lower storeys with wide showcase windows, American merchandise on display even when it's auto parts, hardware, drugstore stuff, remnant rugs, discount furniture. Meridian looks good to Corky's quick-assessing eye—that new Kmart taking up practically a city block, a renovated SuperValue Foods, both with monster parking lots, and one of those CineMax theaters showing six or eight or ten films, Corky feels a nanosecond's pang of regret *Nobody to go to the movies with* he'd used to go with Thalia sometimes when there was something special she'd wanted to see and when between the ages of maybe eleven and fourteen she didn't have or hadn't wanted friends her own age, always so mysterious that kid, subterranean currents her step-Daddy could never fathom nor even her mother poor Charlotte admitting to him once drunk and weeping I never really wanted to have a baby I thought it was something a woman *did.*

No wonder the bitch never had his kid like she'd promised. No wonder, aged forty-three and feeling like he's ready to kick the bucket any hour now, Corky Corcoran's got no children. Not even a daughter.

Northeast on Seneca and Corky's quick eye counts off FOR RENT, FOR SALE signs, three of them the red-white-blue of Drummond Realty, this is a good reliable commercial stretch though hard hit by Bush's recession and what he'll do Corky's plotting is tomorrow maybe go see the old man before the fund-raiser in Chateauguay and put the bite on him for a loan as Corky's done in the past both with and without Charlotte knowing. As Ross Drummond says don't confuse the ladies with finances they think with their cunts.

Crude old bastard for a guy of such monied background, WASP family, foul-mouthed as some of Corky's own male relatives though a gentleman for sure in the presence of women of his social class. Hell, Corky likes old Ross. Misses him. He's smiling thinking of the s.o.b. Like a father to Corky, when Corky hadn't even exactly known he'd needed a father. That day in the office laying his hand heavy on Corky's skinny shoulder and breathing in Corky's face in utmost confidence of his power, *I like you a lot, kid!—I might just change your life.*

Corky's ascending the hill to Mount Moriah Cemetery which he's managed to avoid for years since most of the funerals he attends are Catholic and this is a Protestant/nondenominational cemetery and not the classiest one in Union City. Driving first through the residential neighborhood of middle-income houses ringing the hill Corky's thinking why doesn't *he* live in a place like this, his old friend Nick Daugherty lives in a place like this, Average USA, "ranch" houses, "colonials," on a grid of narrow streets with names like Locust, Elm, Cedar, Maple, Juniper, sleek aluminum siding and fake redwood facades and shrines to the Virgin Mary and antlered deer statues in the identical-sized front yards and in the driveways boats covered in blue plastic on U-Haul rigs. Tomorrow, Memorial Day, unless it's raining hard, the boats will be out on the river, there'll be barbecues in the back yards. Portable TVs on the terraces. Kids shooting baskets in the driveways, playing soccer in the streets. Guys washing their cars. Mount Moriah is ninety-five percent white working-class and homeowners take pride in that fact. Corky's been seeing WARNING: PATROLLED BY MOUNT MORIAH WATCH meaning private citizens in vigilante squads, these guys are serious and licensed to carry firearms, Berettas like the UCPD. (And in fact a high percentage of white cops live in Mount

Moriah, restricted by city law to live within the city limits.) Corky Corcoran would be one of them, riding shotgun with his neighbors drinking
beer out of cans and maybe passing a joint alert to black faces that don't
belong in this crummy little enclave as an owl's alert to prey moving on
the ground. A number of Irish Hill residents relocated to Mount Moriah,
guys Corky went to grade school with, on each of these streets there's
probably somebody he knows, or knew, and who knows him. *Hey Corky,
welcome home!*

Instead, he's a millionaire with a five-bedroom house in Maiden Vale.
Living alone.

Mount Moriah the so-called "mountain" is in fact a "drumlin" formed
in the Ice Age by glaciers like most of the weird-shaped and precipitous hills
in the region. As a kid Corky'd been taught the local geology and like every
other kid forgot most of it except he remembers "Mount Moriah"—one
of the Jesuits at St. Thomas describing its particular "ovoid" shape then
speaking unexpectedly and with vehemence of the crematorium located
there, built after World War I as a private enterprise and taken over by Mohawk County in the 1940s after much local controversy and ill feeling for of
course cremation is forbidden by the Catholic Church: how can your body
be resurrected on Judgment Day if in fact it's been burnt totally to hell?

At St. Thomas, teachers and students pondered such theological problems with the gravity, passion, and ingenuity for which the Society of
Jesus has been renowned through the centuries.

So Corky's intrigued by the idea of the crematorium, a forbidden
place still in some deep crevice of his mind, though it's nothing he really
wants to think about, it makes him uneasy enough to think about regular
burial, any kind of burial, the rites of necessity serving Death. Passing the
graveled mud-puddled drive leading up to the crematorium, following the
main graveled mud-puddled drive beneath a wrought-iron arch MT. MORIAH
CEMETERY into a sudden hush of damp rich green and birdsong that affects
him strangely—he *wants* to feel peaceful here, he *deserves* to feel peaceful
here if only for a few minutes, only just can't, quite.

Driving around aimlessly, at five miles an hour waiting for the Plummer procession to arrive. There are a few other cars in the cemetery so
Corky figures he won't be noticed, recognized. At least if he keeps his
distance.

He's still pissed off by that broad from WWTC coming on to him the way she did. In the relations between man and woman isn't man supposed to be the aggressor, for Christ's sake!

Females like that, you can't fuck gentle you'd have to fuck rough so it hurts. And then they respect you.

Corky's staring at the rows of graves, so many. Jesus, an entire new section of the cemetery's been opened up since the last time he was here! You'd think, in the business Corky Corcoran's in, any familiar landscape developed wouldn't be a surprise but for some reason it always is, he's surprised, something in him's offended, by the sight of change. The evidence of change. At least, change in the landscape that doesn't bring him any profit.

Corky arrives at the cemetery at 5:15 P.M. and the funeral procession headed by the big black hearse arrives at 5:28 P.M. After it passes the drive where he's parked he waits a discreet minute or so then follows after. There are eleven cars in the procession not counting the hearse. The second car is a black stretch limo containing, Corky assumes, Marilee's parents and closest relatives, the windows are dark-tinted so he can't see even the glimmer of an outline of a face. The other cars are bearing men and women unknown to Corky or so he assumes, he doesn't dare look at them too closely.

Marilee Plummer's gravesite isn't far away. Corky drives slowly past the now parked cars observing covertly out of the corner of his eye what he can—the mourners getting out of their cars, an elderly ashy-skinned woman in dark purple clothes being helped out of the limo, a middle-aged woman in a black turban who might be Marilee's mother, or an aunt—young men—teenaged kids—one of the burly black men who'd looked to be guarding the front of the church from the media people.

Those leeches, Corky's relieved to see, haven't followed the mourners to the cemetery.

He's the only outsider.

Driving slowly to higher ground like a man intent upon his own private grief then parking close by a ten-foot ivory marble obelisk like a giant prick stained yellow with time and birdshit, climbing out of his car and lighting another cigarette with shaky excited fingers and taking from the trunk a pair of binoculars so rarely used the lenses are gummy requiring spit and tissue to clean, and so out of focus he's muttering "Fuck! Fuck! *Fuck!*" adjusting them, finally able to see the Plummer mourners as if close up as if he's among their party invisible thus undetected. Corky watches as the pallbearers slide the heavy coffin out of the rear of the hearse and lift it with a tremulous strength he can feel in his own muscles' sinews and bear it aloft to the freshly dug grave in a hillside and the minister who's a thickset man in his sixties with skin the color of horse chestnuts speaks to the mourners his cheeks glistening with tears and the faces of the mourners Corky can make out are glistening with tears, some of the faces showing anger, grief, shock like the faces of cattle stunned by blows to the head yet not dead nor even brought yet to their knees. Corky's staring at these people as he's never stared at anyone in his life or so he believes. Corky's staring from a distance of approximately two hundred feet utterly absorbed, fascinated and his mind struck blank. Staring at the woman in the black turban in black drapery regal and stiff in grief as the figurehead of a ship who's possibly Marilee's mother and the elderly ashy-skinned woman in purple leaning on the other's arm who's possibly Marilee's grandmother and the brown-skinned black man in his early twenties who's possibly Marilee's younger brother if she had a younger brother for if she did he'd look exactly like that kid with his hooded eyes, solid jaw and angry sullen face which not even tears can soften. And staring at the others, backs of heads, faces in two-thirds profile, never has Corky been so lost in concentration in contemplation in the very intensity of being as if every molecule in him is straining to press through the binocular's lenses as the pulley apparatus lowers the coffin bearing the invisible body slowly and with sickening finality into the moist earthy rectangular hole that's a grave but might as easily be a mouth of very earth poised to swallow what it is given to receive.

"Jesus!—" Corky mutters aloud. Feeling the terrible lurch of the coffin that's suddenly *in*.

He lowers the binoculars dazed and dizzy. The gravesite falls back into the distance, the mourners are mere figures in the distance. No faces. No grief.

Why are you spying on these people, you honky motherfucker?

I'm not spying on them, I'm one of them.

One of them! You're white, asshole, you're not one of *them*.

Corky glances around guiltily. Like he's been jerking off in a public place and sure somebody's been watching but, so far as he can gauge, nobody has.

Honky motherfucker, what makes you think you're one of *anybody?*

Back in the Caddy driving down from the cemetery careful not to exceed the fifteen-mile-an-hour speed limit Corky's thinking of an interlude he's all but forgotten, how he'd felt then too this shame-faced sense of having narrowly escaped some catastrophe while half wishing for it. White man! White skin! Devil!—at the same time protesting indignantly, But why? What have *I* done? The occasion was the first clamorous meeting of the City Council some months ago following the refusal of the Union City Police Department's Internal Affairs Division to dismiss and condemn Sergeant Dwayne Pickett who'd shot the twelve-year-old Devane Johnson between the shoulder blades and Marcus Steadman before the Council president could even call the meeting to order rose to his feet magisterial in fury denouncing the UCPD and all of City Hall and his fellow Council members as racist pigs and cowards not sparing even the moderate black members of the Council and in the visitors' gallery on their feet as well were about thirty men and women shouting and cursing and threatening to set fire to City Hall and the UCPD guards of whom there were a dozen on duty that evening unholstered their guns and advanced upon the gallery shouting too and cursing and Corky Corcoran and his fellow Council members (except for Steadman, on his feet and ranting) sat frozen in their cushioned swivel chairs in terror of a sudden eruption of gunfire in which they would die as quickly and as significantly as a flame is snuffed out and Corky's eye desperately measured the space beneath the Council president's desk calculating if he dove into that space if he forced the president's legs out if he drew his knees tight up against his chest if he pushed his chin down onto his chest he could fit in there just fine.

On his way out of the cemetery Corky feels a sudden sharp pinch of his bladder, an urgent need to piss. It strikes him so unexpectedly and with a sensation so close to pain, like a memory of something shameful, he grunts aloud. "God damn!"—next, his prostate's going. Is that it?

Turns off then for expediency's sake onto a narrow bumpy puddled drive he doesn't realize leads to the crematorium until a hundred yards or so along there's the sudden sign MT. MORIAH CREMATORIUM above an open gate, Corky decides what the hell he'll drive on in and park, there are a half dozen cars in front of the building plus a shiny metallic-gray Toyota van marked MT. MORIAH CEMETERY ASSOCIATION. Nobody's around, Corky can stroll to the rear and take a leak and that's that.

Though he's lived in Union City all his life, Corky Corcoran has never seen the Mount Moriah Crematorium up close. From below, you can make out the tall weatherworn brick chimney that's flared at the top, and much of the turreted roof, that's like the roof of a fairy tale castle; the building is a Union City landmark, more visible in winter than when trees are thick-leafed as now. An architectural oddity of dubious distinction akin to several other local buildings of its era, pre–and post–World War I, the Masonic temple on Grand Boulevard (with the pair of stone lions guarding its gate that the nuns at Our Lady of Mercy parish school warned their pupils might one day wake and come after little Catholic children and make "living martyrs" of them), the Arts Club at the farther end of Summit Park, the Proxmire "manor" house on Lake Ontario which Corky's seen only in photos. These old buildings are eyesores, but you've got to love them. Part Victorian Gothic, part Richardsonian Romanesque, some neoclassical features tossed in—ornamental columns and pillars and arches, turrets, gables, heavy slate or hammered copper roofs, cornices, carved pediments, gargoyles. Gargoyles! Corky squints upward seeing an impish bearded face squinting down at him from a drainpipe, like a long-lost Corcoran cousin. "Hiya, buster. How's tricks?" The crematorium has a clock tower, too—stained old orangey-buff brick, that color Corky loves, it's like a setting sun is reflected in it perpetually. And faintly cracked but still elegant pink limestone. The ornate clock face, which can be seen for miles on a clear day, is the color of a jaundiced eyeball and the spidery black Gothic hands are frozen at 12:02 of some lost day.

Corky shivers, though it's a balmy humid day. Automatically checks his watch, he's a guy who lives by his watch—Jesus, already 5:57 P.M.?

(Corky feels a twinge of guilt. Is Charlotte waiting for him? He seems to remember there was a vague agreement of some kind he'd come to see her, she's under a lot of stress about Thalia, but Corky isn't sure how binding it is. And he's got an important dinner date with Vic and Sandra Slattery tonight—*that*, he isn't going to miss.)

The heavy oak front doors to the crematorium are shut, the steep granite steps are covered in rotted maple seeds, nobody's in view and though there's a sign PRIVATE: NO ADMITTANCE BEYOND THIS POINT Corky casually strolls around to the rear, trailing smoke over his shoulder. He's well dressed, looks like money and class, brand-new shirt and polished shoes and what the hell, Corky Corcoran goes where he wants especially if he's got to piss. The building is shabbier around back, and unexpectedly big, as deep as it's wide, must measure one hundred feet. Garbage cans, Dumpster bins, trash barrels. Corky has a quick thought immediately suppressed—*they wouldn't be dumping human remains back here, would they?*

In an area of service outbuildings, lawn equipment sheds Corky turns a corner seeing nobody's in sight and unzips and takes out his cock tender and bruised like a banana past its prime and pisses into a mound of broken concrete and purple flowering thistles resolutely not looking at the glittering arc of his piss nor what it's wetting, he's superstitious never looks at any substance liquid or solid excreted from his body in dread of seeing telltale streaks or clots of red. *Scared cards can't win* but fuck that, some things you don't want to know.

What's the prostate gland Corky doesn't exactly want to know either. His Uncle Brendan McClure dying of cancer of the prostate and the word in the neighborhood was, Poor Brendan's dying of cancer of the balls! No respect. Which is the God-damned fucking least you can expect from the world when you're dying of cancer.

Corky's anxious thinking about it. How sudden and sharp his need to piss, sometimes. Waking him out of a deep sleep where in the past in rambling confused dreams he'd be searching for a lavatory for what seemed like hours never finding one in working order or if he did there'd be women present until finally he'd wake up needing to go to the bathroom so the idiotic dreams made sense, but the need wasn't urgent exactly, not painful like this other. And last night!—so drunk he'd pissed his pants. Uncle Hock all over again. At the age of nineteen Corky'd caught a dose of the clap—what Dr. O'Malley pronounced with fastidious disdain "gon-or-rhea"—and he'd had trouble pissing, scared as hell but in a few months the antibiotics worked thank Christ and he hadn't had any trouble again for more than twenty years. But now?

Corky doesn't want to think about it.

(Now he's a bachelor again, no wife nosing into his affairs "for his own good," checking his calendar to make sure he doesn't cancel out on doctor's and dentist's appointments as he's in the habit of doing—Corky's on his own. Going to hell in his own style.)

As the pressure on his bladder lessens Corky's feeling better, by the time he zips up he'll have forgotten these worries. Almost a sweet sensation, pissing. Nothing like it unless it's taking a really good shit, the kind that empties you out practically like coming with your asshole but nobody talks about. Strange the pleasures the body gives nobody talks about.

Is it possible, coming with your asshole?—fucking up the ass, what queers do together, "gays" they call themselves now, buggering it used to be, mysterious. The guys joked about it in school but what was it exactly Corky'd wondered, why'd you want to do such a dirty thing, or have it done to you, like being a cunt. Taking somebody else's jism, in the ass or in the mouth, Jesus, what perverts can think of!—*a guy making himself into a cunt.*

What *he'd* like to do, go back to Kiki Zaller's some night and fuck her in the cunt *and* the ass *and* the mouth then piss all over her and drop a lighted match on her—*her* calling *him* "pervert"!

What hurt is, Corky'd sort of thought the bitch liked him. For sure, he'd been nice to her. All his Irish charm, putting himself out for her, why hadn't it worked?

Plenty of other women have been hot for Corky Corcoran, and there's plenty to come. So fuck Kiki Zaller.

And Marilee Plummer: calling him "Freckhead" why not come out and say "Fuckhead"?

No, but Corky doesn't mean that. It's a terrible thing, it's really shitty, that Marilee's dead. Any beef you've got with anybody, it has to end with Death.

Except Al Fenske: Corky wishes there was a hell, the fucker'd be burning in it.

What he'd like: exhume Fenske's corpse and piss on it.

What he'd like: go back in time and this time he tells them what they want to hear, yes he saw the car yes he saw the license plate yes he swears to God he saw.

You, Jerome. Our only witness.

Not blind for Christ's sake are you?

Not blind.

Corky's feeling a lot better now, anger's a lot better than fear. Zips himself up like he actually has been fucking and feeling good about it and about himself as, God knows, he hasn't been, lately.

Hearing a bird's sweet liquid cry from somewhere in the woods. A solitary sound, wavering, then stronger, rising like a soprano and Corky realizes he's been hearing birds since coming to Mount Moriah, watching the mourners at Marilee's grave, his binoculars bringing him up so close he'd almost think remembering afterward he'd been able to hear the minister's words and the sounds of weeping, yes he'd been *there*.

Corky figures the Plummer mourners are still in the cemetery. You're not in a hurry to leave when it's somebody you care about—leaving them in the ground. When he'd decided to cut out two girls of maybe eleven very dark-skinned and in long black dresses like nightgowns were doing something with a floral display, giant lilies, positioning it at the head of the grave as their elders sang and clapped and prayed. The minister holding a Bible high over his head with both hands.

Corky's whistling strolling back to his car. Undetected, invisible—it's a terrific feeling. That late-night TV movie *The Invisible Man*—Corky'd loved it, as a kid.

So this is the Mount Moriah Crematorium. Great old building. If he had time he'd explore it a little, also the view from up here, it's like you're in a low-flying plane—church spires, water towers, the red-winking WWUC-TV tower, high-rise buildings along Seneca, Meridian, Decatur and Union Boulevard clear to the Chateauguay River and the green-glassy office towers of downtown, the Hyatt, the Marriott, Bank of America, Union Trust and the Dominion Bridge and Fort Pearce, Ontario, hazy with distance and to the east the Chateauguay Valley and to the west Lake Erie flattened like it's a metal sheet out to a horizon dissolving in red mist, cloud banks ribbed like an old-fashioned washboard. Corky sucks in a deep breath. *His* city. Where *he's* known. Where *he's* important to a lot of people.

Nothing like death to revive the living. Right?

Thinking magnanimously he'll drop in on Charlotte after all. Owes that much to her. Poor dumb bitch. See how she's doing as the wife of a legitimately rich man and what kind of house they have *where she'll try to get you to drink: Don't* and maybe Charlotte will have connected with Thalia and the danger's over and if Corky's really lucky Thalia herself will be there with her mother.

The family reunited. It's possible, isn't it?

The orangey-golden glow of the old bricks, the heavy bluish-black slate roof, the kid's-castle look of the turrets and gables and mock battlements, Mount Moriah Crematorium is *something*. Corky has a fantasy some years from now, the building threatened by demolition—there's been talk for at least fifteen years of building a new modern crematorium elsewhere in the city—and Corcoran, Inc., steps in to buy it, rescue it, preserve it as a local historical landmark.

At the rear, though, the crematorium isn't very glamorous or romantic just a shabby old building run by the city. Trash bins and Dumpsters and Corky can't resist peering inside, what kind of trash does a place like this throw out?—the usual papers and cardboard and Styrofoam and plastic sheets but also chunks of what Corky'd swear is *bone*—unless maybe it's broken plaster. Hard to tell. Corky pokes some of it with a finger and it's more porous than it looks. Somebody said, a crematorium doesn't burn a corpse to powder-fine ashes like people think and it's sentimental bullshit to request your ashes "scattered" in some favorite place because there are New York State health laws against that and in fact the crematorium workers clear out the furnaces like anybody does if they can get away with it (and in Union City for sure they're going to get away with it seventy-five percent of the time), shoveling chunks of bone and ashes into bins in the cellar then parceling a certain amount of it out into these tall ebony urns you pay a lot for like it's some big holy deal and you're thinking this is your wife or husband or parents in the urn when obviously it's a mix of strangers including some old bums shipped direct from the morgue to the crematory because nobody gives a shit for them while they're alive but now they're *yours*.

At least, in a grave, Corky's thinking, the old-fashioned way, the way *he* wants to go, there's no confusion who you are. No fucking around with a corpse you can actually see in the coffin and you see the coffin going in the ground.

Corky jerks his hand out of the trash—it's covered in gray dust like gypsum powder. No smell.

Overhead, Corky sees, there's a gargoyle peering down at him from a window ledge. Long skinny face and grinning mouth and slits for eyes like those ornamental plaster masks at the theater where Charlotte's group used to put on their plays. Like a clown face, but not quite.

Around in front there's the Caddy, parked embarrassingly crooked like the driver was practically pissing his pants in a hurry to get out, or a woman driver. Corky runs his eye quick over the car telling himself it doesn't look too bad, the worst scratch is on the other side and the dirt will wash off; in fact there's a car wash on Schoonover on the way to Charlotte's. Corky Corcoran's got too much pride to show up in Chateauguay at his ex-wife's then at Congressman Vic Slattery's house driving a car that looks like half the pigeons in Union City have been shitting on it.

6:06 P.M. Corky's got his car keys in his hand but out of the corner of his eye he's been noticing some new arrivals, drove up in a new-model Lexus, a make of car Corky's impressed with, a party of middle-aged people climbing the granite stairs to the front entrance and next thing he knows Corky's following after, not that he's interested in them, though one of the women, silvery-blond hair like Kim Novak's long ago and a black silk designer suit fitting her high round little ass just right, catches his eye. Corky's curious about the inside of this weird building, now's his chance. He figures a cremation ceremony is about to begin and he'll be mistaken for one of the mourners, in fact he *is* a mourner, that's his business on Mount Moriah today.

Inside, a foyer with a vaulted ceiling, marble floor and voices echoing and a man with a bald pate and gray curling wings of hair in back turning toward him with what looks like, not a smile but a frown of recognition, and Corky in his confusion stammers, "—Father DeLucca?" but in the next instant he sees, asshole, the man doesn't even look that much like his old Jesuit teacher who anyway is dead! Fortunately the old guy doesn't hear Corky, he's an official of the crematorium smooth and unctuous as a funeral parlor host directing people toward the chapel, murmuring to Corky, "You're with the van Heusen party, yes?" and Corky says, "Sure," and passes by.

Father DeLucca! What is this, the second time thinking you've seen a dead man in two days?

Need a drink. A drink? but no drinks in the reception room as far as Corky can see, Jesus what a weird overdecorated place like a nigger brothel as you'd imagine it, bloodstone marble wall panels and bronze bas-relief columns and a chandelier like a Fourth of July sparkler low enough to graze your head, mildewed carpet bright green as AstroTurf. Corky no more than sticks his head in this room before he retreats, feels almost a gagging sensation like he's underground and this is a tomb and these other people, strangers, milling around with him, they're all trapped in the tomb.

Some of these strangers glancing quizzically at Corky Corcoran with that kind of faint smile that means *Do I know you? Am I supposed to know you?* but Corky's a moving target.

He's looking for the silvery-blond in the black silk designer suit. Maybe she's the widow?

Great place to hook up with a well-to-do widow. Anybody who'd buy a Lexus, passing over a Caddy or a Lincoln or a Mercedes, has got dough to toss around; and without giving much of a damn that anybody knows it. *That's* class.

But the reception room's emptying out, the service in the chapel is about to begin. Corky sees the silvery-blond ahead, in the company of some old farts. Is Corky the youngest guy here?

So many years, working as Ross Drummond's right-hand man, and on the City Council, and around town—Corky Corcoran was always the youngest guy in the room. Youngest, best-looking, brashest. Sexiest.

Too bad Corky isn't free to explore the crematorium by himself. See where the oven—ovens?—are. The bone-and-ash bins. The urns. The cadaver storage room. Must be a small morgue, somewhere on the premises. At the rear of the foyer there's a wrought-iron spiral staircase leading— where? A mezzanine landing, and then—the roof? The clock tower? (Corky wouldn't mind locating a men's room, too. Washing a faint odor of urine from his fingers and that suspicious gypsum dust.) The corridor leading to the chapel has a carved oak ceiling curved as in a tunnel; it's windowless, and somberly lit by fake torches held by creepy little stone hands poking out of the walls. Wild! And everywhere there's pink veined marble like fatty beef and Victorian filigree, trompe l'oeil woodsy scenes with nymphs and satyrs, Charlotte would get off on this "antique" crap, the very opposite of the clean stark no-bullshit Frank Lloyd Wright style Corky's architectural tastes were shaped by at Rensselaer.

Christ, it *is* close in here, like a tomb. Humid air in spite of ventilator fans (at least Corky hears a vibrating-rattling in the background: must mean ventilation?) like everybody's breathing everybody else's expelled breaths. Whiffs now and then of nostril-pinching disinfectant and something faintly rancid, meaty-fatty-scorched like a greasy oven when the heat's turned on high—you don't want to know what *that* smell is.

Still, burning's clean. Got to be the most sanitary method. Isn't that what Hindus have done for thousands of years—funeral pyres. Billions and trillions of people, you'd have bodies piled up from here to the moon. Not the respect for the individual soul you get in Christianity, more primitive but it sure is practical.

"Sir?—in here." A porky-faced youngish balding guy is all but plucking at Corky's sleeve, urging him to enter the chapel, must be a crematorium official, Corky gives him a cold unsmiling stare don't touch *me*, fuckface. But the guy just smiles, smiles and looks through him to the next customer. "Sir?—Madam?—in here. Please."

Corky's reminded of *Tales from the Crypt*, lurid comic books he'd read as a kid sometimes scaring himself so he couldn't sleep, what if all of us are being ushered into an actual crematorium oven under the mistaken notion we're just visitors?

Even now, the fiery oven is being stoked up. The oven that isn't at the front of the chapel hidden by those plush red velvet drapes but surrounds the chapel so stepping inside the chapel you're stepping inside the oven, right? And once the doors are closed, no exit.

Corky pauses, annoying fat-face who's eager to get the "van Heusen" party into the chapel, peering at verse engraved in aged ivory on the archway—

With Earth's first clay they did the last man knead,
And then of the last harvest sow'd the seed;

Yea, the first morning of creation wrote
What the last dawn of reckoning shall read.

This is by "Omar Khayyam" of whom Corky's heard. Some Arab? Turk? Corky's impressed by the logic of it, though it's God-damned depressing *First clay, last man*, fuck that, what about *me?*

Whoever "Omar Khayyam" was, he wasn't an American. That's fucking obvious.

Recorded organ music is being piped into the chapel, thunderous chords like grinding your back molars, must be Bach. A fond running joke between him and Christina, any music Corky'd hear on the radio of a certain "baroque" type he'd say *must be Bach*. He's uneasy being herded into a chapel, having to sit in a pew, any kind of religious atmosphere repels him. Too much church as a kid like all Catholic kids so the very look of a churchy interior makes him slightly nauseated but now he's here, he's here, might as well see it through, what the hell.

You'll never guess what I did on the way over here—imagining Charlotte's expression, Sandra's and Vic's. Corky Corcoran, what a character!

Corky settles reluctantly in a rear pew, farthest outside corner, suppressing a nervous yawn. The sweet potato pie is still a fist-sized mound in his gut. The caffeine zinging through his veins is fading fast. *Need a drink, friend?—reach for a Bud.* And he can't smoke in here, fuck it.

Corky Corcoran with not enough grief of his own, insinuating himself into the grief of strangers. Is that what he's doing?

And these strangers, well-heeled and most of them older, are casting him curious looks, welcome but curious, *Hello son! who are* you, *son! why sitting so far away in that corner?* Corky counts twenty-three mourners including new arrivals who are shuffling in, one old guy struggling with a walker (*not* Buck Glover: though looking enough like him to be his brother), two hefty corseted black-clad ladies with their arms linked, a guy Corky's age with a squirrelly head, a younger woman severe-faced as Thalia but not half as good-looking, stiff as a broomstick and as sexy. All these people knowing one another greeting one another in muted little cries and murmurs, handshakes, hugs, not much visible grief as at poor Marilee's grave so Corky guesses the death of this "van Heusen" hadn't come as any surprise or any great loss probably some poor old bastard better off dead. "Van Heusen" means old Dutch family, rich tradesmen on the Chateauguay and property owners in western New York for generations, "van Fleet," "van Roojen," "van Buren"—which reminds Corky, Jesus! he never did call Andy to apologize for fucking up the other night: better do that tonight or Andy will be Corky's enemy for life—"van Tassel," only got bought out by the Japs a few years ago. Corky sees the silvery-blond is sitting almost directly in front of him but there's a bald fatty behind her, fuck it Corky can't see her face but his impression is she's good-looking in that sort of snooty seasoned cosmetic way Charlotte has gotten to be, cool bitches who'll look right through you though they can see you're undressing them in your head.

Corky's 100 percent against any kind of pervert but sometimes you know why a guy will "expose" himself as it's called, just to make some of these bitches *look*. Anything less, they're out of reach.

Corky's old custom from his Catholic boyhood, and it's a custom he knows at least one guy (Nick Daugherty) shared, probably all Catholic males in fact, he'd settle in a pew where he could fix on some sexy girl he could watch through his eyelashes without being detected, drift almost immediately into a dreamy-horny state kissing her fondling her undressing her fucking her doing all sorts of dirty extravagant things with her but nothing rushed, take your time, s-l-o-w, even old Father Sullivan couldn't rattle through the mass in under thirty minutes, a little's got to go a long long way. Corky's prick filling up with blood like a balloon filling with air blown bigger and bigger to the danger point so by the time the bell rang for Holy Communion he'd be slack-jawed and drooling staring glazed-eyed at the object of his lustful thoughts who'd sometimes glance around nervous as if she sensed somebody staring at her in just such a way. And after mass then as soon as he was home Corky'd jerk off violently in the bathroom, almost fainting with the pleasure of it, the terrible paroxysm of the pleasure, nothing like it. Sunday after Sunday, Holy Day after Holy Day for years in dread of Aunt Frances suspecting what was going on, what *he* was, her nephew Jerome she loved like a son.

Do women suspect, Corky wonders. What utter pigs, what filth we are. Do they have half a clue.

The only disadvantage was, every time Corky masturbated after those years, all of his adult life to this very day, he's susceptible to envisioning, not the naked female form, but the interior of a church.

But he can't line up the silvery-haired woman in his sights and the young one who reminds him of Thalia is blowing her nose loudly into a tissue, a real turn-off. It's shitty being so stone cold sober, reality stark as an overexposed photograph. The chapel is ornately decorated like the reception room, oppressive and humid, marble wall panels, bronze bas-relief columns, intricately carved mahogany pews and doors and pillars and velvet tapestries and a ceiling of some undersea-greenish stone. The rose window is garish with color, bright reds bright greens bright blues, decorated with nonsectarian figures like pyramids, unicorns, suns, the Tree of Life. Corky's feeling a little dizzy, taking it all in. Like an underground candy box. Candy box–tomb. He can't stop yawning.

Drink, need a drink. O sweet Christ.

At the front, shaking hands and whispering with the family, there's a middle-aged guy must be their minister. Or does a nonsectarian chaplain come with this deal? The coffin on a riser at the altar (or what would be an altar if this was a real chapel) is offensive to Corky's eye—plain unfinished wood, like a shipping crate. A human body's in *that?* Nothing like what you're used to at a funeral—like Marilee Plummer's coffin for instance which was heavy, solid, ebony-shiny, dignified, not cheap. Corky understands this is only practical since the coffin is going to be burned but there's something insulting about it anyway. Why not zip up the corpse in a body bag. Dump it in one of those dark green plastic garbage bags. *Christ I need a drink.*

The organ music thunders to a close. The minister, or chaplain, introduces himself, a name Corky forgets at once. Bulbous-nosed old guy in polyester black suit and bow tie, earnest and fawning and smiling showing pink gums and rubbing his hands together speaking of the deceased "Jerry van Heusen" beloved by all—"a man of honor"—"a man of integrity"—"an exemplary son, brother, husband, father, grandfather"—"a loyal and good friend"—"a pillar of charity and philanthropy"—"an employer much respected by his employees"—"a selfless public servant"—Corky listens without hearing, doesn't want to hear, it makes him uneasy the dead man's first name is "Jerry" which is the name people call Corky who don't know him well or who want to get his goat.

If Charlotte calls him "Jerry" tonight, Corky's going to give it to her in the mouth. Sometimes it scares him, how angry he is at that bitch. As if it isn't her fault about Thalia screwed up as she is.

Corky shifts his buttocks, the pew's cushioned but he can't get comfortable. There's something wrong with this chapel and only now does Corky get it: no Christ on the cross, no Christ with His sorrowing face and bloody wounds, no Christ blessing His sheep, *no fucking Christ at all.*

Corky's shocked. As if the marble floor has tilted beneath his feet.

The symbols in the rose window and elsewhere in the chapel are only symbols, chump change. What's a pyramid but some asshole tomb the ancient Egyptian pharaohs made slaves build for them so they could live forever!—a joke. What's a sun but a star that's going to burn out, *its history over in milliseconds!* What's the Tree of Life but the Tree of Death without Christ even if you don't believe in Him *for Christ's sake don't you need Him?* Without religion what's the point of any of it?

Corky sees the coffin's hooked to a rubberized belt, the oven must be fired up behind those purple velvet drapes while the old guy in polyester black yaks about "Jerry." They won't really do this, will they? Roast a man like you'd roast a pig? You have to honor the dead even if you don't give a damn about them—don't you? Isn't that how it is? Don't you owe them that respect?

Corky's panicked thinking *That's me. That poor fucker in there, that's me.*

"Wait! No—"

Everybody in the chapel turns to look at Corky Corcoran, who's on his feet shaky and swaying, appalled. The coffin has jerked forward, the velvet drapes are open and the oven door has lifted and there's a muffled roar of fire. Corky stares, sees these strangers staring back at him, fear and dread in their eyes, too. What's he doing making a public asshole of himself? Intruding where he isn't wanted? A flush comes over his face, hot as actual flame. He shakes his head and mutters, "Sorry!—excuse me—" backing off deeply embarrassed as if he'd farted on a speaker's platform or on TV. Jesus, what's wrong with him? He's cracking up.

Corky's on his way out of the chapel but he's lightheaded suddenly needing to sit again, a roaring in his ears *Death is catching Death is catching Death is catching* shutting his eyes willing himself to snap out of it, c'mon Corky for Christ's sake. You've been here before, right? You'll be O.K., right? He sees Christina's face, her frightened eyes. You just need a drink, right? This is the D.T.'s, it isn't *real*. Right?

Then it's over. The service for "Jerry van Heusen" is over. The coffin has vanished like it's never been and the oven door is shut tight and if there's a powerful searing fire inside you have to imagine it, you can't see it. Or smell it. Most of the mourners are on their feet preparing to leave. More embraces, handshakes. Corky wipes his damp face on his sleeve, Christ, he *is* embarrassed, but nobody knows his name here, and nobody's holding his behavior against him, in fact what's Corky but the mystery man at the van Heusen cremation service, the man "Jerry's" family and friends will long recall as that sweet scared stranger who burst out "Wait! No!"—who *was* he?

Corky sees to his horror they're headed for him. Even the elderly, pushing eagerly out of their pews. The man with the narrow squirrel-head. The silvery-blond wet-eyed and fierce staring at Corky as if they're old lost lovers now to be reconciled—except she isn't even middle-aged, she's in her late sixties, hair not silvery blond but just silver, beehived to disguise its thinness. Kim Novak!

On shaky legs Corky manages to slip out of the pew, escape into the corridor. The only one to catch up with him is the little man with the squeezed-in head, a pert squirrel-face—"Why, Mr. Corcoran! Jerome! What a remarkable coincidence! I never realized you were a friend of Jerry's, too."

Is it possible? That pushy little bastard Teague, or Tyde, who's been bugging Corky?—he's *here?* God damn!

"—Maynard Teague, Jerome, we met just the other day at the Athletic Club, unfortunately we didn't have time to talk—" As before, the little man advances familiarly upon Corky extending his hand to be shaken; he must see the hostility in Corky's face, but it seems to make no difference, *he's* smiling warmly. "This is a sad occasion, heaven knows, but—it must be serendipity, eh? Our paths crossing without either of us intending it?"

Corky, backing off, mutters rudely, "Sorry, no time now, I'm in a hurry." Turns and walks away, fighting the urge to run.

"But, Jerome—we have so much to discuss—"

"*No time now.*"

The cremation service was fast and efficient: it's only 6:42 P.M.

Outside at the Caddy that's so weirdly parked fumbling for his keys to get the hell out of here Corky's distracted by movement overhead, beyond the pinnacle of the slate roof: he looks up astonished, sees coils of smoke rushing out of the tall brick chimney, ashy-gray, creamy, dense, writhing as if alive, the air about it and seemingly the very sky itself irradiated with heat.

Rooted to the spot, staring upward, mouth slack, not knowing what he does Corky Corcoran makes the sign of the cross—fingertips to forehead to breast to left shoulder to right shoulder. Slowly.

9

CORKY IN PURSUIT

And then, while smoke still lifts in soundless billowing clouds from the crematory chimney, this happens: Corky is driving down the rutted puddled lane back to the main drive, he's got a cigarette already lit and in his mouth, deep restorative drags, compulsively he's punching radio stations anxious for news, a blast of teen music like shattering glass, a high-pitched ad for Dyer's Discount Drugs, his thoughts leap desperately ahead to the car wash on Schoonover as a man covered in filth fantasizes being cleansed, he's thinking there's nothing so therapeutic so sane so *good* as getting your car washed in one of these places with all the accessories, he'll have the inside vacuumed too, toss out the crap he's been accumulating (except for the begonia plant: he'll visit Aunt Mary Megan tomorrow!), and if only the car wash is open Sunday evenings, how eager Corky is to get off Mount Moriah vowing he's never coming back under any circumstances but especially not in a box, no cremation for *him*, he wants his own plot of Earth and his own fucking grave marker JEROME ANDREW CORCORAN there in Our Lady of Mercy Cemetery with his family if it's only for pigeons to crap on, the Caddy's jolting along at no more than ten miles an hour, a quick turn onto the main drive, where Corky's eye takes in a car parked by the side in the grass and a woman behind the wheel leaning far forward both elbows on the lower rim of the wheel and her fingers pressed against her eyes as if she's exhausted or weeping or both her dark tangled hair all but hiding her face but Corky sees it's a young face a dead-white face the face of an apparition—*Thalia?*

Corky's already past when the realization hits him. But as he jams on his brakes, the other car starts up suddenly, lurching past him. It must be Thalia, who else would so react, desperate and dangerous, Corky sees the car's a Saab 900 S but it's bottle-green and he doesn't remember Thalia's car that color. "Thalia?—wait!"

But of course Thalia doesn't wait, doesn't hear. As Corky stares astonished the Saab's pulling away bouncing and skidding in the bumpy, puddled drive throwing up gravel in its wake, Corky curses under his breath starting off in pursuit, God-damned motherfucker! why didn't he see who it was quick enough to block her! a split second's advantage and Thalia's escaping driving recklessly picking up speed as the Saab hits lower ground, and a paved street, speeding heedlessly into the residential neighborhood of Mount Moriah where the speed limit is twenty miles an hour she must be going fifty, and Corky following, cursing leaning over the wheel gripping the wheel like an Indy driver, the Caddy's tires too skidding and churning mud and gravel then taking hold hitting solid pavement lunging forward like a rocket as Thalia already a block ahead rushes through a four-way stop and Corky hits his brakes when he comes to the stop not willing to risk driving through seeing out of the corner of his eye two boys on bicycles gaping after the Saab and now at the Caddy shuddering to a stop then leaping forward, and at the next intersection Thalia rushes through this time narrowly missing a car just entering the intersection from the left and this car God damn it brakes and skids turning approximately 180 degrees flailing like a stricken beetle so by the time Corky arrives there furious in pursuit and blaring his horn like a maddened bull elephant he's blocked for several precious seconds finally cursing and maneuvering around the car stalled in the intersection (Corky has a quick glimpse of the driver's stunned face: the plumpish face of a young housewife-mother, a child in the seat beside her, two more in the back) and the Caddy's tires screeching in the wake of the bottle-green Saab now a full block away, turning onto a larger street that must be Seneca, as Corky watches Thalia takes a sharp skidding reckless right onto Seneca indifferent to traffic and when seconds later he gets to the corner again he's blocked this time by a fucking city bus, the fucker just pulling out in that slow-wheezing way of Union City Transit buses belching black exhaust from its rear powerful enough to turn Corky's stomach, he's got a choice of waiting till the bus gathers speed and following in its wake gauging when it's safe to pass or simply careening out into the farther left lane to pass it immediately which for a split second Corky's primed to do then comes to his senses seeing in his rearview mirror vehicles hurtling toward him, a man's face contorted in rage behind the windshield of his Cherokee

Jeep blaring his horn at Corky who's only considering cutting him off so Corky hangs back, Corky loses more precious seconds behind the bus and by the time he's able to swing around the fucker pressing down on his accelerator pushing the Caddy from ten miles an hour to fifty in the space of a single indrawn breath the bottle-green Saab's nowhere in sight.

"Fuck! Fuck! *Fuck!*"—Corky's pounding the steering wheel with both fists. But not slackening his speed, God damn he's not going to give up, he's responsible for that crazy cunt and he's not going to give up fuck it if it kills him.

His heart pumping by this time fast and rackety as the fucking Roto-Rooter drain-cleaning pump he'd needed to hire to clear his fucking cellar drains last week after the fucking rainstorms.

Corky speeds south on Seneca reasoning that Thalia must be ahead, he'll catch up with her. The question is will she stay on Seneca leading back into the city or will she turn off onto another street, if it was Corky fleeing in the Saab he'd for sure turn onto Meridian west and hook up with I-190 north and out of the city but he doubts that Thalia knows these streets as he does, his major disadvantage is he has no idea where Thalia's been staying lately thus can't know where she might be heading to hide if at such a desperate time she would even wish to return there. He's driving impatiently maneuvering around slower-moving assholes in his way, passing on the right with a staccato blast of his horn, *Out of my way! out! yeah fuck you too, sister!* risking an accident risking a speeding ticket at sixty miles an hour which is twenty miles over the speed limit but what the hell this is a desperate situation Corky can't let Thalia escape very likely she's got the German Luger with her and he's got to get it back, it's his responsibility as her stepfather and as a citizen, wincing seeing SPEEDERS LOSE LICENSES! SPEEDERS GO TO JAIL! a billboard he's rushing beneath through a railroad underpass and up into the waning daylight where to his surprise he sees the bottle-green Saab only a half-block ahead!—no mistaking it. Corky renews the pursuit certain now he'll catch up with Thalia and when he does she'll see the futility of trying to escape him, he jams down his accelerator daringly cutting in front of a carload of blacks seeing the Saab just rushing through the next traffic light as it turns from yellow to red but Corky's not going to be fucked this time speeding through on the red risking his ass and provoking horns in his wake now seeing the Saab rapidly cutting over unexpectedly into the right-turn lane, is it Meridian?—no, not Meridian—a smaller commercial street, Tuscarora—the Saab turning onto Tuscarora and God damn Corky can't cut over quickly enough to follow, he has to wait till the next street to turn but instead of doubling back onto Tuscarora he keeps on going for a second block and then doubles back reasoning Thalia isn't far ahead, turning a sharp skidding left on Thalia's street and seeing her, or imagining he sees her, a block or so ahead, Corky can't go very fast on Tuscarora which is only two and a half lanes, parking allowed, he's riding his fucking brakes half the time hearing his tires scream in protest seeing the faces of pedestrians and of other drivers turned toward him, not much traffic on this street but enough to obscure his view so though he believes he sees the bottle-green Saab ahead he can't be 100 percent certain so pausing at intersections he glances swiftly left and right to make sure Thalia hasn't turned off again, it's her desperate strategy to lead her pursuer on a zigzag course and so lose him, yes but he sees her, God damn her she *is* turning off, at a Hoagie Haven Corky takes a sharp right, realizes a moment too late that the car that turned is a green Mercury, can't make a U-turn in the street and so has to turn up a drive and jack himself around and so return to the intersection though it's a one-way street but fuck it Corky doesn't have any choice, sounding his horn so oncoming traffic halts for him and he makes his turn continuing on Tuscarora past Fitness Our Bizness past Fin Feathers & Fur Pets past Mykonos Pizza past Taco Bell past Fertility & Sex Counseling Institute past Comfortum Prosthetics "State-of-the-Art Silicone Limbs" past Tuscarora Clinique of Hair Removal past Grimm's Allstate past Leathergirls Ltd. past La Vogue Unisex Hair Salon past Extermino Termite & Pest Control seeing, or thinking he sees, the bottle-green Saab turning right another time, this time in such careless haste the car's right tires jolt over the curb, who else but Thalia so desperate, and within seconds Corky's there turning in pursuit, he's cutting off a Ford mini-van and the van's coming faster than Corky estimates he steels himself for the collision straining against the seat belt but the vehicle veers aside brakes squealing and Corky's miraculously in the clear seeing wincing through his rearview mirror that the van has skidded up onto the sidewalk, sideswiped a parked car—"Jesus!"—an icy sweat breaking out at Corky's every pore but he doesn't so much as pause, *he's* in the clear.

Corky sights the bottle-green Saab about a block ahead weaving in and out of traffic as if the driver is at last losing her strength or her courage or both and follows in close pursuit seeing her turn into the largely empty parking lot of Luxor Mattress & Bedding Emporium and racing through to a one-way alley unpaved and rutted and puddled as the drives on Mount Moriah and though Corky's there within seconds his heart hammering with anticipation as nearing the paroxysm of orgasm he discovers the Caddy's too unwieldy for such close quarters, bloated and clumsy as a cow, there's a sickening bounce and a scraping of the Caddy's axle against the ground and Corky loses his grip on the wheel for a fraction of an instant staring helpless to avert it as his right front fender smashes into and lifts a metal trash can lifting it as lightly as with the flick of a wrist you might toss a Styrofoam cup into the air, and the trash can crashes down onto the Caddy's hood and rolls against and over the windshield and Corky's braking desperately, skidding, coming to a jerky shuddering halt in a scrubby forsythia hedge where over the radio he hasn't been hearing since the start of the chase comes heavy percussive rock of his long-lost youth Mick Jagger's guttural-gravelly black-bluesy voice Corky hasn't heard in years *Time is on my side.*

10

"THE COCK CREW . . ."

might just change your life kid and so took Corky one evening in February 1973 to a production of *La Ronde* performed by the local amateur group the Union City Players, and midway in the play there appeared, as the glamorous mistress of a wealthy older man, a coolly beautiful golden-blond young woman to Corky's bedazzled eye a cross between Grace Kelly and Julie Christie, a gorgeous woman Corky couldn't take his eyes off neglecting to laugh with the rest of the audience at the comic lines delivered in amateur-production fashion with studied pauses for audience response, Christ, Corky hadn't seen a play since high school *he* was an amateur frankly somewhat shocked at the sexual cynicism of *La Ronde* so clearly not romantic, not American, not *nice*. Jerome Andrew Corcoran, "Corky," twenty-seven, the youngest employee of Ross Drummond Realty, Mr. Drummond had an eye for potential, Mr. Drummond creates potential, that's *his* business, and he's no amateur.

Nudging Corky in the ribs as the scene between the golden-blond woman and the wealthy older man went suggestively to black, almost ribald, gloating, "—That girl's my daughter. My daughter Charlotte. Would you like to meet her, kid? Hmmm?"

Yes, Mr. Drummond. Yes I sure would.

And so it came about, Corky's first glimpse of the woman he was to marry.

Troika's Supper Club close by the theater. Champagne and lobster. *Do these people live like this all the time? Is this their life?* And Corky hadn't even seen the Drummonds' house on Lakeshore Drive yet.

On their way into the glitzy supper club near the theater where Drummond had reserved a table, and where, quite clearly, he was known, Corky's boss laid a warm, hammy hand on his shoulder. "Maybe you can cheer up my little girl, son," an edge to his voice meaning he's embarrassed, don't look at his face, "—we're just getting her out from under this class-A shit she married right out of college. I could wring that guy's balls, hurting my little girl like he did! She's over the worst, though—you saw what she looks like, eh?—she's ready now for some laughs, y'know?—happy times. A nice clean-cut guy, a serious no-bullshit kind of guy with a career ahead, y'know?"

Yes, Mr. Drummond. Yes I sure do.

There was a girl, in fact there were two or three girls, Corky was seeing regularly, that's to say screwing regularly, at that time, but his first evening in the company of Charlotte Drummond at Troika's amid the fevered gaiety of theater people, not to mention Ross Drummond paying the $760 bill without batting an eyelash, curtly instructing the waiter to calculate what fifteen percent of the total was and take it for his tip, erased what had passed for Corky's emotional life until that hour.

Corky'd fallen in love during the performance of *La Ronde* and kept waiting anxiously for the mistress of the wealthy man to reappear, disappointed that she never did—the play passed in a blur for him, redeemed only at the end when the cast of ten made their curtain calls, and there was Ross Drummond's daughter again, younger-looking than she'd appeared in her role, smiling happily out into the audience of wildly applauding friends, family, social acquaintances. (The Union City Players, which, for a brief while, Corky Corcoran himself would join, was a company of well-to-do amateur performers whose productions were enthusiastically and uncritically received. Ross Drummond was one of the principal donors.) At Troika's, introduced to Charlotte by her father, encouraged to sit down beside her, Corky was dazzled as a man afflicted with snow blindness. "Oh, yes, 'Jerome Corcoran,'" the lovely girl said hesitantly, "—Pawpaw has been telling me about you I *think*. Is he the one, Pawpaw?"

Corky asked impulsively, "Wh-What's Mr. Drummond been saying about me?"

Shyly Charlotte smiled, biting her luscious cherry-red lower lip. Like the other actors and actresses crowded into the booth, she was still wearing her stage makeup: doll-like crimson cheeks, false eyelashes black and spiky as spiders' legs, elegantly arched eyebrows that seemed to rise quizzically above her natural eyebrows. And she was wearing a creamy-cocoa jersey dress that showed to advantage her shapely bare shoulders and the tops of her full, fleshy breasts at which Corky, already flush-faced, did not allow himself to look. And a single strand of pearls like none of the "cultured" pearls so proudly worn by Corky's female relatives. "Lean over, and I'll tell you," Charlotte said, as much to tease Ross Drummond as Corky, for between father and daughter there was a spirited sort of tension, and so besotted Corky did, inhaling Charlotte's perfume and the special scent of her hair, in full view of Ross Drummond and a table of glamorous strangers, and Charlotte whispered, "—Pawpaw says you're the only salesman in his office he doesn't have to, um—light a fire under his bottom."

Ass, she meant. He meant.

Corky laughed happily. Taking it as the compliment it surely was, the first of numerous compliments.

After that evening Corky began seeing, that's to say "dating," this fascinating young woman, this actress. Though the sexual pull between them was strong, leaving Corky panting and frustrated, they did not sleep together for weeks; until such time as they were speaking of becoming "engaged." (You'd have thought formal engagements had died out in the Sixties but you'd have thought wrong. Not in the social set to which the Drummonds belonged.) All happened swiftly, and deliriously. Corky Corcoran flailing like a man who can't swim in water over his head and loving it, swallowing mouthfuls of water and loving it *Is this real? Am I real?* waking every morning to a hard-on the size and heft of a billy club.

Corky was infatuated with Charlotte Drummond without actually knowing, that's to say realizing, she had a child: an eight-year-old girl from her disastrous marriage. "The Princess"—as Ross Drummond proudly called her. The hour of his first meeting with Thalia, at the elder Drummond's house, when he'd played "Chopsticks" and "Glowworm" on the piano, changed Corky's life, too: *I can be a father to another man's kid.* It wasn't just that the little girl was so beautiful, which she was, or so shy and docile, as she appeared, but Corky felt too a delicious sense of theft. *Kidnapping!*

"You've made quite a conquest, Jerome," Charlotte told Corky thoughtfully, "—usually Thalia hates my—" pausing as if needing to choose the most exquisitely tactful word, "—visitors."

"And what about her father?" Corky asked. "Where's he fit in here?"

Charlotte said vaguely, with a just-perceptible pinching of her nostrils as if Corky'd inadvertently released a bad smell, "*He's* out of the picture. Pawpaw has seen to it. We never talk about *him*."

Corky became engaged to Charlotte without exactly knowing that her divorce suit was being delayed by Braunbeck's inspired diversionary tactics. (One of them, a $1-million nuisance suit against his Drummond in-laws for "slander." Another, a threat of "exposure to the press"— Braunbeck owned photos he'd taken of Charlotte and himself making love, without Charlotte's knowledge or consent. Yet another, the nastiest, a threat of suing for custody of Thalia on the grounds her mother was "promiscuous.") Or that Charlotte was older than she seemed to suggest, and behaved. (She was in fact three years older, as Corky would learn from their marriage certificate.) Nor did Corky know that Charlotte had been "in analysis" for several years with a Manhattan psychoanalyst whom she flew to see every Monday like clockwork, at Ross Drummond's expense. Nor that, though showered with praise, Charlotte was not a very good actress—arch and mannered in her technique, shallow in affect, vain without being ambitious, incapable of following a director's instructions if the instructions were detailed and subtle. Corky, whose idea of great "classic" acting had been shaped by Kirk Douglas in *Spartacus*, a movie he'd seen four times, thought Charlotte was terrific.

Especially he hadn't guessed that, inclined to extreme emotions, as if in emulation of their marketability on the stage, Charlotte was to be jealous of Corky's relations, no matter how casual, neutral, innocent, with other women.

In time, Charlotte would be bitterly jealous too of certain of Corky's male friends—Vic Slattery, for instance. (Though liking it well enough when they were invited as a couple to the Slatterys' occasional small parties, or when singled out for attention by Sandra Slattery.) Corky's "cronies" she would call them, guys Corky'd known since high school; in the case of Nick Daugherty, since grade school. She was jealous of Corky's poker-playing, Corky's bets, whether he won or lost. Jealous of his Irish Hill relatives. (And what a surprise for an upscale WASP, marrying into a lower-middle-class Irish Catholic family. So many relatives! So many temporarily down on their luck, needing a little cash for medical expenses or a kid in school or to tide them over between jobs, for sure it's loan, a loan with interest, God bless you.)

But all that lay in the future. In the early days, weeks, months of Corky's affair with Charlotte Drummond, still at the time legally Mrs. Sherwood Braunbeck, he hadn't been able to see beyond the end of his prick.

Is this real? Oh Jesus.

And wonderful too, how Ross Drummond, the man everybody feared for his unpredictable temper, began to confide more and more in Corky Corcoran. Began to trust him with certain secrets at Drummond Realty & Insurance. A new office for Corky. Salary raises, opportunities for fat commissions. Promotions over the heads of older long-suffering arguably more deserving employees. Stock market tips. Three-martini lunches at Drummond's clubs—the U.C.A.C., the U.C. Golf Club, the Lakeshore Yacht Club. Ross Drummond introducing Corky to his friends, an arm slung heavy and proprietary around Corky's shoulders—"My daughter's fiancé"—"My daughter's husband"—sometimes "my son-in-law." My, mine.

Even before Corky and Charlotte were married, in May 1974, Corky and the old man were a team—as an elephant yoked with a donkey by an ingenious apparatus might be a team, with advantages to each. No bullshitting from this kid, Drummond would boast, so Corky, in his own right a great bullshitter, knew to keep his mouth shut in Ross Drummond's presence. You listened, you learned. You soaked it up. You didn't interfere with the process. Drummond had no son, only a daughter, and now a granddaughter, his was a household, Corky figured, of compliance and acquiescence; an occasional emotional upset, a flirty sort of tension between father and daughter, but no serious disagreements. "You pay the bills, you got the balls, eh?" Drummond liked to boast.

Corky thinks wryly, Not always.

Drummond did in fact resemble a bull elephant, with a bulky, ill-coordinated body, a massive head of tufted, stiff-graying hairs like metal shavings, and rough, leathery, layered-looking facial skin out of which shrewd damp eyes glared. He was in his late fifties when Corky first met him and he'd seemed then not old so much as beyond aging—seasoned, weathered, as if pickled in brine. You would not guess from Drummond's manner that he was a millionaire many times over, and had a B.A. degree from Dartmouth College. You would not guess, hearing his speech when he was in the company of men, that he would be so conspicuously gallant in the company of "ladies." Or that, in any case, he was from a rich Union City family. He was an obsessive golfer, and played competitively; he liked to boast he'd been an Olympic-quality swimmer, though he was too heavy and too easily winded to swim now, except sometimes in his pool at home or off his yacht in tepid, protected waters. Vivid as if it's yesterday Corky remembers the first time Drummond invited him for a family Sunday outing on his fifty-foot dazzling-white Evinrude sloop *The Rustbucket*—a dreamlike cruise in hot May sunshine along the Chateauguay from the Lakeshore Yacht Club north and east to Lake Ontario thirty miles away, and back just after sundown. The old man luxuriant in a deck chair high up front, his coarse layered-elephant skin gleaming with a mucus-like suntan oil, big gut in rolls over the waistband of red polyester swim trunks, genitals hanging swollen inside the snug fabric of the trunks like goiters. Such a sight, Corky himself felt squeamish about seeing. (There were several women, relatives, aboard *The Rustbucket*, in addition to Drummond's wife, daughter, and granddaughter.) Drummond and Corky guzzled beer together, voyage out and voyage back. They had things to discuss, Drummond said. Carelessly scratching his hairy chest, his genitals, as, energized by Corky's presence, by the sympathetic and seemingly uncritical attentiveness of this young good-looking flat-bellied mick kid he'd plucked from nowhere as a sharp-eyed scout might pluck out of somebody else's garbage an item of actual value, Ross Drummond talked, talked. It was not conversation but speech. But it did require the right listener. It required more than listening, it required *absorbing*. Apart from business, Drummond had numerous pet subjects to talk about—politics, of course: he called himself a "Taft Republican," whatever that meant—and Corky not only professed to be interested in the old man's bullshitting, Corky *was* interested.

Knowing by the age of twenty-seven what for years he'd only sensed: a man learns the way of the world from older men who love him. It doesn't matter if they tell you bullshit as long as they tell you something.

Of all subjects it was Sherwood "Tip" Braunbeck (at that time still Ross Drummond's son-in-law) that provoked the old man to a point beyond his characteristic cunning-caution. Speaking of Braunbeck, which Drummond did, with Corky, only when no one else could overhear, his voice thickened with rage and his small damp close-set eyes flashed with madness. Braunbeck was "that fucker," "that psychopath." Braunbeck was a flat-out crook, a conman. A blackmailer. A thug. He deserved to be shot in the knees, he deserved to be shot in the groin. He deserved death. Worse than death: torture. Threatening a custody suit over Thalia, threatening to sell "filthy faked" photographs of his own wife to the papers. Suing his own in-laws. When—this told Corky in confidence, Drummond's fingers gripping Corky's sunburnt arm, and his beery-belchy breath in Corky's face—he, Ross Drummond, had paid out over $30,000 to save Braunbeck's ass from a grand jury investigation and certain indictment for embezzlement. "Can you believe it! Can you! Betraying *me!* Bad enough the son of a bitch screwed around behind my daughter's back, but—betraying *me!*" Drummond scratched his crotch in a fury. Corky inclined his head, nodding, grave.

From Charlotte, Corky'd learned little of Braunbeck other than he was "cruel," "a liar," "a lousy father," "a psychopath." He was now living in Palm Beach with a rich widow "old enough to be his mother." Corky made discreet inquiries around town and discovered that his predecessor was something of a mystery: he'd arrived in Union City in 1964, with a story of having been honorably discharged from the U.S. Marines, Intelligence Division, midway in a Vietnam tour; he'd come from the Southwest, or the Northwest, or Alaska; he was a dark, curly-haired Burt Lancaster, unless he was a dark, curly-haired Charlton Heston. He wore a goatee. He was clean-shaven. Sometimes he wore horn-rimmed glasses. Virtually within days of arriving in Union City, he established contact with a number of well-to-do women associated with the arts, and through them he became acquainted with their businessmen husbands. He joined the Union City Players and performed in several productions, his great success being Sky Masterson in *Guys and Dolls.* His courtship of Charlotte Drummond was spoken of as "romantic"—"old-fashioned." The two were married in the First Episcopal Church and the wedding party, consisting of over three hundred guests, was held at the Chateauguay Country Club. At about that time Braunbeck took over as business manager of the Union City Players and oversaw an ambitious fund-raising drive. He was also selling partnerships in companies with insufficient assets, or no assets at all. He was spoken of as "charismatic" and "a natural leader"; a few years later, when an auditor discovered that $30,000 was missing from the Players account, and the suckers to whom he'd sold partnerships were discovering how they'd been cheated, he was called "unscrupulous," "a criminal type," "a psychopath." It was widely known that his wealthy feather-in-law had bailed him out and bought him out of his marriage. And bribed him to leave Union City.

That Sunday on *The Rustbucket*, fortified by a considerable amount of alcohol, Corky Corcoran listened at length, and absorbed much, of Ross Drummond's tirade against "Tip" Braunbeck—"That fucker I trusted as a son!" He asked no questions, for no questions were welcome. He made no comments other than beery-belchy exclamations of sympathy—"Christ!" "What a shit!" "Y'don't say!" He remembers how, as the yacht cut through choppy roiling friendly waves at dusk and the pale-glimmering pavilion of the Lakeshore Yacht Club and its trademark white stucco lighthouse came into view, Ross Drummond gripped Corky's forearm urgently, and tugged Corky toward him, saying, in a lowered voice, so that none of the others could possibly overhear even if eavesdropping, something so unexpected that for a beat or two Corky could not be sure he'd actually heard. And, even then, he'd had to ask Drummond to repeat himself.

So Drummond said, scowling, sullen, "—Shit, son, just an inquiry. I mean, hell, you hear of the Irish Mafia, eh? Isn't that what it's called? Certain incidents in Irish Hill—when I was growing up—Prohibition—rum-running from Canada—things happened, eh? Double-crossers wound up floating in the canal, eh? You know anything about that, Corky?"

Drummond always called Corky "Corky." Fond-familiar, even in the office, like a dog's name.

Like a man punched in the gut trying not to show it for fear of offending, Corky said slowly, "I've—heard of it. I guess."

He wants me to arrange for Braunbeck to be killed?

He thinks I'm the man who knows how?

There was a long moment's silence. Clumsy, prickly. Drummond scratched at his crotch, his face sagged with displeasure. Corky just sat there dumb-fuck mute. Elsewhere on the yacht, voices and laughter. Corky'd forgotten where he was, why he was here, sunburnt and headachy and far from home. In the company of the Drummond family, he was shy about even looking at Charlotte—gorgeous Charlotte in her white sailor's togs, hair pulled up beneath a wide-brimmed hat, eyes hidden by dark sunglasses—and Charlotte tended to steer clear of Corky, leaving him for man-to-man stuff with her father. The two men who mean the most to me in the whole world, she called them. Darling Jerome, and Pawpaw.

Now Pawpaw stared at Darling Jerome with hooded, assessing eyes. This is a test you're failing, fuckhead. But saying, sighing, shifting his bulk to indicate he's about to heave himself to his feet, "O.K., son, you're an altar boy, and I'm King Farouk. Mum's the word, eh? *'Dominus vobiscum'*"—making the sign of the cross with ribald fingers in Corky's face.

Corky remembers how then he'd finished his last beer of the day, warm as piss. He was sunburnt all over. His, the kind of fair thin Irish skin that doesn't tan, only burns. The warm comforting beer-buzz at the back of his skull had shifted to a dull ache like a thought, a memory, of something awaiting him back on land, beyond the Yacht Club 's fake lighthouse. *He thinks I'm the man who knows how?* And there came running little Thalia in her pink swimsuit, a welcome interruption, thumb in mouth to whisper in Grandpa's ear her shy dark eyes on Corky's face. And behind her, gorgeous Charlotte, with her teasing, melodic voice, that air of playful reproach Corky wasn't to understand for years, "You men! What on earth do you find to *talk* about all the time?"—as if not knowing the subject could only be her.

Afterward, Corky repeated some of this conversation to Charlotte, who said quickly, "Jerome, darling, you're putting the wrong interpretation on Pawpaw's words. He was joking! He would never seriously suggest such a thing." Kissing Corky, curtly, as a schoolmarm might do. "If you knew Pawpaw, you'd *know*."

Driving out to Chateauguay Falls, thinking these thoughts, Corky's in a defensive, close to derisive mood. What a fool he'd been! Falling for *face, tits, ass.* An emphasis upon *ass.*

And what about the old man's dough, fuckhead? What about that? Well.

Always, driving north of Union City into the affluent predominately white suburbs—St. Claire, St. Claire Shores, Riverdale, Chateauguay, Chateauguay Falls—Corky's in this mood: *he's* a city resident, hates the suburbs. These "communities" of middle-and upper-middle-class whites fleeing Union City taking their schools, churches, hospitals, community services with them: fuckers. Real estate value's a teeter-totter: the city's loss is the suburbs' gain. Even in this fucking recession.

Yet so many of Corky's friends and contacts live now in the suburbs. Vic and Sandra have always lived in Chateauguay, and Christina and her husband in Chateauguay Falls. And now Corky's ex-wife. Another man's new wife. *God damn:* Corky's thinking he could forgive Charlotte everything except moving out to Chateauguay Falls with "Gavin" Pierson.

After Schoonover (where he had the car washed, though hadn't had time to get the interior vacuumed) Corky took the Fillmore north to the Chateauguay exit, he's running late, fuck it, not a time to get lost in the curlicues and cul-de-sacs of Quail Ridge Hollow where the Piersons live, a "planned residential community" where the least expensive properties sell for $1 million, but, sure, he gets lost, so it's 7:37 P.M. when at last, cursing under his breath, Corky turns up the sandstone-pebbled driveway to 23 Quail Ridge Pass. Either he's hours late, or isn't expected at all.

Can't remember exactly what they'd decided this morning. Except hadn't Charlotte hung up on him?—as the bitch is always doing. But Corky owes it to her, in this crisis with Thalia, to drop by. Yeah, he misses her. His "wife." And maybe she'll have some news of Thalia.

Corky's smoking another Camel, smoking like he's expecting somebody to snatch it from him. Last time he'd given up, he'd been chain-smoking, four packs a day, a real nicotine junkie. Swigging too from a plastic jug of unsweetened grapefruit juice he's been gripping between his knees as he drives. Unquenchable thirst. Nothing to eat all day but that sweet potato pie heavy and compact in his gut as a chunk of meteorite but quarts of fluids and still the mocking *a drink need a drink?* he's doing his best to ignore. Drains the jug and tosses it into the back seat amid the other debris. Frowns at himself critically in the rearview mirror and sees he looks like—what? The surprise is, for all the shit he's been taking, he doesn't look that bad, actually. Skidding to a stop in the alley he'd banged the underside of his jaw on the steering wheel but if there's a bruise or a bump, it doesn't show. The other bruise, on his forehead, isn't too visible, his hair combed down, damp from sweating like a pig chasing Thalia all over hell then losing her.

Corky's undecided: how much should he tell Charlotte? She's a natural hysteric and what he did was pretty crazy. Dangerous. Fucking car chase like something on TV except unlike TV where everything's hoked up to come out right and to make sense, the pursuer in this case lost the pursued.

Still, Corky's grateful neither he nor Thalia cracked up. He's God-damned grateful the Caddy isn't damaged, much. (Some scratches and scrapes on the hood from the garbage can, a hairline crack on the passenger's side of the windshield, partly crumpled right front fender and bumper—but now the car's washed, if you don't look too closely it looks almost good as new.)

Grateful too he didn't get stopped by a cop when he was driving like a madman, that's all he needs—JEROME CORCORAN, CITY COUNCILMAN, ARRESTED FOR SPEEDING, RECKLESS DRIVING.

Better yet: JEROME CORCORAN, CITY COUNCILMAN, ARRESTED ON CHARGES OF CHILD MOLESTATION, PERVERSION. His photo in the paper shielding his face with handcuffed hands, like Leroy Nickson, page one of the Metro section.

Corky's thinking he'll never forgive Thalia, now. God as my witness, never. His heart's broken.

At the same time thinking *She loves me, it's a mistake. If there's one thing I know, it's Thalia loves me.*

Corky parks the Caddy in the circle drive below a house that does in fact look like a million bucks: split-level contemporary stacked like a post-modernist wedding cake, white brick, fieldstone, glass walls, redwood deck. The three-car garage is open, a single car inside, Charlotte's Mercedes coupe. Evidently Pierson's not home—Corky hopes so. He jokes about the sucker with everybody but that look in Pierson's eyes when he runs into Corky, cringing-guilty like he's done Corky some insult that in Sicily, for instance, would be his death warrant, has begun to bug Corky. Should've punched Pierson in the mouth when he had the chance, in the locker room at the U.C.A.C. Screwing another member's wife, breaking up a marriage, "Gavin" wouldn't have sued. Maybe, even, he'd hoped Corky would hit him?

Maybe that's what we all want. Somebody to hit us hard enough, our guilt's absolved.

When Corky climbs the steps to the massive front door (what's it made of, hammered copper?) he sees guiltily that the door's ajar and Charlotte's waiting for him. Watching for him. How long? Her voice rings out, "Jerome! Hello—" and quickly they greet each other in the way they've cultivated since their estrangement: the crucial thing is not to look into each other's eyes.

A quick shy half-embrace, Charlotte's cheek turned to be kissed, a handshake—that's enough. Corky knows that Charlotte has just set a drink aside (on a shelf, behind a vase, inside a drawer, behind a television set) when his car turned up the drive, he smells the darkish-sweet wine on her breath. Red wine, not white. Not a good sign, but better than the hard stuff.

Charlotte says, staring, "My God, Jerome! Are you smoking?"

And right away Corky's pissed hearing in this a deep exasperated pity, beyond reproach, for Corky and Charlotte had given up smoking together, not once but three or four times; hellish times, worse for Charlotte than for Corky. Charlotte has wished him dead, Corky knows, but—smoking, again? She says huskily, "Jerome, *no*. You *can't* be."

Corky blocks this, smiling. "*You're* looking good. Terrific!"

Which is true, at least that's his blurred first impression. A woman you'd never take for forty-six, more like thirty-six. She's in beige, creamy-brown, white. Silk designer blouse, silk-wool slacks. Sandals. Dull-gold hair close-cropped and lifting from her ears like wings. Glitter of gold earrings, bell-like jangle of thin gold bracelets. A smooth jawline, shadowless eyes, lovely mouth still cherry-red, fleshy. Must be fifteen, even twenty pounds heavier than she'd been when they first met, starving herself in those days, fighting her appetite, instincts. Corky knows his ex-wife's body—breasts, hips, thighs, curving belly—the brunette pubic hair in scratchy-tickly tufts—the slender ankles, child-sized toes—like a man knows the terrain of a mountain he was once stranded on, and survived on. Recalls too as he hasn't for a long time, and hasn't wanted to, how, making love, whatever glamorous ease and laughing good spirits she'd bring to it, this is a woman who ends heaving and thrashing and whimpering and pleading. *Oh! oh! oh! oh! oh! oh God oh!* coming like a mule's kick.

Gavin Pierson with his spindly legs, hairless concave chest and baby's potbelly, prick about the size of Corky's middle finger—Jesus, no, Corky doesn't want to think about it.

Suppose the woman *is* his wife, she'll always *be* his wife. Always, Corky loves her. But here they are pretending otherwise, like a man and a woman on stage. That play—*La Ronde?*

Charlotte says, "And *you*—you're looking good." A moment's hesitation. "In real life, and on TV. Are those for me?"

Corky's brought his ex-wife a dozen blood-red roses, a guilt offering you might call it, he hopes to hell Charlotte won't make a wisecrack along those lines, spoil things immediately as she has a habit of doing. Hands her the bouquet, smiling his boyish-frank smile, sardonic Corky, can't resist—"Actually, they're for Stud: where's he?"

Charlotte takes the roses without acknowledging the wisecrack though Corky can see she's annoyed, frowning as if with deliberation burying her face in the roses Corky has an idea are scentless, not real roses somehow— he'd bought them from a cadaverous white kid of about eighteen hustling from a traffic median on busy Schoonover near the car wash, poor bastard strung out on possibly crack? heroin? risking his neck at the traffic intersection, a crude printed sign 1 DOZ ROSES $10, Corky guesses they're stolen but rolls down his window eager to make a purchase, just the thing for Charlotte. Never goes empty-handed visiting, or almost never.

"Gavin"—Charlotte's pronunciation of the name, a fruity name to Corky's ear, is precise, emphatic—"is in Philadelphia. His mother's been hospitalized for what we hope is a mild case of diverticulitis, he'll be back tomorrow." A little stiffly adding, "Thank you. For these. They're beauti- ful."

Corky grins awkwardly, rebuffed. They're in the foyer of the house, Charlotte's leading him in the direction he supposes of the kitchen, heels clattering on the gleaming tessellated floor. Christ, this place *is* impressive, Corky feels it as a wire-thin pain in his head, *need a drink? a drink? oh God* cathedral ceiling in the living room, fieldstone fireplace and hearth like something in a ski lodge, a wall of plate glass overlooking one of those prissy little Zen gardens, raked pebbles and miniature shrubbery and a single piece of statuary and what looks like driftwood, artsy stuff, the architect who did the house is Korean and must've sold the newlyweds a bill of goods, also the bare tile floors with oatmeal-colored runner-rugs, Charlotte's taste has always been for heavy Oriental carpets. European antiques. It pisses Corky *he's* been left with that crap not to mention the fucking "Georgian Colonial" in Maiden Vale Charlotte had to have, now on a lousy depressed market Corky'd be lucky to get $500,000 for the property, inside the city limits. "Where's the stuff you took from the house?" Corky asks casually. "That big rug—"

"In the guest suite," Charlotte calls back over her shoulder, casually too. "It's perfect there."

Fuck you, thinks Corky, incensed. What was good enough for our living room is only good enough for your "guest suite."

In the kitchen Charlotte fusses with the roses, chooses a vase for them, Corky sees there aren't twelve roses only eleven, God damn that hustler, he hopes Charlotte won't notice. She's smiling a tight strained smile saying she'd been waiting for Corky since about four but it's all right, she's glad he's here now, would he like a drink?—wine, beer?—and Corky makes a snorting noise to indicate, what?—*wine?*—don't you know me any better than to suggest *wine?*—shifting his shoulders inside his coat annoyed this woman is playing dumb-fuck games with him pretending, after their long history together, she doesn't know his tastes, or has forgotten. It's a put-down, Charlotte's innocent little inquiry, nobody overhearing could guess.

Yeah they'd think *paranoid.* That's what they'd think, huh?—this guy's *paranoid.*

"Well," says Charlotte, carefully, not looking at Corky just as Corky isn't looking too directly at her, the two of them watching her with the roses, "—some beer, then? Gavin has, I think, some—you can look in the refrigerator—German beer, or Japanese—" Corky sees a wine bottle on a counter, opened, fruity-heavy Italian red, but no wine glass in sight. He opens the refrigerator conspicuously snubbing the fancy imported bottled beer, chooses instead a can of club soda. At this, Charlotte does look at him, raised eyebrows and widened eyes. "Did you—have an accident? Your car—"

Corky, knowing perfectly his ex-wife's logic, why the sight of him taking a can of club soda not a bottle of beer alarms her, laughs irritably, says, "No, sweetheart, I did not have an accident. My car's in the driveway, you saw it."

"That's all you want, club soda?"

"I'm not staying long."

"I've been waiting for you since—"

"O.K., I'm sorry, I'm late and I'm sorry and we have things to talk about so let's talk about them for Christ's sake," Corky says rudely, he's feeling the pain as a wire tightening around his head now clamping his temples, *a drink need a drink* but as he yanks the pull-top and swigs a mouthful of the club soda even as he's suppressing a belch of sour grapefruit juice he knows this isn't the drink he wants, it isn't sufficient. Jesus, he's got the shakes.

And Charlotte too, spilling water on the counter forcing the roses into a vase with a narrow neck, Charlotte too has the shakes: ex-wife and ex-husband watching this awkward procedure but Corky won't say a word the complaint against him being he was always bossing Charlotte around monitoring her every action when it came to such things, mechanical things, especially critical of her driving, poor Charlotte taking her revenge as a wife will paying not the slightest attention to Corky's advice even when both of them knew he was right which was ninety-seven percent of the time. Tactful Corky looks away from Charlotte's nervous fingers, the manicured red-polished nails so perfect like the fluff-blown gold-rinsed hair, the expensive clothes, when you're a woman of forty-six perfection of this kind must mean everything, at the same time it means exactly nothing, your youth's gone.

And the new ring. Rings. A shock to Corky to see, to realize *his* rings are gone. In their place an emerald-studded wedding band and a diamond big as a grape rimmed with smaller emeralds. *To spite me. All of it, to spite me.*

Corky's gallant pouring Charlotte wine in a fresh glass and discreetly taking the bottle with him as they move out of the kitchen in the direction of, Corky assumes, the splendid living room, though as it turns out he's wrong, both of them registering with relief how gallant too Corky's been *not* saying a word about Charlotte fucking up the roses (two stems broken, left behind on the counter) as he'd have done in the old days. So Charlotte isn't going to push it about the smoking, though Corky, seeing no ashtrays anywhere in this place, is continuing to smoke, scattering ash, and no apologies.

Charlotte, uncharacteristically silent, leads Corky along a lengthy hall then two steps down into a "family"-style room at the rear of the house, this too like a lounge in a ski lodge, long low cushioned leather sofas, a stark-white ceramic stove looking like it's never been used for a fire only for display, a steep wall of plate glass overlooking a redwood deck stretching out of sight in the shadows. Corky feels a touch of vertigo, *where are we? this isn't our house* as Charlotte sets the vase of roses down on a sculpted-mahogany coffee table, invites Corky to sit down—"Even if you can't stay long." He's embarrassed by the significance Charlotte seems to be giving the impulsive gift of his.

This room at least has the look of a room lived in, unlike other parts of the house Corky has been able to glimpse. Big TV with a thirty-inch screen, VCR equipment and dozens of videotapes on a shelf, a surprising number of books and not just Charlotte's best-sellers in their hot candescent jackets. Built-in bookcases covering much of two walls, "Gavin" must be a reader? Corky scans titles, sees historical biographies, Civil War, World War II, some of the same popularized-science books Corky himself owns, wonder if this guy's actually read them? understood them? On the mahogany coffee table there's a copy of *A Brief History of Time* amid copies of *Fortune, Vanity Fair, TV Guide, The Wall Street Journal*. Corky checks "Gavin's" bookmark and sees he's gotten to page eighty. He's sure *he's* gotten farther.

Get sucked into a black hole and you're "recycled" into the Universe as radiation. Jesus, what a comfort!

Corky's sitting, not beside Charlotte on the sofa, but in a hefty leather chair facing her, so low to the floor and so pneumatic it's like the thing is swallowing him alive. And the weird wheezing air released, a combination of whistle and protracted fart. Charlotte narrows her eyes anxiously at Corky over the rim of her wine glass, asks finally, "Have you heard from—Thalia?" and Corky hesitates not knowing what to say, what's wisest. Try as he did to not blame Charlotte for her daughter, "his" by adoption, it's been tough. Maybe if they'd both adopted Thalia, her parentage unknown, they'd have been equally screwed and could take solace in one another? As it was, Corky'd been haunted constantly by the thought of Sherwood "Tip" Braunbeck down in Palm Beach laughing up his sleeve at this sucker Jerome "Corky" Corcoran freely taking on wife, kid, and Pawpaw. For life.

Since the divorce finally came through in January 1974, not a word from, or of, Braunbeck. The prick cut himself off completely from Thalia, not to mention Charlotte, not even birthday cards, never a single telephone call so far as Corky knows.

Corky says evasively, "Not exactly."

"'Not exactly'—? What does that mean?"

"I didn't hear from her but I saw her."

"Saw her?" Charlotte asks with childlike eagerness. "Where?"

"In her car, in Mount Moriah Cemetery," Corky says, shrugging, "—this afternoon after Marilee Plummer's funeral."

"How is she? What did she say?"

"I only saw her, Charlotte. I didn't have a chance to talk to her. She—"

"You saw Thalia, Jerome," Charlotte says, her voice rising, incredulous, "—and you didn't talk to her?"

Corky says defensively, "She wouldn't let me, Charlotte. She drove away. I wasn't near my car, and by the time I got to it—"

Charlotte's leaning forward staring at Corky her face showing the strain, hairline creases in the forehead, bracketing her cherry-red mouth, unflattering tendons visible in her throat. "You let Thalia get away? You saw her, and you let her get away? Thalia who's taken a gun, a gun of yours, a dangerous lethal weapon—*you let her get away?*"

Corky shrugs. Says, smiling, shifting his ass in the leather chair, "I'm your basic dumb-fuck, we all know that."

Charlotte's eyes are bright with tears. Corky hopes she won't cry, her mascara will run, he's seen that too many times. "Jerome, damn you! You *always* say that. You *always* let yourself off that way."

Always? Corky takes this in silence. Rope-a-dope: the strategy of letting your opponent punch himself out on your body.

Need a drink, sweet fucking Christ. But no forcing himself to speak carefully and without recrimination he explains to Charlotte some of the circumstances of that afternoon, not all but some, Thalia sighted him before he saw her, he hadn't recognized her car. And all of it happening so quickly. Unexpectedly. "I wish I'd been able to speak to her, maybe I could have talked her into coming here with me," Corky says, though this wasn't a thought he'd had at the time. But Charlotte's eager to hear it, pathetic how women want to be lied to, it's the least you can do for them.

"How did she . . . look?" Charlotte asks.

"She looked fine."

"Oh, Jerome, you're not thinking: how could she look *fine?* She's desperate."

"As far as I could see . . . Well, I didn't get a very good look at her, as I said."

Charlotte drains her wine glass compulsively, short of breath. Wordless, Corky picks up the bottle to pour her more wine, a husbandly gesture. Shithead-Corky the guy who's always let her down.

"I keep thinking she'll come here. All day today . . . I've been waiting. For her, and for you." Charlotte laughs, touching her fingertips to her eyes. "I keep thinking you'll come here together. That's ridiculous, isn't it."

"Sweetheart, no—"

"Don't call me 'sweetheart,' Jerome. Please. It's condescending and insulting and this isn't the time."

Corky takes this in silence, too. Nicest guy in Union City, N.Y.

The wire around his head's tight, tightening. He feel as if his brain is going to implode. Just alcohol deprivation, a touch of the D.T.'s, what's to worry? Presses the cold can of soda against his forehead *If I can get through the next hour I can get through the rest of it.* Charlotte's speaking quickly, huskily. Telling Corky how she'd made dozens of telephone calls today, trying to track down Thalia, she'd called girls Thalia knew in high school, in most cases not the girls themselves but their parents—"The girls are all grown of course, and gone. It's been years since they've been *daughters.*" She'd called friends, acquaintances, colleagues of Thalia's; spoke with Thalia's former supervisor at Family Services; her director at WWUC-TV, and another young woman who'd worked with her there. Some of these people gave her names, and she called these others, or tried to. "Here are the names and telephone numbers," Charlotte says, handing Corky a handwritten list, twenty-odd items, as if wanting him to validate her effort, "—though nobody could help me, much. It was so depressing, and embarrassing: having to ask people, some of them strangers, if they know how I can find my own daughter. If they can give me any information about my own daughter. And then, when they say, 'Thalia Corcoran?—I haven't heard from her in years.'" Charlotte presses the flat of her hand against her mouth to keep from crying.

Corky leans over to touch her arm, give a little comfort. Poor Charlotte: when he's away from her he seems, so oddly, to reduce her to a few
stylized gestures and expressions; when he's with her, at least some of the
time, he sees a different woman. "None of these people could help at *all?*"
Corky asks, frowning at the names. Male names, female names. Most of
them unknown to him. Except there's "Kiki Zaller"—but Corky's afraid
to ask if Charlotte got through to her. "That's discouraging."

"Well. It's Memorial Day weekend, people are away. I've marked with
an asterisk the people I actually spoke with—only about half. And I drove
down to Thalia's apartment on Highland Avenue, too, Jerome, today.
You said it was the one place in the world Thalia *wouldn't* be, but . . . I
couldn't stay away. I've been desperate."

Corky says, surprised, "*You* went to Highland Avenue? All the way
from 'Quail Ridge Hollow'?"

"Don't be ridiculous, Jerome, it isn't that far! Forty-five minutes. I
know Union City as well as you do, I've lived here all my life."

Corky lets this absurdity pass. He's envisioning Charlotte venturing
into the Highland area by herself, the classy Mercedes coupe pulling up
in front of Thalia's shabby house. Christ, he should have gone with her!
She'd have been frightened, anxious.

Quickly Charlotte says, as if guessing Corky's thoughts, "I *have* been
there in the past, of course. Many times. And, on a Sunday afternoon,
the neighborhood doesn't seem as . . . I mean, it seems perfectly fine. Of
course, you were right, Thalia wasn't there. But I spoke with a nice young
couple who live downstairs from her . . ."

"'Esdras'—?"

"Yes, has Thalia spoken of them to you? The young man is an instruc-
tor at the University in something called 'semiotics'—I think that's it.
They told me they haven't gotten to know Thalia very well, she's very private, they seem to think she's a graduate student and were very surprised,
I don't know why, when I told them I was her mother. I said I hadn't seen
her in some time and was worried about her, living alone in this place,
and they said somebody'd broken into her apartment on Friday evening!
And Thalia was there, she must have been hiding there . . . and refused to
let them call the police. Can you imagine? What *is* her life?" Charlotte's
face glows with indignation, hurt. "They said they hadn't been able to get

a good look at the man, of course it was a man, who broke in, but they didn't think he'd taken anything from the apartment, or did anything to Thalia. They said she's alone most of the time she's there, but she's often not there, she's away for days, a week, then sometimes they'd be under the impression she was gone but in fact she'd be in the apartment all the while, just very . . . still. What do you suppose she's doing, Jerome? Alone like that, hidden away, like a cloistered nun? For days? Reading? *Thinking?* What is there to *think* about, that it has to be done in such solitude! It just makes her hard, these pure-hearted people are hard, they're not human like the rest of us, *we* do the worrying, *we* take the responsibility. I'm so *exhausted* with being a mother to a girl who refuses to be a daughter! If only Thalia would get married . . . When I was twenty-five . . ." Charlotte's voice trails off, angry, bewildered.

Corky says gently, "Hey: when you were twenty-five, you were married to 'Tip.' You told me, you believed your life was over."

"What? That's ridiculous. I never said that. At Thalia's age I had a beautiful little girl, I'd accomplished *that*. No matter who the father was, no matter the mistakes I made, I had Thalia, I loved my little girl, *that* was what I had."

"All right," says Corky. "That's right."

"It *is* right. I had to grow up fast, I became an adult overnight. You wouldn't know."

"What's that s'posed to mean?"

"*You* wouldn't know, you've never been a father."

Like a panicked fighter throwing punches wildly, high, low, to the groin, Charlotte's getting dangerous. Corky thinks, *Just take it. You've been here before.*

Smiling to show he's O.K., draining the absolutely shitty-tasting soda and crumpling the can in his fist, Corky says, "Aw, honey, how're you so sure? I might've been a 'father' long before I met you. We fucked like rabbits in Irish Hill and the Church forbids birth control, *you* know that. Eh?"

"Don't get dirty, Jerome. Just to deflect the subject. That's an old trick of yours, too."

"You're allowed your old tricks, sweetheart, and I'm not allowed mine? Fuck you."

Corky heaves himself out of the farting leather chair and Charlotte cringes as if fearing he's going to hit her but Corky's just going back to the kitchen, if he can find the God-damned kitchen in this maze of a house, he finds it and opens the refrigerator and takes this time a can of Diet Coke yanking the pull-top and beginning to swig thirstily from it before he's even back in the "family" room with Charlotte who's staring at him unmoved from the position, the very cringing posture, she'd been in when he'd left. The Diet Coke tastes of chemicals strong as the lake-water toxins Corky used to swallow as a kid swimming off the Welland Street dock but at least there's caffeine, Corky needs a hit. Lighting a fresh Camel, too, and tossing the burnt-out match on the gleaming mahogany coffee table.

"So what's 'Stud' think about all this? Or is he out of it?"

Charlotte's staring up at Corky her mouth dumb-slack as if truly she's frightened of him, that little spring in his brain. The many times she'd toyed with it, fingered and tickled it, pinched, poked, prodded it, like playing with her own clit, seeing how close to getting him off she could come; and coming herself, too. But then there were those times, increasing the last two years they lived together, when it all went too far and it wasn't exactly fun. As Corky told the judge offhandedly sure he'd slapped his wife around, sometimes. The two of them soused. But only openhanded, never with fists—he's never punched a woman in his life, and never will. Charlotte was the one to use her fists.

"C-Corky, don't. We only have each other."

And it's an old trick of Charlotte's too, at such a pass to call Corky "Corky" not as a dog's name, nor even as a name to placate his unpredictable temper, but, faintly, pleadingly, her eyes welling with tears, as a name of affection. The affection she might have had for him if the side of him that's "Corky" wasn't just too crude too vulgar too Irish Hill too beneath her.

Charlotte begins suddenly to cry, face stiff in this way she's cultivated of crying without wrinkling her skin excessively, there's a deeper wilder kind of crying that overcomes her when things are really bad but this isn't it, at least not yet. Helpless tears, her shoulders shaking inside the silk blouse, Corky has no choice but to sit beside her and slip his arm around her, awkward as hell and he's burning with resentment and embarrassment but there's nobody else at 23 Quail Ridge Pass to comfort this woman, clearly the new husband *is* out of it, smart guy. "Hey c'mon Charlotte, it's O.K., it's going to be O.K., we've been through worse than this, huh?—remember, at Cornell—" so Corky comforts Charlotte, and Charlotte cries, though not so agitatedly she can't gulp down the remainder of her wine, like medicine. And he guesses too she's on her Xanax, the tranquilizer she's been taking for years, *anxious and blue? and also depressed?* but he knows better than to ask. He can sense how she has to resist the powerful urge to bury her face against his neck, grab at him, always it was hard for them, virtually impossible for them, to keep their hands off each other even when, or especially when, hating each other's guts. Like with Christina the other day, fucking her on the floor, pounding her against the floor, cock like a jackhammer and she'd clutched at him wanting it, needing it, the idea must be you deserve some solace some comfort at such a time, no greater solace and no greater comfort than sex, your reward for the misery like dirty sloshing water washing over you you know's going to drown you anyway.

But Corky thinks: *No.*

Recalling those nights, so sad so shameful he hasn't thought of them in years, when, fucked out from some girl he'd come home to poor Charlotte awake reading in bed, one of her glossy women's-porn novels, or watching a late movie on TV, bathed and talcumed and sexy in her lacy nightgown, breasts heavy pale and loose, if there was strain at her mouth she disguised it with her smile, a happy tranquilized-winey-horny smile, swallowing eagerly as you'd never expect of any daughter of Pawpaw Drummond Corky's hastily concocted excuses, anecdotes of late-night meetings at City Hall, an impromptu caucus at the Statler, a campaign strategy debriefing for the inner Slattery circle, it might have been Vic's congressional campaign, it might have been Oscar's mayoral campaign, sometimes Corky Corcoran's own campaign for election, the hysteria of politics, the heat and craziness and appetite. Charlotte swallowed this crap, or tried to; or seemed to; or called into play her actor's technique to make Corky, guilty and part- or fully drunk, believe she did. But murmuring, complaining, the feminine sweetness just slightly forced, she's lonely she misses her Jerome she loves him please let's make love?—so Corky would try to oblige, most obliging guy in Union City, N.Y., use

the bathroom undress climb naked into bed game as a monkey and proceed through the motions or at least the initial moves of lovemaking, for,
for sure, he did love Charlotte, Charlotte's a beautiful sexually desirable
woman and Corky's fully aware of the fact though feeling an acute weari-
ness at the back of his skull and that fatal limpness to his prick craving not
sex but sleep no more sex only sleep the sweet oblivion of sleep the black
hole *not* a cunt we crave to be sucked into forever and ever Amen. And
Charlotte kissing nuzzling nipping at Corky's slack lips, poking her avid
tongue into his mouth he's just rinsed with Listerine gargling frantically
to erase the taste of another female, Charlotte grinding her warm pelvis
against him, now a rosy nipple jammed into his mouth like he's a baby
stubbornly resisting the teat, Darling come on, darling what's wrong,
don't fall asleep, darling!—arms, thighs, hips, belly undulating over him
like a landscape come alive, Oh Jerome, damn you!—shyly at first then
with increasing impatience her fingers stroking clutching rhythmically
massaging Corky's prick that's limp as a balloon from which all helium
has leaked, a sob of disappointment, a grunt of dismay, a determined inhalation of breath as abandoning the customary decorum of her lovemaking Charlotte leans panting over Corky's hairy belly and tentatively, with
an almost palpable revulsion, touches his tender prick with her tongue,
forces a kiss, then a choked-rushed sucking, which succeeds in refilling
the prick with a little helium, a dull surge of blood, before Corky wakes
up appalled that his wife, *his* wife, should do to him unbidden what he so
loves other women to do, and at such a late hour of the night. Seizing her
then gently by the nape of the neck, urging her away from that part of his
body, protective of her as of a blundering child. And forcing himself then
eyes shut as tightly as possible to kneel between her damp fleshy legs that
close about him eager as an alligator's jaws and to kiss, suck, mash, mutter against her cunt that's so sadly lonely, an alive thing, hot-palpitating
and close to shrieking, and with a dozen deft thrusts of his tongue bring
poor Charlotte off gasping and grunting and writhing *Oh! oh! oh! oh!*
her fingers closed in his hair tugging like a drowning woman so Corky's
in terror of being scalped even as, relieved, exhausted, he collapses where
he is between her thighs, begins to sink into sleep like water swirling into
a drain, not minding nor indeed aware of the scratchy-tickly pubic hair
in his face until sobbing in a kind of angry gratitude Charlotte hauls him

up where he belongs, where a proper husband belongs, slack-jawed and already snoring on the pillow beside her as, exhausted too, she switches off the light.

Amen.

Corky wonders how Charlotte remembers those episodes. How many she remembers. If she remembers them at all.

When they began, he's vague about. An amnesiac wash was settled over much of his marriage. Much of his life. What *do* we remember, of the infinity of seconds that constitutes our lives?

The faster you travel, the slower the clock.

Except it wasn't Corky's fault exclusively, the breakup of his marriage. And Thalia's enmity. How was it *his* fault, how's it a man's fault, women coming on to him, PR-glamor girls, TV girls, City Hall professionals, secretaries receptionists "aides" law students politics B.A.'s having a taste of the real thing, meaning politicians, meaning men, and loving it: no sexual turn-on like campaigns, elections. Power. The Seventies: universal birth control pill, no condoms. No herpes, no AIDS. No second thoughts. No "sexual harassment"—it hadn't been discovered yet. One of Corky's first affairs was with a deputy mayor's Vassar-educated assistant who was known to be screwing the deputy mayor and Corky Corcoran and rumor had it Red Pitts at the same general time, and nobody worried about catching anything, never so much as a thought. And little Bonnie whose last name Corky's forgotten, hired by Corcoran, Inc., from a temp service, Corky's first glimpse of Bonnie and she's got a permanent job, frosted-pink lips and jade eyeliner and seriously big hair, wide-eyed kid looking hardly older than Thalia but in fact twenty-four and much practiced, a diaphragm in her cunt for emergency purposes *and* jelly in her leather bag, as hot for her nattily dressed whistling-breezy boss as he's for her. The Seventies: a decade of impromptu screwing on desktops, in the rears of cars, Corky's back aches at the thought of it. In the Eighties, it was posh hotel rooms downtown and out along I-190, sometimes Corky's girl, or woman as they'd begun to want to be called, would even be on expense account, a sales director at Union Trust, the programmer for WWAZ-TV, assistant district attorneys, the assistant curator of the Art Museum, the society editor at the *Journal*. And certain of Charlotte's women friends, loosening up as if with age, their businessman husbands raking in dough in those boom times before October 1987 and their kids grown and moved away and suddenly what's there to save it for?—their grandchildren? And Charlotte one night waiting up for Corky bathed and talcumed and in her lacy nightgown serene as Mother Teresa dosed to the gills with Xanax and alcohol this time asking, Is it another woman, Jerome, I insist upon knowing for the sake of my therapy, it's crucial for me at this stage to know, Dr. Fromme doesn't believe that actual reality is significant in our psychic lives but I believe it is, *are you unfaithful to me?*—and Corky protested, hurt, offended, Charlotte for Christ's sake there *is* only you, you and Thalia, other women don't mean shit to me, and Charlotte said, calmly, Maybe they don't, maybe that only makes it worse: you're incapable of being faithful, aren't you—and Corky'd hesitated just long enough, and gave it away: Faithful *how?*

As if she's aware of Corky's thoughts and not liking them Charlotte pushes herself up from the sofa, excuses herself to get some Kleenex. Corky watches her walk with purposeful steadiness out of the room: shoulders and back erect as she can manage, hips undulating, ass in the silky-wool beige slacks fleshy, a little heftier than Corky recalls, more of a handful. Handfuls. Those classy clothes she's wearing, for him, might be worth $1000 not to mention the jewelry. Weird how it's developed— "civilization"—the whole thing's dependent upon our hiding our nakedness, that's to say our bodies, from one another. Pile on the glitz, the "style." Take a good look, the game's over. That sociobiologist Corky's been reading, Turke, the evolution of *Homo sapiens* in terms of female reproductive physiology, all hinges upon the fact that in the human female there's no perceptible estrus swelling so the male can't tell when the female is ovulating. And that's because females need males around all the time, not just for impregnating them but for food-supplying and protection; and that's because the human baby is born totally helpless—"premature"; and *that's* because if babies were born with brains sufficiently developed for survival, the brain size would kill the mothers in childbirth. Jesus, what a depressing theory! All of civilization, culture, human history, why Corky Corcoran's where he is at this moment in Time, because a woman's ass is designed in a certain way.

And beneath it all, guiding all life on Earth, DNA seeking to replicate itself. Blind, fanatic, no other purpose. Like rabies. Corky read that in *The Selfish Gene.*

When Charlotte returns, she's carrying a bottle of Red Label and two glasses. Her manner's more aggressive, her face looks glossier, more in focus; she's freshened her makeup, repaired the runny mascara. She looks good and she's smiling and Corky says quickly, "I don't want that. I have to be leaving, I've got a dinner engagement at—"

"Don't want what?"—sitting on the sofa beside Corky, as before, pouring whiskey for them both.

"That drink."

"This is Red Label, your favorite."

"I don't want it, Charlotte. Thanks!"

"Don't tell me you're giving up drinking again." Charlotte cuts her eyes at Corky as if he's said something amusing. "That's what you'd call bullshit."

Charlotte hands Corky the glass, he's got no choice but to take it. The amber liquid quivering in his hand. The wire so tight around his head his blood vessels are about to burst. *Don't. No. You can't.*

Charlotte touches her glass to Corky's, and drinks. Shuts her eyes, laughs again, a sighing despairing-luxuriant laugh so Corky realizes she's far along, she's been drinking for hours. "Remember that terrible time after you came close to losing an election, the Republicans were sweeping people in from Reagan on down, and at the victory party at the Mayor's you started drinking and disappeared and three days later I got a call from the Indian Lake police you'd been found dazed, half-naked, your car stolen and your wallet and—"

"Charlotte, for Christ's sake: I didn't come close to losing that fucking election! I got sixty-four percent of the vote."

"—you gave up drinking then. 'Cold turkey.' For eighteen hours." Charlotte's laughing so hard whiskey comes out of her nose, she has to mop herself with a tissue. "Poor 'Corky.'"

Corky remembers this episode as longer, much longer, than a mere eighteen hours. But his pride's been offended—let it stand.

"That first time we met, at Troika's, you got drunk and sang some

Irish songs for us, I'll never forget—'Pawpaw,' I said, 'who *is* this?' All the Players were charmed. What a character!"

Corky says, "I don't remember that." He's set the glass on the coffee table. Gripping then his right hand with his left, to control the shakes, as he takes a drag from his cigarette.

"*I* remember," Charlotte says gaily. As a stage actress she'd had some pretensions of "using" her voice, doing operettas, she begins to sing now, wavering and off-key but to Corky's untrained ear startlingly professional—

> "*The cock crew,*
> *the sky was blue.*
> *The bells in Heaven*
> *were ringing eleven.*
> *Time for this poor soul*
> *to go to Heaven.*"

"*I* sang that? I did not."

"You certainly did. I'd never forget." Charlotte sighs, runs a hand through her hair, touches an earring. Her eyes are still moist. "You were the handsomest man I'd ever seen, up close. Even more than Braunbeck—that bastard."

Corky's touched, but winces with exaggerated pain. "'Were'—?"

"Well," says Charlotte bluntly, "—you were twenty-seven then. That was a long time ago."

Corky recalls that little song . . . oh Jesus, wasn't it one of the nursery tunes his Grandma McClure from Limerick used to sing to him? And Theresa sang it too, giving it a strong Irish inflection. The more pronounced the Irish inflection, the greater the love. *Did* he—? That night—? And a table of bemused strangers his audience, and his boss Ross Drummond sizing him up?

Maybe Corky does remember, vaguely. *The cock crew, the sky was blue* . . . Like a dream not even his own but recounted to him by another.

Charlotte says, sighing, "Yes. The handsomest man I'd ever seen, up close. And if I'd ever seen Paul Newman in person he might not have been so handsome as in his movies."

Ex-wife and ex-husband sit contemplating the rapidly receding past.

Almost twenty years ago. Twenty years! Corky's one of those American guys who never age beyond twenty, so how's this possible? And even so the "past" is flying away from us into space like distant galaxies flying away from one another, all things in the Universe flying away from one another after the Big Bang initiated Time.

Time for this poor soul to go to Heaven.

Suddenly, unexpectedly, as if she's been wrenched back into the present against her will, Charlotte says, "I almost forgot—I saw you on television, Jerome, on the six o'clock news. WWTC. My heart almost stopped . . . 'Jerome Cochrane' that silly woman called you. If I'd been prepared, I could have taped you."

Corky, swigging Diet Coke, almost chokes. "Oh, God. I don't think I want to know about this."

"Don't be silly. You were terrific as usual."

"I was . . . *terrific?*"

Charlotte hesitates. "Well, you were fine. You can *talk.*" Laughing with sudden harshness, that look in her face signaling it's another woman she's zeroing in on. "That awful Peggy Crofton! She's shameless! Hovering like a vulture outside the church, trying to get an interview with Mrs. Plummer on her very way to the cemetery—can you imagine? Asking the mother of a girl who only just committed suicide if she knows *why?* She looks young, but she's my age at least. Her face has been lifted so many times already it's a *mask.* I'd never watch WWTC, it's tabloid TV, except I was switching through the channels, I almost never watch anything more than three minutes now there's the remote control, this constant worry over Thalia has made me frantic." She lifts the glass of amber whiskey and contemplates her finely vibrating hand as if in wonder.

Corky belches something so chemical-toxic the fumes bring actual tears to his eyes. He doesn't want to think about what, confused and stammering, he might have said. Any public utterance by a politician, or even, like Corky, a guy on the periphery of political power, it's for the public record. It's *there.*

Charlotte asks, "Did *you* know, Jerome, that Thalia was involved somehow with this—this Plummer girl? They were friends? *I* didn't. All the ugly publicity about her, that terrible Marcus Steadman, the rape charges—this black girl is a friend of my daughter's? *I never knew.*"

Hesitantly, almost shyly, Corky asks, "What did I say? On the film clip?"

"Well, it was just a clip. Obviously, it had been edited. I mainly remember you saying the death was a 'tragedy' and there should be a police investigation of it. A thorough one, not just routine." Charlotte frowns, sips her drink. "I *think*. It came and went so quickly. I was in a state of shock just seeing you . . ."

Corky doesn't want to consider why his ex-wife was in a state of shock seeing him on local TV but especially he doesn't want to consider that, on TV, he seems to have asked for a "thorough" police investigation of a matter arguably not his business. How's this going to go over with Oscar Slattery, Ben Pike . . . and the rest?

Gazing at the glass of whiskey. Not seeing it, just gazing.

What they'll tell me at AA: one day at a time.

One hour at a time.

One minute at a time.

That's life!

Charlotte's talking of the Plummer death, the Plummer case. Her distress that Thalia is somehow involved, her worry that Thalia, too, is . . . suicidal. "You know, Jerome, despite the rumors, that poor girl did kill herself. There's no doubt about it."

"No doubt—?"

"She did. The Plummer family won't even allow an autopsy—I don't blame them." Charlotte grimaces, involuntarily glancing down at herself, as if imagining herself, the glory of her ripe female-mammalian flesh, eviscerated. "Brrrr! When I think of anyone *I* love—"

"Wait," Corky says, annoyed, "—how do you know Marilee Plummer killed herself 'without a doubt'? Because the coroner says so?"

"No. Because Pawpaw says so."

Pawpaw!—that ridiculous name. Here's a woman forty-six years old and her old man's in his late seventies and she's still calling him *Pawpaw*. It was worth it, Corky'd thought, going through the hell of a divorce, to get out from under a broad who calls her father *Pawpaw*.

Corky says dryly, "So how's 'Pawpaw' know? He read it in the paper?"

Charlotte sips her whiskey slowly. Licking her cherry-red luscious lips. Like a woman enjoying a secret. The drink has brought color out in her

cheeks, she's more relaxed, enjoying herself. Old times with her wayward husband. "Warren Carter's father Lyle told him, they play squash
together—you know. They've been playing squash together for fifty years
except when one or the other was in the hospital. Or, I guess, during the
war."

"Warren Carter's father told him? So what?"

"Yes, but he *really* told him. I mean—there's *no doubt*."

Warren Carter is Union City's district attorney: a moderate Republican with, it's said, actual moral convictions, principles. During the
Reagan-Bush era this is something of an eccentricity in the Republican
party, so Carter's respected, feared. He's long been a political ally, though
never publicly a friend, of Oscar Slattery and his brother William. Corky
knows that deals are constantly being made between City Hall and the
D.A.'s office, he even knows what some of these deals have been, in any
government you're obliged to trade off favors with your rivals or there's
no getting anything done. Still, he'd guess that Carter, for purely selfish
political purposes, would press for a high-profile investigation into the
Plummer death if he believed anything could be made of it: if "homicide,"
not "suicide" was a possibility. So if not, then not. Corky's relieved to
hear this, in fact.

Since Death has been floating like a black dirigible above Union City
released at about the time of the siren Corky heard on Friday morning,
ambulance rushing to a body already dead, Corky's been made to wonder
what the hell is going on at the same time uneasily sensing it might be better for him not to know.

You, Jerome: our only witness.

Well, fuck that. Here's a guy fighting the shakes, the imminent D.T.'s,
mouth parched no matter how much liquid he sloshes down it, and tomorrow evening at the ritzy Chateauguay Country Club he's got to stand up
before an audience of fifteen hundred formally dressed people and say
something warm witty uplifting original and interesting about the only
man in politics today except maybe Cuomo, Bill Bradley, Bill Clinton,
Al Gore, a very few others he actually can bring himself to contemplate
without gagging—that's enough. More than enough.

Corky shrugs. If Pawpaw says so it must be so.

And then this happens: Corky's checking his watch, knows it's time to leave Charlotte if he hopes not to be too late for the Slatterys', God damn it's already 8:08 P.M. and was he due at 8:00?—yes but if he's smart he'll push a little more on the subject of Pawpaw, say he drops by the old man's house tomorrow warming him up for a bite of $138,000—by Wednesday!—he'd better prime the pump now with Charlotte, and before leaving, too, he should call in to listen to his voice mail, what if there's an important message from Thalia but fuck it he isn't going to, fuck Thalia, and seeing this surreptitious gesture Charlotte's suddenly provoked, snatches Corky's cigarette out of his mouth and boldly takes a drag—an inhalation so deep and sensuous her breasts rise, and appear to swell; her eyes take on light, as a smoldering fire flares up when touched by oxygen. In giddy gratitude then murmuring, "Oh God! Did I need that."

Corky's shocked, and looks it. "Charlotte! What are you doing? You were so brave to quit—"

"What's the difference? *You're* smoking."

"I'm not drinking."

Charlotte laughs happily. "Jerome, you're so *funny*. I love you."

Corky's face heats though he hasn't heard this; doesn't want to have heard this. *No. Never.*

In his husbandly scolding mode, Corky says, "Cut the bullshit, Charlotte—" snatching the cigarette back from her, right out from between her lips, and she gives a shrill cry slapping at his hand, and the cigarette goes flying scattering sparks, and Corky curses and strikes her on the shoulder, not hard, with the flat of his hand, as you might discipline an obnoxious child, and Charlotte screams and punches Corky clumsily, striking his jaw. "You shit! You always play rough."

And Corky lets the woman have it in the mouth.

No: Corky restrains himself. Like a gentleman.

Breathing hard, on the brink of losing it, but managing to say calmly, "Look, sweetheart, don't provoke me."

"Don't provoke *me*, 'sweetheart.'"

Charlotte's retrieved the cigarette, she's smoking it defiantly. That tilt of the chin, that arrogance in the eyes, how like Thalia of just the evening before, taunting Corky about his girlie mags. Daughter, mother.

Fuck me, want to fuck me?

Corky swallows hard. Like a man on a high diving board, swaying in the wind. *Yes. No. Just don't. You know, it's a mistake* yet somehow the glass of Red Label is in Corky's trembling hand, somehow he's raised it to his mouth and he's drinking and oh God the first taste irradiates tongue mouth nasal passages and even his teary-rimmed eyes, his throat that's been parched all this long cruel day of mockery and deprivation.

Corky sighs. "God! Did I need that."

Charlotte's been staring at Corky amazed. There's a moment's startled almost reverent silence. Then, in breathy triumph Charlotte murmurs, her fingers closing about Corky's wrist gently, but purposefully, "Oh, Corky—I've been so *lonely*."

Shyness is clumsiness, and how suddenly shy Corky is. Kissing open-mouthed this passionate woman who's suddenly new to him, and intimidating; her very need, hunger, heat a fire he isn't sure he can quench. This warm straining flesh he knows as intimately as his own, yet doesn't: making love to Charlotte after so long is like one of those dreams of elation and terror in which you return home gradually realizing this is not your home but a simulacrum haphazardly and insufficiently willed into being by an imagination not your own.

And if not your own, whose?

They fumble at each other's clothes like kids. Ritual unzipping, unbuttoning. Careful!—don't tear. Repeated whiskey-kisses like vows of confirmation a few seconds' neglect might revoke. Kissing so much more intimate than fucking, Corky has to force himself not to think of the woman he really wants to be kissing, fucking, wouldn't want Charlotte to know, not right now. She's embracing Corky's hips, tugging at his trousers and shorts bravely burying her face in his groin *Love love love oh Corky nobody but you* and Corky's embarrassed and excited hot with urgency now his prick's hardening, he'll be O.K. And she won't ask him to put on a condom, she wants him just as he is. Asking him does he love her and Corky isn't listening, Corky's grunting, *sure*, O.K., he isn't one to talk at such a time, for Christ's sake the point of fucking *is* you don't need to talk isn't it? Trying not to think of Christina, nor of Thalia. Nor of Kiki. God damn! He's losing it. No, he's got it. He's O.K. The ridiculous leather sofa sinking and wheezing beneath them like a partly awakened third party, roused too, sexy. But leather's impractical—his knees skid.

His heated face against a cushion, the skin sticking, slapping. Fuck it! But this lovemaking is so spontaneous, so unpremeditated, thus so innocent neither can reasonably suggest they move somewhere else—to a bed, for instance. In any case it's Charlotte's prerogative as the hostess to make such a suggestion but she's too distracted to do so, lying invitingly beneath Corky, reaching up to frame his face in her beringed hands and to kiss him on the mouth, her eyes shuddering whitely upward in their sockets. Her need, her terrible need. Hungry void that must be filled.

Corky's erect cock is bouncing against his stomach, thighs, like it's alive, rod-hard. *Made me love you. Didn't want to do it.*

Charlotte's fleshy thighs part, then moistly close, Corky now kneeling clumsily between, a boy's supplicant gesture, so embraced, enclamped. He's sucking a fat goosebump of a nipple, face mashed yearning against a breast both softly flaccid and milky-stolid, you'd swear there was a milky liquid inside, fleshing out the contours of the organ as blood flushes out the contours of Corky's penis. *Did you ever want to fuck your own mother like they say you're supposed to,* Corky's roommate that brief semester at Rensselaer once asked him, with a look of bemused disdain—I *sure never did!* and Corky's wise-guy grin froze and after a moment Corky too laughed, in derision—I *sure never did, either!*

Discovering the little tinfoil packet of Trojans under their mattress, rubbing the imprint of the circle wonderingly with his thumb. Always, dirty-minded Corky seemed to know, sniggering with his friends in the boys' entryway at Our Lady of Mercy, words of precious filth *fuck cock cunt cocksucker blow-job* like the words of the rosary, if you're a Catholic kid you seemed always to have known them. Jerking off after confession, after mass. Into the toilet. Corky's milky-filmy semen. A tearing sensation like flame, then the release, the shock of it, you're never prepared. *Bless me Father for I have sinned.*

Corky has moved into his old rhythm making love to Charlotte with his instinct for what she needs, he's a good lover to any woman seeming to know what the woman needs, attentive to the subtlest exertions, responses. But he's annoyed discovering Charlotte less wet than, for all this passion, you'd think she'd be, and tighter too, that coyness that's a matter of vaginal muscles held in and resisting, or seeming to resist, inviting him to force her—just a little. *Oh! oh darling.* Every fuck a rape. But not

every rape a fuck, they say it's not sex but the desire to hurt, to humiliate, to kill. But why isn't *that* sex, too? Women like it, slammed smacked
punched kicked fucked until they scream, sometimes you'd swear they're
bleeding, so soft in there, a silky-rosy glove; something to tear. Coming
like dying: the heart kicks, stops. Then starts again, racing. That first
time, in Corky's bed in his bachelor apartment, the rich man's daughter
screaming, sobbing. The rawness of it, the terrible need, a woman could
break your spine if she was strong enough, madness rushing through her.
Praying mantis, chewing the male's head off. And the male continuing to
copulate, faster and more efficient than before. *Love love love oh Corky
yes like that: oh!*

The thick-rooted stem of his penis nudging her clit, the rest of him
deep inside her, buried to the hilt. Deep in the womb. Sucked in. His
heart expands in tenderness for her—nothing this good between the two
of them for years. Or is he drunk. The Red Label's a warm sweet mist
in his brain within minutes of his having finished his drink as if hours
of steady drinking had been economically, practicably condensed. Rarely
has Corky Corcoran made love to any woman or girl without this comforting mist in his brain. Stone cold sober you see too clearly, everything's
magnified, nerves spine ganglia glans cease functioning. Praying mantises
copulating, their heads chewed off. Nature knows best. You can't quarrel
with Nature. Over the rim of the black hole you're sucked inside and every molecule of your being destroyed so that the very fact of your extinction is itself destroyed, you're obliterated so entirely *you've never been.*

Corky works himself up to a frenzy then stops to catch his breath, this
is the rhythm Charlotte seems to need, he's gripping her soft bunchy ass in
both his hands driving himself into her with increasing force then pausing
panting for breath Jesus what if he has a heart attack! a heart attack screwing his own ex-wife! but don't think of that, now's not the time, again
working up his rhythm, like that Nautilus exercise the stair-climber, start
slow to build up fast, try to conserve your breath. Mouth-panting, and
you're finished. The trick's to breathe through the nose exclusively. The
male has to be in charge, the male's at the helm, penis like a rudder. This
old rhythm to which they're shaped like old shoes to the contours of
feet: misshapen feet, misshapen shoes. But a good fit. Corky swivelling
his hips grinding and pumping and grunting like a monkey, it's returning

to him like tissue-memory in his feet, left jab, tentative right cross when he dreams of boxing or in his fingers striking the piano's keys without pre-meditation *Glow little glowworm glimmer glimmer* no conscious mind intervening: a miracle. Stop to think and you're finished. And Charlotte too, sheer instinct, hunger. Clutching at him a panicked desperation to her cries *Oh! oh! oh!* sharp as birds' cries and her wild white-rimmed eyes flung open blind, pelvis thrusting upward to meet Corky, legs clamped around Corky's laboring ass, ankles crossed but slipping with sweat, Corky at last feels her coming like the breaking of a great wave, poised for a fraction of an instant at its crest, then breaking, a succession of breaking waves, wash-ing over him, powerful enough to wash him away.

Love love love oh Corky oh God don't leave me ever again.

Hey: it's O.K.

Do you still love me?

Sure.

Pauses dazed with exhaustion, his heart racing and breath labored, he's not a kid any longer screwing like a jackhammer, now it's his turn and he's a little scared, this tightness in his chest, the way the woman is clutching, caressing him, hands moving up and down his body, reclaiming it, like she's given birth to him, *I love you I miss you you're my husband*, Corky's cock is the fleshy rod that joins them, without it where's love? Charlotte kisses him full on the mouth, her tongue nudging his, mouths sucking, Corky responds by instinct, Corky's all instinct, stop to think and you're finished and Christ is it flattering, fucking another man's wife yet sensing the shadowy presence of no other man, no cock to compete with his own after all, *he's* the man: Corky Corcoran. What's the secret of fucking but knowing you'll never die?—Corky pushing bravely now to his own orgasm, like swimming through a chaos of frothy heaving water, trying to hold his head above the water, his mouth, bared teeth, tendons in his neck and arteries at his temples at the point of bursting, he's a bal-loon blown up to the point of bursting, forcing himself forward then sud-denly sucked forward, violently: over the rim.

Over, and out.

"What time is it?—holy Jesus!"

Corky stares at his watch. How's it come to be 11:19 P.M.?

Wakened from a groggy sleep entwined with a warm naked sleeping woman not immediately identifiable since their surroundings are wholly unfamiliar. Not the wheezing leather sofa in the "family" room he might be able to recall if he made the effort but a king-sized bed he doesn't remember crawling into. A bedside lamp, its shade askew, is on. An empty bottle of Johnnie Walker Red Label, two empty glasses are on the table. Corky's naked except for his watch reading 11:20 P.M. The sleeping woman is waking, turning to him, "Oh, Corky—don't go, yet"—he sees it's Charlotte, maybe this is a hotel room, they're still married?—maybe this is a dream, of their still being married? Corky's hoping that might be the explanation but the effect of the alcohol has waned, this explanation isn't plausible.

You shithead, now what've you done?

How're you going to get out of this, now?

Charlotte calls after him as hurriedly Corky uses the bathroom, runs cold water and splashes it onto his face, then he's back in the bedroom that's wholly unfamiliar to him and that he has no desire to examine, it's enough to know it isn't his but another man's and Corky has never in his adulterous career fucked any woman in a bedroom in a house the property of another man let alone slept with her for hours in a state of alcoholic oblivion, not just the risk of such an act but the insult: on another male's turf, spilling your semen, it's one tomcat spraying another's territory, it's *dangerous*.

Charlotte's suggesting that Corky stay the night, "Gavin" won't be home until the following afternoon, but Corky's adamant, Corky's insistent upon leaving, mildly panicked recalling he'd undressed in another room, a downstairs room, but where? Charlotte appeals to him as if in an old argument resurfacing, "—I realize you're involved with another woman, that's what I've heard, and it doesn't matter to me, I accept it, I should have accepted it while we were married, that was my mistake," wrapping an ivory silk negligee about herself, not very steady on her feet looking at Corky searchingly, and Corky's gently pushing her hands off him, what the fuck's he gotten himself into now, and drinking again, hard liquor, that's the worst disappointment of all. Panic has made him sober, stone cold sober, not a desirable state when you're bare-assed naked vulnerable as a crustacean without its shell in another man's bedroom in another man's house, the thought crosses his mind that Pierson might have a gun he, Corky, might borrow, but it's a thought too fleeting to be absorbed, in the face of Charlotte's alarming appeal that she and Corky see each other at least once a week—"I've realized how I miss you, how I love you, I *know* you but I love you, Corky—that's a true measure of love."

Corky laughs, shocked. Trying to talk sense into Charlotte without hurting her feelings, "For God's sake, Charlotte! You're married to another man, you're in love with another man, you don't mean what you're saying!"

"I'm not twenty-six years old any longer, I'm forty-six, I mean everything I say," Charlotte protests, as if her integrity has been challenged, "—and lots of things I don't say. Oh, Corky!"

"But what about Gavin? He's so much better for you than I ever was. He's decent, he's kind, he's got money—real money—"

"Oh he is, I suppose he is," Charlotte says quickly, her eyes misting over, "—he's even better for me, as a husband. But he isn't *you*."

Corky, shivering and sweating at the same time, edging toward the door, says, disbelieving, "Charlotte, look: when you had me, you hated me. And with good reason. Don't you remember?"

Charlotte wraps her arms around him and leans her head against his shoulder, clumsy in affection, giddy. "I miss hating you. I miss *you*," she says, hiccuping. "Corky, don't you feel the same way about me? I know you do!"

Corky thinks, *No. Fuck it no* but can't say such words to this woman more open to him now than she'd been with her legs spread, poor sweet Charlotte. He's been a shit to her in the past and maybe he can make it up to her in the future. Maybe.

"Charlotte, we'll talk about it some other time, O.K.? I'll call you. We can get together. Where are my fucking clothes?"

"You do love me, then? At least—a little?"

Corky kisses her roughly, missing her mouth. "Sure."

How else to be led back downstairs to his clothes, how else but to utter that word, stone cold sober.

And in the "family" room Corky dresses hurriedly for the second time in this long day stretching out of sight as to the horizon and beyond to oblivion, throwing his clothes on in undignified haste in the presence of a woman, not the woman he loves but a woman, it might be any woman, Woman. Clothing himself, shielding himself, his limp cock, from her scrutiny. What do they see, seeing us? What do they know? Corky's hands are trembling but he manages. Doesn't bother with his socks, fuck his socks, stuffs them in his coat pocket and jams his bare feet into his shoes and let's get the hell out of here.

Corky would say goodbye to Charlotte at the door but, in her extravagant mood, she insists upon following him outside to his car, wincing barefoot on the pebbled drive, leaning heavily on his arm. It's a cold night for May, dampness and mist rising from the earth. And a moon startlingly bright floating atop a crest of gauzy clouds, a pale-glowering lidless eye. Corky and Charlotte stare up at it, for a moment sobered. Charlotte whispers, "The moon's never been so close to the Earth before—has it?" Corky frowns seeing those thin gauzy strips of cloud so like smoke, pale smoke, a soul turned to smoke and blown by the wind, ascending—where?

Time for this poor soul to go to Heaven.

"Don't exaggerate," Corky says, "—we're not that important."

Corky climbs into his car, thank God for his car, *his*, he's got the key in the ignition even before Charlotte leans voluptuously through the open window to give him a last open-mouthed kiss redolent of whiskey, she's shivering happily crazy cunt naked beneath her flimsy negligee in the driveway of her $1-million split-level home at 23 Quail Ridge Pass, Chateauguay Falls, New York, forearms crossed beneath her big loose breasts supporting their weight and seeming to offer them too to Corky, to be kissed. It seems impolite to start the motor while Charlotte is kissing him, and the kiss goes on for some time.

When at last Charlotte speaks, her words seem pointedly slurred in the moonlight, as if amplified. "You *will*, Jerome? You promise?"

Corky only dimly registers this shift from "Corky" to "Jerome." And he isn't sure what the promise is. But, what the hell—"Sure, sweetheart. I'm your man."

PART IV

MEMORIAL DAY 1992

THE IMPERSONATOR

S ay this is the last day of your life, asshole: how are you going to spend it? *Stone cold sober?*

No. Yes. God damn *yes.*

I'm strong enough, I can do it.

Help me?

Waking in a shabby Days Inn at exit 14 of I-190 in a no-man's-land of fast-food restaurants, gas stations, motels, discount outlets approximately six miles north of the Union City city limits where, the night before, that's to say in the early hours of this morning, Corky'd taken a room for a rock-bottom twenty-nine dollars plus tax. Figuring no one would look for him in such a dump. No one who knew him.

Had to do it. Why?—don't ask. Just a premonition. Couldn't go home. That big echoing house, never really his. A mausoleum. What if the security system's been disconnected, what if, unarmed, he'd stepped into a trap.

Man, yo' sho is gettin parry-noid, ain't yo'!—Roscoe Beechum's mocking voice in Corky's ear.

Suddenly Corky's back in the Zanzibar, pleading. Why won't they serve him food, why not even coffee. He's a friend to blacks but the fuckers won't recognize him—they think he's *white!*

His heart's broken. His civil rights have been violated. He'll get even, somehow.

And him with $1000 in his wallet.

What am I in their eyes, a *nigger?*

Like, you could say, anybody who's fucked is a *cunt?*

Corky shudders, tries to wake up, his heart's pounding he needs to wake up to protect himself but he's paralyzed, locked in that stupor not sleep yet not full wakefulness, the side of his face pressed against a cheap chenille bedspread smelling of damp and must and it's sure to leave sharp red creases in his cheek, *Help me? help?* this state that's maybe what stroke victims experience, conscious but not-conscious, helpless hearing their loved ones debate, Should we pull the plug? Or wait? But why wait?

An organ out of the ceiling thundering Bach. The conveyor belt, the furnace doors. Afterward, smoke lifting skyward. Bone-white, mushroom-shaped.

Scratching his balls, which feel tender. Cool-clammy, like the circulation's dead. Do these things shrink? Prostate "trouble," it's a matter of time. Hey: a woman was stroking him there just a few hours ago . . . or was that a dream?

A bad dream.

How many years of his life he'd used to wake up, that's to say be awakened, by those violent hard-ons, as a kid. A snake down there growing out of his groin, independent-minded. Urgent as the worst need to piss, jerking himself off in a few deft angry strokes saliva drooling down his chin like jism *Bless me Father for I have sinned* forever and ever Amen.

Just those words *Bless me Father for I have sinned* whispered lewdly among the guys in Corky's class, even lining up for communion on special Holy Days when the whole school went, would set them off. Wild helpless giggling, choking. *Bless me Father!*

Except it doesn't go on forever. It's rare now. And wet dreams, rare now. Next birthday he's forty-four if he lives that long, beyond that fifty which frankly he can't imagine, not Corky Corcoran. Nobody teaches you how to grow up. By the time you get where you're going the rest of them are gone, there's no *there*.

Dying for a cigarette!—so he's in this dream (except he seems to know it *is* a dream, thus won't work) lighting up, slow deep drags into his lungs and the tremulous wait for the nicotine to hit. Like the heroin rush: you're Jesus' son.

Hey: d'you love me?

Oh, lover. Oh God.

He's waking. He'll be O.K. Nobody's in the room and nobody's at the door which is chain-latched as well as locked. That rumbling rackety sound—must be I-190, or the wind.

Last night, a pint of Jack Daniel's by moonlight. Parked in his car in a secret place in a tunnel of tall trees to the very horizon. The moon's craters winked. The light became too bright—blinding.

You don't want her to see you're here, mister? Do you?

Sweet Christ, no. Have mercy.

Corky's waking. Through the gash in what appears to be a wall (in fact it's a strip of window jaggedly bared where draw-drapes on their jerry-built runner don't quite close) he sees suddenly, at an upward angle where the sky should be, the uniform corrugated gray of cement that hasn't set right. That ripply-hard surface that burns your ass: you pay the fucking contractor to do a professional job, he fucks up and there's a hassle over the estimate.

But, no: that *is* the sky. Paved over.

Something special about today, fuck it the sky should be *blue*.

Something special Corky's supposed to do today: what?

Follow through on his deals. Don't bullshit. Name your price, refuse to go any higher and refuse to accept any lower. Anybody's dealing with Corcoran, Inc., he's dealing with a real pro.

A sudden memory: riding high in the jolting cab of the cement-mixer truck heavy as a tank. Tim Corcoran behind the wheel grinning down at him. That grinding deafening noise, rotary motion of the wet cement in the rear of the truck. Say the mixer breaks down or even slows there's the danger the cement will harden and the truck will be thrown off balance and overturn but *Don't be afraid, Jerome, Daddy won't let that happen.*

A nice memory. Corky's smiling in his sleep. Tears stinging the corners of his eyes but he's smiling, he's happy. *Daddy? Daddy don't go. Wait.*

Here's a nice memory, too: even before *Homo sapiens* over two hundred thousand years ago there was a species of apeman who buried their dead with ceremony. Not just dragging off the putrid corpses, or dumping them. Or eating them. But taking the time to dig real graves and laying the dead inside and arranging little treasures like flint arrowheads around their bodies, choice haunches of meat, mysterious stones—trinkets. And flat, heavy stones placed at the heads of the graves to protect the dead from scavengers, evil spirits. To commemorate the dead. Corky read this in a paperback titled *Mysteries of Human Evolution: From Where, to Where?*

Maybe they weren't *Homo sapiens* but, fuck it, the apemen *cared*.

Corky's sobbing, Corky's in mortal terror nobody's going to *care*.

Sobbing dry-eyed and without sound like the dry heaves and this at last wakes him up: he sits up with a jolt, he's been lying sideways in his sour-smelling underwear across a motel bed, dim as an undersea cave in here except for the gash at the window, at first he doesn't know where the fuck he is except he's not in his own bed, then he remembers, or starts to. By his watch it's 7:19 A.M. Thank God, early. He'll need every hour of this day, he knows. Out on the expressway traffic is sporadic—not a continuous roar but *thrumps* of vibrating sound. Corky shakes his head to get the kinks out of his neck and that's a mistake—his hangover hits him like lightning. His eyes pop like those plastic eyes in a joke shop. But he's O.K. He's going to be O.K.

To prove it, Corky gets down on the carpet (wincing seeing it's stained: God damn) and does twenty quick push-ups. Well, almost twenty. On his back then and tries for twenty sit-ups. He's winded, his head's reeling. O.K., enough. Tomorrow morning, Tuesday, a weekday, he'll check himself in at the Alcoholics Anonymous Reception Center in the rear of Union City General Hospital. No "Jerome Andrew Corcoran" if you're "anonymous." Right?

Soon as he enrolls, he'll tell Christina. How much she knows about his drinking problem he doesn't know but the woman's obviously smart enough to know he's got a problem. *He can blame his drinking for the crude way he's treated her.*

Groping for his near-empty pack of Camels on the bedside table, on his way swaying, head down, into the bathroom he's already got one lit and while pissing puffs deeply and God-damn gratefully and even while taking a fast clumsy harried shower he leaves the cigarette burning on the top of the toilet tank where, when he feels the need, he can reach it.

Then, this: at an International House of Pancakes on North Decatur Boulevard just outside the city limits where also, among the mostly families with children, he figures he'd never be sighted by anyone who knows him, Corky surprises himself devouring a gut-stretching breakfast of a half dozen banana pancakes so soaked in blueberry syrup they resemble sponges, scrambled eggs and Canadian bacon and butter-soaked toast, a tall glass of orange juice and several cups of black coffee—no idea he's so ravenous with hunger until he starts eating, then almost can't stop. And he's smoking too, and scanning the *Journal*. Actually has to open his belt a notch, and the girl who's been waiting on him, platinum-blond with brown-penciled eyebrows and funky-slutty makeup like Madonna, shakes a forefinger at him with such flirty familiarity Corky's flattered as hell. He laughs, rubbing his stomach ruefully, saying, "—Must be I'm a guy who can't say 'no,'" and the waitress murmurs suggestively, "*That* must get you in a lot of trouble, mister." Corky eyes her frankly—pert little jacked-up breasts, cute little ass even in the sappy uniform, fantastic legs—so she's flattered, too; young, but practiced at this kind of banter with solitary male customers at least like Corky giving a signal, by his clothes if not his bristly jaws, of being a generous tipper, and of not being obviously nuts.

Only a year or two ago Corky might've pursued this a little more, got the girl's telephone number, assuming she'd give it out to a stranger—surprising how many of them do: *he* was a girl or woman in such circumstances, he'd never—and see what might come of it. But not any longer. No thanks.

He's trying not to think about last night. What the consequences will be. The details of what he and Charlotte actually did are woozy—like a film fast-forwarded, without sound, as soon as Corky gave in and picked up that glass of Red Label. God damn! It's the Irish weakness, you lose control completely, wind up doing the exact opposite of what you want to do. Fuck fuck *fuck* Charlotte for getting him to drink, seducing him. Saying she misses him, she loves him—"Oh, Christ." Is that possible? And what's *he* supposed to do about it?

A new concept of alimony, that's for sure. Fucking your own ex-wife, like in installments.

And standing up Vic and Sandra for the second evening in a row. Is he crazy? Is he out of control completely? What's he going to tell them, this time?

All like a dream once he started drinking again like *it happened*, not *I did it*. Still less *I'm responsible*.

After leaving Charlotte, Corky's intentions were certainly to return home. Yet somehow he'd ended up, at midnight, drinking from a pint of Jack Daniel's bought in a Chateauguay Falls liquor store, in his car parked secretly in the street outside the Kavanaughs' house. He can't remember making any decision to drive into the village—Christina and Harry live in the "historic" village of Chateauguay Falls, a few miles from the recently developed suburban subdivision of Quail Ridge Hollow—but he remembers shutting off his ignition, switching off his lights. He remembers sipping from the pint and staring at the facade of the big white brick colonial with the dark shutters—dark green, dark blue, black?—stark as a photograph in black and white in the glaring moonlight. Once, a single time only, he'd been a guest in that house: a large New Year's Day reception. Christina Kavanaugh shaking his hand, lightly kissing his cheek—Corky Corcoran, one of eighty or ninety people. Harry Kavanaugh, the retired federal judge, in his motorized wheelchair, gaunt-cheeked, graying, a ruin of a handsome man, his eyes still sharp, bright, inquisitive, reaching out to shake Corky's hand briskly. They weren't friends, scarcely knew each other, but wished each other Happy New Year vigorously.

Last night, at midnight, most of the house was darkened. A single lighted room on the second floor. *Christina, awake and alone thinking of him. He knew.*

Then, this: except, did it happen?—or did Corky dream it?

The moon wavered like a swaying head, the sparely spaced streetlamps blurred, Corky was blinking astonished as the moon grew brighter and brighter and blinding and suddenly—"What's your business here, mister?"—a private security cop shining his flashlight in Corky's eye cautious and even courteous as no real cop, still less no Union City cop, would be, and Corky stammered, "Th-there's a woman in there, in that house . . . I don't know, officer, I'm just here," his face hot and his voice wan, shamed, resigned, none of his old belligerence, nor even his pride. The cop examined Corky's wallet, his ID, not knowing the name "Jerome Andrew Corcoran," thank God, asked him a few questions which Corky stumblingly answered, this private cop a young guy scarcely thirty who'd obviously never had to use his gun and wanted no trouble that could be avoided or that might, this being the affluent white suburbs, result in a lawsuit; and no doubt he was embarrassed too at the spectacle of a guy Corky's age sitting out in his car like a lovesick kid. Saying, "You don't want this woman to know you're here, do you, mister?"

No, officer. Thank you, officer.

So Corky'd driven sheepishly off, God-damn grateful not to be run in

to the local police station where he'd've had to take, and flunk, a Breathalyzer test, for sure. God-damn grateful it was only a private cop not a
Chateauguay Falls cop, a probable arrest.

Following that, his nerves shot, Corky couldn't drive all the way home
to Summit Avenue. That big empty echoing house. Checked into the Days
Inn at one A.M. and now at eight A.M. he's here reading the *Journal* in a
booth in the smoking section of a tacky International House of Pancakes
on North Decatur, gut still straining against his loosened belt. He's dropping ash on the newspaper's pages anxious and disappointed there's little
news of interest to him, no new developments in the Plummer case, a brief
item on page five that a "small fire of unknown origin" was reported the
night before in the African-American First Church of the Evangelist on
East Huron—Marcus Steadman's church—obvious arson, but minimal
damage, quickly put out by a caretaker. There's a notice on the obituary
page of Marilee Plummer's funeral, and the same photograph the *Journal*
has used before. A private funeral, attended by family and friends of the
deceased. Last rites at the Covenant Evangelical Free Church, burial in
Mount Moriah Cemetery.

On the *Journal*'s front page the big feature is Memorial Day—the oldest veteran to be "marching" (in a wheelchair) in this afternoon's parade
sponsored by the Mohawk County American Legion is ninety-six years
old, a U.S. Army corporal who'd served in World War I, face like a desiccated turtle's and skeletal hand raised in a military salute. Eyes so empty-
looking they might be blind but he's a feisty old guy, you got to give these
old, ancient men and women credit, hanging *on*.

This year's veterans' parade will be the first since 1919 to follow a cur-
tailed route, participation in and attendance at the annual parades have
been in decline since the early 1980s, so instead of a three-mile march
from the World War I Memorial in Union Square, downtown, to the Soldiers' and Sailors' Monument in Lake Erie Park, the parade will begin
at a smaller park a mile and a half east of Lake Erie Park and continue
as usual along that stretch of Union Boulevard. And there will be fewer
units in the parade, fewer veterans marching. Asked why this is so, the
president of the Mohawk County American Legion, a sixty-two-year-old
veteran of the Korean War, is quoted, "The old traditions are dying out, I

guess. Younger people today, they get war on television and in the movies and it isn't real to them, so veterans aren't real to them."

Sad, thinks Corky. Thinking of his father, *his* war.

Thinking too, Is anybody *real* to anybody else?

Quickly skimming the rest of the news. Governor Cuomo, the New York State Legislature, pollution control laws, the old capital punishment debate—the legislators, reflecting the "will of the people," vote *yes* to restore it; Cuomo vetoes the bill. Next governor, if he's a Republican, will be pro–capital punishment, the electric chair will be reclaimed. There's an article Corky'd take the time to read if he had the time on the Justice Department auditing the United Way, including the United Way of Union City—if it turns out the local branch is crooked, too, that means Corky Corcoran's been a sucker, every year he gives $1000 to the United Way courtesy of Corcoran, Inc. It's only one of the charities and organizations Corcoran, Inc., gives money to, all of them local, most of them headed, like the United Way, by people Corky knows, sure he wants to impress them—who doesn't want to impress, being "charitable"?—but he's naturally generous, too. God damn, if he's been taken by these bastards! One of the local ex-officers is a member of the U.C.A.C. and a guy Corky knows, would've said he trusts, here in the *Journal* it says a county grand jury is convening to consider bringing criminal charges against him for transferring $288,000 from a spin-off United Way organization to his own banking account to pay off a mortgage on his house. Corky whispers aloud, "God *damn*."

The one thing that pisses him, is being a sucker, or even *seeming* a sucker.

And more front-page news of this remote country Bosnia—"Serbs" attacking, "Muslim Slav forces" seeking retaliation. "Neo-Nazi" youth culture, vandalism, terrorism in the old East Germany. "Palestinian Kills Rabbi in Gaza—Israelites Retaliate." "Haitian Capital's Worst Week of Violence." There's a city in Brazil where the population has increased eleven-fold since 1940, there's "economic and moral despair" in the old Soviet Union, there's a "renewal of township violence" in South Africa. So much bad news from all around the world would cheer Corky up, *you're an American you're living in the best God-damned country in the world,* except there's rotten news at home too, he isn't even going to read about drug killings, shootouts in New York, Los Angeles, Chicago, you name it, he isn't going to read another fucking human-interest feature on AIDS, or the homeless, or battered children. It's like prodding an aching tooth, to scan the financial section, yes but he can't resist, it's like looking at your X rays dreading the fatal shadow in the lungs, dreading headline news of his asshole investments, asshole big dreams, Greenbaum's ponderous Jew-frog face appears fleetingly before him, there's a guy who got Corky Corcoran's number immediately: *sucker.* Quarterly losses for Delta, United, Chrysler, GM, Dow Chemical—Corky doesn't own stock in any of these, so feels a stab of satisfaction. And Sears: Jesus, can Sears go under? *Sears?* Corky winces seeing this outfit he'd owned stock in not long ago, "American Health Laboratories" they call themselves, is pleading guilty to defrauding government health insurance programs making false claims for tests measuring cholesterol and iron, might be indicted for negligence resulting in hundreds of heart patients' deaths—"The cocksuckers." On the advice of a broker-friend Corky bought 200 shares of stock in the company at twenty-eight dollars which turned out to be the high, almost at once it started going down and Corky hung on like a dope finally bailing out at nine dollars—remembers those days vividly, around the time Thalia was having trouble with that psychopath stalking her.

Much of the *Journal*'s politics, like TV these days. The presidential election's over five months away but there's this feverish interest in it, Corky's in a fever too, or would be if he had time to think about it right now. Damn, that shit with "Gennifer" Flowers really hurt Clinton, makes a fool of him if nothing else—a cunt's got no power except to throw shame on a man, that's *her* power. Corky reads there's a mood of "skepticism" in the country, there's a "widespread voters' revolt" in the offing, polls show that Americans are "fed up" with their politicians. Yet, also in the polls, voters still favor George Bush over Bill Clinton by a big majority. Clinton will win the Democratic presidential nomination but won't win the election—it's possible he won't get many more votes, if as many, as this weirdo out of nowhere who's never been elected to any public office in his life, Ross Perot. What a humiliation for the Democrats! Another Republican sweep! The shits could run Reagan again, even Nixon—they'd win. Corky's sick reading such crap, by November second he'll really be sick.

Here's George Bush on the front page of the *Journal* giving a speech at the U.S. Naval Academy in Annapolis in praise of "jobs, family, peace, and the need to maintain the world's highest standards of military might." Here's fucking Quayle on page three saying the same thing at the Air Force Academy in Pueblo, Colorado. The lead editorial—who writes this shit, anyway? Corky knows most of the *Journal* editors, they seem like reasonable men—is a MEMORIAL DAY SALUTE to all veterans past present and future of all American wars and a special salute to President George Bush for his "decisive, inspiring leadership" in Operation Desert Storm where American military power not only ruled the day but made such a powerful impression on the Soviets, *the USSR's disintegration thus the defeat of world communism was assured by it.*

Corky crumples the paper, lets the pages scatter in the booth. Knows, just knows, in his gut, that Clinton won't win the election in November, the Blue Jays won't win the American League championship in October. *He's* fucked. He *knows.*

Then, this: on his way out of the International House of Pancakes Corky goes to pay his bill seeing the cashier and his waitress whispering, giggling together casting him significant glances, he's flattered but a little uneasy, what's up? His waitress doesn't even know yet the size of the tip he's left for her, a five-dollar bill under his coffee cup, more than twice what she's probably expecting, so that isn't it. Corky pays his bill, takes a toothpick to clean the worst crud out of his teeth, and still these flirty broads are eyeing him so he gives them a quizzical look, and the one who's the cashier, a plumpish-pretty woman in her mid-thirties, says, "—Oh, mister, we're just wondering: who *are* you? We saw you on TV yesterday we *think*—"

Must be, Corky's expecting this. Giving the girls a wry-resigned smile, already halfway to the door, "Sorry, you're mistaking me for some local shithead politician, it's always happening. *I'm* a private citizen."

And so right out the door, toothpick in his mouth. And these sweet dumb broads blinking after him now *really* not knowing what to think.

Then, this: at 8:25 A.M. finally arriving home at the house on Summit Avenue he's been dreading, a tightness in his chest as he exits from the Fillmore west a mile on Seneca and across Ninth Street into Maiden Vale—

that abruptly, you're *in* it: this old prestigious neighborhood like an island in Union City where the houses are large and stately and many of them of "historical" significance, the lots too large, deep, artfully landscaped, and the property and school taxes reflect these facts—and so along Summit Park which is looking brilliantly green, sumptuous after a season of rain, Corky passes the Museum of Fine Arts, the Annandale Foundation for Medical Research, a Congregationalist church all white floating like something in a dream this misty-porous morning, then Corky's "neighbors" whose names he barely knows, these handsome old houses overlooking the park, each with ten-foot wrought-iron fences or brick or stone walls and state-of-the-art security systems just like his own. Homesick, Corky's coming home. Seeing his home, the home that's *his*, he feels a stab of angry melancholy like he's been cheated, only doesn't know why, or by who. *I want my real home, where the fuck is it!*

And pulling into his driveway he sees a UCPD squad car parked in front of the house—"Oh, Christ."

Something has happened to Thalia.

Corky brakes to a lurching stop, climbs out of the Caddy sick and shaking and there's Budd Yeager looking at him, hand raised in greeting, a guarded smile like you'd give somebody you like well enough but might have to hurt. Corky sees that Yeager isn't just in the act of descending the front steps like he's rung the doorbell and given up waiting for an answer, he seems to have been just standing there beneath the portico, waiting. No reason for him to assume Corky will be pulling into the driveway, he's just waiting.

Yeager calls out, "Hey Corky, how's it going?" giving a forced-cheery tone to this encounter but Corky's unable to smile back, anxious eyes snatching at Yeager's. Corky can hardly stammer, "What's w-wrong?"

They're shaking hands. Corky's begun to sweat. He knows, just knows, it's Thalia: she's killed herself. With his Luger. That's it.

Yeager's volunteered to come over personally to tell Corky the bad news. They're poker buddies, that's the connection? Corky stares seeing this bullet-headed guy staring at him calculated and regretful and Corky's thinking he's never hated anybody's guts more than he hates Yeager's. "—What's wrong?"

Thinking, even in this panic, If he doesn't want us to go inside, sit down, it might not be bad news. Not the worst kind of bad news.

And there's a younger cop, in uniform, in the squad car, behind the wheel. Listening to the radio, not looking at Corky. What's this mean? They don't expect him to faint? Have a bad reaction?

Seeing how scared Corky is, Yeager lays his hand, warm and meaty, on Corky's shoulder to comfort him. His smile's more quizzical now, bemused. "I don't know, Corky," he says, "—*you* tell me. Some friends are a little worried about you lately, that's all."

"Worried about me? What the fuck? Who?"

"They think you've been acting strange, the last couple of days. Not yourself, y'know?" Yeager shrugs to indicate *he* isn't one who's concerned. Doesn't know anything about it.

Corky's asking. "What the hell do you mean, Budd?" like this is a preposterous exchange. Like he's close to being seriously insulted. "What's going on?"

Yeager's looking thoughtfully at Corky. Outweighs him by forty pounds at least. A chesty bull-necked guy with pewter-gray eyes and pewter-gray hair so short it looks almost shaved, and that blunt hard head he could use, like a pro wrestler, for ramming an opponent in the gut and feeling no pain. You'd think a UCPD detective wearing an off-the-rack brown suit from Macy's, cheap flashy fake-leather shoes, would be intimidated by a big Georgian Colonial house on Summit Park but Yeager isn't, much. *Don't bullshit me, Corcoran. Come clean.*

At the same time, Corky wants to think they're friends. That sweet way, the other day, at the U.C.A.C., his hand clamping down on Corky's shoulder, he'd slipped $900 into Corky's pocket for a $780 debt. One man to another. Cutting Greenbaum out. See?—*we're* brothers.

But Corky *is* scared. A cop can pull his gun and shoot you dead and who's to say it wasn't self-defense? or he thought it was self-defense, seeing you reach inside your coat to pull your gun? and maybe providing the gun for you, fingerprints and all, after you're dead? and a history of the gun? And two cops make one eyewitness to what happened.

Budd Yeager laughs as if he can read Corky's mind. Strolls away casually to look at Corky's car, it's a cop's second nature to examine things without even seeming to know he's doing so, and a car like this Cadillac De Ville naturally draws attention—the windshield cracked like a spiderweb, the crumpled front fender and part of the bumper, numerous scratches and scrapes on the elegant cocoa-and-cream finish. Corky's shamed as if he's dropped his trousers in public. Yeager says conversationally, "—Looks like you've had some bumpy rides lately, Corky, Eh? And flowers—" he's peering into the back seat, "—for Marilee Plummer, maybe? I heard you were out there yesterday."

"Out where?"

"At the cemetery." Yeager pauses, glancing over at Corky. "At the funeral, then the cemetery. Were you invited by the family?"

"No."

"You just went?"

"I just went."

"You were at the morgue, too? Asking about the coroner's report?"

"What's this, Yeager? An interrogation?"

Corky's getting pissed. He's scared, and excited, and sweating inside his clothes. Now he knows it isn't Thalia, and he isn't going to be arrested—if they'd come for that, the other cop wouldn't just be sitting on his ass in the squad car—the sight of Budd Yeager just *looking* at Corky's car, standing there in Corky's driveway, sets him off. Now he realizes people have been spying on him, reporting on him to one another, maybe laughing at him!

"Hey c'mon, Corky," Yeager says, surprised, smiling like Corky's the one being unreasonable, "—why'd anybody interrogate *you?* This is just a visit. Don't be an asshole."

"*I'm* an asshole? What about you, Yeager?"

Corky's so nervous by now, lighting a cigarette he lets the burning match get blown from his fingers to the ground. Fuck it, he's losing it. He's having a caffeine reaction, all that black coffee. Must've drunk six cups.

Yeager says, protesting, "I'm just an intermediary. Hell, I'm a friend. You're in some kind of trouble, or hassle—I'd like to know." He's back beside Corky, eyeing him curiously. Six feet tall, with that bull neck, pitted cheeks, gray eyes—a man who makes you want to know what's on his mind. Just the fact he *exists* in proximity to you, you want to know. But saying unexpectedly, frowning, "Hey, I thought you gave up smoking, Corky?"

Corky's surprised at this remark then remembers how, a few years ago, at one of Oscar's Friday-night poker games, he and Yeager got to talking seriously about giving up smoking: Yeager'd given up too, after twenty years of three packs a day. He'd seen his father die of lung cancer.

Jesus, the guy remembers: maybe he *is* my friend?

"Yeah, well. I started again. Temporarily."

"Something going on? You're worried about something?"

"I just don't like being interrogated, Budd. You can relate to that, right?"

"It's just a friendly inquiry, Corky. Some things we've been hearing—"

Corky says, "Fuck it, what things? I feel sorry for the girl, I go the funeral, I don't even *go* to the funeral I sit outside in my car, in the street! I go to the cemetery—so what? I didn't know her but she was a friend of my stepdaughter's and I felt sorry for her, that's all. That's *all*."

"Corky, why're—"

"I *wasn't* fucking her, or any of them," Corky says angrily, "—I have my own personal private life, I'm maybe going to get married—remarried— sometime—it's my own business, right?"

"Sure, Corky. That's fine. But—"

"Whatever that asshole at the morgue told you—what a creep! what a grade-A jerk-off cocksucker creep!—don't believe it. He wouldn't know his ass from a hole in the ground. And your buddy Beck—what's *he* been saying? I stopped at Pendle Hill Village to see what was going on, I didn't know whose place it was, for sure I didn't know Marilee Plummer lived there—I didn't know *her*. It was just an accident, me stopping there. I admit, I was poking my nose in where it wasn't wanted—a dumb-fuck thing to do, but I was curious. I'm an elected city official, you guys are accountable to me. I might be the next president of the City Council. I'm fucking *interested* in what's going on in this fucking city."

Corky's been advancing on Budd Yeager who's been staring at him bemused and mildly apprehensive as a German shepherd might be mildly apprehensive, if only out of disbelief, of a feisty little dachshund snapping at his knees. Yeager says, "Why're you getting your back up, Corky? This is in your own best interest. You seem a little excitable."

Corky says, "Fuck you, I'm not excitable! These are my premises. This is my private property you're on. What'll the neighborhood think, I'm being arrested? On my front lawn? You saw me come home just now, I didn't get home last night, I'm under a lot of pressure, it's a family crisis and nobody's business—" A new, infuriating thought occurs to Corky. "—This bitch Kiki, she's in on it, too?"

"Who?"

Corky thinks better of this. Fuck it you never give a cop information unless he already has it. He says, quickly backpedaling, "The thing is, Budd, I'm in a rush right now. I've got appointments. Those flowers in the car—no, they're not for who you said, they're for an aunt of mine in the hospital. A fucking *nun*. In Holy Reedemer. You want to check? You doubt me, you want to check? I'm going to see my uncle who lives in Irish Hill, right now—Sean Corcoran—and take him to the park, to the Memorial Day service. That's a crime?" Corky's speaking so loudly, the young cop in the squad car is watching him now. "You want to give me a fucking Breathalyzer test?"

Even in the midst of the running at the mouth Corky's thinking how in other circumstances he'd welcome Yeager, invite him and the young cop in, offer them something to drink—beer for Yeager if he's off duty, coffee for the kid if he's on. The Corky Corcoran Yeager knows, or thinks he knows. This nerved-up unshaven guy with the shakes, bloodshot eyes, all but ordering a police officer and old poker buddy off his property, who's *he?*

Guilty as hell. Guilty of what?

Guilty, and needing to be punished.

So Corky tries a new tack, relenting, half-apologetic, as frank as he can manage, he knows it's going O.K. when the young cop turns back to the radio, and Yeager nods, frowning and sympathetic—"Budd, it's true I'm a little rattled right now. You caught me at a bad time. A family crisis—my stepdaughter, my ex-wife. Nothing to do with any kind of police business, absolutely not. This stepdaughter of mine, my ex-wife—" telling Yeager a vague confused incredulous hurt resentful story meant to evoke shared indignation; man-to-man stuff—*my stepdaughter, my ex-wife*—the cunts are wearing us out, doing us in; isn't Yeager a veteran of the divorce court himself, for sure he can relate to this. And, Christ knows, the essence of what Corky is saying is true. "My ex-wife, did you ever meet her?—no?—Charlotte Drummond, Ross Drummond's daughter—God-damned confused bitch wanted the divorce, now she thinks it's a mistake, *I* don't know, maybe she doesn't think it's a mistake, I can't figure her—I'm a shit whatever I do, or don't do—" Once Corky gets talking, talking and gesturing, it's like this other self takes over, he'll be O.K. now he's more in control, and bullshitting another guy always gives pleasure. Like making a political speech, you shuffle around truths and part-truths and what comes out *is* true, yet isn't—just talking, gesturing, grinning, and "making eye contact" makes it phony somehow.

Still, Corky wonders how much Yeager knows. Yeager and anybody else. He did break into Thalia's apartment the other night—maybe it *was* reported? Maybe Esdras or his wife did get a look at him, could identify him? Is that possible?

And vindictive Kiki—Corky wouldn't put it past her, to make trouble for him. Maybe she has reported him to the police, for attempted rape? *Actual* rape? Is that possible?

But Yeager seems to be listening to Corky sympathetically, uncritically. With a poker player, even a medium-level player like Yeager, you never can tell absolutely. But Corky thinks it's O.K. They talk for maybe twenty minutes, out on Corky's front step. It's one of those misty spring days, a silvery sheen to the air, low visibility but a wind picking up off the lake—the sky could be blown clear of rain clouds. Rain's predicted for this afternoon, for the parade, but this is western New York, weather can change from hour to hour depending upon the wind. Corky's feeling better now, and hopeful. Seeing that Budd Yeager who's got a reputation as a hard-nosed son of a bitch is treating him with respect. That bemused edge to his smile, like he knows more than he's letting on, and knows Corky knows—but, hell, that's Yeager's style. You don't get to be UCPD chief of detectives for being a Boy Scout.

Corky's feeling good too about the house, the lawn—*he* might look like hell at the moment, and his car a bit beat up, but this is a terrific Maiden Vale house he isn't inviting Budd Yeager inside of, proof if further proof's required, that Corky Corcoran has really made it in this town. Even his lawn, *his* lawn, that he's never so much as walked across to the sidewalk, let alone mowed, or raked, or fertilized, or planted things in, or trimmed them—Luigi's Lawn Service takes care of all that, and not cheaply—looks terrific. Budd Yeager, a lieutenant on the force, drawing a salary of under $50,000, living probably in some tacky neighborhood like Mount Moriah, can appreciate Corky's achievement, right? And his rank?

Corky isn't going to ask, though, why Yeager slipped him $900 instead of $780. Why the careless-seeming generosity. There might be a purpose, and there might not. It's small potatoes. Don't push it.

Never ask a cop a question to get him thinking.

Nor ask who's been worrying about Corky enough to enlist Budd Yeager to drop by off duty. Must be Oscar, who else but the boss hearing from Vic *Corky Corcoran's been behaving strangely lately*—two nights in a row he didn't show up at Vic's and Sandra's where he's never missed an invitation in all their years of friendship.

Nearing nine A.M. and Yeager's on his way. Corky's affable enough now he's calmed down considerably, and the men have been joking together, they're going to part on friendly terms but Corky wants to get on with the morning, needs to get inside the house. (Needs to use the toilet, for one thing. Jesus!) So he shakes hands with Yeager, each says he hopes he'll be seeing the other soon, it's time for another poker night, right? And Corky like the lord of the manor is walking Yeager to the squad car. And Yeager's about to climb inside but pauses, shaking his head, a sudden grin signaling Corky this is a joke, this is far out, don't blame *me*. "One more thing, Corky."

"Sure."

"You'll laugh like hell it's fucking weird, Corky."

"I will?"

"—Not a charge or anything, not even a complaint just a—what you'd call a rumor. I don't even remember who I heard it from exactly but it's making the round of the Department, you know how news travels—"

"What news?"

"People saying there's this spade down on Welland making out like you were down there yesterday—impersonating a UCPD undercover detective." Yeager laughs a hoarse phlegmy cough but isn't looking at Corky.

For a beat Corky isn't actually sure he's heard this.

"I was—what?"

Says Yeager amiably, "Like I said, Corky—it's not a charge or anything. It's nothing anybody's taking seriously except it got passed along, I thought you might like to know. Weird, huh?"

"*I was impersonating a UCPD undercover detective?*"

Now Yeager does glance at Corky, steely ghost-eyes the color of his crewcut and that kind of skin that looks like beneath the surface layer it's metal. "Hell, just some spade shooting off his mouth," Yeager says, "—proprietor of a nigger dive called 'Zanzibar.' You ever heard of it, or him?"

2

THE KISS

Those years. He believed mystery inhabited her body and that she like the priests was the custodian of secrets no words could express. And then when he was older, after his father's death, he understood that the mystery was her very body and that she, whom others called Theresa but whom he called Mommy, was as helpless in the face of that mystery as he who was her son born of that body. And that the words they were obliged to speak—Theresa, even before the death, had a way of talking in wild skittering rifts punctuated with laughter like icicles breaking that made you shiver: you laughed with her not knowing why—were inadequate to convey or even to suggest that mystery. As that afternoon she came to take Jerome out of school offering no explanation to the startled nuns except *it's time* and by Greyhound bus they fled to the countryside north of Indian Lake rural scrubland in those days where there was at first the vague hope of staying with relatives Theresa trusted not to betray them, then did not trust, the fear that these relatives (whom Jerome did not know, was never even to glimpse) would call the Corcorans or worse yet the police or even the men who pursued them to murder them. *Don't show your face*, Theresa warned him—*you have your father's face.* And there was a day and a night of hiding. By day at the rear of the Indian Lake Free Library in an aged clapboard house where there were rust-stained toilet facilities mother and son could use and where the elderly wall-eyed librarian was too frightened of Theresa's hard bright lipsticked smiles and stony serenity to eject them except when the library closed at 5 P.M. of a windy thunderous April day. Theresa whispered to the old woman *All right: but if you tell them we've been here you'll regret it!* By night yet more vividly as the boy was to remember on top of a roof, out-of-doors as in a child's dream where wishes come true but are not as you'd expected—*They won't find us here, nobody will find us here, but hurry!* From somewhere, a quart bottle of syrupy-sweet Mogen David wine, a crackling bag of potato chips, and what Theresa called her "meds"—the chunky pills that, taken several times a day, kept her bright, alert, optimistic and serene yet at the same time suspicious of all strangers and cunning with the logic of the desperate-doomed thus capable at least temporarily (even Theresa did not imagine their escape would be permanent) of eluding the murderers who pursued not so much Theresa the widowed wife of Tim Corcoran as twelve-year-old Jerome who was Tim Corcoran's only child. The building to which Theresa brought them by chance, it had to be by chance since she knew nothing of Indian Lake so far as Jerome could determine though pretending otherwise for his sake, was a derelict warehouse of three floors with a fire escape that swung like an amusement ride as they climbed, Theresa pushing Jerome up before her *Hurry! Go on! It's safe for us!* The roof opened up flat, puddled with rainwater, encrusted with the bird droppings of decades. A harsh wet rain blew. But it was already dusk, and they could not be seen, Theresa was right, they *were* safe. She claimed to have been in this place before claiming that Daddy had brought her here to prepare her and there was a shelter atop the roof which in fact there might once have been, for rotted boards with protruding spikes, torn strips of tarpaper, crates, barrels were strewn about. A rich fecund smell of rotting leaves, the wind in the trees roaring like a freight train. Its loudness hypnotic, reassuring. Theresa laughed and scolded cajoling Jerome into helping her fix a makeshift shelter for the night out of the debris. An upended barrel, propped-up boards. Tarpaper softly pliant enough to be, if not torn, bent by hand. Overhead high clouds were blown wild, scattered like strips of bright rag. Rain came in gusts but sometimes the moon was visible, like a staring eye. Theresa prayed rapidly and carelessly as if saying the rosary to get the rosary said and held Jerome warning *Don't let the cold get inside you, honey!* She drank from the bottle of Mogen David then pressed it to Jerome's lips and he lifted it and drank from it thirstily seeming to know when in the morning the world returned he would tell Theresa frankly and bluntly and unpityingly she was crazy, there was nobody after them, he would himself make the telephone call from town (the phone to be answered at once by Aunt Frances, sleepless with worry about them) to bring them back to Union City but that night he believed, he understood completely and unquestioningly *Don't let the cold get inside you* hunched beneath the tarpaper as Theresa moaned and rocked from side to side holding him in her thin, strong arms, and kissed him wetly, hotly, with a terrible hunger, on the mouth, and he began to fight her as always he did at such times but then abruptly ceased, it was to be the last kiss between them and thus the last struggle and she wept over him *Don't let it happen! if it does I can't save you! I'm not strong enough!* and a single heart beat between them.

He remembers.

3

"MAY THE ROAD RISE UP TO MEET YOU . . ."

And now so abruptly so unexpectedly, when, as he'd told Yeager, he had other plans, Corky's on his way to a *communion breakfast*.

Not that he's going to mass and to communion, for sure not, hasn't been to mass still less to communion in years except for certain funerals he can't get out of, God damn how you wind up resenting the elderly and not-so-elderly relatives for croaking and screwing up a morning's plans not to mention a morning's promise: a high requiem mass leaves a taste you can't get rid of even with Johnnie Walker Red Label even with fucking Listerine for Christ's sake. Just the thought of it, and the memory of it, pisses Corky off.

He dies, he wants family and friends to have a party. Good old-fashioned Irish wake except that's it—no church service.

Not that Corky's thinking about dying, he isn't. Kept putting off his and Charlotte's wills, Charlotte nagging him for years and now they're divorced and *that* pressure's off. Corky fully intends to get the will drawn up, however. This spring. Or summer. When things calm down. When he can find a lawyer he can trust not one of these mercenary shits you call them on the phone and the meter starts clicking at their end like a taxicab.

Here's what: call Greenbaum, ask *him* for a referral. The first step in a friendship, you ask advice of a guy; you take the advice seriously; you follow through. *He* likes that, and next thing you know he's asking advice of you. You and him and your mutual friend meet for drinks, lunch.

Like Pawpaw says *Never trust a Jew unless you have him in your pocket.*

It's 10:20 A.M. Radio-weather girl announcing there's hope for no rain, deferred showers, this afternoon. Corky sees the sky's almost cleared in the east, the wind's so God-damned strong, pale dilated light flooding everywhere. Driving south on the Fillmore toward downtown past fucking-familiar sights ordinarily he wouldn't see Corky's struck how the air looks moist, glistening. Billboards, buildings, church spires, gold-glinting dome of the Byzantine church and the blue-choppy river and even the Canadian shore a mile away—sharp, hard, clean edges. Shit, a man's got a chance!

(Weird thoughts that come to you sometimes in your car—like it isn't you but the good sense of the car, the soul of the car, that's talking.)

Corky's feeling if not exactly terrific, hopeful. Stone cold sober and that's the way it's going to be. Charlotte really pissed him off laughing at him, bullshit he'd only quit for eighteen hours that time. And this time it's permanent. *Once an alcoholic always an alcoholic*, sure. It figures. It's in the genes. But tonight at the Chateauguay Country Club there'll be Corky Corcoran trim and looking good in his tux giving his speech about Congressman Vic Slattery and the one thing certain assholes are going to say to one another is, Corcoran hasn't had a drink all evening, what's up?

Sure he can do it. Won't need any of that scary stuff Antabuse, either, makes you puke if you drink even beer, wine. Sean was into that for a while and it does things to your head.

His head, nobody's going to fuck with.

Should've told Yeager to get off his property unless he had a warrant, preserve his self-respect. Nobody fucks with *me*.

Except: Yeager *is* his friend. Corky could see that in the guy's eyes.

And behind Yeager there's Oscar Slattery himself: Oscar who for sure is Corky Corcoran's friend, going back almost thirty years. Absolutely no doubt about that. (It's Oscar's place he's headed for now, the Mayor's residence, Stuyvesant House. Invited to a communion breakfast Oscar is hosting.) Not only a friend but a kind of son, like with Vic he's a kind of brother. Right?

Telling Vic certain things about his father's death, and about his mother. Vic's sympathy, Vic's silence. You knew you could trust Vic who'd wanted to be a Jesuit but gave it up thinking he wasn't "pure" enough. Not "worthy."

Need a drink? a drink crouched in front of the liquor cabinet in the room Charlotte called the library staring at the bottles for how long he didn't know after the squad car drove off. Nobody talks of the life we live in dreams, the other life that's deeper, richer. The life in drinking. Drunk. *There's* the fucking soul.

Like the female body you just can't talk about. You can't. Theresa hugging him so tight against her the breath went out of him like a blow, his ribs cracked open. That last time. They'd both seemed to know it was the last time. Kissing him hot and wet and so hungry on the mouth like nobody's ever kissed him since. Nor ever will. And nobody so beautiful. Schizzy, crazy—the pupils of her eyes like pinpricks, and the eyeballs shiny. The radiant heat of the dead-white skin. Nobody so beautiful. Her cries like the wind crazy too in the trees, oh Jesus how wonderful to hear it and feel it and know you might be dead someday but right now sweet fucking Jesus *you're alive*.

The rest of his life, this "Corky" life—shit! Just searching what's left of the world for it.

Some of these things, Corky'd told Vic Slattery, once. Or, not these things exactly, for of course Corky'd never told another living soul about that madness with Theresa, solitary in his knowledge even while his mother remained alive since she would not have remembered it or, remembering it, would not have been capable of distinguishing it from any dream or apparition in her head. Corky said, *It's something about women, women's bodies, what is it,* his voice trailing off in adolescent anguish and resentment and wonder, and Vic said, serious, even solemn, in that way of his both childlike and prematurely adult, *No, it's anybody's body, it's our own bodies, like Christ came to earth and became a body too, it blows your mind knowing we're alive but never knowing what alive is.*

And yet more earnestly, saying, *Corky, I think that's what it is: not sex. Just being alive.*

That year, when Jerome became "Corky." The world wasn't bounded by the perimeters of Irish Hill, he had a new life, *he* was new. Even "Irish" up in the Lakeshore district was different!

That year, Corky's first year at St. Thomas Aquinas Academy for Boys. The debate team, and the boxing team, and student government—which suited "Corky's" talents and ambition just fine.

He was still living on Roosevelt Street with his aunt and uncle, for sure. But it wasn't the same, it would never be the same again. He hadn't known it at the time, but he'd hoped.

After Yeager left Corky'd felt like his head was a clay pot somebody was beating sticks against. Staggering inside the house groping his way to the nearest bathroom, a "guest" bathroom on the first floor so little used now Mrs. Krauss jokes she has to dust the fancy carved perfumed soap. Dropping his trousers, sitting on the toilet amid gleaming black porcelain and gleaming brass fixtures and Portuguese floor tiles, Corky's voiding his bowels as if *The faster you travel, the slower the clock* the enormous breakfast he'd consumed hardly an hour before had already been digested, its superfluities turned to shit. Everything's accelerated, rushing past. His life, what he'd thought was *his*. Past, present—future? Thinking of how that time in biology class Corky'd asked Father Ober why, no matter what you eat, it comes out the same color and smell? and the class rocking with laughter thinking Corky's being a wise guy when, he swears, he wasn't. *What the fuck's so funny?*

Trying to comprehend what Budd Yeager's visit means. If it's just what it is, the Slatterys concerned about him; or if it's something more. Could they be fearful of him, too? Poking his nose where it isn't wanted, like in fact he is impersonating a cop. And that's dangerous.

Knowing he's been spied on is bad enough, humiliating to know that that ghoul Wiegler must've made a goofy story of it, "Jerome Andrew Corcoran" passing out in the morgue like a woman, *that's* bad enough, but—*impersonating a cop!* Corky can't get over it.

How many times he'd insisted at the Zanzibar he *wasn't* a cop, *isn't* a cop! Why wouldn't Roscoe Beechum believe him! Why wouldn't Roscoe Beechum look and see *him!*

Corky could cry, it's so unjust.

Flushing the toilet, his nostrils pinched against the stink of his own shit, rinsing his hands with cold water since he's in a rush and doesn't want to use the expensive French soap nor even the dainty embroidered Irish linen hand towels—God damn! Corky's a guest in his own house.

Prowling the downstairs rooms then checking for . . . he doesn't know what. Nobody's broken in here, obviously. These rooms he'd last seen in Thalia's presence. The silence a pressure on his eardrums. And that smell—emptiness acquires a smell, unmistakable. Dusty-gritty, with an undercurrent of body stink. *Married again? You? It's too late for you.* One thing Corky knows now, he'll have to sell this house. Can't bear living here any longer. Prestige, pride, assuring that jealous assholes like Donnelly, Philly Dowd get their noses rubbed in it—not enough. Also the elder Drummonds approved. Fuck the elder Drummonds. Buying The Bull's Eye on a crazy impulse like he did, putting 33 Summit Avenue on the market with a list price of let's say $550,000—Corky's life will be turning 180 degrees. If the house was in Chateauguay, even in St. Claire, he'd ask a cool $1 million and get it, but it isn't. So fuck that. He'll get his price.

And maybe he and Christina Kavanaugh will get married, and maybe they won't. Corky can't make up his mind if he loves the woman or wishes she and Harry Kavanaugh were both dead.

In the kitchen toast crumbs scattered on the tile floor and the same dishes, cups stacked in the sink and crap spilling out of the trash basket beneath the sink and in the solarium the Sunday paper looking like the wind blew it, Corky's Rolodex, cordless phone. And sunshine spilling through the tinted glass like acid. Corky lifts the phone receiver and quickly dials his ten-digit voice mail code but when he hears the beginning of the first call, anxious concerned Sandra Slattery, "Corky? Is something wrong? It's after eight-thirty, we were expecting you at—" Corky hangs up guiltily.

Upstairs, first thing, Corky enters his bedroom and checks the bedside table drawer another time—of course it's empty. What's he thinking, Thalia would've crept back repentant and replaced it?

"Dream on, asshole."

Stripping his clothes. Throwing them down. Like he could strip off his skin. Sour-smelling underwear he'd had to put back on after showering at the motel. Nothing he hates worse. Sniffing his shorts he thinks he smells Charlotte's perfume. Poor Charlotte, a beautiful woman like that, all-American girl, she deserves better than *him.*

Proof, if more proof's required, women think with their cunts and their cunts can't think.

In the corner of the bedroom there's a forty-pound dumbbell, Corky picks it up in his right hand and lifts it a half dozen times then transfers it to his left hand already panting, winded. A sign of alcohol deprivation he's sweating and shivering plus the D.T.'s always a possibility at the corner of his eye, giant roaches set to GO across the ceiling. *I'm an alcoholic, help me.*

Bare-assed and anxious Corky calls in for his voice mail. Listens while lifting, or trying to lift, the dumbbell that's heavier than it's ever been before. *Forty* pounds? He remembers that compulsive phase of weight lifting, guys at St. Thomas, Vic methodically building up his muscles like they were armature, Cassius Clay was their hero, fantastic black heavyweight quick and wily on his feet as a middle-weight, the boxing team coach showing them tapes, drilling them. Now boxing's not an option at St. Thomas. Too dangerous, lowlife.

". . . Corky? This is Vic calling, it's a little after nine and Sandra and I are wondering if you've forgotten?—you were going to have dinner with us?" Vic's voice concerned, but easy, not a sign of being annoyed, pissed at Corky's rudeness, the Slatterys set aside an evening for Corky and this is how he values it, and could they know he was balling his ex-wife the two of them blotto drunk *what would they think?* The next call's from both Vic and Sandra, both of them on the line but Sandra does most of the talking, now she does sound anxious, "—almost eleven, Corky—we're afraid something has happened to you, please call when you can?—" and Corky feels like a real shit letting the dumbbell slip from his damp fingers to bounce on the bed *what the fuck is wrong with you!*

A fourth call clicks on, and there's a husky, breathy voice, for a hopeful moment Corky thinks it's Christina, but, no, not Christina, Charlotte instead, ". . . Jerome? Darling? You've just left and I'm missing you already . . . but you're with me, too . . . inside me . . . I feel . . ." A long pause, Corky's embarrassed, poor Charlotte drunk and maudlin-sexy not knowing how she sounds by acid-bright daylight, the moon and its romantic-hazy aura long gone. By "inside me" Charlotte means Corky's semen in her vagina, is that what she means?—Corky grimaces fastidiously and punches "3" to erase the message.

You'd think a woman of forty-six would know better, for Christ's sake.

Thick-tongued and contrite Corky calls the Slatterys to apologize for the night before. Talks first to Sandra, then Vic lifts a second receiver and it's a three-way conversation, gratifying to Corky how relieved they are to hear from him at last and to hear he's all right. They're not angry with him! They're not judging him harshly! He can't remember exactly what he told Sandra the day before so he's vague, elusive, it's a "personal matter"— "family crisis"—he hopes they aren't fed up with him completely. Sandra says quickly, "Corky, don't be silly, a dinner's just a dinner—we can do that any time we're in Union City. Or you can come down to Washington. We were worried about you." And Vic says, "—You *are* all right, Corky? Is there anything we can do?" and Corky says, sighing, "Jesus, Vic, I wish there was." There's a pause, and Vic says, "Well, maybe there is, try us." And there's another pause, and Corky says, slowly, "I need to talk to you sometime, before tonight if that's possible." Not knowing he's going to say this until he says it. Not knowing even what he means by saying it.

It's then that Vic invites Corky to the communion breakfast. This breakfast has become a Memorial Day custom since Oscar became Mayor but it isn't an official affair in any way, just family and friends, nine o'clock mass at St. Stanislaus and a buffet breakfast at Stuyvesant House but lots of people come to the breakfast who haven't attended mass—"Sandra and I promised Dad we'd drop in, so *you* come, too, Corky. Dad will be delighted to see you, no question about it."

Corky's naturally flattered as hell to be invited, even so casually. Any occasion at the Mayor's residence is an honor. He hesitates for maybe three seconds before saying, "Great! Thanks! I'll be there."

Breakfast! But maybe he won't have to eat.

By 10:28 A.M. Corky's coming off the ramp of the City Center-Dominion Bridge exit, he'd turn right if he was going to Nott Street but he turns left taking cobbled Front Street downhill to the river to the Van Dusen Dorf district which is the oldest part of Union City, settled by Dutch traders in the 1600s. Jesus, what a long time ago! Corky's glad he doesn't live in Europe, ancestors going back forever, no way to measure even a century let alone your own puny life. Here, it's exhausting enough. You have to love these old ugly buildings, the squarebuilt stone Lutheran Church still in use, General Schuyler's house one of those boring domestic museums mainly furniture and spinning wheels, butter churns. There's the ruin of a gunpowder shed preserved like it's sacred ground. And the aged pockmarked stone jail with the slots for windows. And the square behind the jail where the scaffold used to be—where, in 1883, a Corcoran from County Kerry, a kid in his early twenties, was not only hanged but decapitated. What a sight *that* must've been for the gaping assholes in the crowd.

And the ancient Van Dusen Dorf cemetery kept up now like a theme park. As if history's something you can see. And small-scaled—the graves look like they're made for dwarves. Tilting weatherworn markers thin as pancakes. Even a decrepit old plane tree is propped up by crutches. In observation of Memorial Day a dozen foot-high American flags are fluttering in the cemetery but skeptical Corky thinks, Is that right?—any veterans buried there, they're none of *ours*.

Stuyvesant House, deeded to the city in lieu of taxes in the Depression, is a red brick colonial mansion on a narrow two-acre peninsula in the Chateauguay River; even so, it's surrounded by a twelve-foot brick wall topped with electrified razor wire. There's a security guard on duty in a kiosk just inside the granite gateposts of the entrance and this guy insists upon checking Corky's ID and scanning the list of guests frowning pinch-faced not finding *Corcoran* at first, which burns Corky's ass—as if he hasn't been a guest at the Mayor's many times since Oscar's inaugural party! "Look at the bottom of the list, or turn it over—I'm invited," Corky says hotly, "—I was just invited this morning, I'm a special guest of Vic Slattery's, my fucking name's *there*." So finally the guard locates *Corcoran, Jerome* and waves Corky through, cocksucker eyeing the Caddy's crumpled fender and bumper. Corky says, "Thanks, buddy!" in a voice heavy with sarcasm.

A moment later rebuking himself: that asshole's a potential *voter*.

Corky parks his car, wincing a little in the bright May sunshine but feeling good, optimistic. Meeting the Slatterys at Stuyvesant House, Memorial Day morning: just the kind of impromptu invitation Corky's grown to expect from these people. They pick you up, they sometimes set you down—sure, there've been dry spells when the Slattery's, both Vic and Oscar, seemed to have forgotten Corky Corcoran's existence—but they pick you up again.

How's it feel, kid, to be established in this town?

Looming like a rift in the sky a quarter-mile away is the Dominion Bridge to Canada. And across the way, details of its shoreline distinct, even the winking glare of sunshine on the windows of the high-rise Holi-day Inn, is Fort Pearce, Ontario. Corky remembers, in high school, how they'd drive over to Fort Pearce on weekend nights sometimes—six or seven guys crowded into a car, Heinz Meuller driving, or Eddy Darn-ton, sometimes Vic in the big canary-yellow Caddy convertible, looking for action, girls. Those adventures that'd seemed wild to them, Catholic schoolboys, now tame in retrospect, childish. Most of the time.

In the graveled parking lot Corky meets up with the city comptrol-ler Fats Pickering, heavyset good-natured guy in his fifties Corky's got a special feeling for, the sucker's dropped $500 in Corky's lap not once but twice backing the Bills for the Super Bowl. Pickering's attitude toward Corky is more complex so while he's grinning and clamping a hand on Corky's shoulder wishing him a good morning he's also quick to get in, before Corky can respond, "Saw you on TV yesterday, kid—you really fucked up, eh?" laughing like gravel being shoveled.

Corky wilts under his friend's arm like he wants to disappear.

Inside Stuyvesant House Corky's dismayed seeing so many old and middle-aged men, and Vic nowhere in sight. And no women. Must be the occasion is a Holy Name Society breakfast?—did Vic get the details wrong? (It wouldn't be the first time: Vic's so dependent upon his office staff to deal with things like places, times, the actual nature of events, he can fuck up ordinary matters. God damn!) Oscar Slattery is greeting guests in the reception room and Corky heads for him but he's cut off by Red Pitts swinging by, Pitts sees Corky and freezes, even the wide affable smile on his face freezes, and the two men look at each other, and finally Pitts says, "Corky, hello—what are *you* doing here?" not hostile but for sure not friendly, and Corky says, flaring up, "What do you think?—I was invited," and Pitts says, as if without thinking, "*You* were invited? To *this?*" and this really pisses Corky who says, "Vic asked me to meet him here. That's a problem with you?" Pitts contemplates Corky as the men, in the entrance to the reception room, are being jostled on all sides, decides against whatever he's going to say and shrugs and moves on and Corky grabs his arm, and repeats, "That's a problem with you, Pitts?" and Pitts glares down at him, he's half a head taller than Corky and out-weighs him by fifty pounds, and not bemused by him like Yeager, nor certainly apprehensive of him, screwing up his face, saying, "Don't go sucking up to Oscar right now, Corcoran, he's pissed at you," and Corky says, "Why?" though knowing why: it's the TV interview, him running at the mouth the way he did.

Pitts is walking away, Corky's mouthing after him, "Why? Why's he pissed? *I'm* pissed—I'm the one!"

Desperate now to get to Oscar as a son to a father he believes has judged him correctly as rebellious yet must present himself as misjudged, but, fuck it, Corky's way is blocked, all these old farts crowded in here, and moving in a shuffling flow into the dining room where the breakfast buffet's set up, and tables draped in white linen with shining cutlery and foot-high American flags as centerpieces. Corky's dry-mouthed, scared. Angry. Seeing Father Vincent O'Brien handsome and regal in his priest's costume working the room like a seasoned politician, there's Bishop Malley white-haired and palsied in an earnest conversation with Oscar's older brother William—but hadn't the Bishop had a stroke, wasn't he non compos mentis? Corky's sure he's heard this, but the report must have been exaggerated. And in the buffet line getting his plate heaped with steaming food is Father Creighton the St. Stanislaus parish priest, an old friend of the Slatterys. Too many priests! Corky's feeling oppressed, a tightness in his chest.

"Corky Corcoran! How the hell's it going?"—and Corky's hand is being briskly shaken, Corky switches to automatic pilot, talking with Hatch the deputy mayor in charge of public school funding, and Aickley the Fourth Ward Democratic boss, and Spitzer the head of Oscar's Finances and Appropriations Office, and Leo Boner the chief attorney for Lloyd, Weber, and Marty MacLeod the middle-aged son of the man who owns the *Union City Journal*, Marty who's something of an asshole but a good-natured guy always glad-handing Corky and suggesting with a lewd snigger the two of them take a Vegas weekend together—"Hit the casinos, and bang the broads, and have a helluva great time, eh Corky?" And there's an octogenarian Democratic donor from the Edgewater district where the elder Slatterys live, one of those elderly multimillionaires with a New Deal—Great Society social conscience, an old friend and long-time supporter of the Slatterys and he's got Corky buttonholed apparently mistaking him for a nephew of Oscar's rattling on excitedly spittle gleaming in the corners of his slack lips about some issue Corky can't follow though he's furrow-browed, respectful making an effort, *a drink? need a drink?*—seeing with horror it's only 10:48 A.M., how's he going to get through the day? At last in desperation grabbing the elbow of a man he scarcely knows except *he's* a relative of Oscar's and the owner of WWUC-TV and gets the sucker caught like tarbaby on the old man and adroitly detaches himself with a wave and a grin and pushes his way to the beverage bar and gets a glass of tomato juice, nice and chilled, he can pretend is a Bloody Mary. There's even a sprig of celery in it.

And where the hell's Vic? Sandra? Nowhere in sight.

Serve Corky right if his friends stand *him* up, now.

Corky's face lights up seeing Oscar Slattery headed in his direction, Oscar's plumpish-pale with that ghostly pious look in the eyes men of a certain temperament and girth get when they've *fasted* and *taken Holy Communion* and everybody knows it. Oscar seems to see Corky yet doesn't recognize him intensely involved in a conversation with several other men well dressed and groomed like himself, these faces familiar to Corky, multimillionaire donors and supporters they are most likely. St. Stanislaus parish is the most wealthy Union City parish, located in the northeast Edgewater district, taking in St. Thomas Aquinas Academy for Boys and the Marymount Academy of the Sacred Heart for Girls. Oscar and his companions are going into the dining room to the head table but Corky's going to waylay them, put his hand on Oscar's arm and say hello but just at that moment, fuck it, here's Petey Zubkow putting *his* hand on Corky's arm and chortling, with that perpetually drunk-sounding wheezing laugh, "Corcoran! Long time no see! How's the ol' pecker holding up?" so Corky's thrown off balance like a boxer caught by a smart jab he didn't see coming but he's going to pretend he did, saying, grinning, "Zubkow! How's the bunchy-fatty ass?" And the two men laugh, laugh.

Damn, Oscar and his friends slip away. Without a glance at Corky Corcoran.

Corky quickly shakes Zubkow who's a longtime political appointee of Oscar's in the Department of Public Transport, one of those crafty-sleazy-unfailingly loyal types even a mayor of such integrity as Oscar Slattery keeps around him. Following in the wake of Oscar as, now, everybody remaining in the reception room follows him, it's time for breakfast to formally begin though (Corky sees, with disdain) a number of guests have begun to eat hungrily. Corky counts fifteen tables, round tables set for twelve; plus the head table, set for eight, on a raised dais against the rear wall. Behind the head table are French doors opened upon a garden of gorgeous big crimson-blooming flowers like orchids—that classy shrub, Corky can never remember the name, Charlotte's favorite, rhododendron? Jesus, what a room! What a house, Stuyvesant House! Herringbone wood floors, thirteen-foot ceilings in the downstairs public rooms, intricate plaster moldings, a total of eleven fireplaces. In here, French silk wallpaper a bronzey-radiant shade like sunshine's coming out of it, almost the same color as the bricks of the Mount Moriah Crematorium—real class. Corky always has a great feeling about this house since, when Oscar decided to renovate it, after his second election as Mayor, when he'd won with enough of a majority to buck the tide of criticism from his detractors, he'd asked Corky for advice; and if he didn't exactly follow it, he listened.

Corky knows better but, hell, even a City Councilman in a place like this, you can't help fantasizing *What if, someday . . . me?*

The Slatterys' private quarters are on the second and third floors, and from what Corky's seen of them, admittedly not much, they're pretty classy, too.

Of course, the Slatterys have maintained their private house in Edgewater. Oscar will run for another mayoral term and he's sure to win and beyond that who knows, maybe yet another term, or maybe retirement. But he won't be Mayor of Union City forever.

Corky's watching Oscar and two of his companions step up to take their places at the head table where Bishop Malley, Father O'Brien, and Father Creighton in their Roman collars, regal black suits are just settling in. Silky American flags in the background, a podium, a microphone. This evening, at the Chateauguay Country Club, Jerome Andrew Corcoran will be at the head table, in a larger and even more politically, charged setting than this: Oscar Slattery's *Union City*; Vic Slattery's *Washington*.

The smell of breakfast food—especially crispy bacon, greasy sausage links—*is* mouthwatering; though Corky isn't in a mood to eat just now.

Seeing then, with a stab of resentment, that prick McElroy easing past with some well-dressed paunchy guys, Jesus, is McElroy a member of St. Stanislaus parish now, and in the Holy Name Society? Corky wouldn't put it past the conniving bastard. Talk about sucking up to the big boys, McElroy's the one! Corky's feeling not just disgust but hurt realizing McElroy for sure saw him, and walked right past.

McElroy's wearing an expensive-looking three-piece suit, those executive pinstripes, gray, not much imagination but he does look like a sharpie lawyer of the high-paid kind. And the shoes. Corky has a pair just like them exactly, he knows the price. Fucker with his yuppie haircut, a ring on his left hand meaning he's married which Corky must've known, but forgot. And McElroy has kids, too—no doubt. Sons he'll send to St. Thomas, daughters he'll send to Marymount. A Catholic wife, *not* from Irish Hill, who's at this moment attending a luncheon of the St. Stanislaus Sodality of Mary at, let's say, the Edgewater Inn.

Corky thinks, mollified, that time in the swimming pool in Dundonald, my friends and me, we half-drowned the jerk-off, *I* got a knee in his balls.

Corky's going to drift back to the front of the house to see if possibly Vic and Sandra are waiting there, though it doesn't seem likely, when Zubkow and a City Hall pal come swinging by and inveigle him into going through the buffet line with them, so Corky does, not that he's hungry but he lets the smiling black waiters in their dazzling white outfits heap his plate with food, it's their job and they seem to enjoy it, Corky's a guy who hates to say no, somebody wants to give you something it's against human nature to say no, isn't it—or just Irish nature? *Do you need to fuck every woman who makes it known she's available* Charlotte used to rage, suddenly past the age of forty Charlotte began using the word *fuck*, must've been in the air so much she decided why the hell not why let her husband throw the word in her face to insult her thus to disempower her like the very word's an extension of his prick she's supposed to be envious of, and inferior to?—*fuck that.*

Whatever Corky told Charlotte, he's forgotten, more or less. But the truth of it was, and is, assuming a woman's attractive, and the circumstances are right, Corky can't say no.

Even since getting serious about Christina Kavanaugh, and seeing her every chance he can, Corky's had a few one-night stands, not that he'd want Christina to know about them, Jesus, it's just hard to resist.

It's a sumptuous buffet, what you'd expect from Oscar Slattery, but

Corky declines the eggs Benedict, ditto the breakfast ham, O.K. for a piece of French toast and maple syrup, O.K. for some hash browns and some bacon, sausage links he'll douse with catsup, no strawberry pancakes, *no thanks!*—but maybe a single blueberry-and-cream waffle, a waffle's not a pancake exactly. The smiling black waiter with a gold-glinting front tooth seems to be pushing scrambled eggs with smoked salmon, looks disappointed when Corky says no so Corky says yes, but then no thanks to a fruit cup of fresh pineapple and yogurt, no thanks to a bowl of what looks like tapioca pudding unless it's some fancy kind of oatmeal but, O.K., sure, he's got a sweet tooth and he won't be eating until the fund-raiser tonight, why not a piece of cherry Danish. Waiters are serving coffee at the tables, more tomato juice if he wants it, Corky's laughing in good spirits screwing around joking with Zubkow and the other guy who really are asking for Bloody Marys and the black waiter's stopped short like either he doesn't know what this is or he's pretending not to mumbling he'll check with the kitchen, so everybody at the table laughs. It's a festive occasion, Memorial Day breakfast at the Mayor's, a select group of citizens, why not enjoy it? Nobody's getting any younger.

And it's O.K. to light up here, too—this is a private party, not a public one. Any Union City or New York State official event or event held on public property, smoking's outlawed, but not here, this is 100 percent men. Lots of these old guys carrying cigars.

More laughter, this muffled, throughout the dining room, as Father Creighton rises solemnly to say grace, and the clattering of silverware abruptly ceases, *Bless us O Lord and these thy gifts which we are about to receive from thy bounty through Christ our Lord Amen and on this Memorial Day special gratitude . . .* that lilting droning priestly voice, the "singing" voice of the mass, weird, almost beautiful like a woman's. Corky's heard it in so many priests strangers to one another he guesses it's something that happens to them? But the Church really fucked up, though, ditching Latin for English. Now you can understand the mass, its asshole simplicity, there's nothing *there*. The muffled laughter's because half the guys in the room were already eating and had to quick stop, bow their heads, mumble grace.

Old geezers sixty, seventy years old giggling like schoolkids. Christ, thinks Corky, don't we ever grow up?

He's laughing at Zubkow's nonstop wisecracks, dirty asides and sniggers, crude grade-school stuff but funny—*What's the pilot's seat in a plane called when there's an all-girl crew?—a cuntpit!*—maybe not too funny but everybody at the table roars laughing except one old guy blinking quizzically, must be deaf and that makes it funnier yet when Zubkow has to repeat *cuntpit!* raising his voice so he's heard at other tables. So they're all laughing, Corky's sputtering his scrambled eggs and smoked salmon, feeling a hell of a lot better now that shit with Yeager's pushed to the back of his mind, he'll worry about the implications some other time, now's not the time.

Corky's eating all the food on his plate surprising himself he *is* hungry even after that enormous breakfast at the Pancake House. Yes but you could say this is lunch—it's 11:20 A.M. and time's moving fast. Waiters coming along with coffee, huge steaming silver pots of fresh-brewed coffee, caffeine-charged. The French toast is Goddamned delicious: Corky remembers how Aunt Frances used to make them French toast on Sunday sometimes, especially if they went to high mass at 9:00 A.M. instead of regular mass at 8:00, Peter, Lois, Tess and Jerome all of them starving by the time they sat down to breakfast . . . Uncle Sean stopped going to mass, since Tim's death he had a hard time taking any of it seriously he said but Aunt Frances said: Don't let the children hear you! Jerome at the kitchen table his eyes watering like his mouth for the delicious food that's never going to be enough to fill his empty belly, shovel it in, chew and tamp it down, unloosen your belt another notch, never enough. *And he loves Aunt Frances for feeding him like he was her own not another woman's son that woman has ceased to cook for, loves Aunt Frances but will never tell her so: never.*

His cousins resented him. Sure. No secret. Especially Peter—*he's* the son in the family, the big deal. Lois was always bossing him around, Tess was O.K., now they don't keep in touch except for Lois laying a guilt trip on Corky about Sean, how long's it been since you've seen him the bitch is always asking. Who's counting?

Corky's thinking if he sees his uncle today, takes him to the parade, maybe if there's time to see Aunt Megan in the hospital—*that* should square it.

Of course, Corky's cousins don't know how he's supplementing the old man's pension from the city. Fuck if he'd ever tell them.

Just the kind of thing Tim Corcoran did on a grander scale. For elderly or sick relatives, his and Theresa's both. In Union City and back in Ireland, too. But helping out people's no good if you humble them, humiliate them in the process.

Like Oscar Slattery, secretly providing scholarship money for Tim Corcoran's boy Jerome. The man's kindness, generosity. Tact.

Corky's laughing, having a great time, almost forgetting why he's here—a *communion breakfast?* Stomach's unpleasantly bloated, has to surreptitiously loosen his belt by another notch. Once he starts his AA regimen back to bench pressing, too, get rid of the flab, embarrassing when a woman glances down, sees—*What a slob!* she'd be thinking if she had common sense. Corky's got one eye on the head table like a pining lover (*why* doesn't Oscar Slattery acknowledge Corky?—Corky who's glancing his way smiling and alert?) and one eye on Zubkow who's been talking about "Preacher Marcus Steadman" giving the credulous table the lowdown on him, wild-kinky stuff Corky's never heard before and guesses might be invented the way that shit about Corky Corcoran impersonating a police officer was invented but it's funny, nasty and funny, what more can you ask. And everybody at the table is Caucasian, in fact everybody at the communion breakfast is Caucasian, so there's no offense. As long as Zubkow lowers his voice so the waiters can't hear.

A weird guy, Petey Zubkow: a sleaze, perpetually on the make, any woman with half her brains should know but the guy's got these longlashed sloe eyes, Russian-Slavic cheekbones, he's Corky's age at least but like Corky looks younger, and though married for half his life to the same woman, with near grown-up kids, he's got girlfriends mad for him to hear him tell it—must be the City Hall atmosphere, a crisis every week, sometimes every day, and then there's election time when everybody goes crazy. Politics *is* sex, you want to screw. The closer to election day, the hornier you get. Except nothing satisfies the craving. Corky remembers the hottest campaign, 1988, Oscar's early lead in the polls was shrinking and by November 1 he was only ten points ahead of his Republican rival a youngish federal attorney, Bush-endorsed, and there was Marcus Steadman running as a spoiler, ceaseless shit going on in the local media, daily accusations, calls for reform, Democrats and Republicans at a stalemate blackmailing one another (not that the public knew this—for sure, the public didn't) and Steadman taking potshots at everybody, and nerves were so high-strung it was like a perpetual Red Alert—even Corky Corcoran, with no one running against him for the Council, was antsy all the time, couldn't concentrate and couldn't sleep and one night at campaign headquarters in the Statler Zubkow introduced Corky to a girlfriend of his and her friend, both of them working as assistants, and they went out drinking together and had a great time and wound up at four in the morning in Zubkow's office at City Hall where Zubkow screwed his girl in his inner office where there was a sofa, and Corky screwed his in the outer office atop a desk where she passed out giggling and hiccuping, and after a while Zubkow came out saying *his* had passed out, too, so let's switch, so they did, and Corky goes into Zubkow's office where it's dark stumbling over practically onto the girl and she's faintly protesting pushing him away saying she wants to go home but she's so obviously drunk she doesn't know where the hell she is or what she wants, then Corky's inside her where she's already wet and dilated from Zubkow and he's making it interesting for her, Corky'd take bets any day he's a superior fuck to Zubkow, so the girl starts responding, grabs the cheeks of his ass with both hands, he gets her to come and it's like a sudden scared sneeze all over her body and she likes it O.K. but afterward when they're both getting their breath she says, sullen in the dark, "It isn't funny, what you and Petey did, you shits, fuck you both," starting to cry she's so pissed off, and Corky says, the first thing he's said till now, innocent-seeming, "How'd you know I wasn't Petey?" and the girl says, this line that cracks Corky up, "*He's* got a bunchy-fatty ass, the bastard." So ever after they've got this joke between them, Corky and Zubkow: Zubkow's "bunchy-fatty ass." *Funny!*

Every time they meet, or, like now, Zubkow sees Corky grinning at him, the memory passes between them and Zubkow actually blushes a little and laughs—what the hell, it's like they're bonded brothers or something. Even should the men hate each other's guts Corky's a decent enough guy and a reliable friend never to tell any third party about the episode which would embarrass Zubkow who's vain about his looks, his body, his reputation.

The waiters are coming around now with strawberry cream tarts and tiny cups of Irish coffee, it's early in the day for Irish coffee but, Christ, hard to resist, so Corky takes a cup, also a tart, but vows inwardly he isn't going to drink any of the coffee nor eat more than a few forkfuls of the tart, he *is* stuffed, almost like he's been drinking and it's 11:47 P.M. not 11:47 A.M. There's a clicking of glasses, Oscar Slattery's on his feet beaming at the roomful of men he knows are his friends, men he can trust, men like himself, Corky sees Oscar still looks a little pale which is unusual for him, and his eyes ringed in shadow like he hasn't been sleeping well lately, must be tough to be under constant scrutiny, knowing your enemies are waiting for you to fuck up like wolves snapping at your heels, yes but Oscar Slattery's an old pro now saying, "Gentlemen! Excuse me! May I say a few words about this day—a secular holiday, but sacred in our hearts?—but first, a toast, if I may—" lifting his tiny cup of Irish coffee in a spirit of playful festivity so everybody in the room lifts his, Corky included, "—An old Irish toast that to my mind has never been bettered: 'May the road rise up to meet you, may the wind be always at your back, may the sunshine be warm on your face, and may you be safe in Heaven before the devil knows you're dead!'"

Always, at this toast, there's appreciative laughter as there is now, and Corky laughs, too, though moved by the familiar words—hell, he *is* proud of being Irish, it's a grand race. A sorrowful history and an uncertain future God knows, but St. Patrick too was a slave, never forget. The Irish are God's special people like the Jews which is maybe why He has sent them so much suffering and ignominy, fuck Him.

Zubkow nudges Corky in the arm, "—your coffee? Aren't you drinking it?" grinning and suspicious like he's got Corky's number, knows Corky's on the wagon cautious about sipping even a little whiskey-warmed coffee, even some frothy whipped cream, and Corky plays it cool saying, "Jesus, Petey, I'm stuffed."

Not even a thimbleful of whiskey—this time, Corky's serious.

This is part of your education, lads: learning the difference between yourselves and real fighters.

That first time, meeting Oscar Slattery. Knowing who Oscar was, and his older, then more powerful brother William, talked of with envious admiration in Irish Hill. Where few could claim to know them personally. Corky was fifteen, on the boxing team at St. Thomas, a junior lightweight at 125 pounds; Vic Slattery a heavyweight at 178 pounds, the star of the team. Both boys were baby-faced and intense and erratically talented depending upon the ineptitude of their opponents. Intramural bouts, Corky and Vic always won their matches; away from home, things were chancy. Amateur boxing more resembles fencing than it resembles professional boxing, judged by the quantity of points—"hits"—rather than the actual force of the blows; knockouts are infrequent, and may be accidental. Yet what glamor in being picked to be on the St. Thomas team, and Corky only a sophomore! Skinny-scrappy Corky Corcoran who'd grown up in Irish Hill liking to hit other guys and used to being hit in turn, what sport better suited for *him*. In the ring, you only fight guys your own weight.

Corky modeled himself after Henry Armstrong, Kid Gavilan, Carmen Basilio he'd seen in films shown by the boxing coach, Vic modeled himself after Joe Louis, Rocky Marciano trying patiently for that big right hand but also Cassius Clay—"Muhammad Ali"—quick and cunning and unpredictable on his feet. Corky knows in retrospect he was a lousy boxer even for an amateur, throwing punches in rapid windmill fashion when he panicked, with a percussive but near-strengthless left jab and not much real power in his flashy right, fast on his feet and a classic amateur imagining he's got the will to fight, the warrior's blood-lust, when it's only an American kid's desire to compete in a sport, be one of the guys on a team. And Vic, too intelligent to fight by instinct, ponderous, studied, then suddenly reckless in his ring style, capable of throwing what the coach called "bombshells" in his left hook but missing half his shots, wasn't much better. He'd confessed to Corky he wanted to win his matches but not to *hurt* his opponent so Corky laughed incredulously in his face—"Jesus, Vic, hurting them's the point, isn't it?"

Corky thought Vic's reason was, too, he didn't want to be hurt himself. Wasn't used to it. His family, nobody hauled off and slammed a kid, ever. Whereas Corky Corcoran didn't mind, much. Maybe his pain threshold, so-called, was higher.

Corky could never figure why Vic liked him, Corky can never figure through his life why the hell anybody likes *him*, it's a puzzle so many people do. Girls and women, most of them are such dopes they're easily fooled, but guys like Vic Slattery? This big-boned sweet-faced kid, good-looking tawny-blond with wide intelligent brown eyes and strong

jaws and a nose that bled at the mildest blow from a twelve-ounce boxing glove—Vic was a rich man's son, something of a momma's boy (so it
was said: Corky never thought so), smutty-minded like all kids his age
but religious, too; he'd embarrass his friends, talking suddenly of Catholic theology he took seriously enough to question—whether the Trinity
of Father, Son, and Holy Ghost was "there from the beginning"—why
it might happen that, if you slashed the sanctified Host with a knife it
would bleed, being the body and blood of Jesus, but when you allow it to
dissolve in your mouth after communion it doesn't bleed—"Or, if it does,
you can't taste it." Corky would've jeered at such crap except it was Vic
anxious to know what was true, what was *real*.

Also you never know, as a Catholic born into the faith, whether what
you think is crap *is* real, and it will all be on your head someday, your
derision.

At the new school Corky—still, then, "Jerome"—hadn't any real
friends until Vic Slattery, and after that, quick as Blackstone's magic, he
had lots of friends. Start at the top, Corky knew even as a fifteen-year-
old, and everything else follows. Kids who wouldn't piss on you will rush
to be your friends if you're friends with a big shot—"social life" is as
simple as that. He'd set his sights on Vic because Vic was tops. Also Vic
was good-natured, generous, the kind of A student who has to work for
his grades, not dumb but sometimes dumb-seeming, innocent. (Corky
understood exactly how it could happen, years later when Vic was suspended for a semester from Villanova for being involved in a "cheating
episode." Vic had lent a friend his chemistry notes, the asshole took the
notes into the final exam, and got caught. And years after that when Vic
was a freshman congressman just getting to know the ropes his career
had been almost permanently fucked by the media digging up dirt about
contributions to his campaign, all of it the fault of the campaign manager
he'd inherited from Oscar Slattery—a smart guy, a guy you'd want on
your side in a campaign, unless he gets caught.) Corky's strategy with Vic
was just to be around him a lot, at crucial times; to be the kind of guy Vic
would naturally like, but with some surprises, too—Corky's Irish Hill
tough-guy manner played for laughs. *If you can make people laugh you
can make them like you:* a motto of Corky Corcoran's. Working on Vic
Slattery whose old man was in Democratic politics and a part owner of

a big Union City department store wasn't any harder than working on trigonometry homework for a kid with a mind like Corky's, and a hell of a lot more rewarding.

Also, Corky loves Vic. Vic's his man.

And what an occasion, that first meeting with Oscar Slattery!—Vic's father showed up unexpected at a boxing meet at St. Loyola High School, in Troy, just in time to see Vic win—barely, but win—his match, and to see feisty little Corky Corcoran win his match, both boys scoring points while taking punches to the face and body, and looking as much like losers as winners. Vic's nose was swollen and bleeding, Corky's thin-skinned face red as if he'd been scraped with sandpaper. Oscar Slattery was a magnanimous man warmly congratulating the coach and taking everybody out for steak suppers then driving Vic and Corky back to Union City that night so they'd be spared the school bus—he'd come to Troy in a chauffeur-driven Lincoln Town Car, a deep mahogany color, flashing chrome and tinted windows and about the most beautiful thing Corky'd ever seen, stopped dead in his tracks knowing *he* was going to ride in it.

Of the nine guys on the boxing team, *he'd* been singled out as Vic Slattery's close friend.

The embarrassment of being dropped off at his uncle's shabby-shingled house on Roosevelt Street amid a neighborhood of similar, even shabbier houses was hours away, not to be contemplated yet.

It was during this drive along the nighttime Thruway from Troy to Union City that Oscar Slattery told Vic and Corky, kindly, if bluntly, that they weren't boxers, still less fighters; just amateurs lucky enough not to meet opponents outside the Catholic boys' school league, Negroes especially—how carefully Oscar Slattery pronounced that tricky word: "Ne-groes"—who'd take their heads off. Sitting in the front seat of the Lincoln, smoking a cigar, thoughtful, smiling, happy, a good-looking man with plump clean-shaven cheeks and steely-gray hair, not complicated-seeming as, later, Corky would know he was, *is*; a father who loved his son so much some of the love spilled over onto his son's friend.

"This is part of your education, lads," Oscar Slattery said, looking from one to the other in the rear seat, "—you're learning the difference between yourselves and real fighters. You're learning how hard the real thing is, how you can lose even while 'winning.'" He paused, sucking on his cigar, to let that sink in. "You're not hungry enough, either of you—and God help you, if you were."

Calling them *lads*—that word Corky'd last heard on his Grandfather Liam's lips, years before.

Corky didn't learn until graduation that Oscar Slattery had paid for his three years at St. Thomas—arranged for his "scholarship." And that not from Oscar but from one of Corky's Jesuit teachers. Corky'd been stunned, astonished. There was no connection he knew, nor ever was to know, between Oscar Slattery and Tim Corcoran. Never could he ask *why* for fear of revealing his own uncharitable heart.

Several times Corky tried to write a letter thanking his mysterious benefactor, sweating over the God-damned thing, writing and rewriting and tearing it up and finally one day at the Slatterys' house he'd started to thank Oscar in person, blushing and tongue-tied, and Oscar curtly cut him off, "Hell, kid, us micks have got to stick together, eh?"

The communion breakfast is breaking up, photographers from local papers are taking pictures of Oscar and his VIP guests outside on the peninsula of lawn, Corky Corcoran not included. It's almost noon.

And here comes Red Pitts looking like he's got a corkscrew up his ass. That's a smile?

Pitts tells Corky that Vic and Sandra are waiting for him in Oscar's private office. They don't want anybody to know they're on the premises who doesn't need to know—"So keep it to yourself, Corky, will you?"

"Thanks, Red," says Corky, stubbing out his cigarette in the remains of somebody's waffle, in a plate on a trolley heaped with dirty dishes and cutlery, "—fuck you, Red. Terrific."

"Sure," says Pitts, calling after Corky, Corky can't see but knows the fucker's shiny-eyed clenching his fists, "—any time, Corky. You name it."

Corky's heart's pounding like he and Red have actually been swinging at each other. Jesus, do they hate each other's guts! Not even knowing why.

Except Corky remembers Red Pitts talking with Thalia: looming over her, leaning close.

Oscar Slattery's private office is a spacious walnut-paneled room off the front foyer, converted from a gentleman's library for Oscar's use—part of it's a home office, but it opens into a billiard room with a wet bar, sumptuous leather furniture, a flagstone fireplace with a ten-foot hearth. The rear windows are twelve-foot Thermopane looking out onto a strip of lawn and the Chateauguay River.

It's in this room, at a round table beneath a low-hanging porcelain chandelier, that Oscar's poker games take place. Always on a Friday night, but on an unpredictable schedule. At least, so far as Corky Corcoran knows, it's an unpredictable schedule.

Corky lives in dread of being dropped from these games. Not that he'd want to admit it!—fuck, he's got too much pride.

Fuck, what's he care if he *is* dropped? He's finished with politics anyway.

Corky enters Oscar's office with a quick shy knock on the door and steps inside seeing Sandra Slattery sitting long-legged and poised on a couch, Vic Slattery pacing between Oscar's big glass-topped desk and a window. On the wall above Oscar's desk is the framed hand-lettered quote that's a favorite of Oscar's, Steve Owen of the Giants—FOOTBALL IS A GAME PLAYED DOWN IN THE DIRT, AND ALWAYS WILL BE.

Corky's first impression of Vic and Sandra is they're talking together earnestly in low voices. And the way, when he enters, their eyes swing onto him.

"Corky! At last!"

Vic shakes Corky's hand practically crushing it, and Sandra rising with a cheerleader's bounce to kiss Corky on the cheek says warmly, with that air of flirty feminine reproach Corky loves, "But you look *fine*, Corky, really you do!"—to reassure him, after all he'd spilled to her of his misery over the phone.

It's a weird fact of Corky's life, though he feels like shit much of the time, in others' eyes, if he shaves, combs his hair, dresses in his usual dapper style, he looks good.

(What the hell *did* Corky tell Sandra over the phone?—he can't remember, exactly. Has only a vague shamed memory of breaking down, crying. God damn!)

(Once you confide in a woman she'll never let it go like a dog with a bone but if you confide in a man, next time he sees you he'll pretend to have forgotten.)

Vic is saying, frowning, "—sorry we interrupted your breakfast,

Corky. We meant to get here to join you but, as always, something came up—I was on the phone for forty minutes. Sorry!"

Quickly Corky says, "Hell, no, breakfast's over," grinning and patting his stomach kidding around like he's bloated when, in fact, painfully, he *is*. "Your father put on a fantastic spread and I had all I want. I'm fine."

"You're sure, Corky?" Sandra asks doubtfully. "You did manage to get something to eat?"

"I'm fine. I'm not that hungry."

Sandra Slattery, of a height with Corky in her smart patent leather medium-heeled pumps, looks him level in the eye in that way of hers she seems to have cultivated for Corky Corcoran alone, direct, sisterly, solicitous. Her voice is husky, sexy. She's been a teacher, a college professor, there's a brusque familiar just slightly condescending tone to her remarks, a kind of nudge in Corky's ribs. "This bachelor life is hard on you, Corky, I can tell. You have too much freedom—you don't eat regular meals and you don't sleep . . ." Sandra's voice trails off nervously without lessening its pitch.

And Vic cuts in, solicitous too, concerned, "Well, it's a relief to see you, Corky. We'd been wondering, these last couple of days—"

"—Why *have* you been avoiding us?"

Corky stares at Sandra. The question is more playful and flirty than accusatory, but what's he to make of it? It's never occurred to him that the Slatterys might interpret his behavior as an avoidance of *them*.

"Are you serious?" Corky protests. "*Me*, avoiding *you?*"

Quickly Vic says, "No, Sandra isn't serious. But she's been worried."

Glancing at Sandra reprovingly, as Sandra chatters nervously on, Corky can see Vic's a little pissed at her—Vic's become, over the years, the kind of public man, the larger-than-life public presence, who can register near-imperceptible annoyance to an aide or a spouse even as he remains affable and smiling and squeezing your arm signaling all's well. Like Oscar Slattery beaming into an audience while with a quirk of his eyebrow he's sending a signal to one or another assistant, Red Pitts for instance, he's furious, he'll explode in a rage in the limo.

The Slatterys have been drinking coffee in Vic's father's office, there's a cup for Corky too, no thanks says Corky again rubbing his stomach above the sharp indentation of his belt, but he sits down at their invitation, facing a window, whitish-sun-lit and the river more slate-colored than blue, and to his side, prominent on the wall in its campy-ornate frame, FOOTBALL IS A GAME PLAYED DOWN IN THE DIRT, of course it's POLITICS IS A GAME PLAYED DOWN IN THE DIRT that's Oscar's secret meaning.

As they talk, Corky senses there's been some disagreement between Vic and Sandra, tension in the air. Corky Corcoran can't be the cause but can maybe be the pretext.

As, when a marriage is beginning to go down, or a public career about to explode, the first thing that comes along can be the pretext.

Corky's flattered at the Slatterys' concern. The way, as Vic looks on somber and nodding, Sandra guides the conversation, deft, friendly, tactful. Corky hears himself apologizing again for standing them up, two evenings in a row, Christ he's sorry, he *is* sorry, of course he wasn't avoiding them, far from it—"I'd a helluva lot rather been with you two, than where I was, that's for sure." Playing his Irish-kid bit, the melancholy beneath, he *has* been through some rough times and there's more to come. "Someday I'll explain in more detail when we have time, and you're in the mood for some laughs."

"Maybe you can come visit us in Washington, stay with us for a weekend, next month?"—Sandra's smiling at Corky like all's forgiven.

"Sure," says Corky. "I'd like that."

Sandra Slattery's in her early forties, but still a striking-looking woman—wheat-blond hair, a round wide-cheeked face, eyes a resolute green-brown, intelligent, watchful. She doesn't wear much makeup, unlike Charlotte who wears, in public, a flawless cosmetic mask, there are fine white wrinkles fanning out at the corners of her eyes, a puffiness beneath her eyes, faint shadows like she's been crying. (Why? Has it anything to do with Marilee Plummer's death, did Sandra know Marilee from Vic's campaign? Better not ask.) When, just out of Georgetown Law, Vic introduced Corky to the girl from Washington he was going to marry, he took care to enunciate her name—"Sandra Birney"—as if halfconsciously he'd thought Corky might confuse her with Sandy Sherman who'd been Vic's devoted girlfriend through high school, whom he'd outgrown after a few months at Villanova. Those Marymount girls, sweet dumb virgins you wanted to die for, how quickly boring they became, like

D.A. haircuts, outmoded fashions and slang of the day. Corky'd been in love with Sandy Sherman and might've fallen in love with Sandra Birney except she's a little too sharp-edged for him, watchful; too smart. The rap on Sandra Slattery since Vic's been elected to the House is she's the brains behind his career but Corky, who's known since high school how serious, smart, dedicated, determined, if sometimes wooden-slow Vic can be, knows this is bullshit.

Still, as Vic's friend, supporter, sometime advisor, Corky wishes to hell that Sandra would keep more in the background. Not seem so often to be interfering, pushing. She's got a Ph.D. from Johns Hopkins in something trendy like urban planning, or is it public health policy, writes articles for newspapers, national magazines like *Newsweek*, appears on TV forums, teaches part-time at George Mason University—Sandra's been throwing herself into this like it's *her* career, not Vic's. Which lots of people, friends of Vic's, resent.

Vic's telling Corky what an excellent job the organizers for tonight's fund-raiser have done, how grateful he is, terrific news it's completely sold out. Cuomo has promised to try to come, and the Lieutenant Governor is definitely coming, also Moynihan's right-hand man, also Archbishop O'Dwyer, the chancellor of SUNY Union City, CEOs from AT&T, GM, Squibb, the chairman of the board at Ewing Trust who'd been a locally prominent Reagan man, the dean of Syracuse Law School, the president of Cornell, a good number of state legislators including Whit Post the majority leader, plus the vice-president of the American Council of Education—Vic's ticking these off with an enthusiasm that strikes Corky as a little forced, if you know Vic, but he goes along with it saying, "Great!" and "Terrific!" God knows *he's* enthusiastic, too. There's sure to be guaranteed-friendly media coverage upstate, Vic Slattery's a favorite son of the region and since the energy bill out of the Energy and Commerce Committee passed with such a majority in the House, and Vic was central in drafting it, he's been the object of some national attention, too—"Great timing, if accidental," Vic says.

Corky says, not knowing what the hell he's saying, "Nothing's accidental! You've earned it!"

Remembering then the inexplicable complaint of Oscar's *My son doesn't know how to campaign. He's afraid to get his hands dirty.*

Vic makes a confession: he hasn't exactly finished writing his speech yet. Corky says laughing, he hasn't exactly finished writing *his*—"But I promise to keep it under eight minutes."

There's a pause. Some odd tension. Corky can't figure it.

Then Sandra says dryly, touching Vic's shoulder, "Vic's never kept anything under eight minutes. Not over a microphone."

Vic laughs self-consciously, there's a sullen-wry twist to his mouth. Then a pause again, Corky can almost feel the strain, like charged air before a storm.

Which of them, Corky's wondering, is going to mention Marilee Plummer first?

It's true, Vic Slattery, giving speeches, at any podium, starts off John Kennedy–style like every youngish good-looking liberal Democrat tries for, then something sets in like lockjaw and he turns wooden, ponderous, his forehead actually furrowing with thoughts bombarding him in the interstices of his typed text, so he's got to speak extemporaneously to expand, explain, illustrate, qualify. It's all but impossible for him to make a simple declarative statement. In politics you have to take sides, everything's black or white, in the voting booth it's just one lever for one office, any shithead can figure it except sweet-dumb Vic Slattery with his Jesuit hairsplitting morality—but even the Jesuits lost patience with him sometimes. You can think too much, you can trip over your own feet. In the boxing ring where Vic was trying to figure out his opponent's strategy when most of the time his opponent didn't have any strategy, on the debate team where he'd spend too much time qualifying his position. Basically, Vic said, he couldn't believe in Aristotle's logic—a thing can't be both X and non-X at the same time. His idea of "reality" was things are a lot more mixed up than that.

His heroes were Thomas Jefferson, Daniel Webster, Abraham Lincoln, FDR, Thomas Merton, Adlai Stevenson. For a Catholic-school kid, naming Stevenson (so infamously divorced and fucked over in public by his ex-wife) was what you'd call *daring*.

As they talk, a little more relaxed now, Vic taking over, Corky sees not wanting to see that his friend is looking his age: no, older than forty-four: fifty, at least. Christ, it's sad! The strain showing around the eyes, the cheeks flushed and looser-jowled than Corky recalls, a drinker's skin,

Corky wonders how much Vic's been drinking lately, what it means. Since high school Vic hasn't grown more than a couple of inches in height but he's put on at least thirty pounds, not fat exactly but that fatty-muscled bulk of an ex-athlete, thickening in the shoulders, torso, waist. His thighs, in shorts, are big as hams. His tawny-blond hair is thinning more rapidly than Corky's, and shading to gray. Yet there's that boy's face innocent-seeming and perplexed inside the other. *Hey, tell me! Explain to me! I want to know! My heart is pure, my intentions are pure, I want to do good: how?*

Corky notes that both Slatterys are dressed for the occasion of a communion breakfast at Stuyvesant House though for some reason they missed the breakfast. Sandra in a yellow linen suit, white silk blouse and bow at her throat, medium-heeled patent leather shoes, here's a woman not out to display her legs but she *is* feminine—to a point. A good wholesome signal. Vic's in one of his typical suits, custom-made but nothing out of the ordinary, somber dark blue tropical wool, plain dark tie, trousers wrinkled at the knees, thighs. A middle-of-the-road Democrat, a Trust-Me appeal to Republicans, businessmen.

By contrast, Corky Corcoran's dressed like he's hoping somebody will take his picture. No wop designer clothes for today, today he's All-American in a Macy's double-breasted navy blue blazer with brass buttons if you're nearsighted you'd mistake for a Marine dress uniform. A red-sheen necktie that's actually an Enzio Cenci silk at $75 but looks like American issue. White cotton shirt, starched. And the almost-new Florsheims polished and gleaming sending a signal *you can trust this man.*

(Except: through the window beyond Sandra's pert attentive head there's the Mayor and the favored VIPs of the day still being photographed. Corky counts six, seven men, most of them known to him, millionaire Party donors. So it figures. And the priests, toothy Father Vincent, *that* figures.)

One of the black waiters returns smiling with a fresh pot of coffee and this time Corky says O.K., he'll have some. Purely black, and hot, bitter on the tongue. And lighting up a cigarette to calm his nerves clattering *A drink, why not a drink? you've earned it* though knowing he's risking Sandra Slattery's disapproval. But he's been dying for a smoke. A smoke and *a drink: it's past noon* the well-stocked wet bar's close by in the bil-

liard room and never absolutely never has Corky Corcoran been in the
Mayor's residence so God-damned long without being offered a drink.
God damn!

So he lights up a Camel, and at once Sandra cries, "Corky, no!"—like
he's personally insulted her. "You're smoking—again? How can you!"
Eyes fierce and intolerant and lips damply parted in that affronted way
that, in good-looking women, Corky finds sexy as hell. In homely women,
it's repulsive.

Vic, who hasn't smoked in fifteen years, grins wistfully-reproachfully
at Corky. His old teammate, sneaking a cigarette against Coach's orders.
*If I catch any of you smoking, if I hear of any of you smoking—there'll
be hell to pay. Got it?*

Sandra's been known to boast, *she's* never smoked. Nor even cared to
experiment as a teenager.

Corky shrugs, annoyed. "It's just temporary, till the pressure's off. If it
bothers you, I'll put it out."

"But why begin?" Sandra demands. "You're too smart for such ignorant behavior, Corky!"

Sandra's fierce, dazzling. The intensity of her concern is disconcerting:
Corky's made to realize how rare it is, how rare it's going to be, that anybody gives a damn about him. Whether he smokes, drinks, dies in a car
wreck . . . gets his head blown off.

Protesting, "Christ, Sandra, I *have* quit drinking, don't I get any
credit?"

Sandra doesn't hear. She's lecturing Corky, bombarding him with statistics, four thousand Americans die every day of cancer! of which thirty
percent are attributable to smoking! which means twelve hundred need-
less deaths a day! even with the Surgeon General's warning! what's to be
done if people like him—! Corky's listening, isn't listening, drawing a
toxic hit deep into his lungs, but wishing he could swallow the smoke and
not provoke this excitable woman who's leaning toward him so urgently.
Corky's never seen Sandra Slattery so high-pitched, aggressive. Usually
she's poised, careful, cautious—the seasoned politician's wife—even in
private company.

Vic says, embarrassed, "Hey Sandra, let's not upset Corky right now.
We can talk about it another time."

Sandra says recklessly, "There might not be another time!"

This is such an extravagant statement the three of them laugh.

Corky exaggerates being chastised, like a child quickly stubbing out his cigarette—"O.K.! Sorry." He stubs out the cigarette in a brass ashtray on Oscar's desk, sees several wrapped cigars close by, Macanud, and a big stub of another in the ashtray. Atop the desk are scattered documents Corky isn't in a position to read without being obvious about it but he recognizes the distinctive laser printout of City Council memos and reports, must be the forty-page committee report on the Civilian Complaint Review Board proposal that's on Corky's desk, too, at home. Not exactly read but thumbed through.

Now Corky has capitulated to Sandra, like most women she's immediately conciliatory. They don't want to seem, to *be* bossy, even when they are. Getting their own way makes them feel guilty, maybe? Sandra takes Corky's hands in hers, how cold her hands are, thin-boned, saying, "It's because we love you, Corky. We don't want you to endanger your health. We *care*."

Bullshit, thinks Corky.

No, in fact he's moved. He'd make a joke of such lavish talk but he *is* moved. And Vic looking on frowning, inscrutable.

As if on cue then Sandra excuses herself to make a telephone call, the men are left alone together. Abrupt and disorienting, and Corky feels uneasy. Since they were in their twenties, Corky and Vic have rarely been alone together; have rarely talked together as they'd used to do in high school. Corky's thinking he should leave soon . . . if he wants to get to Uncle Sean's this afternoon. Can't break his promise another time.

To take the edge off their awkwardness with each other, Vic and Corky have been observing the photo session outside the window, now breaking up. Vic identifies the men Corky doesn't know, one of them a new presence in Union City—a partner at Niagara Frontier Commodities, from Dallas. Another Reagan man disillusioned with Bush. And he's bought tickets for tonight.

"Great," says Corky. Then, since this doesn't sound enthusiastic enough, "Terrific."

Vic says, emphatically if a little flatly, "It's the wave of the future. It's the way the country will be going. After Clinton wins the nomination—"

That roaring sound like a freight train barreling overhead—it's the wind. Late May in upstate New York, a reasonably clear-blue day, but, as always, that fucking wind out of Canada. On its thirty-foot pole at the tip of the grassy-manicured peninsula a giant American flag is whipping in fierce convulsive gusts. The river's surface is choppy and pocked, you'd never know which way the current is going. Corky smiles meanly seeing one of the men in Oscar's party trying to tamp his hair down—he's grown it long on one side of his head to comb it over his bald pate but the wind keeps dislodging it. *Sad*.

Corky vows, *he'll* never resort to that.

Vic shifts in his seat, uncrosses his legs, seems about to say something further then decides against it. "Corky, my man!—what can I get you? Scotch?" Suddenly ebullient, Vic's on his feet headed for the wet bar recessed in the wall, and Corky feels almost a stab of panic, he *is* dying for a drink.

How hard it is to sit still with a friend, a male friend, without a drink in hand, and talk. Best at a bar, standing up, with a lot of other people around.

"No thanks, Vic."

"Red Label, eh?"

"Thanks, *no*."

Vic looks through Oscar's bottles, whistling thinly. Corky's mouth is actually watering: he's wondering if it isn't just thirst, a strange kind of thirst, not alcohol deprivation that's taken him over.

The document on Oscar's desk, Corky sees it *is* the report on the Civilian Complaint Review Board. Must be coming up next Thursday, unavoidable. Corky'd been nominated for the committee but managed to get out of it, more shit he doesn't need in his life, a no-win situation. The proposal, in the parlance of City Hall, is a class-A fucker. You push for the review board, you make enemies of the UCPD and their supporters; you vote it down, or stonewall it, you make enemies of the "ethnic minorities" and their supporters. The shrewdest strategy, which Corky guesses Oscar will work on behind the scenes, though Oscar hasn't discussed it with Corky yet, is to dilute the proposal qualifying its actual legal power to challenge the UCPD Internal Affairs Division and get it passed before the Pickett trial. After that, depending on the verdict—God knows.

Corky thinks of bringing this subject up with Vic, finagling around to the subject of the UCPD, did Vic happen to see or to hear about Corky on TV the day before getting boxed into a corner by that cunt saying things he didn't exactly mean to say at least in that context without controlling the situation *Yes but in fact you meant it: don't bullshit* and is Oscar angry with him?—but why should Oscar be angry with him, the Mayor himself should be calling for a thorough police investigation.

God damn Marilee Plummer: killing yourself *is* revenge.

Corky lights up a fresh cigarette, why the hell not. Now Sandra's out of the room, why the hell not.

One thing a man can't stand, it's a woman, any woman, your own or anybody else's, trying to tell you what to do.

Whistling, seemingly in a good mood, Vic pours drinks for himself and Corky both, Corky sees to his dismay it *is* Red Label. In other circumstances he'd have to laugh, the coincidence of, twice within twelve hours, somebody close to him pressing upon him the identical brand of poison.

But Corky isn't going to drink, and when Vic returns, handing him his glass, Corky sets it down on a table. "Thanks, Vic, but didn't I tell you?—I've quit."

"Yes," says Vic, "—but you're not serious."

Corky laughs, his friend's got his number. That's how you know your friends: the guys who've got your number.

Vic raises his glass, murmurs, "Cheers!—thanks for coming, and for tonight," and takes a small quick sip, then sets his glass down too. Eyeing Corky with a wan rueful smile, seeing Corky smoking but making no comment except, obliquely—"Sandra's father died of lung cancer last year, maybe you remember? Poor man, it was a horrible death. She hasn't gotten over it yet, entirely."

Corky, intimate friend of the Slatterys, isn't sure that he knew about this death. He exhales smoke through both nostrils, in grim acknowledgment.

Vic says, "I'm sorry Sandra came down quite so hard on you, Corky. She thinks, as I do, that so much of what happens to us we can't control, what we *can*, we should." He pauses. His breath is audible as if he's been exercising. "At least, it's an ideal principle."

Corky nods. It's a principle with him, too.

After an awkward pause, Vic asks after Corky's family and Corky asks after Vic's family as the men do whenever they meet, though it isn't clear what either means by "family"—with the rapid passage of years, the original conceptions have changed many times. Vic's questions about Corky's ex-wife and estranged daughter are guarded, and Corky doesn't press it about Oscar, accepting it that Oscar's "well" and "busy as usual"—in any case, Corky knows that Vic Slattery isn't privy to his father's most intimate thoughts. The Mayor plays his cards close to his chest, and deadpan. If Corky's on Oscar Slattery's shit list for running his mouth in public, seeming to be critical of City Hall, Corky will find out soon enough on his own.

Another awkward pause, and Corky's nerved up purposefully not looking at the glass of scotch so temptingly within reach, fuck it he *isn't* going to take that first drink of the day no matter how thirsty he is and how his hands are trembling; or would be trembling, if he didn't hold them firm. He gets the idea then to ask Vic about the energy bill, and Vic's grateful, animated in replying, and at length, as if for an interview, speaking of the pressure he and other liberal Democrats were under for weeks to compromise on certain controversial issues—price increases for natural gas, offshore drilling restrictions. Corky'd forgotten there are forty-two members on the House Energy and Commerce Committee—*forty-two!*—a bipartisan group with a Democratic majority but working in uneasy anticipation of what Bush's Energy Secretary Watkins will say, and what the Senate will do when it gets the bill; eventually, how the President will react—if negotiations fall through, if there's some abrupt seismic swing in political consciousness, for instance more trouble from Iraq, with the Chief Executive taking charge again, and soaring in the polls, Bush *could* veto. Corky listens sympathetically as Vic speaks, how passionate his friend is, how genuine he is in caring, politics isn't an abstract principle to him but an immediate reality, charged with emotion.

Vic's voice trails off as if midsentence he's forgotten what he's talking about. Rubbing his eyes, and when he looks up at Corky his vision appears bruised. "It's a peculiar life, isn't it—needing to be liked for your livelihood. That's what it reduces to, basically—in a democracy, a politician derives power from being *liked*." For some reason this strikes Vic as funny: he laughs soundlessly, without mirth. His broad white smile is whiter than Corky remembers.

Corky mumbles, embarrassed, "Well—we all want to be liked, I guess.

Even before we're politicians. Maybe we think—" hesitating wanting to say *then we'll live forever*, but saying instead, "—it will make a difference."

But this isn't what Corky wants to say, either.

Outside, Oscar and his companions have disappeared from view. The wind is louder, a high, hollow-sounding roar. Nothing to draw Corky's and Vic's attention except the grassy tip of the peninsula, the high fence with its military look, the choppy, agitated, slate-colored river. The gaudy striped American flag whipping in frantic gusts.

Then, this: Corky's staring at his watch calculating how long it will take to get to Roosevelt Street, can't let his uncle down another time. *A drink? a drink, Jesus!* his throat's parched but he won't, fuck it he will *not*. And out of his resolution a sudden question put to his friend point-blank, without warning, "Vic, look—I need to know: were you involved with Marilee Plummer?"

Vic lowers his glass of whiskey in silence. Afterward Corky will think *Was he expecting this? Sure* though at the time interpreting his friend's reaction as surprise, hurt.

Vic says quietly, unhesitatingly, "In the way you mean, no I was not."

"There's just one way I mean," Corky says, blundering, crude, "—were you fucking her?"

Again calmly Vic says, "No, Corky, I was not."

Corky feels the blood rush into his face, knows he's turning beet-red. And this sinking sensation in his bowels he's really fucked up now, now you've done it asshole, you dumb shit killing the friendship that means the most to you in the world but Vic's being a gentleman, hurt, maybe indignant but trying not to show it. Corky says, stammering, "I'm sorry as hell to be asking, Vic, but I—I've heard some things around town. And Thalia gave me this." Corky's taken out his wallet and carefully removes the snapshot taken at Rooney's summer place of Vic, Marilee, Presson; Thalia and the unidentified man in the background. He hands it over to Vic who takes it wordlessly and stares at it without expression. A sleaze-bag lawyer's trick, Vic will never forgive him. Corky says, quickly, "—It's just a party. Letting off steam. We go to parties all the time with and without our wives and what the hell, it doesn't mean anything." Continuing, in the face of Vic's silence, "—Who's that guy with Thalia in the background? She claimed not to remember."

Vic, examining the snapshot, doesn't seem to have heard. Like a man who's taken a low blow but isn't going to show it. How can Corky pull this shit on his friend? As evidence it *is* nothing. Vic hands it back and Corky sees he's angry, and upset. His eyes suddenly bloodshot. "Whatever there was between Marilee and me is private," he says carefully, "—but it was not sexual. She was my friend, and I like to think I was hers. During the campaign we saw each other almost every day but we were rarely alone together—quite possibly, never alone together. Then after the election she went to work for a PR firm, I think. Then for the historical museum." He pauses, breathing quickly. "Sandra and I are devastated by what's happened to her—it's a terrible tragedy. But I can't—"

Can't get involved, sure. Corky understands.

In a democracy, a politician needs to be liked. Trusted. If not you don't get the vote, if you don't get the vote you don't get in office. Your good intentions are worth shit.

Corky feels sorry for Vic, he's sure it's as Vic says—*he* could tell if Vic was lying. Doesn't want to push it but has to ask, "What about after the Steadman business, then? After she went public, filed charges? Did you see Marilee then, were you in contact with her then?"

Vic says slowly, rubbing the bridge of his nose, "—I spoke with Marilee on the phone, but I don't believe I saw her. We helped arrange for a lawyer for her—Steadman was threatening a suit for defamation of character, slander—she was under terrible pressure. I was in Washington most of the time, I wasn't—here. And we'd about lost contact by then." Vic begins to pace, his voice rising. "That bastard, Steadman!—that racist! He did it deliberately, I'm sure—raped Marilee, humiliated her—taunted her with being 'white.' If there's any justice he should be charged for her murder, too." Vic's speaking so loudly Corky's worried somebody will hear him outside the door. Those hundreds of guests milling around.

Corky remembers how after Vic was elected senior class president at St. Thomas he'd disappeared and they found him in the chapel praying—so grateful he'd won, tears on his cheeks. You had to love a guy like that, eighteen years old and still believing in God, Jesus Christ, the Virgin Mary and St. Joseph—the whole campaign crew.

When Corky was elected treasurer of his class, the next year, he'd thanked the guys who'd helped him win; thanking too those he guessed hadn't voted for him but in the aftermath of his victory would pretend they had. Everybody loves a winner, so you want to be a good winner. A good winner hides his grudges.

Corky would like to ask Vic pointblank *were you screwing Kiki?—Thalia?*—but he can't. He's through with his questions. Guessing that, if Vic was involved with Marilee Plummer in some ambiguous way, it wasn't recently and it's nobody's business in fact, why tell Corky any of it. Lamely Corky says not meaning this as a joke but it comes out dumb-fuck funny, "—*I* tried to make her—Marilee—and her friend Kiki, too—I have to admit. But those girls hosed me out on my ass."

Vic's wiping his face with a handkerchief and glances over at Corky, not smiling, quizzical. Why tell *me?*

Vic takes up the glasses, goes to the bar to wash them, brisk and business-like, wanting to hide the evidence of drinking from Sandra. Corky who'd been thinking of just maybe having a drink after all watches with dismay the premium whiskey meant for him alone poured down the sink with a blast of water behind it. God damn! *Stone cold sober* is a pitiless existence.

Corky says hesitantly, like a chagrined kid, "Vic, you're pissed off at me, aren't you?" and Vic shrugs, no, of course not, and Corky says, "I had to ask, that's all," and Vic says bemused, "*Did* you," and Corky says, honestly, "I had to, yes," and Vic says, turned away, wiping the glasses with a towel and setting them back on the shelf amid the gleaming bottles, "Corky, if people are saying things about me and Marilee Plummer, I'm grateful to know. But don't tell me who they are. We can end it right here."

So the men shake hands at the door. It's 12:29 P.M. Memorial Day 1992. Vic Slattery says, amiably enough, "See you tonight, Corky," and Corky grins back, "See you tonight, Vic!—terrific." And only out in the crowded foyer dazed like a lightweight who's managed to slip a heavy-weight's punches for several rounds but has exhausted himself in the effort thinking *We can end it right here, what's that mean?* Feeling sick wondering if he's lost his best friend and for what reason?—*why?*

Corky can't remember.

4

COLDCOCKED

And then, on his way out of Stuyvesant House, three more things happen to Corky Corcoran.

The first, and quickest, is: he's pushing through this crowd of men most of them older, potbellied, known to him but no friends of his, head lowered, preoccupied, not watching where he's going when he feels a heavy hand descending on his left shoulder like a karate chop deflected just by inches from breaking his neck, and it's of all people Oscar Slattery—"Corky Corcoran! How the hell are *you?*"—and a beaming-jovial smile, eyes boring into his, but before Corky can reply the Mayor's barreled past, he's in the company of that slick operator Father O'Brien and that new man in town the former Reagan Republican now a partner in Niagara Frontier Commodities Corp., and no time for Corky right now. So Corky, blinking, stunned as a dog who's anticipated being kicked who's been roughly fondled instead, can only call after, weakly, "Oscar! How the hell are *you?*"

So Corky's *not* on Oscar Slattery's shit list, after all! He's been forgiven?

That's it?

And then, before he can think this through, see how it might be fitted together with what Vic's told him, there's Sandra Slattery in her dazzling-daffodil suit, stepping forward unexpectedly too amid the crowd of departing guests, she lays a hand on Corky's sleeve and says, reprovingly, "Corky!"—for of course Corky's smoking, sucking at his cigarette like a baby sucking its mother's teat, exhaling poisonous blue clouds of smoke; but then, in a softer tone, with a squeeze of his wrist that excites his prick, it feels so intimate, "Corky?—can I speak with you for a few minutes, in private?"

Corky thinks, feeling a chill: Bad news.

And in a rear corridor of the Mayor's residence Corky learns just how bad, how bizarre and unexpected it is: according to Sandra Slattery, Thalia has been "harassing" Vic for months.

"She seems to have become fixated on him," Sandra says, embarrassed, "—she calls him at home here, and at the office in Washington; she sends him, and sometimes me, clippings, and cryptic little cards; she's shown up unannounced in Washington wanting to talk to Vic about legislation— animal rights, abortion rights—she's been following the Energy and Commerce Committee closely. We didn't want to worry you or Char-lotte, we're fond of Thalia and don't want to humiliate her. You know what she's like—passionate, and intelligent, and devoted to causes, only just not quite focused. Vic doesn't know I'm telling you, he thinks Thalia will lose interest eventually. But this came about eight days ago, to our Chateauguay house, addressed to 'Congressman V. Slattery and Ms. S. Slattery'—I didn't show it to Vic." Sandra takes out of her purse a small ob-ject wrapped in tissue paper, Corky can't believe his eyes seeing it's a turn-of-the-century porcelain doll he'd bought Thalia for her sixteenth birthday. About eight inches long, with waved brunette hair the color of Thalia's, and a pretty-vacuous painted-on face, wide blue eyes and a rosebud mouth. The doll is wearing an aged yellowed lace nightgown and there's a jagged crack in its forehead that wasn't there the last time Corky saw it.

Corky whispers, "Jesus!" feeling for a scary moment he's about to keel over.

Sandra says, "The note that accompanied it was 'I perished—of De-light.' I think it must be Emily Dickinson, but I'm not sure. It sounds like Dickinson."

Corky's straining to make sense of this. "Dickinson—who?"

"Oh, never mind, Corky, a poet, a nineteenth-century woman poet, it isn't important. What's upsetting is getting it—trying to decode Thalia's meaning."

Corky has the doll in his fingers, turning it dumbly. How could Thalia give away *his* present to her?—she'd loved it so, or seemed to, when she was sixteen.

Sandra goes on to say that Thalia seems to assume there's a special relationship between her and Vic, but Vic insists there isn't, there never has been, it's in Thalia's imagination exclusively. Sandra says she believes

Vic. Sandra says yes she knows that Vic was in a phase for a while in the 1970s, the early 1980s when he had affairs—fleeting affairs—with young women—women who threw themselves at him—but Vic no longer has these affairs, he's sworn to her and Sandra believes him. So Corky mustn't think what it's probably in his head to think—because it isn't so.

Corky hasn't been following all this, exactly. He's lost the thread. Turning the porcelain doll in his fingers, staring at it stunned. How the fuck *do* you decode such a thing? Corky's in over his head.

Sandra takes pity on Corky, she's pained at the sick sliding look on his face. Impulsively she hugs him, kisses him wetly on the side of his mouth. They stumble together like drunken dancers just as, as chance would have it, two uniformed black waiters pass by carrying something between them; if the waiters see they give no sign, nor do they murmur together, or laugh.

The worst of it is, dumping this news in Corky's lap, handing him the cracked-head doll, Sandra Slattery now says she has to leave. She and Vic must get back to Chateauguay, there are a thousand last-minute things to be done between now and seven P.M. when the cocktail reception begins.

Sandra pulls away, and Corky takes hold of her wrist, they're panting, warm. Sandra's elegantly coiffed hair has become disheveled and her purse, hanging from a strap on her arm, is hanging open, about to spill its contents. "Wait," Corky says, desperate, incredulous, "—you're telling me my daughter's been harassing you and Vic, and you kept it a secret? For how long?" and Sandra says, apologetically, "Oh, Corky, we didn't want to worry you, you're so excitable. And it hasn't been continuous. And some of it has been playful—more what you'd call eccentric behavior," and Corky says. "'Eccentric behavior'?—you mean, *crazy!* What you're saying is *crazy!*" and Sandra protests, "Oh, Corky, no, not really, I shouldn't have used the word 'harassing'—that's too extreme," and Corky says, still holding Sandra's wrist, though she's backing away from him, and he's following, in the direction of the public rooms at the front of the house, "Sandra, wait: are you sure Vic wasn't involved with Thalia? Maybe just a single time," and Sandra tries to wrench her arm away, her face tightening, "*She's* fixated on *him*, and it isn't reciprocated, that's why she's so—persistent," and Corky says, "Whatever Vic tells you, or tells me, it might be true and it might not, he isn't an altar boy any longer, don't hand me that crap," and Sandra says, "Corky, I'm sorry. I know you're upset, but let me go!"—managing to get free of him, and turning, walking swiftly away not looking back.

So here's Corky Corcoran standing staring after Sandra Slattery who's hurrying away breathless and disheveled as if they've been struggling together, staring muttering, "Fuck. Fuck. *Fuck*," under his breath.

A porcelain doll in a lace nightgown in his hand?

Better then for Corky to leave Stuyvesant House immediately. But he doesn't.

Pleading with Sandra Slattery, Corky hasn't noticed Red Pitts at the far end of the corridor but Pitts has been watching them, and when Sandra approaches him hurried and distracted Pitts asks what's going on, Mrs. Slattery?—has that guy been bothering you?—and Sandra says no, it's nothing, thanks Red, in no mood right now to so much as pause to talk with hulking Red Pitts her father-in-law's devoted bodyguard, Sandra's aroused, fierce-eyed, gratified too, God-damned happy she's dumped such distressing news in Corky Corcoran's lap, let Corky deal with it, let Corky try to calculate how seriously Thalia's accusations can be taken—all this Corky will learn, or figure out, in the future. At the moment the poor guy's concerned with finding a lavatory, at the rear of Stuyvesant House preferably, his bowels have turned to liquid shit and there's no time for speculation.

Corky locates a lavatory beyond the kitchen area, MEN STAFF painted in black on the door. Inside, just two stalls, and both empty, and in one of the toilets he voids his bowels for the second time in a few hours trembling and shivering as scalding liquid cascades from what seems a raw tear, a fissure in his very flesh, *O Jesus have mercy*. But it's done. It's done and he wipes himself with fistfuls of toilet paper and flushes the toilet, then at the sink furiously washing his hands staring in hollow-eyed contempt at the pathetic prick in the mirror in his Macy's blazer, his patterned Enzio Cenci necktie, when the door behind him is shoved rudely open, and there's Red Pitts framed in the doorway.

Corky's first thought is a taunting *Red, my man!*—but he says nothing. Not a word, the two men looking at each other in the mirror above the sink. Red steps inside, lets the door close. Corky's crouched over the plain white sink head lowered, face dripping water where he's splashed it. Crude as a twelve-year-old-boy, screwing his face up against the odor, which the ventilating system's been defeated in carrying away, Red says, "Phew, what a stink!—that's *you*, 'Corky'?" seeing too in that instant the antique doll balanced on the mirror's ledge and laughing derisively, "What's that—your *baby?*" Corky reaches for a wad of paper towels to dry his face nervously aware he's in actual danger from Red Pitts, a guy the size of a pro fullback, and hotheaded, and packing a gun. So Corky doesn't say anything except, "Fuck you, 'Red,'" under his breath.

Corky hasn't caught on that Red Pitts has come in the lavatory *for* him. He thinks it's just coincidence.

Red Pitts, the pimp. Corky Corcoran, the gentleman.

But Red's advancing upon Corky big-jawed with that twitchy smile, eyes like steel filings, "I saw you and Mrs. Slattery out there—what the fuck were you doing with that lady? *I saw you*," and Corky says excitedly, "What? What did you see? You're following me around? You're spying on me?" crouched watching Red Pitts behind him, through the mirror, the pug nose, the beefy face and dumb-fuck blow-dried hair in an Elvis sweep across the forehead—*that's* a new style, for Red. Corky's heart is pounding like a sparrow's in the presence of a hawk, Corky knows if the two of them were alone together somewhere remote and unobserved this man would crack Corky's skull against the sink like an eggshell. Red says, incredulous, "What the fuck's wrong with you, Corcoran? Molesting Vic Slattery's wife? On these premises? You got a screw loose? You drunk? That's it, huh, you're drunk? And impersonating a cop?—you, you dumb little shit, you sawed-off dwarf-freak, you—*impersonating a cop?*"

What happens then Corky won't recall exactly, he's still crouched and watching Red Pitts through the mirror, he sees, or thinks he sees, Red starting to swing at him, a crude roundhouse right to land between Corky's shoulder blades and drive his jaw against the sink and his lower teeth into his upper teeth, so quick-on-his-feet Corky Corcoran the Irish Henry Armstrong slips this blow, or the trajectory of the blow if it was actually on its way, dodges and ducks and sends a desperate and unerring right straight from the shoulder with the pent-up fury of years into Red Pitts' groin.

Red Pitts' eyes fly open. A grunting sound like a rug struck by a wire rugbeater seems to issue not from his mouth but from his body. He doubles over grabbing his crotch and he sinks to his knees on the lavatory floor and long before he recovers even enough to stagger to his feet Corky Corcoran is gone.

5

"PLEASE FORGIVE ME, I LOVE YOU . . ."

Like a figure in a film run swiftly and comically backward Corky Corcoran retraces his steps to the parking lot adjacent to Stuyvesant House, hurriedly in the Caddy backs around throwing up gravel beneath the fenders, nursing his right hand which is already beginning to swell at the knuckles but *sweet fucking Jesus did that feel good! better than any fuck, any day!* and laughing to himself, out of the corner of his eye he sees, but isn't going to acknowledge, Fats Pickering and Mort McNamara Oscar's campaign manager walking together, he's headed for the security kiosk to get the hell out of here though reasoning that Red Pitts even should he recover quickly enough from being coldcocked in time to alert Security won't do so: won't in his pride tell a living soul what happened, preferring to get his revenge, and for sure Red Pitts will, as a private citizen.

Still, Corky hauls his ass off the Stuyvesant House grounds at quadruple the speed he arrived.

At the kiosk there's no hassle. In fact the prick who gave him a hard time coming in is actually smiling at him now, waves him through like Corky Corcoran's a dignitary, Corky's feeling so good he grins and waves back, yelling out the Caddy window, "Happy Memorial Day!"

How's it feel, kid?

Terrific!

Then on Van Dusen speeding to the Fillmore he'll be taking south to Irish Hill feeling the first mild tinge of regret, also, fuck it, he left Thalia's doll in the lavatory, *that* he'd wanted to hang onto to confront her with, shake in her face, *This is all you care about me?—giving away my present you said you loved?—running around town telling shit-faced lies I'm a pervert?*—but he has to laugh, a good belly laugh like he hasn't had in days, that look on Pitts' face, that grunt that erupted out of him, Corky hasn't coldcocked another guy since a parking lot fight at the old Cloverleaf before he was married, which is too long ago. He can't believe how sweet, driving his fist into Red Pitts' balls, it's like the boxing commentators say, deadpan—*That got his attention.*

But a mild tinge of regret like the beginning of a toothache. If Oscar finds *this* out.

Yes, but Oscar won't. This is between Red and you, and nobody else.

But if Oscar does. And Vic, and Sandra. What then?

Self-defense. It *was* self-defense.

And what about Red, what's *he* going to do? The guy's a psycho waiting to spring.

Worry about that when the time comes.

Time's on *my* side.

Hire two goons like with Thalia's stalker, $500 up front and $500 on delivery, beat the shit out of Red Pitts before he gets his hands on you O.K. but what if they kill him?—what then?

Sucking on his swelling knuckles but still laughing Corky swings off Van Dusen taking a sharp left against traffic signs to get over into the right-hand lane of the access ramp to the Fillmore, not acknowledging he's cutting off some middle-aged guy and his old lady blinking at him through the windshield of one of those crappy budget imports, then up the ramp flying onto the Expressway like flying into the sky, seeing high-blown clouds like horses' manes so beautiful and that pale washed-looking blue beyond he'd stare at from the attic of his uncle's house on Roosevelt where he'd sneak away to stand for long wordless minutes as a boy waiting for the release of his brain from its ceaseless toil of thought: and his soul then turning to vapor, rising into that sky.

"Terrific!"—the latest weather bulletin on WWAZ between blasts of commercials predicts no rain until this evening. So the parade, scheduled to begin at two P.M., will go as planned.

This word Corky's been saying repeatedly, compulsively, like tiny bubbles fizzing in his brain—"Terrific!"

He's a little punch-drunk, after Stuyvesant House. But he'll be O.K.

Then, next happens what Corky could never have anticipated, nor even hoped for in his wildest fantasies, never: as, at the poker table, better yet at craps, you do truly enter sometimes that incalculable dimension called *luck*, or *a winning streak:* he decides to call in for his voice mail on his way to Irish Hill—and his anxiety of the past twenty-four hours vanishes as if it has never been.

First, there's another call, throaty and intimate, from Charlotte, which at once impatient guilty and embarrassed for her Corky cuts off with his thumb on "3," for erase; then, an abrupt hangup—Corky'd like to think this is Christina calling him; then, a second hangup—*this* has got to be Christina; then, to Corky's astonishment, so like an answered prayer as he listens with the receiver pressed up tight against his ear he slackens the Caddy's speed unconsciously until he's traveling at below forty miles per hour in the farthest left-hand lane and other drivers begin honking, it's Thalia—"Hello, Corky, this is . . . I guess you know who this is . . . I'm calling to say how sorry I am for the way I've been behaving, will you forgive me? Please forgive me . . ." a pause, a sound that might be muffled laughter, or sobbing, ". . . Since Marilee did what she did . . . what she'd say she had to do . . . *I* don't judge . . . I haven't been in control of my thoughts. Whoever is, I don't know. Marilee shared certain confidences with me in the secrecy of sisterhood-blood that transcends the blood of 'race' . . . 'identity' . . . I can never betray her. I believed I would enact her revenge for her from out of the grave but I have come to the conclusion now that I have no right. Corky, there *is* God . . ." another pause, so long Corky thinks the message might be over, then Thalia's breathy murmurous voice continues, ". . . I have been unfair to you, Corky . . . I know you love me, I know you are a good man and God resides in your heart despite you . . . I love Mother, too, and will write to her from where I am going . . . from the *western ranges* . . ." these words, *western ranges*, uttered in a curious melodic voice, ". . . to explain and to beg forgiveness for my cruelty but above all my ignorance. And I beg forgiveness from the Slatterys too, by now maybe you know of my shame how I . . . misunderstood, and made a fool of myself . . . I do love him . . . but my love will never again make any claim . . . there need be no reciprocation . . . as, loving God, we must not expect God to love us in turn nor even to know us." And another pause, and then with more force, confidence, "Corky, I have thrown your gun into the river. The temptation of evil is gone forever. Don't be angry with me, Corky! Forgive me! Please forgive me, I love you . . ."

By this time Corky's braked to a stop on the Expressway shoulder.

Tears in his eyes, O Christ he's relieved!

Punches "1" to have Thalia's message repeated. And then another time. Can't believe it. His good fortune. So unexpected. And just at the right time.

Thalia, sweetheart! Sure I forgive you. Sure I love you too.

Corky listens to the tape four times in all each time steeling himself for hearing different words, or, in Thalia's breathy voice, a touch of mockery, trickery—it's hard to trust her, after all. But this is the real thing. He'll call Charlotte right away and give her his voice-mail code so she can call in and hear the tape herself.

The *western ranges*—what's that mean? Corky thinks he remembers a friend of Thalia's from Cornell, family owned a big ranch in Wyoming. Or Montana. A girlfriend, and they'd been close. Must be this friend, this ranch, Wyoming, or Montana, the *western ranges* Thalia means.

Right now Corky's not going to think about it, Corky's so happy so relieved it's like he's filled with helium gas knowing now he *can* visit his Uncle Sean and tonight he *can* speak in honor of Vic Slattery he loves like a brother—what's life but a celebration?

6

RAT'S NEST

And if Dermott Corcoran hanged *and* beheaded aged twenty-two, and not Gahern his younger brother, had been destined from the start of Time to be Corky Corcoran's ancestor, what then?

Every other story, you don't exist. Only in this story, you exist. So long as the story continues.

Praying to God in Whom since the age of eleven he has not believed.

Praying to God with a kid's snotty arrogance. *I hate You, I blame You.*

And why wasn't he strong enough, why wasn't it in him. To identify his father's murderers with a simple lie—he who, all the years of his life afterward, would be capable of any kind of bullshit when it suited him.

And why not strong enough to save his mother. Letting her go, finally. Sure he'd been relieved. Got drunk after the funeral, got laid, and that very night a dose of the clap.

Old fart-in-a-bottle O'Malley telling him he had "gon-or-rhea" and should be grateful it's 1967 and not 1867. And Corky said, Yeah?—well it *is* 1967, Doctor. So fix me up.

Theresa angry, weeping over him, *I can't! can't save you! I'm not strong enough!* But he keeps trying, any woman almost, might be the one.

That hot wet claiming kiss, full on the mouth. Piercing his groin like a knife blade.

And that sudden-shuddering waking to something raw against his eyelids: the sky. Knowing you're out-of-doors, not safe inside, still less in a bed. Nothing between you and the sky.

How light winked like beads of water. The puddled roof, the tarpaper smell. Crows shrieking in a field. Then a rattling freight train. And faded letters on a water tower a mile away just coming into focus in the mist. INDIAN LAKE, N.Y.

He'd told Theresa she was crazy but never told her how he loved her.

That craziness. Realizing yesterday morning waking after his worst drunk in recent memory flat on his back in gravel by the Expressway and the black kid bug-eyed squatting over him to determine is this honky dead or is he alive, realizing then it's this waking, the rawness of first light, the sky glaring down at him that's drawing him up into it. *So fucking lonely.*

And the black kid calling over bemused and contemptuous to his momma not giving a damn if Corky hears, *Just some drunk.*

It's 12:46 P.M. Corky's on his way to Roosevelt Street to visit Sean Corcoran. At last.

Though a little pissed off, he's just called the old man to say for sure he *is* coming, be there in ten minutes sharp, and what's the old man do but grumble he won't be holding his breath.

Meant to be a joke. Typical Irish wit.

Corky isn't going to let it get him down, though. What's life for but to celebrate.

And all these flags flapping—State Street, Union Boulevard, Erie. All over the city and all over the United States of America flags flying, Memorial Day, try to get in the mood. *Kiss me America, I'm your boy.*

Corky heads south on Erie, crosses the canal at Dalkey this time instead of Welland, he'll *never* drive on Welland past Club Zanzibar as long as he lives, black racist shit, you meet them halfway, and more than halfway, your good intentions shoved up your ass. This canal bridge too is narrow, shaky, but in better repair than the other, this section of Irish Hill not so run-down. Corky slows his car squinting east along the canal where the surface is wind-rippled, shot with light like shivering. He's feeling so good so relieved so fucking grateful about Thalia, he could cry. Like it's a reward for not drinking. For running his ass off these last few days.

Next, he'll settle it with Christina. The situation's simple: Harry Kavanaugh knows, so he doesn't have to be told. So Christina can get a divorce, and marry Corky. What's the problem?

He's sure now, he loves *her.* Around that fact, like the steel structure of a building, other facts can fall into place.

Up-canal, the rear of the old Dundonald Cannery Co., where relatives of Corky's worked, Judd Donnelly's father a manager, Corky as a kid had a summer job, one of many. Now boarded up, for sale for years, no buyer. Across the canal, brown-brick rowhouses. Must be mainly blacks, Hispanics. Clotheslines, laundry hanging out to dry, rear yards weedy and heaped with trash except here and there one kept clear, somebody's planted a garden, probably a woman, there's more hope in them somehow, the species without hope would die out in a generation. Heat death of the sun. Entropy?—things winding down. But all that's bullshit if you know what *you* want.

Up-canal at the next bridge, the Dundonald Street Bridge, just visible from here, there's the City Pride Bakery which is still in business. North on Dundonald, where Parish intersects, Grandpa Liam's lumberyard he'd started as a kid practically, in his mid-twenties, at the farther corner Corcoran Brothers Construction Co., now the site of a tacky mini-mart but Corky won't be driving in that direction.

Nor past 1191 Barrow Street, the old house. Whoever lives there now has added a front porch with a green-plastic roof, aluminum fixtures, fake-brick asphalt siding. Last time Corky cruised by, there was a young mother on the porch with a baby, small children, the skin color might've been white or light-skinned black, Hispanic.

Couldn't make himself look closely. Just couldn't.

You made me love you. Didn't want to do it.

The canal looks shallow along this stretch but that's deceptive—it's deep. A few miles north the canal sides are as high as thirty feet at the uptown locks, made of rock and nightmare-looking but in Irish Hill the banks are grassy, footpaths trail along the sides, you can walk right to the edge. Plenty of drownings over the years, in Corky's memory alone. An uncle of a kid at school, a priest visiting his family, out drinking with his old friends and returning from the Cloverleaf after it closed they'd decided to go swimming and two of them drowned including the priest. And Nick Daugherty that time, pushed in by some kid he was fighting with, and Corky and some other guys managed to haul him out, would've drowned otherwise. How old?—around the time the Bishop came to Our Lady of Mercy to confirm their class, eighth grade it must have been, thirteen years old.

And Tim's Great-uncle Stanislaus, the captain of the Irish Hill precinct, what a scandal, dumped in the canal bloated and his nose and groin shot away. *That* was no drowning.

The first wave of relatives came over from County Kerry in the 1820s to work digging the canal. Of six or seven Corcoran brothers and a number of Donnellys, Dowds, McClures only a few survived the digging of the canal and the rough times to follow. No direct ancestors of Corky's but blood kin from Dingle Bay, wonder did any of them look like him? Genes, DNA, through the decades? He'd always wanted a brother, could you have a brother close as a twin born in the wrong century? Living and dying so long ago these young men were not recalled in any family tales. Nor buried in Our Lady of Mercy Cemetery. Buried instead where they'd died of dysentery, yellow fever, influenza, beatings and stabbings and shootings, buried in the muck along the canal banks. Living in tents, what kind of food were they fed, what kind of sanitation did New York State provide, must've died like flies.

Irish and Chinese laborers mainly. Why Chinese, so long ago?—*they're a smart race.*

Why the Church has always forbidden birth control, abortion. The more Catholics born, the more chance of a few surviving. Holy Mother Church—like Mother Nature not giving a damn for the individual only the species. Thirteen brothers and sisters in Theresa's mother's family! Corky's Dowd cousins, fifteen of them at least, how many still living he's lost track. Also the Donnellys but some of them are long gone from Union City.

No more big Irish families, even in Ireland the population's in decline. Scarcely four million. Maybe a race can wear out, lose faith in itself. Northern Ireland, Protestants outnumber Catholics is it two to one? The IRA, poor suckers, a lost cause.

Corky continues on Dalkey past the Dalkey Street Elementary School past a row of stores he wouldn't know except in his memory seeing them as they were twenty-five years ago, this intersection with Decatur a thriving commercial zone at that time. But there's a drugstore exactly where there'd been a Rexall's. And Dignam's Funeral Home is still a funeral home, the name's now W. Young & Sons.

The Corcorans had always used Donnelly's of course. On Erie. Still in business, run by the sons.

The Ship of Death they'd called it, the cholera barge traveling north from New York City then westward from Albany past towns along the canal where they weren't allowed to dock—Irish immigrants mainly, in the 1880s. Yet some survived. Three Corcoran brothers of how many brothers, sisters, cousins and these too from Dingle Bay coming to live with family and work in the Moneghan Pottery Works. Dermott, Joseph, Gahern bearing the gift of life.

Corky's approaching Roosevelt where Sean lives beginning to feel that sickish excitement, dread. The fact is, in his dreams he often visits that house. Never dreams of the first house, on Barrow, nor even of the house on Schuyler where his father died and his mother's screams rent the air. But waking within a dream in his old room shared with his cousin Pete, or upstairs in the attic where since that first time after his father's funeral he'd gotten drunk, and knew the solace of drink. Like *drunk* is a place you can go to, a bucket you can lower down to a deep secret subterranean spring.

Except no longer. Corky's never going to taste alcohol again.

Never?

The last time Corky visited the old man he'd brought him home half-crocked after a funeral and the two sat in the dim-lit shabby parlor in front of a TV watching the Mohawks play a crappy game losing to the Athletics and killing two six-packs of Molson's between them. And even at the commercial breaks they hadn't talked, weird like Corky wasn't even there. Corky gearing himself up to ask for twenty-five years *Why did my father die? Is there some secret nobody's ever told me? Why wasn't Fenske, or any of them, arrested?* but has never asked waiting, must be, for the right moment. But when's the right moment? You'd think, the two of them getting soused together might be it but suddenly near the end of the game there's a whistling snort from Sean and Corky sees the old man's passed out in his ratty chair, head back and jaw slack as a corpse's, a tusk of spit hanging from his chin.

That's you, Corky my man, in thirty years' time.

Corky used the bathroom, made enough noise on the creaky stairs to wake the dead. Still the old man slept, snored. So Corky gave up. Left five twenty-dollar bills atop the TV, pocket money for his uncle (who'd been complaining, at the funeral mass, how seriously Corky didn't know, of not having enough money to get his suit dry-cleaned, his shoes repaired) and what happens?—next day, that cunt Lois calls Corky at his office to give him hell for getting her father drunk, "That's just like you, 'Corky,' isn't it! Just what we've learned to expect!"

And no mention of the $100. No mention!

Typical Irish gratitude.

Corky's losing it, his high. *A drink?* God damn *no.* His knuckles hurt, you wouldn't think busting somebody in the crotch would be like busting him in the jaw, of course Corky'd caught some bone there, fucker's pelvis.

Wonder will Red be there tonight, at the Chateauguay Country Club.

If Oscar Slattery's there, and it's not likely Oscar Slattery would stay away, Red will be there, too. Don't kid yourself he won't.

"Hey, fuck it!—watch out!" Corky calls out his car window not exactly wanting to yell, riding his brakes as three black kids high school age cross the street against traffic, strutting unhurried and unseeing. Buzz-cut hair, razor-carved initials, rattails—it's like Zululand, some kind of primitive tribe. Except these guys are wearing expensive Reeboks, gold chains, wraparound mirror sunglasses, skintight black spandex bicycle pants that even Corky, who's disgusted, and no queer, can't help staring at—buttocks like melons, genitals showcased like for a male stripper show. Corky feels a wave of frustration, rage. Remembers how, before things started to change in the late 1960s, Dundonald Park was off-limits to blacks, gangs of white kids like Corky and his friends made sure of it, and the cops, who were mainly Irish cops from the neighborhood, looked the other way. And now, who would believe it?

It isn't just Corky's white, these flashy fucks ignore traffic, take over the sidewalk so everybody's quick to get out of their way.

Yesterday, at the Zanzibar: that tall menacing kid suddenly smiling at Corky handing him sweet potato pie, an emissary of Roscoe Beechum's so it was O.K., Corky's O.K. and in no danger. Like when they see white skin it isn't automatic it's *white,* or *white* exclusively. If another black man, one with big bucks and authority, like Beechum, sanctifies you, you're O.K.

Corky has to admit, it felt good, that kid yesterday looking at him with respect. And it surely did hurt, Roscoe Beechum turning him away seeing *white,* seeing *cop,* never seeing *him.*

Corky swings around to Dundonald, not much of a boulevard any-more, drives past Our Lady of Mercy which looks mostly unchanged—weatherworn pebble-colored brick and a steeple not nearly so high as Corky remembers, also the rose window not so big, if he had time he'd go inside for a few minutes, in any Catholic church it's nice to see the stained glass from the inside. And that smell of a Catholic church, incense, votive candles. Flowers at the Virgin Mary's feet, white lilies against the blue plaster robes.

He's lonely, he misses it. Homesick?

Yes but it's all crap. Even as a kid you figured it out.

One of his aunts saying in a slow halting voice after a typical funeral these days, *It used to be so nice in Latin, we didn't have to know what it meant* meaning how simple, like for children, wish-fulfillment fantasy, God loves you and you're all set for Heaven. And confession's different now, too, Corky knows though he hasn't gone in thirty years. No power any longer to make you God-damned *scared*.

This section of Irish Hill is mixed white, black, Hispanic, of course the Hispanics are Catholic so the parish is holding its own. Hispanic priest now, Corky'd heard, or at least somebody who can speak Spanish. Won-der what the ratio is, Irish parishioners to Hispanic now. Some blacks, too—that's always struck Corky as weird. Old Father Sullivan who'd speak somberly of "coloreds" and people "wanting to live with their own kind," he'd turn over in his grave could he know.

Sean Corcoran saying mean and aggrieved, at the wake *No reason for any nigger to come to Irish Hill, except he helped get my brother killed.*

As long as he's this close, Corky decides to drive into Dundonald Park. Hasn't been here in years. He's surprised it looks so good, from what he's heard and read, drugs, crime, vandalism, no more waterfowl on the pond because they'd been killed or mutilated by kids, and the sunken rose garden, the pride of Irish Hill, hundreds of rosebushes fanning out from the World War II monument, long gone. Driving past the swimming pool, the wading pool, basketball courts, Corky doesn't see too much different except of course most of the people in sight are black, at the picnic tables too, here and there some white faces but it's rare. And that fucking graffiti all over, an insult to the eye, Day-Glo scrawls on sidewalks, walls, even trees—supposed to be gang colors, declarations of turf.

Still the park looks O.K. The sun's out, or almost; it's spring; every-thing bright green from all the rain they've been having, and in bloom. That kind of golden-fuzzy stuff, must be seeds, on certain trees, birches. White-fuzzy stuff on other trees. And lilac. Lots of lilac, must grow wild.

Please forgive me, I love you.

O.K. *honey I love you.*

Corky cruises, turns. What time is it? A potholed lane through the woods, what's left of the woods, then out behind the pond, what they'd called the duck pond, litter floating on its surface and in fact there are ducks, but that fucking graffiti, bright orange so for a second it looks like flame, on the war monument. Corky's dreamy remembering how summer nights, in the park, he'd make out with girls. After swimming. And after softball games. Corky's first girlfriend, the first time he'd made it with any girl, if you could call it that, Marianne Bannon after the Holy Redeemer picnic, Corky was twelve years old and hot-skinned Marianne a year or so older. Corky mashing his mouth against Marianne's, grinding his frantic little cock against her belly and closed thighs, coming in his pants with a puppy's yelp of astonishment—never forget. And afterward, other nights, in the woods beyond the refreshment concessions, she'd actually take him in her fingers and he'd come. But she'd never let Corky do it to her.

Why, Corky didn't know. He'd thought maybe girls were scared of it. Or embarrassed. Or Marianne was laughing at him, at the look on his face.

Marianne Bannon, her old man a butcher. And in fact a drinking buddy of Sean Corcoran's. If Bannon had known he'd've torn Corky's ass up the seam, not to say what he'd've done to Marianne. She'd had to drop out of St. John's suddenly in ninth grade, married some guy years older, in the Navy. Living now in Mount Moriah, her three or four kids grown up, *really* grown up—Corky'd been surprised as hell, and not pleasantly, ran into Marianne at a mall and bought her a drink at the Mauna Loa and Marianne's still looking good, tough and sexy and giggling at the look on Corky's face when she happens to mention she's a grandma.

And her granddaughter's eight years old!

Saying, a flirty poke of her pink tongue, *You* could be a grandpa, too, Corky, you might not even know it.

That possibility, the possibility he's actually fathered kids, somewhere along the line and never knew it, never was informed—that depresses Corky like hell. Like his genes, DNA, the stream of life flowing invisibly through him played a dirty trick on him behind his back. Who's to know?

The most profound difference between the sexes, that makes them, Corky's thinking, as un-alike as two different species, a woman for sure *knows*.

Should turn back and get to Sean's before he's late, *I won't hold my breath* but Corky finds himself cruising past the softball field where three yellow school buses are loading up, SOUTH UNION CITY HIGH SCHOOL MARCHING BAND, must be organizing for the parade. A few adults but mainly teenagers, whites, blacks, Hispanics, even Asians, dark Mideast-looking types, more of a mix than you'd expect in Irish Hill, Corky's surprised. They're all wearing green-and-white satin uniforms with American-flag epaulettes, everybody in trousers except, Jesus! drum majorettes in miniskirts showing their panties and knee-high white vinyl boots like junior hookers. Boys and girls in about equal numbers carrying musical instruments, Corky envies them, surprising to see a good-looking white girl with a trumpet, other girls with horns, drums, there's a sleepy-looking black boy square-built as Mike Tyson delicately carrying one of those fancy brass horns, French horn?—another black kid, tall, rangy, mean-dude-style with flattop hair, razor-cut initials, gold in both ears carrying a sax, big fattish baby-face Irish kid hauling a tuba, lots of drums, snare drums?—and that hefty booming kind that drowns out all competition, you can see why no soft-sounding instruments in a band, violins for instance, woodwinds, or *are* there woodwinds? Kids trotting by with cymbals—that'd be fun, a deafening noise. But wonder: bad on the eardrums? Or do they wear earplugs?

Kids carrying flags, some of them on six-foot poles, must be God-damned heavy over a distance. How long the parade?—three miles? Plus the big banner-flag. Plus the school banners. But everybody's in high spirits, at this age a Memorial Day parade's *fun*.

Sure, Corky envies them. So young. *He* was that age, every day at the rich boys' school was a hustle.

On the far side of the parking lot on a grassy strip there's an impromptu drum majorette drill, Corky cruises by slowing, braking to a stop to watch though it's almost one P.M., can't resist the sight of a dozen girls in sexy-satiny costumes tossing gleaming batons up into the air, up up up into the air, twirling and ducking the batons under their shapely legs like quick flashes of sword, all the while holding their bodies self-conscious on display as strippers, pointy tits, tight-rounded asses, some of them fairly plump, no anorexics here. And no feminists. Corky's amazed at these bimbo-looking girls capable of such feats of dexterity, the great Harry Blackstone would admire, and more than admire. Faces made up all bright lipstick and teased-tousled hair, could be 1962 not 1992. The girls begin to notice Corky eyeing them sucking on his cigarette exhaling smoke in lecherous clouds, must be used to men watching, what point to the display otherwise, they're giggling together one even drops her baton on the ground liking his attention? *not* liking it? but if they don't like masculine attention why dress to provoke it? The majorette leading the drill is a tall good-looking girl with a skin the color of the cocoa finish of Corky's Cadillac De Ville, can't be older than eighteen but looks in her mid-twenties stacked like a *Playboy* centerfold, hair in a frizzy cascade to her shoulders, sexy as hell purse-kissing her lips smiling sly at Corky like there's a lowdown secret between them. She tosses, twirls, catches her spinning baton fluid as a waterfall, up in the air one long shapely-muscled leg and fuck-me boot giving Corky a good eyeful of white-satin cunt, then the baton's in her fist she's thrusting it toward Corky jerking it upward so Corky's blinking grinning as the rest of the girls laugh and his face burns pleasantly and he drives on and only after a few minutes as he's cruising the area for the second time to watch the drill (but no: it's over) does Corky catch on: the bitch was giving him the finger.

At her age! And on Memorial Day!

God damn! damn Corky's muttering to himself royally pissed off and antsy *I need a fucking drink* turning onto the short, hilly block of Roosevelt where Sean Corcoran lives around the corner from the old house on Barrow, two blocks over there's Our Lady of Mercy and the church bells ringing for one o'clock, a sweet-fading sound Corky listens to, as if it's a message. Church bells you only notice when you've lived away from the neighborhood and have returned. Growing up in Irish Hill you rarely heard like rarely smelling the yeasty aroma of the bakery or the cruder earthy-bloody smell of the old slaughteryards or the stink of Cayuga Fertilizers, this *is* home. Corky's actually sweating.

Yet seeing quickly, his eyes snatching for evidence, the block looks about the same, these old decent two-storey brick houses cramped in together on less-than-acre lots, typical of the old Union City residential neighborhoods in general as if owning too much land, too much grass to mow, was a liability. Corky notices how much damned *cement* there is here, double driveways between houses and double sidewalks, twelve-inch strips of grass dividing properties, so different from the suburbs where younger families live now. Those passionate neighborhood feuds lasting for years over not who owned the grassy median between properties but who didn't own it, thus was spared the chore of mowing it, digging out crab-grass.

Corky's Aunt Frances did all she could not to get into disagreements with neighbors. The quarrelsome Culligans next door, the Paynes, who were actually blood kin of hers, across the street and two doors over—not disciplining their younger son, that little bastard. She'd tried to get along with everybody. Even after Tim's death when Sean so quickly turned sour, mean. And started to drink heavily.

Corky parks his car in front of the sand-colored weatherworn brick house at 1043 Roosevelt where he'd lived from the age of eleven to the age of eighteen. Is he late? He isn't. Yet the house looks accusing. On this balmy May afternoon, everybody in the neighborhood out, it's shut up tighter than a drum: front door shut, and no screen door at all; window blinds drawn; nobody waiting for Corky on the front porch, as he'd expected Sean would be, reading the newspaper, sucking ale.

The next wrong thing, the sky's more evident than Corky remembers. It looks as if the city has chainsawed down diseased trees by the curb, just ugly stumps left. Elms? Oaks? Corky can see them in his mind's eye, too fucking bad, Aunt Frances would be heartbroken loved those trees, and the ones in the back yard. Now everything's too exposed, the house looks smaller, seedier, even the fresh caulking around the porch foundation looks cheesy. Like there's a rent in the sky, raw light pouring through.

Corky trots up to the front stoop to ring the doorbell, cheerful, whistling, anybody sees him arriving to visit his Uncle Sean he's in a good mood for sure. Jerome Andrew Corcoran the City Councilman, used to live in this house. Note his spiffy clothes, his car.

Except, does anybody who might be watching recognize Corky? The Culligans are long gone, ditto the Paynes. Next door at 1041 Roosevelt where a family named Hennessey lived while Corky was growing up, and two elderly Hennessey sisters lived alone together for years, there's a stranger, a dumpy woman in a housedress and bedroom slippers, fussing over a squalling child on her front porch. An Appalachian look to the woman, Corky figures she's from south Irish Hill below Dalkey where the poor whites, the ones everybody called white trash, lived. Must be the old-lady Hennesseys died, the property was sold and Sean never mentioned it to Corky.

This woman is staring at Corky, almost slack-jawed. The Caddy must look good to her, considering the piece of shit parked in her driveway.

"Uncle Sean?—hey, it's me, Corky." Like who the fuck else would it be?

Corky uses the knocker on the door, three sharp raps, the old man's half-deaf but won't wear a hearing aid, refuses. And maybe the doorbell's broken. "Uncle Sean?—hey."

It burns Corky's ass, the old man keeping him waiting on purpose, for sure that's what he's doing. Mean old son of a bitch.

Corky sees, close up, the brick looks grimy. You'd have to have it sandblasted to clean it, not worth the cost. And the stumpy front porch, dirty, in fact filthy, last year's rotted leaves never swept away. Aunt Frances used to keep the porch tidy like any room of the house, wicker chairs and waterproof cushions, potted geraniums on the railings, all the women, the housewives, on Roosevelt took such care. The past few years, Sean hasn't even bothered to put an aluminum lawn chair on the porch to sit on. Hardly uses the porch at all.

Corky tries the doorknob but of course it's locked. Goes to peer through the front windows but the blinds are drawn to the sills. He raps loudly on the glass. "Hey, you in there? Uncle Sean?"

No answer. Corky tries the door knocker again. Fuck it, he's getting scared. Just talked to Sean about a half hour ago but maybe something's happened since?

Old people living alone in Irish Hill are special targets for break-ins.

Kids as young as twelve are crack addicts, need cash. Corky knows from his cousin Lois that the house has been broken into at least twice, there've been muggings, murders in the neighborhood, but Sean refuses to discuss it. Refuses to think of moving. Move where? he'd asked Corky last time they were together, baring his yellowed teeth in a sardonic smile. Up to Maiden Vale, with *you*?

Corky must have looked so scared at the prospect, Sean burst into laughter.

Corky descends the steps, sees the steps too have been newly repaired, freshly caulked, *that's* a good sign. Though the asphalt driveway and the sidewalks are riddled with cracks, the scrubby front lawn is mottled crabgrass and dandelions. And dandelions in sunny profusion growing in the median between this property and the property next door.

Corky calls over to the woman, who's been staring at him all this while, "You seen my uncle Sean Corcoran anywhere around today? I'm supposed to meet him."

Both the woman and the kid stare at Corky like they've never seen anything like him. They're pasty-faced, doughy-pale, bleached-looking blond hair and close-set ferret eyes. Every door and window in their house is wide open and there's what looks like a yellow chenille bedspread hanging like a curtain through one of the porch windows, blowing in the wind. Corky sees the kid is actually two kids, the smaller no older than two, little boy bare-assed naked. The woman calls over what sounds like, "Ain't seen him, no sir," shaking her head vehemently and turning away.

Hillbillies, for sure. Probably on welfare. Wonder what they paid for the house, or maybe do they rent. Yes, probably, they rent, big family with lots of kids, they'll let the property go all to hell then blacks will buy it. Or, nobody will buy it, it'll stand empty, be used by gangs as a crack house.

Corky strolls up the driveway peering at the windows, can't see a Goddamned thing through the blinds, or whatever it is over the windows— along the side here it looks like sheets of plywood. The basement windows are thick with grime and there appear to be bars, boards nailed horizontally, across them. Can't blame the old guy, protecting himself against break-ins, or trying to. Wonder does he have a burglar alarm yet, Corky tried to talk him into it, offered to pay for it but Sean refused, God knows why. At the back Corky sees the rear yard is scrubby and bright with dandelions like the front. Aunt Frances' hollyhocks are still growing tall beside the garage, must be a kind of weed, like sunflowers. The little vegetable garden, Aunt Frances' victory garden she called it, back by the fence—vanished as if it'd never been.

She'd grown tomatoes, green beans, carrots, onions, that short bright yellow-orange crinkly flower, sharp-smelling, petunias?—marigolds? Encouraged Corky to plant seeds a few times too but nothing much came up for him but weeds. Once, clumsy asshole, he'd helped his aunt set tiny plants in the soil then turned around and stepped on some of them squashing them flat.

Corky sees the old rotting wood fence has been replaced by a ten-foot chain-link fence with razor wire on top.

That must've cost Sean. And you got to wonder, would it really keep those black kids out if they're determined to break in.

Corky ascends the steps of the small back porch, a wood porch, and pretty shaky; knocks at the door, rattles the knob. "Uncle Sean? Fuck it, open up! You know who this is."

Just Corky's luck: now the danger from Thalia's past, and he might have had a great time at the fund-raiser tonight, something's happened to his uncle.

Recalling that crude joke one of his drinking buddies once told Corky on their way into the Seneca House, pointing to some dog shit on the sidewalk asking did Corky know what that was? and when Corky said no he did not—"The luck of the Irish."

Truer words never spoken.

Corky doesn't know whether to be scared or angry. Should he hang around awhile, or try to call Sean; or call the cops. Or try to break in.

About five minutes have passed since he first knocked on the front door. It's just possible Sean has been in the bathroom, and hasn't heard; he *is* deaf in one ear. Or he's pissed off at Corky and pretending not to hear. Won't be holding my breath.

Corky returns to his car, calls his uncle's number on the phone and this time there's no answer. Which he'd expected.

Now, next door, there's a bare-chested skinny kid in his twenties with long straggly hair, biker's leather pants, a can of beer in his hand, plus the woman and two kids, staring over at Corky.

Corky trots around to the rear of the house. The door's shut tight and probably chain-locked. But there's a window opening into a hall, and that hall into the kitchen; the window's covered with a sheet of plywood so Corky can't see in, but he remembers this rear hall has become filled with junk since Aunt Frances died, including stacks of newspapers. If he's going to break in this is the most practical place! Nobody's watching, so far as he can tell: the back yards of both neighboring houses are empty.

The second time Corky Corcoran's breaking in a relative's place in a few days. What are the odds against such a thing, considering how, in all of his life up until now, he's never been so desperate as to do such a thing before?

So Corky tries the window. Pushing, grunting. It's locked of course but the kind of lock not hard to break. If he was just strong enough, hasn't been lifting his weights very regularly lately, muscles go quickly to fat if you stop. Arm, shoulder muscles. For a smallish man it's crucial to keep fit: any chance, remove coat, a snug-fitting shirt, muscles defined. Women's eyes shift, virtually light up—he'd swear he's seen.

Even classy Christina, that first time she saw him without his coat, stroking his arms. Her eyes warm and assessing she's got just a little more than, back in the Maiden Vale Library, she'd imagined she was getting. And Corky didn't disappoint.

Corky's panting and losing patience about to break the God-damned window when the plywood sheet is dislodged and falls and he freezes staring at what's inside no more than eighteen inches away on the other side of the dusty pane—"Sweet fucking Christ!"

Unable to believe at first he's seeing what he's seeing.

Three years ago Christmas, the time before last Corky visited his Uncle Sean, he'd drifted bored around the house looking for things that needed fixing; something useful beyond just helping the old guy guzzle the bottle of Johnnie Walker he'd brought, uncle and nephew sitting in front of the TV with nothing much to say to each other. There was plenty in the house that needed cleaning, straightening up, but that was women's work not Corky's. He'd screwed some kitchen shelves tighter, shored up a tilting water heater in the basement, strengthened some steps. A born carpenter and handyman like Tim Corcoran, happiest at such times. Whistle while you work. Then climbing excited to the attic to stare from the window, that view down Dalkey hill to the lake that's imprinted so vivid in his memory he can see it sometimes not exactly meaning to, see it like it's before him so he stood there for possibly ten minutes just looking, thinking of nothing but just looking, and then as thirty years before the lights on Dalkey were bright dipping steeply downhill and traffic on the Fillmore Expressway and beyond that Lake Erie vaporous and indistinct so you needed to know it was a lake, it was *there*. Always, it would be *there*.

Then it came to Corky slowly, reluctantly he was hearing some scurrying sounds behind him in the dense clutter of the attic, smelling that unmistakable gamey-dirty smell of rodents. So rummaging about back beneath the eaves he discovered of all things to blow the mind, in this house his Aunt Frances once kept so scrupulously clean, a rat's nest.

"Sweet fucking Christ—!"

As an owner of urban properties some of which might be designated substandard, Corky'd seen rats' nests in the past but always at a reasonable distance, and always when there were workmen in his hire to clean them out. Never had Corky actually examined a rat's nest up close squatting over the thing, appalled but admiring, and the more he looked the more admiring, for what an amazing thing this was: basketball-sized, finely and you could say lovingly woven, all these weird things together not just twine, string, rags, scraps of newspaper which you'd expect but here were feathers and glittering wire and Christmas tinsel and a half dozen buttons and bits of colored glass and plastic and part of a child's rubber Donald Duck and a badly tarnished silver medal on a delicate chain and a pair of broken wire eyeglasses and, most amazing of all, the metallic-phosphorescent face of the Big Ben alarm clock he and Pete had had in their room.

Corky was so absorbed in the nest, dragging it into the light to see it, he didn't think how lucky he was the baby rats were gone from the nest for the mother rat would have attacked him for sure. Going for his bare hands and face.

Never feel quite the same way about a rat again, once you see a nest like this. Poor buggers, Corky felt like a shit cleaning them out. But after all a rat's a *rat*. It's them or us.

When Corky carried the nest downstairs to show to his uncle who was dozing in front of the TV, Sean sat up alert opening his eyes wide for the first time in Corky's recent memory. And his eyes then filling with tears, and his hand finely trembling tugging the tarnished medal on its chain out of the dense-woven nest—a religious medal, the Holy Virgin Mary, once belonging to Frances Corcoran, long vanished.

It's with the same awe Corky examined the rat's nest in the attic he's staring at the double-barreled shotgun aimed at his head. The thing is on a stepladder, secured with twine, and twine looped around both triggers a hairsbreadth from being pulled if a heavy iron frying pan falls from the window ledge where it doesn't seem to be balanced very securely. Corky was within seconds of getting his head blown off.

Just then rushing cursing to the door his trousers but partway zipped there's Sean Corcoran who unlatches the door, fumbles with the lock, and a chain too, then opens the door in a fury and glares at his nephew who's gone dead-white in the face shaking so badly, his knees turned to water, he can't immediately react. The old man is taller and thicker in the torso than Corky remembers, he's flush-faced angry and his stubbly chin glinting harshly like steel filings embedded in the flesh—"You! What the hell are you doing jimmying this window? Are you crazy? Is this some kid's game? God *damn!*" Sean Corcoran's so disgusted, the color up in his face, red-lidded eyes like pulpy grapes gleaming with purpose, it's like he's actually enjoying this.

It comes back to Corky in a rush: Sean Corcoran looming over him giving him hell deserved or undeserved, the spit-edged words, the rising voice, the more emotional the more Irish-inflected.

But Corky recovers, pissed as hell, too. Pushing past his jabbering uncle going to examine the shotgun—*shotgun!*—double-barreled twelve-gauge W. & C. Scott *shotgun!*—fixed by twine to the stepladder, and attached to the handle of the frying pan on the windowsill. It's a Rube Goldberg contraption, Corky's never seen anything like it. "What the fuck's this gun here? Where'd you get a shotgun? Is this *real?* Real shells? Rigged to go off? Blow somebody's head off?"

Sean's nudging Corky back from the stepladder like he could protect the gun, or prevent Corky from actually seeing it. He says, furious, "I'm asking *you*, you little pisspot: what the hell're you doing breaking in this house?"

"Look, I knocked! God damn it I knocked on every fucking door and window in this fucking house! And you didn't answer! I was worried about you!"

"God-damn fool doesn't know his asshole from a hole in the ground! God *damn!*"

"You knew I was coming for Christ's sake—I just talked to you on the phone. Where the fuck were you?"

"Get away from that gun! Get the hell out of here! I don't need you poking your nose around here! I don't need your pisspot charity!"

"—I knocked! I telephoned from the car! I asked your hillbilly neighbors where the fuck you were! I was worried about you!"

"You think I need you, any of you?—I don't! This is my house, and this is my property, and anybody I don't care the color of the bugger's skin tries to break in here one more time I know how to protect myself."

"Uncle Sean, are you crazy? This is a deadly weapon! This is a murder weapon! Guys who've done things like this, killing some twelve-year-old black kid—they're arrested for murder. It's premeditated murder. You go on *trial*. You go to *jail*."

Sean laughs contemptuously, pulling at Corky's arm as Corky shakes him off, "Not in this town you don't. Not on this street, not in Irish Hill, you don't, not for killing a nigger you don't, oh no"—shaking his head so his neck-wattles shiver, "—oh no, my lad, you *don't*."

"Uncle Sean, it's fucking 1992 not 1942! You kill anybody black with a booby trap like this, you're dead meat! It's the law—you can only shoot in self-defense! This contraption—"

"This *is* self-defense! Go on get the hell out of here, nobody's asked your opinion, what're you, you little pisspot"—this word hissing from Sean Corcoran's spittled lips *pisspot little pisspot* how many times as a kid he'd been called this name, and not always in anger but sometimes with gruff-grudging manly affection, "—you're a hot-shit lawyer or something? Eh? Go on!"

"I'm telling you what's so—it *is* the law. You can't just blow somebody's head off for breaking in a house. And why the fuck didn't you answer the door? You knew I was coming for Christ's sake why didn't you answer the door?"

"Because I was in the toilet! A man's got a right to take a shit when he needs to in his own house don't he!—without some Goddamned fool jimmying his window! Eh? Go on!"

"I'm not going anywhere until I dismantle this crazy thing—"

"I said, God damn your soul to hell, get away—"

It happens like this: Corky pushes the old man, and the old man pushes back with a demented child's flailing fury, uncle and nephew panting hotbreathed in each other's contorted Corcoran face, Sean muttering now in a hurt aggrieved voice, "I said get out! Out! You think I need you? any of you?—oh no my lad, I don't! Hot-shit 'Jerome Andrew Corcoran'— showing up in this house once a year! Two years! Well, nobody wants your pisspot charity so get the hell out! I said—*out!*" snatching at Corky's hands as, with more force, elbowing the hefty old bastard aside, Corky lunges for the shotgun but in so doing sets the stepladder wobbling, teetering and it begins to overturn taking up as in slow motion the slack of the twine so the heavy frying pan is tugged, then crashes from the sill to the floor and in the same instant quick as ten million trillion neutrinos speeding through the Earth's body the shotgun explodes, both barrels blast, a deafening noise and the very air shaken as the dusty windowpane shatters into myriad glass-fragments flying outward along with much of the window frame.

Following which, the rest of Corky's visit with his Uncle Sean Corcoran goes relatively peacefully.

7

IN MEMORIAM

A *drink? dying for a drink* but before leaving for Lake Erie Park Corky and Sean Corcoran barricade the blown-out window at the rear of 1043 Roosevelt, nephew and uncle working deftly and, as the minutes pass, companionably as a team replacing the flimsy sheet of plywood and across the plywood nailing boards horizontally, like bars. It's as if the two, working wordlessly, have operated as a team of carpenters pressed into emergency service together in the past: the younger, the nephew, lifting boards each in turn and holding them steady across the plywood sheet while with quick short expert blows of his hammer the elder, the uncle, drives two-inch spikes into the boards securing them in place. Bang! Bang! Bang!—the harsh happy percussive hammer blows, the pleasantly mild sweat of short-term carpentry. When the job doesn't require more than two bottles of ale, there's nothing like it.

Sean Corcoran had once been a union bricklayer but an expert carpenter too. Like Tim Corcoran. Like many of the Corcoran men. When Corky lifts a hammer, it feels good. Like he's come home. The weight of the hammer in the hand, the smell of fresh-sawed lumber, that good sensation of hammering in nails, spikes: how swiftly can you lay boards in without slackening your rhythm a single time without a single bent nail or missed blow.

Corky remembers his father working sometimes with his carpenters, the nonunion men, removing his coat rolling up his shirtsleeves but not taking off his tie. The sound of the men talking together, laughing. The banging hammer blows, the smell of the wood, fresh-sawed pine.

Stone cold sober? You poor prick.

Sean Corcoran who'd been drinking ale for hours before Corky's arrival is drinking ale now, a bottle of Molson's close by as he's hammering; he tells Corky, when at last he's willing to speak directly to Corky, to get a bottle for himself out of the icebox—Sean's of a generation rapidly vanishing still says "icebox." Poor Corky swallowing hard mumbles, a dip in his voice like he's embarrassed, no thanks I don't want an ale right now, so Sean says, a beer, then? and Corky mumbles no, not right now and at this point Sean actually pauses in his hammering to look at his nephew, making no comment except by way of the stare of his pale-blue eyes, that expression of disbelief, disdain with which one seasoned alcoholic regards another wishing to deny the bond between them.

Corky considers telling his uncle he's going to sign up for AA in the morning. But, the way the old man's looking at him on the verge of a scornful laugh, he doesn't have the nerve.

Sean snorts bemusement or disapproval, reaches for another spike. The moment passes.

The spikes Corky's uncle is using are used, not new, like these fairly filthy boards of uneven length discovered in a disorderly cobwebbed stack in the garage. (The garage!—such a mess of ancient accumulated trash, there's no doubt rats have infested it.) So there's no smell of fresh-sawed lumber nor any tactile pleasure in stroking these splintery boards but, when the job's finished, the bars in place, both men stand looking at it with approval.

Corky doesn't want to think how crazy and sad this is, how pathetic an old man nearing eighty barricading himself in his house, but it's preferable to the Rube Goldberg shotgun at least. So he's enthusiastic when Sean says, with a chuckle, "Let's see the black buggers break in my house *now.*"

Corky manages a weak laugh. The next logical step is to barricade every first-floor window, and why not the second-floor windows too since burglars can use ladders but best not to think of that. He says, agreeing, "Yeah, it's a real deterrent." Pausing eyeing his uncle with that air of incredulity tinged with respect Corky's grown into with the old man, the way you'd approach a stallion long past its prime but capable still of outbursts of temper and violence—"So you won't need the shotgun, right? You can keep it where it is, right?"

After the accidental explosion, in a panicked flurry believing that one of the neighbors would call the police, or come over to investigate, Sean removed the shotgun from the ladder, took up the shells, and, paying no heed to Corky who was trying to talk sense to him, hid everything—gun, shells, twine, ladder—in the trash-filled basement beneath a tarpaulin stiff with dirt.

Strange: no neighbor called the police, apparently. Still less came over to investigate.

How Irish Hill has changed. Christ!

Sean who's wiping his sweat-beaded face on his shirtsleeve, finishing up his bottle of ale with quick thirsty gulps maybe hears this and maybe doesn't. For a long time, since his fifties at least, he's been partly deaf in one ear, or seems so; hearing what he wishes to hear and not hearing the rest. But if you raise your voice he'll be pissed as hell. Once cutting his daughter Lois to tears when she'd spoken loudly and clearly at him so Corky doesn't want to risk that now, now he's on the old guy's good side apparently.

Still, before they go to wash up, Corky brings up the subject of the shotgun again, asking Sean where he got the gun, does he have a permit for it? Has he ever used it? Sean shrugs off these questions like they're gnats swirling around his head and Corky persists would he really want to use a double-barreled twelve-gauge shotgun on another human being, and it could be a kid, knowing the kind of damage it would inflict?— seeing again in his mind's eye vivid and terrible as if it had been yesterday his father's collapsed and bleeding body, and believing that Sean must be envisioning that sight, imagining it, too. But Sean pauses in heading up-stairs, affable-seeming, bemused, now his hot temper has been temporar-ily quelled, lays a hand on Corky's shoulder and says, "Corky, you've got a good heart, but you don't know shit."

Corky stares up at the old man climbing the stairs favoring his left leg too surprised and hurt even to mutter under his breath *Fuck you too.*

He *is* hurt, that's the one thing he prides himself on: his savvy.

And he'd thought, God damn it, his family especially the older ones really admired that in him—how he'd raised himself up from practically nothing, how he'd made himself "Corky Corcoran" the way you'd make yourself an athlete by training, endurance, sheer stubborn inviolable will. Not to mention his business success—he's a millionaire! And his political success. And his social success. *He's an intimate friend of the Slatterys.*

Fuming, planning to ask Sean what the fuck he meant by that remark when the old guy comes back downstairs but, when he does, spruced up for their outing together—Sean's wetted and brushed his steely-white hair, hasn't shaved but has washed his face so it's pink-glowing in the cheeks where the capillaries have broken decades ago, and he's wearing an almost-fresh white cotton shirt, a snap-on moss-colored bow tie that looks as if it's made of vinyl, the same baggy gabardine trousers but a blue serge suit coat that looks as if, many years ago, it might have buttoned across his hard little potbelly—*and* he's carrying a straw fedora with a red band—Corky hasn't the heart.

Shit, why provoke a quarrel? Corky guesses he loves the old bastard.

When, at 1:43 P.M., Corky and Sean climb into Corky's car parked at the curb, it's like they're on TV being watched by any number of neighbors: across the street, next door in the former Culligan house, and, at 1041 Roosevelt, where on the crumbling brick porch and in the cracked asphalt driveway are standing not only the dumpy woman with the two small children and the bare-chested young man in biker's leather but a fat teen-aged girl with breasts like muskmelons sagging in a halter top and a squat bald suspicious-squinting guy of about Corky's age.

So many onlookers, a dozen or more, having heard a shotgun go off in a neighbor's house, but not calling the cops. Don't want to get involved—that's it?

Irish Hill's changed. Forever.

Corky who on principle believes you should always be on civil terms with your neighbors, or get them to think so, smiles and waves at the hillbillies next door who stare impassively at him, not a flicker of response. Sean growls disapproval.

Corky says, "So the Hennesseys sold their house, too? D'you know your new neighbors?"

Sean makes a snorting noise. Half-sullen and half-prideful, buckling his seat belt fumblingly, "Don't know nobody anymore, and nobody knows *me*."

Christ, that's depressing. Corky wants to make a joke but can't think of one.

The first time Sean Corcoran's been a passenger in Corky's new Cadillac and he peers about, frowning. His nostrils, wide, bristling with stiff white hairs, inhale deeply the rich leathery interior. But taking in too the cracked windshield, the scraped hood that looks as if a giant cat has scratched it. No comment, but Corky knows the old man's thinking he banged it up drunk-driving.

Corky says, "I've been having a fucking rotten time lately. But I think my luck's changing. In fact, I know it is."

Sean makes a snorting noise like he's bemused. Like saying, No shit!

Corky drives west along Roosevelt to Dalkey down the hill to South Erie. Keeping up a bright cheerful line of inquiry with his uncle—how's he been, how's the family, grandchildren, aunts, uncles Corky hasn't seen in years—and Sean responds with grunts, shrugs, silence. Not much to say about his children, nor even the grandchildren but he always was hard to talk to like you needed a secret key to open him up. After Tim's death. Losing the business, going to work for the city, on the payroll until retirement. Drinking. Aunt Frances' sickness, death. At the funeral Sean was sullen-drunk and Corky vowed he'd never see the s.o.b. again in his life but here we are. Fewer of us now. Soon no one to remember.

Why did my father die, why did it happen the way it did.

Did it happen the only way it could or was it a way that might have been altered. Tell me!

An infinity of alternative universes. But if you're in this one this is the one you're *in*.

Corky's plan for today's outing is to treat Sean to lunch at the Seneca House where Sean knows the owner, an old Irish-American of his generation, it's convenient since the Seneca House is near Lake Erie Park where they can watch the parade and attend the Memorial Day ceremony; then they can swing around to Our Lady of Mercy Cemetery which Corky hasn't visited in a long long time; then to Holy Redeemer Hospital to visit Corky's Aunt Mary Megan. (Corky telephoned another of his Dowd aunts to determine, under the guise of asking whether Aunt Mary Megan is seeing visitors, whether she's still alive.) Uncle Sean seems agreeable to all this, nodding and shrugging as if giving himself up to Corky for the day. Or maybe there's an ironic cast to his passivity like Corky's doing too little for him, and too late.

You little pisspot. Who wants your charity.

When, after about ten minutes, Corky's questions run out, Sean ceases speaking. Stingy with words as he'd been stingy with affection through his life. And stingy with money, even when he'd had it. Lois and Tess playing up to him, saw him mainly at meals, and Pete for a while, until Pete dropped out of high school and went to work at Curtiss Wright, started making more money than his old man. Corky never tried to suck up to Sean Corcoran: not *his* son.

Aunt Frances was the one who'd loved him: Jerome. No blood relation of hers but she'd loved him, who knows why. Skinny-homely kid, freckle-faced, reddish monkey-fuzz covering his body. Young-looking for his age but that's deceptive. Never was *young* after his father's death only young-seeming. His body sprouted hair under his arms and at his crotch, his genitals grew like tropical fruit, filthy thoughts clotted his brain but you're my good boy Jerome, you're my sweet boy aren't you Jerome, Aunt Frances said, and she'd meant it. Not knowing him. If she'd known she'd been revulsed but she hadn't known, women never do. The weakness of women, no civilization without it. Why Corky loves them, pities them. *Jesus I'm dying for a drink.*

Wanting to jack himself off, too—that young cow with the tits hanging practically out of her, what's it, halter top. And her ass in tight blue jeans. IQ maybe a moron's, moony look to her staring at Corky Corcoran in his spiffy clothes, fancy Cadillac. Corky thinks maybe if he could see himself, like on TV, a fleeting image, he'd respect himself. Envy?

But gnawing his lower lip, he's feeling sad. So suddenly. Uncle Sean beside him at last and nothing to say. Those years, lost. Half his life lost. Remembering Pete, their room together, the Big Ben alarm clock, you'd never think the clock face was detachable from the mechanism, the very hands, but of course that makes sense. A human face, too, detachable from its brain.

Poor bastard Pete: a serious drinker, too. Runs in the family, no escaping it. *But I'm going to escape it.* Laid off from Curtiss Wright just a kid in his mid-twenties with a wife, sweet-dumb Catholic girl and they'd had three babies in rapid sequence just like the Church ordered then the marriage broke up, Pete enlisted in the Army, went to Vietnam where he really got fucked up. Now out in Fresno, CA, working, Corky guesses, as a laborer though Lois and Tess are careful to call it "in construction."

Out of the silence like nerves strung tight Corky hears himself saying in a bright-ebullient voice like he's fielding questions at an open session of the Council, "It's been a helluva long time since we've gotten together, eh? My fault I guess I'm always so damned busy—" as Sean Corcoran, straw fedora now on his head pulled down just a little too far, sits stiff staring out the web-cracked windshield, "—but I think of you a lot, Uncle Sean. I really do. All you did for me. When I was a kid. When—" squinting ahead, he's on South Erie approaching Grand Boulevard why's it taking so fucking long to get to the Seneca House, "—after—it happened. And you and Aunt Frances took me in. Maybe I couldn't appreciate it then exactly, you know how kids are, how I was, but, Jesus, I know *now*. Which is why—" *stone cold sober you'll never get through the afternoon, you sorry prick*, "—I'm kind of worried about you, these days? Living alone in the old house? I know this is none of my business, Uncle Sean, for sure it isn't, I know I've butted my nose in where it wasn't wanted in the past but like I said I'm kind of—worried. If you wanted to sell the house and move I can help you, no commission, we can list it without putting a For Sale sign out front—the neighbors don't need to know your business, right?" a long pause as Corky's stalled in traffic at the intersection with Grand, traffic's being rerouted because of the fucking parade and Sean stares out frowning, there's that weird fierce look of an old man's eyebrows where individual wiry-white hairs spring vertically out of wiry-gray-grizzled horizontal hairs, *look at me! talk to me! God damn you! I love you!*—"I agree with you the neighborhood *is* dangerous, but— rigging a shotgun like that! Even having a shotgun in the house! That's dangerous, too. You can't shoot people even burglars without just cause and assuming they're black kids it's your ass that's going to burn, believe me. So I was thinking—put your house on the market, I'll try to get you the best price possible, and—"

There's Dequindre, thank God the Seneca House is in the next block, Corky's running at the mouth not knowing what the fuck he's saying wanting to make it up to his uncle, years of ignoring him, taking offense at the old guy's remarks, easy to do. The way he'd written Charlotte off without telling her when, in Miami Beach, he'd needed to fly back to see his aunt and Charlotte hadn't wanted to come, though might have come if he'd explained to her what it meant to him, what Frances Corcoran meant to him, now she's dying and I'll never see her again and I'm losing it. He'd written Charlotte off, and he'd written Sean off. Cold-hearted s.o.b., Corky Corcoran.

Turning into the cinder drive of the fake-redwood Seneca House unable to acknowledge what his eyes immediately absorb: parking lot's empty, fucking place must be closed. Memorial Day afternoon and the fucking Seneca House is closed!

"Shit!" Corky says. "This is disappointing."

Glancing sidelong at Sean who does in fact look disappointed—sulky. Like a kid who's been hiding his hopes, you only learn it when his hopes are dashed.

This famous, or notorious, old Irish tavern dating back to the early 1900s and before that a stagecoach stop, once a favorite hangout of Tim Corcoran's, one of Corky's places too though no use kidding himself it's anything now but a crummy neighborhood saloon. Shabby exterior, dandelions pushing up through cracks in the pavement, even the unlit red-neon SENECA HOUSE is peeling its paint. It occurs to Corky suddenly, his uncle's old friend Davy Kiernan is long dead!

Corky, asshole, has been mixing him up with his son. Who's no spring chicken, either.

Sean Corcoran sighs, makes a snuffling sound. Like this is what he'd expected. The straw fedora, new to Corky's eye, gives the old man a jaunty-arrogant look. At first glance you think here's a dapper dude, if Caucasian, then you look closer and see his age—the flushed-wrinkled face, wattled throat, pursy lips. Why do the lips of the elderly begin to *retract?* Yet, Corky's thinking, you have to hand it to Sean—for an old guy soused two-thirds of his life he doesn't look bad. Not bad at all. Came close to croaking a half dozen times, weeklong benders and a few arrests for drunk and disorderly and hospitalized and detoxed (supposedly) and discharged and off the bottle for anywhere between six months and six days then back again, curse of the Irish. Drinking makes you a better man until that hour it makes you a shithead-loser, like love gone wrong but for Christ's sake can you live without love? You can't. And if you can, it's not worth it. And in any case Sean Corcoran has outlived his good wife who drank rarely and never smoked and he's still going strong and Corky'd bet ten to one *he* isn't going to make it to age seventy-seven.

Sean shrugs. Bares his smoky-looking straggly teeth at Corky, smiles and says, "What the hell, lad, there's a hundred places in Union City better than this dump."

How it happened exactly, there are two versions. How Dermott Corcoran was hanged.

There were three young Corcoran brothers who emigrated to Union City, New York, in the spring of 1880, from County Kerry, Ireland. Living at first with relatives in Irish Hill and toiling alongside them at the Moneghan Pottery Works making decent wages (by Irish standards) roughly one-fifth of which were sent back home—at least at the start. Dermott was the eldest, nineteen years old when processed through Castle Garden; Joseph was eighteen; Gahern, sixteen. Were they high-spirited fun-loving lads for whom the discipline of tending kilns in even the summer heat (and how much hotter upstate New York than County Kerry, Ireland! even into late September, temperatures pitilessly high as ninety-five degrees Fahrenheit) proved insufferable; or were they hotheaded hard-drinking rebellious lads with no patience, once out from under their father's rule, for taking orders from priests, relatives, or foremen? Very soon Dermott Corcoran quit, or was discharged, from the pottery works; followed soon after by his brothers Joseph and Gahern. All three worked at whatever jobs came their way, however briefly—mule drivers on the Erie Canal, bargemen on the Great Lakes, slaughterers in the Union City stockyards, dockside laborers. Dermott Corcoran was also a stone quarrier, a teamster driving a horse-drawn truck, a popular local prizefighter. He was never married and if, as probably he did, he sired any number of bastard children in upstate New York in the short period of time he lived there, no records were kept of them; no Corcoran lineage maintained. Dermott was a tall bull-necked red-haired young man with a hotter temper than either of his brothers; his expectations for himself were grander. On the *other side*, as America was spoken of with both reverence and apprehension back in County Kerry, a man with pride has a right to expect anything he can envision.

Bare-knuckle fighting, sometimes to the very death, was a specialty of the Irish in America. It was one of the things they were good at, and good for. In some cases they fought for actual monetary rewards in the "prize ring" though in most cases, being Irish, they fought for fighting's sake, usually in saloons or close by saloons. Dermott Corcoran exhibited a natural talent for such fighting and soon became a crowd-pleaser in towns and settlements along the Erie Canal. He was known as the "Irish Charger"—a heavyweight blindly ferocious as a young bull when provoked, all offense and no defense. He was undaunted even when his face was streaming blood, nose broken and teeth loosened in his jaws. In the sixty-odd bouts of his foreshortened career liquor fueled his best performances; liquor was at once the stimulant, the balm, and the reward. It seemed he must feel less pain than the average man—in the ring, he could be relied upon to stagger to his feet after being knocked down repeatedly, returning for more punishment until, as often happened, his opponent punched himself out on Dermott's very body. His youth was like a Fourth of July rocket—consuming itself in its display. Next to the pleasure of feeling his opponent's nose or jaw shatter against his skinned, bloody knuckles, Dermott loved the applause of the crowd. He was a man among men, and would live forever.

Asked if he wasn't afraid in the ring, especially against an opponent bigger and more experienced than he, Dermott Corcoran sincerely professed bewilderment—for what was there to be afraid of other than turning coward, and running away? And *that* no Corcoran would ever do.

His purses were as low as $25, and as high as $1000. In his career he may have earned—the estimate was his brother Gahern's—as much as $4500, of which virtually all was spent, lost, or stolen. After a winning bout, when Dermott was in his happiest state, drinking until he collapsed, he sometimes gave all his money away to his companions, and when, waking sober, a day or two later, he realized what he'd done, he would weep and insist upon going to a priest to take confession and be absolved of his sins. Rarely, in America, did Dermott take communion—he would wait, he vowed, until he was ready. Until he was heavyweight champion of the world.

The Corcorans of County Kerry, Ireland, were anxious about Dermott who sent them money only intermittently.

In November 1882, in Albany, Dermott was matched with the heavy-

weight title-holder himself—John L. Sullivan. The purse was an extraordinary $4000—winner take all. It did not occur to Dermott that he might
lose, so the stark terms of the stake were satisfactory. In fact, Dermott
was so certain he would win, he made numerous bets on himself, using
up what little money he'd saved. He encouraged his brothers Joseph and
Gahern to bet, too. A contingent of male Corcorans journeyed to Albany
for the fight, of whom some did not return to Union City for days. One of
them, a father of nine young children, disappeared entirely and was never
heard of again.

Every Irish family knows these griefs, like a secret rosary. Every Irish
family has said this rosary. The saintly who die young, the drinkers and
shouters and abusers who live into old age. The hardworking silent ones
who die of heart attacks where they stand, uncomplaining. The good girls
who run off and return home pregnant and humiliated and their young
lives ruined forever. Or who never return, and are lost forever. The seminary student, passionate for God, who inflames the lust of one of his supe-
riors and ends trying to commit suicide. The nun, safe in the convent, who
goes laughing-mad and is sent back home again. The mother of six, or nine,
or eleven children who dies of the last-born, mother and infant burning
up together in fever, given the sacrament of extreme unction by the parish
priest, and buried together. *Forever and ever, amen.*

At the start of his match with the great John L. Sullivan, who outweighed
him by twenty pounds, the Irish Charger performed heroically—he did not
turn back when hit punishing blows against the head, the solar plexus, the
midriff, the groin; he did not seem exactly to register these blows, as a vase,
struck hard, finely cracking, might not shatter and fall into pieces immediately. By accident, in his desperate flailing, Dermott managed to strike some
telling blows against his opponent, to the great excitement of the crowd.
But at about the eighteenth round, Dermott had used up his youthful energy against the older, cunning, and more vicious fighter; by the thirty-first
round, reeling and groggy on his feet, one eye completely shut, streaming
blood from countless cuts, Dermott was overcome by a powerful right
hand to the heart, fell heavily to the ground, and could not be roused for
nearly an hour afterward. The evening was to be the pinnacle of the Irish
Charger's career. He was twenty-one.

Following this, Dermott Corcoran began to lose as many fights as he won. And often with younger, less experienced men—emigrated Irishmen like himself, hot-tempered and with a weakness for alcohol. Though he flailed as madly with his fists as ever, he often missed his target completely; he made the crowd laugh by tripping over his own feet; often he failed to see a punch coming straight at him, as if, even at the start of a fight, his vision was impaired. His former admirers, many of them women, pitied him, or scorned him, or forgot him, for there was a steady supply of young prizefighters out of Irish Hill.

At this time Dermott's younger brothers Joseph and Gahern were working in a slaughterhouse off the Dundonald Road. And in the slaughterhouse there were many rough, illiterate, hard-drinking men, some of whom had been dismissed by other employers—by the Moneghan Pottery Works, for example. Joseph was continually harassed by one of his coworkers who had taken a special dislike to him for being the brother of Dermott Corcoran; one day, he was forced to fight this man against his will, and, with Gahern looking on helplessly, fell like a shot when struck a blow to the temple, and died in convulsions. It was widely rumored that his opponent, a fellow Irishman, had boasted beforehand of meaning to kill him in the guise of a fair fight, and that he'd closed his fist around a rock; and whether true or not, Joseph was dead at the age of twenty. When he heard the news, Dermott tracked down his brother's killer in a canalside saloon and beat him mercilessly with his fists until, with dozens of witnesses looking on, he too died.

So Dermott was arrested, tried, and found guilty of murder in the county court; sentenced to die by hanging, as an example to the "lawless" "drunken" "anarchic" Irishmen of the western New York region of whom there were, in 1883, many thousands, and the threat of more all the time.

Now the history of Dermott Corcoran, as recalled, and told and retold by the family, begins to become more ambiguous.

In one version, young Dermott, only twenty-two at the time of his death, was courageous to the very end. He did not insist upon his innocence, and was too proud to beg for his life. Especially in a court, and before a judge, disdainful of the Irish. On the morning of his execution he shook off his jailers to approach the scaffold, ascending the steps by himself, wrists bound tightly behind his back and his legs awkwardly shackled but his handsome red-haired head held high. Here was the "Irish

Charger" as all would remember him through their lives—the man from Irish Hill, Union City, who had fought, and fought bravely, the great John L. Sullivan. A murmur of pity and terror rippled through the crowd of hundreds densely gathered in the barren square behind the county jail. Several young women hid their faces, weeping as if their hearts were broken. A priest approached Dermott to bless him with shaking fingers. The sheriff himself was grim-faced. Even the hangman went about his duty reluctantly.

Dermott Corcoran stood on the scaffold unflinchingly. He refused to allow the black hood to be lowered over his head—it was soiled, having been used many times in the past. He did not require being shielded from seeing the trapdoor beneath his feet, the noose as it was lowered over his head and tightened around his neck. Nor did he allow the priest to get close to him—he had no need of the Catholic Church, he said, where he was going.

The execution was set for eight A.M. As the bells of the nearby Lutheran Church began to toll, the hangman released the trapdoor, and Dermott fell through to jerk horribly at the end of the eight-foot rope. But Dermott's muscular young body was so heavy that his head was torn from his body—there was a geyser-like torrent of blood from the neck as the body fell to the ground, followed by the head which bounced, and rolled, its eyes starkly open and, according to some onlookers, *seeing*.

Everyone screamed and recoiled in horror, even Dermott Corcoran's executioners. The headless body, its heart still frantically pumping, sent out streams of bright red blood for another six seconds.

But in another account of the execution of Dermott Corcoran, the condemned man was so sick with dysentery he had to be half-carried out of his jail cell, and lifted to the scaffold in a chair. His face was so wasted and yellow, he looked so aged, the few friends and fewer relatives who'd come to watch could scarcely recognize him. Was *that* Dermott Corcoran?— *that*? The "Irish Charger" who'd once brought such pride to Irish Hill by fighting the great John L. Sullivan?

In this account, poor Dermott clutched at the priest's black robe and begged for his life. The priest, who knew of Dermott Corcoran only by his reputation, and who strongly disapproved of him and his kind, for bringing such shame to decent law-abiding Irish, told him sternly that it was too late for his life—he should be thinking now of his soul.

By the expression on Dermott Corcoran's contorted face, it was clear that here was a man, or the semblance of a man, without a soul.

Again, the Lutheran bells began to toll the hour of eight A.M. Again, the trapdoor fell open. But poor Dermott was so emaciated from his illness that when he fell, the soiled black hood on his head, the noose tightened around his neck, his body wasn't heavy enough to snap his neck. Instead, he writhed and kicked at the end of the rope, strangling. Hideous sounds erupted from his mouth. He shat his trousers. The hood was dislodged in his desperate struggle, like a worm on a hook as onlookers afterward reported, and his face was exposed—the eyes bulging, skin beet-red, blood trickling from mouth, nose, ears. There were shouts of "God have mercy!" and "Cut the boy down!" For two or three minutes the executioners stood paralyzed not knowing what to do as Dermott continued to struggle piteously. By now, the rope binding his wrists together had come undone, and he was clawing frantically at the noose. Witnesses close enough to hear would swear afterward they could make out him crying "Help me! Help me!" Finally, the sheriff came to his senses and gave the order "Pull his legs!" and he and two deputies rushed forward to grab hold of Dermott's frenzied legs, and tug downward at them, but so hard, putting so much weight into it, that Dermott's body was torn away from his head—there was a geyser-like torrent of blood from the neck as the body fell to the ground, followed by the head which bounced, and rolled, eyes starkly open and sightless. The body continued to pump bright red blood, in ever-decreasing quantities, for another six seconds.

In both accounts of the execution, many in the crowd fainted dead away, and many more were violently sick to their stomachs. It was a fact that the hangman immediately quit his job and never did another public hanging in Union City or elsewhere. And no one ever forgot the spectacle of a man's head and body torn asunder though in time, and probably, for most, fairly quickly, they forgot Dermott Corcoran's name and his local renown.

Says Corky with a grim laugh, "Jesus. You can always depend upon a mick to entertain, eh?"

Sean Corcoran laughs with uncharacteristic bluster. He's had a few ales, he's feeling mellow. Telling a story, you're in charge. Telling a story, you're listened to. If the story isn't something your listener already knows and judging by Sean's nephew's face he hadn't known this, only maybe vaguely. It isn't a Corcoran story the Corcorans and their kin have been proud of. Too sad and, if you're a Corcoran, too convincing. Poor bastard carried up to be hanged in a chair—to Corky, *that's* convincing.

As far as Sean's concerned it's just a story by now—1992. He'd first heard it when he was a kid of ten or eleven, that long ago. To him it's like something he'd seen on television, flicking through the channels as he does now, never watching anything, even the news, for more than a minute or two. Or something in a movie many years ago when, sometimes, he went to movies. Which version of the story is truer than the other, or whether Dermott Corcoran died in some other, untold way, Sean doesn't know. Except one thing's for sure: Dermott Corcoran *did* die in Van Dusen Dorf Square, and his head *was* torn from his body.

And Gahern Corcoran, only nineteen years old at the time, was a witness.

Gahern, himself a sturdy-bodied young man, inclined to rough living and drinking, was so shaken by the deaths of both Dermott and Joseph, he never drank again, not even beer. Nor could he return to the slaughterhouse, in terror of the sight and smell of blood. He wrote impassioned letters to his father back in County Kerry asking to be allowed to return to Ireland and enter a Franciscan monastery—he wanted to consecrate his soul to God. But his father ordered him to stay in America, where he belonged. And to continue to send money home.

Which Gahern did. Within a year of Dermott's execution he married a pious Catholic woman eleven years older than himself who lived with her parents and helped them run a small drygoods store on lower Dalkey Street. These were the Dowds of County Clare: proudly "lace curtain" and not "shanty" Irish. In their presence, Gahern told no tales of the Corcorans, especially not of the "Irish Charger." Few questions were asked, for Gahern was a handsome, able-bodied young man, and himself pious too, to a degree. Rare for an Irishman, he did not drink, and did not fight. He had no temper, it was marveled—no strong emotions at all. He went to mass faithfully on Sundays and Holy Days and never spoke critically of the Church, rare too for an Irishman. When his father-in-law died, Gahern capably took over the store: by then, he was the father of five children of whom the youngest, born in 1891, was Liam.

Liam Corcoran, the father of Sean and Timothy, Corky's grandfather.

Corky who's been listening to this for some reason tense, worried how it's going to turn out, says, "Grandpa Liam!—thank God he *got* born."

Corky and his Uncle Sean are in a restaurant close by Lake Erie Park called Blackhawk Barbecue: a new, noisy, tacky-slick place really a fast-food joint though with more pretensions, and higher prices. One advantage is it's *open*; another, it serves drinks, so Sean can have ale with his chili dog, French fries, and soupy coleslaw. Corky, smoking, and drinking Canada Dry, has been so absorbed in his uncle's story, recounted in a dry, droll, ironic voice, he hasn't even been annoyed much by the bleeps and blips and chirps and percussive farts of a video arcade behind the row of booths they're sitting in. He hasn't been hungry for lunch but, to keep his uncle company, he's been eating a few French fries, dipping them in catsup and chewing quickly as if to get the pulpy stuff down before he's revulsed by it. Sean has bummed a cigarette from Corky so both men are smoking and the plastic ashtray between them is heaped with ash.

Corky says, "Uncle Sean, you make it sound as if it had to happen that way. Jesus!" He's cheerful suddenly, laying his hand on the old man's forearm which is ropey-hard with muscle.

Sean screws up his face at Corky. "What the hell other way could it've happened, lad?"

And while they stand together among a thinned-out crowd stretched along the main road through Lake Erie Park, watching the Memorial Day parade, the companionable feeling between Corky and his Uncle Sean continues. Corky's making wisecracks to combat a melancholy mood that's beginning to come over him like those cobwebbed clouds over the silvery-blue sky *all these old men in uniform! and Tim Corcoran would be among them if he was still alive! and he, Corky, what a shithead, Corky, what a coward, never served his country never wore his country's uniform not even the uniform of the National Guard!* and Sean half-soused from his numerous ales is sardonic and witty like a white-haired old character actor on TV in dapper straw hat and blue serge suit coat and moss-green vinyl bow tie saying, when the oldest living veteran in the parade, the ninety-six-year-old ex-Army corporal from World War II is pushed past in his flag-festooned wheelchair, "—*I get that age, take me out to the town dump and shoot me. Both barrels!*"

Corky manages a cracked-sounding laugh as if this is funny. Others, overhearing, turn toward Sean and grin.

Liking the attention, Sean says again, in a louder voice, "Yessir—I get that age, take me out and shoot me! Va-va-*voom!*"

Next comes an American Legion marching band, "My Country 'Tis of Thee," deafening brass bugles and trumpets and too many drums imperfectly coordinated, Corky grates his jaws resisting the impulse to put his hands over his ears: not that he gives a damn about being rude but somebody's sure to recognize him.

In a democracy, every shithead's a potential vote.

You're a politician, however small-time, you don't forget *that*.

Pathetic little squad of pom-pom girls, must be the Legionnaires' granddaughters, O.K.-looking in the faces but flat-chested or chubby-assed or thick-legged, so few women really look good showing their bodies so why the hell risk it? These poor kids in their red-white-and-blue miniskirt costumes, more of those slick-cheap imitation leather boots, one of the pom-pom girls is on the fat side and some guys whistle at her jeering and crude so she's almost in tears but, for Christ's sake, you're a fat-assed pom-pom girl who isn't even pretty, *get out of our faces.*

Next, military vehicles. Decked up in flags, banners. Officers saluting one another. Hot shit, eh? The highest rank in the parade is supposed to be some Air Force lieutenant-general, World War II. These are World War II veterans now, shocking to see how old, some of them in wheelchairs too, in their uniforms. A row or so of U.S. Army, then U.S. Navy, Air Force, Marine Corps, Coast Guard. Corky loses count somewhere beyond thirty, old guys in their seventies but proud-looking, not marching exactly in step but marching. Every year fewer of them, must be depressing as hell. Can't help but figure next time *you* might not be here, the parade goes on without you.

Corky asks Sean, who's a World War II vet himself, does he know any of these men, but Sean shrugs as if to say, *Who cares?*

"Well," says Corky, "—they look pretty good for their age. They're holding up almost as well as you, Sean." Feeling he should defend the veterans, his uncle's attitude worries him.

Sean Corcoran had fought in the Philippines as a Private First Class in the U.S. Army and was honorably discharged in 1945 but so far as Corky can remember he never spoke of it. Never. Unlike his younger brother Tim who talked so much about Korea, who'd seemed in a way fixated upon Korea, his platoon buddies there, what had happened to him. Sean had not been wounded in the war like Tim, nor taken prisoner by the enemy. He'd almost died of malaria, he'd maybe had a nervous collapse, or, Corky guesses, he'd spent some time in the stockade; there was some secret about his uncle's wartime service nobody would speak of, not even Aunt Frances. Of course, his children would never have dared ask him, or his nephew Jerome.

Sean had never marched in the Memorial Day parade and was said to have thrown out his Army uniform as soon as he got home, even his dog tags. Kept no mementos which is maybe a healthy thing sometimes?

Though Corky thinks it's a futile gesture, to try to erase history by an act of will.

Next comes another marching band, the National Anthem played off-key but in high spirits, a Marine guard bearing tall impressive flags and a showy contingent of drum majorettes, not bad, a honey-blond tossing a flirty smile Corky's way is especially not bad, though just slightly bowlegged, and an ass like a boy's. Corky's remembering poor Charlotte the night before clutching at him *How I miss you how I love you oh Corky!*—so sad, a woman closing her eyes lifting her face to be kissed, opening her legs to be fucked, so sad. How sad how *serious* to be a woman in a man's world, he'd probably cut his throat, or bloat up to three hundred pounds if he had to be a woman that's the fucking truth.

Even Christina Kavanaugh: likes to think she's independent, a "feminist," uses her maiden name and has that loft and has her work such as it is and had Corky Corcoran as a lover but all the while she's somebody's *wife*, thinks of herself as somebody's *wife*. *He's my husband I share most of my life with him.*

Next come the Korean War veterans. Old guys too, trying to march like they're kids. Two of them in wheelchairs. One, Corky recognizes, last name's Mulvaney, an old friend of Tim Corcoran's. And there's a black man, burly, somber, in gold-rimmed eyeglasses looking like a school-teacher. Corky's staring at these vets swallowing hard, blinking tears out of his eyes. It pisses him off nobody's paying much attention to them, nobody knows them, old guys in uniforms stepping along only eleven of them, fewer than the others, strange, well maybe not strange: Korea was never a *war* was it. Next in the parade is a hook-and-ladder truck asshole firemen sounding their siren, God damn.

Corky says to Sean, casually, as if this is just making conversation, "—Dad would probably be marching here, if he was alive."

Sean makes no reply. Maybe hasn't heard.

Corky's feeling again that sharp painful sensation of a son seeing his father *out there*. He'd be standing with Theresa clasping his hand, the excitement and worry was almost more than he could bear. A tall broad-shouldered good-looking man in a private's uniform, with medals, a Silver Star, a Purple Heart, fancy epaulettes, a smart visored hat—his dad. Je-rome standing rigid staring so Theresa laughed and nudged him—*There's Daddy!* but even then he'd felt shy, doubtful. He knew that tall red-haired man marching with the others was Daddy but could he be *sure?*

Even when Daddy saw him, grinned and waved at him, even then could he be *sure?*

Corky remembers soldiers on horseback. Funeral wreaths carried alongside the American flags. A solitary trumpeter playing that slow, sad song "Taps." The Memorial Day parade so much bigger, so much more of an event, than it is now. The World War II vets were still youth-ful, and there were a lot of them, and the Korean vets were *young*. Young and vigorous and good-looking even the crippled ones nobody had to feel sorry for them exactly, they were important, they mattered, *they were the real thing.*

That's all a man wants, no matter what it costs him. *To be the real thing.*

Jesus, Corky can't help thinking, if Tim Corcoran was alive and marching in this unit today he'd be just another of these sad old guys in their tight uniforms, trying to march in step, eyes restlessly scanning the faces of onlookers hoping to see somebody, anybody, familiar so they can smile, wave, salute.

Corky surprises his Uncle Sean by grinning and waving at the Korean vets, like he's the one who's been drinking. He calls out to the marchers, "Great, guys! Terrific! Keep it up! Congratulations! You're almost there!"—meaning the Soldiers' and Sailors' Monument a half-mile away. Startled, squinting, most of the vets wave back at Corky. His enthusiasm starts a wave of enthusiasm close around him and others are waving and calling out too, it's a good feeling even if it's over almost before it's begun.

The next, noisy unit, drawing much more attention, is the Union City Firemen's Association Marching Band. Flags, drums, majorettes in skin-tight gold lamé with the glossy-shellacked glamor of grade-B hookers, followed by a shiny-red fire engine emitting teasing squeals of siren, each of them deafening. Kids are jumping up and down yelling with excitement as uniformed firemen, grinning like bozos, toss candy from the rear of the truck. Demeaning crap, Corky thinks, offended. What's it doing in a Memorial Day parade? Isn't a Memorial Day parade about the *dead?* It's fucking disgusting to see children, some of them just old enough to make it on their own, rushing out like greedy rats to pick up candy from the pavement. Corky Corcoran would never let any kid of his participate in such shit.

Glancing surreptitiously at his watch. Already past three P.M. The parade was slow getting started, it looks now as if it's maybe going to rain. Quick chill gusts of wind from the lake and that sulfurous smell that makes Corky's nostrils pinch that shift in the barometer *something's going to happen.* You can't grow up in Union City, New York, without getting to like that smell, that sensation. Like an addict, liking it a lot.

Next is Vietnam, guys Corky's age and, yes, he knows a few of them but keeps back just far enough so if they're scanning the crowd they don't see him. Only twenty-two men. A row of Army uniforms, a row of Navy, a row of Marines. A bugler with a ponytail—*that's* shocking. Poor dumbfuck leftover of the Sixties, Corky's embarrassed for him but nobody looking much cares, or even notices. One of the Marine officers is a guy Corky knows from the old neighborhood, Billy Brannon, the rumor was he'd gotten hooked on heroin in Vietnam but he looks clean now, walks with a slight limp but like it's a badge of pride—Vietnam's a long time ago, all's forgiven.

Corky makes sure Brannon doesn't catch his eye. They run into each other around town, sometimes at City Hall where Brannon shows up occasionally, he's a high school principal.

Vietnam: Corky Corcoran's war, if he'd gone.

Should have, maybe. His dad would have been ashamed of him doing all he could to stay out. *A man among men:* he'd missed it forever. Why Corky runs off at the mouth so much, maybe. Chasing pussy like he's desperate to prove something. That's it?

Next comes the brassy-percussive noise of another marching band belting out in quickstep time what sounds like the theme song from *Rocky:* it's the South Union City High School Marching Band and this is a unit everybody's waiting for, cheers whistles catcalls wild applause for the marchers bearing the American flag and just behind it the school colors Day-Glo green-and-white most of all for the teenaged majorettes looking just as terrific to Corky's yearning eye as they'd looked in Dundonald Park, a glisten of sweat on their faces, upper chests, half-moons of sweat darkened beneath their arms, Corky's thinking Jesus how he'd love to lick them there, the tall gorgeous black girl first, then between the legs, that sweaty-cunty smell, that heat, nothing like it. Clapping and whistling like every other fuckhead as the girls strut past swinging their cute little asses, poking out their tits, to the *boom! boom! boom!* of big drums and the manic crash of cymbals the gleaming-silver batons fly up into the air, turn and flash and drop still turning and are unhesitantly caught and twirled and tossed up again, so sexy Corky's getting a hard-on *just watching the fucking batons let alone the girls.*

Helpless Corky stares after the majorettes strutting away sad-hearted as if they're leaving him stuck somewhere to die. Those satin asses, smooth-gleaming young thighs and buttocks you can be sure have no trace of that veiny-fatty cellulite that's in older women, poor Charlotte's ample ass now riddled with it, even Christina's firmer thighs beginning to show it, fine-cracked flesh like it's been crumpled. Corky's looking after the high school girls wondering if he'd really screwed up misreading the black girl's *fuck you* gesture with the baton, maybe it was really *fuck me,* maybe it's a way the kids have of communicating with one another, he's out of it: too old. Actually shocked when, at the Council, the public health people come to demand money for condoms for not just high school kids but for junior high too, for the "sexually active" as they're called. No use pretending they're not screwing like rabbits, mothers as young as thirteen mostly black girls but not in every case, the ones that get pregnant are the innocent ones, the ones that get caught.

Also the threat of AIDS, spreading if they don't use condoms. Kids think they're going to live forever, that's why the Army can recruit, that's why wars, no end to wars, young guys eager to put on the uniform, grab the gun, that cruel ancient bullshit: *A man among men.*

Doggy-Corky wiping his face, blowing his nose. Has Uncle Sean picked up on him, staring at the black majorette?—does *he* feel it, too? Or is he old enough to be out of it?

Dryly Sean remarks, nudging Corky in the ribs like they're two young studs surveying the field together, "—Not bad, eh? Except for the smell, maybe."

Corky's frankly shocked by this dumb-fuck racist remark from his own uncle but, shit, laughs to go along with it, only just not very loud or very enthusiastically so Uncle Sean can take a hint. But being half-soused and feeling cocky in his straw hat and blue serge, Uncle Sean isn't in a mood to take any hint. At least lowering his gravelly voice so he won't be overheard by a black family a few yards away, saying, with a sardonic grin, "—Saw you on TV yesterday, Corky—why'd you turn up at that whore's funeral?—*those people are not your friends.*"

Amazed Corky stares at his uncle. "What? What 'whore'? You mean—Marilee Plummer? *What people?*"

Sean screws up his face regarding Corky with pale washed-out blue eyes, blood-veined, yellowish. That look of sour wisdom, old-mannish scorn. And the grizzled eyebrows jutting over, it registers in Corky's memory bank, he gets old he's got to remember to have the barber trim his eyebrows, yes and the nostril hairs, wiry hairs sprouting out of the ears. Can't let himself go, the next stop's dead meat.

Sean's looking at him like *he*, Corky, is the asshole.

Corky repeats, "What 'whore'? *What people?*"

Shrugging Sean says, "Lad, don't play dumb." Looking back at the parade, saying, indifferently, "—The whore was on the take, they paid her fifty thousand dollars to lie about that nigger minister what's-his-name, everybody knows it."

Corky can't believe how his uncle tosses this off, such a remark, such an accusation, what he's saying is that Oscar Slattery bribed Marilee Plummer to bring false charges of rape, sodomy, against Steadman, to perjure herself to a grand jury, the way it's tossed *everybody knows* like there's nothing to discuss. Typical neighborhood bullshitting, Christ knows where he picked it up, doesn't go to church any longer, does he? Corky opens his mouth to protest with a kid's incredulous whine then figures what the hell, no point in trying to argue with his uncle when his uncle doesn't know shit only what he thinks he knows.

Corky makes a joke about the TV interview hoping to hear Sean say he sounded good but Sean's not listening, must be Corky'd offended him so obviously not believing his inside dope, well too bad, fuck that, Corky's face is smarting and his heart beating hard *those people are not your friends* what the hell does this ignorant old rummy know about Corky Corcoran's life?—about anything?

Irish Hill, in the old days: big grins, laughter, like it was an accomplishment of one of their own, and Corky's own relatives for instance Joe Donnelly his uncle calling out right on Dalkey Street to Corky *Great news, eh?*—when news of the assassination of Martin Luther King first hit the neighborhood.

Even Aunt Frances, such a goodhearted woman, her face going stiff watching TV seeing the demonstrations, burnings, Detroit Los Angeles Newark Philadelphia, it's the Jews put them up to it, it's the Jews give them money, now look.

Corky stubs out a cigarette in the grass, and lights up another.

Decides to keep his mouth shut. Let Uncle Sean think whatever crap he wants, *he's* never going to be interviewed on TV.

Next comes a solemn contingent of mostly middle-aged and older women in white and gold-trimmed capes, caps, pleated skirts and rubber-soled walking shoes, nobody's paying much attention to them craning their necks impatient to see what's next, the Gulf War vets the real glamor stars of the parade are at the end and a military marching band pounding out "Stars and Stripes Forever" and National Guard motorcyclists bringing up the rear. Distracted Corky his mouth God-damned parched by now watches these good ladies trudging along visibly tired after three miles much of it uphill, poor old biddies bearing American flags like claiming they're American, too, they're in this parade, too, carrying floral funeral wreaths and photographs of what you'd guess to be dead sons, don't look at me, lady, *I* didn't kill your precious son. The fluttering satin banner AMERICAN GOLD STAR MOTHERS stirs some scattered applause, Corky doesn't think it's jeering or derisive though the American Gold Star Mothers aren't walking fast enough to suit the crowd *C'mon ladies get a move on!*—trailing after the quickstepping South Union High School Marching Band whose noise is still dominant as if amplified, broadcast downward, out of the very sky.

Afterward wondering why for fuck's sake he hadn't asked Sean more about it, what he'd said about Marilee Plummer, for instance where did the specific sum $50,000 come from?—for in fact none of this was common knowledge nor even common gossip at this time. Afterward wondering why he'd been so hurt, so pissed, was it because he'd expected his uncle to be impressed with him on TV like maybe his own father might've been, instead the old bastard was critical, bad-mouthing him to his face *those people are not your friends.*

Is that Nick Daugherty?—Nick, with one of his kids, on the far side of the crowd at the Soldiers' and Sailors' Monument? Corky tries to catch his eye, he's sure it *is* Nick, staring straight at the speakers' platform not noticing Corky. His old friend, once closest-friend Corky.

Dying for a drink but here's good-sport Corky Corcoran beside his Uncle Sean in a sparse crowd of about one hundred people at the fifty-foot tower-like Soldiers' and Sailors' Monument at the northernmost edge of Lake Erie Park, the quick-waning afternoon of Memorial Day 1992. More military music, an hour of speeches, eulogies. *This day of sacred remembrance. That they might not die in vain. The dead we cherish, may they live forever in our hearts and minds.* The high point of the ceremony is the unveiling of a memorial honoring the single soldier from Union City to die in Bush's Gulf War, an Army helicopter pilot, the novelty is she's female, twenty-five years old when she died, crashed in Northern Saudi Arabia in a noncombat accident the day *after* the cease-fire. Can't be much consolation to the parents, their daughter dead and this chunk of granite and a copper plaque with her "likeness" stamped on it, but they're up there on the platform being noble being photographed and on

TV blinking tears from their eyes as the president of the Mohawk County American Legion reads off a citation followed by one of the Mayor's aides reading off another followed by one of Cuomo's aides reading off a statement by the Governor, *We honor you who by your sacrifice honor us.*

Bullshit, but it sounds good.

A drink sweet Jesus do I need a drink his throat parched despite the Canada Dry he'd swigged this terrible thirst *never make it cold stone sober: never* in his shaky state close to crying when the granite memorial is finally unveiled.

Doesn't Nick Daugherty see Corky? Sure, he must. Corky's been craning his neck trying to get his friend's attention for the past twenty minutes.

Of the $5000 Nick was able to make only a couple of payments that first year and then ran into financial problems—more problems. Three years now, or is it four? No hurry about repaying the loan Corky insisted, embarrassed. A handshake's enough, between friends. And no interest either, of course. What d'you think I am, a Jew? Hey Nick here's your old friend Corky Corcoran, O.K.?

A distant shuddering of thunder, light bleeding through matted layers of cloud above Lake Erie. Corky's nostrils arch like a horse's smelling something's going to happen.

Why'd you turn up at that whore's funeral.

Those people are not your friends.

Get him to sign. Talk's talk.

Greenbaum looking at him, those shrewd turtle's eyes, like Corky's a terminal case. Any asshole can figure, you lend a guy up to his ass in debt money charging no interest he'll pay back his creditors who are charging him interest, not you. You're the last on his list. You're maybe not even on the list.

Hasn't seen Nick in maybe a year. But Corky's slow to believe.

Christ, that promissory note Greenbaum prepared for Corky to take to Nick, on Corky's desk at home, couldn't bring himself to read it through. *Pay me back when you can* he'd said. A way of boasting *Hey I'm rich: look what I can afford.*

The last time the Daughertys invited him out to dinner, Deborah redeyed and weepy in the kitchen, taking Corky's hands in hers whispering thanks, soft so Nick in the other room couldn't hear. Deborah saying lifting her earnest pretty face to Corky's you don't know how much this means to Nick, it's a real boost to him he's been feeling so low your faith in him your friendship oh Corky thank you! A wet breathless kiss like a dog's daringly on Corky's mouth meant to seem impulsive but Corky guessed she'd been planning it for days, weeks. And Corky blushing embarrassed saying O.K., shit it's O.K., Nick would do the same for me.

That, Corky still believes. For sure.

"—If the dead could speak to us today, instead of us presuming to speak for them, we might be shocked at what they would say: no more 'heroic' deaths, no more 'sacrifice,' no more wars, no more Memorial Days!"

This final speech of the afternoon is being given, over ominous rolls of thunder, by former U.S. Marine First Lieutenant Billy Brannon. Brannon's been introduced impressively as a veteran of two tours in Vietnam, seriously wounded near My Lai and several times decorated for bravery in combat, president of the Great Lakes Veterans' Association and principal of North Decatur High School. Corky listens to Brannon's high, reedy, impassioned voice, he's envious, hell he's jealous, but admiring, too—Brannon's the real thing. Daring to say what he's saying, practically coming out and telling the crowd that war is bullshit, all the while maintaining his respect for his listeners—that's true leadership. Corky's thinking *he* might've been up there in Brannon's place, *he* might've been a man of integrity, a man with a true mission, if circumstances had been otherwise. If he hadn't been a coward.

Coward: that night when Heinz Meuller was driving after a basketball game, six or seven of them crammed into the car on their way downtown to The Bull's Eye and everybody including Vic Slattery drunk on beer they'd smuggled into the gym and Heinz sighted some black kids on the sidewalk in front of the Palace Theatre crying *Hey watch this!* laying on the horn and aiming the car for the sidewalk so the kids turned, screamed and scattered their eyes wild and faces like dark leaves lifted and blown in a furious wind, *Run niggers!* Heinz yelled and some of the others *Run run run niggers!* laughing wildly and Corky in the back seat staring his face locked in an idiotic grin as Heinz's car, a heavy Olds, began to skid, its rear wheels veering to the right even as the black kids ran in desperation one of them falling and scrambling to his feet and managing to escape even as the car jolted up onto the sidewalk but bounced back into the street again like a car in a child's cartoon lethal-seeming but harmless and only a joke harmless as Heinz brought it under control and continued on Grand Boulevard at forty miles an hour all the guys laughing like they're about to piss their pants and Corky was gripping the seat in front of him thinking he'd be sick to his stomach and at The Bull's Eye his terrible worry was there wouldn't be room enough for him in the booth, what if, what then, yes but there was plenty of room for Corky Corcoran that night, he was O.K.

Brannon's winding up his speech. Pretty strong stuff, criticizing the Gulf War, asking why weren't sanctions tried, what of the Iraqi dead and wounded victims of their mad leader, must the United States be a party to such madness?

"—We must learn to transcend the old way of thinking *our dead* are to be memorialized, *their dead* are to be tallied," Brannon is saying urgently, "—there are no winners in any war, we are all losers! Those of us who have killed no less than those of us who have died!"

It's at this point that Brannon's voice begins to shake. He breaks off, rubs his eyes inside his glasses, for an awkward moment he's silent then mutters what sounds like "Thank you" and turns away from the microphone. At that moment there's a high rumbling roll of thunder like faint laughter and a gust of wind shakes tree limbs over the reviewing stand, loosening fuzzy-golden seeds like rain. At the edge of the crowd where people have been drifting away there's a pause, nobody seems to know if Brannon's speech is over, or what the hell's going on, so Corky, embarrassed for Brannon, begins to clap, lifting his hands over his head so others join in, though the applause is scattered and sporadic and never builds up much momentum before the military band swings into "The Battle Hymn of the Republic" in what sounds like polka time.

Sean turns to Corky, annoyed. "Sounds like a Communist, that one. How in hell'd *he* get on the program?"

Says Corky, "Shit, Billy Brannon's an old buddy of mine."

At that moment remembering: Nick Daugherty!

The crowd is breaking and scattering. Corky pushes through to see Nick and his teenaged son walking away. Hasn't Nick seen him? Corky shouts, "Nick? Hey, it's Corky—" as he sees, or thinks he sees, his friend glancing nervously over his shoulder even as he continues without slackening his speed, eager to escape Lake Erie Park.

8

OUR LADY OF MERCY CEMETERY

Trying to recall how many times but he could not. He must have been between the ages of six and eleven. And would it have continued? Each Memorial Day morning before the parade Daddy solemn and passionate, clean-shaven, in suit, white shirt and tie, polished shoes and insisting that Mommy dress Jerome too as if for church, this is more important than church and don't you ever forget it. Taking Jerome by the hand, Daddy's callused hand, firm, even rough, an impatient edge to Daddy's patience you never wanted to test the way you'd test Mommy. Never. In Our Lady of Mercy Cemetery behind the church under the arch and into the grassy graveyard where sometimes a cold drizzle fell and sometimes it was steamy hot prematurely hot as summer the sun swollen in the sky by nine A.M. so beads of sweat formed at Daddy's hairline and ran in slow trickles down his face. Like tears. And there were tears too, sometimes. Which Daddy didn't hide. And Daddy's nose running, which he didn't seem to notice. You didn't want to see and you'd never tell and when Mommy asked afterward was it all right? was it nice in the cemetery? were there lots of other people there? you knew she really meant had he scared you so you said yes it was nice, it was just Daddy and you it *was* nice.

In Our Lady of Mercy Cemetery Daddy and Jerome walked slowly along the rows of graves and at veterans' graves they stuck six-inch American flags into the earth sometimes beside other flags already there, and beside pots of bright-blossoming azaleas, begonias, geraniums. Tim Corcoran bought a small bundle of these flags at fifty cents apiece, and so did other veterans and the parents, widows, or children of veterans who had died in service. So a single grave might have several flags. Most of the dead veterans in Our Lady of Mercy in the 1950s had died in World War II but there were quite a few graves from World War I. And fresher ones, from Korea. Whenever they came to one of these it was always a man Daddy knew, sometimes a man Daddy had been friends with in school and Daddy would say, *This could be my grave*. And, *If I was lucky this would be my grave but probably it would've been in the prison camp I died, or alongside the road, and they'd have buried me like they did the others, in a ditch. That was how they did it. So I guess this wouldn't be my grave after all. I wouldn't be here, at all.*

The mystery of that: Daddy wouldn't be here, at all.

So Jerome wondered, *Then where?*

Not in Our Lady of Mercy Cemetery but at home sometimes when he'd been drinking Daddy would tell of how in October 1951 when he was twenty-eight years old and in Korea for only one month his platoon was attacked above the Naktong River. Of how shrapnel hit him in the small of his back and in his right knee. Of how he, and the other surviving members of his platoon, endured a three-week march north of the river and seven weeks of imprisonment in a rural compound before they were liberated. Repeatedly Daddy told of how, had it not been for a young black soldier from Georgia named Lucius Prudhomme who'd helped him walk, almost carried him at times, he would have died along the road. Others died, you'd have thought they weren't as bad off as him, but they died and were left beside the road. It wasn't just twenty-two-year-old Private First Class Lucius Prudhomme who'd helped him, it was other soldiers, too, and some of these others black, too. Black men who'd be regarded as "niggers" in the United States, in the North as well as in the South, and in Irish Hill where not a one of them would dare try to live, nor even walk at certain hours of the day or night.

Lucius Prudhomme died in the prison camp. Timothy Corcoran did not die but was airlifted out with other injured men and hospitalized in Seoul and shipped back home with two Purple Hearts and a Silver Star though he was not a hero, hadn't done anything heroic except get through. But one thing he'd learned, it was not to take any shit from anybody. Know who your friends are, and who your enemies are. And never confuse them.

Once, when Jerome was very young, Mommy went with them to Our Lady of Mercy Cemetery on Memorial Day morning wearing white gloves and a hat with a veil, one of her pretty hats she wore to church. And white high-heeled shoes that sank into the soft damp gravel and grass. Mommy held Jerome's hand until he pulled away. Her eyes were restless, drawn upward from the graves to the green-budding trees, to the sky. She too was shy of Daddy in this strange place. It was Daddy, but maybe not. Like when he'd come home smelling of beer, or whiskey—it was Daddy, but not always the same Daddy. When, in the cemetery, Daddy stood quiet at one of the graves you let him alone, you didn't tease or act silly to get attention. You didn't sulk. With Mommy and Grandma and the other women you could act any way you wanted but with Daddy, no. If he touched you to take your hand and pull you along that was all right but you wouldn't want to touch him to interrupt him from his thoughts. His eyes glistening-wet, the glare of them swinging around. That moment when he didn't know who the hell you were. And where this was.

Our Lady of Mercy Cemetery. Memorial Day 1992. Corky sees by his watch it's 4:20 P.M. anxious the day's sliding by and *something's going to happen* but, Jesus, not prepared for, when he and Uncle Sean come to the Corcoran family plot, that first sight of the paired markers—

TIMOTHY PATRICK CORCORAN
1923-1959
THERESA AGNES CORCORAN
1927-1967

—and Corky astonishes and embarrasses his Uncle Sean, Jesus! and himself, bursting into tears like a woman.

Just stands there, crying. Wracking sobs, out of control. His chest like there's a band tightening around it about to crack his ribs, his breath choked, a fierce heat in his face and his throat actually *hurting*. It's been so long since Corky's cried must be twenty years, he's forgotten how crying *hurts*. A sharp cramped pain in the throat like you'd imagine cancer.

Sean's staring at him like he's gone nuts. And Sean fearful too, like *he* might start in.

Corky tries to get himself back together. Saying, between sobs, "Shit, I'm sorry—" and "—I don't know what this *is*—" then breaking down again, blowing his nose in a tissue, hands shaking so he's in a panic this really is the start of the D.T.'s, he'll have to be taken away in an ambulance, put in a straitjacket. He's trying not to think exactly why he's crying trying not to think of his father Tim Corcoran, his mother Theresa Corcoran, Jerome's lost young parents trying not to think *Daddy! Mommy!* surrendering to the terror of grief recalling those Memorial Day mornings here in Our Lady of Mercy Cemetery he'd believed as a child because he had no reason not to believe would go on forever.

Somebody's stuck a six-inch American flag in the moist earth at the head of Tim Corcoran's grave—maybe that set off Corky's crying jag. And scattered throughout the cemetery there are others. Veterans still make it a practice to come around, the way Corky's father did, to mark other veterans' graves. What good people they are, Corky's thinking. What good people in the world it isn't all just shit and double-dealing.

Corky's brought the potted pink begonia to place between his father's and mother's graves. Since he and Uncle Sean won't be getting to Holy Redeemer today after all to see Aunt Mary Megan.

In the Blackhawk Barbecue parking lot Corky'd glanced into the back seat of the Caddy and hadn't seen the begonia at first, thinking somebody'd stolen the plant, God damn must've been those hillbillies on Roosevelt Street!—then he found it upside down on the floor where the pot must've tumbled from the seat one of the times he'd used his brakes; he'd more or less forgotten about it. Brushing off the crumbled earth, picking off the broken and wilted buds. Then took the plant back into the restaurant to get some water for it, hoping it will be O.K. and not die in a day or two. Some of these badly wilted buds, maybe they'll never open. Still, it's a beautiful plant. Beautiful flowers. Sean thought so, too.

Corky stoops to place the begonia plant on the grassy earth between the graves. Theresa always liked flowers, she'd like these. The worst of his crying jag's over. He hopes. Staring at the grave markers which are smooth-faced pinkish-gray granite with rough edges, expensive-looking, hefty, measuring about three feet by four. But the gravesites are so small. When you consider. Final resting place, about the size of one of those Johnny-on-the-Spot portable toilets. That's a fact you never get used to— big as people are in life, extended through time, the space they take up in the earth is finally so fucking *small*.

Still, it's better than being cremated. Must be.

Corky's hiccuping, blowing his nose in a sopping tissue. So far gone for the moment he isn't even thinking how he needs a drink, how stone cold sober he isn't going to make it. Sean says, "Corky—?" eyeing him cautiously, touching his arm. Not knowing what to do or say, all his life Sean Corcoran's disliked touching people or being touched, maybe not all his life exactly but since his brother was murdered. Probably he's thinking he doesn't really know Jerome—"Corky"—at all. His brother's son who lived for years under his roof like a son of his own, he doesn't know him at all. Grown up into this wise-ass character, small-time politician and hustler, a look in his face on even his best days like he's bet every penny at the track and he's watching the horses come in and the news is not going to be good.

Also, at his age Sean Corcoran's used to strong-seeming people suddenly cracking. And once they crack, Christ knows if they can get it back together again. All Sean can think to tell his nephew staring at these graves like a man in a dream is, soberly, yet with an air of subtle avuncular reproach as if any fuckhead should be able to figure this out for himself, "Lad, I'd say you need a drink."

Corky makes a snorting noise that might be a sob or a laugh. But he's grinning when he says, "Shit, I can't ever drink again, Uncle Sean. I'm dead meat if I do."

"What the hell? Sure you can."

"No. I know it."

Sean's got his arm around Corky's shoulders to steady him. It's an awkward and painful stance and now this remark of Corky's is God-damned embarrassing as a fart let at the wrong moment but Sean's committed to the gesture and can't just step away. Mumbling as if ashamed for his nephew Sean says, "*That's* what the fuckers brainwash you into thinking. You believe it, you're off your head."

"Who?"

"The AA people."

"I haven't been there yet. I'm checking in tomorrow morning."

"Hell you are."

"Hell I'm *not*. I need help."

Now Sean does release him. The men stand side by side breathing quickly not looking at each other. A gust of wind ripples the cemetery's dense grass, there's a shivering sound in the leaves overhead. A rainfall of those fuzzy-golden seeds. Corky says, "Tell me about my father, Uncle Sean. Why he died, how he died—anything. Tell me anything."

Sean says quickly, as if he's been expecting this, "There's nothing you don't know. There's nothing to say."

"Why didn't Fenske ever get arrested? Or the men he hired? *Was* it Fenske who had Daddy killed?"

The first time Corky Corcoran has uttered aloud the word *Daddy* in thirty years. He's fumbling for his pack of Camels his hands shaking so he almost can't get a cigarette out and, in the gusty air, lighted.

Sean's cursing under his breath—"God damn! Son of a bitch!" Turning his heel in the graveled path, puffing like a fat man. An angry fat man.

Sean begins to say something, then stops; begins again, and stops. Corky's exhaling smoke watching him worriedly not knowing what the fuck he might do if his uncle just walks away—run after him? He's in a state so close to flipping, if the old bastard turns his back on him he might just kick him in the ass.

So Sean surprises Corky saying finally, slowly, "Yes—you could say it was Fenske. It *was* Fenske. Sure. Like everybody knew except we couldn't prove it. *You* know that." Pausing not looking at Corky to let that sink in. "And the fucker paid for it, only not right away. They got him a couple of years later. Remember?"

Corky says quickly, "Sure, I remember. But who's 'they'?"

Sean shrugs. "The next guy, taking over the union. There's always a next guy. Or was. The trade unions had everybody over a barrel then— now, they're shit. Al Fenske had Tim Corcoran killed but it wasn't like he had any choice, his back was against the wall. It didn't have to happen."

Sean speaks bitterly, with an air of satisfaction. He isn't looking at Corky but at the straw hat he's turning in his hand.

Corky asks, "What? What didn't have to happen?"

"Your father getting killed. Like he did. Hit. God damn, it *wouldn't* have happened, if he'd listened to me."

"If who'd listened to you?"

Sean cuts his eyes at Corky exasperated. "Your father! Who the hell else? We're talking about 'Daddy,' aren't we talking about 'Daddy'? Eh?"

"I—don't know what we're talking about," Corky says. His breath is coming so quick and shallow, it's like he's about to keel over. Like the ground is tilting beneath his feet. "You tell *me*."

Sean turns his hat in his hand not seeming to know what he's doing. His rheumy-blue eyes glaring at Corky. And there's a sudden dip to his voice, he gestures toward Theresa's grave marker, "Your mother was a lovely woman, Corky. She never should have married into the Corcorans. Never should've married *him*."

"What? *Why?*"

"Because it upped the ante. Because they were crazy about each other and it blew things out of proportion—how Tim saw himself, or wanted to see himself. How he had to play things out, with her looking on. Like in the war, too, he never got over that. Everything meant too much!" Sean's speaking more and more rapidly, shaking his head so his jowls tremble. His voice takes on a tone of bitter mockery. "Like nothing could be the way other people did it, running a business where you compromise, make deals, get along. The way everybody else did it including our own father—that's why! Because he got himself killed, that's fucking why! Never thought it could really happen like he was some hot-shit hero in a movie, just couldn't believe what everybody else knew including me but would he listen? So all of it, everything that happened afterward, Buck Glover and those other cocksuckers selling us out, the family losing the business, Theresa breaking down—*it was your father's fault.* Don't look at me like some asshole, you hear what I'm saying?"

Scared Corky says, stammering, "I—don't know. What—?"

"—Because it wasn't like we hadn't paid Fenske, and a dozen other guys, before. Like our father did, and everybody else. It wasn't any different from paying taxes, you hear what I'm saying? Commissions you pay some fancy fucking broker for a piece of paper going over his desk, fees, percentages, 'kickbacks'—it's just a word. It's shit. How'd you think we got the contract for the City Hall addition?—we weren't the low bid. So it wasn't like Tim couldn't play the hand like everybody else. Sure, he could. If he couldn't, I could. I did. You pay them, and they pay you. *You* know this, you're not a jerk-off kid any longer. Right? It's business and it's got to run like on a greased track and even if there's a D.A. making a stink about it once in a while that's got to run smooth, too, you hear what I'm saying? So if somebody fucks it up grandstanding like Tim Corcoran he's got to be talked to seriously and if he doesn't listen he's got to be stopped. Simple as that. *I* talked to him, myself. Fensake talked to me, and I talked to Tim not once but a dozen times, it was about all we were talking about at the end, not him hiring nonunion niggers but him not paying Fenske what Fenske asked for that privilege, which would've been to our advantage anyway, which *he* knew, but there he was so proud, hot-shit buying a new house borrowing a hundred thousand dollars from the bank to buy into Maiden Vale like nobody's know where he came from if he could just get there by the Union City Golf Club maybe they'd vote him in, eh?—*him!* A Corcoran! A mick from Irish Hill! What a laugh!" Sean screws up his face like he's going to spit. Corky has never seen his uncle so passionate.

"Wait," says Corky. "What're you telling me? I always thought—"

"You always thought 'Daddy' was a big deal, 'Daddy' was a hero," Sean says contemptuously. "Well, it's like that Lieutenant What's-his-name was saying just now, his speech—maybe we don't need no more big deals, heroes, people getting killed when they don't need to get killed and the rest of us cleaning up the mess. Maybe it's a lot of bullshit, dying when you don't need to."

"But—"

"Look, I loved him, too. I loved my brother. I don't even think of him like he's dead—" gesturing toward Tim Corcoran's grave, crinkling his face, "—that's just what *happened*. That isn't *him*. I loved him but he wouldn't listen to me, like I say I talked to him a dozen times and the last time, it was the morning he was killed, I said to him, 'You're pushing Al in a corner, he's got no way out except to hurt you,' and *he* said, like it's a joke, 'Nobody's going to hurt me, not in this town'—because we were in tight with Glover, or he thought we were. We *were*, but it didn't last. After you're dead all your deals are canceled, you hear what I'm saying?"

Forlornly, sucking at his cigarette like it's a straw to the air and he's a drowning man, Corky says, "I—guess I do." Though really he doesn't. His instinct is to push past his uncle and run out of the cemetery and get in his car and escape. Anywhere!

Sean says bitterly, "The things Tim said to me, maybe he was joking but *I* never laughed, calling me a 'mick scumbag' and pat-slapping me on the cheek like I was a woman—I'd've killed him myself, if he'd pulled that shit in front of witnesses! In front of your mother, for instance. All that crap I had to take that Tim was my *younger* brother, and *he's* the smart one, *he's* got the ideas, *he's* the boss—I swallowed it to keep peace, we were building up the business. And we'd have done O.K. except *he* always wanted more. Expanding operations, buying more equipment, borrowing money. He'd take on more work than we could do, take the client's money and start digging then move on to another job and juggle the two and then it's three, sure everybody in the trade does it but Tim really pushed. And his personal style—he always had to throw money around, whether he had it or not. At restaurants, clubs. Paying the bills for guys who really had dough. Had to be in tight with City Hall and cops and every realtor and lawyer he thought had influence and ward heelers and gamblers and bookies and sucks! Him and Al Fenske, they were two of a kind, they came up at about the same time never letting each other out of their sight like two boxers in the same weight division fighting other opponents but knowing they're going to fight each other eventually—which they did." Sean's puffing, turning his straw hat in his hands not knowing what he's doing then clamps it on his head, hard, almost breaking the brim. "So they both lost."

Corky says, "What the fuck, they both lost?—Fenske killed my father!"

But must be he's looking so dazed and pleading the old man takes pity on him and shuts up. Turns, and walks away. And Corky's standing there like a man trying to decipher the meaning of a sound so loud it's deafening, it's blown him away without his knowing.

Then, this: uncle and nephew talk together in Corky's car for the next hour until the first hard splotches of rain strike the Caddy's cobweb-cracked windshield at 5:20 P.M. Reluctant to take the old man home Corky drives the sloping streets of Irish Hill slowly and with the air of a dazed or drunken man to whom the navigation of the physical world is not merely a challenge but a tonic, a stimulant. Clamoring in his ears the drumbeat *A drink! a drink!* he no longer hears as we no longer hear the blood's pulse in the ears. Yet at the same time managing to ask pertinent questions, intelligent and even shrewd questions. And Sean Corcoran's replies are intelligent too, detailed and passionate. All this happened so long ago: thirty years. Yesterday.

Corky learns what he seems not to have known nor even guessed: Tim Corcoran brought his own death upon himself, yet not intentionally, seeming not to know he would die, even as he seems to have willed his death.

An inevitable death. Yet in its way accidental.

Corky learns that Corcoran Brothers Construction Co. refused to pay an unofficial "fee" to the president of the Western New York Trade Union Council that would have exempted them from being required to employ union help. The payment of such "fees" was strictly illegal, in violation of trade union legislation, for it allowed certain companies to hire nonunion workers at lower wages and for fewer benefits thus putting them in the position of being able to underbid legitimate competitors—the union of-ficials were selling out their own men. In refusing the deal, Tim Corcoran put himself at a double disadvantage: in hiring (nonunion) black work-ers, he was defying the union; yet, since ninety to ninety-five percent of his workers were in fact (union) whites, he had to pay competitive wages including time-and-a-half for overtime and Saturdays. And so his bids for jobs were higher than they might have been, or, if lower, disadvan-tageously lower. To get a lucrative government contract, Tim had to pay "fees" to government officials, which seemed to him a different matter from paying "fees" to trade union officials who were selling out their own men. But the ultimate advantage of Corcoran Brothers' integrity—in Tim Corcoran's eyes at least—was that he maintained good relations with the trade unions' rank-and-file membership, the men who actually worked; they, and their sons, would understand his position, and respect him, and in the future when the current corrupt union officials lost power, and were replaced by others more liberal and more democratic, less racially bigoted, the advantage would be his.

His mistake, says Sean, was he wouldn't live that long.

Getting killed was something Tim Corcoran hadn't factored in.

And afterward: Union City government officials and the district at-torney made a deal with union officials—and the mob behind the unions?—to go easy on the investigation into the killing in return for political support from the unions; and with the promise that, within a year or two, Al Fenske, the president of the Western New York Trade Union Council, would be out. If records of the Trade Union Council were subpoenaed by the D.A.'s office they were "lost"—the prosecution never presented a case to the county grand jury. Informers gave police conflicting accounts of who had hired who to do the killing and their testimonies were considered proof of the difficulty of the case—conflicting, contradictory, thus canceling one another out, thus worthless in court. Fenske and his men were questioned by police but always in the presence of their lawyers and there were never to be any arrests, still less any indictments.

So far as Sean knew, there was no deal made with Fenske himself—for Fenske, having ordered Tim Corcoran killed, had sealed his own death warrant. The question was simply when, and how.

In Irish Hill, it was commonly believed that the Mayor of Union City, Buck Glover, himself of Irish Hill, had betrayed his own people. Yet those with some inside knowledge understood that in fact the prosecution had no case—there were no eyewitnesses to the crime, and there were no reliable informers. There was certainly no evidence linking Al Fenske to the killing.

At 4:20 P.M. of December 24, 1959, Fenske was in Miami Beach, at the Fontainebleau. He and his family and a half dozen relatives booked in for a solid week.

Months later, Sean Corcoran himself publicly supported Buck Glover and his administration, when the Mayor came to Irish Hill to answer questions from voters. This, for the look of things. While secretly he hated Glover's guts. Hated all of them. They sold us out, Sean tells Corky. And that goes for the Slatterys, too—Bill, and Oscar—just getting in solid in the party at that time. They gave money, they got involved in a big way, backing Glover and the old-line Democrats, using them until they could dump them and take control for themselves.

That's what a politician is, Sean tells Corky. A guy who uses you then dumps you then climbs on your dead body to raise himself.

But maybe you know that already?

And then in a different voice entirely Sean speaks of Theresa so Corky understands his uncle was in love with his mother, and he wonders if Theresa knew this, or if Sean Corcoran himself knew, or knows. Sean speaks of how it hadn't had to happen, none of it had to happen, and just to blame Tim is maybe wrong, but to blame Theresa in any way is certainly wrong. Because the love that was between Tim and Theresa—so far as he, an outsider, could know—was so much *between* them, and nobody else exactly mattered to them, except their kid who was you, Jerome, the only kid they ever had though they tried, God knows they tried, but it didn't work out. Sean doesn't speak at much length of Theresa, he's silent for long moments working his mouth, drawing his sleeve roughly across his nostrils, saying several times she was a lovely woman he'd known her as a girl so he doesn't think of her as *dead* exactly even now for when you're his age so many people you've known and loved are *dead* it's like the center of gravity is somewhere else that's more real than where you are. So you don't give a name to it, to diminish it. For to diminish it is to diminish yourself.

Corky listens, nods. He's been driving slowly up Dalkey hill from the deserted warehouse district at the lakeshore back up into the neighborhood listening to his uncle with such concentration he hardly knows where he is, or why; what this day is, and where it began; where it will lead. Except as always that panicked sensation he has somewhere else to be, soon. *Somewhere else he has to be, and soon.*

Sean has asked to be let off, not at his house, but at a tavern up ahead. One of the old neighborhood taverns, so many of them in Irish Hill, never less than one and often two taverns on every commercial block. This is Killian's Red Star where Corky used to drop in but hasn't for a long time, in fact years. Actually he's surprised to see Killian's Red Star is still there at the corner of Dalkey and Ontario. Front door wide open, rummy-looking oldish white guys lounging in the doorway. An invitation *in*.

Sean's thanking Corky for the afternoon, not shaking his hand because the Corcorans don't do that, but gripping his forearm with surprising strength, and Corky, still emotional, grips his uncle's forearm in turn. Sean says, "At my age you learn to get used to people looking through you unless they're going to mug you, or crack your head. Once you get old it happens you're invisible and if you don't have money you don't have power and even to people who like you O.K. you're not worth shit and it's a matter of getting used to it, you hear what I'm saying? I'm not complaining!" chuckling so Corky who's been nodding sympathetically, guiltily doesn't know what the hell he's agreeing with, puts him in an awkward position. As Sean slides out the door, turning back for a moment, "—Yes, lad, and I appreciate you giving me advice about the house, too. I'll look into that. I don't know what I'll do but I'll look into it. At my age God damn it you hate like hell to be pushed out of your own home by—" pausing frowning what's he mean to say, *niggers? hillbillies?* then giving up on it and heaving himself up out of the Caddy, and goodbye.

Corky leans over watching Sean walk toward the darkened interior of Killian's Red Star. Bulky-chested old guy thin in the legs, some stiffness in the walk but good posture for his age, and that dapper straw hat, he'll outlive me. Greeting the old rummies in the doorway and being greeted by them like they're long-lost brothers then turning to wave at Corky. Must be Sean's bragging to the other old men that that's his nephew in the Caddy, his big-shot nephew so the old men wave at Corky, too.

9

CORKY'S PRICE

Corky in his tux by Valentino makes his first mistake of the evening swinging by 19 Lakeshore Drive to see Ross Drummond on his way to the Chateauguay Country Club. *Put the bite on the old bastard, why the hell not. Fucker owes me.* He'd set up this quick meeting at the last minute and now wishes he hadn't, his heart isn't in it, too much to think about, his Uncle Sean's words ringing in his ears and his old passion for The Bull's Eye quaintly remote to him now—6:40 P.M.—as the memory of one of those numerous girls he was crazy for as a teenager then couldn't remember her name a few months later. *Because he got himself killed. It was your father's fault. You hear what I'm saying?* Corky shakes his head to clear it. Except he can't.

Also, Lakeshore Drive is out of the way, an extra eight miles or so, and as usual he's running late. With commingled excitement and dread anticipating the speech he's obliged to give tonight in honor of Vic Slattery his oldest and dearest friend which he might not be giving; and hasn't in any case prepared, as Mike Rooney feared. Incapable of sitting at his desk nor even of standing in one place to skim through the fifty or more pages of PR material U.S. CONGRESSMAN VIC SLATTERY: A PROFILE Rooney sent him by messenger the other day.

Too much to think about, his head's going to explode. One thing at a time as, in the handball court, or in the ring, it's one move at a time, and your eye never leaving your opponent. Not for a split second for it's in that split second you're fucked.

And here's Corky's ex-father-in-law Ross Drummond greeting him in the doorway of his house before Corky even presses the doorbell.

But too late to turn back. As soon as you register danger, already it's too late.

"Corky, come in! Good to see you!"—Drummond's reaching out to shake Corky's hand in that special bone-crushing grip of his that signals to business rivals and rivalrous friends alike all's well, you can trust Ross Drummond, what a great guy. "It's been a while, eh? Too long."

Says Corky, forcing a grin, "Too damned long."

"But I hear you've been renegotiating with my daughter and grand-daughter, eh?"—wagging his forefinger at Corky, another lewd grin, as, in that way he has, rudely abrupt, Drummond turns on his heel and walks away leaving Corky to close the front door and follow him into the interior of the house.

Though Corky and Ross Drummond have met a few times for drinks downtown since the breakup of Corky's marriage to Charlotte, this is the first time he's been in this house in years. He's completely estranged from his ex-mother-in-law Hilda (who's certainly home, and won't come downstairs to meet him) who despises him as an adulterer.

More than sixteen years since Corky was first a guest in this house. That evening he met Thalia, eight years old staring up at him like it's love at first sight which maybe, Christ knows, it was.

Passing the doorway of the enormous living room, Corky sees the Steinway grand in a farther corner. His impulse is to run over and strike the keys, for the hell of it banging "Chopsticks"—"Glow, Little Glowworm"—to see if he can still do it.

Not much seems to have changed in the Drummonds' house since the last time Corky was here. That evening too he was wearing a tux, and Charlotte was wearing one of her $1000 designer dresses so classy-sexy Corky wondered why, why the hell, so sad to wonder, not to know the answer, he couldn't get it up for her anymore worth shit; and her looking at him knowing his thoughts, staring at him boldly knowing his thoughts telling the old man we only have ten minutes Pawpaw I'd like vodka on the rocks.

"You're looking pretty spiffy tonight, Corky," says Drummond with his sliding grin, a lewd wink to one eye, "—like a maitre d' in a fancy French restaurant," pausing to wait for Corky's response, which is a faint forced laugh, "—where're you headed? Your own funeral?" and laughing himself, richly, yet not unkindly, rubbing his hands together and moving in the direction of his liquor cabinet. Corky's allowed himself to be pushed down into a cushioned leather chair in Drummond's study, already he's having trouble breathing and he's only been here ten seconds. Drummond chats in his high blustery way, the way of a man who in fact spends most of his life in his head, ceaselessly formulating theorems by which his already enormous fortune can be increased, but Corky's only intermittently listening. A clamorous pulse *A drink! a drink!* almost drowning out Drummond's repeated query, "—drink, kid? Red Label as per usual—?"

"Thanks, Ross, but no. I'm cutting back."

"Hell you are! *You?*"—which is maybe a joke, but Corky's not in the mood to find it funny.

Declining too Drummond's offer of wine, yes thanks a club soda, Corky's hand visibly shaking as he reaches for the tumbler which Drummond surely sees but, out of tact, or sympathy, or surprise, says nothing. *Pawpaw is always kidding around and Pawpaw is always deadly serious.*

Drummond splashes a good three inches of whiskey into a tumbler of his own, sits close by Corky and strikes his glass to Corky's—"Cheers!"—drinks and sighs, small bright close-set eyes fixed hungrily on Corky's face. His dentures grin and wink with a humor of their own. His skin, creased, leathery, freckled with liver spots, has an odd twitchy motility, like a living thing. He's shinily bald across the crown of his head with a fringe of fine gray curls that give him the look of a merry, debauched Roman emperor. In recent years Drummond has had ulcer surgery, prostate surgery, a fairly serious cardiac "episode." According to Charlotte he's forever revising his will; he upsets his wife with his worries about failing health, imminent death, the collapse of the American economy. Yet Corky knows he works at his downtown office the same exhausting eighty-hour week he'd worked when Corky first met him twenty years ago; he's as tireless in his business dealings, as dogged in his campaigns against his enemies. When Corky was Ross Drummond's son-in-law *and* his employee he'd wake from strangled dreams in which the old man was literally sitting on his chest. Jesus!

What the hell, Corky's always admired Ross Drummond. A first-rate businessman, if a little too secretive and inclined to paranoia. A generous guy, if you're on his good side. Scrupulously decorous and attentive to his wife, as to all "ladies" of a certain age and class. Except out of their earshot vulgar and funny, as, now, grinning at Corky, he says, "Just like old times, eh? You and me, and the broads in the kitchen." As if Hilda

Drummond, with a household staff of two or three, has ever worked in her own kitchen.

As if, at this moment, Charlotte, as Corky's wife, is here in this house. Sad. Must be, he misses me.

So put the bite on the old fart. Now's the hour!

Corky laughs uneasily to go along with this, drinking his club soda, a cigarette burning in his fingers he doesn't remember lighting. And Drummond's puffing thoughtfully on a cigar now on the subject of Memorial Day, confessing to Corky he's been haunted all day—hell, for years—by the memory of certain men who'd died in the war who were his friends, platoon buddies but he's long forgotten their names, some of them he'd actually witnessed die struck by shrapnel or bombs and dead now for fifty years—so hard to believe: fifty years!—and *he*, Ross Drummond, still alive—and how astonishing that is, how guilty you feel, how in a way you never become accustomed to being alive once you see somebody die in your presence as if it had been meant to be you who died except you cheated Death, and even if Death one day catches up with you, still you cheated Death. "So I say a prayer for them," Drummond tells Corky, almost shyly, "—shut my eyes tight and say a prayer for them, they're not forgotten."

There's a pause. Corky, knowing Drummond's quicksilver shifts of mood, doesn't quite trust him; waits for a sly wisecrack; says, "—I was just at the Memorial Day parade, and the ceremony in Erie Park, it *was* touching—" thinking then of Our Lady of Mercy Cemetery and how he'd broken down, Christ that's scary, what if he breaks down tonight at Chateauguay?

But Drummond isn't much interested in the Memorial Day parade and ceremony. He's still contemplating the past, nodding, sighing and working his lips, his leathery, layered-looking face creased with thought. "You know who I admire from those years, son?—Harry S. Truman. Not for his politics—you Democrats, your politics S-T-I-N-K—but for his common sense. There was a man who had the guts to drop the A-bomb, just the right time and just the right place. Knew he'd take shit for it, which he did, but here's a man with courage enough to do what had to be done. 'Thank God the bomb has come to us and not our enemies,' Truman said. Truer words never spoken." Drummond seems genuinely moved.

He sighs and puffs on his cigar and exhales a cloud of bluish smoke that drifts into, and overcomes, Corky's thinner cloud of white smoke. His hand, heavy, meaty-warm, and roughly affectionate, is on Corky's black silk-wool tuxedo sleeve. "You may be too young to know about this watershed in history, Corky, but *I* know; *I* was there. I was on a troop transport ship headed for fucking Nippon myself when the A-bomb was dropped on Hiroshima—might've been killed, like hundreds, thousands of other guys in my position. But the A-bomb exploded, and we were saved. Truer words never spoken: 'Thank God the bomb has come to us'—to America—'and not our enemies.'" A fierce moist laugh escapes his rubbery lips turning high-pitched, almost a snigger. *"To America. And not our enemies."*

Pleasure in the emotion of this moment like Corky and his ex-father-in-law are alone together on the sleek white *Rustbucket* riding the waves of an anonymous river, hearing the harsh comforting slap of the waves and feel-ing the muscular ease of the powerful craft beneath them. Corky's inhal-ing smoke deep into his lungs needing to think how to begin, how to most shrewdly yet tactfully bring up the subject of The Bull's Eye, it isn't the first time in his relationship with Ross Drummond he's come to the older man for help but he's forgotten how in the past he handled it. A misstep with Drummond and you can be on your ass before you know it.

Slyly Drummond says he'd heard Corky dropped in to visit Charlotte and Gavin the other evening. Laying his forefinger alongside his nose like a lewd Santa Claus—"But Gavin wasn't home, eh?"

Corky thinks, Did she tell you we fucked?

Saying aloud, playing it straight and earnest like a good son-in-law, "Yeah. Charlotte and I've both been worried about Thalia. But it's O.K. now—at least, it isn't so crucial." Wondering if Drummond knows about the stolen Luger. By the look in Drummond's face, part serious and part playful, he guesses no. Charlotte doesn't tell Pawpaw everything. "Thalia left a message for me this morning, at home. She's going to stay with a friend somewhere out West—'the western ranges,' she says. Do you know anything about it, Ross?"

Drummond says quickly, "Of course. Thalia tells me everything. She confides in her granddaddy."

"Where's she going?" Corky asks. "Charlotte thought Wyoming, or Montana—"

Stiffly Drummond cuts him off, "As I said, Thalia confides in me. And in her grandmother. But we can't violate her trust."

Bullshit, thinks Corky. You know less than I do.

Sitting then in an awkward silence. Corky's eyes move restlessly about the handsomely furnished room *you'll never see again: this is your last visit* pressing the lukewarm bottle of soda against his forehead that feels feverish. And his cheeks, jaws. Burning aching eyes. No time to shower before coming here but he'd shaved fast and distractedly holding his right hand with his left but even so it shook and he nicked himself not once but several times *fuck it!* blood trickling swiftly down his chin and he'd had a hell of a time staunching it then hurrying to put on his tux, fumbling the fucking studs and the tiny clamps in the bow tie so he'd almost thought he couldn't do it, couldn't dress himself and would have to (his mind moving through its limited possibilities like a computer in slow dazed time) drop by at Charlotte's to get her help before going to the country club, might have to remarry his wife to ensure that over the years he'll be able to get dressed for formal affairs or maybe at all. And Charlotte can't betray him with her husband *because he's her husband whether they are married or not.* And thinking too he's got to move his ass and get out to Chateauguay which is at least a twenty-minute drive and he's got to speak with Vic in privacy for the second time in a single day though Vic isn't his brother just as this devious old man isn't his father but he's got to speak with him, too. And drawing a shaky breath he's prepared to say outright he's in need of emergency financial aid when Ross Drummond gets to it first.

Saying, baring his beaming dentures in a rapacious smile, "Corky, it's great to see you again, I've been missing you! Like Hilda says, you're lots of laughs. But I know why you've taken time out from your busy social life to drop in here tonight, and I'm sorry as hell to have to disappoint you—my answer is 'no.'"

Corky stares, uncomprehending. Ross Drummond's small moist pinwheel eyes radiate amusement. Clearly, Drummond's enjoying this, the way, fishing off his yacht, he'd enjoyed hauling fish into the air squirming and writhing at the end of his line letting them flop around spasmodically on the deck before tossing them back overboard, their mouths torn and bleeding from the hook.

"'No'—what?" Corky asks in dread.

"Don't play dumb, kid. We're talking about a four-hundred-sixty-thousand-dollar property. At least, that's the price you're paying for The Bull's Eye, of which one hundred thirty-eight thousand is the down payment which I understand you've already paid with a check postdated for tomorrow?" Drummond's frowning, mock solicitous. Shaking his head gravely. "Were you going to ask me for the full one hundred thirty-eight thousand, Corky, or do you have some spare cash of your own not 'tied up in investments'?"

Corky's astonished. This echo of Corky's own past words is so cruel, he almost can't believe it.

Corky stammers, "I—I'm not sure. I thought we could discuss—"

"Now? In fifteen minutes? On your way to a black-tie evening at the Chateauguay Country Club? In your monkey suit? You're doing your old father-in-law a big favor dropping by at his house on your way to better things giving him the chance to lend you one hundred thirty-eight thousand dollars—at what interest?"

"—That's what I thought we c-could discuss—"

"There's nothing to discuss," Drummond says curtly. Sitting back now in his chair, crossing one stumpy leg over the other, his barrel torso quivering in indignation and his eyes fixed sadistically on Corky's face. "That dump—'The Bull's Eye'"—the name rolls off Drummond's tongue with a particular zestful contempt—"isn't worth a hundred thirty-eight thousand dollars all together. I know—I'm the realtor who listed it. Didn't my office manager tell you it's been on the market for *years?* I know what the offers have been—how few, and how low. How much renovation's got to be done. What you didn't think of, I guess, is the place has been exempt from bringing its facilities up to the new state code for 'handicapped access' but you, sucker, buying in 1992, you're responsible for making sure cripples in wheelchairs can not only get in the front door and out an exit if there's a fire but can take a crap when they need to—and each crap is going to cost you. I'd estimate a minimum of one hundred thousand dollars just to bring the facilities up to code. Plus you need a complete electrical overhaul. And the basement—the basement's substandard. Maybe you're thinking the Downtown Refurbishing Project's going to save your ass, drive the value up? Sorry, kid, I happen to know that project's dead— absolutely belly up." Drummond makes a slashing gesture across his throat. "Your best bet would be to raze the dump and build a parking garage. That's my advice, too bad you didn't ask it a few days ago."

"Wait," says Corky, "—how do you know about the Project? *I'm* on the Council—"

"*I'm* on the Committee. And we just voted to kill it."

Corky just stares at Ross Drummond. The bottle of whatever tasteless crap it is he's drinking almost falling from his fingers.

Now Drummond's warmed up, really gets into it. So Corky's made to realize *this* is why Drummond agreed to see him tonight, not for the purpose Corky'd planned. The old man is hurt, angry, face darkened with blood and lips sputtering saliva—"*Why* didn't you call me first, before committing yourself to that hag 'Chantal Crowe'? I heard you were so drunk Saturday night you pissed your pants and they had to send you home in a taxi, is that so? Here I'm on hand to give you advice, for Christ's sake, I'm your friend, there's nobody knows anything more about Union City real estate than Ross Drummond, I've been in the business for fifty-five years, and you, you dumb shit, you don't ask! What if it's thought around town you *do* ask, and it's my advice you're taking!" Seeing the sick panicked look in Corky's face, Drummond leans closer to trap him in his chair. "Who've you been talking to, your City Hall scumbag buddies? You'd trust Oscar Slattery? Anybody with the name 'Slattery'? Your Jew money man? You'd trust *him?*" Drummond's elephantine head is bobbing, he's stabbing a fat forefinger dangerously close to Corky's eyes. "So you think you can go it alone, eh? Without the old man? The 'father-in-law'—eh? Well, you're wrong, kid. You don't know shit. This latest money man of yours—Greenbaum—Howard Greenbaum, eh?—he's slick as they come. You should've stuck with dopes you can handle. I bet Greenbaum's sold you on this roll-up scam at Viquinex, eh? Did he?"

Corky says defensively, "Why's it a 'scam'? I thought—"

"Well, did he?"

"He explained it, and—"

"Did he explain the cost of the roll-up is paid by the investors? And it could run as high as five thousand dollars per hundred-thousand-dollar investment?"

"I think so, yes—"

"And did he explain he gets a commission as broker, from the company, for every investor of his who votes 'yes' but no commission for anybody who votes 'no'?"

"He—what?"

Drummond laughs, a series of short barking walrus-laughs, delighted at the sick drowning look in Corky's face. "He didn't tell you, and you didn't ask, eh? Why didn't you ask? Greenbaum's a broker, isn't he? What'd you think he is—a rabbi?"

Corky's feeling nauseated. Got to get out of here: got to breathe.

With gusto Drummond polishes off his tumbler of whiskey and wipes his mouth on the back of his hand. His beady little eyes shine up alertly at Corky calculating has he gone too far. He says, almost kindly, "How much are you in for, with Viquinex? Maybe I could help you out. The SEC is going to be investigating these sons of bitches by September—maybe we could scare 'em with a lawsuit—"

Corky manages to push himself to his feet staggering and swaying headed for the door. Saying weakly, "Ross, thanks. It's been great. It's been . . . great. We'll have to do this again soon."

Now, regretful, Drummond heaves himself up, almost blocks Corky's way out. "You're leaving so soon? You just arrived. Wait'll I go get Hilda, she'll be hurt if you leave without saying hello to her."

Corky runs his hands through his hair, a faint coughing laugh issues from him like he's been kicked hard in the ass but he's a good sport willing to see the humor of it. In the foyer saying, "Just give Hilda my love, Ross, will you? Tell her I miss her as much as she misses me."

Drummond laughs uproariously, spittle flying from his rubbery lips.

"Corky, c'mon! Don't go away mad."

This, then: in the foyer a brief though seemingly protracted tugging match, clumsy, panting, as Drummond pulls on Corky's arm, and Corky pulls away red-faced, trying to be as polite as respectful as possible: Ross Drummond *is* old, older than Sean Corcoran, and worth a helluva lot more money. Saying, laughing, "Corky, what the hell—? Did I call you a dumb shit?—you know me, I didn't mean it. I maybe meant dumb mick—"

laughing again uproariously, so that, Corky imagines, his ex-mother-in-law Hilda is straining to hear somewhere close by in wonderment, disapproval, envy, "—hey, no: it's all in the family, you know that. What's the big deal?" as Corky pushes past him to the door, desperate to escape this place as a suffocating man desperate for air, "—Come back inside and sit down, for Christ's sake," Drummond says, "—we need to discuss these matters seriously. Corcoran, Inc., is in trouble. I can put pressure on that Crowe broad to tear up your check but if she won't, maybe we can work something out. What you need, if you're investing in an enterprise like The Bull's Eye, is a partner who knows the real demographics of—"

Old bastard seems genuinely contrite but can't trust him, never will again.

"Fuck you, Ross," says Corky, "—your price is too high."

At the door, as Corky's got it open, Drummond's virtually blocking him, breath labored and mean little eyes enlarged, alarmed—must be, he can't believe the dumb mick is actually walking out. "Corky, you're too hotheaded, c'mon back inside and have a drink and cut this bullshit. You want Corcoran, Inc., to go belly up?—that's what you want?"

"I said fuck you, Ross, and thanks," says Corky as amiable as he can manage, outside and walking to his car hoping he won't slip and fall on his ass on the rain-slick flagstone walk, at the driveway he turns to wave back at Drummond astonished on the doorstep of the French Normandy mansion glistening in the rain and ludicrous in its outsized proportions as a painted house in a children's fairytale book, and the old man shrunken in height if not in girth, staring after Corky Corcoran, that leathery face, that shiny-scaly scalp, that vacant death's-head grin that's the last sight Corky will have of his wealthy ex-father-in-law.

And Corky in his tux by Valentino arriving at the Chateauguay Country Club at 7:27 P.M. makes his second mistake of the evening arriving there at all.

Stone cold sober in his elegant black silk-wool coat and trousers, black satin cummerbund, black bow tie, impeccably starched dazzling-white pleated-front shirt with gold studs, gold cuff links, and $240 Bally dress shoes, not only stone cold sober but determined, resolute he isn't going to fuck up tonight except by his own decision, if he so decides, *he's* the one to decide: *the one in control* and seeing as soon as he pulls the Caddy up to the white stucco portico of the county club who else but Mike Rooney outside beneath the canopy among the uniformed parking attendants *waiting for him.*

Rooney!—that bastard!

The way Rooney's grim eyes snatch at Corky through the Caddy's windshield, that accusing anxious-furious *Drunk aren't you! Drunk!* the very set of his head, neck, shoulders in his tux—Corky sees.

Seeing too how Rooney takes in the Caddy's battered front fender and bumper, the myriad scratches, dents, pockmarks in the finish, yes and the fine-cracked windshield exposed like an X ray of Corky Corcoran's brain—Corky registers this insult, too.

On the way out to Chateauguay—speeding north along Lakeshore Drive to Edgewater Boulevard, past the handsome gray stone buildings of St. Thomas Aquinas Academy for Boys, north into the suburbs of St. Claire, St. Claire Shores, across the river on the gleaming metallic bridge of I-190 in hard-hissing splashes of rain into a sky dissolving in darkness as if giant dark-feathered wings were opening obscuring the sun—Corky's been thinking *This is it! it will be decided* not knowing exactly what will be decided, if he is thinking of Vic Slattery, or of Christina Kavanaugh (if she isn't here tonight, it is finished between them—absolutely), or of his father who need not have died, thus of the course of his own life which need not have been invented, lived. And thinking *Why am I here, why am I doing whatever it is I believe I am doing thinking is it a vow I've taken? to see things through? but why me? and why such—not giving a word to it: desperation, destiny.* Seeing then before him on the left side of Bloomfield Road the manicured-green undulating hills of the Chateauguay Country Club's golf course eerily iridescent in the fading light like a cinematic set reduced to the size of a tabletop yet, magnified by an illusion of optics, faithful in every particular as if it were real. And there, emerging out of the green, the tall pillar-like gateposts with their discreet warning sign CHATEAUGUAY COUNTRY CLUB PRIVATE MEMBERS ONLY.

Corky Corcoran isn't a member of the country club (you have to figure: they haven't gotten around to inviting him yet; or, he's so associated with Union City, downtown, even his close Chateauguay friends don't think of him as a likely candidate for a club so suburban) but of course he's been invited here many times. Not just for political reasons, for social reasons, too.

Yet feeling the stab of that warning, fine-engraved letters on brass PRIVATE MEMBERS ONLY as, entering here, though always by invitation, Corky can't help feeling.

And so, seeing Rooney waiting for him so conspicuously, staring grim and unsmiling and not raising a hand in welcome as Corky pulls up, Corky thinks *Don't lose it: see it through.* Stone cold sober and dignified in his tux if slightly flush-faced and his eyes like a poached fish's Corky hands over his ignition key to the young Latino parking attendant, approaches the entrance to the club unhurried even as Rooney approaches him saying, "Corky, for Christ's sake where were you? We've been waiting for forty minutes! You knew about the press conference! You promised not to be late!" and for a beat or two Corky's all right but then Rooney like a vexed brother unable to keep from pushing it keeps on, clearly he's upset and maybe there's a legitimate reason but this isn't the way to handle Corky Corcoran and particularly not in the near-presence of others (guests are entering the club in a discontinuous stream, some of them known to and known by both Corky Corcoran and Mike Rooney), saying, accusing, "Where the hell *were* you? Getting tanked up?" like an angry wasp flying straight into Corky's face, so, without breaking his stride, Corky veers at Rooney and grabs his front, black satin lapels, starched-pleated fancy shirt in his fists shaking the little prick saying, "Fuck you, Rooney! I'm not late! It's just seven-thirty! *I'm not late and I'm not drunk!*"—grabbing and releasing Rooney in virtually the same gesture, no threat of violence to it but Rooney's staggering backward into the dripping shrubbery white-faced and absolutely astonished, as stunned as if Corky had walked up to him and fired a bullet through his brain.

Yet regaining his dignity then Corky walks quickly on, past men in tuxedos, women in shimmering dresses, faces turned toward him in astonishment too and in certain of the faces recognition which, in his state of exemplary dignity, Corky need not see; isn't required to see; blinded as if striding through walls of fire. *And now, and now—what?* still believing, after the accelerated motion of the past several days, that *I'm in control: stone cold sober* and actually pausing, to catch his breath, inside the club amid the high-chattering clamor of cocktail-wielding guests to shake a few hands, a dozen hands, to kiss women's warm proffered cheeks and to have his own kissed in turn, exchanging greetings *Hello! How are you!*

Quite an occasion isn't it! A part of Corky's mind detached, even fatal-
istic as he glances rapidly around the crowded space not seeing Christina
Kavanaugh though glimpsing at a short distance a tuxedo-clad man in
a wheelchair his back to Corky so Corky can't identify him: ex-Judge
Harry Kavanaugh?

As if there would be only a single man in a wheelchair in all of Chateauguay.

As if, if Harry Kavanaugh *is* here, at a fund-raiser for Vic Slattery, his
presence can have any significance for Corky Corcoran.

Yet here's Corky suddenly determined threading his way through the
crowd smiling his sunny heedless smile into faces turned toward him in
recognition without seeming to recognize them in turn, passing by the
bar and the lavish hors d'oeuvres tables where chattering laughing people
are jammed in together like cattle bound for slaughter headed for the reception lounge into which, with several others, the man in the wheelchair
has rolled. *I will shake his hand, declare myself to him* even as voices call
out sharply, "Jerome! Jerome Corcoran!" and it's Andy van Buren's assistant Maggie, and Vic's assistant Kimberly, and now these women have got
Corky Corcoran by both arms they're not going to let him go.

Leading him with hard strained smiles into the dining room, empty
yet of guests, where a vast sea of elegantly decorated tables has been set
up each with its number prominent on a sign incorporating too a small
tasteful American flag, not scolding but informing him that the rest of the
people involved in the program have been here since six-thirty. "Vic was
getting a little worried, Jerome," says Kimberly who's a young aggressive
thirty, new on Vic's staff and disapproving of much of what she knows of
Jerome Corcoran yet even now subtly coming on to him, baring her gums
in a sexy-combative smile, "—evidently you got in some kind of accident
with your car this morning? Or yesterday morning—"

Corky lets this pass. Or maybe doesn't register it.

The main dining room of the Chateauguay Country Club is an immense space much of which is glass, including vaulting skylights, and
at the far end technicians are adjusting a microphone at a flower-and-
flag-bedecked podium at the center of the head table; this long table on a
raised platform so the diner-dignitaries have to face out. *They've dropped
me from the head table* Corky thinks almost calmly but no: he checks

the place cards, there's JEROME CORCORAN between SANDRA SLATTERY and ANDREW VAN BUREN the Mohawk County Democratic chairman. First time in Corcoran's career he's been so publicly so visibly *raised*.

The sound technicians are being instructed by a middle-aged man in tux, red carnation in his lapel, it's Andy van Buren himself who happens to glance down to see Corky and he's wordless for a moment then says loudly, "Corky Corcoran!—at last. Good to see you," reaching down to shake Corky's hand and the handshake seems sincere on both sides, "—great you've showed up. Speech all prepared?" grinning at Corky with his mouth and the realization floods over Corky *He hates me for some reason: why?* but the effort of remembering is too much. Corky grins back at van Buren saying, "Sure. All prepared," even as the women tug him away. Corky winks at van Buren shrugging as if to indicate how cooperative he is, what a good sport, these pushy broads dragging him around.

Leading him into the adjoining Rotunda Room where Vic Slattery and Sandra Slattery and some others are standing, Corky guesses it's the end of a photography session, the Slatterys posed with the evening's organizers and top donors, several photographers are packing up their gear to leave and seeing Corky Sandra hurries at once to hug him, kiss his cheek, how warm Sandra Slattery is and how breathless murmuring into Corky's ear like he's an old lover, "Corky, hello! But you seem feverish." Corky hugs Sandra in turn, more roughly than he intends. He's got a cigarette in his hand and this pisses her off but she doesn't say anything, Corky shrugs amiably, "—*You* seem feverish, Sandra." And Vic shaking Corky's hand smiling warmly at him his eyes not smiling but unlike van Buren's betraying no anger nor even anxiety but instead that glisten of blank perplexity with which young boxers confront their opponents in the ring—not the insolence of the pro who has come to do injury but the wonderment of the amateur who, in this space where he suddenly finds himself, can have no idea what will happen to him, or by way of him. Saying, "Corky, hello!" As if not lovers but brothers. For the second time, Corky's thinking, in twelve hours.

Corky screws it up into a joke, "—Heard you were worried I might not make it," he says, "—but what's this shit about me having an accident with the car? I don't have accidents." There's some nervous laughter, enough to encourage Corky to push it, "Red Pitts has accidents with cars: they run over him."

This remark, senseless, yet meets with moderate laughter, you can count on laughter if you say even senseless things in the right tone of voice.

The photographer from the *Journal* who knows Jerome Corcoran by name, face, reputation insists upon a quick shot of Corky and Vic, so they pose obligingly together against a glassy wall beyond which tennis courts float in twilit wind-slanted rain: this photograph, to be published in the next day's newspaper, on the front page, showing both men to advantage though Corky looks dazed and bleached out standing at his full height yet still two full inches shorter than Vic.

Vic Slattery, handsome in his tux. In his photographs you don't see the signs of strain bracketing the eyes, the oily enlarged pores of the nose, the faint rosy flush of broken capillaries in the cheeks. In his photographs he's got a burnished look. Intelligence, pride, humility and capability in equal measure. Corky says in an undertone, "Vic, before the dinner begins I need to talk to you."

"But that's right now."

"Right. Right now."

Vic hesitates. His mouth works. From somewhere he takes up his glass of whiskey. Leading Corky into a hallway outside the Rotunda Room as Corky's smoke trails behind. Sandra watches after them with worried eyes and seems about to follow but does not.

Corky's tongue is suddenly swollen and numb. He has to speak with unnatural care. "Vic, just tell me: did Marilee Plummer lie about Steadman? Is that the deal?"

Vic winces but doesn't reply. Nor does he look at Corky. His whiskey glass is raised to his mouth and he drinks, this gesture too performed with care. Corky sees his friend's hand is no steadier than his own.

Persisting, still in that slow, careful voice, "Vic, I'm asking you: did Marilee Plummer lie about Steadman? Did Oscar pay her off? Is that what it's about, all this shit? Marilee killed herself because she got in over her head, she couldn't deal with it?"

Corky's looking desperately at Vic but Vic, frowning and eyes downcast, isn't looking at him.

Corky explodes, "For Christ's sake tell me, Vic! You owe that to me, don't you? I'm your friend! I thought I was your friend!"

"You *are* my friend, Corky—"

"But—? But what?"

"But we can't talk about it now. This isn't the time."

"This is the time!"

Vic doesn't answer, or can't. Corky says in a fury, accusing, "And you'd let Steadman take the blame for that, too! For her killing herself, too! Oscar set it up, Oscar or somebody working for him, and it went too far, is that it? And Marilee was paid? How much? And put on a payroll?—at the history museum? Sure! It's obvious! I just can't believe you and your father would lie to *me*. You'd do such a thing, or be a party to such a thing, and then lie to *me*."

Vic's gaze slides onto Corky's, such misery such anguish *What can I say? don't ask!* Corky rocks back on his heels. His skin in a fever.

Corky's about to walk away, and Vic stops him, and seems about to speak but does not speak, and Corky shrugs off his hand, and again Vic seems about to speak, and this time manages to speak, his voice hoarse and cracked, shamed, "Corky, it isn't like that—exactly. It's far more complicated. As soon as this—tonight—is over, I promise I will—"

"Look, she *did* kill herself, didn't she? It wasn't—arranged?"

"Corky, for God's sake what do you think my father is! He isn't a—"

"If not him, people around him. Red Pitts, for instance—"

"Don't insult my father, God damn you! Who are *you* to insult my father!"

"Fuck your father, Vic, the girl's *dead*. What about her?"

Vic says slowly, "Corky, if there was anything I could do to bring Marilee back, I would do it. If there was anything—"

"That's bullshit. She's dead, and people need to know why. You think you can keep the lid on all this? That's what you think?"

"Corky, please—"

Now Corky does shove away from Vic, slamming along the corridor past the bright-lit bustling kitchen with its myriad aromas swirling to nausea in his stomach, he pushes out a rear door to stand cursing *Fuck! fuck! fuck!* trembling in the rain staring at the straight lines and planes of the clay tennis courts, the greeny twilight of sloping hills beyond. And

gigantic clotted brain-like masses of clouds in the sky, shot with the light
of the setting sun, orangey-red, radiant as illuminated arteries he's staring
at unseeing and uncomprehending. There's a sensation in his head like a
rubber band being pulled tighter and tighter to the point of bursting yet
not bursting but at that point, that tremulous point so he fumbles to light
another cigarette which falls from his fingers to the pavement and which
he dares not retrieve for the pulsing tension in his head and so takes out
another cigarette and lights it instead aware of the door behind him shut,
and no one coming after.

And so he's free, safe. *Just walk away.*

And yet: some minutes later Corky Corcoran enters the dining room
alone amid a dense stream of guests, now pale in the face and damp-
haired and his tuxedo damp and bow tie drunkenly crooked so a woman
acquaintance (whose familiar face, name, Corky doesn't register, but who
will remember him, *the pupils of his eyes like pinpricks!* she'll say telling
of him, of what happened, afterward) stops him to adjust it matter-of-fact
as any wife; and Corky walks on murmuring thanks which he himself
doesn't hear. He's sighted another time the man in the wheelchair—or is
this another man, in another wheelchair—now in profile and it's a strong
dignified profile, heavy head, steely-gray hair and there's a woman walking beside him, slender in black, black hair: Christina?—but the two are
moving away from Corky to a distant table, he can't be certain.

Thinking, *She loves me! I'm the one.*

Thinking, *No. Let her go. Don't involve her.*

And thinking too, *You can still leave: just walk out of here.*

Yet for some reason Corky doesn't leave the Chateauguay Country
Club but continues making his way forward, in fact passing close by
Father Vincent O'Brien with whom he shakes hands, exchanges brisk
friendly greetings though not remembering this exchange even ten seconds
afterward. Yet more remarkably Corky encounters his ex-wife Charlotte
and her new husband Gavin Pierson with whom too he exchanges warm
greetings yet within a few seconds he's forgotten them, perhaps even as he
speaks with them he's forgetting.

Corky's attention is riveted upon Vic Slattery a few yards away.

Vic is still on his feet, shaking hands, talking with Mario Cuomo, the Governor must also be seated at the head table but for the moment both men are on ground level as hundreds of guests drift into the dining room to locate their tables, a slow surging Brownian movement that always requires more time than organizers calculate for already it's 8:12 P.M. and the dinner was scheduled to begin promptly at 8 P.M. and Andy van Buren has yet to make his ebullient welcoming remarks standing stiff behind the podium compulsively cleaning his glasses and smiling blindly out into the sea of faces. Uniformed attendants are ushering the guests along. Photographers' cameras flash. Beneath the affable high-pitched din a string quartet from the local Riverdale Academy of Music plays invisibly from a mezzanine, something fiercely bright and baroque to which no one listens and if Corky Corcoran chanced to hear he might have thought it a bright-mad plucking and sawing of strings inside his own brain. *Just walk out of here. You don't even need to denounce them.* Yet unable to turn back.

Instead pushing forward as if drawn, tugged by gravity. As if transfixed by the figure of Vic Slattery, tall broad-shouldered tawny-blond head, smiling at Cuomo, taller too than Cuomo by two or three inches, Corky doesn't even hear Sandra Slattery calling gaily down to him from her seat at the raised table, come sit down Corky, here's your seat Corky, he's watching though not hearing Vic Slattery and Mario Cuomo talking earnestly together, the two men are political allies yet not friends precisely for there's the awkward matter of Oscar Slattery between them, the rough history of Union City Democratic politics since the time of Buck Glover. Corky presses forward, and now Vic has seen him, blinking and staring at him distracted for the instant from his conversation with the Governor, and even at this point Corky is irresolute not knowing if he's going to take his seat at the head table and if so, what will follow, what will he say, what words will spring unbidden from him though the sensation of a rubber band straining tighter and tighter inside his head urges him onward *You can't go back; Time moves in one direction only.*

Pausing then as if by chance Corky turns, scanning the crowd, there's a cigarette burning in his fingers though on his way into the dining room somebody's asked him please to put it out, it might be he's looking for Oscar Slattery, and also Red Pitts, a cruel laughter stirring his very groin at the memory of Red Pitts doubled over that look of absolute astonishment in his face *Take that! pimp!* and so by chance at 8:13 P.M. Corky sees a tall dark-haired young woman making her way forward through the crowd with the urgent yet unhurried grace of a sleepwalker, solitary and unaccompanied and knowing her destination unlike most of the others around her and it's this determination in her manner that catches Corky's eye even before he recognizes her: Thalia.

Thalia!

Corky's so astonished seeing his stepdaughter here, emerging out of a sea of faces that deathly-pale grimly beautiful and ecstatic face, he doesn't wonder why she's here; to what mad purpose she's here; and wearing Corky's own white silk Christian Dior shirt!—the one he'd left for her on the bed.

Wearing this elegant shirt that's too big for her, shoulders drooping, cuffs covering half her slender hands, and what looks like an ankle-length shapeless black skirt of some cheap layered muslin material purchased off a rack of sale items at an East Indian emporium, and no doubt she's bare-legged, in scruffy leather sandals or even black aerobic shoes. And she's carrying an awkward-sized leather handbag conspicuously different from the tiny silk or sequined evening bag every other woman in the place is carrying. And she's shining-eyed, and staring straight ahead. Transfixed, too. Not seeing, as if he's invisible, her own stepfather Corky Corcoran gesturing frantically at her. It's Vic Slattery she's looking at.

It happens like this, though so swiftly Corky will never register it, as if a series of electronic flashes have gone off in his face: Thalia moves in a straight unerring line toward Vic Slattery removing from her bag the Luger she'd stolen from Corky's bedside table, lifting the long-barreled heavy weapon with her right hand and steadying it with her left in a pose, a gesture practiced to grim perfection, her expression is stony yet radiant as Corky remembers in the hospital in Ithaca when she'd seemed to be peering over the rim of the very Earth into Death, and liking what she saw. And in this same instant calling out "Vic Slattery! Murderer!" in a voice high, soprano-clear, unwavering as if much practiced, too.

Corky shouts, "Thalia! Don't!"—stepping by instinct toward her as if to disarm her or with his bare hands impede the bullets, he's no more than three feet from her blocking her aim thus shielding Vic Slattery from the bullets that erupt in deafening succession the first striking Corky in the chest with the impact of a sledgehammer slamming him backward even as the second bullet shatters the wristbones of his uplifted left arm and the third bullet grazes his skull as he falls as his legs vanish beneath him as if erased by a quick careless stroke of a blackboard's chalk marks, Corky's fallen heavily to the floor amid the panicked screams of men and women he can no longer see nor even imagine seeing blinding lights spin wildly like water sucked down a drain by a force greater than mere gravity yet no pain nor terror not even alarm only surprise and a mild curiosity as he's sucked away *So this is it. And where*

EPILOGUE

May 25, 1992–May 28, 1992

EPILOGUE

ever race a train that was his mistake maybe but he never took seriously he might die, and he didn't die. For the knowledge of Death refutes Death for no one who has died possesses such knowledge.

Yet, God damn: to visit a patient in the intensive care unit of the Chateauguay Medical Center even in this private room where Jerome Corcoran has been moved following his six-hour surgery you must be a relative or a spouse but this unwanted visitor they're telling him is hanging around outside the door wanting to see him is no relative of Corky's and he's pissed as hell anybody might think so trying to explain to these white-clad figures he can see only through a tunnel reduced in size to thumbs and their faces with that glare of faces reflected in toasters or in the chrome trim of a car so you understand sure the faces are *real* but so what?—so reduced in size.

—No don't let the fucker in, not now and not ever.

Trying to explain too to his aunt Sister Mary Megan of the Order of St. Ursula come to visit him to give comfort, a weird coincidence *she's* just discharged from Holy Redeemer and *he's* just been admitted to wherever this is he's in, she was waiting in her nun's habit, stark white-starched wimple and gentle eyes when at last he woke from the coma into which he'd sunk during the surgery to remove the bullet from his shattered left lung, one of the pulmonary arteries of his heart shattered too and midway in the surgery this organ abruptly ceased but was electrically stimulated to begin again to start its beat again and if Corky Corcoran had knowledge of this fact he felt no alarm not even especial concern explaining wryly to Aunt Mary Megan he isn't a hypochondriac and thank sweet Christ he's insured, ninety percent medical coverage through Corcoran, Inc.'s, pension plan. Unless those cocksuckers at the IRS take him to court.

—Excuse me, my mouth, damn I'm sorry—but Aunt Mary Megan just smiles shaking her head growing up in Irish Hill so long ago she's used to such language. And worse. And maybe in the convent and at St. Ursula's where she'd taught English for fifty-four years misses it? Dignified old woman in her habit and the dangling rattling shiny-black beads at her waist he'd thought as a kid at Our Lady of Mercy looked like cockroaches. Corky starts to explain to Aunt Mary Megan about the IRS challenging his pension plan but he can't seem to remember the details nor even the name of the man, the Jew money man who's also his friend, who's going to save his ass and fight them. And it's then one of the windowpanes cracks or maybe the pane's been cracked all along and he hadn't noticed, cold black air seeping in and Corky in his tender skinned state feels it like he's mere meat on bones, and there's a danger of his fingers and toes being frostbitten. Shivering so violently the bed vibrates so Aunt Mary Megan calls Nurse! nurse! come help us, nurse! bring a blanket please! and Corky's pissed thinking at these prices, he'd guess a minimum of $4000 a day, you deserve better. Aunt Mary Megan takes Corky's hands in hers rubbing them briskly to bring the circulation back, then she takes his feet in her hands rubbing the toes briskly to bring the circulation back, with frostbite there's the danger of toes and fingers snapping off. Aunt Mary Megan assures Corky who's beginning now to be a little scared he *is* going to live he *is* going to be all right the doctors intend to take him off the respirator in the morning if he has a good night except Corky's thinking morning looks the same as night in this place with no name they've brought him. Beyond the window there's nothing. *Jesus, Mary, and Joseph pray for us* Aunt Mary Megan says quietly bowing her head. Corky's vision clears for a stark moment and he's surprised to see inside the old woman's ashy-creased face a girl's sweet face, a girl he'd known, blue Irish eyes and fair-freckled milky skin of her lost youth. *Jesus, Mary, and Joseph pray for us* he's embarrassed being prayed over like somebody on his deathbed but his aunt's an old lady and a nun and if it makes her happy it's O.K. with him.

Too young at forty-three to take any of this seriously. Though losing his hair, God damn.

Whoever it was lifted him from the bloody-slippery floor of the Chateau-guay Country Club he never saw. Lifted and bore him on a stretcher away inside a speeding ambulance inside a siren's high-pitched scream which in fact Corky didn't hear, at least has no memory of hearing and now his inner ears are filling up with fluid it's a puzzle for him to comprehend what *hearing* is. But they were traveling fast. Fast as the speed of light. For if you die, you get there first. Wherever you're going you're already there. Sucked over the rim of the Earth. Except, no: *the event horizon, the boundary of the black hole, is like the edge of a shadow—the shadow of impending doom* but that hasn't happened yet. And won't.

On the operating table beneath the blinding laser lights Corky lay as on a marble slab not so much as flinching as they strapped him down and with a saw through his breastbone and instruments sharp and thin as icepicks and a bar resembling a tire iron opened his wounded chest cavity as a butcher by manual force might open a side of beef preparatory to sawing it into pieces. The .38-caliber bullet Thalia had shot into him from his own gun was removed and the damaged lung mended and the feebly beat-ing heart mended too like magic so it seemed that Jerome A. Corcoran had not died at all, his heart had not stopped its purposeful beat and there was the promise you won't remember any of this shit when you're out of here. And if you don't remember, it didn't happen as after Harry Black-stone hypnotized Jerome as a child and he denied this ever afterward thus hadn't been hypnotized.

Except: he'd seen the head ripped from the body, can't erase the sight. The body plummeting to the ground spouting blood and the loose head falling to the ground and bouncing and rolling the eyes wide-staring and affrighted. *You dumb-fuck Corcoran, that's your face! Sure.* And what they did with the head, and the body leaking blood, Corky can't remember. Must've been buried. Where?

They'd lifted him, and carried him away, and he never needed to wake as they threaded him stitching him tight. The lung, the arteries, the damaged tissue. The skull, the wristbones. He's in this cobweb tight-stitched and bars on the bed for his own safety. Tremors in his body like shouts he can't hear, still less control. They'd inserted by force a tube between two of his ribs on the left side to drain blood and fluids from his pulmonary cavity and another tube to siphon off air. Through his grotesquely distended right nostril a straw-sized tube attached to a respirator now breathing for him in ceaseless indefatigable unvarying rhythm like a slow march. An IV dripping into the bruised flesh at the crook of his right arm and wires to monitor his brain and his heart and other vital organs and none of these he can feel nor can he feel the catheter under the sheet piercing his sad shrunken cock to drain wastes from his body of which he has no knowledge thus no embarrassment. Nor does he smell himself or the sheets so quickly soiled. Though sometimes the shadow of a white-clad figure above him panics him to wakefulness and twitching and struggling and yelling in gagged strangulated moans he rips one of the heart monitor wires loose and thus has to be restrained.

On a TV monitor descending from the ceiling electronic patterns move ceaselessly like saw-notched waves from left to right, left to right, left to right in sometimes erratic rhythms. One of the video games in Club Zanzibar, *Total Terminator II*.

Another day, his elderly aunt-who's-a-nun has gone and in the doorway whispering, excited murmuring and Corky squints through the gauze seeing—is it Uncle Sean irresolute there in the doorway?—and beside him taller than he a red-haired man with no face or rather a dream-blurred forbidden face so Corky knows *It's him! it's Daddy* but the spell will be broken if he reveals he knows. So he lies absolutely still swaddled tight in the cobweb and the bars of the bed like a crib shameful to him but it can't be helped. At the same time knowing Tim Corcoran is probably not there though Uncle Sean *is* there, turning his straw fedora anxiously in his hands. Old man's terrified of him.

—Hey fuck it, Uncle Sean—I'm O.K. I'm not going to die.

Now right in front of him speaking slowly staring down at him as if not recognizing him or not wanting to recognize him. Corky can't see his uncle very well. Nor hear him. He's pissed at something, or maybe just tired. The cold air wears you down. Bitch never brought an extra blanket. Where the bullet tore across his head tearing out hair, skin, bloody scalp like a hook and fracturing the bone of the skull there's a big clot of something foreign and in fact much of Corky's head he's beginning to realize is wound up in something foreign, heavy as crockery on the pillow and so impossible to move.

—I said don't worry, what the hell—I'll be out of here by next week.

Thalia too is hospitalized. Corky seems to know this without knowing anything further—where she's hospitalized, for instance. Maybe somebody told him. Or he saw it on the TV screen over the bed. The promise is she'll be O.K., too.

The front page of Tuesday morning's *Journal*, photo of Vic and Corky grinning into the camera's flash above big black headlines GUN ATTEMPT ON SLATTERY'S LIFE, FRIEND INTERVENES.

The Medical Center's deluged with messages for Jerome A. Corcoran, telephone calls, cards, flowers. So many God-damned flowers! Nowhere to put them, flowers aren't allowed in intensive care. Corky tells the pretty blond nurse Sharon take them home, they're yours.

Never less than sixty-four percent of the vote. That's a fact. Now they're talking of Jerome A. Corcoran for Mayor of Union City, now Oscar Slattery is resigning but screw that Corky's thinking *he's* finished with Union City politics, too. And no more TV interviews—unless he gets to see the questions beforehand.

Waking to see Red Pitts above him impassive staring down at him the men contemplating each other in silence until like a bull with an injured knee

Pitts walks out leaving on the aluminum table beside Corky's bed a small object which at first Corky can't make out, can't see until at last it comes into dreamlike focus: the antique porcelain doll with the waved brunette hair, round empty eyes and rosebud mouth. *I'll be waiting for you.*

At the far end of the tunnel that's like a telescope turned around he's watching the white-clad figures working over him. Sticking him with needles extracting blood, fluids, bone marrow from his unresisting body. And out of that marrow iron dust from the farthest stars of the Universe which is trackless and has no perimeter and is isotopic meaning identical in all directions and it scares Corky to realize he's going to die never understanding. The iron dust of the Big Bang in the very marrow of his bones and he's going to die never understanding.

Telling Christina it's the saddest God-damned thing, or maybe the funniest. You live and you die and never understand where the fuck you've come from let alone where you're going, or why.

What *is* passing so swiftly so irrevocably into what *was*.

How many times Christina has been here, and how many hours standing at his bed Corky doesn't know. Must have explained to reception who she is, what her special connection to the patient is, she's carrying a pass so it's O.K. Staring at Corky who's smiling at her but it's through a barrier of some kind like scratched plastic he can see *her* and she sees him but isn't somehow seeing *him*. *Oh Corky!—my God.*

—Hey c'mon sweetheart, it isn't that bad. Give me a kiss?

This woman leaning over him shielding him from the cold with her warm body. Dark shining hair spilling in his face so he can't see but unmistakably it's her, he's forgotten her name but knows it's her, *she's the one*. And the house in the suburbs, and the kids. She's rubbing his frostbitten fingers in her hands and then the frostbitten toes. And finally with tremulous fingers the sad bruised shrunken cock. *Love love love you Corky please don't die.* Kissing the cock's tip, caressing the shriveled veins so they stir feebly with blood. Stooping over him to suck him sucking life into him sucking him hard so it hurts *Love love love love you darling.*

The monitors continue. The IV tube drips into a fresh vein in Corky's other arm. The respirator breathes for him in perfect unvarying robot rhythm. He asks one of the doctors can a respirator keep a corpse breathing, too?—laughing at the look on the guy's face. And day and night identical beneath the fluorescent lights. And outside the window—nothing.

The cold is getting worse. The broken windowpane nobody notices except him. Slow seeping air. Fuck it, Corky Corcoran doesn't like to whine but you never brought me the God-damned blanket. Theresa has warned *Don't let the cold get inside you!*

Cunning Corky: beneath his pillow he's hidden the promissory note for Nick Daugherty to sign. Nick's dropping by to see him tomorrow and Corky's going to take the document out and shove it in his face saying O.K. pal let's cut the bullshit. This is for *you*. And Nick's got no option but to sign. If you don't sign a promissory note you're saying outright you're a crook, a bum, you'd steal from your own best friend, you'd take advantage of a good-hearted dumb-shit's trust. And if you do sign but don't pay up your friend's got the legal means to sue *you*.

Hell, they'll have a good laugh over it afterward. When Corky gets out of the hospital. When Corky's himself again. A few ales at Killian's Red Star like old times.

Except: Corky and Nick are at the bar, talking and laughing together but there's this other guy, this third party, unwanted, intrusive, trying to elbow in. *Excuse me Mr. Corcoran?—Jerome?* Pushy little bastard with the squeezed-in head, squirrelly teeth. Pop eyes blinking inside his glasses. *Excuse me, my name is—*

Corky's agitated thrashing around pulling at the monitor wires, the IV tube and the tube in his nose so there's the danger they will be pulled out. He can't remember what the fucker's name is, Teague, or Tyde, what the fucker wants from him exactly. When Miriam comes by the next time he'll ask, Miriam's been here to visit Corky a half dozen times keeping him in close contact with the office but he never remembers to ask. Got more important things on his mind than some dumb amateur asshole scheme. Union City Mausoleum of the Dead—that's the scam! Money from Corcoran, Inc., the use of Corky Corcoran's name well fuck that.

Artie Fleischman and the other cop he'd met at Bobby Ray's, Fats Pickering, Mike Donnelly, Petey Zubkow, Budd Yeager, one or two other guys whose faces he can't see—one night they all show up together, to pay off bets they owe to Corky Corcoran! Jesus, what a commotion pushing through the intensive care unit, what a lot of laughs! Good-natured horsing around counting out bills onto Corky's bed from thick money wads, Corky you lucky prick, you s.o.b. how's one guy pick so many winners?—these guys crowding into the room around Corky's bed jiggling the bed laughing loud and smoking so the place fills up with smoke like Corky's bed is filling up with money, and Nick's here too, in fact Nick Daugherty's here too, he's got the dough he owes Corky and he's grinning counting it out getting lots of laughs from the guys counting out single $100 bills—so many of them: must be forty—so the guys are wisecracking what'd Corcoran sucker *you* into betting on? Somebody sneaks a cigarette to Corky who's dying for a smoke, and here's a bottle of Twelve Horse Ale haven't had one of these in a long time eh Corky? so Corky pulls the God-damned tubes and the aspirator out of his mouth, how many weeks he's been trapped in this place, hasn't been able to eat or taste or talk or breathe normally hasn't been able to see nor can he hear well fuck that shit he's had enough of doctors telling him what to do and his buddies are grinning saying *Right on, Corky! You tell 'em, Corky!*

Walking away trying not to run though yes he *is* scared. Knowing somebody or something's after them climbing the swaying fire escape to the roof, flecks of rust coming off on their hands. Theresa says *Go first! go first!* so if he falls she can catch him in her arms. And on the roof smelling of wet tarpaper and decaying leaves they're crouched together behind a tall blackened brick chimney. Theresa's excited holding Jerome in her arms *Don't let the cold get inside you!* and Jerome says he won't and Theresa says *But yes you are, I can feel it in you: the cold* and Jerome says trying not to cry no he's all right and Theresa seems to accept this or anyway holds him tight so he feels a powerful sensation of being loved wash over him and waking from his dream—this, he knows *is* a dream—lying for a long time dazed suspended in relief turning over and over in his mind what has happened to him and where he is and by slow degrees feeling stronger, more in control as in fact he hasn't felt for years or possibly in his entire life until now, it takes something like this to make you *think* for Christ's sake, to make you assess your life realizing too he's completely over his need for drinking and even the bittersweet memory of that need so won't be going to AA after all, and he's completely over his nicotine addiction that's been like a fever these past few days understanding and appreciating that what they've been doing here is detoxing him cleaning him out the way you'd hose down a filthy sidewalk washing the crap into the gutter, and gone. And he's still young, only forty-three. Plenty of time to get married, have another kid or two with Charlotte, no not the blond one the black-haired one he's so crazy for, can't think of her name, yes it's Christina, and maybe after all he *will* run for Mayor if it isn't just bullshit the Party getting seriously behind Jerome A. Corcoran.

He's telling one of the doctors this and the guy's impressed. And a young Jewish-looking intern wearing one of those little things—skull caps?—on the back of his head. And nurses including the blond with the cute bouncy ass, respectful of their celebrity-patient. Tomorrow morning you'll be off the respirator, we hope by tomorrow afternoon you'll be on another floor and you can have visitors. And Corky's thanking them, and shaking hands. Never hurts to shake hands. Not just these people are voters but they've done a good job. He's God-damned fucking grateful, they've done a good job. This emergency medicine, this fancy medical technology—it costs you, but it's worth it. And he's insured thank Christ. And he's feeling he can bring his life back under control again. And he's sure this time he won't let the good feeling go. So glimpsing that little prick Teague, or Tyde, out in the corridor waiting to see him for days, weeks, God knows how long he's been waiting for what he's got in that briefcase to show Corky, Corky gives him a wave.

—Hell, come on in, I'm Corky Corcoran, I'm your man.

May 28, 1992, 4:43 A.M.